P9-CLB-671

Praise for Alice Munro

"Munro's stories abound ... in such insights: within any story, within any human being, there may be a dangerous treasure, a priceless ruby. A heart's desire."

—from the Introduction by Margaret Atwood

"Alice Munro has a strong claim to being the best fiction writer now working in North America."

—*The New York Times Book Review*

"It is her genius to know when to pull back and bow to oblivion, when to insert her wilful self into stories both historical and deeply personal: maps of a pioneering writer's heart."

—*O, The Oprah Magazine*

"The living writer most likely to be read in a hundred years."

—*The Atlantic*

"When reading her work it is difficult to remember why the novel was ever invented."

—*The Times*

"Cynthia Ozick has said of Munro that she is our Chekhov ... But she is our Flaubert, too. We couldn't ask for more."

—*The Globe and Mail*

"The pre-eminent master of the short story ... all delivered in her spare, wonderful prose."

—*The Independent on Sunday*

"Munro's genius ... has to do with her exceptional openness to other people's words."

—*London Review of Books*

"Munro's powers are at their peak … she continues to charge forward, shining a light on what is most fearsome and true."

—*Chicago Tribune*

"Munro is the illusionist whose trick can never be exposed. And that is because there is no smoke, there are no mirrors. Munro really does know magic: how to summon the spirits and the emotions that animate our lives."

—*The Washington Post*

"The power of Munro's storytelling never falters."

—*Sunday Telegraph*

"Munro proves that the short story should never be deemed as the uninspiring younger sibling of the novel."

—*Financial Times*

PENGUIN CANADA

MY BEST STORIES

ALICE MUNRO grew up in Wingham, Ontario, and attended the University of Western Ontario. She has published many books, including *Dance of the Happy Shades; Lives of Girls and Women; Something I've Been Meaning to Tell You; Who Do You Think You Are?; The Moons of Jupiter; The Progress of Love; Friend of My Youth; Open Secrets; The Love of a Good Woman; Hateship, Friendship, Courtship, Loveship, Marriage; Runaway;* and *The View from Castle Rock.*

During her distinguished career, Munro has been the recipient of many awards and prizes, including the W.H. Smith Award in the United Kingdom and, in the United States, the National Book Critics Circle Award, the PEN/Malamud Award for Excellence in Short Fiction, the Lannan Literary Award, and the Rea Award for the Short Story. *Away from Her*, the film version of Munro's "The Bear Came Over the Mountain," won seven Genie Awards and was nominated for two Academy Awards.

In Canada, her prize-winning record is extraordinary: three Governor General's Awards, two Giller Prizes, the Trillium Book Award, the Jubilee Prize, and the Libris Award. Abroad, acclaim continues to pour in. Both *Runaway* and *Hateship, Friendship, Courtship, Loveship, Marriage* won the Commonwealth Writers' Prize Best Book Award, Caribbean and Canada region, and were chosen as Books of the Year by *The New York Times.* In 2005 Munro was included in *Time* magazine's list of the world's one hundred most influential people and in 2009 she won the Man Booker International Prize for her lifetime body of work.

Alice Munro's stories appear regularly in *The New Yorker*, as well as in *The Atlantic* and *The Paris Review.* She and her husband divide their time between Clinton, Ontario, and Comox, British Columbia.

ALSO BY ALICE MUNRO

ALICE MUNRO

MY BEST STORIES

WITH AN INTRODUCTION
BY MARGARET ATWOOD

PENGUIN
CANADA

PENGUIN CANADA

Published by the Penguin Group

Penguin Group (Canada), 90 Eglinton Avenue East, Suite 700, Toronto, Ontario, Canada M4P 2Y3
(a division of Pearson Canada Inc.)

Penguin Group (USA) Inc., 375 Hudson Street, New York, New York 10014, U.S.A.
Penguin Books Ltd, 80 Strand, London WC2R 0RL, England
Penguin Ireland, 25 St Stephen's Green, Dublin 2, Ireland (a division of Penguin Books Ltd)
Penguin Group (Australia), 250 Camberwell Road, Camberwell, Victoria 3124, Australia
(a division of Pearson Australia Group Pty Ltd)
Penguin Books India Pvt Ltd, 11 Community Centre, Panchsheel Park, New Delhi – 110 017, India
Penguin Group (NZ), 67 Apollo Drive, Rosedale, North Shore 0745, Auckland, New Zealand
(a division of Pearson New Zealand Ltd)
Penguin Books (South Africa) (Pty) Ltd, 24 Sturdee Avenue, Rosebank, Johannesburg 2196, South Africa

Penguin Books Ltd, Registered Offices: 80 Strand, London WC2R 0RL, England

Published in the United States in the Everyman's Library by Alfred A. Knopf, 2006
First published in Canada by McClelland & Stewart Ltd., 2006
Published in this edition, 2009

2 3 4 5 6 7 8 9 10 (WEB)

Copyright © Alice Munro, 2006
Introduction copyright © Margaret Atwood, 2006

The stories in this collection originally appeared in the following works published by Alfred A. Knopf:

The Beggar Maid, copyright © 1977, 1978 by Alice Munro
The Moons of Jupiter, copyright © 1977, 1979, 1980, 1981, 1982 by Alice Munro
The Progress of Love, copyright © 1985, 1986 by Alice Munro
Friend of My Youth, copyright © 1990 by Alice Munro
Open Secrets, copyright © 1994 by Alice Munro
The Love of a Good Woman, copyright © 1998 by Alice Munro
Hateship, Friendship, Loveship, Courtship, Marriage, copyright © 2001 by Alice Munro
Runaway, copyright © 2004 by Alice Munro

All rights reserved. Without limiting the rights under copyright reserved above, no part of this publication may
be reproduced, stored in or introduced into a retrieval system, or transmitted in any form or by any means
(electronic, mechanical, photocopying, recording or otherwise), without the prior written permission of both
the copyright owner and the above publisher of this book.

*Publisher's note: This book is a work of fiction. Names, characters, places and incidents either are the product
of the author's imagination or are used fictitiously, and any resemblance to actual persons living or dead, events,
or locales is entirely coincidental.*

Manufactured in Canada.

LIBRARY AND ARCHIVES CANADA CATALOGUING IN PUBLICATION

Munro, Alice, 1931–
My best stories / Alice Munro.

Short stories.
ISBN 978-0-14-317039-6

I. Title.

PS8576.U57A6 2009   C813'.54   C2009-904116-2

Visit the Penguin Group (Canada) website at **www.penguin.ca**

Special and corporate bulk purchase rates available; please see
www.penguin.ca/corporatesales or call 1-800-810-3104, ext. 477 or 474

CONTENTS

———

INTRODUCTION

——

Alice Munro is among the major writers of English fiction of our time. She's been accorded armfuls of super-superlatives by critics in both North America and the United Kingdom, she's won many awards, and she has a devoted international readership. Among writers themselves, her name is spoken in hushed tones. Most recently she's been used as a stick to flog the enemy with, in various inter-writerly combats. "You call this writing?" the floggers say, in effect. "Alice Munro! Now *that's* writing!" She's the kind of writer about whom it is often said—no matter how well-known she becomes—that she ought to be better known.

None of this happened overnight. Alice Munro has been writing since the 1960s, and her first collection—*Dance of the Happy Shades*—appeared in 1968. To date she has published eleven collections, averaging nine or ten stories each. Though her fiction has been a regular feature of *The New Yorker* since the 1970s, her recent elevation to international literary sainthood took as long as it did partly because of the form in which she writes. She is a writer of stories—"short stories," as they used to be called, or "short fiction," which is now more common. Though many American and British and Canadian writers of the first rank have practised this form, there is still a widespread but false tendency to equate length with importance.

Thus Alice Munro has been among those writers subject to periodic rediscovery, at least outside Canada. It's as if she jumps out of a cake— *Surprise!*—and then has to jump out of it again, and then again. Readers don't see her name in lights on every billboard. They come across her as if by accident or fate, and are drawn in, and then there is an outbreak of wonder and excitement, and incredulity—*Where did Alice Munro come from? Why didn't anybody tell me? How can such excellence have sprung from nowhere?*

*

But Alice Munro did not spring from nowhere. She sprang—though it's a verb her characters would find overly sprightly, and indeed pretentious—from Huron County, in south-western Ontario.

Ontario is the large province of Canada that stretches from the Ottawa River to the western end of Lake Superior. This is a huge and varied space, but south-western Ontario is a distinct part of it. It was named Sowesto by the painter Greg Curnoe, a name that has stuck. Curnoe's view was that Sowesto was an area of considerable interest, but also of considerable psychic murkiness and oddity, a view shared by many. Robertson Davies, also from Sowesto, used to say, "I know the dark folk-ways of my people," and Alice Munro knows them, too. You are likely to run into quite a few signs in Sowesto wheat fields telling you to be prepared to meet your God, or else your doom—felt to be much the same thing.

Lake Huron lies at the western edge of Sowesto, Lake Erie to the south. The country is mostly flat farmland, cut by several wide, winding rivers prone to flooding, and on the rivers—because of the available boat transport, and the power provided by water-driven mills—a number of smaller and larger towns grew up in the nineteenth century. Each has its red-brick town hall (usually with a tower), each its post-office building and its handful of churches of various denominations, each its main street and its residential section of gracious homes, and its other residential section on the wrong side of the tracks. Each has its families with long memories and stashes of bones in the closets.

Sowesto contains the site of the famous Donnelly Massacre of the nineteenth century, when a large family was slaughtered and their home burnt as a result of political resentments carried over from Ireland. Lush nature, repressed emotions, respectable fronts, hidden sexual excesses, outbreaks of violence, lurid crimes, long-held grudges, strange rumours—none are ever far away in Munro's Sowesto, partly because all have been provided by the real life of the region itself.

Oddly enough, a number of writers have come from Sowesto. Oddly, because when Alice Munro was growing up in the 1930s and '40s, the idea of a person from Canada—but especially one from small-town south-western Ontario—thinking they could be a writer to be taken seriously in the world at large was laughable. Even by the '50s and '60s there were very few publishers in Canada, and these were mostly text-book publishers who imported whatever so-called literature was to be had from England and the United States. There might be some amateur theatre—high-school performances, Little Theatre groups. There was, however, the radio, and in the '60s Alice Munro got her start through a CBC programme called *Anthology,* produced by Robert Weaver.

But very few Canadian writers of any sort were known to an inter-national readership, and it was taken for granted that if you had han-kerings of that kind—hankerings about which you would of course feel defensive and ashamed, because art was not something a grown-up morally credible person would fool around with—it would be best for you if you left the country. Everyone knew that writing was not a thing you could ever expect to make your living at.

It might be marginally acceptable to dabble around the edges of water-colour painting or poetry if you were a certain kind of man, described by Munro in "The Turkey Season": "There were homosexu-als in town, and we knew who they were: an elegant, light-voiced, wavy-haired paperhanger who called himself an interior decorator; the minister's widow's fat, spoiled only son, who went so far as to enter baking contests and had crocheted a tablecloth; a hypochondriacal church organist and music teacher who kept the choir and his pupils in line with screaming tantrums." Or you could do art as a hobby, if you were a woman with time on your hands, or you could scrape out a living at some poorly paid quasi-artistic job. Munro's stories are sprinkled with women like this. They go in for piano-playing, or write chatty newspa-per columns. Or—more tragically—they have a real though small talent, like Almeda Roth in "Meneseteung," but there is no context for them. Almeda produces one volume of minor verse, published in 1873, called *Offerings:*

> The local paper, the *Vidette,* referred to her as "our poetess." There
> seems to be a mixture of respect and contempt, both for her calling
> and for her sex—or for their predictable conjuncture.

At the beginning of the story Almeda is a maiden lady whose family has died. She lives alone, preserves her good name, and does charitable works. But by the end, the dammed-up river of art has overflowed—helped on by hefty doses of laudanum-laced painkiller—and it sweeps her rational self away:

> Poems, even. Yes, again, poems. Or one poem. Isn't that the idea—one very great poem that will contain everything and, oh, that will make all the other poems, the poems she has written, inconsequential, mere trial and error, mere rags? . . . The name of the poem is the name of the river. No, in fact it is the river, the Meneseteung . . . Almeda looks deep, deep into the river of her mind and into the tablecloth, and she sees the crocheted roses floating.

This seemed to be the fate of an artist—of necessity, a minor artist—in the small Sowesto towns of yore: silence enforced by the need for respectability, or else an eccentricity verging on madness.

If you moved to a larger Canadian city, you might at least find a few others of your ilk, but in the small towns of Sowesto you'd be on your own. Nevertheless, John Kenneth Galbraith, Robertson Davies, Marian Engel, Graeme Gibson, and James Reaney all came out of Sowesto; and Alice Munro herself—after a spell on the west coast—moved back there, and lives at present not far from Wingham, the prototype of the various Jubilees and Walleys and Dalgleishes and Hanrattys in her stories.

Through Munro's fiction, Sowesto's Huron County has joined Faulkner's Yoknapatawpha County as a slice of land made legendary by the excellence of the writer who has celebrated it, though in both cases "celebrated" is not quite the right word. "Anatomized" might be closer to what goes on in the work of Munro, though even that term is too clinical. What should we call the combination of obsessive scrutiny, archeological unearthing, precise and detailed recollection, the wallowing in the seamier and meaner and more vengeful undersides of human nature, the telling of erotic secrets, the nostalgia for vanished miseries, and rejoicing in the fullness and variety of life, stirred all together?

At the end of Munro's *Lives of Girls and Women* (1971), her only novel and a *bildungsroman*—a novel of development, in this case a portrait of the artist as a young girl—there's a telling passage. Del Jordan of Jubilee, who has by now—true to her last name—crossed over into the promised land of womanhood and also of writerhood, says of her adolescence:

> It did not occur to me then that one day I would be so greedy for Jubilee. Voracious and misguided as Uncle Craig out at Jenkin's Bend, writing his history, I would want to write things down.
>
> I would try to make lists. A list of all the stores and businesses going up and down the main street and who owned them, a list of family names, names on the tombstones in the cemetery and any inscriptions underneath . . .
>
> The hope of accuracy we bring to such tasks is crazy, heartbreaking.
>
> And no list could hold what I wanted, for what I wanted was every last thing, every layer of speech and thought, stroke of light on bark or walls, every smell, pothole, pain, crack, delusion, held still and held together—radiant, everlasting.

As a programme for a life's work this is daunting. Nevertheless it's a programme Alice Munro was to follow over the next thirty-five years with remarkable fidelity.

*

Alice Munro was born Alice Laidlaw, in 1931, which means that she was a small child during the Depression. She was eight in 1939, the year Canada entered the Second World War, and she attended university—the University of Western Ontario, in London—in the postwar years. She was twenty-five and a young mother when Elvis Presley first became famous, and thirty-eight at the time of the flower-child revolution and the advent of the women's movement in 1968–9, a moment in time that saw the publication of her first book. In 1981 she was fifty. Her stories are set mainly over these years—the '30s to the '80s—or even before then, in the time of ancestral memory.

Her own ancestry was partly Scotch Presbyterian: she can trace her family back to James Hogg, the Ettrick Shepherd, friend of Robert Burns and the Edinburgh literati of the late eighteenth century, and author of *The Confessions of a Justified Sinner,* which could itself be a Munro title. On the other side of the family there were Anglicans, for whom the worst sin is said to consist of using the wrong fork at dinner. Munro's acute consciousness of social class, and of the minutiae and sneers separating one level from the next, is honestly come by, as is—from the Presbyterians— her characters' habit of rigorously examining their own deeds, emotions, motives, and consciences, and finding them wanting. In a traditional Protestant culture, such as that of small-town Sowesto, forgiveness is not easily come by, punishments are frequent and harsh, potential humiliation and shame lurk around every corner, and nobody gets away with much.

But this tradition also contains the doctrine of justification by faith alone: grace descends upon us without any action on our part. In Munro's work, grace abounds, but it is strangely disguised: nothing can be predicted. Emotions erupt. Preconceptions crumble. Surprises proliferate. Astonishments leap out. Malicious acts can have positive consequences. Salvation arrives when least expected, and in peculiar forms.

But as soon as you make such a pronouncement about Munro's writing—or any other such analysis, inference, or generalization about it—you're aware of that mocking commentator so often present in a Munro story—the one who says, in essence, *Who do you think you are? What gives you the right to think you know anything about me, or about anyone else for that matter?* Or, to quote from *Lives of Girls and Women* again, "People's lives . . . were dull, simple, amazing and unfathomable—deep caves paved with kitchen linoleum." The key word here is "unfathomable."

*

The first two stories in this selection, "Royal Beatings" and "The Beggar Maid," are from a book with two different titles. In Canada it was called—after a term of peevish accusation used to let the air out of somebody else's puffed-up head—*Who Do You Think You Are?* In the United States and England it was called, romantically, *The Beggar Maid.* The stories in this enigmatically-titled book have a common protagonist— Rose, who grows up in a poorer section of a town called Hanratty with her father and her stepmother Flo, then goes to university on scholarship, marries a man from a social level far above hers and later runs away from him, and then, later still, becomes an actress—a cardinal sin and cause for shame in the Hanratty still inhabited by Flo. *Who Do You Think You Are?* is thus another *bildungsroman*—an account of the formation of its heroine—and another portrait of the artist.

What is fakery, what is authenticity? Which emotions and modes of behaviour and speech are honest and true, which pretended or pretentious? Or can they be separated? Munro's characters think frequently about such matters.

As in art, so in life. Hanratty society is divided in two by the river that flows through the town:

> In Hanratty the social structure ran from doctors and dentists and lawyers down to foundry workers and factory workers and draymen; in West Hanratty it ran from factory workers and foundry workers down to large improvident families of casual bootleggers and prostitutes and unsuccessful thieves.

Each half of the town claims jeering rights against the other. Flo goes across to Hanratty, the better part of town, to shop, but also

> to see people, and listen to them. Among the people she listened to were Mrs. Lawyer Davies, Mrs. Anglican Rector Henley-Smith, and Mrs. Horse-Doctor McKay. She came home and imitated their flibberty voices. Monsters, she made them seem, of foolishness, and showiness, and self-approbation.

But when Rose goes to college and boards with a lady professor and becomes engaged to Patrick, son of a West Coast department-store tycoon, and gets a look at upper middle-class surroundings, Flo in turn becomes monstrous in Rose's eyes, and Rose is divided against herself. Patrick's visit to Rose's home town is a disaster for Rose:

> She felt ashamed on more levels than she could count. She was ashamed of the food and the swan and the plastic tablecloth; ashamed for Patrick,

the gloomy snob, who made a startled grimace when Flo passed him the toothpick-holder; ashamed for Flo with her timidity and hypocrisy and pretensions; most of all ashamed of herself. She didn't even have any way that she could talk, and sound natural.

Yet as soon as Patrick begins to criticize her town and family, Rose feels "a layer of loyalty and protectiveness . . . hardening around every memory she had . . ."

This state of divided allegiance applies to Munro's vocation as well as to considerations of social status. Her fictional world is peopled with secondary characters who despise art and artifice, and any kind of pretentiousness or showing off. It's against these attitudes and the self-mistrust they inspire that her central characters must struggle in order to free themselves enough to create anything at all.

At the same time her writer protagonists share this scorn of the artificial side of art, and the distrust of it. What should be written about? How should one write? How much of art is genuine, how much just a bag of cheap tricks—imitating people, manipulating their emotions, making faces? How can one affirm anything about another person—even a made-up person—without presumption? Above all, how should a story end? (Munro often provides one ending, then questions or revises it. Or else she simply distrusts it, as in the final paragraph of "Meneseteung" where the narrator says, "I may have got it wrong.") Isn't the very act of writing an act of arrogance, isn't the pen a broken reed? A number of stories— "Friend of My Youth," "Carried Away," "Wilderness Station," "Hateship, Friendship, Courtship, Loveship, Marriage"—contain letters that display the vanity or falsity or even the malice of their writers. If the writing of letters can be so devious, what about writing itself?

This tension has remained with her: as in "The Moons of Jupiter," Munro's artistic characters are punished for not succeeding, but they are punished also for success. The woman writer, thinking about her father, says:

I could hear him saying, Well, I didn't see anything about you in *Maclean's*. And if he had read something about me, he would say, Well, I didn't think too much of that write-up. His tone would be humorous and indulgent but would produce in me a familiar dreariness of spirit. The message I got from him was simple: Fame must be striven for, then apologized for. Getting or not getting it, you will be to blame.

*

"Dreariness of spirit" is one of the great Munro enemies. Her characters do battle with it in every way they can, fighting against stifling mores and other people's deadening expectations and imposed rules of behaviour, and every possible kind of muffling and spiritual smothering. Given a choice between being a person who does good works but has inauthentic feelings and is numb at heart and one who behaves badly but is true to what she really feels and is thus alive to herself, a Munro woman is likely to choose the latter; or, if she chooses the former, she will then comment on her own slipperiness, guile, wiliness, slyness, and perversity. Honesty, in Munro's work, is not the best policy: it is not a policy at all, but an essential element, like air. The characters must get hold of at least some of it, by fair means or foul, or—they feel—they will go under.

The battle for authenticity is waged most significantly in the field of sex. The Munro social world—like most societies in which silence and secrecy are the norm in sexual matters—carries a high erotic charge, and this charge extends like a neon penumbra around each character, illuminating landscapes, rooms, and objects. A rumpled bed says more, in the hands of Munro, than any graphic in-out, in-out depiction of genitalia ever could. Even if a story is not primarily about a love affair or sexual encounter, men and women are always aware of one another as men and women, positively or negatively, recognizing sexual attraction and curiosity or else sexual revulsion. Women are immediately attuned to the sexual power of other women, and are wary of it, or envious. Men show off and preen and flirt and seduce and compete.

Munro's characters are as alert as dogs in a perfume store to the sexual chemistry in a gathering—the chemistry among others, as well as that of their own visceral responses. Falling in love, falling in lust, sneaking around on spouses and enjoying it, telling sexual lies, doing shameful things they feel compelled to do out of irresistible desire, making sexual calculations based on social desperation—few writers have explored such processes more thoroughly, and more ruthlessly. Pushing the sexual boundaries is distinctly thrilling for many a Munro woman; but in order to trespass you have to know exactly where the fence is, and Munro's universe is criss-crossed with meticulously defined borders. Hands, chairs, glances—all are part of an intricate inner map strewn with barbed wire and booby traps, and secret paths through the shrubbery.

For women of Munro's generation, sexual expression was a liberation and a way out. But out of what? Out of the denial and limiting scorn she describes so well in "The Turkey Season":

> Lily said she never let her husband come near her if he had been drinking. Marjorie said since the time she nearly died with a hemorrhage she never let her husband come near her, period. Lily said quickly that it was only when he'd been drinking that he tried anything. I could see that it was a matter of pride not to let your husband come near you, but I couldn't quite believe that "come near" meant "have sex."

For older women like Lily and Marjorie, to enjoy sex would have been a humiliating defeat. For women like Rose, in "The Beggar Maid," it's a matter for pride and celebration, a victory. For later generations of women—post Sexual Revolution—enjoying sex was to become simply a duty, the perfect orgasm yet another thing to add to the list of required accomplishments; and when enjoyment becomes a duty, we're back in the land of "dreariness of spirit." But for a Munro character in the throes of sexual exploration, the spirit may be confused and ashamed and tormented, even cruel and sadistic—some of the couples in her stories get pleasure out of torturing each other emotionally, just like some real people—but it is never dreary.

In some of the later stories, sex can be less impetuous, more calculated. For example, Grant, in "The Bear Came Over The Mountain," uses it as the decisive element in an astonishing feat of emotional commodities-trading. His beloved wife Fiona has dementia, and has become attached to a similarly-afflicted man in her care facility. When this man is taken home by his hard-bitten, practical wife, Marian, Fiona pines and stops eating. Grant wants to persuade Marian to put her husband back in the institution, but Marian refuses: it would cost too much. However, Grant detects that Marian is lonely and sexually available. She has a wrinkled-up face, but her body is still attractive. Like an adroit sales-man, Grant moves in to close the deal. Munro knows full well that sex can be a glory and a torment, but it can also be a bargaining chip.

*

The society Munro writes about is a Christian one. This Christianity is not often overt; it's merely the general background. Flo in "The Beggar Maid" decorates the walls with "a number of admonitions, pious and cheerful and mildly bawdy:"

THE LORD IS MY SHEPHERD
BELIEVE IN THE LORD JESUS CHRIST AND THOU SHALT BE SAVED

Why did Flo have those, when she wasn't even religious? They were what people had, common as calendars.

Christianity is "what people had"—and in Canada, church and state were never separated along the lines laid down in the United States. Prayers and Bible readings were daily fare in publicly funded schools. This cul-tural Christianity has provided ample material for Munro, but it is also connected with one of the most distinctive patterns in her image-making and storytelling.

The central Christian tenet is that two disparate and mutually exclu-sive elements—divinity and humanity—got jammed together in Christ, neither annihilating the other. The result was not a demi-god, or a God in disguise: God became totally a human being while remaining at the same time totally divine. To believe that Christ was only a man or to believe he was simply God were both declared heretical by the early Christian church. Christianity thus depends on a denial of either/or clas-sifying logic and an acceptance of both-at-once mystery. Logic says that A cannot be both itself and non-A at the same time, Christianity says it can. The formulation "A but also non-A" is indispensable to it.

Many of Munro's stories resolve themselves—or fail to resolve themselves—in precisely this way. The example that first comes to mind—though there are many—is from *Lives of Girls and Women,* in which the teacher who'd staged the high school's airy and joyful operettas drowns herself in the river.

> Miss Farris in her velvet skating costume . . . Miss Farris *con brio* . . . Miss Farris floating face down, unprotesting, in the Wawanash River, six days before she was found. Though there is no plausible way of hanging those pictures together—if the last one is true then must it not alter the others?—they are going to have to stay together now.

For Munro, a thing can be true, but not true, but true nonetheless. "It is real and dishonest," thinks Georgia, of her remorse, in "Differently." "How hard it is for me to believe that I made that up," says the narrator of "The Progress of Love." "It seems so much the truth it is the truth; it's what I believe about them. I haven't stopped believing it." The world is profane *and* sacred. It must be swallowed whole. There is always more to be known about it than you can ever know.

*

In a story called "Something I've Been Meaning to Tell You," jealous Et describes her sister's former lover—a promiscuous ladies' man—and the look he gives to every woman, a look "that made him seem to want to be a deep-sea diver diving down, down through all the emptiness and cold and wreckage to discover the one thing he had set his heart on, something small and precious, hard to locate, as a ruby maybe on the ocean floor."

Munro's stories abound in such questionable seekers and well-fingered ploys. But they abound also in such insights: within any story, within any human being, there may be a dangerous treasure, a priceless ruby. A heart's desire.

Margaret Atwood

MARGARET ATWOOD is the author of *The Handmaid's Tale, The Blind Assassin,* and *Oryx and Crake.*

MY BEST STORIES

ROYAL BEATINGS

ROYAL BEATING. That was Flo's promise. You are going to get one Royal
Beating.

The word *Royal* lolled on Flo's tongue, took on trappings. Rose had
a need to picture things, to pursue absurdities, that was stronger than
the need to stay out of trouble, and instead of taking this threat to
heart she pondered: How is a beating royal? She came up with a tree-
lined avenue, a crowd of formal spectators, some white horses and black
slaves. Someone knelt, and the blood came leaping out like banners.
An occasion both savage and splendid. In real life they didn't approach
such dignity, and it was only Flo who tried to supply the event with
some high air of necessity and regret. Rose and her father soon got
beyond anything presentable.

Her father was king of the royal beatings. Those Flo gave never
amounted to much; they were quick cuffs and slaps dashed off while
her attention remained elsewhere. You get out of my road, she would
say. You mind your own business. You take that look off your face.

They lived behind a store in Hanratty, Ontario. There were four of
them: Rose, her father, Flo, Rose's young half brother, Brian. The store
was really a house, bought by Rose's father and mother when they
married and set up here in the furniture- and upholstery-repair business.
Her mother could do upholstery. From both parents Rose should have
inherited clever hands, a quick sympathy with materials, an eye for the
nicest turns of mending, but she hadn't. She was clumsy, and when something broke she couldn't wait to sweep it up and throw it away.

Her mother had died. She said to Rose's father during the afternoon,
"I have a feeling that is so hard to describe. It's like a boiled egg in my
chest, with the shell left on." She died before night, she had a blood clot
on her lung. Rose was a baby in a basket at the time, so of course could

not remember any of this. She heard it from Flo, who must have heard it from her father. Flo came along soon afterward, to take over Rose in the basket, marry her father, open up the front room to make a grocery store. Rose, who had known the house only as a store, who had known only Flo for a mother, looked back on the sixteen or so months her parents spent here as an orderly, far gentler and more ceremonious time, with little touches of affluence. She had nothing to go on but some eggcups her mother had bought, with a pattern of vines and birds on them, delicately drawn as if with red ink; the pattern was beginning to wear away. No books or clothes or pictures of her mother remained. Her father must have got rid of them, or else Flo would. Flo's only story about her mother, the one about her death, was oddly grudging. Flo liked the details of a death: the things people said, the way they protested or tried to get out of bed or swore or laughed (some did those things), but when she said that Rose's mother mentioned a hard-boiled egg in her chest she made the comparison sound slightly foolish, as if her mother really was the kind of person who might think you could swallow an egg whole.

Her father had a shed out behind the store, where he worked at his furniture repairing and restoring. He caned chair seats and backs, mended wickerwork, filled cracks, put legs back on, all most admirably and skillfully and cheaply. That was his pride: to startle people with such fine work, such moderate, even ridiculous charges. During the Depression people could not afford to pay more, perhaps, but he continued the practice through the war, through the years of prosperity after the war, until he died. He never discussed with Flo what he charged or what was owing. After he died she had to go out and unlock the shed and take all sorts of scraps of paper and torn envelopes from the big wicked-looking hooks that were his files. Many of these she found were not accounts or receipts at all but records of the weather, bits of information about the garden, things he had been moved to write down.

Ate new potatoes 25th June. Record.
Dark Day, 1880's, nothing supernatural. Clouds of ash from forest fires.
Aug 16, 1938. Giant thunderstorm in evng. Lightning str. Pres.
    Church, Turberry Twp. Will of God?

Scald strawberries to remove acid.
All things are alive. Spinoza.

Flo thought Spinoza must be some new vegetable he planned to grow, like broccoli or eggplant. He would often try some new thing. She showed the scrap of paper to Rose and asked, did she know what Spinoza was? Rose did know, or had an idea – she was in her teens by that time – but she replied that she did not. She had reached an age where she thought she could not stand to know any more, about her father, or about Flo; she pushed any discovery aside with embarrassment and dread.

There was a stove in the shed, and many rough shelves covered with cans of paint and varnish, shellac and turpentine, jars of soaking brushes and also some dark sticky bottles of cough medicine. Why should a man who coughed constantly, whose lungs took in a whiff of gas in the war (called, in Rose's earliest childhood, not the First, but the Last, War), spend all his days breathing fumes of paint and turpentine? At the time, such questions were not asked as often as they are now. On the bench outside Flo's store several old men from the neighborhood sat gossiping, drowsing, in the warm weather, and some of these old men coughed all the time too. The fact is they were dying, slowly and discreetly, of what was called, without any particular sense of grievance, "the foundry disease." They had worked all their lives at the foundry in town, and now they sat still, with their wasted yellow faces, coughing, chuckling, drifting into aimless obscenity on the subject of women walking by, or any young girl on a bicycle.

From the shed came not only coughing but speech, a continual muttering, reproachful or encouraging, usually just below the level at which separate words could be made out. Slowing down when her father was at a tricky piece of work, taking on a cheerful speed when he was doing something less demanding, sandpapering or painting. Now and then some words would break through and hang clear and nonsensical on the air. When he realized they were out, there would be a quick bit of cover-up coughing, a swallowing, an alert, unusual silence.

"Macaroni, pepperoni, Botticelli, beans–"

What could that mean? Rose used to repeat such things to herself. She could never ask him. The person who spoke these words and the person who spoke to her as her father were not the same, though they seemed to occupy the same space. It would be the worst sort of taste to acknowledge the person who was not supposed to be there; it would not be forgiven. Just the same, she loitered and listened.

The cloud-capped towers, she heard him say once.

"The cloud-capped towers, the gorgeous palaces."

That was like a hand clapped against Rose's chest, not to hurt, but astonish her, to take her breath away. She had to run then, she had to get away. She knew that was enough to hear, and besides, what if he caught her? It would be terrible.

This was something the same as bathroom noises. Flo had saved up and had a bathroom put in, but there was no place to put it except in a corner of the kitchen. The door did not fit, the walls were only beaverboard. The result was that even the tearing of a piece of toilet paper, the shifting of a haunch, was audible to those working or talking or eating in the kitchen. They were all familiar with each other's nether voices, not only in their more explosive moments but in their intimate sighs and growls and pleas and statements. And they were all most prudish people. So no one ever seemed to hear, or be listening, and no reference was made. The person creating the noises in the bathroom was not connected with the person who walked out.

They lived in a poor part of town. There was Hanratty and West Hanratty, with the river flowing between them. This was West Hanratty. In Hanratty the social structure ran from doctors and dentists and lawyers down to foundry workers and factory workers and draymen; in West Hanratty it ran from factory workers and foundry workers down to large improvident families of casual bootleggers and prostitutes and unsuccessful thieves. Rose thought of her own family as straddling the river, belonging nowhere, but that was not true. West Hanratty was where the store was and they were, on the straggling tail end of the main street. Across the road from them was a blacksmith shop, boarded up about the time the war started, and a house that had been another store at one time. The Salada Tea sign had never been taken out of the front window;

it remained as a proud and interesting decoration though there was no Salada Tea for sale inside. There was just a bit of sidewalk, too cracked and tilted for roller-skating, though Rose longed for roller skates and often pictured herself whizzing along in a plaid skirt, agile and fashionable. There was one streetlight, a tin flower; then the amenities gave up and there were dirt roads and boggy places, front-yard dumps and strange-looking houses. What made the houses strange-looking were the attempts to keep them from going completely to ruin. With some the attempt had never been made. These were gray and rotted and leaning over, falling into a landscape of scrub hollows, frog ponds, cattails, and nettles. Most houses, however, had been patched up with tarpaper, a few fresh shingles, sheets of tin, hammered-out stovepipes, even cardboard. This was, of course, in the days before the war, days of what would later be legendary poverty, from which Rose would remember mostly low-down things – serious-looking anthills and wooden steps, and a cloudy, interesting, problematical light on the world.

THERE WAS A LONG truce between Flo and Rose in the beginning. Rose's nature was growing like a prickly pineapple, but slowly, and secretly, hard pride and skepticism overlapping, to make something surprising even to herself. Before she was old enough to go to school, and while Brian was still in the baby carriage, Rose stayed in the store with both of them – Flo sitting on the high stool behind the counter, Brian asleep by the window; Rose knelt or lay on the wide creaky floorboards, working with crayons on pieces of brown paper too torn or irregular to be used for wrapping.

People who came to the store were mostly from the houses around. Some country people came too, on their way home from town, and a few people from Hanratty, who walked across the bridge. Some people were always on the main street, in and out of stores, as if it was their duty to be always on display and their right to be welcomed. For instance, Becky Tyde.

Becky Tyde climbed up on Flo's counter, made room for herself beside an open tin of crumbly jam-filled cookies.

"Are these any good?" she said to Flo, and boldly began to eat one. "When are you going to give us a job, Flo?"

"You could go and work in the butcher shop," said Flo innocently. "You could go and work for your brother."

"Roberta?" said Becky with a stagey sort of contempt. "You think I'd work for him?" Her brother who ran the butcher shop was named Robert but often called Roberta, because of his meek and nervous ways. Becky Tyde laughed. Her laugh was loud and noisy like an engine bearing down on you.

She was a big-headed loud-voiced dwarf, with a mascot's sexless swagger, a red velvet tam, a twisted neck that forced her to hold her head on one side, always looking up and sideways. She wore little polished high-heeled shoes, real lady's shoes. Rose watched her shoes, being scared of the rest of her, of her laugh and her neck. She knew from Flo that Becky Tyde had been sick with polio as a child, that was why her neck was twisted and why she had not grown any taller. It was hard to believe that she had started out differently, that she had ever been normal. Flo said she was not cracked, she had as much brains as anybody, but she knew she could get away with anything.

"You know I used to live out here?" Becky said, noticing Rose. "Hey! What's-your-name! Didn't I used to live out here, Flo?"

"If you did it was before my time," said Flo, as if she didn't know anything.

"That was before the neighborhood got so downhill. Excuse me saying so. My father built his house out here and he built his slaughterhouse and we had half an acre of orchard."

"Is that so?" said Flo, using her humoring voice, full of false geniality, humility even. "Then why did you ever move away?"

"I told you, it got to be such a downhill neighborhood," said Becky. She would put a whole cookie in her mouth if she felt like it, let her cheeks puff out like a frog's. She never told any more.

Flo knew anyway, and who didn't. Everyone knew the house, red brick with the veranda pulled off and the orchard, what was left of it, full of the usual outflow – car seats and washing machines and bedsprings and junk. The house would never look sinister, in spite of what had happened in it, because there was so much wreckage and confusion all around.

Becky's old father was a different kind of butcher from her brother, according to Flo. A bad-tempered Englishman. And different from Becky in the matter of mouthiness. His was never open. A skinflint, a family tyrant. After Becky had polio he wouldn't let her go back to school. She was seldom seen outside the house, never outside the yard. He didn't want people gloating. That was what Becky said, at the trial. Her mother was dead by that time and her sisters married. Just Becky and Robert at home. People would stop Robert on the road and ask him, "How about your sister, Robert? Is she altogether better now?"

"Yes."

"Does she do the housework? Does she get your supper?"

"Yes."

"And is your father good to her, Robert?"

The story being that the father beat them, had beaten all his children and beaten his wife as well, beat Becky more now because of her deformity, which some people believed he had caused (they did not understand about polio). The stories persisted and got added to. The reason that Becky was kept out of sight was now supposed to be her pregnancy, and the father of the child was supposed to be her own father. Then people said it had been born, and disposed of.

"What?"

"Disposed of," Flo said. "They used to say go and get your lamb chops at Tyde's, get them nice and tender! It was all lies in all probability," she said regretfully.

Rose could be drawn back – from watching the wind shiver along the old torn awning, catch in the tear – by this tone of regret, caution, in Flo's voice. Flo telling a story – and this was not the only one, or even the most lurid one, she knew – would incline her head and let her face go soft and thoughtful, tantalizing, warning.

"I shouldn't even be telling you this stuff."

More was to follow.

Three useless young men, who hung around the livery stable, got together – or were got together, by more influential and respectable men in town – and prepared to give old man Tyde a horsewhipping, in the interests of public morality. They blacked their faces. They were provided with whips and a quart of whisky apiece, for courage. They were: Jelly Smith, a horse-racer and a drinker; Bob Temple, a ballplayer and strong-man; and Hat Nettleton, who worked on the town dray, and had his nickname from a bowler hat he wore, out of vanity as much as for the comic effect. He still worked on the dray, in fact; he had kept the name if not the hat, and could often be seen in public – almost as often as Becky Tyde – delivering sacks of coal, which blackened his face and arms. That should have brought to mind his story, but didn't. Present time and past, the shady melodramatic past of Flo's stories, were quite separate, at least for Rose. Present people could not be fitted into the past. Becky herself, town oddity and public pet, harmless and malicious, could never match the butcher's prisoner, the cripple daughter, a white streak at the window: mute, beaten, impregnated. As with the house, only a formal connection could be made.

The young men primed to do the horsewhipping showed up late, out-side Tyde's house, after everybody had gone to bed. They had a gun, but they used up their ammunition firing it off in the yard. They yelled for the butcher and beat on the door; finally they broke it down. Tyde con-cluded they were after his money, so he put some bills in a handkerchief and sent Becky down with them, maybe thinking those men would be touched or scared by the sight of a little wry-necked girl, a dwarf. But that didn't content them. They came upstairs and dragged the butcher out from under his bed, in his nightgown. They dragged him outside and stood him in the snow. The temperature was four below zero, a fact noted later in court. They meant to hold a mock trial but they could not remember how it was done. So they began to beat him and kept beating him until he fell. They yelled at him, *Butcher's meat!* and continued beating him while his nightgown and the snow he was lying in turned red. His son Robert said in court that he had not watched the beating. Becky said that Robert had watched at first but had run away and hid. She herself had watched all the way through. She watched the men leave at last and her father make his delayed bloody progress through the snow and up the steps of the veranda. She did not go out to help him, or open the door until he got to it. Why not? she was asked in court, and she said she did not go out because she just had her nightgown on, and she did not open the door because she did not want to let the cold into the house.

Old man Tyde then appeared to have recovered his strength. He sent Robert to harness the horse, and made Becky heat water so that he could wash. He dressed and took all the money and with no explanation to his children got into the cutter and drove to Belgrave where he left the horse tied in the cold and took the early-morning train to Toronto. On the train he behaved oddly, groaning and cursing as if he was drunk. He was picked up on the streets of Toronto a day later, out of his mind with fever, and was taken to a hospital, where he died. He still had all the money. The cause of death was given as pneumonia.

But the authorities got wind, Flo said. The case came to trial. The three men who did it all received long prison sentences. A farce, said Flo. Within a year they were all free, had all been pardoned, had jobs waiting for them. And why was that? It was because too many higher-ups were in on it. And it seemed as if Becky and Robert had no interest in seeing justice done. They were left well-off. They bought a house in Hanratty. Robert went into the store. Becky after her long seclusion started on a career of public sociability and display.

That was all. Flo put the lid down on the story as if she was sick of it. It reflected no good on anybody.

"Imagine," Flo said.

Flo at this time must have been in her early thirties. A young woman. She wore exactly the same clothes that a woman of fifty, or sixty, or seventy, might wear: print housedresses loose at the neck and sleeves as well as the waist; bib aprons, also of print, which she took off when she came from the kitchen into the store. This was a common costume, at the time, for a poor though not absolutely poverty-stricken woman; it was also, in a way, a scornful deliberate choice. Flo scorned slacks, she scorned the outfits of people trying to be in style, she scorned lipstick and permanents. She wore her own black hair cut straight across, just long enough to push behind her ears. She was tall but fine-boned, with narrow wrists and shoulders, a small head, a pale, freckled, mobile, monkeyish face. If she had thought it worthwhile, and had the resources, she might have had a black-and-pale, fragile, nurtured sort of prettiness; Rose realized that later. But she would have to have been a different person altogether; she would have to have learned to resist making faces, at herself and others.

Rose's earliest memories of Flo were of extraordinary softness and hardness. The soft hair, the long, soft, pale cheeks, soft almost invisible fuzz in front of her ears and above her mouth. The sharpness of her knees, hardness of her lap, flatness of her front.

When Flo sang:

> "Oh the buzzin' of the bees in the cigarette trees
> And the soda-water fountain . . ."

Rose thought of Flo's old life before she married her father, when she worked as a waitress in the coffee shop in Union Station, and went with her girlfriends Mavis and Irene to Centre Island, and was followed by men on dark streets and knew how pay phones and elevators worked. Rose heard in her voice the reckless dangerous life of cities, the gum-chewing sharp answers.

And when she sang:

> "Then slowly, slowly, she got up
> And slowly she came nigh him
> And all she said, that she ever did say,
> Was young man, I think you're dyin'!"

Rose thought of a life Flo seemed to have had beyond that, earlier than that, crowded and legendary, with Barbara Allan and Becky Tyde's father and all kinds of outrages and sorrows jumbled up together in it.

THE ROYAL BEATINGS. What got them started?

Suppose a Saturday, in spring. Leaves not out yet but the doors open to the sunlight. Crows. Ditches full of running water. Hopeful weather. Often on Saturdays Flo left Rose in charge of the store — it's a few years now, these are the years when Rose was nine, ten, eleven, twelve — while she herself went across the bridge to Hanratty (going uptown they called it) to shop and see people, and listen to them. Among the people she listened to were Mrs. Lawyer Davies, Mrs. Anglican Rector Henley-Smith, and Mrs. Horse-Doctor McKay. She came home and imitated their flibberty voices. Monsters, she made them seem, of foolishness, and showiness, and self-approbation.

When she finished shopping she went into the coffee shop of the Queen's Hotel and had a sundae. What kind? Rose and Brian wanted to know when she got home, and they would be disappointed if it was only pineapple or butterscotch, pleased if it was a Tin Roof, or Black and White. Then she smoked a cigarette. She had some ready-rolled that she carried with her, so that she wouldn't have to roll one in public. Smoking was the one thing she did that she would have called showing off in anybody else. It was a habit left over from her working days, from Toronto. She knew it was asking for trouble. Once, the Catholic priest came over to her right in the Queen's Hotel, and flashed his lighter at her before she could get her matches out. She thanked him but did not enter into conversation, lest he should try to convert her.

Another time, on the way home, she saw at the town end of the bridge a boy in a blue jacket, apparently looking at the water. Eighteen, nineteen years old. Nobody she knew. Skinny, weakly-looking, something the matter with him, she saw at once. Was he thinking of jumping? Just as she came up even with him, what does he do but turn and display himself, holding his jacket open, also his pants. What he must have suffered from the cold, on a day that had Flo holding her coat collar tight around her throat.

When she first saw what he had in his hand, Flo said, all she could think of was What is he doing out here with a baloney sausage?

She could say that. It was offered as truth; no joke. She maintained that she despised dirty talk. She would go out and yell at the old men sitting in front of her store.

"If you want to stay where you are you better clean your mouths out!"

Saturday, then. For some reason Flo is not going uptown, has decided to stay home and scrub the kitchen floor. Perhaps this has put her in a bad mood. Perhaps she was in a bad mood anyway, due to people not paying their bills, or the stirring-up of feelings in spring. The wrangle with Rose has already commenced, has been going on forever, like a dream that goes back and back into other dreams, over hills and through doorways, maddeningly dim and populous and familiar and elusive. They are carting all the chairs out of the kitchen preparatory to the scrubbing, and they have also got to move some extra provisions for the store, some cartons of canned goods, tins of maple syrup, coal-oil cans, jars of vinegar. They take these things out to the woodshed. Brian, who is five or six by this time, is helping drag the tins.

"Yes," says Flo, carrying on from our lost starting point. "Yes, and that filth you taught to Brian."

"What filth?"

"And he doesn't know any better."

There is one step down from the kitchen to the woodshed, a bit of carpet on it so worn Rose can't ever remember seeing the pattern. Brian loosens it, dragging a tin.

"Two Vancouvers," she says softly.

Flo is back in the kitchen. Brian looks from Flo to Rose and Rose says again in a slightly louder voice, an encouraging singsong, "Two Vancouvers–"

"Fried in snot!" finishes Brian, not able to control himself any longer.

"Two pickled arseholes–"

"–tied in a knot!"

There it is. The filth.

> *Two Vancouvers fried in snot!*
> *Two pickled arseholes tied in a knot!*

Rose has known that for years, learned it when she first went to school. She came home and asked Flo, what is a Vancouver?

"It's a city. It's a long ways away."

"What else besides a city?"

Flo said, what did she mean, what else? How could it be fried, Rose said, approaching the dangerous moment, the delightful moment, when she would have to come out with the whole thing.

"Two Vancouvers fried in snot!/Two pickled arseholes tied in a knot!"

"You're going to get it!" cried Flo in a predictable rage. "Say that again and you'll get a good clout!"

Rose couldn't stop herself. She hummed it tenderly, tried saying the innocent words aloud, humming through the others. It was not just the words *snot* and *arsehole* that gave her pleasure, though of course they did. It was the pickling and tying and the unimaginable Vancouvers. She saw them in her mind shaped rather like octopuses, twitching in the pan. The tumble of reason; the spark and spit of craziness.

Lately she has remembered it again and taught it to Brian, to see if it has the same effect on him, and of course it has.

"Oh, I heard you!" says Flo. "I heard that! And I'm warning you!"

So she is. Brian takes the warning. He runs away, out the woodshed door, to do as he likes. Being a boy, free to help or not, involve himself or not. Not committed to the household struggle. They don't need him anyway, except to use against each other, they hardly notice his going. They continue, can't help continuing, can't leave each other alone. When they seem to have given up they really are just waiting and building up steam.

Flo gets out the scrub pail and the brush and the rag and the pad for her knees, a dirty red rubber pad. She starts to work on the floor. Rose sits on the kitchen table, the only place left to sit, swinging her legs. She can feel the cool oilcloth, because she is wearing shorts, last summer's tight faded shorts dug out of the summer-clothes bag. They smell a bit moldy from winter storage.

Flo crawls underneath, scrubbing with the brush, wiping with the rag. Her legs are long, white, and muscular, marked all over with blue veins as if somebody had been drawing rivers on them with an indelible pencil. An abnormal energy, a violent disgust, is expressed in the chewing of the brush at the linoleum, the swish of the rag.

What do they have to say to each other? It doesn't really matter. Flo speaks of Rose's smart-aleck behavior, rudeness and sloppiness and conceit. Her willingness to make work for others, her lack of gratitude. She mentions Brian's innocence, Rose's corruption. Oh, don't you think you're somebody, says Flo, and a moment later, Who do you think you are? Rose contradicts and objects with such poisonous reasonableness and mildness, displays theatrical unconcern. Flo goes beyond her ordinary scorn and self-possession and becomes amazingly theatrical herself, saying it was for Rose that she sacrificed her life. She saw her father saddled with a baby daughter and she thought, What is that man going to do? So she married him, and here she is, on her knees.

At that moment the bell rings, to announce a customer in the store. Because the fight is on, Rose is not permitted to go into the store and wait on whoever it is. Flo gets up and throws off her apron, groaning – but not communicatively; it is not a groan whose exasperation Rose is allowed to share – and goes in and serves. Rose hears her using her normal voice.

"About time! Sure is!"

She comes back and ties on her apron and is ready to resume.

"You never have a thought for anybody but your ownself! You never have a thought for what I'm doing."

"I never asked you to do anything. I wish you never had. I would have been a lot better off."

Rose says this smiling directly at Flo, who has not yet gone down on her knees. Flo sees the smile, grabs the scrub rag that is hanging on the side of the pail, and throws it at her. It may be meant to hit her in the face but instead it falls against Rose's leg and she raises her foot and catches it, swinging it negligently against her ankle.

"All right," says Flo. "You've done it this time. All right."

Rose watches her go to the woodshed door, hears her tramp through the woodshed, pause in the doorway, where the screen door hasn't yet been hung, and the storm door is standing open, propped with a brick. She calls Rose's father. She calls him in a warning, summoning voice, as if against her will preparing him for bad news. He will know what this is about.

The kitchen floor has five or six different patterns of linoleum on it. Ends, which Flo got for nothing and ingeniously trimmed and fitted together, bordering them with tin strips and tacks. While Rose sits on the table waiting, she looks at the floor, at this satisfying arrangement of rectangles, triangles, some other shape whose name she is trying to remember. She hears Flo coming back through the woodshed, on the creaky plank walk laid over the dirt floor. She is loitering, waiting too. She and Rose can carry this no further by themselves.

Rose hears her father come in. She stiffens, a tremor runs through her legs, she feels them shiver on the oilcloth. Called away from some peaceful, absorbing task, away from the words running in his head, called out of himself, her father has to say something. He says, "Well? What's wrong?"

Now comes another voice of Flo's. Enriched, hurt, apologetic, it seems to have been manufactured on the spot. She is sorry to have called him from his work. Would never have done it if Rose was not driving her to distraction. How to distraction? With her back talk and impudence and her terrible tongue. The things Rose has said to Flo are such that if Flo had said them to her mother, she knows her father would have thrashed her into the ground.

Rose tries to butt in, to say this isn't true.

What isn't true?

Her father raises a hand, doesn't look at her, says, "Be quiet."

When she says it isn't true, Rose means that she herself didn't start this, only responded, that she was goaded by Flo, who is now, she believes, telling the grossest sort of lies, twisting everything to suit herself. Rose puts aside her other knowledge that whatever Flo has said or done, whatever she herself has said or done, does not really matter at all. It is the struggle itself that counts, and that can't be stopped, can never be stopped, short of where it has got to now.

Flo's knees are dirty, in spite of the pad. The scrub rag is still hanging over Rose's foot.

Her father wipes his hands, listening to Flo. He takes his time. He is slow at getting into the spirit of things, tired in advance, maybe, on the verge of rejecting the role he has to play. He won't look at Rose, but at any sound or stirring from Rose, he holds up his hand.

"Well, we don't need the public in on this, that's for sure," Flo says, and she goes to lock the door of the store, putting in the store window the sign that says BACK SOON, a sign Rose made for her with a great deal of fancy curving and shading of letters in black and red crayon. When she comes back she shuts the door to the store, then the door to the stairs, then the door to the woodshed.

Her shoes have left marks on the clean wet part of the floor.

"Oh, I don't know," she says now, in a voice worn down from its emotional peak. "I don't know what to do about her." She looks down and sees her dirty knees (following Rose's eyes) and rubs at them viciously with her bare hands, smearing the dirt around.

"She humiliates me," she says, straightening up. There it is, the explanation. "She humiliates me," she repeats with satisfaction. "She has no respect."

"I do not!"

"Quiet, you!" says her father.

"If I hadn't called your father you'd still be sitting there with that grin on your face! What other way is there to manage you?"

Rose detects in her father some objections to Flo's rhetoric, some embarrassment and reluctance. She is wrong, and ought to know she is wrong, in thinking that she can count on this. The fact that she knows about it, and he knows she knows, will not make things any better. He is beginning to warm up. He gives her a look. This look is at first cold and challenging. It informs her of his judgment, of the hopelessness of her position. Then it clears, it begins to fill up with something else, the way a spring fills up when you clear the leaves away. It fills with hatred and pleasure. Rose sees that and knows it. Is that just a description of anger, should she see his eyes filling up with anger? No. Hatred is right. Pleasure is right. His face loosens and changes and grows younger, and he holds up his hand this time to silence Flo.

"All right," he says, meaning that's enough, more than enough, this part is over, things can proceed. He starts to loosen his belt.

Flo has stopped anyway. She has the same difficulty Rose does, a difficulty in believing that what you know must happen really will happen, that there comes a time when you can't draw back.

"Oh, I don't know, don't be too hard on her." She is moving around nervously as if she has thoughts of opening some escape route. "Oh, you don't have to use the belt on her. Do you have to use the belt?"

He doesn't answer. The belt is coming off, not hastily. It is being grasped at the necessary point. *All right you.* He is coming over to Rose. He pushes her off the table. His face, like his voice, is quite out of character. He is like a bad actor, who turns a part grotesque. As if he must savor and insist on just what is shameful and terrible about this. That is not to say he is pretending, that he is acting, and does not mean it. He is acting, and he means it. Rose knows that, she knows everything about him.

She has since wondered about murders, and murderers. Does the thing have to be carried through, in the end, partly for the effect, to prove to the audience of one – who won't be able to report, only register, the lesson – that such a thing can happen, that there is nothing that can't happen, that the most dreadful antic is justified, feelings can be found to match it?

She tries again looking at the kitchen floor, that clever and comforting geometrical arrangement, instead of looking at him or his belt. How can this go on in front of such daily witnesses – the linoleum, the calendar with the mill and creek and autumn trees, the old accommodating pots and pans?

Hold out your hand!

Those things aren't going to help her, none of them can rescue her. They turn bland and useless, even unfriendly. Pots can show malice, the patterns of linoleum can leer up at you, treachery is the other side of dailiness.

At the first, or maybe the second, crack of pain, she draws back. She will not accept it. She runs around the room, she tries to get to the doors. Her father blocks her off. Not an ounce of courage or of stoicism in her, it would seem. She runs, she screams, she implores. Her father is after her, cracking the belt at her when he can, then abandoning it and using his hands. Bang over the ear, then bang over the other ear. Back and forth, her head ringing. Bang in the face. Up against the wall and bang in the face again. He shakes her and hits her against the wall, he kicks her legs. She is incoherent, insane, shrieking. *Forgive me! Oh please, forgive me!*

Flo is shrieking too. *Stop, stop!*

Not yet. He throws Rose down. Or perhaps she throws herself down. He kicks her legs again. She has given up on words but is letting out a noise, the sort of noise that makes Flo cry, *Oh, what if people can hear her?* The very last-ditch willing sound of humiliation and defeat it is, for it seems Rose must play her part in this with the same grossness, the same exaggeration, that her father displays, playing his. She plays his victim with a self-indulgence that arouses, and maybe hopes to arouse, his final, sickened contempt.

They will give this anything that is necessary, it seems, they will go to any lengths.

Not quite. He has never managed really to injure her, though there are times, of course, when she prays that he will. He hits her with an open hand, there is some restraint in his kicks.

Now he stops, he is out of breath. He allows Flo to move in, he grabs Rose up and gives her a push in Flo's direction, making a sound of disgust. Flo retrieves her, opens the stair door, shoves her up the stairs.

"Go on up to your room now! Hurry!"

Rose goes up the stairs, stumbling, letting herself stumble, letting herself fall against the steps. She doesn't bang her door because a gesture like that could still bring him after her, and anyway, she is weak. She lies on the bed. She can hear through the stovepipe hole Flo snuffling and remonstrating, her father saying angrily that Flo should have kept quiet then, if she did not want Rose punished she should not have recommended it. Flo says she never recommended a hiding like that.

They argue back and forth on this. Flo's frightened voice is growing stronger, getting its confidence back. By stages, by arguing, they are being drawn back into themselves. Soon it's only Flo talking; he will not talk anymore. Rose has had to fight down her noisy sobbing, so as to listen to them, and when she loses interest in listening, and wants to sob some more, she finds she can't work herself up to it. She has passed into a state of calm, in which outrage is perceived as complete and final. In this state events and possibilities take on a lovely simplicity. Choices are mercifully clear. The words that come to mind are not the quibbling, seldom the conditional. "Never" is a word to which the right is suddenly established. She will never speak to them, she will never look at them with anything but loathing, she will never forgive them. She will punish them; she will finish them. Encased in these finalities, and in her bodily pain, she floats in curious comfort, beyond herself, beyond responsibility.

Suppose she dies now? Suppose she commits suicide? Suppose she runs away? Any of these things would be appropriate. It is only a matter of choosing, of figuring out the way. She floats in her pure superior state as if kindly drugged.

And just as there is a moment, when you are drugged, in which you feel perfectly safe, sure, unreachable, and then without warning and right next to it a moment in which you know the whole protection has fatally cracked, though it is still pretending to hold soundly together, so there is a moment now – the moment, in fact, when Rose hears Flo step on the stairs – that contains for her both present peace and freedom and a sure knowledge of the whole down-spiralling course of events from now on.

Flo comes into the room without knocking, but with a hesitation that shows it might have occurred to her. She brings a jar of cold cream. Rose is hanging on to advantage as long as she can, lying face down on the bed, refusing to acknowledge or answer.

"Oh, come on," Flo says uneasily. "You aren't so bad off, are you? You put some of this on and you'll feel better."

She is bluffing. She doesn't know for sure what damage has been done. She has the lid off the cold cream. Rose can smell it. The intimate, baby-ish, humiliating smell. She won't allow it near her. But in order to avoid it, the big ready clot of it in Flo's hand, she has to move. She scuffles, resists, loses dignity, and lets Flo see there is not really much the matter.

"All right," Flo says. "You win. I'll leave it here and you can put it on when you like."

Later still a tray will appear. Flo will put it down without a word and go away. A large glass of chocolate milk on it, made with Vita-Malt from the store. Some rich streaks of Vita-Malt around the bottom of the glass. Little sandwiches, neat and appetizing. Canned salmon of the first quality and reddest color, plenty of mayonnaise. A couple of butter tarts from a bakery package, chocolate biscuits with a peppermint filling. Rose's favorites, in the sandwich, tart, and cookie line. She will turn away, refuse to look, but left alone with these eatables will be miserably tempted; roused and troubled and drawn back from thoughts of suicide or flight by the smell of salmon, the anticipation of crisp chocolate, she will reach out a finger, just to run it around the edge of one of the sandwiches (crusts cut off!) to get the overflow, get a taste. Then she will decide to eat one, for strength to refuse the rest. One will not be noticed. Soon, in helpless corruption, she will eat them all. She will drink the chocolate milk, eat the tarts, eat the cookies. She will get the malty syrup out of the bottom of the glass with her finger, though she sniffles with shame. Too late.

Flo will come up and get the tray. She may say, "I see you got your appetite still," or, "Did you like the chocolate milk, was it enough syrup in it?" depending on how chastened she is feeling, herself. At any rate, all advantage will be lost. Rose will understand that life has started up again, that they will all sit around the table eating again, listening to the radio news. Tomorrow morning, maybe even tonight. Unseemly and unlikely as that may be. They will be embarrassed, but rather less than you might expect considering how they have behaved. They will feel a queer lassitude, a convalescent indolence, not far off satisfaction.

One night after a scene like this they were all in the kitchen. It must have been summer, or at least warm weather, because her father spoke of the old men who sat on the bench in front of the store.

"Do you know what they're talking about now?" he said, and nodded his head toward the store to show who he meant, though of course they were not there now, they went home at dark.

"Those old coots," said Flo. "What?"

There was about them both a geniality not exactly false but a bit more emphatic than was normal, without company.

Rose's father told them then that the old men had picked up the idea somewhere that what looked like a star in the western sky, the first star that came out after sunset, the evening star, was in reality an airship hovering over Bay City, Michigan, on the other side of Lake Huron. An American invention, sent up to rival the heavenly bodies. They were all in agreement about this, the idea was congenial to them. They believed it to be lit by ten thousand electric light bulbs. Her father had ruthlessly disagreed with them, pointing out that it was the planet Venus they saw, which had appeared in the sky long before the invention of an electric light bulb. They had never heard of the planet Venus.

"Ignoramuses," said Flo. At which Rose knew, and knew her father knew, that Flo had never heard of the planet Venus either. To distract them from this, or even apologize for it, Flo put down her teacup, stretched out with her head resting on the chair she had been sitting on and her feet on another chair (somehow she managed to tuck her dress modestly between her legs at the same time), and lay stiff as a board, so that Brian cried out in delight, "Do that! Do that!"

Flo was double-jointed and very strong. In moments of celebration or emergency she would do tricks.

They were silent while she turned herself around, not using her arms at all but just her strong legs and feet. Then they all cried out in triumph, though they had seen it before.

Just as Flo turned herself Rose got a picture in her mind of that airship, an elongated transparent bubble, with its strings of diamond lights, floating in the miraculous American sky.

"The planet Venus!" her father said, applauding Flo. "Ten thousand electric lights!"

There was a feeling of permission, relaxation, even a current of happiness, in the room.

YEARS LATER, many years later, on a Sunday morning, Rose turned on the radio. This was when she was living by herself in Toronto.

Well, sir.

It was a different kind of place in our day. Yes, it was.

It was all horses then. Horses and buggies. Buggy races up and down the main street on the Saturday nights.

"Just like the chariot races," says the announcer's, or interviewer's, smooth encouraging voice.

I never seen a one of them.

"No, sir, that was the old Roman chariot races I was referring to. That was before your time."

Musta been before my time. I'm a hunerd and two years old.

"That's a wonderful age, sir."

It is so.

She left it on, as she went around the apartment kitchen, making coffee for herself. It seemed to her that this must be a staged interview, a scene from some play, and she wanted to find out what it was. The old man's voice was so vain and belligerent, the interviewer's quite hopeless and alarmed, under its practiced gentleness and ease. You were surely meant to see him holding the microphone up to some toothless, reckless, preening centenarian, wondering what in God's name he was doing here, and what would he say next?

"They must have been fairly dangerous."

What was dangerous?

"Those buggy races."

They was. Dangerous. Used to be the runaway horses. Used to be a-plenty of accidents. Fellows was dragged along on the gravel and cut their face open. Wouldna matter so much if they was dead. Heh.

Some of them horses was the high-steppers. Some, they had to have the mustard under their tail. Some wouldn step out for nothin. That's the thing it is with the horses. Some'll work and pull till they drop down dead and some wouldn pull your cock out of a pail of lard. Hehe.

It must be a real interview after all. Otherwise they wouldn't have put that in, wouldn't have risked it. It's all right if the old man says it. Local color. Anything rendered harmless and delightful by his hundred years.

Accidents all the time then. In the mill. Foundry. Wasn't the precautions.

"You didn't have so many strikes then, I don't suppose? You didn't have so many unions?"

Everybody taking it easy nowadays. We worked and we was glad to get it. Worked and was glad to get it.

"You didn't have television."

Didn't have no TV. Didn't have no radio. No picture show.

"You made your own entertainment."

That's the way we did.

"You had a lot of experiences young men growing up today will never have."

Experiences.

"Can you recall any of them for us?"

I eaten groundhog meat one time. One winter. You wouldna cared for it. Heh.

There was a pause, of appreciation, it would seem, then the announcer's voice saying that the foregoing had been an interview with Mr. Wilfred Nettleton of Hanratty, Ontario, made on his hundred and second birthday, two weeks before his death, last spring. A living link with our past.

Mr. Nettleton had been interviewed in the Wawanash County Home for the Aged.

Hat Nettleton.

Horsewhipper into centenarian. Photographed on his birthday, fussed over by nurses, kissed no doubt by a girl reporter. Flashbulbs popping at him. Tape recorder drinking in the sound of his voice. Oldest resident. Oldest horsewhipper. Living link with our past.

Looking out from her kitchen window at the cold lake, Rose was longing to tell somebody. It was Flo who would enjoy hearing. She thought of her saying *Imagine!* in a way that meant she was having her worst suspicions gorgeously confirmed. But Flo was in the same place Hat Nettleton had died in, and there wasn't any way Rose could reach her. She had been there even when that interview was recorded, though she would not have heard it, would not have known about it. After Rose put her in the Home, a couple of years earlier, she had stopped talking. She had removed herself, and spent most of her time sitting in a corner of her crib, looking crafty and disagreeable, not answering anybody, though she occasionally showed her feelings by biting a nurse.

THE BEGGAR MAID

PATRICK BLATCHFORD was in love with Rose. This had become a fixed, even furious, idea with him. For her, a continual surprise. He wanted to marry her. He waited for her after classes, moved in and walked beside her, so that anybody she was talking to would have to reckon with his presence. He would not talk when these friends or classmates of hers were around, but he would try to catch her eye, so that he could indicate by a cold incredulous look what he thought of their conversation. Rose was flattered, but nervous. A girl named Nancy Falls, a friend of hers, mispronounced Metternich in front of him. He said to her later, "How can you be friends with people like that?"

Nancy and Rose had gone and sold their blood together, at Victoria Hospital. They each got fifteen dollars. They spent most of the money on evening shoes, tarty silver sandals. Then because they were sure the bloodletting had caused them to lose weight, they had hot fudge sundaes at Boomers. Why was Rose unable to defend Nancy to Patrick?

Patrick was twenty-four years old, a graduate student, planning to be a history professor. He was tall, thin, fair, and good-looking, though he had a long pale-red birthmark, dribbling like a tear down his temple and his cheek. He apologized for it, but said it was fading as he got older. When he was forty, it would have faded away. It was not the birthmark that cancelled out his good looks, Rose thought. (Something did cancel them out, or at least diminish them, for her; she had to keep reminding herself they were there.) There was something edgy, jumpy, disconcerting about him. His voice would break under stress – with her, it seemed he was always under stress – he knocked dishes and cups off tables, spilled drinks and bowls of peanuts, like a comedian. He was not a comedian; nothing could be further from his intentions. He came from British Columbia. His family was rich.

He arrived early to pick Rose up, when they were going to the movies. He wouldn't knock, he knew he was early. He sat on the step outside Dr. Henshawe's door. This was in the winter, it was dark out, but there was a little coach lamp beside the door.

"Oh, Rose! Come and look!" called Dr. Henshawe, in her soft, amused voice, and they looked down together from the dark window of the study. "The poor young man," said Dr. Henshawe tenderly. Dr. Henshawe was in her seventies. She was a former English professor, fastidious and lively. She had a lame leg, but a still youthfully, charmingly tilted head, with white braids wound around it.

She called Patrick poor because he was in love, and perhaps also because he was a male, doomed to push and blunder. Even from up here he looked stubborn and pitiable, determined and dependent, sitting out there in the cold.

"Guarding the door," Dr. Henshawe said. "Oh, Rose!"

Another time she said disturbingly, "Oh, dear, I'm afraid he is after the wrong girl."

Rose didn't like her saying that. She didn't like her laughing at Patrick. She didn't like Patrick sitting out on the steps that way, either. He was asking to be laughed at. He was the most vulnerable person Rose had ever known; he made himself so, didn't know anything about protecting himself. But he was also full of cruel judgments, he was full of conceit.

"YOU ARE A SCHOLAR, Rose," Dr. Henshawe would say. "This will interest you." Then she would read aloud something from the paper, or, more likely, something from *Canadian Forum* or the *Atlantic Monthly*. Dr. Henshawe had at one time headed the city's school board, she was a founding member of Canada's Socialist Party. She still sat on committees, wrote letters to the paper, reviewed books. Her father and mother had been medical missionaries; she had been born in China. Her house was small and perfect. Polished floors, glowing rugs, Chinese vases, bowls, and landscapes, black carved screens. Much that Rose could not appreciate, at the time. She could not really distinguish between the little jade animals on Dr. Henshawe's mantelpiece and the ornaments displayed in the jewelry-store window in Hanratty, though she could now distinguish between either of these and the things Flo bought from the five-and-ten.

She could not really decide how much she liked being at Dr. Henshawe's. At times she felt discouraged, sitting in the dining room with a linen napkin on her knee, eating from fine white plates on blue placemats. For one thing, there was never enough to eat, and she had taken to buying doughnuts and chocolate bars and hiding them in her room. The canary swung on its perch in the dining-room window and Dr. Henshawe directed conversation. She talked about politics, about writers. She mentioned Frank Scott and Dorothy Livesay. She said Rose must read them. Rose must read this, she must read that. Rose became sullenly determined not to. She was reading Thomas Mann. She was reading Tolstoy.

Before she came to Dr. Henshawe's, Rose had never heard of the working class. She took the designation home.

"This would have to be the last part of town where they put the sewers," Flo said.

"Of course," Rose said coolly. "This is the working-class part of town."

"*Working* class?" said Flo. "Not if the ones around here can help it."

Dr. Henshawe's house had done one thing. It had destroyed the naturalness, the taken-for-granted background, of home. To go back there was to go quite literally into a crude light. Flo had put fluorescent lights in the store and the kitchen. There was also, in a corner of the kitchen, a floor lamp Flo had won at Bingo; its shade was permanently wrapped in wide strips of cellophane. What Dr. Henshawe's house and Flo's house did best, in Rose's opinion, was discredit each other. In Dr. Henshawe's charming rooms there was always for Rose the raw knowledge of home, an indigestible lump, and at home now her sense of order and modulation elsewhere exposed such embarrassing sad poverty in people who never thought themselves poor. Poverty was not just wretchedness, as Dr. Henshawe seemed to think, it was not just deprivation. It meant having those ugly tube lights and being proud of them. It meant continual talk of money and malicious talk about new things people had bought and whether they were paid for. It meant pride and jealousy flaring over something like the new pair of plastic curtains, imitating lace, that Flo had bought for the front window.

That as well as hanging your clothes on nails behind the door and being able to hear every sound from the bathroom. It meant decorating your walls with a number of admonitions, pious and cheerful and mildly bawdy.

THE LORD IS MY SHEPHERD

BELIEVE IN THE LORD JESUS CHRIST AND THOU SHALL
BE SAVED

Why did Flo have those, when she wasn't even religious? They were what people had, common as calendars.

THIS IS MY KITCHEN AND I WILL DO AS I DARNED PLEASE

MORE THAN TWO PERSONS TO A BED IS DANGEROUS
AND UNLAWFUL

Billy Pope had brought that one. What would Patrick have to say about them? What would someone who was offended by a mispronunciation of Metternich think of Billy Pope's stories?

Billy Pope worked in Tyde's Butcher Shop. What he talked about most frequently now was the D.P., the Belgian, who had come to work there, and got on Billy Pope's nerves with his impudent singing of French songs and his naive notions of getting on in this country, buying a butcher shop of his own.

"Don't you think you can come over here and get yourself ideas," Billy Pope said to the D.P. "It's *youse* workin' for *us,* and don't think that'll change into *us* workin' for *youse.*" That shut him up, Billy Pope said.

Patrick would say from time to time that since her home was only fifty miles away he ought to come up and meet Rose's family.

"There's only my stepmother."

"It's too bad I couldn't have met your father."

Rashly, she had presented her father to Patrick as a reader of history, an amateur scholar. That was not exactly a lie, but it did not give a truthful picture of the circumstances.

"Is your stepmother your guardian?"

Rose had to say she did not know.

"Well, your father must have appointed a guardian for you in his will. Who administers his estate?"

His *estate*. Rose thought an estate was land, such as people owned in England.

Patrick thought it was rather charming of her to think that.

"No, his money and stocks and so on. What he left."

"I don't think he left any."

"Don't be silly," Patrick said.

AND SOMETIMES Dr. Henshawe would say, "Well, you are a scholar, you are not interested in that." Usually she was speaking of some event at the college: a pep rally, a football game, a dance. And usually she was right; Rose was not interested. But she was not eager to admit it. She did not seek or relish that definition of herself.

On the stairway wall hung graduation photographs of all the other girls, scholarship girls, who had lived with Dr. Henshawe. Most of them had got to be teachers, then mothers. One was a dietician, two were librarians, one was a professor of English, like Dr. Henshawe herself. Rose did not care for the look of them, for their soft-focused meekly smiling gratitude, their large teeth and maidenly rolls of hair. They seemed to be urging on her some deadly secular piety. There were no actresses among them, no brassy magazine journalists; none of them had latched on to the sort of life Rose wanted for herself. She wanted to perform in public. She thought she wanted to be an actress but she never tried to act, was afraid to go near the college drama productions. She knew she couldn't sing or dance. She would really have liked to play the harp, but she had no ear for music. She wanted to be known and envied, slim and clever. She told Dr. Henshawe that if she had been a man she would have wanted to be a foreign correspondent.

"Then you must be one!" cried Dr. Henshawe alarmingly. "The future will be wide open for women. You must concentrate on languages. You must take courses in political science. And economics. Perhaps you could get a job on the paper for the summer. I have friends there."

Rose was frightened at the idea of working on a paper, and she hated the introductory economics course; she was looking for a way of dropping it. It was dangerous to mention things to Dr. Henshawe.

SHE HAD GOT to live with Dr. Henshawe by accident. Another girl had been picked to move in but she got sick; she had t.b., and went instead to a sanatorium. Dr. Henshawe came up to the college office on the second day of registration to get the names of some other scholarship freshmen.

Rose had been in the office just a little while before, asking where the meeting of the scholarship students was to be held. She had lost her notice. The Bursar was giving a talk to the new scholarship students, telling them of ways to earn money and live cheaply and explaining the high standards of performance to be expected of them here if they wanted their payments to keep coming.

Rose found out the number of the room, and started up the stairs to the first floor. A girl came up beside her and said, "Are you on your way to three-oh-twelve, too?"

They walked together, telling each other the details of their scholarships. Rose did not yet have a place to live, she was staying at the Y. She did not really have enough money to be here at all. She had a scholarship for her tuition and the county prize to buy her books and a bursary of three hundred dollars to live on; that was all.

"You'll have to get a job," the other girl said. She had a larger bursary, because she was in science (that's where the money is, the money's all in science, she said seriously), but she was hoping to get a job in the cafeteria. She had a room in somebody's basement. How much does your room cost? How much does a hot plate cost? Rose asked her, her head swimming with anxious calculations.

This girl wore her hair in a roll. She wore a crêpe blouse, yellowed and shining from washing and ironing. Her breasts were large and sagging. She probably wore a dirty-pink hooked-up-the-side brassiere. She had a scaly patch on one cheek.

"This must be it," she said.

There was a little window in the door. They could look through at the other scholarship winners already assembled and waiting. It seemed to Rose that she saw four or five girls of the same stooped and matronly type as the girl who was beside her, and several bright-eyed, self-satisfied, babyish-looking boys. It seemed to be the rule that girl scholarship winners looked about forty and boys about twelve. It was not possible, of course, that they all looked like this. It was not possible that in one glance through the windows of the door Rose could detect traces of eczema, stained underarms, dandruff, moldy deposits on the teeth, and crusty flakes in the corners of the eyes. That was only what she thought. But there was a pall over them, she was not mistaken, there was a true terrible pall of eagerness and docility. How else could they have supplied so many right answers, so many pleasing answers, how else distinguished themselves and got themselves here? And Rose had done the same.

"I have to go to the john," she said.

She could see herself working in the cafeteria. Her figure, broad enough already, broadened out still more by the green cotton uniform, her face red and her hair stringy from the heat. Dishing up stew and fried chicken for those of inferior intelligence and handsomer means. Blocked off by the steam tables, the uniform, by decent hard work that nobody need be ashamed of, by publicly proclaimed braininess and poverty. Boys could get away with that, barely. For girls it was fatal. Poverty in girls is not attractive unless combined with sweet sluttishness, stupidity. Braininess is not attractive unless combined with some signs of elegance; *class.* Was this true, and was she foolish enough to care? It was; she was.

She went back to the first floor where the halls were crowded with ordinary students who were not on scholarships, who would not be expected to get A's and be grateful and live cheap. Enviable and innocent, they milled around the registration tables in their new purple-and-white blazers, their purple Frosh beanies, yelling reminders to each other, confused information, nonsensical insults. She walked among them feeling bitterly superior and despondent. The skirt of her green corduroy suit kept falling back between her legs as she walked. The material was limp; she should have spent more and bought the heavier weight. She thought now that the jacket was not properly cut either, though it had looked all right at home. The whole outfit had been made by a dress-maker in Hanratty, a friend of Flo's, whose main concern had been that there should be no revelations of the figure. When Rose asked if the skirt couldn't be made tighter this woman had said, "You wouldn't want your b.t.m. to show, now would you?" and Rose hadn't wanted to say she didn't care.

Another thing the dressmaker said was "I thought now you was through school you'd be getting a job and help out at home."

A woman walking down the hall stopped Rose.

"Aren't you one of the scholarship girls?"

It was the Registrar's secretary. Rose thought she was going to be reprimanded for not being at the meeting, and she was going to say she felt sick. She prepared her face for this lie. But the secretary said, "Come with me, now. I've got somebody I want you to meet."

Dr. Henshawe was making a charming nuisance of herself in the office. She liked poor girls, bright girls, but they had to be fairly good-looking girls.

"I think this could be your lucky day," the secretary said, leading Rose. "If you could put a pleasanter expression on your face."

Rose hated being told that, but she smiled obediently.

Within the hour she was taken home with Dr. Henshawe, installed in the house with the Chinese screens and vases, and told she was a scholar.

SHE GOT A JOB working in the library of the college, instead of in the cafeteria. Dr. Henshawe was a friend of the Head Librarian. Rose worked on Saturday afternoons. She worked in the stacks, putting books away. On Saturday afternoons in the fall the library was nearly empty, because of the football games. The narrow windows were open to the leafy campus, the football field, the dry fall country. The distant songs and shouts came drifting in.

The college buildings were not old at all, but they were built to look old. They were built of stone. The Arts Building had a tower, and the library had casement windows, which might have been designed for shooting arrows through. The buildings and the books in the library were what pleased Rose most about the place. The life that usually filled it, and that was now drained away, concentrated around the football field, letting loose those noises, seemed to her inappropriate and distracting. The cheers and songs were idiotic, if you listened to the words. What did they want to build such dignified buildings for if they were going to sing songs like that?

She knew enough not to reveal these opinions. If anybody said to her, "It's awful you have to work Saturdays and can't get to any of the games," she would fervently agree.

Once a man grabbed her bare leg, between her sock and her skirt. It happened in the Agriculture section, down at the bottom of the stacks. Only the faculty, graduate students, and employees had access to the stacks, though someone could have hoisted himself through a ground-floor window if he was skinny. She had seen a man crouched down looking at the books on a low shelf, further along. As she reached up to push a book into place he passed behind her. He bent and grabbed her leg, all in one smooth startling motion, and then was gone. She could feel for quite a while where his fingers had dug in. It didn't seem to her a sexual touch; it was more like a joke, though not at all a friendly one. She heard him run away, or felt him running; the metal shelves were vibrating. Then they stopped. There was no sound of him. She walked around looking between the stacks, looking into the carrels. Suppose she did see him, or bumped into him around a corner, what did she intend to do? She did not know. It was simply necessary to look for him, as in some tense childish game. She looked down at the sturdy pinkish calf of her leg. Amazing, that out of the blue somebody had wanted to blotch and punish it.

There were usually a few graduate students working in the carrels, even on Saturday afternoons. More rarely, a professor. Every carrel she looked into was empty, until she came to one in the corner. She poked her head in freely, by this time not expecting anybody. Then she had to say she was sorry.

There was a young man with a book on his lap, books on the floor, papers all around him. Rose asked him if he had seen anybody run past. He said no.

She told him what had happened. She didn't tell him because she was frightened or disgusted, as he seemed afterward to think, but just because she had to tell somebody; it was so odd. She was not prepared at all for his response. His long neck and face turned red, the flush entirely absorbing a birthmark down the side of his cheek. He was thin and fair. He stood up without any thought for the book in his lap or the papers in front of him. The book thumped on the floor. A great sheaf of papers, pushed across the desk, upset his ink bottle.

"How vile," he said.

"Grab the ink," Rose said. He leaned to catch the bottle and knocked it onto the floor. Fortunately the top was on, and it did not break.

"Did he hurt you?"

"No, not really."

"Come on upstairs. We'll report it."

"Oh, no."

"He can't get away with that. It shouldn't be allowed."

"There isn't anybody to report to," Rose said with relief. "The librarian goes off at noon on Saturdays."

"It's disgusting," he said in a high-pitched, excitable voice. Rose was sorry now that she had told him anything, and said she had to get back to work.

"Are you really all right?"

"Oh, yes."

"I'll be right here. Just call me if he comes back."

That was Patrick. If she had been trying to make him fall in love with her, there was no better way she could have chosen. He had many chivalric notions, which he pretended to mock, by saying certain words and phrases as if in quotation marks. "The fair sex," he would say, and "damsel in distress." Coming to his carrel with that story, Rose had turned herself into a damsel in distress. The pretended irony would not fool anybody; it was clear that he did wish to operate in a world of knights and ladies; outrages; devotions.

She continued to see him in the library, every Saturday, and often she met him walking across the campus or in the cafeteria. He made a point of greeting her with courtesy and concern, saying, "How are you?" in a way that suggested she might have suffered a further attack, or might still be recovering from the first one. He always flushed deeply when he saw her, and she thought that this was because the memory of what she had told him so embarrassed him. Later she found out it was because he was in love.

He discovered her name, and where she lived. He phoned her at Dr. Henshawe's house and asked her to go to the movies. At first when he said, "This is Patrick Blatchford speaking," Rose could not think who it was, but after a moment she recognized the high, rather aggrieved and tremulous voice. She said she would go. This was partly because Dr. Henshawe was always saying she was glad Rose did not waste her time running around with boys.

Rather soon after she started to go out with him, she said to Patrick, "Wouldn't it be funny if it was you who grabbed my leg that day in the library?"

He did not think it would be funny. He was horrified that she would think such a thing.

She said she was only joking. She said she meant that it would be a good twist in a story, maybe a Maugham story, or a Hitchcock movie. They had just been to see a Hitchcock movie.

"You know, if Hitchcock made a movie out of something like that, you could be a wild insatiable leg-grabber with one half of your personality, and the other half could be a timid scholar."

He didn't like that either.

"Is that how I seem to you, a timid scholar?" It seemed to her he deepened his voice, introduced a few growling notes, drew in his chin, as if for a joke. But he seldom joked with her; he didn't think joking was suitable when you were in love.

"I didn't say you were a timid scholar or a leg-grabber. It was just an idea."

After a while he said, "I suppose I don't seem very manly."

She was startled and irritated by such an exposure. He took such chances; had nothing ever taught him not to take such chances? But maybe he didn't, after all. He knew she would have to say something reassuring. Though she was hoping not to, she longed to say judiciously, "Well, no. You don't."

But that would not actually be true. He did seem masculine to her. Because he took those chances. Only a man could be so careless and demanding.

"We come from two different worlds," she said to him, on another occasion. She felt like a character in a play, saying that. "My people are poor people. You would think the place I lived in was a dump."

Now she was the one who was being dishonest, pretending to throw herself on his mercy, for of course she did not expect him to say, "Oh, well, if you come from poor people and live in a dump, then I will have to withdraw my offer."

"But I'm glad," said Patrick. "I'm glad you're poor. You're so lovely. You're like the Beggar Maid."

"Who?"

"'King Cophetua and the Beggar Maid.' You know. The painting. Don't you know that painting?"

Patrick had a trick – no, it was not a trick, Patrick had no tricks – Patrick had a way of expressing surprise, fairly scornful surprise, when people did not know something he knew, and similar scorn, similar surprise, whenever they had bothered to know something he did not. His arrogance and humility were both oddly exaggerated. The arrogance, Rose decided in time, must come from being rich, though Patrick was never arrogant about that in itself. His sisters, when she met them, turned out to be the same way, disgusted with anybody who did not know about horses or sailing, and just as disgusted by anybody knowing about music, say, or politics. Patrick and they could do little together but radiate disgust. But wasn't Billy Pope as bad, wasn't Flo as bad, when it came to arrogance? Maybe. There was a difference, though, and the difference was that Billy Pope and Flo were not protected. Things could get at them: D.P.'s; people speaking French on the radio; changes. Patrick and his sisters behaved as if things could never get at them. Their voices, when they quarrelled at the table, were astonishingly childish; their demands for food they liked, their petulance at seeing anything on the table they didn't like, were those of children. They had never had to defer and polish themselves and win favor in the world, they never would have to, and that was because they were rich.

Rose had no idea at the beginning how rich Patrick was. Nobody believed that. Everybody believed she had been calculating and clever, and she was so far from clever, in that way, that she really did not mind if they believed it. It turned out that other girls had been trying, and had not struck, as she had, the necessary note. Older girls, sorority girls, who had never noticed her before began to look at her with puzzlement and respect. Even Dr. Henshawe, when she saw that things were more serious than she had supposed, and settled Rose down to have a talk about it, assumed that she would have an eye on the money.

"It is no small triumph to attract the attentions of the heir to a mercantile empire," said Dr. Henshawe, being ironic and serious at the same time. "I don't despise wealth," she said. "Sometimes I wish I had some of it." (Did she really suppose she had not?) "I am sure you will learn how to put it to good uses. But what about your ambitions, Rose? What about your studies and your degree? Are you going to forget all that so soon?"

"Mercantile empire" was a rather grand way of putting it. Patrick's family owned a chain of department stores in British Columbia. All Patrick had said to Rose was that his father owned some stores. When she said *two different worlds* to him she was thinking that he probably lived in some substantial house like the houses in Dr. Henshawe's neighborhood. She was thinking of the most prosperous merchants in Hanratty. She could not realize what a coup she had made because it would have been a coup for her if the butcher's son had fallen for her, or the jeweller's; people would say she had done well.

She had a look at that painting. She looked it up in an art book in the library. She studied the Beggar Maid, meek and voluptuous, with her shy white feet. The milky surrender of her, the helplessness and gratitude. Was that how Patrick saw Rose? Was that how she could be? She would need that king, sharp and swarthy as he looked, even in his trance of passion, clever and barbaric. He could make a puddle of her, with his fierce desire. There would be no apologizing with him, none of that flinching, that lack of faith, that seemed to be revealed in all transactions with Patrick.

She could not turn Patrick down. She could not do it. It was not the amount of money but the amount of love he offered that she could not ignore; she believed that she felt sorry for him, that she had to help him out. It was as if he had come up to her in a crowd carrying a large, simple, dazzling object – a huge egg, maybe, of solid silver, something of doubtful use and punishing weight – and was offering it to her, in fact thrusting it at her, begging her to take some of the weight of it off him. If she thrust it back, how could he bear it? But that explanation left something out. It left out her own appetite, which was not for wealth but for worship. The size, the weight, the shine, of what he said was love (and she did not doubt him) had to impress her, even though she had never asked for it. It did not seem likely such an offering would come her way again. Patrick himself, though worshipful, did in some oblique way acknowledge her luck.

She had always thought this would happen, that somebody would look at her and love her totally and helplessly. At the same time she had thought that nobody would, nobody would want her at all, and up until now nobody had. What made you wanted was nothing you did, it was something you had, and how could you ever tell whether you had it? She would look at herself in the glass and think: Wife, sweetheart. Those mild lovely words. How could they apply to her? It was a miracle; it was a mistake. It was what she had dreamed of; it was not what she wanted.

She grew very tired, irritable, sleepless. She tried to think admiringly of Patrick. His lean, fair-skinned face was really very handsome. He must know a number of things. He graded papers, presided at examinations, he was finishing his thesis. There was a smell of pipe tobacco and rough wool about him that she liked. He was twenty-four. No other girl she knew who had a boyfriend had one as old as that.

Then without warning she thought of him saying, "I suppose I don't seem very manly." She thought of him saying, "Do you love me? Do you really love me?" He would look at her in a scared and threatening way. Then when she said yes he said how lucky he was, how lucky they were; he mentioned friends of his and their girls, comparing their love affairs unfavorably to his and Rose's. Rose would shiver with irritation and misery. She was sick of herself as much as him, she was sick of the picture they made at this moment, walking across a snowy downtown park, her bare hand snuggled in Patrick's, in his pocket. Some outrageous and cruel things were being shouted inside her. She had to do something, to keep them from getting out. She started tickling and teasing him.

Outside Dr. Henshawe's back door, in the snow, she kissed him, tried to make him open his mouth, she did scandalous things to him. When he kissed her his lips were soft; his tongue was shy; he collapsed over rather than held her, she could not find any force in him.

"You're lovely. You have lovely skin. Such fair eyebrows. You're so delicate."

She was pleased to hear that, anybody would be. But she said warningly, "I'm not so delicate, really. I'm quite large."

"You don't know how I love you. There's a book I have called *The White Goddess.* Every time I look at the title it reminds me of you."

She wriggled away from him. She bent down and got a handful of snow from the drift by the steps and clapped it on his head.

"My White God."

He shook the snow out. She scooped up some more and threw it at him. He didn't laugh; he was surprised and alarmed. She brushed the snow off his eyebrows and licked it off his ears. She was laughing, though she felt desperate rather than merry. She didn't know what made her do this.

"Dr. *Hen*-shawe," Patrick hissed at her. The tender poetic voice he used for rhapsodizing about her could entirely disappear, could change to remonstrance, exasperation, with no steps at all between.

"Dr. Henshawe will hear you!"

"Dr. Henshawe says you are an honorable young man," Rose said dreamily. "I think she's in love with you." It was true; Dr. Henshawe had said that. And it was true that he was. He couldn't bear the way Rose was talking. She blew at the snow in his hair. "Why don't you go in and deflower her? I'm sure she's a virgin. That's her window. Why don't you?" She rubbed his hair, then slipped her hand inside his overcoat and rubbed the front of his pants. "You're hard!" she said triumphantly. "Oh, Patrick! You've got a hard-on for Dr. Henshawe!" She had never said anything like this before, never come near behaving like this.

"Shut up!" said Patrick, tormented. But she couldn't. She raised her head and in a loud whisper pretended to call toward an upstairs window,

"Dr. Henshawe! Come and see what Patrick's got for you!" Her bullying hand went for his fly.

To stop her, to keep her quiet, Patrick had to struggle with her. He got a hand over her mouth, with the other hand beat her away from his zipper. The big loose sleeves of his overcoat beat at her like floppy wings. As soon as he started to fight she was relieved – that was what she wanted from him, some sort of action. But she had to keep resisting, until he really proved himself stronger. She was afraid he might not be able to.

But he was. He forced her down, down, to her knees, face down in the snow. He pulled her arms back and rubbed her face in the snow. Then he let her go, and almost spoiled it.

"Are you all right? Are you? I'm sorry. Rose?"

She staggered up and shoved her snowy face into his. He backed off.

"Kiss me! Kiss the snow! I love you!"

"Do you?" he said plaintively, and brushed the snow from a corner of her mouth and kissed her, with understandable bewilderment. "*Do* you?"

Then the light came on, flooding them and the trampled snow, and Dr. Henshawe was calling over their heads.

"Rose! Rose!"

She called in a patient, encouraging voice, as if Rose was lost in a fog nearby, and needed directing home.

"DO YOU LOVE HIM, Rose?" said Dr. Henshawe. "No, think about it. Do you?" Her voice was full of doubt and seriousness. Rose took a deep breath and answered as if filled with calm emotion, "Yes, I do."

"Well, then."

In the middle of the night Rose woke up and ate chocolate bars. She craved sweets. Often in class or in the middle of a movie she started thinking about fudge cupcakes, brownies, some kind of cake Dr. Henshawe bought at the European Bakery; it was filled with dollops of rich bitter chocolate that ran out on the plate. Whenever she tried to think about herself and Patrick, whenever she made up her mind to decide what she really felt, these cravings intervened.

She was putting on weight, and had developed a nest of pimples between her eyebrows.

Her bedroom was cold, being over the garage, with windows on three sides. Otherwise it was pleasant. Over the bed hung framed photographs of Greek skies and ruins, taken by Dr. Henshawe herself on her Mediterranean trip.

She was writing an essay on Yeats's plays. In one of the plays a young bride is lured away by the fairies from her sensible unbearable marriage. "Come away, O human child . . ." Rose read, and her eyes filled up with tears for herself, as if she was that shy elusive virgin, too fine for the bewildered peasants who have entrapped her. In actual fact she was the peasant, shocking high-minded Patrick, but he did not look for escape.

She took down one of those Greek photographs and defaced the wallpaper, writing the start of a poem which had come to her while she ate chocolate bars in bed and the wind from Gibbons Park banged at the garage walls.

> *Heedless in my dark womb*
> *I bear a madman's child . . .*

She never wrote any more if it, and wondered sometimes if she had meant headless. She never tried to rub it out, either.

PATRICK SHARED AN apartment with two other graduate students. He lived plainly, did not own a car or belong to a fraternity. His clothes had an ordinary academic shabbiness. His friends were the sons of teachers and ministers. He said his father had all but disowned him for becoming an intellectual. He said he would never go into business.

They came back to the apartment in the early afternoon when they knew both the other students would be out. The apartment was cold. They undressed quickly and got into Patrick's bed. Now was the time. They clung together, shivering and giggling. Rose was doing the giggling. She felt a need to be continually playful. She was terrified that they would not manage it, that there was a great humiliation in store, a great exposure of their poor deceits and stratagems. But the deceits and stratagems were only hers. Patrick was never a fraud; he managed, in spite of gigantic embarrassment, apologies; he passed through some amazed pantings and flounderings, to peace. Rose was no help, presenting instead of an honest passivity much twisting and fluttering eagerness, unpracticed counterfeit of passion. She was pleased when it was accomplished; she did not have to counterfeit that. They had done what others did, they had done what lovers did. She thought of celebration. What occurred to her was something delicious to eat, a sundae at Boomers, apple pie with hot cinnamon sauce. She was not at all prepared for Patrick's idea, which was to stay where they were and try again.

When pleasure presented itself, the fifth or sixth time they were together, she was thrown out of gear entirely, her passionate carrying-on was silenced.

Patrick said, "What's the matter?"

"Nothing!" Rose said, turning herself radiant and attentive once more. But she kept forgetting, the new developments interfered, and she had finally to give in to that struggle, more or less ignoring Patrick. When she could take note of him again she overwhelmed him with gratitude; she was really grateful now, and she wanted to be forgiven, though she could not say so, for all her pretended gratitude, her patronizing, her doubts.

Why should she doubt so much, she thought, lying comfortably in the bed while Patrick went to make some instant coffee. Might it not be possible, to feel as she pretended? If this sexual surprise was possible, wasn't anything? Patrick was not much help; his chivalry and self-abasement, next door to his scoldings, did discourage her. But wasn't the real fault hers? Her conviction that anyone who could fall in love with her must be hopelessly lacking, must finally be revealed as a fool? So she took note of anything that was foolish about Patrick, even though she thought she was looking for things that were masterful, admirable. At this moment, in his bed, in his room, surrounded by his books and clothes, his shoe brushes and typewriter, some tacked-up cartoons – she sat up in bed to look at them, and they really were quite funny, he must allow things to be funny when she was not here – she could see him as a likable, intelligent, even humorous person; no hero; no fool. Perhaps they could be ordinary. If only, when he came back in, he would not start thanking and fondling and worshipping her. She didn't like worship, really; it was only the idea of it she liked. On the other hand, she didn't like it when he started to correct and criticize her. There was much he planned to change.

Patrick loved her. What did he love? Not her accent, which he was trying hard to alter, though she was often mutinous and unreasonable, declaring in the face of all evidence that she did not have a country accent, everybody talked the way she did. Not her jittery sexual boldness (his relief at her virginity matched hers at his competence). She could make him flinch at a vulgar word, a drawling tone. All the time, moving and speaking, she was destroying herself for him, yet he looked right through her, through all the distractions she was creating, and loved some obedient image that she herself could not see. And his hopes were high. Her accent could be eliminated, her friends could be discredited and removed, her vulgarity could be discouraged.

What about all the rest of her? Energy, laziness, vanity, discontent, ambition? She concealed all that. He had no idea. For all her doubts about him, she never wanted him to fall out of love with her.

They made two trips.

They went to British Columbia, on the train, during the Easter holidays. His parents sent Patrick money for his ticket. He paid for Rose, using up what he had in the bank and borrowing from one of his roommates. He told her not to reveal to his parents that she had not paid for her own ticket. She saw that he meant to conceal that she was poor. He knew nothing about women's clothes, or he would not have thought that possible. Though she had done the best she could. She had borrowed Dr. Henshawe's raincoat for the coastal weather. It was a bit long, but otherwise all right, due to Dr. Henshawe's classically youthful tastes. She had sold more blood and bought a fuzzy angora sweater, peach-colored, which was extremely messy and looked like a small-town girl's idea of dressing up. She always realized things like that as soon as a purchase was made, not before.

Patrick's parents lived on Vancouver Island, near Sidney. About half an acre of clipped green lawn – green in the middle of winter; March seemed like the middle of winter to Rose – sloped down to a stone wall and a narrow pebbly beach and salt water. The house was half stone, half stucco-and-timber. It was built in the Tudor style, and others. The windows of the living room, the dining room, the den, all faced the sea, and because of the strong winds that sometimes blew onshore, they were made of thick glass, plate glass Rose supposed, like the windows of the automobile showroom in Hanratty. The seaward wall of the dining room was all windows, curving out in a gentle bay; you looked through the thick curved glass as through the bottom of a bottle. The sideboard too had a curving, gleaming belly, and seemed as big as a boat. Size was noticeable everywhere and particularly thickness. Thickness of towels and rugs and handles of knives and forks, and silences. There was a terrible amount of luxury and unease. After a day or so there Rose became so discouraged that her wrists and ankles felt weak. Picking up her knife and fork was a chore; cutting and chewing the perfect roast beef was almost beyond her; she got short of breath climbing the stairs. She had never known before how some places could choke you off, choke off your very life. She had not known this in spite of a number of very unfriendly places she had been in.

The first morning, Patrick's mother took her for a walk on the grounds, pointing out the greenhouse, the cottage where "the couple" lived: a charming, ivied, shuttered cottage, bigger than Dr. Henshawe's house. The couple, the servants, were more gentle-spoken, more discreet and dignified, than anyone Rose could think of in Hanratty, and indeed they were superior in these ways to Patrick's family.

Patrick's mother showed her the rose garden, the kitchen garden. There were many low stone walls.

"Patrick built them," said his mother. She explained anything with an indifference that bordered on distaste. "He built all these walls."

Rose's voice came out full of false assurance, eager and inappropriately enthusiastic.

"He must be a true Scot," she said. Patrick was a Scot, in spite of his name. The Blatchfords had come from Glasgow. "Weren't the best stonemasons always Scotsmen?" (She had learned quite recently not to say "Scotch.") "Maybe he had stonemason ancestors."

She cringed afterward, thinking of these efforts, the pretense of ease and gaiety, as cheap and imitative as her clothes.

"No," said Patrick's mother. "No. I don't think they were stonemasons." Something like fog went out from her: affront, disapproval, dismay. Rose thought that perhaps she had been offended by the suggestion that her husband's family might have worked with their hands. When she got to know her better – or had observed her longer; it was impossible to get to know her – she understood that Patrick's mother disliked anything fanciful, speculative, abstract, in conversation. She would also, of course, dislike Rose's chatty tone. Any interest beyond the factual consideration of the matter at hand – food, weather, invitations, furniture, servants – seemed to her sloppy, ill-bred, and dangerous. It was all right to say, "This is a warm day," but not, "This day reminds me of when we used to–" She hated people being *reminded*.

She was the only child of one of the early lumber barons of Vancouver Island. She had been born in a vanished northern settlement. But whenever Patrick tried to get her to talk about the past, whenever he asked her for the simplest sort of information – what steamers went up the coast, what year was the settlement abandoned, what was the route of the first logging railway – she would say irritably, "I don't know. How would I know about that?" This irritation was the strongest note that ever got into her words.

Neither did Patrick's father care for this concern about the past. Many things, most things, about Patrick seemed to strike him as bad signs.

"What do you want to know all that for?" he shouted down the table. He was a short square-shouldered man, red-faced, astonishingly belligerent. Patrick looked like his mother, who was tall, fair, and elegant in the most muted way possible, as if her clothes, her makeup, her style, were chosen with an ideal neutrality in mind.

"Because I am interested in history," said Patrick in an angry, pompous, but nervously breaking voice.

"Because-I-am-interested-in-history," said his sister Marion in an immediate parody, break and all. "History!"

45

The sisters Joan and Marion were younger than Patrick, older than Rose. Unlike Patrick they showed no nervousness, no cracks in self-satisfaction. At an earlier meal they had questioned Rose.

"Do you ride?"

"No."

"Do you sail?"

"No."

"Play tennis? Play golf? Play badminton?"

No. No. No.

"Perhaps she is an intellectual genius, like Patrick," the father said. And Patrick, to Rose's horror and embarrassment, began to shout at the table in general an account of her scholarships and prizes. What did he hope for? Was he so witless as to think such bragging would subdue them, would bring out anything but further scorn? Against Patrick, against his shouted boasts, his contempt for sports and television, his so-called intellectual interests, the family seemed united. But this alliance was only temporary. The father's dislike of his daughters was minor only in comparison with his dislike of Patrick. He railed at them too, when he could spare a moment; he jeered at the amount of time they spent at their games, complained about the cost of their equipment, their boats, their horses. And they wrangled with each other on obscure questions of scores and borrowings and damages. All complained to the mother about the food, which was plentiful and delicious. The mother spoke as little as possible to anyone and to tell the truth Rose did not blame her. She had never imagined so much true malevolence collected in one place. Billy Pope was a bigot and a grumbler, Flo was capricious, unjust, and gossipy, her father, when he was alive, had been capable of cold judgments and unremitting disapproval; but compared to Patrick's family, all Rose's people seemed jovial and content.

"Are they always like this?" she said to Patrick. "Is it me? They don't like me."

"They don't like you because I chose you," said Patrick with some satisfaction.

They lay on the stony beach after dark, in their raincoats, hugged and kissed and uncomfortably, unsuccessfully, attempted more. Rose got seaweed stains on Dr. Henshawe's coat. Patrick said, "You see why I need you? I need you so much!"

SHE TOOK HIM to Hanratty. It was just as bad as she had thought it would be. Flo had gone to great trouble, and cooked a meal of scalloped potatoes, turnips, big country sausages which were a special present from Billy Pope, from the butcher shop. Patrick detested coarse-textured food, and made no pretense of eating it. The table was spread with a plastic cloth, they ate under the tube of fluorescent light. The centerpiece was new and especially for the occasion. A plastic swan, lime green in color, with slits in the wings, in which were stuck folded, colored paper napkins. Billy Pope, reminded to take one, grunted, refused. Otherwise he was on dismally good behavior. Word had reached him, word had reached both Flo and Billy, of Rose's triumph. It had come from their superiors in Hanratty; otherwise they could not have believed it. Customers in the butcher shop – formidable ladies, the dentist's wife, the veterinarian's wife – had said to Billy Pope that they heard Rose had picked herself up a millionaire. Rose knew Billy Pope would go back to work tomorrow with stories of the millionaire, or millionaire's son, and that all these stories would focus on his – Billy Pope's – forthright and unintimidated behavior in the situation.

"We just set him down and give him some sausages, don't make no difference to us what he comes from!"

She knew Flo would have her comments too, that Patrick's nervousness would not escape her, that she would be able to mimic his voice and his flapping hands that had knocked over the ketchup bottle. But at present they both sat hunched over the table in miserable eclipse. Rose tried to start some conversation, talking brightly, unnaturally, rather as if she was an interviewer trying to draw out a couple of simple local people. She felt ashamed on more levels than she could count. She was ashamed of the food and the swan and the plastic tablecloth; ashamed for Patrick, the gloomy snob, who made a startled grimace when Flo passed him the toothpick-holder; ashamed for Flo with her timidity and hypocrisy and pretensions; most of all ashamed for herself. She didn't even have any way that she could talk, and sound natural. With Patrick there, she couldn't slip back into an accent closer to Flo's, Billy Pope's, and Hanratty's. That accent jarred on her ears now, anyway. It seemed to involve not just a different pronunciation but a whole different approach to talking. Talking was shouting; the words were separated and emphasized so that people could bombard each other with them. And the things people said were like lines from the most hackneyed rural comedy. *Wal, if a feller took a notion to,* they said. They really said that. Seeing them through Patrick's eyes, hearing them through his ears, Rose too had to be amazed.

She was trying to get them to talk about local history, some things she thought Patrick might be interested in. Presently, Flo did begin to talk; she could only be held in so long, whatever her misgivings. The conversation took another line from anything Rose had intended.

"The line I lived on when I was just young," Flo said, "it was the worst place ever created for suiciding."

"A line is a concession road. In the township," Rose said to Patrick. She had doubts about what was coming, and rightly so, for then Patrick got to hear about a man who cut his own throat, *his own throat,* from ear to ear; a man who shot himself the first time and didn't do enough damage, so he loaded up and fired again and managed it; another man who hanged himself using a chain, the kind of chain you hook on a tractor with, so it was a wonder his head was not torn off.

Tore off, Flo said.

She went on to a woman who, though not a suicide, had been dead in her house a week before she was found, and that was in the summer. She asked Patrick to imagine it. All this happened, said Flo, within five miles of where she herself was born. She was presenting credentials, not trying to horrify Patrick, at least not more than was acceptable in a social way; she did not mean to disconcert him. How could he understand that?

"You were right," said Patrick as they left Hanratty on the bus. "It is a dump. You must be glad to get away."

Rose felt immediately that he should not have said that.

"Of course that's not your real mother," Patrick said. "Your real parents can't have been like that." Rose did not like his saying that either, though it was what she believed herself. She saw that he was trying to provide for her a more genteel background, perhaps something like the homes of his poor friends: a few books about, a tea tray, and mended linen, worn good taste; proud, tired, educated people. What a coward he was, she thought angrily, but she knew that she herself was the coward, not knowing any way to be comfortable with her own people or the kitchen or any of it. Years later she would learn how to use it, she would be able to amuse or intimidate right-thinking people at dinner parties with glimpses of her early home. At the moment she felt confusion, misery.

Nevertheless her loyalty was starting. Now that she was sure of getting away, a layer of loyalty and protectiveness was hardening around every memory she had, around the store and the town, the flat, somewhat scrubby, unremarkable countryside. She would oppose this secretly to Patrick's views of mountains and ocean, his stone-and-timbered mansion. Her allegiances were far more proud and stubborn than his.

But it turned out he was not leaving anything behind.

PATRICK GAVE HER a diamond ring and announced that he was giving up being a historian for her sake. He was going into his father's business.

She said she thought he hated his father's business. He said that he could not afford to take such an attitude now that he would have a wife to support.

It seemed that Patrick's desire to marry, even to marry Rose, had been taken by his father as a sign of sanity. Great streaks of bounty were mixed in with all the ill will in that family. His father at once offered a job in one of the stores, offered to buy them a house. Patrick was as incapable of turning down this offer as Rose was of turning down Patrick's, and his reasons were as little mercenary as hers.

"Will we have a house like your parents'?" Rose said. She really thought it might be necessary to start off in that style.

"Well, maybe not at first. Not quite so—"

"I don't want a house like that! I don't want to live like that!"

"We'll live however you like. We'll have whatever kind of house you like."

Provided it's not a dump, she thought nastily.

Girls she hardly knew stopped and asked to see her ring, admired it, wished her happiness. When she went back to Hanratty for a weekend, alone this time, thank God, she met the dentist's wife on the main street.

"Oh, Rose, isn't it wonderful! When are you coming back again? We're going to give a tea for you, the ladies in town all want to give a tea for you!"

This woman had never spoken to Rose, never given any sign before of knowing who she was. Paths were opening now, barriers were softening. And Rose – oh, this was the worst, this was the shame of it – Rose, instead of cutting the dentist's wife, was blushing and skittishly flashing her diamond and saying yes, that would be a lovely idea. When people said how happy she must be she did think herself happy. It was as simple as that. She dimpled and sparkled and turned herself into a fiancée with no trouble at all. Where will you live, people said, and she said, Oh, in British Columbia! That added more magic to the tale. Is it really beautiful there, they said, is it never winter?

"Oh, yes!" cried Rose. "Oh, no!"

SHE WOKE UP EARLY, got up and dressed, and let herself out the side door of Dr. Henshawe's garage. It was too early for the buses to be running. She walked through the city to Patrick's apartment. She walked across the park. Around the South African War Memorial a pair of greyhounds were leaping and playing, an old woman standing by, holding their leashes. The sun was just up, shining on their pale hides. The grass was wet. Daffodils and narcissus in bloom.

Patrick came to the door, tousled, frowning sleepily, in his gray-and-maroon striped pajamas.

"Rose! What's the matter?"

She couldn't say anything. He pulled her into the apartment. She put her arms around him and hid her face against his chest and, in a stagy voice, said, "Please, Patrick. Please let me not marry you."

"Are you sick? What's the matter?"

"Please let me not marry you," she said again, with even less conviction.

"You're crazy."

She didn't blame him for thinking so. Her voice sounded so unnatural, wheedling, silly. As soon as he opened the door and she faced the fact of him, his sleepy eyes, his pajamas, she saw that what she had come to do was enormous, impossible. She would have to explain everything to him, and of course she could not do it. She could not make him see her necessity. She could not find any tone of voice, any expression of the face, that would serve her.

"Are you upset?" said Patrick. "What's happened?"

"Nothing."

"How did you get here anyway?"

"Walked."

She had been fighting back a need to go to the bathroom. It seemed that if she went to the bathroom she would destroy some of the strength of her case. But she had to. She freed herself. She said, "Wait a minute, I'm going to the john."

When she came out Patrick had the electric kettle going, was measuring out instant coffee. He looked decent and bewildered.

"I'm not really awake," he said. "Now. Sit down. First of all, are you premenstrual?"

"No." But she realized with dismay that she was, and that he might be able to figure it out, because they had been worried last month.

"Well, if you're not premenstrual, and nothing's happened to upset you, then what is all this about?"

"I don't want to get married," she said, backing away from the cruelty of *I don't want to marry you.*

"When did you come to this decision?"

"Long ago. This morning."

They were talking in whispers. Rose looked at the clock. It was a little after seven.

"When do the others get up?"

"About eight."

"Is there milk for the coffee?" She went to the refrigerator.

"Quiet with the door," said Patrick, too late.

"I'm sorry," she said, in her strange silly voice.

"We went for a walk last night and everything was fine. You come this morning and tell me you don't want to get married. *Why* don't you want to get married?"

"I just don't. I don't want to be married."

"What else do you want to do?"

"I don't know."

Patrick kept staring at her sternly, drinking his coffee. He who used to plead with her *do you love me, do you really,* did not bring the subject up now.

"Well, I know."

"What?"

"I know who's been talking to you."

"Nobody has been talking to me."

"Oh, no. Well, I bet Dr. Henshawe has."

"No."

"Some people don't have a very high opinion of her. They think she has an influence on girls. She doesn't like the girls who live with her to have boyfriends. Does she? You even told me that. She doesn't like them to be normal."

"That's not it."

"What did she say to you, Rose?"

"She didn't say anything." Rose began to cry.

"Are you sure?"

"Oh, Patrick, listen, please, I can't marry you, please, I don't know why, I can't, please, I'm sorry, believe me, I can't," Rose babbled at him, weeping, and Patrick saying, "Shh! You'll wake them up!" lifted or dragged her out of the kitchen chair and took her to his room, where she sat on the bed. He shut the door. She held her arms across her stomach, and rocked back and forth.

"What is it, Rose? What's the matter? Are you sick?"

"It's just so hard to tell you!"

"Tell me what?"

"What I just did tell you!"

"I mean have you found out you have to or something?"

"No!"

"Is there something in your family you haven't told me about? Insanity?" said Patrick encouragingly.

"No!" Rose rocked and wept.

"So what is it?"

"I don't love you!" she said. "I don't love you. I don't love you." She fell on the bed and put her head in the pillow. "I'm so sorry. I'm so sorry. I can't help it."

After a moment or two Patrick said, "Well. If you don't love me you don't love me. I'm not forcing you to." His voice sounded strained and spiteful, against the reasonableness of what he was saying. "I just wonder," he said, "if you know what you do want. I don't think you do. I don't think you have any idea what you want. You're just in a state."

"I don't have to know what I want to know what I don't want!" Rose said, turning over. This released her. "I never loved you."

"Shh. You'll wake them. We have to stop."

"I never loved you. I never wanted to. It was a mistake."

"All right. All right. You made your point."

"Why am I supposed to love you? Why do you act as if there was something wrong with me if I didn't? You despise me. You despise my family and my background and you think you are doing me a *great favor*—"

"I fell in love with you," Patrick said. "I don't despise you. Oh, Rose. I worship you."

"You're a sissy," Rose said. "You're a prude." She jumped off the bed with great pleasure as she said this. She felt full of energy. More was coming. Terrible things were coming.

"You don't even know how to make love right. I always wanted to get out of this from the very first. I felt sorry for you. You won't look where you're going, you're always knocking things over, just because you can't be bothered, you can't be bothered noticing anything, you're wrapped up in yourself, and you're always bragging, it's so stupid, you don't even know how to brag right, if you really want to impress people you'll never do it, the way you do it all they do is laugh at you!"

Patrick sat on the bed and looked up at her, his face open to whatever she would say. She wanted to beat and beat him, to say worse and worse, uglier and crueller, things. She took a breath, drew in air, to stop the things she felt rising in her from getting out.

"I don't want to see you, ever!" she said viciously. But at the door she turned and said in a normal and regretful voice, "Goodbye."

PATRICK WROTE HER a note: *I don't understand what happened the other day and I want to talk to you about it. But I think we should wait for two weeks and not see or talk to each other and find out how we feel at the end of that time.*

Rose had forgotten all about giving him back his ring. When she came out of his apartment building that morning she was still wearing it. She couldn't go back, and it seemed too valuable to send through the mail. She continued to wear it, mostly because she did not want to have to tell Dr. Henshawe what had happened. She was relieved to get Patrick's note. She thought that she could give him back the ring then.

She thought about what Patrick had said about Dr. Henshawe. No doubt there was some truth in that, else why should she be so reluctant to tell Dr. Henshawe she had broken her engagement, so unwilling to face her sensible approval, her restrained, relieved congratulations?

She told Dr. Henshawe that she was not seeing Patrick while she studied for her exams. Rose could see that even that pleased her.

She told no one that her situation had changed. It was not just Dr. Henshawe she didn't want knowing. She didn't like giving up being envied; the experience was so new to her.

She tried to think what to do next. She could not stay on at Dr. Henshawe's. It seemed clear that if she escaped from Patrick, she must escape from Dr. Henshawe too. And she did not want to stay on at the college, with people knowing about her broken engagement, with the girls who now congratulated her saying they had known all along it was a fluke, her getting Patrick. She would have to get a job.

The Head Librarian had offered her a job for the summer but that was perhaps at Dr. Henshawe's suggestion. Once she moved out, the offer might not hold. She knew that instead of studying for her exams she ought to be downtown, applying for work as a filing clerk at the insurance offices, applying at Bell Telephone, at the department stores. The idea frightened her. She kept on studying. That was the one thing she really knew how to do. She was a scholarship student after all.

On Saturday afternoon, when she was working at the library, she saw Patrick. She did not see him by accident. She went down to the bottom floor, trying not to make noise on the spiralling metal staircase. There was a place in the stacks where she could stand, almost in darkness, and see into his carrel. She did that. She couldn't see his face. She saw his long pink neck and the old plaid shirt he wore on Saturdays. His long neck. His bony shoulders. She was no longer irritated by him, no longer frightened by him; she was free. She could look at him as she would look at anybody. She could appreciate him. He had behaved well. He had not tried to rouse her pity, he had not bullied her, he had not molested her with pitiful telephone calls and letters. He had not come and sat on Dr. Henshawe's doorstep. He was an honorable person, and he would never know how she acknowledged that, how she was grateful for it. The things she had said to him made her ashamed now. And they were not even true. Not all of them. He did know how to make love. She was so moved, made so gentle and wistful, by the sight of him, that she wanted to give him something, some surprising bounty, she wished to undo his unhappiness.

Then she had a compelling picture of herself. She was running softly into Patrick's carrel, she was throwing her arms around him from behind, she was giving everything back to him. Would he take it from her, would he still want it? She saw them laughing and crying, explaining, forgiving. *I love you. I do love you, it's all right, I was terrible, I didn't mean it, I was just crazy, I love you, it's all right.* This was a violent temptation for her; it was barely resistible. She had an impulse to hurl herself. Whether it was off a cliff or into a warm bed of welcoming grass and flowers, she really could not tell.

It was not resistible, after all. She did it.

*   *   *

WHEN ROSE AFTERWARD reviewed and talked about this moment in her life – for she went through a period, like most people nowadays, of talking freely about her most private decisions, to friends and lovers and party acquaintances whom she might never see again, while they did the same – she said that comradely compassion had overcome her, she was not proof against the sight of a bare bent neck. Then she went further into it, and said greed, greed. She said she had run to him and clung to him and overcome his suspicions and kissed and cried and reinstated herself simply because she did not know how to do without his love and his promise to look after her; she was frightened of the world and she had not been able to think up any other plan for herself. When she was seeing life in economic terms, or was with people who did, she said that only middle-class people had choices anyway, that if she had had the price of a train ticket to Toronto her life would have been different.

Nonsense, she might say later, never mind that, it was really vanity, it was vanity pure and simple, to resurrect him, to bring him back his happiness. To see if she could do that. She could not resist such a test of power. She explained then that she had paid for it. She said that she and Patrick had been married ten years, and that during that time the scenes of the first breakup and reconciliation had been periodically repeated, with her saying again all the things she had said the first time, and the things she had held back, and many other things which occurred to her. She hopes she did not tell people (but thinks she did) that she used to beat her head against the bedpost, that she smashed a gravy boat through a dining-room window; that she was so frightened, so sickened by what she had done that she lay in bed, shivering, and begged and begged for his forgiveness. Which he granted. Sometimes she flew at him; sometimes he beat her. The next morning they would get up early and make a special breakfast; they would sit eating bacon and eggs and drinking filtered coffee, worn out, bewildered, treating each other with shamefaced kindness.

What do you think triggers the reaction? they would say.

Do you think we ought to take a holiday? A holiday together? Holidays alone?

A waste, a sham, those efforts, as it turned out. But they worked for the moment. Calmed down, they would say that most people probably went through the same things like this, in a marriage, and indeed they seemed to know mostly people who did. They could not separate until enough damage had been done, until nearly mortal damage had been done, to keep them apart. And until Rose could get a job and make her own money, so perhaps there was a very ordinary reason after all.

What she never said to anybody, never confided, was that she sometimes thought it had not been pity or greed or cowardice or vanity but something quite different, like a vision of happiness. In view of everything else she had told she could hardly tell that. It seems very odd; she can't justify it. She doesn't mean that they had perfectly ordinary, bearable times in their marriage, long busy stretches of wallpapering and vacationing and meals and shopping and worrying about a child's illness, but that sometimes, without reason or warning, happiness, the possibility of happiness, would surprise them. Then it was as if they were in different though identical-seeming skins, as if there existed a radiantly kind and innocent Rose and Patrick, hardly ever visible, in the shadow of their usual selves. Perhaps it was that Patrick she saw when she was free of him, invisible to him, looking into his carrel. Perhaps it was. She should have left him there.

SHE KNEW THAT was how she had seen him; she knows it, because it happened again. She was in Toronto Airport, in the middle of the night. This was about nine years after she and Patrick were divorced. She had become fairly well known by this time, her face was familiar to many people in this country. She did a television program on which she interviewed politicians, actors, writers, *personalities,* and many ordinary people who were angry about something the government or the police or a union had done to them. Sometimes she talked to people who had seen strange sights, UFOs, or sea monsters, or who had unusual accomplishments or collections, or kept up some obsolete custom.

She was alone. No one was meeting her. She had just come in on a delayed flight from Yellowknife. She was tired and bedraggled. She saw Patrick standing with his back to her, at a coffee bar. He wore a raincoat. He was heavier than he had been, but she knew him at once. And she had the same feeling that this was a person she was bound to, that by a certain magical yet possible trick, they could find and trust each other, and that to begin this all that she had to do was go up and touch him on the shoulder, surprise him with his happiness.

She did not do this, of course, but she did stop. She was standing still when he turned around, heading for one of the little plastic tables and curved seats grouped in front of the coffee bar. All his skinniness and academic shabbiness, his look of prim authoritarianism, was gone. He had smoothed out, filled out, into such a modish and agreeable, responsible, slightly complacent-looking man. His birthmark had faded. She thought how haggard and dreary she must look, in her rumpled trenchcoat, her long, graying hair fallen forward around her face, old mascara smudged under her eyes.

He made a face at her. It was a truly hateful, savagely warning, face; infantile, self-indulgent, yet calculated; it was a timed explosion of disgust and loathing. It was hard to believe. But she saw it.

Sometimes when Rose was talking to someone in front of the television cameras she would sense the desire in them to make a face. She would sense it in all sorts of people, in skillful politicians and witty liberal bishops and honored humanitarians, in housewives who had witnessed natural disasters and in workmen who had performed heroic rescues or been cheated out of disability pensions. They were longing to sabotage themselves, to make a face or say a dirty word. Was this the face they all wanted to make? To show somebody, to show everybody? They wouldn't do it, though; they wouldn't get the chance. Special circumstances were required. A lurid unreal place, the middle of the night, a staggering unhinging weariness, the sudden, hallucinatory appearance of your true enemy.

She hurried away then, down the long varicolored corridor, shaking. She had seen Patrick; Patrick had seen her; he had made that face. But she was not really able to understand how she could be an enemy. How could anybody hate Rose so much, at the very moment when she was ready to come forward with her good will, her smiling confession of exhaustion, her air of diffident faith in civilized overtures?

Oh, Patrick could. Patrick could.

THE TURKEY SEASON
To Joe Radford

WHEN I WAS FOURTEEN I got a job at the Turkey Barn for the Christmas season. I was still too young to get a job working in a store or as a part-time waitress; I was also too nervous.

I was a turkey gutter. The other people who worked at the Turkey Barn were Lily and Marjorie and Gladys, who were also gutters; Irene and Henry, who were pluckers; Herb Abbott, the foreman, who superintended the whole operation and filled in wherever he was needed. Morgan Elliott was the owner and boss. He and his son, Morgy, did the killing.

Morgy I knew from school. I thought him stupid and despicable and was uneasy about having to consider him in a new and possibly superior guise, as the boss's son. But his father treated him so roughly, yelling and swearing at him, that he seemed no more than the lowest of the workers. The other person related to the boss was Gladys. She was his sister, and in her case there did seem to be some privilege of position. She worked slowly and went home if she was not feeling well, and was not friendly to Lily and Marjorie, although she was, a little, to me. She had come back to live with Morgan and his family after working for many years in Toronto, in a bank. This was not the sort of job she was used to. Lily and Marjorie, talking about her when she wasn't there, said she had had a nervous breakdown. They said Morgan made her work in the Turkey Barn to pay for her keep. They also said, with no worry about the contradiction, that she had taken the job because she was after a man, and that the man was Herb Abbott.

All I could see when I closed my eyes, the first few nights after working there, was turkeys. I saw them hanging upside down, plucked and stiffened, pale and cold, with the heads and necks limp, the eyes and nostrils clotted with dark blood; the remaining bits of feathers – those

59

dark and bloody too – seemed to form a crown. I saw them not with aversion but with a sense of endless work to be done.

Herb Abbott showed me what to do. You put the turkey down on the table and cut its head off with a cleaver. Then you took the loose skin around the neck and stripped it back to reveal the crop, nestled in the cleft between the gullet and the windpipe.

"Feel the gravel," said Herb encouragingly. He made me close my fingers around the crop. Then he showed me how to work my hand down behind it to cut it out, and the gullet and windpipe as well. He used shears to cut the vertebrae.

"Scrunch, scrunch," he said soothingly. "Now, put your hand in."

I did. It was deathly cold in there, in the turkey's dark insides.

"Watch out for bone splinters."

Working cautiously in the dark, I had to pull the connecting tissues loose.

"Ups-a-daisy." Herb turned the bird over and flexed each leg. "Knees up, Mother Brown. Now." He took a heavy knife and placed it directly on the knee knuckle joints and cut off the shank.

"Have a look at the worms."

Pearly-white strings, pulled out of the shank, were creeping about on their own.

"That's just the tendons shrinking. Now comes the nice part!"

He slit the bird at its bottom end, letting out a rotten smell.

"Are you educated?"

I did not know what to say.

"What's that smell?"

"Hydrogen sulfide."

"Educated," said Herb, sighing. "All right. Work your fingers around and get the guts loose. Easy. Easy. Keep your fingers together. Keep the palm inwards. Feel the ribs with the back of your hand. Feel the guts fit into your palm. Feel that? Keep going. Break the strings – as many as you can. Keep going. Feel a hard lump? That's the gizzard. Feel a soft lump? That's the heart. Okay? Okay. Get your fingers around the gizzard. Easy. Start pulling this way. That's right. That's right. Start to pull her out."

It was not easy at all. I wasn't even sure what I had was the gizzard. My hand was full of cold pulp.

"Pull," he said, and I brought out a glistening, liverish mass.

"Got it. There's the lights. You know what they are? Lungs. There's the heart. There's the gizzard. There's the gall. Now, you don't ever want to break that gall inside or it will taste the entire turkey." Tactfully, he scraped out what I had missed, including the testicles, which were like a pair of white grapes.

"Nice pair of earrings," Herb said.

Herb Abbott was a tall, firm, plump man. His hair was dark and thin, combed straight back from a widow's peak, and his eyes seemed to be slightly slanted, so that he looked like a pale Chinese or like pictures of the Devil, except that he was smooth-faced and benign. Whatever he did around the Turkey Barn — gutting, as he was now, or loading the truck, or hanging the carcasses — was done with efficient, economical movements, quickly and buoyantly. "Notice about Herb — he always walks like he had a boat moving underneath him," Marjorie said, and it was true. Herb worked on the lake boats, during the season, as a cook. Then he worked for Morgan until after Christmas. The rest of the time he helped around the poolroom, making hamburgers, sweeping up, stopping fights before they got started. That was where he lived: he had a room above the poolroom on the main street.

In all the operations at the Turkey Barn it seemed to be Herb who had the efficiency and honor of the business continually on his mind; it was he who kept everything under control. Seeing him in the yard talking to Morgan, who was a thick, short man, red in the face, an unpredictable bully, you would be sure that it was Herb who was the boss and Morgan the hired help. But it was not so.

If I had not had Herb to show me, I don't think I could have learned turkey gutting at all. I was clumsy with my hands and had been shamed for it so often that the least show of impatience on the part of the person instructing me could have brought on a dithering paralysis. I could not stand to be watched by anybody but Herb. Particularly, I couldn't stand to be watched by Lily and Marjorie, two middle-aged sisters, who were very fast and thorough and competitive gutters.

They sang at their work and talked abusively and intimately to the turkey carcasses.

"Don't you nick me, you old bugger!"

"Aren't you the old crap factory!"

I had never heard women talk like that.

Gladys was not a fast gutter, though she must have been thorough; Herb would have talked to her otherwise. She never sang and certainly she never swore. I thought her rather old, though she was not as old as Lily and Marjorie; she must have been over thirty. She seemed offended by everything that went on and had the air of keeping plenty of bitter judgments to herself. I never tried to talk to her, but she spoke to me one day in the cold little washroom off the gutting shed. She was putting pancake makeup on her face. The color of the makeup was so distinct from the color of her skin that it was as if she were slapping orange paint over a whitewashed, bumpy wall.

She asked me if my hair was naturally curly.

I said yes.

"You don't have to get a permanent?"

"No."

"You're lucky. I have to do mine up every night. The chemicals in my system won't allow me to get a permanent."

There are different ways women have of talking about their looks. Some women make it clear that what they do to keep themselves up is for the sake of sex, for men. Others, like Gladys, make the job out to be a kind of housekeeping, whose very difficulties they pride themselves on. Gladys was genteel. I could see her in the bank, in a navy-blue dress with the kind of detachable white collar you can wash at night. She would be grumpy and correct.

Another time, she spoke to me about her periods, which were profuse and painful. She wanted to know about mine. There was an uneasy, prudish, agitated expression on her face. I was saved by Irene, who was using the toilet and called out, "Do like me, and you'll be rid of all your problems for a while." Irene was only a few years older than I was, but she was recently – tardily – married, and heavily pregnant.

Gladys ignored her, running cold water on her hands. The hands of all of us were red and sore-looking from the work. "I can't use that soap. If I use it, I break out in a rash," Gladys said. "If I bring my own soap in here, I can't afford to have other people using it, because I pay a lot for it – it's a special anti-allergy soap."

I think the idea that Lily and Marjorie promoted – that Gladys was after Herb Abbott – sprang from their belief that single people ought to be teased and embarrassed whenever possible, and from their interest in Herb, which led to the feeling that somebody ought to be after him. They wondered about him. What they wondered was, How can a man want so little? No wife, no family, no house. The details of his daily life, the small preferences, were of interest. Where had he been brought up? (Here and there and all over.) How far had he gone in school? (Far enough.) Where was his girlfriend? (Never tell.) Did he drink coffee or tea if he got the choice? (Coffee.)

When they talked about Gladys's being after him they must have really wanted to talk about sex – what he wanted and what he got. They must have felt a voluptuous curiosity about him, as I did. He aroused this feeling by being circumspect and not making the jokes some men did, and at the same time by not being squeamish or gentlemanly. Some men, showing me the testicles from the turkey, would have acted as if the very existence of testicles were somehow a bad joke on me, something a girl could be taunted about; another sort of man would have been embarrassed and would have thought he had to protect me from embarrassment. A man who didn't seem to feel one way or the other was an oddity – as much to older women, probably, as to me. But what was so welcome to me may have been disturbing to them. They wanted to jolt him. They even wanted Gladys to jolt him, if she could.

There wasn't any idea then – at least in Logan, Ontario, in the late forties – about homosexuality's going beyond very narrow confines. Women, certainly, believed in its rarity and in definite boundaries. There were homosexuals in town, and we knew who they were: an elegant, light-voiced, wavy-haired paperhanger who called himself an interior decorator; the minister's widow's fat, spoiled only son, who went so far as to enter baking contests and had crocheted a tablecloth;

a hypochondriacal church organist and music teacher who kept the choir and his pupils in line with screaming tantrums. Once the label was fixed, there was a good deal of tolerance for these people, and their talents for decorating, for crocheting, and for music were appreciated – especially by women. "The poor fellow," they said. "He doesn't do any harm." They really seemed to believe – the women did – that it was the penchant for baking or music that was the determining factor, and that it was this activity that made the man what he was – not any other detours he might take, or wish to take. A desire to play the violin would be taken as more a deviation from manliness than would a wish to shun women. Indeed, the idea was that any manly man would wish to shun women but most of them were caught off guard, and for good.

I don't want to go into the question of whether Herb was homosexual or not, because the definition is of no use to me. I think that probably he was, but maybe he was not. (Even considering what happened later, I think that.) He is not a puzzle so arbitrarily solved.

THE OTHER PLUCKER, who worked with Irene, was Henry Streets, a neighbor of ours. There was nothing remarkable about him except that he was eighty-six years old and still, as he said of himself, a devil for work. He had whisky in his thermos, and drank it from time to time through the day. It was Henry who said to me, in our kitchen, "You ought to get yourself a job at the Turkey Barn. They need another gutter." Then my father said at once, "Not her, Henry. She's got ten thumbs," and Henry said he was just joking – it was dirty work. But I was already determined to try it – I had a great need to be successful in a job like that. I was almost in the condition of a grown-up person who is ashamed of never having learned to read, so much did I feel my ineptness at manual work. Work, to everybody I knew, meant doing things I was no good at doing, and work was what people prided themselves on and measured each other by. (It goes without saying that the things I was good at, like schoolwork, were suspect or held in plain contempt.) So it was a surprise and then a triumph for me not to get fired, and to be able to turn out clean turkeys at a rate that was not disgraceful. I don't know if I really understood how much Herb Abbott was responsible for this, but he would sometimes say, "Good girl," or pat my waist and say, "You're getting to be a good gutter – you'll go a long ways in the world," and when I felt his quick, kind touch through the heavy sweater and bloody smock I wore, I felt my face glow and I wanted to lean back against him as he stood behind me. I wanted to rest my head against his wide, fleshy shoulder. When I went to sleep at night, lying on my side, I would run my cheek against the pillow and think of that as Herb's shoulder.

I was interested in how he talked to Gladys, how he looked at her or noticed her. This interest was not jealousy. I think I wanted something to happen with them. I quivered in curious expectation, as Lily and Marjorie did. We all wanted to see the flicker of sexuality in him, hear it in his voice, not because we thought it would make him seem more like other men but because we knew that with him it would be entirely different. He was kinder and more patient than most women, and as stern and remote, in some ways, as any man. We wanted to see how he could be moved.

If Gladys wanted this too, she didn't give any signs of it. It is impossible for me to tell with women like her whether they are as thick and deadly as they seem, not wanting anything much but opportunities for irritation and contempt, or if they are all choked up with gloomy fires and useless passions.

Marjorie and Lily talked about marriage. They did not have much good to say about it, in spite of their feeling that it was a state nobody should be allowed to stay out of. Marjorie said that shortly after her marriage she had gone into the woodshed with the intention of swallowing Paris green.

"I'd have done it," she said. "But the man came along in the grocery truck and I had to go out and buy the groceries. This was when we lived on the farm."

Her husband was cruel to her in those days, but later he suffered an accident – he rolled the tractor and was so badly hurt he would be an invalid all his life. They moved to town, and Marjorie was the boss now.

"He starts to sulk the other night and say he don't want his supper. Well, I just picked up his wrist and held it. He was scared I was going to twist his arm. He could see I'd do it. So I say, 'You *what?*' And he says, 'I'll eat it.'"

They talked about their father. He was a man of the old school. He had a noose in the woodshed (not the Paris green woodshed – this would be an earlier one, on another farm), and when they got on his nerves he used to line them up and threaten to hang them. Lily, who was the younger, would shake till she fell down. This same father had arranged to marry Marjorie off to a crony of his when she was just sixteen. That was the husband who had driven her to the Paris green. Their father did it because he wanted to be sure she wouldn't get into trouble.

"Hot blood," Lily said.

I was horrified, and asked, "Why didn't you run away?"

"His word was law," Marjorie said.

They said that was what was the matter with kids nowadays – it was the kids that ruled the roost. A father's word should be law. They brought up their own kids strictly, and none had turned out bad yet. When Marjorie's son wet the bed she threatened to cut off his dingy with the butcher knife. That cured him.

They said ninety percent of the young girls nowadays drank, and swore, and took it lying down. They did not have daughters, but if they did and caught them at anything like that they would beat them raw. Irene, they said, used to go to the hockey games with her ski pants slit and nothing under them, for convenience in the snowdrifts afterward. Terrible.

I wanted to point out some contradictions. Marjorie and Lily themselves drank and swore, and what was so wonderful about the strong will of a father who would insure you a lifetime of unhappiness? (What I did not see was that Marjorie and Lily were not unhappy altogether – could not be, because of their sense of consequence, their pride and style.) I could be enraged then at the lack of logic in most adults' talk – the way they held to their pronouncements no matter what evidence might be presented to them. How could these women's hands be so gifted, so delicate and clever – for I knew they would be as good at dozens of other jobs as they were at gutting; they would be good at quilting and darning and painting and papering and kneading dough and setting out seedlings – and their thinking so slapdash, clumsy, infuriating?

Lily said she never let her husband come near her if he had been drinking. Marjorie said since the time she nearly died with a hemorrhage she never let her husband come near her, period. Lily said quickly that it was only when he'd been drinking that he tried anything. I could see that it was a matter of pride not to let your husband come near you, but I couldn't quite believe that "come near" meant "have sex." The idea of Marjorie and Lily being sought out for such purposes seemed grotesque. They had bad teeth, their stomachs sagged, their faces were dull and spotty. I decided to take "come near" literally.

THE TWO WEEKS before Christmas was a frantic time at the Turkey Barn. I began to go in for an hour before school as well as after school and on weekends. In the morning, when I walked to work, the streetlights would still be on and the morning stars shining. There was the Turkey Barn, on the edge of a white field, with a row of big pine trees behind it, and always, no matter how cold and still it was, these trees were lifting their branches and sighing and straining. It seems unlikely that on my way to the Turkey Barn, for an hour of gutting turkeys, I should have experienced such a sense of promise and at the same time of perfect, impenetrable mystery in the universe, but I did. Herb had something to do with that, and so did the cold snap – the series of hard, clear mornings. The truth is, such feelings weren't hard to come by then. I would get them but not know how they were to be connected with anything in real life.

One morning at the Turkey Barn there was a new gutter. This was a boy eighteen or nineteen years old, a stranger named Brian. It seemed he was a relative, or perhaps just a friend, of Herb Abbott's. He was staying with Herb. He had worked on a lake boat last summer. He said he had got sick of it, though, and quit.

What he said was "Yeah, fuckin' boats, I got sick of that."

Language at the Turkey Barn was coarse and free, but this was one word never heard there. And Brian's use of it seemed not careless but flaunting, mixing insult and provocation. Perhaps it was his general style that made it so. He had amazing good looks: taffy hair, bright blue eyes,

67

ruddy skin, well-shaped body – the sort of good looks nobody disagrees about for a moment. But a single, relentless notion had got such a hold on him that he could not keep from turning all his assets into parody. His mouth was wet-looking and slightly open most of the time, his eyes were half shut, his expression a hopeful leer, his movements indolent, exaggerated, inviting. Perhaps if he had been put on a stage with a microphone and a guitar and let grunt and howl and wriggle and excite, he would have seemed a true celebrant. Lacking a stage, he was unconvincing. After a while he seemed just like somebody with a bad case of hiccups – his insistent sexuality was that monotonous and meaningless.

If he had toned down a bit, Marjorie and Lily would probably have enjoyed him. They could have kept up a game of telling him to shut his filthy mouth and keep his hands to himself. As it was, they said they were sick of him, and meant it. Once, Marjorie took up her gutting knife. "Keep your distance," she said. "I mean from me and my sister and that kid."

She did not tell him to keep his distance from Gladys, because Gladys wasn't there at the time and Marjorie would probably not have felt like protecting her anyway. But it was Gladys Brian particularly liked to bother. She would throw down her knife and go into the washroom and stay there ten minutes and come out with a stony face. She didn't say she was sick anymore and go home, the way she used to. Marjorie said Morgan was mad at Gladys for sponging and she couldn't get away with it any longer.

Gladys said to me, "I can't stand that kind of thing. I can't stand people mentioning that kind of thing and that kind of – gestures. It makes me sick to my stomach."

I believed her. She was terribly white. But why, in that case, did she not complain to Morgan? Perhaps relations between them were too uneasy, perhaps she could not bring herself to repeat or describe such things. Why did none of us complain – if not to Morgan, at least to Herb? I never thought of it. Brian seemed just something to put up with, like the freezing cold in the gutting shed and the smell of blood and waste. When Marjorie and Lily did threaten to complain, it was about Brian's laziness.

He was not a good gutter. He said his hands were too big. So Herb took him off gutting, told him he was to sweep and clean up, make packages of giblets, and help load the truck. This meant that he did not have to be in any one place or doing any one job at a given time, so much of the time he did nothing. He would start sweeping up, leave that and mop the tables, leave that and have a cigarette, lounge against the table bothering us until Herb called him to help load. Herb was very busy now and spent a lot of time making deliveries, so it was possible he did not know the extent of Brian's idleness.

"I don't know why Herb don't fire you," Marjorie said. "I guess the answer is he don't want you hanging around sponging on him, with no place to go."

"I know where to go," said Brian.

"Keep your sloppy mouth shut," said Marjorie. "I pity Herb. Getting saddled."

ON THE LAST school day before Christmas we got out early in the afternoon. I went home and changed my clothes and came in to work at about three o'clock. Nobody was working. Everybody was in the gutting shed, where Morgan Elliott was swinging a cleaver over the gutting table and yelling. I couldn't make out what the yelling was about, and thought someone must have made a terrible mistake in his work; perhaps it had been me. Then I saw Brian on the other side of the table, looking very sulky and mean, and standing well back. The sexual leer was not altogether gone from his face, but it was flattened out and mixed with a look of impotent bad temper and some fear. That's it, I thought, Brian is getting fired for being so sloppy and lazy. Even when I made out Morgan saying "pervert" and "filthy" and "maniac," I still thought that was what was happening. Marjorie and Lily, and even brassy Irene, were standing around with downcast, rather pious looks, such as children get when somebody is suffering a terrible bawling out at school. Only old Henry seemed able to keep a cautious grin on his face. Gladys was not to be seen. Herb was standing closer to Morgan than anybody else. He was not interfering but was keeping an eye on the cleaver. Morgy was blubbering, though he didn't seem to be in any immediate danger.

Morgan was yelling at Brian to get out. "And out of this town – I mean it – and don't you wait till tomorrow if you still want your arse in one piece! Out!" he shouted, and the cleaver swung dramatically towards the door. Brian started in that direction but, whether he meant to or not, he made a swaggering, taunting motion of the buttocks. This made Morgan break into a roar and run after him, swinging the cleaver in a stagy way. Brian ran, and Morgan ran after him, and Irene screamed and grabbed her stomach. Morgan was too heavy to run any distance and probably could not have thrown the cleaver very far, either. Herb watched from the doorway. Soon Morgan came back and flung the cleaver down on the table.

"All back to work! No more gawking around here! You don't get paid for gawking! What are you getting under way at?" he said, with a hard look at Irene.

"Nothing," Irene said meekly.

"If you're getting under way get out of here."

"I'm not."

"All right, then!"

We got to work. Herb took off his blood-smeared smock and put on his jacket and went off, probably to see that Brian got ready to go on the suppertime bus. He did not say a word. Morgan and his son went out to the yard, and Irene and Henry went back to the adjoining shed, where they did the plucking, working knee-deep in the feathers Brian was supposed to keep swept up.

"Where's Gladys?" I said softly.

"Recuperating," said Marjorie. She too spoke in a quieter voice than usual, and *recuperating* was not the sort of word she and Lily normally used. It was a word to be used about Gladys, with a mocking intent.

They didn't want to talk about what had happened, because they were afraid Morgan might come in and catch them at it and fire them. Good workers as they were, they were afraid of that. Besides, they hadn't seen anything. They must have been annoyed that they hadn't. All I ever found out was that Brian had either done something or shown something to

Gladys as she came out of the washroom and she had started screaming and having hysterics.

Now she'll likely be laid up with another nervous breakdown, they said. And he'll be on his way out of town. And good riddance, they said, to both of them.

I HAVE A PICTURE of the Turkey Barn crew taken on Christmas Eve. It was taken with a flash camera that was someone's Christmas extravagance. I think it was Irene's. But Herb Abbott must have been the one who took the picture. He was the one who could be trusted to know or to learn immediately how to manage anything new, and flash cameras were fairly new at the time. The picture was taken about ten o'clock on Christmas Eve, after Herb and Morgy had come back from making the last delivery and we had washed off the gutting table and swept and mopped the cement floor. We had taken off our bloody smocks and heavy sweaters and gone into the little room called the lunchroom, where there was a table and a heater. We still wore our working clothes: overalls and shirts. The men wore caps and the women kerchiefs, tied in the wartime style. I am stout and cheerful and comradely in the picture, transformed into someone I don't ever remember being or pretending to be. I look years older than fourteen. Irene is the only one who has taken off her kerchief, freeing her long red hair. She peers out from it with a meek, sluttish, inviting look, which would match her reputation but is not like any look of hers I remember. Yes, it must have been her camera; she is posing for it, with that look, more deliberately than anyone else is. Marjorie and Lily are smiling, true to form, but their smiles are sour and reckless. With their hair hidden, and such figures as they have bundled up, they look like a couple of tough and jovial but testy workmen. Their kerchiefs look misplaced; caps would be better. Henry is in high spirits, glad to be part of the work force, grinning and looking twenty years younger than his age. Then Morgy, with his hangdog look, not trusting the occasion's bounty, and Morgan very flushed and bosslike and satisfied. He has just given each of us our bonus turkey. Each of these turkeys has a leg or a wing missing, or a malformation of some kind, so none of them are salable at the full price. But Morgan has been at pains to tell us that you often get the best meat off the gimpy ones, and he has shown us that he's taking one home himself.

We are all holding mugs or large, thick china cups, which contain not the usual tea but rye whisky. Morgan and Henry have been drinking since suppertime. Marjorie and Lily say they only want a little, and only take it at all because it's Christmas Eve and they are dead on their feet. Irene says she's dead on her feet as well but that doesn't mean she only wants a little. Herb has poured quite generously not just for her but for Lily and Marjorie too, and they do not object. He has measured mine and Morgy's out at the same time, very stingily, and poured in Coca-Cola. This is the first drink I have ever had, and as a result I will believe for years that rye-and-Coca-Cola is a standard sort of drink and will always ask for it, until I notice that few other people drink it and that it makes me sick. I didn't get sick that Christmas Eve, though; Herb had not given me enough. Except for an odd taste, and my own feeling of consequence, it was like drinking Coca-Cola.

I don't need Herb in the picture to remember what he looked like. That is, if he looked like himself, as he did all the time at the Turkey Barn and the few times I saw him on the street – as he did all the times in my life when I saw him except one.

The time he looked somewhat unlike himself was when Morgan was cursing out Brian and, later, when Brian had run off down the road. What was this different look? I've tried to remember, because I studied it hard at the time. It wasn't much different. His face looked softer and heavier then, and if you had to describe the expression on it you would have to say it was an expression of shame. But what would he be ashamed of? Ashamed of Brian, for the way he had behaved? Surely that would be late in the day; when had Brian ever behaved otherwise? Ashamed of Morgan, for carrying on so ferociously and theatrically? Or of himself, because he was famous for nipping fights and displays of this sort in the bud and hadn't been able to do it here? Would he be ashamed that he hadn't stood up for Brian? Would he have expected himself to do that, to stand up for Brian?

All this was what I wondered at the time. Later, when I knew more, at least about sex, I decided that Brian was Herb's lover, and that Gladys really was trying to get attention from Herb, and that that was why Brian had humiliated her – with or without Herb's connivance and consent. Isn't it true that people like Herb – dignified, secretive, honorable people – will often choose somebody like Brian, will waste their helpless love on some vicious, silly person who is not even evil, or a monster, but just some importunate nuisance? I decided that Herb, with all his gentleness and carefulness, was avenging himself on us all – not just on Gladys but on us all – with Brian, and that what he was feeling when I studied his face must have been a savage and gleeful scorn. But embarrassment as well – embarrassment for Brian and for himself and for Gladys, and to some degree for all of us. Shame for all of us – that is what I thought then.

Later still, I backed off from this explanation. I got to a stage of backing off from the things I couldn't really know. It's enough for me now just to think of Herb's face with that peculiar, stricken look; to think of Brian monkeying in the shade of Herb's dignity; to think of my own mystified concentration on Herb, my need to catch him out, if I could ever get the chance, and then move in and stay close to him. How attractive, how delectable, the prospect of intimacy is, with the very person who will never grant it. I can still feel the pull of a man like that, of his promising and refusing. I would still like to know things. Never mind facts. Never mind theories, either.

When I finished my drink I wanted to say something to Herb. I stood beside him and waited for a moment when he was not listening to or talking with anyone else and when the increasingly rowdy conversation of the others would cover what I had to say.

"I'm sorry your friend had to go away."

"That's all right."

Herb spoke kindly and with amusement, and so shut me off from any further right to look at or speak about his life. He knew what I was up to. He must have known it before, with lots of women. He knew how to deal with it.

Lily had a little more whisky in her mug and told how she and her best girlfriend (dead now, of liver trouble) had dressed up as men one time and gone into the men's side of the beer parlor, the side where it said MEN ONLY, because they wanted to see what it was like. They sat in a corner drinking beer and keeping their eyes and ears open, and nobody looked twice or thought a thing about them, but soon a problem arose.

"Where were we going to go? If we went around to the other side and anybody seen us going into the ladies,' they would scream bloody murder. And if we went into the men's somebody'd be sure to notice we didn't do it the right way. Meanwhile the beer was going through us like a bugger!"

"What you don't do when you're young!" Marjorie said.

Several people gave me and Morgy advice. They told us to enjoy ourselves while we could. They told us to stay out of trouble. They said they had all been young once. Herb said we were a good crew and had done a good job but he didn't want to get in bad with any of the women's husbands by keeping them there too late. Marjorie and Lily expressed indifference to their husbands, but Irene announced that she loved hers and that it was not true that he had been dragged back from Detroit to marry her, no matter what people said. Henry said it was a good life if you didn't weaken. Morgan said he wished us all the most sincere Merry Christmas.

When we came out of the Turkey Barn it was snowing. Lily said it was like a Christmas card, and so it was, with the snow whirling around the streetlights in town and around the colored lights people had put up outside their doorways. Morgan was giving Henry and Irene a ride home in the truck, acknowledging age and pregnancy and Christmas. Morgy took a shortcut through the field, and Herb walked off by himself, head down and hands in his pockets, rolling slightly, as if he were on the deck of a lake boat. Marjorie and Lily linked arms with me as if we were old comrades.

"Let's sing," Lily said. "What'll we sing?"

"'We Three Kings'?" said Marjorie. "'We Three Turkey Gutters'?"

"'I'm Dreaming of a White Christmas.'"

"Why dream? You got it!"

So we sang.

THE MOONS OF JUPITER

I FOUND MY FATHER in the heart wing, on the eighth floor of Toronto General Hospital. He was in a semi-private room. The other bed was empty. He said that his hospital insurance covered only a bed in the ward, and he was worried that he might be charged extra.

"I never asked for a semi-private," he said.

I said the wards were probably full.

"No. I saw some empty beds when they were wheeling me by."

"Then it was because you had to be hooked up to that thing," I said. "Don't worry. If they're going to charge you extra, they tell you about it."

"That's likely it," he said. "They wouldn't want those doohickeys set up in the wards. I guess I'm covered for that kind of thing."

I said I was sure he was.

He had wires taped to his chest. A small screen hung over his head. On the screen a bright jagged line was continually being written. The writing was accompanied by a nervous electronic beeping. The behavior of his heart was on display. I tried to ignore it. It seemed to me that paying such close attention – in fact, dramatizing what ought to be a most secret activity – was asking for trouble. Anything exposed that way was apt to flare up and go crazy.

My father did not seem to mind. He said they had him on tranquilizers. You know, he said, the happy pills. He did seem calm and optimistic.

It had been a different story the night before. When I brought him into the hospital, to the emergency room, he had been pale and close-mouthed. He had opened the car door and stood up and said quietly, "Maybe you better get me one of those wheelchairs." He used the voice he always used in a crisis. Once, our chimney caught on fire; it was on a Sunday afternoon and I was in the dining room pinning together a dress I was making. He came in and said in that same matter-of-fact, warning voice, "Janet. Do you know where there's some baking powder?" He wanted it to throw on the fire. Afterwards he said, "I guess it was your fault – sewing on Sunday."

I had to wait for over an hour in the emergency waiting room. They summoned a heart specialist who was in the hospital, a young man. He called me out into the hall and explained to me that one of the valves of my father's heart had deteriorated so badly that there ought to be an immediate operation.

I asked him what would happen otherwise.

"He'd have to stay in bed," the doctor said.

"How long?"

"Maybe three months."

"I meant, how long would he live?"

"That's what I meant too," the doctor said.

I went to see my father. He was sitting up in bed in a curtained-off corner. "It's bad, isn't it?" he said. "Did he tell you about the valve?"

"It's not as bad as it could be," I said. Then I repeated, even exaggerated, anything hopeful the doctor had said. "You're not in any immediate danger. Your physical condition is good, otherwise."

"Otherwise," said my father gloomily.

I was tired from the drive – all the way up to Dalgleish, to get him, and back to Toronto since noon – and worried about getting the rented car back on time, and irritated by an article I had been reading in a magazine in the waiting room. It was about another writer, a woman younger, better-looking, probably more talented than I am. I had been in England for two months and so I had not seen this article before, but it crossed my mind while I was reading that my father would have. I could hear him saying, Well, I didn't see anything about you in *Maclean's*. And if he had read something about me he would say, Well, I didn't think too much of that write-up. His tone would be humorous and indulgent but would produce in me a familiar dreariness of spirit. The message I got from him was simple: Fame must be striven for, then apologized for. Getting or not getting it, you will be to blame.

I was not surprised by the doctor's news. I was prepared to hear something of the sort and was pleased with myself for taking it calmly, just as I would be pleased with myself for dressing a wound or looking down from the frail balcony of a high building. I thought, Yes, it's time; there has to be something, here it is. I did not feel any of the protest I would have felt twenty, even ten, years before. When I saw from my father's face that he felt it — that refusal leapt up in him as readily as if he had been thirty or forty years younger — my heart hardened, and I spoke with a kind of badgering cheerfulness. "Otherwise is plenty," I said.

THE NEXT DAY he was himself again.

That was how I would have put it. He said it appeared to him now that the young fellow, the doctor, might have been a bit too eager to operate. "A bit knife-happy," he said. He was both mocking and showing off the hospital slang. He said that another doctor had examined him, an older man, and had given it as his opinion that rest and medication might do the trick.

I didn't ask what trick.

"He says I've got a defective valve, all right. There's certainly some damage. They wanted to know if I had rheumatic fever when I was a kid. I said I didn't think so. But half the time then you weren't diagnosed what you had. My father was not one for getting the doctor."

The thought of my father's childhood, which I always pictured as bleak and dangerous — the poor farm, the scared sisters, the harsh father — made me less resigned to his dying. I thought of him running away to work on the lake boats, running along the railway tracks, toward Goderich, in the evening light. He used to tell about that trip. Somewhere along the track he found a quince tree. Quince trees are rare in our part of the country; in fact, I have never seen one. Not even the one my father found, though he once took us on an expedition to look for it. He thought he knew the crossroad it was near, but we could not find it. He had not been able to eat the fruit, of course, but he had been impressed by its existence. It made him think he had got into a new part of the world.

The escaped child, the survivor, an old man trapped here by his leaky heart. I didn't pursue these thoughts. I didn't care to think of his younger selves. Even his bare torso, thick and white – he had the body of a working-man of his generation, seldom exposed to the sun – was a danger to me; it looked so strong and young. The wrinkled neck, the age-freckled hands and arms, the narrow, courteous head, with its thin gray hair and mustache, were more what I was used to.

"Now, why would I want to get myself operated on?" said my father reasonably. "Think of the risk at my age, and what for? A few years at the outside. I think the best thing for me to do is go home and take it easy. Give in gracefully. That's all you can do, at my age. Your attitude changes, you know. You go through some mental changes. It seems more natural."

"What does?" I said.

"Well, death does. You can't get more natural than that. No, what I mean, specifically, is not having the operation."

"That seems more natural?"

"Yes."

"It's up to you," I said, but I did approve. This was what I would have expected of him. Whenever I told people about my father I stressed his independence, his self-sufficiency, his forbearance. He worked in a factory, he worked in his garden, he read history books. He could tell you about the Roman emperors or the Balkan wars. He never made a fuss.

JUDITH, MY YOUNGER daughter, had come to meet me at the Toronto Airport two days before. She had brought the boy she was living with, whose name was Don. They were driving to Mexico in the morning, and while I was in Toronto I was to stay in their apartment. For the time being, I live in Vancouver. I sometimes say I have my headquarters in Vancouver.

"Where's Nichola?" I said, thinking at once of an accident or an overdose. Nichola is my older daughter. She used to be a student at the Conservatory, then she became a cocktail waitress, then she was out of work. If she had been at the airport, I would probably have said something wrong. I would have asked her what her plans were, and she would have gracefully brushed back her hair and said, "Plans?" – as if that was a word I had invented.

"I knew the first thing you'd say would be about Nichola," Judith said.

"It wasn't. I said hello and I—"

"We'll get your bag," Don said neutrally.

"Is she all right?"

"I'm sure she is," said Judith, with a fabricated air of amusement. "You wouldn't look like that if I was the one who wasn't here."

"Of course I would."

"You wouldn't. Nichola is the baby of the family. You know, she's four years older than I am."

"I ought to know."

Judith said she did not know where Nichola was exactly. She said Nichola had moved out of her apartment (that dump!) and had actually telephoned (which is quite a deal, you might say, Nichola phoning) to say she wanted to be incommunicado for a while but she was fine.

"I told her you would worry," said Judith more kindly on the way to their van. Don walked ahead carrying my suitcase. "But don't. She's all right, believe me."

Don's presence made me uncomfortable. I did not like him to hear these things. I thought of the conversations they must have had, Don and Judith. Or Don and Judith and Nichola, for Nichola and Judith were sometimes on good terms. Or Don and Judith and Nichola and others whose names I did not even know. They would have talked about me. Judith and Nichola comparing notes, relating anecdotes; analyzing, regretting, blaming, forgiving. I wished I'd had a boy and a girl. Or two boys. They wouldn't have done that. Boys couldn't possibly know so much about you.

I did the same thing at that age. When I was the age Judith is now I talked with my friends in the college cafeteria or, late at night, over coffee in our cheap rooms. When I was the age Nichola is now I had Nichola herself in a carry-cot or squirming in my lap, and I was drinking coffee again on all the rainy Vancouver afternoons with my one neighborhood friend, Ruth Boudreau, who read a lot and was bewildered by her situation, as I was. We talked about our parents, our childhoods, though for some time we kept clear of our marriages. How thoroughly we dealt with our fathers and mothers, deplored their marriages, their mistaken ambitions or fear of ambition, how competently we filed them away, defined them beyond any possibility of change. What presumption.

I looked at Don walking ahead. A tall ascetic-looking boy, with a St. Francis cap of black hair, a precise fringe of beard. What right did he have to hear about me, to know things I myself had probably forgotten? I decided that his beard and hairstyle were affected.

Once, when my children were little, my father said to me, "You know those years you were growing up – well, that's all just a kind of a blur to me. I can't sort out one year from another." I was offended. I remembered each separate year with pain and clarity. I could have told how old I was when I went to look at the evening dresses in the window of Benbow's Ladies' Wear. Every week through the winter a new dress, spotlit – the sequins and tulle, the rose and lilac, sapphire, daffodil – and me a cold worshipper on the slushy sidewalk. I could have told how old I was when I forged my mother's signature on a bad report card, when I had measles, when we papered the front room. But the years when Judith and Nichola were little, when I lived with their father – yes, *blur* is the word for it. I remember hanging out diapers, bringing in and folding diapers; I can recall the kitchen counters of two houses and where the clothesbasket sat. I remember the television programs – *Popeye the Sailor, The Three Stooges, Funorama*. When *Funorama* came on it was time to turn on the lights and cook supper. But I couldn't tell the years apart. We lived outside Vancouver in a dormitory suburb: Dormir, Dormer, Dormouse – something like that. I was sleepy all the time then; pregnancy made me sleepy, and the night feedings, and the west coast rain falling. Dark dripping cedars, shiny dripping laurel; wives yawning, napping, visiting, drinking coffee, and folding diapers; husbands coming home at night from the city across the water. Every night I kissed my homecoming husband in his wet Burberry and hoped he might wake me up; I served up meat and potatoes and one of the four vegetables he permitted. He ate with a violent appetite, then fell asleep on the living-room sofa. We had become a cartoon couple, more middle-aged in our twenties than we would be in middle age.

Those bumbling years are the years our children will remember all their lives. Corners of the yards I never visited will stay in their heads.

"Did Nichola not want to see me?" I said to Judith.

"She doesn't want to see anybody, half the time," she said. Judith moved ahead and touched Don's arm. I knew that touch – an apology, an anxious reassurance. You touch a man that way to remind him that you are grateful, that you realize he is doing for your sake something that bores him or slightly endangers his dignity. It made me feel older than grandchildren would to see my daughter touch a man – a boy – this way. I felt her sad jitters, could predict her supple attentions. My blunt and stocky, blond and candid child. Why should I think she wouldn't be susceptible, that she would always be straightforward, heavy-footed, self-reliant? Just as I go around saying that Nichola is sly and solitary, cold, seductive. Many people must know things that would contradict what I say.

In the morning Don and Judith left for Mexico. I decided I wanted to see somebody who wasn't related to me, and who didn't expect anything in particular from me. I called an old lover of mine, but his phone was answered by a machine: "This is Tom Shepherd speaking. I will be out of town for the month of September. Please record your message, name, and phone number."

Tom's voice sounded so pleasant and familiar that I opened my mouth to ask him the meaning of this foolishness. Then I hung up. I felt as if he had deliberately let me down, as if we had planned to meet in a public place and then he hadn't shown up. Once, he had done that, I remembered.

I got myself a glass of vermouth, though it was not yet noon, and I phoned my father.

"Well, of all things," he said. "Fifteen more minutes and you would have missed me."

"Were you going downtown?"

"Downtown Toronto."

He explained that he was going to the hospital. His doctor in Dalgleish wanted the doctors in Toronto to take a look at him, and had given him a letter to show them in the emergency room.

"Emergency room?" I said.

"It's not an emergency. He just seems to think this is the best way to handle it. He knows the name of a fellow there. If he was to make me an appointment, it might take weeks."

"Does your doctor know you're driving to Toronto?" I said.

"Well, he didn't say I couldn't."

The upshot of this was that I rented a car, drove to Dalgleish, brought my father back to Toronto, and had him in the emergency room by seven o'clock that evening.

Before Judith left I said to her, "You're sure Nichola knows I'm staying here?"

"Well, I told her," she said.

Sometimes the phone rang, but it was always a friend of Judith's.

"WELL, IT LOOKS like I'm going to have it," my father said. This was on the fourth day. He had done a complete turnaround overnight. "It looks like I might as well."

I didn't know what he wanted me to say. I thought perhaps he looked to me for a protest, an attempt to dissuade him.

"When will they do it?" I said.

"Day after tomorrow."

I said I was going to the washroom. I went to the nurses' station and found a woman there who I thought was the head nurse. At any rate, she was gray-haired, kind, and serious-looking.

"My father's having an operation the day after tomorrow?" I said.

"Oh, yes."

"I just wanted to talk to somebody about it. I thought there'd been a sort of decision reached that he'd be better not to. I thought because of his age."

"Well, it's his decision and the doctor's." She smiled at me without condescension. "It's hard to make these decisions."

"How were his tests?"

"Well, I haven't seen them all."

I was sure she had. After a moment she said, "We have to be realistic. But the doctors here are very good."

When I went back into the room my father said, in a surprised voice, "*Shore*-less seas."

"What?" I said. I wondered if he had found out how much, or how little, time he could hope for. I wondered if the pills had brought on an untrustworthy euphoria. Or if he had wanted to gamble. Once, when he was talking to me about his life, he said, "The trouble was I was always afraid to take chances."

I used to tell people that he never spoke regretfully about his life, but that was not true. It was just that I didn't listen to it. He said that he should have gone into the Army as a tradesman – he would have been better off. He said he should have gone on his own, as a carpenter, after the war. He should have got out of Dalgleish. Once, he said, "A wasted life, eh?" But he was making fun of himself, saying that, because it was such a dramatic thing to say. When he quoted poetry too, he always had a scoffing note in his voice, to excuse the showing-off and the pleasure.

"Shoreless seas," he said again. "'Behind him lay the gray Azores, / Behind the Gates of Hercules; / Before him not the ghost of shores, / Before him only shoreless seas.' That's what was going through my head last night. But do you think I could remember what kind of seas? I could not. Lonely seas? Empty seas? I was on the right track but I couldn't get it. But there now when you came into the room and I wasn't thinking about it at all, the word popped into my head. That's always the way, isn't it? It's not all that surprising. I ask my mind a question. The answer's there, but I can't see all the connections my mind's making to get it. Like a computer. Nothing out of the way. You know, in my situation the thing is, if there's anything you can't explain right away, there's a great temptation to – well, to make a mystery out of it. There's a great temptation to believe in – You know."

"The soul?" I said, speaking lightly, feeling an appalling rush of love and recognition.

"Oh, I guess you could call it that. You know, when I first came into this room there was a pile of papers here by the bed. Somebody had left them here – one of those tabloid sort of things I never looked at. I started reading them. I'll read anything handy. There was a series running in them on personal experiences of people who had died, medically speaking – heart arrest, mostly – and had been brought back to life. It was what they remembered of the time when they were dead. Their experiences."

"Pleasant or un-?" I said.

"Oh, pleasant. Oh, yes. They'd float up to the ceiling and look down on themselves and see the doctors working on them, on their bodies. Then float on further and recognize some people they knew who had died before them. Not see them exactly but sort of sense them. Sometimes there would be a humming and sometimes a sort of – what's that light that there is or color around a person?"

"Aura?"

"Yes. But without the person. That's about all they'd get time for; then they found themselves back in the body and feeling all the mortal pain and so on – brought back to life."

"Did it seem – convincing?"

"Oh, I don't know. It's all in whether you want to believe that kind of thing or not. And if you are going to believe it, take it seriously, I figure you've got to take everything else seriously that they print in those papers."

"What else do they?"

"Rubbish – cancer cures, baldness cures, bellyaching about the younger generation and the welfare bums. Tripe about movie stars."

"Oh, yes. I know."

"In my situation you have to keep a watch," he said, "or you'll start playing tricks on yourself." Then he said, "There's a few practical details we ought to get straight on," and he told me about his will, the house, the cemetery plot. Everything was simple.

"Do you want me to phone Peggy?" I said. Peggy is my sister. She is married to an astronomer and lives in Victoria.

He thought about it. "I guess we ought to tell them," he said finally. "But tell them not to get alarmed."

"All right."

"No, wait a minute. Sam is supposed to be going to a conference the end of this week, and Peggy was planning to go along with him. I don't want them wondering about changing their plans."

"Where is the conference?"

"Amsterdam," he said proudly. He did take pride in Sam, and kept track of his books and articles. He would pick one up and say, "Look at that, will you? And I can't understand a word of it!" in a marvelling voice that managed nevertheless to have a trace of ridicule.

"Professor Sam," he would say. "And the three little Sams." This is what he called his grandsons, who did resemble their father in braininess and in an almost endearing pushiness – an innocent energetic showing-off. They went to a private school that favored old-fashioned discipline and started calculus in Grade 5. "And the dogs," he might enumerate further, "who have been to obedience school. And Peggy . . ."

But if I said, "Do you suppose she has been to obedience school too?" he would play the game no further. I imagine that when he was with Sam and Peggy he spoke of me in the same way – hinted at my flightiness just as he hinted at their stodginess, made mild jokes at my expense, did not quite conceal his amazement (or pretended not to conceal his amazement) that people paid money for things I had written. He had to do this so that he might never seem to brag, but he would put up the gates when the joking got too rough. And of course I found later, in the house, things of mine he had kept – a few magazines, clippings, things I had never bothered about.

Now his thoughts travelled from Peggy's family to mine. "Have you heard from Judith?" he said.

"Not yet."

"Well, it's pretty soon. Were they going to sleep in the van?"

"Yes."

"I guess it's safe enough, if they stop in the right places."

I knew he would have to say something more and I knew it would come as a joke.

"I guess they put a board down the middle, like the pioneers?"

I smiled but did not answer.

"I take it you have no objections?"

"No," I said.

"Well, I always believed that too. Keep out of your children's business. I tried not to say anything. I never said anything when you left Richard."

"What do you mean, 'said anything'? Criticize?"

"It wasn't any of my business."

"No."

"But that doesn't mean I was pleased."

I was surprised – not just at what he said but at his feeling that he had any right, even now, to say it. I had to look out the window and down at the traffic to control myself.

"I just wanted you to know," he added.

A long time ago, he said to me in his mild way, "It's funny. Richard when I first saw him reminded me of what my father used to say. He'd say if that fellow was half as smart as he thinks he is, he'd be twice as smart as he really is."

I turned to remind him of this, but found myself looking at the line his heart was writing. Not that there seemed to be anything wrong, any difference in the beeps and points. But it was there.

He saw where I was looking. "Unfair advantage," he said.

"It is," I said. "I'm going to have to get hooked up too."

We laughed, we kissed formally; I left. At least he hadn't asked me about Nichola, I thought.

THE NEXT AFTERNOON I didn't go to the hospital, because my father was having some more tests done, to prepare for the operation. I was to see him in the evening instead. I found myself wandering through the Bloor Street dress shops, trying on clothes. A preoccupation with fashion and my own appearance had descended on me like a raging headache. I looked at the women in the street, at the clothes in the shops, trying to discover how a transformation might be made, what I would have to buy. I recognized this obsession for what it was but had trouble shaking it. I've had people tell me that waiting for life-or-death news they've stood in front of an open refrigerator eating anything in sight – cold boiled potatoes, chili sauce, bowls of whipped cream. Or have been unable to stop doing crossword puzzles. Attention narrows in on something – some distraction – grabs on, becomes fanatically serious. I shuffled clothes on the racks, pulled them on in hot little changing rooms in front of cruel mirrors. I was sweating; once or twice I thought I might faint. Out on the street again, I thought I must remove myself from Bloor Street, and decided to go to the museum.

I remembered another time, in Vancouver. It was when Nichola was going to kindergarten and Judith was a baby. Nichola had been to the doctor about a cold, or maybe for a routine examination, and the blood test revealed something about her white blood cells – either that there were too many of them or that they were enlarged. The doctor ordered further tests, and I took Nichola to the hospital for them. Nobody mentioned leukemia but I knew, of course, what they were looking for. When I took Nichola home I asked the babysitter who had been with Judith to stay for the afternoon and I went shopping. I bought the most daring dress I ever owned, a black silk sheath with some laced-up arrangement in front. I remembered that bright spring afternoon, the spike-heeled shoes in the department store, the underwear printed with leopard spots.

I also remembered going home from St. Paul's Hospital over the Lions Gate Bridge on the crowded bus and holding Nichola on my knee. She suddenly recalled her baby name for *bridge* and whispered to me, "Whee – over the whee." I did not avoid touching my child – Nichola was slender and graceful even then, with a pretty back and fine dark hair – but realized I was touching her with a difference, though I did not think it could ever be detected. There was a care – not a withdrawal exactly but a care – not to feel anything much. I saw how the forms of love might be maintained with a condemned person but with the love in fact measured and disciplined, because you have to survive. It could be done so discreetly that the object of such care would not suspect, any more than she would suspect the sentence of death itself. Nichola did not know, would not know. Toys and kisses and jokes would come tumbling over her; she would never know, though I worried that she would feel the wind between the cracks of the manufactured holidays, the manufactured normal days. But all was well. Nichola did not have leukemia. She grew up – was still alive, and possibly happy. Incommunicado.

I could not think of anything in the museum I really wanted to see, so I walked past it to the planetarium. I had never been to a planetarium. The show was due to start in ten minutes. I went inside, bought a ticket, got in line. There was a whole class of schoolchildren, maybe a couple of classes, with teachers and volunteer mothers riding herd on them. I looked around to see if there were any other unattached adults.

Only one – a man with a red face and puffy eyes, who looked as if he might be here to keep himself from going to a bar.

Inside, we sat on wonderfully comfortable seats that were tilted back so that you lay in a sort of hammock, attention directed to the bowl of the ceiling, which soon turned dark blue, with a faint rim of light all around the edge. There was some splendid, commanding music. The adults all around were shushing the children, trying to make them stop crackling their potato-chip bags. Then a man's voice, an eloquent professional voice, began to speak slowly, out of the walls. The voice reminded me a little of the way radio announcers used to introduce a piece of classical music or describe the progress of the Royal Family to Westminster Abbey on one of their royal occasions. There was a faint echo-chamber effect.

The dark ceiling was filling with stars. They came out not all at once but one after another, the way the stars really do come out at night, though more quickly. The Milky Way appeared, was moving closer; stars swam into brilliance and kept on going, disappearing beyond the edges of the sky-screen or behind my head. While the flow of light continued, the voice presented the stunning facts. A few light-years away, it announced, the sun appears as a bright star, and the planets are not visible. A few dozen light-years away, the sun is not visible, either, to the naked eye. And that distance – a few dozen light-years – is only about a thousandth part of the distance from the sun to the center of our galaxy, one galaxy, which itself contains about two hundred billion suns. And is, in turn, one of millions, perhaps billions, of galaxies. Innumerable repetitions, innumerable variations. All this rolled past my head too, like balls of lightning.

Now realism was abandoned, for familiar artifice. A model of the solar system was spinning away in its elegant style. A bright bug took off from the earth, heading for Jupiter. I set my dodging and shrinking mind sternly to recording facts. The mass of Jupiter two and a half times that of all the other planets put together. The Great Red Spot. The thirteen moons. Past Jupiter, a glance at the eccentric orbit of Pluto, the icy rings of Saturn. Back to Earth and moving in to hot and dazzling Venus. Atmospheric pressure ninety times ours. Moonless Mercury rotating three times while circling the sun twice; an odd arrangement, not as satisfying as what they used to tell us – that it rotated once as it circled the sun. No perpetual darkness after all. Why did they give out such confident information, only to announce later that it was quite wrong? Finally, the picture already familiar from magazines: the red soil of Mars, the blooming pink sky.

When the show was over I sat in my seat while the children clambered across me, making no comments on anything they had just seen or heard. They were pestering their keepers for eatables and further entertainments. An effort had been made to get their attention, to take it away from canned pop and potato chips and fix it on various knowns and unknowns and horrible immensities, and it seemed to have failed. A good thing too, I thought. Children have a natural immunity, most of them, and it shouldn't be tampered with. As for the adults who would deplore it, the ones who promoted this show, weren't they immune themselves to the extent that they could put in the echo-chamber effects, the music, the churchlike solemnity, simulating the awe that they supposed they ought to feel? Awe – what was that supposed to be? A fit of the shivers when you looked out the window? Once you know what it was, you wouldn't be courting it.

Two men came with brooms to sweep up the debris the audience had left behind. They told me that the next show would start in forty minutes. In the meantime, I had to get out.

"I WENT TO THE show at the planetarium," I said to my father. "It was very exciting – about the solar system." I thought what a silly word I had used: *exciting.* "It's like a slightly phony temple," I added.

He was already talking. "I remember when they found Pluto. Right where they thought it had to be. Mercury, Venus, Earth, Mars," he recited. "Jupiter, Saturn, Nept – no, Uranus, Neptune, Pluto. Is that right?"

"Yes," I said. I was just as glad he hadn't heard what I said about the phony temple. I had meant that to be truthful, but it sounded slick and superior. "Tell me the moons of Jupiter."

"Well, I don't know the new ones. There's a bunch of new ones, isn't there?"

"Two. But they're not new."

"New to us," said my father. "You've turned pretty cheeky now I'm going under the knife."

"'Under the knife.' What an expression."

He was not in bed tonight, his last night. He had been detached from his apparatus, and was sitting in a chair by the window. He was bare-legged, wearing a hospital dressing gown, but he did not look self-conscious or out of place. He looked thoughtful but good-humored, an affable host.

"You haven't even named the old ones," I said.

"Give me time. Galileo named them. Io."

"That's a start."

"The moons of Jupiter were the first heavenly bodies discovered with the telescope." He said this gravely, as if he could see the sentence in an old book. "It wasn't Galileo named them, either; it was some German. Io, Europa, Ganymede, Callisto. There you are."

"Yes."

"Io and Europa, they were girlfriends of Jupiter's, weren't they? Ganymede was a boy. A shepherd? I don't know who Callisto was."

"I think she was a girlfriend too," I said. "Jupiter's wife – Jove's wife – changed her into a bear and stuck her up in the sky. Great Bear and Little Bear. Little Bear was her baby."

The loudspeaker said that it was time for visitors to go.

"I'll see you when you come out of the anesthetic," I said.

"Yes."

When I was at the door, he called to me, "Ganymede wasn't any shepherd. He was Jove's cupbearer."

WHEN I LEFT THE planetarium that afternoon, I had walked through the museum to the Chinese garden. I saw the stone camels again, the warriors, the tomb. I sat on a bench looking toward Bloor Street. Through the evergreen bushes and the high grilled iron fence I watched people going by in the late-afternoon sunlight. The planetarium show had done what I wanted it to after all – calmed me down, drained me.

I saw a girl who reminded me of Nichola. She wore a trenchcoat and carried a bag of groceries. She was shorter than Nichola — not really much like her at all — but I thought that I might see Nichola. She would be walking along some street maybe not far from here — burdened, pre-occupied, alone. She was one of the grown-up people in the world now, one of the shoppers going home.

If I did see her, I might just sit and watch, I decided. I felt like one of those people who have floated up to the ceiling, enjoying a brief death. A relief, while it lasts. My father had chosen and Nichola had chosen. Someday, probably soon, I would hear from her, but it came to the same thing.

I meant to get up and go over to the tomb, to look at the relief carvings, the stone pictures, that go all the way around it. I always mean to look at them and I never do. Not this time, either. It was getting cold out, so I went inside to have coffee and something to eat before I went back to the hospital.

THE PROGRESS OF LOVE

I GOT A CALL at work, and it was my father. This was not long after I was divorced and started in the real-estate office. Both of my boys were in school. It was a hot enough day in September.

My father was so polite, even in the family. He took time to ask me how I was. Country manners. Even if somebody phones up to tell you your house is burning down, they ask first how you are.

"I'm fine," I said. "How are you?"

"Not so good, I guess," said my father, in his old way – apologetic but self-respecting. "I think your mother's gone."

I knew that *gone* meant *dead*. I knew that. But for a second or so I saw my mother in her black straw hat setting off down the lane. The word *gone* seemed full of nothing but a deep relief and even an excitement – the excitement you feel when a door closes and your house sinks back to normal and you let yourself loose into all the free space around you. That was in my father's voice too – behind the apology, a queer sound like a gulped breath. But my mother hadn't been a burden – she hadn't been sick a day – and far from feeling relieved at her death, my father took it hard. He never got used to living alone, he said. He went into the Netterfield County Home quite willingly.

He told me how he found my mother on the couch in the kitchen when he came in at noon. She had picked a few tomatoes, and was setting them on the windowsill to ripen; then she must have felt weak, and lain down. Now, telling this, his voice went wobbly – meandering, as you would expect – in his amazement. I saw in my mind the couch, the old quilt that protected it, right under the phone.

"So I thought I better call you," my father said, and he waited for me to say what he should do now.

*   *   *

MY MOTHER PRAYED on her knees at midday, at night, and first thing in the morning. Every day opened up to her to have God's will done in it. Every night she totted up what she'd done and said and thought, to see how it squared with Him. That kind of life is dreary, people think, but they're missing the point. For one thing, such a life can never be boring. And nothing can happen to you that you can't make use of. Even if you're wracked by troubles, and sick and poor and ugly, you've got your soul to carry through life like a treasure on a platter. Going upstairs to pray after the noon meal, my mother would be full of energy and expectation, seriously smiling.

She was saved at a camp meeting when she was fourteen. That was the same summer that her own mother – my grandmother – died. For a few years, my mother went to meetings with a lot of other people who'd been saved, some who'd been saved over and over again, enthusiastic old sinners. She could tell stories about what went on at those meetings, the singing and hollering and wildness. She told about one old man getting up and shouting, "Come down, O Lord, come down among us now! Come down through the roof and I'll pay for the shingles!"

She was back to being just an Anglican, a serious one, by the time she got married. She was twenty-five then, and my father was thirty-eight. A tall good-looking couple, good dancers, good cardplayers, sociable. But serious people – that's how I would try to describe them. Serious the way hardly anybody is anymore. My father was not religious in the way my mother was. He was an Anglican, an Orangeman, a Conservative, because that's what he had been brought up to be. He was the son who got left on the farm with his parents and took care of them till they died. He met my mother, he waited for her, they married; he thought himself lucky then to have a family to work for. (I have two brothers, and I had a baby sister who died.) I have a feeling that my father never slept with any woman before my mother, and never with her until he married her. And he had to wait, because my mother wouldn't get married until she had paid back to her own father every cent he had spent on her since her mother died. She had kept track of everything – board, books, clothes – so that she could pay it back. When she married, she had no nest egg, as teachers usually did, no hope chest, sheets, or dishes. My father used to say, with a sombre, joking face, that he had hoped to get a woman with money in the bank. "But you take the money in the bank, you have to take the face that goes with it," he said, "and sometimes that's no bargain."

THE HOUSE WE lived in had big, high rooms, with dark-green blinds on the windows. When the blinds were pulled down against the sun, I used to like to move my head and catch the light flashing through the holes and cracks. Another thing I liked looking at was chimney stains, old or fresh, which I could turn into animals, people's faces, even distant cities. I told my own two boys about that, and their father, Dan Casey, said, "See, your mom's folks were so poor, they couldn't afford TV, so they got these stains on the ceiling – your mom had to watch the stains on the ceiling!" He always liked to kid me about thinking poor was anything great.

WHEN MY FATHER was very old, I figured out that he didn't mind people doing new sorts of things – for instance, my getting divorced – as much as he minded them having new sorts of reasons for doing them.

Thank God he never had to know about the commune.

"The Lord never intended," he used to say. Sitting around with the other old men in the Home, in the long, dim porch behind the spirea bushes, he talked about how the Lord never intended for people to tear around the country on motorbikes and snowmobiles. And how the Lord never intended for nurses' uniforms to be pants. The nurses didn't mind at all. They called him "Handsome," and told me he was a real old sweetheart, a real old religious gentleman. They marvelled at his thick black hair, which he kept until he died. They washed and combed it beautifully, wet-waved it with their fingers.

Sometimes, with all their care, he was a little unhappy. He wanted to go home. He worried about the cows, the fences, about who was getting up to light the fire. A few flashes of meanness – very few. Once, he gave me a sneaky, unfriendly look when I went in; he said, "I'm surprised you haven't worn all the skin off your knees by now."

I laughed. I said, "What doing? Scrubbing floors?"

"Praying!" he said, in a voice like spitting.

He didn't know who he was talking to.

I DON'T REMEMBER my mother's hair being anything but white. My mother went white in her twenties, and never saved any of her young hair, which had been brown. I used to try to get her to tell what color brown.

"Dark."

"Like Brent, or like Dolly?" Those were two workhorses we had, a team.

"I don't know. It wasn't horsehair."

"Was it like chocolate?"

"Something like."

"Weren't you sad when it went white?"

"No. I was glad."

"Why?"

"I was glad that I wouldn't have hair anymore that was the same color as my father's."

Hatred is always a sin, my mother told me. Remember that. One drop of hatred in your soul will spread and discolor everything like a drop of black ink in white milk. I was struck by that and meant to try it, but knew I shouldn't waste the milk.

ALL THESE THINGS I remember. All the things I know, or have been told, about people I never even saw. I was named Euphemia, after my mother's mother. A terrible name, such as nobody has nowadays. At home they called me Phemie, but when I started to work, I called myself Fame. My husband, Dan Casey, called me Fame. Then in the bar of the Shamrock Hotel, years later, after my divorce, when I was going out, a man said to me, "Fame, I've been meaning to ask you, just what is it you are famous for?"

"I don't know," I told him. "I don't know, unless it's for wasting my time talking to jerks like you."

After that I thought of changing it altogether, to something like Joan, but unless I moved away from here, how could I do that?

IN THE SUMMER of 1947, when I was twelve, I helped my mother paper the downstairs bedroom, the spare room. My mother's sister, Beryl, was coming to visit us. These two sisters hadn't seen each other for years. Very soon after their mother died, their father married again. He went to live in Minneapolis, then in Seattle, with his new wife and his younger daughter, Beryl. My mother wouldn't go with them. She stayed on in the town of Ramsay, where they had been living. She was boarded with a childless couple who had been neighbors. She and Beryl had met only once or twice since they were grown up. Beryl lived in California.

The paper had a design of cornflowers on a white ground. My mother had got it at a reduced price, because it was the end of a lot. This meant we had trouble matching the pattern, and behind the door we had to do some tricky fitting with scraps and strips. This was before the days of pre-pasted wallpaper. We had a trestle table set up in the front room, and we mixed the paste and swept it onto the back of the paper with wide brushes, watching for lumps. We worked with the windows up, screens fitted under them, the front door open, the screen door closed. The country we could see through the mesh of screens and the wavery old window glass was all hot and flowering – milkweed and wild carrot in the pastures, mustard rampaging in the clover, some fields creamy with the buckwheat people grew then. My mother sang. She sang a song she said her own mother used to sing when she and Beryl were little girls.

> *"I once had a sweetheart, but now I have none.*
> *He's gone and he's left me to weep and to moan.*
> *He's gone and he's left me, but contented I'll be,*
> *For I'll get another one, better than he!"*

I was excited because Beryl was coming, a visitor, all the way from California. Also because I had gone to town in late June to write the Entrance Examinations, and was hoping to hear soon that I had passed with honors. Everybody who had finished Grade 8 in the country schools had to go into town to write those examinations. I loved that – the rustling sheets of foolscap, the important silence, the big stone high-school building, all the old initials carved in the desks, darkened with varnish. The first burst of summer outside, the green and yellow light, the townlike chestnut trees, and honeysuckle. And all it was was this same town, where I have lived now more than half my life. I wondered at it. And at myself, drawing maps with ease and solving problems, knowing quantities of answers. I thought I was so clever. But I wasn't clever enough to understand the simplest thing. I didn't even understand that examinations made no difference in my case. I wouldn't be going to high school. How could I? That was before there were school buses; you had to board in town. My parents didn't have the money. They operated on very little cash, as many farmers did then. The payments from the cheese factory were about all that came in regularly. And they didn't think of my life going in that direction, the high-school direction. They thought that I would stay at home and help my mother, maybe hire out to help women in the neighborhood who were sick or having a baby. Until such time as I got married. That was what they were waiting to tell me when I got the results of the examinations.

You would think my mother might have a different idea, since she had been a schoolteacher herself. But she said God didn't care. God isn't interested in what kind of job or what kind of education anybody has, she told me. He doesn't care two hoots about that, and it's what He cares about that matters.

This was the first time I understood how God could become a real opponent, not just some kind of nuisance or large decoration.

MY MOTHER'S NAME as a child was Marietta. That continued to be her name, of course, but until Beryl came I never heard her called by it. My father always said Mother. I had a childish notion – I knew it was childish – that Mother suited my mother better than it did other mothers. Mother, not Mama. When I was away from her, I could not think what my mother's face was like, and this frightened me. Sitting in school, just over a hill from home, I would try to picture my mother's face. Sometimes I thought that if I couldn't do it, that might mean my mother was dead. But I had a sense of her all the time, and would be reminded of her by the most unlikely things – an upright piano, or a tall white loaf of bread. That's ridiculous, but true.

Marietta, in my mind, was separate, not swallowed up in my mother's grown-up body. Marietta was still running around loose up in her town of Ramsay, on the Ottawa River. In that town, the streets were full of horses and puddles, and darkened by men who came in from the bush on weekends. Loggers. There were eleven hotels on the main street, where the loggers stayed, and drank.

The house Marietta lived in was halfway up a steep street climbing from the river. It was a double house, with two bay windows in front, and a wooden trellis that separated the two front porches. In the other half of the house lived the Sutcliffes, the people Marietta was to board with after her mother died and her father left town. Mr. Sutcliffe was an Englishman, a telegraph operator. His wife was German. She always made coffee instead of tea. She made strudel. The dough for the strudel hung down over the edges of the table like a fine cloth. It sometimes looked to Marietta like a skin.

Mrs. Sutcliffe was the one who talked Marietta's mother out of hanging herself.

Marietta was home from school that day, because it was Saturday. She woke up late and heard the silence in the house. She was always scared of that – a silent house – and as soon as she opened the door after school she would call, "Mama! Mama!" Often her mother wouldn't answer. But she would be there. Marietta would hear with relief the rattle of the stove grate or the steady slap of the iron.

That morning, she didn't hear anything. She came downstairs, and got herself a slice of bread and butter and molasses, folded over. She opened the cellar door and called. She went into the front room and peered out the window, through the bridal fern. She saw her little sister, Beryl, and some other neighborhood children rolling down the bit of grassy terrace to the sidewalk, picking themselves up and scrambling to the top and rolling down again.

"Mama?" called Marietta. She walked through the house to the back yard. It was late spring, the day was cloudy and mild. In the sprouting vegetable gardens, the earth was damp, and the leaves on the trees seemed suddenly full-sized, letting down drops of water left over from the rain of the night before.

"Mama?" calls Marietta under the trees, under the clothesline.

At the end of the yard is a small barn, where they keep firewood, and some tools and old furniture. A chair, a straight-backed wooden chair, can be seen through the open doorway. On the chair, Marietta sees her mother's feet, her mother's black laced shoes. Then the long, printed cotton summer work dress, the apron, the rolled-up sleeves. Her mother's shiny-looking white arms, and neck, and face.

Her mother stood on the chair and didn't answer. She didn't look at Marietta, but smiled and tapped her foot, as if to say, "Here I am, then. What are you going to do about it?" Something looked wrong about her, beyond the fact that she was standing on a chair and smiling in this queer, tight way. Standing on an old chair with back rungs missing, which she had pulled out to the middle of the barn floor, where it teetered on the bumpy earth. There was a shadow on her neck.

The shadow was a rope, a noose on the end of a rope that hung down from a beam overhead.

"Mama?" says Marietta, in a fainter voice. "Mama. Come down, please." Her voice is faint because she fears that any yell or cry might jolt her mother into movement, cause her to step off the chair and throw her weight on the rope. But even if Marietta wanted to yell she couldn't. Nothing but this pitiful thread of a voice is left to her — just as in a dream when a beast or a machine is bearing down on you.

"Go and get your father."

That was what her mother told her to do, and Marietta obeyed. With terror in her legs, she ran. In her nightgown, in the middle of a Saturday morning, she ran. She ran past Beryl and the other children, still tumbling down the slope. She ran along the sidewalk, which was at that time a boardwalk, then on the unpaved street, full of last night's puddles. The street crossed the railway tracks. At the foot of the hill, it intersected the main street of the town. Between the main street and the river were some warehouses and the buildings of small manufacturers. That was where Marietta's father had his carriage works. Wagons, buggies, sleds were made there. In fact, Marietta's father had invented a new sort of sled to carry logs in the bush. It had been patented. He was just getting started in Ramsay. (Later on, in the States, he made money. A man fond of hotel bars, barbershops, harness races, women, but not afraid of work – give him credit.)

Marietta did not find him at work that day. The office was empty. She ran out into the yard where the men were working. She stumbled in the fresh sawdust. The men laughed and shook their heads at her. No. Not here. Not a-here right now. No. Why don't you try up-street? Wait. Wait a minute. Hadn't you better get some clothes on first?

They didn't mean any harm. They didn't have the sense to see that something must be wrong. But Marietta never could stand men laughing. There were always places she hated to go past, let alone into, and that was the reason. Men laughing. Because of that, she hated barbershops, hated their smell. (When she started going to dances later on with my father, she asked him not to put any dressing on his hair, because the smell reminded her.) A bunch of men standing out on the street, outside a hotel, seemed to Marietta like a clot of poison. You tried not to hear what they were saying, but you could be sure it was vile. If they didn't say anything, they laughed and vileness spread out from them – poison – just the same. It was only after Marietta was saved that she could walk right past them. Armed by God, she walked through their midst and nothing stuck to her, nothing scorched her; she was safe as Daniel.

Now she turned and ran, straight back the way she had come. Up the hill, running to get home. She thought she had made a mistake leaving her mother. Why did her mother tell her to go? Why did she want her father? Quite possibly so that she could greet him with the sight of her own warm body swinging on the end of a rope. Marietta should have stayed – she should have stayed and talked her mother out of it. She should have run to Mrs. Sutcliffe, or any neighbor, not wasted time this way. She hadn't thought who could help, who could even believe what she was talking about. She had the idea that all families except her own lived in peace, that threats and miseries didn't exist in other people's houses, and couldn't be explained there.

A train was coming into town. Marietta had to wait. Passengers looked out at her from its windows. She broke out wailing in the faces of those strangers. When the train passed, she continued up the hill – a spectacle, with her hair uncombed, her feet bare and muddy, in her nightgown, with a wild, wet face. By the time she ran into her own yard, in sight of the barn, she was howling. "Mama!" she was howling. "Mama!"

Nobody was there. The chair was standing just where it had been before. The rope was dangling over the back of it. Marietta was sure that her mother had gone ahead and done it. Her mother was already dead – she had been cut down and taken away.

But warm, fat hands settled down on her shoulders, and Mrs. Sutcliffe said, "Marietta. Stop the noise. Marietta. Child. Stop the crying. Come inside. She is well, Marietta. Come inside and you will see."

Mrs. Sutcliffe's foreign voice said, "Mari-et-cha," giving the name a rich, important sound. She was as kind as could be. When Marietta lived with the Sutcliffes later, she was treated as the daughter of the household, and it was a household just as peaceful and comfortable as she had imagined other households to be. But she never felt like a daughter there.

In Mrs. Sutcliffe's kitchen, Beryl sat on the floor eating a raisin cookie and playing with the black-and-white cat, whose name was Dickie. Marietta's mother sat at the table, with a cup of coffee in front of her.

"She was silly," Mrs. Sutcliffe said. Did she mean Marietta's mother or Marietta herself? She didn't have many English words to describe things.

Marietta's mother laughed, and Marietta blacked out. She fainted, after running all that way uphill, howling, in the warm, damp morning. Next thing she knew, she was taking black, sweet coffee from a spoon held by Mrs. Sutcliffe. Beryl picked Dickie up by the front legs and offered him as a cheering present. Marietta's mother was still sitting at the table.

HER HEART WAS broken. That was what I always heard my mother say. That was the end of it. Those words lifted up the story and sealed it shut. I never asked, Who broke it? I never asked. What was the men's poison talk? What was the meaning of the word *vile?*

Marietta's mother laughed after not hanging herself. She sat at Mrs. Sutcliffe's kitchen table long ago and laughed. Her heart was broken.

I always had a feeling, with my mother's talk and stories, of something swelling out behind. Like a cloud you couldn't see through, or get to the end of. There was a cloud, a poison, that had touched my mother's life. And when I grieved my mother, I became part of it. Then I would beat my head against my mother's stomach and breasts, against her tall, firm front, demanding to be forgiven. My mother would tell me to ask God. But it wasn't God, it was my mother I had to get straight with. It seemed as if she knew something about me that was worse, far worse, than ordinary lies and tricks and meanness; it was a really sickening shame. I beat against my mother's front to make her forget that.

My brothers weren't bothered by any of this. I don't think so. They seemed to me like cheerful savages, running around free, not having to learn much. And when I just had the two boys myself, no daughters, I felt as if something could stop now – the stories, and griefs, the old puzzles you can't resist or solve.

AUNT BERYL said not to call her Aunt. "I'm not used to being anybody's aunt, honey. I'm not even anybody's momma. I'm just me. Call me Beryl."

Beryl had started out as a stenographer, and now she had her own typing and bookkeeping business, which employed many girls. She had arrived with a man friend, whose name was Mr. Florence. Her letter had said that she would be getting a ride with a friend, but she hadn't said whether the friend would be staying or going on. She hadn't even said if it was a man or a woman.

Mr. Florence was staying. He was a tall, thin man with a long, tanned face, very light-colored eyes, and a way of twitching the corner of his mouth that might have been a smile.

He was the one who got to sleep in the room that my mother and I had papered, because he was the stranger, and a man. Beryl had to sleep with me. At first we thought that Mr. Florence was quite rude, because he wasn't used to our way of talking and we weren't used to his. The first morning, my father said to Mr. Florence, "Well, I hope you got some kind of a sleep on that old bed in there." (The spare-room bed was heavenly, with a feather tick.) This was Mr. Florence's cue to say that he had never slept better.

Mr. Florence twitched. He said, "I slept on worse."

His favorite place to be was in his car. His car was a royal-blue Chrysler, from the first batch turned out after the war. Inside it, the upholstery and floor covering and roof and door padding were all pearl gray. Mr. Florence kept the names of those colors in mind and corrected you if you said just "blue" or "gray."

"Mouse skin is what it looks like to me," said Beryl rambunctiously. "I tell him it's just mouse skin!"

The car was parked at the side of the house, under the locust trees. Mr. Florence sat inside with the windows rolled up, smoking, in the rich new-car smell.

"I'm afraid we're not doing much to entertain your friend," my mother said.

"I wouldn't worry about him," said Beryl. She always spoke about Mr. Florence as if there was a joke about him that only she appreciated. I wondered long afterward if he had a bottle in the glove compartment and took a nip from time to time to keep his spirits up. He kept his hat on.

Beryl herself was being entertained enough for two. Instead of staying in the house and talking to my mother, as a lady visitor usually did, she demanded to be shown everything there was to see on a farm. She said that I was to take her around and explain things, and see that she didn't fall into any manure piles.

I didn't know what to show. I took Beryl to the icehouse, where chunks of ice the size of dresser drawers, or bigger, lay buried in sawdust. Every few days, my father would chop off a piece of ice and carry it to the kitchen, where it melted in a tin-lined box and cooled the milk and butter.

Beryl said she had never had any idea ice came in pieces that big. She seemed intent on finding things strange, or horrible, or funny.

"Where in the world do you get ice that big?"

I couldn't tell if that was a joke.

"Off of the lake," I said.

"Off of the lake! Do you have lakes up here that have ice on them all summer?"

I told her how my father cut the ice on the lake every winter and hauled it home, and buried it in sawdust, and that kept it from melting.

Beryl said, "That's amazing!"

"Well, it melts a little," I said. I was deeply disappointed in Beryl.

"That's really amazing."

Beryl went along when I went to get the cows. A scarecrow in white slacks (this was what my father called her afterward), with a white sun hat tied under her chin by a flaunting red ribbon. Her fingernails and toenails – she wore sandals – were painted to match the ribbon. She wore the small, dark sunglasses people wore at that time. (Not the people I knew – they didn't own sunglasses.) She had a big red mouth, a loud laugh, hair of an unnatural color and a high gloss, like cherry wood. She was so noisy and shiny, so glamorously got up, that it was hard to tell whether she was good-looking, or happy, or anything.

We didn't have any conversation along the cowpath, because Beryl kept her distance from the cows and was busy watching where she stepped. Once I had them all tied in their stalls, she came closer. She lit a cigarette. Nobody smoked in the barn. My father and other farmers chewed tobacco there instead. I didn't see how I could ask Beryl to chew tobacco.

"Can you get the milk out of them or does your father have to?" Beryl said. "Is it hard to do?"

I pulled some milk down through the cow's teat. One of the barn cats came over and waited. I shot a thin stream into its mouth. The cat and I were both showing off.

"Doesn't that hurt?" said Beryl. "Think if it was you."

I had never thought of a cow's teat as corresponding to any part of myself, and was shaken by this indecency. In fact, I could never grasp a warm, warty teat in such a firm and casual way again.

*   *   *

BERYL SLEPT IN a peach-colored rayon nightgown trimmed with écru lace. She had a robe to match. She was just as careful about the word *écru* as Mr. Florence was about his royal blue and pearl gray.

I managed to get undressed and put on my nightgown without any part of me being exposed at any time. An awkward business. I left my underpants on, and hoped that Beryl had done the same. The idea of sharing my bed with a grownup was a torment to me. But I did get to see the contents of what Beryl called her beauty kit. Hand-painted glass jars contained puffs of cotton wool, talcum powder, milky lotion, ice-blue astringent. Little pots of red and mauve rouge – rather greasy-looking. Blue and black pencils. Emery boards, a pumice stone, nail polish with an overpowering smell of bananas, face powder in a celluloid box shaped like a shell, with the name of a dessert – Apricot Delight.

I had heated some water on the coal-oil stove we used in summertime. Beryl scrubbed her face clean, and there was such a change that I almost expected to see makeup lying in strips in the washbowl, like the old wallpaper we had soaked and peeled. Beryl's skin was pale now, covered with fine cracks, rather like the shiny mud at the bottom of puddles drying up in early summer.

"Look what happened to my skin," she said. "Dieting. I weighed a hundred and sixty-nine pounds once, I took it off too fast and my face fell in on me. Now I've got this cream, though. It's made from a secret formula and you can't even buy it commercially. Smell it. See, it doesn't smell all perfumy. It smells serious."

She was patting the cream on her face with puffs of cotton wool, patting away until there was nothing to be seen on the surface.

"It smells like lard," I said.

"Christ Almighty, I hope I haven't been paying that kind of money to rub lard on my face. Don't tell your mother I swear."

She poured clean water into the drinking glass and wet her comb, then combed her hair wet and twisted each strand round her finger, clamping the twisted strand to her head with two crossed pins. I would be doing the same myself, a couple of years later.

"Always do your hair wet, else it's no good doing it up at all," Beryl said. "And always roll it under even if you want it to flip up. See?"

When I was doing my hair up – as I did for years – I sometimes thought of this, and thought that of all the pieces of advice people had given me, this was the one I had followed most carefully.

We put the lamp out and got into bed, and Beryl said, "I never knew it could get so dark. I've never known a dark that was as dark as this." She was whispering. I was slow to understand that she was comparing country nights to city nights, and I wondered if the darkness in Netterfield County could really be greater than that in California.

"Honey?" whispered Beryl. "Are there any animals outside?"

"Cows," I said.

"Yes, but wild animals? Are there bears?"

"Yes," I said. My father had once found bear tracks and droppings in the bush, and the apples had all been torn off a wild apple tree. That was years ago, when he was a young man.

Beryl moaned and giggled. "Think if Mr. Florence had to go out in the night and he ran into a bear!"

NEXT DAY WAS Sunday. Beryl and Mr. Florence drove my brothers and me to Sunday school in the Chrysler. That was at ten o'clock in the morning. They came back at eleven to bring my parents to church.

"Hop in," Beryl said to me. "You too," she said to the boys. "We're going for a drive."

Beryl was dressed up in a satiny ivory dress with red dots, and a red-lined frill over the hips, and red high-heeled shoes. Mr. Florence wore a pale-blue summer suit.

"Aren't you going to church?" I said. That was what people dressed up for, in my experience.

Beryl laughed. "Honey, this isn't Mr. Florence's kind of religion."

I was used to going straight from Sunday school into church, and sitting for another hour and a half. In summer, the open windows let in the cedary smell of the graveyard and the occasional, almost sacrilegious sound of a car swooshing by on the road. Today we spent this time driving through country I had never seen before. I had never seen it, though it was less than twenty miles from home. Our truck went to the cheese factory, to church, and to town on Saturday nights. The nearest thing to a drive was when it went to the dump. I had seen the near end of Bell's Lake, because that was where my father cut the ice in winter. You couldn't get close to it in summer; the shoreline was all choked up with bulrushes. I had thought that the other end of the lake would look pretty much the same, but when we drove there today, I saw cottages, docks and boats, dark water reflecting the trees. All this and I hadn't known about it. This too was Bell's Lake. I was glad to have seen it at last, but in some way not altogether glad of the surprise.

Finally, a white frame building appeared, with verandas and potted flowers, and some twinkling poplar trees in front. The Wildwood Inn. Today the same building is covered with stucco and done up with Tudor beams and called the Hideaway. The poplar trees have been cut down for a parking lot.

On the way back to the church to pick up my parents, Mr. Florence turned in to the farm next to ours, which belonged to the McAllisters. The McAllisters were Catholics. Our two families were neighborly but not close.

"Come on, boys, out you get," said Beryl to my brothers. "Not you," she said to me. "You stay put." She herded the little boys up to the porch, where some McAllisters were watching. They were in their raggedy home clothes, because their church, or Mass, or whatever it was, got out early. Mrs. McAllister came out and stood listening, rather dumbfounded, to Beryl's laughing talk.

Beryl came back to the car by herself. "There," she said. "They're going to play with the neighbor children."

Play with McAllisters? Besides being Catholics, all but the baby were girls.

"They've still got their good clothes on," I said.

"So what? Can't they have a good time with their good clothes on? I do!"

My parents were taken by surprise as well. Beryl got out and told my father he was to ride in the front seat, for the legroom. She got into the back, with my mother and me. Mr. Florence turned again onto the Bell's

Lake road, and Beryl announced that we were all going to the Wildwood Inn for dinner.

"You're all dressed up, why not take advantage?" she said. "We dropped the boys off with your neighbors. I thought they might be too young to appreciate it. The neighbors were happy to have them." She said with a further emphasis that it was to be their treat. Hers and Mr. Florence's.

"Well, now," said my father. He probably didn't have five dollars in his pocket. "Well, now. I wonder do they let the farmers in?"

He made various jokes along this line. In the hotel dining room, which was all in white – white tablecloths, white painted chairs – with sweating glass water pitchers and high, whirring fans, he picked up a table napkin the size of a diaper and spoke to me in a loud whisper, "Can you tell me what to do with this thing? Can I put it on my head to keep the draft off?"

Of course he had eaten in hotel dining rooms before. He knew about table napkins and pie forks. And my mother knew – she wasn't even a country woman, to begin with. Nevertheless this was a huge event. Not exactly a pleasure – as Beryl must have meant it to be – but a huge, unsettling event. Eating a meal in public, only a few miles from home, eating in a big room full of people you didn't know, the food served by a stranger, a snippy-looking girl who was probably a college student working at a summer job.

"I'd like the rooster," my father said. "How long has he been in the pot?" It was only good manners, as he knew it, to joke with people who waited on him.

"Beg your pardon?" the girl said.

"Roast chicken," said Beryl. "Is that okay for everybody?"

Mr. Florence was looking gloomy. Perhaps he didn't care for jokes when it was his money that was being spent. Perhaps he had counted on something better than ice water to fill up the glasses.

The waitress put down a dish of celery and olives, and my mother said, "Just a minute while I give thanks." She bowed her head and said quietly but audibly, "Lord, bless this food to our use, and us to Thy service, for Christ's sake. Amen." Refreshed, she sat up straight and passed the dish to me, saying, "Mind the olives. There's stones in them."

Beryl was smiling around at the room.

The waitress came back with a basket of rolls.

"Parker House!" Beryl leaned over and breathed in their smell. "Eat them while they're hot enough to melt the butter!"

Mr. Florence twitched, and peered into the butter dish. "Is that what this is – butter? I thought it was Shirley Temple's curls."

His face was hardly less gloomy than before, but it was a joke, and his making it seemed to convey to us something of the very thing that had just been publicly asked for – a blessing.

"When he says something funny," said Beryl – who often referred to Mr. Florence as "he" even when he was right there – "you notice how he always keeps a straight face? That reminds me of Mama. I mean of our mama, Marietta's and mine. Daddy, when he made a joke you could see it coming a mile away – he couldn't keep it off his face – but Mama was another story. She could look so sour. But she could joke on her deathbed. In fact, she did that very thing. Marietta, remember when she was in bed in the front room the spring before she died?"

"I remember she was in bed in that room," my mother said. "Yes."

"Well, Daddy came in and she was lying there in her clean nightgown, with the covers off, because the German lady from next door had just been helping her take a wash, and she was still there tidying up the bed. So Daddy wanted to be cheerful, and he said, 'Spring must be coming. I saw a crow today.' This must have been in March. And Mama said quick as a shot, 'Well, you better cover me up then, before it looks in that window and gets any ideas!' The German lady – Daddy said she just about dropped the basin. Because it was true, Mama was skin and bones; she was dying. But she could joke."

Mr. Florence said, "Might as well when there's no use to cry."

"But she could carry a joke too far, Mama could. One time, one time, she wanted to give Daddy a scare. He was supposed to be interested in some girl that kept coming around to the works. Well, he was a big good-looking man. So Mama said, 'Well, I'll just do away with myself, and you can get on with her and see how you like it when I come back and haunt you.' He told her not to be so stupid, and he went off downtown. And Mama went out to the barn and climbed on a chair and put a rope around her neck. Didn't she, Marietta? Marietta went looking for her and she found her like that!"

My mother bent her head and put her hands in her lap, almost as if she was getting ready to say another grace.

"Daddy told me all about it, but I can remember anyway. I remember Marietta tearing off down the hill in her nightie, and I guess the German lady saw her go, and she came out and was looking for Mama, and somehow we all ended up in the barn – me too, and some kids I was playing with – and there was Mama up on a chair preparing to give Daddy the fright of his life. She'd sent Marietta after him. And the German lady starts wailing, 'Oh, missus, come down missus, think of your little *kindren*' – '*kindren*' is the German for 'children' – 'think of your *kindren*,' and so on. Until it was me standing there – I was just a little squirt, but I was the one noticed that rope. My eyes followed that rope up and up and I saw it was just hanging over the beam, just flung there – it wasn't tied at all! Marietta hadn't noticed that, the German lady hadn't noticed it. But I just spoke up and said, 'Mama, how are you going to manage to hang yourself without that rope tied around the beam?'"

Mr. Florence said, "That'd be a tough one."

"I spoiled her game. The German lady made coffee and we went over there and had a few treats, and, Marietta, you couldn't find Daddy after all, could you? You could hear Marietta howling, coming up the hill, a block away."

"Natural for her to be upset," my father said.

"Sure it was. Mama went too far."

"She meant it," my mother said. "She meant it more than you give her credit for."

"She meant to get a rise out of Daddy. That was their whole life together. He always said she was a hard woman to live with, but she had a lot of character. I believe he missed that, with Gladys."

"I wouldn't know," my mother said, in that particularly steady voice with which she always spoke of her father. "What he did say or didn't say."

"People are dead now," said my father. "It isn't up to us to judge."

"I know," said Beryl. "I know Marietta's always had a different view."

My mother looked at Mr. Florence and smiled quite easily and radiantly. "I'm sure you don't know what to make of all these family matters."

The one time that I visited Beryl, when Beryl was an old woman, all knobby and twisted up with arthritis, Beryl said, "Marietta got all Daddy's looks. And she never did a thing with herself. Remember her wearing that old navy-blue crêpe dress when we went to the hotel that time? Of course, I know it was probably all she had, but did it have to be all she had? You know, I was scared of her somehow. I couldn't stay in a room alone with her. But she had outstanding looks." Trying to remember an occasion when I had noticed my mother's looks, I thought of the time in the hotel, my mother's pale-olive skin against the heavy white, coiled hair, her open, handsome face smiling at Mr. Florence – as if he was the one to be forgiven.

I DIDN'T HAVE a problem right away with Beryl's story. For one thing, I was hungry and greedy, and a lot of my attention went to the roast chicken and gravy and mashed potatoes laid on the plate with an ice-cream scoop and the bright diced vegetables out of a can, which I thought much superior to those fresh from the garden. For dessert, I had a butterscotch sundae, an agonizing choice over chocolate. The others had plain vanilla ice cream.

Why shouldn't Beryl's version of the same event be different from my mother's? Beryl was strange in every way – everything about her was slanted, seen from a new angle. It was my mother's version that held, for a time. It absorbed Beryl's story, closed over it. But Beryl's story didn't vanish; it stayed sealed off for years, but it wasn't gone. It was like the knowledge of that hotel and dining room. I knew about it now, though I didn't think of it as a place to go back to. And indeed, without Beryl's or Mr. Florence's money, I couldn't. But I knew it was there.

The next time I was in the Wildwood Inn, in fact, was after I was married. The Lions Club had a banquet and dance there. The man I had married, Dan Casey, was a Lion. You could get a drink there by that time. Dan Casey wouldn't have gone anywhere you couldn't. Then the place was remodelled into the Hideaway, and now they have strippers every night but Sunday. On Thursday nights, they have a male stripper. I go there with people from the real-estate office to celebrate birthdays or other big events.

THE FARM WAS sold for five thousand dollars in 1965. A man from Toronto bought it, for a hobby farm or just an investment. After a couple of years, he rented it to a commune. They stayed there, different people drifting on and off, for a dozen years or so. They raised goats and sold the milk to the health-food store that had opened up in town. They painted a rainbow across the side of the barn that faced the road. They hung tie-dyed sheets over the windows, and let the long grass and flowering weeds reclaim the yard. My parents had finally got electricity in, but these people didn't use it. They preferred oil lamps and the woodstove, and taking their dirty clothes to town. People said they wouldn't know how to handle lamps or wood fires, and they would burn the place down. But they didn't. In fact, they didn't manage badly. They kept the house and barn in some sort of repair and they worked a big garden. They even dusted their potatoes against blight – though I heard that there was some sort of row about this and some of the stricter members left. The place actually looked a lot better than many of the farms round about that were still in the hands of the original families. The McAllister son had started a wrecking business on their place. My own brothers were long gone.

I knew I was not being reasonable, but I had the feeling that I'd rather see the farm suffer outright neglect – I'd sooner see it in the hands of hoodlums and scroungers – than see that rainbow on the barn, and some letters that looked Egyptian painted on the wall of the house. They seemed a mockery. I even disliked the sight of those people when they came to town – the men with their hair in ponytails, and with holes in their overalls that I believed were cut on purpose, and the women with long hair and no makeup and their meek, superior expressions. What do you know about life, I felt like asking them. What makes you think you can come here and mock my father and mother and their life and their poverty? But when I thought of the rainbow and those letters, I knew they weren't trying to mock or imitate my parents' life. They had displaced that life, hardly knowing it existed. They had set up in its place these beliefs and customs of their own, which I hoped would fail them.

That happened, more or less. The commune disintegrated. The goats disappeared. Some of the women moved to town, cut their hair, put on makeup, and got jobs as waitresses or cashiers to support their children. The Toronto man put the place up for sale, and after about a year it was sold for more than ten times what he had paid for it. A young couple from Ottawa bought it. They have painted the outside a pale gray with oyster trim, and have put in skylights and a handsome front door with carriage lamps on either side. Inside, they've changed it around so much that I've been told I'd never recognize it.

I did get in once, before this happened, during the year that the house was empty and for sale. The company I work for was handling it, and I had a key, though the house was being shown by another agent. I let myself in on a Sunday afternoon. I had a man with me, not a client but a friend – Bob Marks, whom I was seeing a lot at the time.

"This is that hippie place," Bob Marks said when I stopped the car. "I've been by here before."

He was a lawyer, a Catholic, separated from his wife. He thought he wanted to settle down and start up a practice here in town. But there already was one Catholic lawyer. Business was slow. A couple of times a week, Bob Marks would be fairly drunk before supper.

"It's more than that," I said. "It's where I was born. Where I grew up." We walked through the weeds, and I unlocked the door.

He said that he had thought, from the way I talked, that it would be farther out.

"It seemed farther then."

All the rooms were bare, and the floors swept clean. The woodwork was freshly painted – I was surprised to see no smudges on the glass. Some new panes, some old wavy ones. Some of the walls had been stripped of their paper and painted. A wall in the kitchen was painted a deep blue, with an enormous dove on it. On a wall in the front room, giant sunflowers appeared, and a butterfly of almost the same size.

Bob Marks whistled. "Somebody was an artist."

"If that's what you want to call it," I said, and turned back to the kitchen. The same woodstove was there. "My mother once burned up three thousand dollars," I said. "She burned three thousand dollars in that stove."

He whistled again, differently. "What do you mean? She threw in a check?"

"No, no. It was in bills. She did it deliberately. She went into town to the bank and she had them give it all to her, in a shoebox. She brought it home and put it in the stove. She put it in just a few bills at a time, so it wouldn't make too big a blaze. My father stood and watched her."

"What are you talking about?" said Bob Marks. "I thought you were so poor."

"We were. We were very poor."

"So how come she had three thousand dollars? That would be like thirty thousand today. Easily. More than thirty thousand today."

"It was her legacy," I said. "It was what she got from her father. Her father died in Seattle and left her three thousand dollars, and she burned it up because she hated him. She didn't want his money. She hated him."

"That's a lot of hate," Bob Marks said.

"That isn't the point. Her hating him, or whether he was bad enough for her to have a right to hate him. Not likely he was. That isn't the point."

"Money," he said. "Money's always the point."

"No. My father letting her do it is the point. To me it is. My father stood and watched and he never protested. If anybody had tried to stop her, he would have protected her. I consider that love."

"Some people would consider it lunacy."

I remember that that had been Beryl's opinion, exactly.

I went into the front room and stared at the butterfly, with its pink-and-orange wings. Then I went into the front bedroom and found two human figures painted on the wall. A man and a woman holding hands and facing straight ahead. They were naked, and larger than life size.

"It reminds me of that John Lennon and Yoko Ono picture," I said to Bob Marks, who had come in behind me. "That record cover, wasn't it?"

I didn't want him to think that anything he had said in the kitchen had upset me.

Bob Marks said, "Different color hair."

That was true. Both figures had yellow hair painted in a solid mass, the way they do it in the comic strips. Horsetails of yellow hair curling over their shoulders and little pigtails of yellow hair decorating their not so private parts. Their skin was a flat beige pink and their eyes a staring blue, the same blue that was on the kitchen wall.

I noticed that they hadn't quite finished peeling the wallpaper away before making this painting. In the corner, there was some paper left that matched the paper on the other walls – a modernistic design of intersecting pink and gray and mauve bubbles. The man from Toronto must have put that on. The paper underneath hadn't been stripped off when this new paper went on. I could see an edge of it, the cornflowers on a white ground.

"I guess this was where they carried on their sexual shenanigans," Bob Marks said, in a tone familiar to me. That thickened, sad, uneasy, but determined tone. The not particularly friendly lust of middle-aged respectable men.

I didn't say anything. I worked away some of the bubble paper to see more of the cornflowers. Suddenly I hit a loose spot, and ripped away a big swatch of it. But the cornflower paper came too, and a little shower of dried plaster.

"Why is it?" I said. "Just tell me, why is it that no man can mention a place like this without getting around to the subject of sex in about two seconds flat? Just say the words *hippie* or *commune* and all you guys can think about is screwing! As if there wasn't anything at all behind it but orgies and fancy combinations and non-stop screwing! I get so sick of that – it's all so stupid it just makes me sick!"

IN THE CAR, on the way home from the hotel, we sat as before – the men in the front seat, the women in the back. I was in the middle, Beryl and my mother on either side of me. Their heated bodies pressed against me, through cloth; their smells crowded out the smells of the cedar bush we passed through, and the pockets of bog, where Beryl exclaimed at the water lilies. Beryl smelled of all those things in pots and bottles. My mother smelled of flour and hard soap and the warm crêpe of her good dress and the kerosene she had used to take the spots off.

"A lovely meal," my mother said. "Thank you, Beryl. Thank you, Mr. Florence."

"I don't know who is going to be fit to do the milking," my father said. "Now that we've all ate in such style."

"Speaking of money," said Beryl – though nobody actually had been – "do you mind my asking what you did with yours? I put mine in real estate. Real estate in California – you can't lose. I was thinking you could get an electric stove, so you wouldn't have to bother with a fire in summer or fool with that coal-oil thing, either one."

All the other people in the car laughed, even Mr. Florence.

"That's a good idea, Beryl," said my father. "We could use it to set things on till we get the electricity."

"Oh, Lord," said Beryl. "How stupid can I get?"

"And we don't actually have the money, either," my mother said cheerfully, as if she was continuing the joke.

But Beryl spoke sharply. "You wrote me you got it. You got the same as me."

My father half turned in his seat. "What money are you talking about?" he said. "What's this money?"

"From Daddy's will," Beryl said. "That you got last year. Look, maybe I shouldn't have asked. If you had to pay something off, that's still a good use, isn't it? It doesn't matter. We're all family here. Practically."

"We didn't have to use it to pay anything off," my mother said. "I burned it."

Then she told how she went into town in the truck, one day almost a year ago, and got them to give her the money in a box she had brought along for the purpose. She took it home, and put it in the stove and burned it.

My father turned around and faced the road ahead.

I could feel Beryl twisting beside me while my mother talked. She was twisting, and moaning a little, as if she had a pain she couldn't suppress.

At the end of the story, she let out a sound of astonishment and suffering, an angry groan.

"So you burned up money!" she said. "You burned up money in the stove."

My mother was still cheerful. "You sound as if I'd burned up one of my children."

"You burned their chances. You burned up everything the money could have got for them."

"The last thing my children need is money. None of us need his money."

"That's criminal," Beryl said harshly. She pitched her voice into the front seat: "Why did you let her?"

"He wasn't there," my mother said. "Nobody was there."

My father said, "It was her money, Beryl."

"Never mind," Beryl said. "That's criminal."

"Criminal is for when you call in the police," Mr. Florence said. Like other things he had said that day, this created a little island of surprise and a peculiar gratitude.

Gratitude not felt by all.

"Don't you pretend this isn't the craziest thing you ever heard of," Beryl shouted into the front seat. "Don't you pretend you don't think so! Because it is, and you do. You think just the same as me!"

MY FATHER DID not stand in the kitchen watching my mother feed the money into the flames. It wouldn't appear so. He did not know about it – it seems fairly clear, if I remember everything, that he did not know about it until that Sunday afternoon in Mr. Florence's Chrysler, when my mother told them all together. Why, then, can I see the scene so clearly, just as I described it to Bob Marks (and to others – he was not the first)? I see my father standing by the table in the middle of the room – the table with the drawer in it for knives and forks, and the scrubbed oil-cloth on top – and there is the box of money on the table. My mother is carefully dropping the bills into the fire. She holds the stove lid by the blackened lifter in one hand. And my father, standing by, seems not just to be permitting her to do this but to be protecting her. A solemn scene, but not crazy. People doing something that seems to them natural and necessary. At least, one of them is doing what seems natural and necessary, and the other believes that the important thing is for that person to be free, to go ahead. They understand that other people might not think so. They do not care.

How hard it is for me to believe that I made that up. It seems so much the truth it is the truth; it's what I believe about them. I haven't stopped believing it. But I have stopped telling that story. I never told it to anyone again after telling it to Bob Marks. I don't think so. I didn't stop just because it wasn't, strictly speaking, true. I stopped because I saw that I had to give up expecting people to see it the way I did. I had to give up expecting them to approve of any part of what was done. How could I even say that I approved of it myself? If I had been the sort of person who approved of that, who could do it, I wouldn't have done all I have done – run away from home to work in a restaurant in town when I was fifteen, gone to night school to learn typing and book-keeping, got into the real-estate office, and finally become a licensed agent. I wouldn't be divorced. My father wouldn't have died in the county home. My hair would be white, as it has been naturally for years, instead of a color called Copper Sunrise. And not one of these things would I change, not really, if I could.

Bob Marks was a decent man – good-hearted, sometimes with imagination. After I had lashed out at him like that, he said, "You don't need to be so tough on us." In a moment, he said, "Was this your room when you were a little girl?" He thought that was why the mention of the sexual shenanigans had upset me.

And I thought it would be just as well to let him think that. I said yes, yes, it was my room when I was a little girl. It was just as well to make up right away. Moments of kindness and reconciliation are worth having, even if the parting has to come sooner or later. I wonder if those moments aren't more valued, and deliberately gone after, in the setups some people like myself have now, than they were in those old marriages, where love and grudges could be growing underground, so confused and stubborn, it must have seemed they had forever.

MILES CITY, MONTANA

MY FATHER CAME across the field carrying the body of the boy who had been drowned. There were several men together, returning from the search, but he was the one carrying the body. The men were muddy and exhausted, and walked with their heads down, as if they were ashamed. Even the dogs were dispirited, dripping from the cold river. When they all set out, hours before, the dogs were nervy and yelping, the men tense and determined, and there was a constrained, unspeakable excitement about the whole scene. It was understood that they might find something horrible.

The boy's name was Steve Gauley. He was eight years old. His hair and clothes were mud-colored now and carried some bits of dead leaves, twigs, and grass. He was like a heap of refuse that had been left out all winter. His face was turned in to my father's chest, but I could see a nostril, an ear, plugged up with greenish mud.

I don't think so. I don't think I really saw all this. Perhaps I saw my father carrying him, and the other men following along, and the dogs, but I would not have been allowed to get close enough to see something like mud in his nostril. I must have heard someone talking about that and imagined that I saw it. I see his face unaltered except for the mud — Steve Gauley's familiar, sharp-honed, sneaky-looking face — and it wouldn't have been like that; it would have been bloated and changed and perhaps muddied all over after so many hours in the water.

To have to bring back such news, such evidence, to a waiting family, particularly a mother, would have made searchers move heavily, but what was happening here was worse. It seemed a worse shame (to hear people talk) that there was no mother, no woman at all — no grandmother or aunt, or even a sister — to receive Steve Gauley and give him his due of grief. His father was a hired man, a drinker but not a drunk, an erratic man without being entertaining, not friendly but not exactly a troublemaker. His fatherhood seemed accidental, and the fact that the child had been left with him when the mother went away, and that they continued living together, seemed accidental. They lived in a steep-roofed, gray-shingled hillbilly sort of house that was just a bit better than a shack – the father fixed the roof and put supports under the porch, just enough and just in time – and their life was held together in a similar manner; that is, just well enough to keep the Children's Aid at bay. They didn't eat meals together or cook for each other, but there was food. Sometimes the father would give Steve money to buy food at the store, and Steve was seen to buy quite sensible things, such as pancake mix and macaroni dinner.

I had known Steve Gauley fairly well. I had not liked him more often than I had liked him. He was two years older than I was. He would hang around our place on Saturdays, scornful of whatever I was doing but unable to leave me alone. I couldn't be on the swing without him wanting to try it, and if I wouldn't give it up he came and pushed me so that I went crooked. He teased the dog. He got me into trouble – deliberately and maliciously, it seemed to me afterwards – by daring me to do things I wouldn't have thought of on my own: digging up the potatoes to see how big they were when they were still only the size of marbles, and pushing over the stacked firewood to make a pile we could jump off. At school, we never spoke to each other. He was solitary, though not tormented. But on Saturday mornings, when I saw his thin, self-possessed figure sliding through the cedar hedge, I knew I was in for something and he would decide what. Sometimes it was all right. We pretended we were cowboys who had to tame wild horses. We played in the pasture by the river, not far from the place where Steve drowned. We were horses and riders both, screaming and neighing and bucking and waving whips of tree branches beside a little nameless river that flows into the Saugeen in southern Ontario.

The funeral was held in our house. There was not enough room at Steve's father's place for the large crowd that was expected because of the circumstances. I have a memory of the crowded room but no picture of Steve in his coffin, or of the minister, or of wreaths of flowers. I remember that I was holding one flower, a white narcissus, which must have come from a pot somebody forced indoors, because it was too early for even the forsythia bush or the trilliums and marsh marigolds in the woods. I stood in a row of children, each of us holding a narcissus. We sang a children's hymn, which somebody played on our piano: "When He Cometh, When He Cometh, to Make Up His Jewels." I was wearing white ribbed stockings, which were disgustingly itchy, and wrinkled at the knees and ankles. The feeling of these stockings on my legs is mixed up with another feeling in my memory. It is hard to describe. It had to do with my parents. Adults in general but my parents in particular. My father, who had carried Steve's body from the river, and my mother, who must have done most of the arranging of this funeral. My father in his dark-blue suit and my mother in her brown velvet dress with the creamy satin collar. They stood side by side opening and closing their mouths for the hymn, and I stood removed from them, in the row of children, watching. I felt a furious and sickening disgust. Children sometimes have an access of disgust concerning adults. The size, the lumpy shapes, the bloated power. The breath, the coarseness, the hairiness, the horrid secretions. But this was more. And the accompanying anger had nothing sharp and self-respecting about it. There was no release, as when I would finally bend and pick up a stone and throw it at Steve Gauley. It could not be understood or expressed, though it died down after a while into a heaviness, then just a taste, an occasional taste – a thin, familiar misgiving.

TWENTY YEARS OR so later, in 1961, my husband, Andrew, and I got a brand-new car, our first – that is, our first brand-new. It was a Morris Oxford, oyster-colored (the dealer had some fancier name for the color) – a big small car, with plenty of room for us and our two children. Cynthia was six and Meg three and a half.

Andrew took a picture of me standing beside the car. I was wearing white pants, a black turtleneck, and sunglasses. I lounged against the car door, canting my hips to make myself look slim.

"Wonderful," Andrew said. "Great. You look like Jackie Kennedy." All over this continent probably, dark-haired, reasonably slender young women were told, when they were stylishly dressed or getting their pictures taken, that they looked like Jackie Kennedy.

Andrew took a lot of pictures of me, and of the children, our house, our garden, our excursions and possessions. He got copies made, labelled them carefully, and sent them back to his mother and his aunt and uncle in Ontario. He got copies for me to send to my father, who also lived in Ontario, and I did so, but less regularly than he sent his. When he saw pictures he thought I had already sent lying around the house, Andrew was perplexed and annoyed. He liked to have this record go forth.

That summer, we were presenting ourselves, not pictures. We were driving back from Vancouver, where we lived, to Ontario, which we still called "home," in our new car. Five days to get there, ten days there, five days back. For the first time, Andrew had three weeks' holiday. He worked in the legal department at B. C. Hydro.

On a Saturday morning, we loaded suitcases, two thermos bottles – one filled with coffee and one with lemonade – some fruit and sandwiches, picture books and coloring books, crayons, drawing pads, insect repellent, sweaters (in case it got cold in the mountains), and our two children into the car. Andrew locked the house, and Cynthia said ceremoniously, "Goodbye, house."

Meg said, "Goodbye, house." Then she said, "Where will we live now?"

"It's not goodbye forever," said Cynthia. "We're coming back. Mother! Meg thought we weren't ever coming back!"

"I did not," said Meg, kicking the back of my seat.

Andrew and I put on our sunglasses, and we drove away, over the Lions Gate Bridge and through the main part of Vancouver. We shed our house, the neighborhood, the city, and – at the crossing point between Washington and British Columbia – our country. We were driving east across the United States, taking the most northerly route, and would cross into Canada again at Sarnia, Ontario. I don't know if we chose this route because the Trans-Canada Highway was not completely finished at the time or if we just wanted the feeling of driving through a foreign, a very slightly foreign, country – that extra bit of interest and adventure.

We were both in high spirits. Andrew congratulated the car several times. He said he felt so much better driving it than our old car, a 1951 Austin that slowed down dismally on the hills and had a fussy-old-lady image. So Andrew said now.

"What kind of image does this one have?" said Cynthia. She listened to us carefully and liked to try out new words such as *image*. Usually she got them right.

"Lively," I said. "Slightly sporty. It's not show-off."

"It's sensible, but it has class," Andrew said. "Like my image."

Cynthia thought that over and said with a cautious pride, "That means like you think you want to be, Daddy?"

As for me, I was happy because of the shedding. I loved taking off. In my own house, I seemed to be often looking for a place to hide — sometimes from the children but more often from the jobs to be done and the phone ringing and the sociability of the neighborhood. I wanted to hide so that I could get busy at my real work, which was a sort of wooing of distant parts of myself. I lived in a state of siege, always losing just what I wanted to hold on to. But on trips there was no difficulty. I could be talking to Andrew, talking to the children and looking at whatever they wanted me to look at — a pig on a sign, a pony in a field, a Volkswagen on a revolving stand — and pouring lemonade into plastic cups, and all the time those bits and pieces would be flying together inside me. The essential composition would be achieved. This made me hopeful and lighthearted. It was being a watcher that did it. A watcher, not a keeper.

We turned east at Everett and climbed into the Cascades. I showed Cynthia our route on the map. First I showed her the map of the whole United States, which showed also the bottom part of Canada. Then I turned to the separate maps of each of the states we were going to pass through. Washington, Idaho, Montana, North Dakota, Minnesota, Wisconsin. I showed her the dotted line across Lake Michigan, which was the route of the ferry we would take. Then we would drive across Michigan to the bridge that linked the United States and Canada at Sarnia, Ontario. Home.

Meg wanted to see too.

"You won't understand," said Cynthia. But she took the road atlas into the back seat.

"Sit back," she said to Meg. "Sit still. I'll show you."

I could hear her tracing the route for Meg, very accurately, just as I had done it for her. She looked up all the states' maps, knowing how to find them in alphabetical order.

"You know what that line is?" she said. "It's the road. That line is the road we're driving on. We're going right along this line."

Meg did not say anything.

"Mother, show me where we are right this minute," said Cynthia.

I took the atlas and pointed out the road through the mountains, and she took it back and showed it to Meg. "See where the road is all wiggly?" she said. "It's wiggly because there are so many turns in it. The wiggles are the turns." She flipped some pages and waited a moment. "Now," she said, "show me where we are." Then she called to me, "Mother, she understands! She pointed to it! Meg understands maps!"

It seems to me now that we invented characters for our children. We had them firmly set to play their parts. Cynthia was bright and diligent, sensitive, courteous, watchful. Sometimes we teased her for being too conscientious, too eager to be what we in fact depended on her to be. Any reproach or failure, any rebuff, went terribly deep with her. She was fair-haired, fair-skinned, easily showing the effects of the sun, raw winds, pride, or humiliation. Meg was more solidly built, more reticent – not rebellious but stubborn sometimes, mysterious. Her silences seemed to us to show her strength of character, and her negatives were taken as signs of an imperturbable independence. Her hair was brown, and we cut it in straight bangs. Her eyes were a light hazel, clear and dazzling.

We were entirely pleased with these characters, enjoying their contradictions as well as the confirmations of them. We disliked the heavy, the uninventive, approach to being parents. I had a dread of turning into a certain kind of mother – the kind whose body sagged, who moved in a woolly-smelling, milky-smelling fog, solemn with trivial burdens. I believed that all the attention these mothers paid, their need to be burdened, was the cause of colic, bed-wetting, asthma. I favored another approach – the mock desperation, the inflated irony of the professional mothers who wrote for magazines. In those magazine pieces, the children were splendidly self-willed, hard-edged, perverse, indomitable. So were the mothers, through their wit, indomitable. The real-life mothers I warmed to were the sort who would phone up and say, "Is my embryo Hitler by any chance over at your house?" They cackled clear above the milky fog.

We saw a dead deer strapped across the front of a pickup truck.

"Somebody shot it," Cynthia said. "Hunters shot the deer."

"It's not hunting season yet," Andrew said. "They may have hit it on the road. See the sign for deer crossing?"

"I would cry if we hit one," Cynthia said sternly.

I had made peanut-butter-and-marmalade sandwiches for the children and salmon-and-mayonnaise for us. But I had not put any lettuce in, and Andrew was disappointed.

"I didn't have any," I said.

"Couldn't you have got some?"

"I'd have had to buy a whole head of lettuce just to get enough for sandwiches, and I decided it wasn't worth it."

This was a lie. I had forgotten.

"They're a lot better with lettuce."

"I didn't think it made that much difference." After a silence, I said, "Don't be mad."

"I'm not mad. I like lettuce on sandwiches."

"I just didn't think it mattered that much."

"How would it be if I didn't bother to fill up the gas tank?"

"That's not the same thing."

"Sing a song," said Cynthia. She started to sing:

> *"Five little ducks went out one day,*
> *Over the hills and far away.*
> *One little duck went*
> *'Quack-quack-quack.'*
> *Four little ducks came swimming back."*

Andrew squeezed my hand and said, "Let's not fight."

"You're right. I should have got lettuce."

"It doesn't matter that much."

I wished that I could get my feelings about Andrew to come together into a serviceable and dependable feeling. I had even tried writing two lists, one of things I liked about him, one of things I disliked — in the cauldron of intimate life, things I loved and things I hated — as if I hoped by this to prove something, to come to a conclusion one way or the other. But I gave it up when I saw that all it proved was what I already knew — that I had violent contradictions. Sometimes the very sound of his footsteps seemed to me tyrannical, the set of his mouth smug and mean, his hard, straight body a barrier interposed — quite consciously, even dutifully, and with a nasty pleasure in its masculine authority — between me and whatever joy or lightness I could get in life. Then, with not much warning, he became my good friend and most essential companion. I felt the sweetness of his light bones and serious ideas, the vulnerability of his love, which I imagined to be much purer and more straightforward than my own. I could be greatly moved by an inflexibility, a harsh propriety, that at other times I scorned. I would think how humble he was, really, taking on such a ready-made role of husband, father, breadwinner, and how I myself in comparison was really a secret monster of egotism. Not so secret, either — not from him.

At the bottom of our fights, we served up what we thought were the ugliest truths. "I know there is something basically selfish and basically untrustworthy about you," Andrew once said. "I've always known it. I also know that that is why I fell in love with you."

"Yes," I said, feeling sorrowful but complacent.

"I know that I'd be better off without you."

"Yes. You would."

"You'd be happier without me."

"Yes."

And finally — finally — wracked and purged, we clasped hands and laughed, laughed at those two benighted people, ourselves. Their grudges, their grievances, their self-justification. We leapfrogged over them. We declared them liars. We would have wine with dinner, or decide to give a party.

I haven't seen Andrew for years, don't know if he is still thin, has gone completely gray, insists on lettuce, tells the truth, or is hearty and disappointed.

WE STAYED THE night in Wenatchee, Washington, where it hadn't rained for weeks. We ate dinner in a restaurant built about a tree – not a sapling in a tub but a tall, sturdy cottonwood. In the early-morning light, we climbed out of the irrigated valley, up dry, rocky, very steep hillsides that would seem to lead to more hills, and there on the top was a wide plateau, cut by the great Spokane and Columbia rivers. Grainland and grassland, mile after mile. There were straight roads here, and little farming towns with grain elevators. In fact, there was a sign announcing that this county we were going through, Douglas County, had the second-highest wheat yield of any county in the United States. The towns had planted shade trees. At least, I thought they had been planted, because there were no such big trees in the countryside.

All this was marvellously welcome to me. "Why do I love it so much?" I said to Andrew. "Is it because it isn't scenery?"

"It reminds you of home," said Andrew. "A bout of severe nostalgia." But he said this kindly.

When we said "home" and meant Ontario, we had very different places in mind. My home was a turkey farm, where my father lived as a widower, and though it was the same house my mother had lived in, had papered, painted, cleaned, furnished, it showed the effects now of neglect and of some wild sociability. A life went on in it that my mother could not have predicted or condoned. There were parties for the turkey crew, the gutters and pluckers, and sometimes one or two of the young men would be living there temporarily, inviting their own friends and having their own impromptu parties. This life, I thought, was better for my father than being lonely, and I did not disapprove, had certainly no right to disapprove. Andrew did not like to go there, naturally enough, because he was not the sort who could sit around the kitchen table with the turkey crew, telling jokes. They were intimidated by him and contemptuous of him, and it seemed to me that my father, when they were around, had to be on their side. And it wasn't only Andrew who had trouble. I could manage those jokes, but it was an effort.

I wished for the days when I was little, before we had the turkeys. We had cows, and sold the milk to the cheese factory. A turkey farm is nothing like as pretty as a dairy farm or a sheep farm. You can see that the turkeys are on a straight path to becoming frozen carcasses and table meat. They don't have the pretense of a life of their own, a browsing idyll, that cattle have, or pigs in the dappled orchard. Turkey barns are long, efficient buildings – tin sheds. No beams or hay or warm stables. Even the smell of guano seems thinner and more offensive than the usual smell of stable manure. No hints there of hay coils and rail fences and songbirds and the flowering hawthorn. The turkeys were all let out into one long field, which they picked clean. They didn't look like great birds there but like fluttering laundry.

Once, shortly after my mother died, and after I was married – in fact, I was packing to join Andrew in Vancouver – I was at home alone for a couple of days with my father. There was a freakishly heavy rain all night. In the early light, we saw that the turkey field was flooded. At least, the low-lying parts of it were flooded – it was like a lake with many islands. The turkeys were huddled on these islands. Turkeys are very stupid. (My father would say, "You know a chicken? You know how stupid a chicken is? Well, a chicken is an Einstein compared with a turkey.") But they had managed to crowd to higher ground and avoid drowning. Now they might push each other off, suffocate each other, get cold and die. We couldn't wait for the water to go down. We went out in an old rowboat we had. I rowed and my father pulled the heavy, wet turkeys into the boat and we took them to the barn. It was still raining a little. The job was difficult and absurd and very uncomfortable. We were laughing. I was happy to be working with my father. I felt close to all hard, repetitive, appalling work, in which the body is finally worn out, the mind sunk (though sometimes the spirit can stay marvellously light), and I was homesick in advance for this life and this place. I thought that if Andrew could see me there in the rain, red-handed, muddy, trying to hold on to turkey legs and row the boat at the same time, he would only want to get me out of there and make me forget about it. This raw life angered him. My attachment to it angered him. I thought that I shouldn't have married him. But who else? One of the turkey crew?

And I didn't want to stay there. I might feel bad about leaving, but I would feel worse if somebody made me stay.

Andrew's mother lived in Toronto, in an apartment building looking out on Muir Park. When Andrew and his sister were both at home, his mother slept in the living room. Her husband, a doctor, had died when the children were still too young to go to school. She took a secretarial course and sold her house at Depression prices, moved to this apartment, managed to raise her children, with some help from relatives – her sister Caroline, her brother-in-law Roger. Andrew and his sister went to private schools and to camp in the summer.

"I suppose that was courtesy of the Fresh Air Fund?" I said once, scornful of his claim that he had been poor. To my mind, Andrew's urban life had been sheltered and fussy. His mother came home with a headache from working all day in the noise, the harsh light of a department-store office, but it did not occur to me that hers was a hard or admirable life. I don't think she herself believed that she was admirable – only unlucky. She worried about her work in the office, her clothes, her cooking, her children. She worried most of all about what Roger and Caroline would think.

Caroline and Roger lived on the east side of the park, in a handsome stone house. Roger was a tall man with a bald, freckled head, a fat, firm stomach. Some operation on his throat had deprived him of his voice – he spoke in a rough whisper. But everybody paid attention. At dinner once in the stone house – where all the dining-room furniture was enormous, darkly glowing, palatial – I asked him a question. I think it had to do with Whittaker Chambers, whose story was then appearing in the *Saturday Evening Post*. The question was mild in tone, but he guessed its subversive intent and took to calling me Mrs. Gromyko, referring to what he alleged to be my "sympathies." Perhaps he really craved an adversary, and could not find one. At that dinner, I saw

Andrew's hand tremble as he lit his mother's cigarette. His Uncle Roger had paid for Andrew's education, and was on the board of directors of several companies.

"He is just an opinionated old man," Andrew said to me later. "What is the point of arguing with him?"

Before we left Vancouver, Andrew's mother had written, *Roger seems quite intrigued by the idea of your buying a small car!* Her exclamation mark showed apprehension. At that time, particularly in Ontario, the choice of a small European car over a large American car could be seen as some sort of declaration – a declaration of tendencies Roger had been sniffing after all along.

"It isn't that small a car," said Andrew huffily.

"That's not the point," I said. "The point is, it isn't any of his business!"

WE SENT THE second night in Missoula. We had been told in Spokane, at a gas station, that there was a lot of repair work going on along Highway 2, and that we were in for a very hot, dusty drive, with long waits, so we turned onto the interstate and drove through Coeur d'Alene and Kellogg into Montana. After Missoula, we turned south toward Butte, but detoured to see Helena, the state capital. In the car, we played Who Am I?

Cynthia was somebody dead, and an American, and a girl. Possibly a lady. She was not in a story. She had not been seen on television. Cynthia had not read about her in a book. She was not anybody who had come to the kindergarten, or a relative of any of Cynthia's friends.

"Is she human?" said Andrew, with a sudden shrewdness.

"No! That's what you forgot to ask!"

"An animal," I said reflectively.

"Is that a question? Sixteen questions!"

"No, it is not a question. I'm thinking. A dead animal."

"It's the deer," said Meg, who hadn't been playing.

"That's not fair!" said Cynthia. "She's not playing!"

"What deer?" said Andrew.

I said, "Yesterday."

"The day before," said Cynthia. "Meg wasn't playing. Nobody got it."

"The deer on the truck," said Andrew.

"It was a lady deer, because it didn't have antlers, and it was an American and it was dead," Cynthia said.

Andrew said, "I think it's kind of morbid, being a dead deer."

"I got it," said Meg.

Cynthia said, "I think I know what morbid is. It's depressing."

Helena, an old silver-mining town, looked forlorn to us even in the morning sunlight. Then Bozeman and Billings, not forlorn in the slightest – energetic, strung-out towns, with miles of blinding tinsel fluttering over used-car lots. We got too tired and hot even to play Who Am I? These busy, prosaic cities reminded me of similar places in Ontario, and I thought about what was really waiting there – the great tombstone furniture of Roger and Caroline's dining room, the dinners for which I must iron the children's dresses and warn them about forks, and then the other table a hundred miles away, the jokes of my father's crew. The pleasures I had been thinking of – looking at the countryside or drinking a Coke in an old-fashioned drugstore with fans and a high, pressed-tin ceiling – would have to be snatched in between.

"Meg's asleep," Cynthia said. "She's so hot. She makes me hot in the same seat with her."

"I hope she isn't feverish," I said, not turning around.

What are we doing this for, I thought, and the answer came – to show off. To give Andrew's mother and my father the pleasure of seeing their grandchildren. That was our duty. But beyond that we wanted to show them something. What strenuous children we were, Andrew and I, what relentless seekers of approbation. It was as if at some point we had received an unforgettable, indigestible message – that we were far from satisfactory, and that the most commonplace success in life was probably beyond us. Roger dealt out such messages, of course – that was his style – but Andrew's mother, my own mother and father couldn't have meant to do so. All they meant to tell us was "Watch out. Get along." My father, when I was in high school, teased me that I was getting to think I was so smart I would never find a boyfriend. He would have forgotten that in a week. I never forgot it. Andrew and I didn't forget things. We took umbrage.

"I wish there was a beach," said Cynthia.

"There probably is one," Andrew said. "Right around the next curve."

"There isn't any curve," she said, sounding insulted.

"That's what I mean."

"I wish there was some more lemonade."

"I will just wave my magic wand and produce some," I said. "Okay, Cynthia? Would you rather have grape juice? Will I do a beach while I'm at it?"

She was silent, and soon I felt repentant. "Maybe in the next town there might be a pool," I said. I looked at the map. "In Miles City. Anyway, there'll be something cool to drink."

"How far is it?" Andrew said.

"Not so far," I said. "Thirty miles, about."

"In Miles City," said Cynthia, in the tones of an incantation, "there is a beautiful blue swimming pool for children, and a park with lovely trees."

Andrew said to me, "You could have started something."

BUT THERE WAS a pool. There was a park too, though not quite the oasis of Cynthia's fantasy. Prairie trees with thin leaves – cottonwoods and poplars – worn grass, and a high wire fence around the pool. Within this fence, a wall, not yet completed, of cement blocks. There were no shouts or splashes; over the entrance I saw a sign that said the pool was closed every day from noon until two o'clock. It was then twenty-five after twelve.

Nevertheless I called out, "Is anybody there?" I thought somebody must be around, because there was a small truck parked near the entrance. On the side of the truck were these words: *We have Brains, to fix your Drains. (We have Roto-Rooter too.)*

A girl came out, wearing a red lifeguard's shirt over her bathing suit. "Sorry, we're closed."

"We were just driving through," I said.

"We close every day from twelve until two. It's on the sign." She was eating a sandwich.

"I saw the sign," I said. "But this is the first water we've seen for so long, and the children are awfully hot, and I wondered if they could just dip in and out – just five minutes. We'd watch them."

A boy came into sight behind her. He was wearing jeans and a T-shirt with the words *Roto-Rooter* on it.

I was going to say that we were driving from British Columbia to Ontario, but I remembered that Canadian place names usually meant nothing to Americans. "We're driving right across the country," I said. "We haven't time to wait for the pool to open. We were just hoping the children could get cooled off."

Cynthia came running up barefoot behind me. "Mother. Mother, where is my bathing suit?" Then she stopped, sensing the serious adult negotiations. Meg was climbing out of the car – just wakened, with her top pulled up and her shorts pulled down, showing her pink stomach.

"Is it just those two?" the girl said.

"Just the two. We'll watch them."

"I can't let any adults in. If it's just the two, I guess I could watch them. I'm having my lunch." She said to Cynthia, "Do you want to come in the pool?"

"Yes, please," said Cynthia firmly.

Meg looked at the ground.

"Just a short time, because the pool is really closed," I said. "We appreciate this very much," I said to the girl.

"Well, I can eat my lunch out there, if it's just the two of them." She looked toward the car as if she thought I might try to spring some more children on her.

When I found Cynthia's bathing suit, she took it into the changing room. She would not permit anybody, even Meg, to see her naked. I changed Meg, who stood on the front seat of the car. She had a pink cotton bathing suit with straps that crossed and buttoned. There were ruffles across the bottom.

"She *is* hot," I said. "But I don't think she's feverish."

I loved helping Meg to dress or undress, because her body still had the solid unself-consciousness, the sweet indifference, something of the milky smell, of a baby's body. Cynthia's body had long ago been pared

135

down, shaped and altered, into Cynthia. We all liked to hug Meg, press and nuzzle her. Sometimes she would scowl and beat us off, and this forthright independence, this ferocious bashfulness, simply made her more appealing, more apt to be tormented and tickled in the way of family love.

Andrew and I sat in the car with the windows open. I could hear a radio playing, and thought it must belong to the girl or her boyfriend. I was thirsty, and got out of the car to look for a concession stand, or perhaps a soft-drink machine, somewhere in the park. I was wearing shorts, and the backs of my legs were slick with sweat. I saw a drinking fountain at the other side of the park and was walking toward it in a roundabout way, keeping to the shade of the trees. No place became real till you got out of the car. Dazed with the heat, with the sun on the blistered houses, the pavement, the burnt grass, I walked slowly. I paid attention to a squashed leaf, ground a Popsicle stick under the heel of my sandal, squinted at a trash can strapped to a tree. This is the way you look at the poorest details of the world resurfaced, after you've been driving for a long time – you feel their singleness and precise location and the forlorn coincidence of your being there to see them.

Where are the children?

I turned around and moved quickly, not quite running, to a part of the fence beyond which the cement wall was not completed. I could see some of the pool. I saw Cynthia, standing about waist-deep in the water, fluttering her hands on the surface and discreetly watching something at the end of the pool, which I could not see. I thought by her pose, her discretion, the look on her face, that she must be watching some byplay between the lifeguard and her boyfriend. I couldn't see Meg. But I thought she must be playing in the shallow water – both the shallow and deep ends of the pool were out of my sight.

"Cynthia!" I had to call twice before she knew where my voice was coming from. "Cynthia! Where's Meg?"

It always seems to me, when I recall this scene, that Cynthia turns very gracefully toward me, then turns all around in the water – making me think of a ballerina on pointe – and spreads her arms in a gesture of the stage. "Dis-ap-peared!"

Cynthia was naturally graceful, and she did take dancing lessons, so these movements may have been as I have described. She did say "Disappeared" after looking all around the pool, but the strangely artificial style of speech and gesture, the lack of urgency, is more likely my invention. The fear I felt instantly when I couldn't see Meg – even while I was telling myself she must be in the shallower water – must have made Cynthia's movements seem unbearably slow and inappropriate to me, and the tone in which she could say "Disappeared" before the implications struck her (or was she covering, at once, some ever-ready guilt?) was heard by me as quite exquisitely, monstrously self-possessed.

I cried out for Andrew, and the lifeguard came into view. She was pointing toward the deep end of the pool, saying, "What's that?"

There, just within my view, a cluster of pink ruffles appeared, a bouquet, beneath the surface of the water. Why would a lifeguard stop and point, why would she ask what that was, why didn't she just dive into the water and swim to it? She didn't swim; she ran all the way around the edge of the pool. But by that time Andrew was over the fence. So many things seemed not quite plausible – Cynthia's behavior, then the lifeguard's – and now I had the impression that Andrew jumped with one bound over this fence, which seemed about seven feet high. He must have climbed it very quickly, getting a grip on the wire.

I could not jump or climb it, so I ran to the entrance, where there was a sort of lattice gate, locked. It was not very high, and I did pull myself over it. I ran through the cement corridors, through the disinfectant pool for your feet, and came out on the edge of the pool.

The drama was over.

Andrew had got to Meg first, and had pulled her out of the water. He just had to reach over and grab her, because she was swimming somehow, with her head underwater – she was moving toward the edge of the pool. He was carrying her now, and the lifeguard was trotting along behind. Cynthia had climbed out of the water and was running to meet them. The only person aloof from the situation was the boyfriend, who had stayed on the bench at the shallow end, drinking a milkshake. He smiled at me, and I thought that unfeeling of him, even though the danger was past. He may have meant it kindly. I noticed that he had not turned the radio off, just down.

Meg had not swallowed any water. She hadn't even scared herself. Her hair was plastered to her head and her eyes were wide open, golden with amazement.

"I was getting the comb," she said. "I didn't know it was deep."

Andrew said, "She was swimming! She was swimming by herself. I saw her bathing suit in the water and then I saw her swimming."

"She nearly drowned," Cynthia said. "Didn't she? Meg nearly drowned."

"I don't know how it could have happened," said the lifeguard. "One moment she was there, and the next she wasn't."

What had happened was that Meg had climbed out of the water at the shallow end and run along the edge of the pool toward the deep end. She saw a comb that somebody had dropped lying on the bottom. She crouched down and reached in to pick it up, quite deceived about the depth of the water. She went over the edge and slipped into the pool, making such a light splash that nobody heard – not the life-guard, who was kissing her boyfriend, or Cynthia, who was watching them. That must have been the moment under the trees when I thought, Where are the children? It must have been the same moment. At that moment, Meg was slipping, surprised, into the treacherously clear blue water.

"It's okay," I said to the lifeguard, who was nearly crying. "She can move pretty fast." (Though that wasn't what we usually said about Meg at all. We said she thought everything over and took her time.)

"You swam, Meg," said Cynthia, in a congratulatory way. (She told us about the kissing later.)

"I didn't know it was deep," Meg said. "I didn't drown."

WE HAD LUNCH at a takeout place, eating hamburgers and fries at a picnic table not far from the highway. In my excitement, I forgot to get Meg a plain hamburger, and had to scrape off the relish and mustard with plastic spoons, then wipe the meat with a paper napkin, before she would eat it. I took advantage of the trash can there to clean out the car. Then we resumed driving east, with the car windows open in front. Cynthia and Meg fell asleep in the back seat.

Andrew and I talked quietly about what had happened. Suppose I hadn't had the impulse just at that moment to check on the children? Suppose we had gone uptown to get drinks, as we had thought of doing? How had Andrew got over the fence? Did he jump or climb? (He couldn't remember.) How had he reached Meg so quickly? And think of the lifeguard not watching. And Cynthia, taken up with the kissing. Not seeing anything else. Not seeing Meg drop over the edge.

Disappeared.

But she swam. She held her breath and came up swimming.

What a chain of lucky links.

That was all we spoke about – luck. But I was compelled to picture the opposite. At this moment, we could have been filling out forms. Meg removed from us, Meg's body being prepared for shipment. To Vancouver – where we had never noticed such a thing as a graveyard – or to Ontario? The scribbled drawings she had made this morning would still be in the back seat of the car. How could this be borne all at once, how did people bear it? The plump, sweet shoulders and hands and feet, the fine brown hair, the rather satisfied, secretive expression – all exactly the same as when she had been alive. The most ordinary tragedy. A child drowned in a swimming pool at noon on a sunny day. Things tidied up quickly. The pool opens as usual at two o'clock. The lifeguard is a bit shaken up and gets the afternoon off. She drives away with her boyfriend in the Roto-Rooter truck. The body sealed away in some kind of shipping coffin. Sedatives, phone calls, arrangements. Such a sudden vacancy, a blind sinking and shifting. Waking up groggy from the pills, thinking for a moment it wasn't true. Thinking if only we hadn't stopped, if only we hadn't taken this route, if only they hadn't let us use the pool. Probably no one would ever have known about the comb.

There's something trashy about this kind of imagining, isn't there? Something shameful. Laying your finger on the wire to get the safe shock, feeling a bit of what it's like, then pulling back. I believed that Andrew was more scrupulous than I about such things, and that at this moment he was really trying to think about something else.

When I stood apart from my parents at Steve Gauley's funeral and watched them, and had this new, unpleasant feeling about them, I thought that I was understanding something about them for the first time. It was a deadly serious thing. I was understanding that they were implicated. Their big, stiff, dressed-up bodies did not stand between me and sudden death, or any kind of death. They gave consent. So it seemed. They gave consent to the death of children and to my death not by anything they said or thought but by the very fact that they had made children – they had made me. They had made me, and for that reason my death – however grieved they were, however they carried on – would seem to them anything but impossible or unnatural. This was a fact, and even then I knew they were not to blame.

But I did blame them. I charged them with effrontery, hypocrisy. On Steve Gauley's behalf, and on behalf of all children, who knew that by rights they should have sprung up free, to live a new, superior kind of life, not to be caught in the snares of vanquished grownups, with their sex and funerals.

Steve Gauley drowned, people said, because he was next thing to an orphan and was let run free. If he had been warned enough and given chores to do and kept in check, he wouldn't have fallen from an untrustworthy tree branch into a spring pond, a full gravel pit near the river – he wouldn't have drowned. He was neglected, he was free, so he drowned. And his father took it as an accident, such as might happen to a dog. He didn't have a good suit for the funeral, and he didn't bow his head for the prayers. But he was the only grownup that I let off the hook. He was the only one I didn't see giving consent. He couldn't prevent anything, but he wasn't implicated in anything, either – not like the others, saying the Lord's Prayer in their unnaturally weighted voices, oozing religion and dishonor.

AT GLENDIVE, not far from the North Dakota border, we had a choice – either to continue on the interstate or head northeast, toward Williston, taking Route 16, then some secondary roads that would get us back to Highway 2.

We agreed that the interstate would be faster, and that it was important for us not to spend too much time – that is, money – on the road. Nevertheless we decided to cut back to Highway 2.

"I just like the idea of it better," I said.

Andrew said, "That's because it's what we planned to do in the beginning."

"We missed seeing Kalispell and Havre. And Wolf Point. I like the name."

"We'll see them on the way back."

Andrew's saying "on the way back" was a surprising pleasure to me. Of course, I had believed that we would be coming back, with our car and our lives and our family intact, having covered all that distance, having dealt somehow with those loyalties and problems, held ourselves up for inspection in such a foolhardy way. But it was a relief to hear him say it.

"What I can't get over," said Andrew, "is how you got the signal. It's got to be some kind of extra sense that mothers have."

Partly I wanted to believe that, to bask in my extra sense. Partly I wanted to warn him – to warn everybody – never to count on it.

"What I can't understand," I said, "is how you got over the fence."

"Neither can I."

So we went on, with the two in the back seat trusting us, because of no choice, and we ourselves trusting to be forgiven, in time, for everything that had first to be seen and condemned by those children: whatever was flippant, arbitrary, careless, callous – all our natural, and particular, mistakes.

FRIEND OF MY YOUTH

With thanks to R.J.T.

I USED TO DREAM about my mother, and though the details in the dream varied, the surprise in it was always the same. The dream stopped, I suppose, because it was too transparent in its hopefulness, too easy in its forgiveness.

In the dream I would be the age I really was, living the life I was really living, and I would discover that my mother was still alive. (The fact is, she died when I was in my early twenties and she in her early fifties.) Sometimes I would find myself in our old kitchen, where my mother would be rolling out piecrust on the table, or washing the dishes in the battered cream-colored dishpan with the red rim. But other times I would run into her on the street, in places where I would never have expected to see her. She might be walking through a handsome hotel lobby, or lining up in an airport. She would be looking quite well – not exactly youthful, not entirely untouched by the paralyzing disease that held her in its grip for a decade or more before her death, but so much better than I remembered that I would be astonished. Oh, I just have this little tremor in my arm, she would say, and a little stiffness up this side of my face. It is a nuisance but I get around.

I recovered then what in waking life I had lost – my mother's liveliness of face and voice before her throat muscles stiffened and a woeful, impersonal mask fastened itself over her features. How could I have forgotten this, I would think in the dream – the casual humor she had, not ironic but merry, the lightness and impatience and confidence? I would say that I was sorry I hadn't been to see her in such a long time – meaning not that I felt guilty but that I was sorry I had kept a bugbear in my mind, instead of this reality – and the strangest, kindest thing of all to me was her matter-of-fact reply.

Oh, well, she said, better late than never. I was sure I'd see you someday.

*   *   *

WHEN MY MOTHER was a young woman with a soft, mischievous face and shiny, opaque silk stockings on her plump legs (I have seen a photograph of her, with her pupils), she went to teach at a one-room school, called Grieves School, in the Ottawa Valley. The school was on a corner of the farm that belonged to the Grieves family – a very good farm for that country. Well-drained fields with none of the Precambrian rock shouldering through the soil, a little willow-edged river running alongside, a sugar bush, log barns, and a large, unornamented house whose wooden walls had never been painted but had been left to weather. And when wood weathers in the Ottawa Valley, my mother said, I do not know why this is, but it never turns gray, it turns black. There must be something in the air, she said. She often spoke of the Ottawa Valley, which was her home – she had grown up about twenty miles away from Grieves School – in a dogmatic, mystified way, emphasizing things about it that distinguished it from any other place on earth. Houses turn black, maple syrup has a taste no maple syrup produced elsewhere can equal, bears amble within sight of farmhouses. Of course I was disappointed when I finally got to see this place. It was not a valley at all, if by that you mean a cleft between hills; it was a mixture of flat fields and low rocks and heavy bush and little lakes – a scrambled, disarranged sort of country with no easy harmony about it, not yielding readily to any description.

The log barns and unpainted house, common enough on poor farms, were not in the Grieveses' case a sign of poverty but of policy. They had the money but they did not spend it. That was what people told my mother. The Grieveses worked hard and they were far from ignorant, but they were very backward. They didn't have a car or electricity or a telephone or a tractor. Some people thought this was because they were Cameronians – they were the only people in the school district who were of that religion – but in fact their church (which they themselves always called the Reformed Presbyterian) did not forbid engines or electricity or any inventions of that sort, just cardplaying, dancing, movies, and, on Sundays, any activity at all that was not religious or unavoidable.

My mother could not say who the Cameronians were or why they were called that. Some freak religion from Scotland, she said from the perch of her obedient and lighthearted Anglicanism. The teacher always boarded with the Grieveses, and my mother was a little daunted at the thought of going to live in that black board house with its paralytic Sundays and coal-oil lamps and primitive notions. But she was engaged by that time, she wanted to work on her trousseau instead of running around the country having a good time, and she figured she could get home one Sunday out of three. (On Sundays at the Grieveses' house, you could light a fire for heat but not for cooking, you could not even boil the kettle to make tea, and you were not supposed to write a letter or swat a fly. But it turned out that my mother was exempt from these rules. "No, no," said Flora Grieves, laughing at her. "That doesn't mean you. You must just go on as you're used to doing." And after a while my mother had made friends with Flora to such an extent that she wasn't even going home on the Sundays when she'd planned to.)

Flora and Ellie Grieves were the two sisters left of the family. Ellie was married, to a man called Robert Deal, who lived there and worked the farm but had not changed its name to Deal's in anyone's mind. By the way people spoke, my mother expected the Grieves sisters and Robert Deal to be middle-aged at least, but Ellie, the younger sister, was only about thirty, and Flora seven or eight years older. Robert Deal might be in between.

The house was divided in an unexpected way. The married couple didn't live with Flora. At the time of their marriage, she had given them the parlor and the dining room, the front bedrooms and staircase, the winter kitchen. There was no need to decide about the bathroom, because there wasn't one. Flora had the summer kitchen, with its open rafters and uncovered brick walls, the old pantry made into a narrow dining room and sitting room, and the two back bedrooms, one of which was my mother's. The teacher was housed with Flora, in the poorer part of the house. But my mother didn't mind. She immediately preferred Flora, and Flora's cheerfulness, to the silence and sickroom atmosphere of the front rooms. In Flora's domain it was not even true that all amusements were forbidden. She had a crokinole board – she taught my mother how to play.

The division had been made, of course, in the expectation that Robert and Ellie would have a family, and that they would need the room. This hadn't happened. They had been married for more than a dozen years and there had not been a live child. Time and again Ellie had been pregnant, but two babies had been stillborn, and the rest she had miscarried. During my mother's first year, Ellie seemed to be staying in bed more and more of the time, and my mother thought that she must be pregnant again, but there was no mention of it. Such people would not mention it. You could not tell from the look of Ellie, when she got up and walked around, because she showed a stretched and ruined though slack-chested shape. She carried a sickbed odor, and she fretted in a childish way about everything. Flora took care of her and did all the work. She washed the clothes and tidied up the rooms and cooked the meals served in both sides of the house, as well as helping Robert with the milking and separating. She was up before daylight and never seemed to tire. During the first spring my mother was there, a great housecleaning was embarked upon, during which Flora climbed the ladders herself and carried down the storm windows, washed and stacked them away, carried all the furniture out of one room after another so that she could scrub the woodwork and varnish the floors. She washed every dish and glass that was sitting in the cupboards supposedly clean already. She scalded every pot and spoon. Such need and energy possessed her that she could hardly sleep – my mother would wake up to the sound of stovepipes being taken down, or the broom, draped in a dish towel, whacking at the smoky cobwebs. Through the washed uncurtained windows came a torrent of unmerciful light. The cleanliness was devastating. My mother slept now on sheets that had been bleached and starched and that gave her a rash. Sick Ellie complained daily of the smell of varnish and cleansing powders. Flora's hands were raw. But her disposition remained top-notch. Her kerchief and apron and Robert's baggy overalls that she donned for the climbing jobs gave her the air of a comedian – sportive, unpredictable.

My mother called her a whirling dervish.

"You're a regular whirling dervish, Flora," she said, and Flora halted. She wanted to know what was meant. My mother went ahead and explained, though she was a little afraid lest piety should be offended.

(Not piety exactly – you could not call it that. Religious strictness.) Of course it wasn't. There was not a trace of nastiness or smug vigilance in Flora's observance of her religion. She had no fear of heathens – she had always lived in the midst of them. She liked the idea of being a dervish, and went to tell her sister.

"Do you know what the teacher says I am?"

Flora and Ellie were both dark-haired, dark-eyed women, tall and narrow-shouldered and long-legged. Ellie was a wreck, of course, but Flora was still superbly straight and graceful. She could look like a queen, my mother said – even riding into town in that cart they had. For church they used a buggy or a cutter, but when they went to town they often had to transport sacks of wool – they kept a few sheep – or of produce, to sell, and they had to bring provisions home. The trip of a few miles was not made often. Robert rode in front, to drive the horse – Flora could drive a horse perfectly well, but it must always be the man who drove. Flora would be standing behind holding on to the sacks. She rode to town and back standing up, keeping an easy balance, wearing her black hat. Almost ridiculous but not quite. A gypsy queen, my mother thought she looked like, with her black hair and her skin that always looked slightly tanned, and her lithe and bold serenity. Of course she lacked the gold bangles and the bright clothes. My mother envied her her slenderness, and her cheekbones.

RETURNING IN THE fall for her second year, my mother learned what was the matter with Ellie.

"My sister has a growth," Flora said. Nobody then spoke of cancer.

My mother had heard that before. People suspected it. My mother knew many people in the district by that time. She had made particular friends with a young woman who worked in the Post Office; this woman was going to be one of my mother's bridesmaids. The story of Flora and Ellie and Robert had been told – or all that people knew of it – in various versions. My mother did not feel that she was listening to gossip, because she was always on the alert for any disparaging remarks about Flora – she would not put up with that. But indeed nobody offered any.

Everybody said that Flora had behaved like a saint. Even when she went to extremes, as in dividing up the house – that was like a saint.

Robert came to work at Grieveses' some months before the girls' father died. They knew him already, from church. (Oh, that church, my mother said, having attended it once, out of curiosity – that drear building miles on the other side of town, no organ or piano and plain glass in the windows and a doddery old minister with his hours-long sermon, a man hitting a tuning fork for the singing.) Robert had come out from Scotland and was on his way west. He had stopped with relatives or people he knew, members of the scanty congregation. To earn some money, probably, he came to Grieveses'. Soon he and Flora were engaged. They could not go to dances or to card parties like other couples, but they went for long walks. The chaperone – unofficially – was Ellie. Ellie was then a wild tease, a long-haired, impudent, childish girl full of lolloping energy. She would run up hills and smite the mullein stalks with a stick, shouting and prancing and pretending to be a warrior on horseback. That, or the horse itself. This when she was fifteen, sixteen years old. Nobody but Flora could control her, and generally Flora just laughed at her, being too used to her to wonder if she was quite right in the head. They were wonderfully fond of each other. Ellie, with her long skinny body, her long pale face, was like a copy of Flora – the kind of copy you often see in families, in which because of some carelessness or exaggeration of features or coloring, the handsomeness of one person passes into the plainness – or almost plainness – of the other. But Ellie had no jealousy about this. She loved to comb out Flora's hair and pin it up. They had great times, washing each other's hair. Ellie would press her face into Flora's throat, like a colt nuzzling its mother. So when Robert laid claim to Flora, or Flora to him – nobody knew how it was – Ellie had to be included. She didn't show any spite toward Robert, but she pursued and waylaid them on their walks; she sprung on them out of the bushes or sneaked up behind them so softly that she could blow on their necks. People saw her do it. And they heard of her jokes. She had always been terrible for jokes and sometimes it had got her into trouble with her father, but Flora had protected her. Now she put thistles in Robert's bed. She set his place at the table with the knife and fork the wrong way around. She switched the milk pails to give him the old one with the hole in it. For Flora's sake, maybe, Robert humored her.

The father had made Flora and Robert set the wedding day a year ahead, and after he died they did not move it any closer. Robert went on living in the house. Nobody knew how to speak to Flora about this being scandalous, or looking scandalous. Flora would just ask why. Instead of putting the wedding ahead, she put it back – from next spring to early fall, so that there should be a full year between it and her father's death. A year from wedding to funeral – that seemed proper to her. She trusted fully in Robert's patience and in her own purity.

So she might. But in the winter a commotion started. There was Ellie, vomiting, weeping, running off and hiding in the haymow, howling when they found her and pulled her out, jumping to the barn floor, running around in circles, rolling in the snow. Ellie was deranged. Flora had to call the doctor. She told him that her sister's periods had stopped – could the backup of blood be driving her wild? Robert had had to catch her and tie her up, and together he and Flora had put her to bed. She would not take food, just whipped her head from side to side, howling. It looked as if she would die speechless. But somehow the truth came out. Not from the doctor, who could not get close enough to examine her, with all her thrashing about. Probably, Robert confessed. Flora finally got wind of the truth, through all her high-mindedness. Now there had to be a wedding, though not the one that had been planned.

No cake, no new clothes, no wedding trip, no congratulations. Just a shameful hurry-up visit to the manse. Some people, seeing the names in the paper, thought the editor must have got the sisters mixed up. They thought it must be Flora. A hurry-up wedding for Flora! But no – it was Flora who pressed Robert's suit – it must have been – and got Ellie out of bed and washed her and made her presentable. It would have been Flora who picked one geranium from the window plant and pinned it to her sister's dress. And Ellie hadn't torn it out. Ellie was meek now, no longer flailing or crying. She let Flora fix her up, she let herself be married, she was never wild from that day on.

Flora had the house divided. She herself helped Robert build the necessary partitions. The baby was carried full term – nobody even pretended that it was early – but it was born dead after a long, tearing labor. Perhaps Ellie had damaged it when she jumped from the barn beam and rolled in the snow and beat on herself. Even if she hadn't done that, people would have expected something to go wrong, with that child or maybe one that came later. God dealt out punishment for hurry-up marriages – not just Presbyterians but almost everybody else believed that. God rewarded lust with dead babies, idiots, harelips and withered limbs and clubfeet.

In this case the punishment continued. Ellie had one miscarriage after another, then another stillbirth and more miscarriages. She was constantly pregnant, and the pregnancies were full of vomiting fits that lasted for days, headaches, cramps, dizzy spells. The miscarriages were as agonizing as full-term births. Ellie could not do her own work. She walked around holding on to chairs. Her numb silence passed off, and she became a complainer. If anybody came to visit, she would talk about the peculiarities of her headaches or describe her latest fainting fit, or even – in front of men, in front of unmarried girls or children – go into bloody detail about what Flora called her "disappointments." When people changed the subject or dragged the children away, she turned sullen. She demanded new medicine, reviled the doctor, nagged Flora. She accused Flora of washing the dishes with a great clang and clatter, out of spite, of pulling her – Ellie's – hair when she combed it out, of stingily substituting water-and-molasses for her real medicine. No matter what she said, Flora soothed her. Everybody who came into the house had some story of that kind to tell. Flora said, "Where's my little girl, then? Where's my Ellie? This isn't my Ellie, this is some crosspatch got in here in place of her!"

In the winter evenings after she came in from helping Robert with the barn chores, Flora would wash and change her clothes and go next door to read Ellie to sleep. My mother might invite herself along, taking whatever sewing she was doing, on some item of her trousseau. Ellie's bed was set up in the big dining room, where there was a gas lamp over the table. My mother sat on one side of the table, sewing, and Flora sat on the other side, reading aloud. Sometimes Ellie said, "I can't hear you." Or if Flora paused for a little rest Ellie said, "I'm not asleep yet."

What did Flora read? Stories about Scottish life – not classics. Stories about urchins and comic grandmothers. The only title my mother could remember was *Wee Macgregor*. She could not follow the stories very well, or laugh when Flora laughed and Ellie gave a whimper, because so much was in Scots dialect or read with that thick accent. She was surprised that Flora could do it – it wasn't the way Flora ordinarily talked, at all.

(But wouldn't it be the way Robert talked? Perhaps that is why my mother never reports anything that Robert said, never has him contributing to the scene. He must have been there, he must have been sitting there in the room. They would only heat the main room of the house. I see him black-haired, heavy-shouldered, with the strength of a plow horse, and the same kind of sombre, shackled beauty.)

Then Flora would say, "That's all of that for tonight." She would pick up another book, an old book written by some preacher of their faith. There was in it such stuff as my mother had never heard. What stuff? She couldn't say. All the stuff that was in their monstrous old religion. That put Ellie to sleep, or made her pretend she was asleep, after a couple of pages.

All that configuration of the elect and the damned, my mother must have meant – all the arguments about the illusion and necessity of free will. Doom and slippery redemption. The torturing, defeating, but for some minds irresistible pileup of interlocking and contradictory notions. My mother could resist it. Her faith was easy, her spirits at that time robust. Ideas were not what she was curious about, ever.

But what sort of thing was that, she asked (silently), to read to a dying woman? This was the nearest she got to criticizing Flora.

The answer – that it was the only thing, if you believed it – never seemed to have occurred to her.

BY SPRING A NURSE had arrived. That was the way things were done then. People died at home, and a nurse came in to manage it.

The nurse's name was Audrey Atkinson. She was a stout woman with corsets as stiff as barrel hoops, marcelled hair the color of brass candlesticks, a mouth shaped by lipstick beyond its own stingy outlines. She drove a car into the yard – her own car, a dark-green coupé, shiny and smart. News of Audrey Atkinson and her car spread quickly. Questions were asked. Where did she get the money? Had some rich fool altered his will on her behalf? Had she exercised influence? Or simply helped herself to a stash of bills under the mattress? How was she to be trusted?

Hers was the first car ever to sit in the Grieveses' yard overnight.

Audrey Atkinson said that she had never been called out to tend a case in so primitive a house. It was beyond her, she said, how people could live in such a way.

"It's not that they're poor, even," she said to my mother. "It isn't, is it? That I could understand. Or it's not even their religion. So what is it? They do not care!"

She tried at first to cozy up to my mother, as if they would be natural allies in this benighted place. She spoke as if they were around the same age – both stylish, intelligent women who liked a good time and had modern ideas. She offered to teach my mother to drive the car. She offered her cigarettes. My mother was more tempted by the idea of learning to drive than she was by the cigarettes. But she said no, she would wait for her husband to teach her. Audrey Atkinson raised her pinkish-orange eyebrows at my mother behind Flora's back, and my mother was furious. She disliked the nurse far more than Flora did.

"I knew what she was like and Flora didn't," my mother said. She meant that she caught a whiff of a cheap life, maybe even of drinking establishments and unsavory men, of hard bargains, which Flora was too unworldly to notice.

Flora started into the great housecleaning again. She had the curtains spread out on stretchers, she beat the rugs on the line, she leapt up on the stepladder to attack the dust on the molding. But she was impeded all the time by Nurse Atkinson's complaining.

"I wondered if we could have a little less of the running and clattering?" said Nurse Atkinson with offensive politeness. "I only ask for my patient's sake." She always spoke of Ellie as "my patient" and pretended that she was the only one to protect her and compel respect. But she was not so respectful of Ellie herself. "Allee-oop," she would say, dragging the poor creature up on her pillows. And she told Ellie she was not going to stand for fretting and whimpering. "You don't do yourself any good that way," she said. "And you certainly don't make me come any quicker. What you just as well might do is learn to control yourself." She exclaimed at Ellie's bedsores in a scolding way, as if they were a further disgrace of the house. She demanded lotions, ointments, expensive soaps – most of them, no doubt, to protect her own skin, which she claimed suffered from the hard water. (How could it be hard, my mother asked her – sticking up for the household when nobody else would – how could it be hard when it came straight from the rain barrel?)

Nurse Atkinson wanted cream too – she said that they should hold some back, not sell it all to the creamery. She wanted to make nourishing soups and puddings for her patient. She did make puddings, and jellies, from packaged mixes such as had never before entered this house. My mother was convinced that she ate them all herself.

Flora still read to Ellie, but now it was only short bits from the Bible. When she finished and stood up, Ellie tried to cling to her. Ellie wept, sometimes she made ridiculous complaints. She said there was a horned cow outside, trying to get into the room and kill her.

"They often get some kind of idea like that," Nurse Atkinson said. "You mustn't give in to her or she won't let you go day or night. That's what they're like, they only think about themselves. Now, when I'm here alone with her, she behaves herself quite nice. I don't have any trouble at all. But after you been in here I have trouble all over again because she sees you and she gets upset. You don't want to make my job harder for me, do you? I mean, you brought me here to take charge, didn't you?"

"Ellie, now, Ellie dear, I must go," said Flora, and to the nurse she said, "I understand. I do understand that you have to be in charge and I admire you, I admire you for your work. In your work you have to have so much patience and kindness."

My mother wondered at this – was Flora really so blinded, or did she hope by this undeserved praise to exhort Nurse Atkinson to the patience and kindness that she didn't have? Nurse Atkinson was too thick-skinned and self-approving for any trick like that to work.

"It is a hard job, all right, and not many can do it," she said. "It's not like those nurses in the hospital, where they got everything laid out for them." She had no time for more conversation – she was trying to bring in "Make-Believe Ballroom" on her battery radio.

My mother was busy with the final exams and the June exercises at the school. She was getting ready for her wedding in July. Friends came in cars and whisked her off to the dressmaker's, to parties, to choose the invitations and order the cake. The lilacs came out, the evenings lengthened, the birds were back and nesting, my mother bloomed in everybody's attention, about to set out on the deliciously solemn adventure of marriage. Her dress was to be appliquéd with silk roses, her veil held by a cap of seed pearls. She belonged to the first generation of young women who saved their money and paid for their own weddings – far fancier than their parents could have afforded.

On her last evening, the friend from the Post Office came to drive her away, with her clothes and her books and the things she had made for her trousseau and the gifts her pupils and others had given her. There was great fuss and laughter about getting everything loaded into the car. Flora came out and helped. This getting married is even more of a nuisance than I thought, said Flora, laughing. She gave my mother a dresser scarf, which she had crocheted in secret. Nurse Atkinson could not be shut out of an important occasion – she presented a spray bottle of cologne. Flora stood on the slope at the side of the house to wave goodbye. She had been invited to the wedding, but of course she had said she could not come, she could not "go out" at such a time. The last my mother ever saw of her was this solitary, energetically waving figure in her housecleaning apron and bandanna, on the green slope by the black-walled house, in the evening light.

"Well, maybe now she'll get what she should've got the first time round," the friend from the Post Office said. "Maybe now they'll be able to get married. Is she too old to start a family? How old is she, anyway?"

My mother thought that this was a crude way of talking about Flora and replied that she didn't know. But she had to admit to herself that she had been thinking the very same thing.

*　　*　　*

WHEN SHE WAS married and settled in her own home, three hundred miles away, my mother got a letter from Flora. Ellie was dead. She had died firm in her faith, Flora said, and grateful for her release. Nurse Atkinson was staying on for a little while, until it was time for her to go off to her next case. This was late in the summer.

News of what happened next did not come from Flora. When she wrote at Christmas, she seemed to take for granted that information would have gone ahead of her.

You have in all probability heard, wrote Flora, *that Robert and Nurse Atkinson have been married. They are living on here, in Robert's part of the house. They are fixing it up to suit themselves. It is very impolite of me to call her Nurse Atkinson, as I see I have done. I ought to have called her Audrey.*

Of course the Post Office friend had written, and so had others. It was a great shock and scandal and a matter that excited the district – the wedding as secret and surprising as Robert's first one had been (though surely not for the same reason), Nurse Atkinson permanently installed in the community, Flora losing out for the second time. Nobody had been aware of any courtship, and they asked how the woman could have enticed him. Did she promise children, lying about her age?

The surprises were not to stop with the wedding. The bride got down to business immediately with the "fixing up" that Flora mentioned. In came the electricity and then the telephone. Now Nurse Atkinson – she would always be called Nurse Atkinson – was heard on the party line lambasting painters and paperhangers and delivery services. She was having everything done over. She was buying an electric stove and putting in a bathroom, and who knew where the money was coming from? Was it all hers, got in her deathbed dealings, in shady bequests? Was it Robert's, was he claiming his share? Ellie's share, left to him and Nurse Atkinson to enjoy themselves with, the shameless pair?

All these improvements took place on one side of the house only. Flora's side remained just as it was. No electric lights there, no fresh wallpaper or new venetian blinds. When the house was painted on the outside – cream with dark-green trim – Flora's side was left bare. This strange open statement was greeted at first with pity and disapproval, then with less sympathy, as a sign of Flora's stubbornness and eccentricity (she could have bought her own paint and made it look decent), and finally as a joke. People drove out of their way to see it.

There was always a dance given in the schoolhouse for a newly married couple. A cash collection – called "a purse of money" – was presented to them. Nurse Atkinson sent out word that she would not mind seeing this custom followed, even though it happened that the family she had married into was opposed to dancing. Some people thought it would be a disgrace to gratify her, a slap in the face to Flora. Others were too curious to hold back. They wanted to see how the newlyweds would behave. Would Robert dance? What sort of outfit would the bride show up in? They delayed a while, but finally the dance was held, and my mother got her report.

The bride wore the dress she had worn at her wedding, or so she said. But who would wear such a dress for a wedding at the manse? More than likely it was bought specially for her appearance at the dance. Pure-white satin with a sweetheart neckline, idiotically youthful. The groom was got up in a new dark-blue suit, and she had stuck a flower in his buttonhole. They were a sight. Her hair was freshly done to blind the eye with brassy reflections, and her face looked as if it would come off on a man's jacket, should she lay it against his shoulder in the dancing. Of course she did dance. She danced with every man present except the groom, who sat scrunched into one of the school desks along the wall. She danced with every man present – they all claimed they had to do it, it was the custom – and then she dragged Robert out to receive the money and to thank everybody for their best wishes. To the ladies in the cloakroom she even hinted that she was feeling unwell, for the usual newlywed reason. Nobody believed her, and indeed nothing ever came of this hope, if she really had it. Some of the women thought that she was lying to them out of malice, insulting them, making them out to be so credulous. But nobody challenged her, nobody was rude to her – maybe because it was plain that she could summon a rudeness of her own to knock anybody flat.

Flora was not present at the dance.

"My sister-in-law is not a dancer," said Nurse Atkinson. "She is stuck in the olden times." She invited them to laugh at Flora, whom she always called her sister-in-law, though she had no right to do so.

My mother wrote a letter to Flora after hearing about all these things. Being removed from the scene, and perhaps in a flurry of importance due to her own newly married state, she may have lost sight of the kind of person she was writing to. She offered sympathy and showed outrage, and said blunt disparaging things about the woman who had – as my mother saw it – dealt Flora such a blow. Back came a letter from Flora saying that she did not know where my mother had been getting her information, but that it seemed she had misunderstood, or listened to malicious people, or jumped to unjustified conclusions. What happened in Flora's family was nobody else's business, and certainly nobody needed to feel sorry for her or angry on her behalf. Flora said that she was happy and satisfied in her life, as she always had been, and she did not interfere with what others did or wanted, because such things did not concern her. She wished my mother all happiness in her marriage and hoped that she would soon be too busy with her own responsibilities to worry about the lives of people that she used to know.

This well-written letter cut my mother, as she said, to the quick. She and Flora stopped corresponding. My mother did become busy with her own life and finally a prisoner in it.

But she thought about Flora. In later years, when she sometimes talked about the things she might have been, or done, she would say, "If I could have been a writer – I do think I could have been; I could have been a writer – then I would have written the story of Flora's life. And do you know what I would have called it? 'The Maiden Lady.'"

The Maiden Lady. She said these words in a solemn and sentimental tone of voice that I had no use for. I knew, or thought I knew, exactly the value she found in them. The stateliness and mystery. The hint of derision turning to reverence. I was fifteen or sixteen years old by that time, and I believed that I could see into my mother's mind. I could see what she would do with Flora, what she had already done. She would make her into a noble figure, one who accepts defection, treachery, who forgives and stands aside, not once but twice. Never a moment of complaint. Flora goes about her cheerful labors, she cleans the house and shovels out the cow byre, she removes some bloody mess from her sister's bed, and when at last the future seems to open up for her – Ellie will die and Robert will beg forgiveness and Flora will silence him with the proud gift of herself – it is time for Audrey Atkinson to drive into the yard and shut Flora out again, more inexplicably and thoroughly the second time than the first. She must endure the painting of the house, the electric lights, all the prosperous activity next door. "Make-Believe Ballroom," "Amos 'n' Andy." No more Scottish comedies or ancient sermons. She must see them drive off to the dance – her old lover and that coldhearted, stupid, by no means beautiful woman in the white satin wedding dress. She is mocked. (And of course she has made over the farm to Ellie and Robert, of course he has inherited it, and now everything belongs to Audrey Atkinson.) The wicked flourish. But it is all right. It is all right – the elect are veiled in patience and humility and lighted by a certainty that events cannot disturb.

That was what I believed my mother would make of things. In her own plight her notions had turned mystical, and there was sometimes a hush, a solemn thrill in her voice that grated on me, alerted me to what seemed a personal danger. I felt a great fog of platitudes and pieties lurking, an incontestable crippled-mother power, which could capture and choke me. There would be no end to it. I had to keep myself sharp-tongued and cynical, arguing and deflating. Eventually I gave up even that recognition and opposed her in silence.

This is a fancy way of saying that I was no comfort and poor company to her when she had almost nowhere else to turn.

I had my own ideas about Flora's story. I didn't think that I could have written a novel but that I would write one. I would take a different tack. I saw through my mother's story and put in what she left out. My Flora would be as black as hers was white. Rejoicing in the bad turns done to her and in her own forgiveness, spying on the shambles of her sister's life. A Presbyterian witch, reading out of her poisonous book. It takes a rival ruthlessness, the comparatively innocent brutality of the thick-skinned nurse, to drive her back, to flourish in her shade. But she is driven back; the power of sex and ordinary greed drive her back and shut her up in her own part of the house with the coal-oil lamps. She shrinks, she caves in, her bones harden and her joints thicken, and – oh, this is it, I see the bare beauty of the ending I will contrive! – she becomes crippled herself, with arthritis, hardly able to move. Now Audrey Atkinson comes into her full power – she demands the whole house. She wants those partitions knocked out that Robert put up with Flora's help when he married Ellie. She will provide Flora with a room, she will take care of her. (Audrey Atkinson does not wish to be seen as a monster, and perhaps she really isn't one.) So one day Robert carries Flora – for the first and last time he carries her in his arms – to the room that his wife Audrey has prepared for her. And once Flora is settled in her well-lit, well-heated corner Audrey Atkinson undertakes to clean out the newly vacated rooms, Flora's rooms. She carries a heap of old books out into the yard. It's spring again, housecleaning time, the season when Flora herself performed such feats, and now the pale face of Flora appears behind the new net curtains. She has dragged herself from her corner, she sees the light-blue sky with its high skidding clouds over the watery fields, the contending crows, the flooded creeks, the reddening tree branches. She sees the smoke rise out of the incinerator in the yard, where her books are burning. Those smelly old books, as Audrey has called them. Words and pages, the ominous dark spines. The elect, the damned, the slim hopes, the mighty torments – up in smoke. There was the ending.

To me the really mysterious person in the story, as my mother told it, was Robert. He never has a word to say. He gets engaged to Flora. He is walking beside her along the river when Ellie leaps out at them. He finds Ellie's thistles in his bed. He does the carpentry made necessary by his and Ellie's marriage. He listens or does not listen while Flora reads. Finally he sits scrunched up in the school desk while his flashy bride dances by with all the men.

So much for his public acts and appearances. But he was the one who started everything, in secret. He *did it to* Ellie. He did it to that skinny wild girl at a time when he was engaged to her sister, and he did it to her again and again when she was nothing but a poor botched body, a failed childbearer, lying in bed.

He must have done it to Audrey Atkinson, too, but with less disastrous results.

Those words, *did it to* – the words my mother, no more than Flora, would never bring herself to speak – were simply exciting to me. I didn't feel any decent revulsion or reasonable indignation. I refused the warning. Not even the fate of Ellie could put me off. Not when I thought of that first encounter – the desperation of it, the ripping and striving. I used to sneak longing looks at men in those days. I admired their wrists and their necks and any bit of their chests a loose button let show, and even their ears and their feet in shoes. I expected nothing reasonable of them, only to be engulfed by their passion. I had similar thoughts about Robert.

What made Flora evil in my story was just what made her admirable in my mother's – her turning away from sex. I fought against everything my mother wanted to tell me on this subject; I despised even the drop in her voice, the gloomy caution, with which she approached it. My mother had grown up in a time and in a place where sex was a dark undertaking for women. She knew that you could die of it. So she honored the decency, the prudery, the frigidity, that might protect you. And I grew up in horror of that very protection, the dainty tyranny that seemed to me to extend to all areas of life, to enforce tea parties and white gloves and all other sorts of tinkling inanities. I favored bad words and a breakthrough, I teased myself with the thought of a man's reck-lessness and domination. The odd thing is that my mother's ideas were in line with some progressive notions of her times, and mine echoed the notions that were favored in my time. This in spite of the fact that we both believed ourselves independent, and lived in backwaters that did not register such changes. It's as if tendencies that seem most deeply rooted in our minds, most private and singular, have come in as spores on the prevailing wind, looking for any likely place to land, any welcome.

NOT LONG BEFORE she died, but when I was still at home, my mother got a letter from the real Flora. It came from that town near the farm, the town that Flora used to ride to, with Robert, in the cart, holding on to the sacks of wool or potatoes.

Flora wrote that she was no longer living on the farm.

Robert and Audrey are still there, she wrote. *Robert has some trouble with his back but otherwise he is very well. Audrey has poor circulation and is often short of breath. The doctor says she must lose weight but none of the diets seem to work. The farm has been doing very well. They are out of sheep entirely and into dairy cattle. As you may have heard, the chief thing nowadays is to get your milk quota from the government and then you are set. The old stable is all fixed up with milking machines and the latest modern equipment, it is quite a marvel. When I go out there to visit I hardly know where I am.*

She went on to say that she had been living in town for some years now, and that she had a job clerking in a store. She must have said what kind of a store this was, but I cannot now remember. She said nothing, of course, about what had led her to this decision – whether she had in fact been put off her own farm, or had sold out her share, apparently not to much advantage. She stressed the fact of her friendliness with Robert and Audrey. She said her health was good.

I hear that you have not been so lucky in that way, she wrote. *I ran into Cleta Barnes who used to be Cleta Stapleton at the post office out at home, and she told me that there is some problem with your muscles and she said your speech is affected too. This is sad to hear but they can do such wonderful things nowadays so I am hoping that the doctors may be able to help you.*

An unsettling letter, leaving so many things out. Nothing in it about God's will or His role in our afflictions. No mention of whether Flora still went to that church. I don't think my mother ever answered. Her fine legible handwriting, her schoolteacher's writing, had deteriorated, and she had difficulty holding a pen. She was always beginning letters and not finishing them. I would find them lying around the house. *My dearest Mary,* they began. *My darling Ruth, My dear little Joanne (though I realize you are not little anymore), My dear old friend Cleta, My lovely Margaret.* These women were friends from her teaching days, her Normal School days, and from high school. A few were former pupils. I have friends all over the country, she would say defiantly. I have dear, dear friends.

I remember seeing one letter that started out: *Friend of my Youth.* I don't know whom it was to. They were all friends of her youth. I don't recall one that began with *My dear and most admired Flora.* I would always look at them, try to read the salutation and the few sentences she had written, and because I could not bear to feel sadness I would feel an impatience with the flowery language, the direct appeal for love and pity. She would get more of that, I thought (more from myself, I meant), if she could manage to withdraw with dignity, instead of reaching out all the time to cast her stricken shadow.

I had lost interest in Flora by then. I was always thinking of stories, and by this time I probably had a new one on my mind.

But I have thought of her since. I have wondered what kind of a store. A hardware store or a five-and-ten, where she has to wear a coverall, or a drugstore, where she is uniformed like a nurse, or a Ladies' Wear, where she is expected to be genteelly fashionable? She might have had to learn about food blenders or chain saws, negligees, cosmetics, even condoms. She would have to work all day under electric lights, and operate a cash register. Would she get a permanent, paint her nails, put on lipstick? She must have found a place to live – a little apartment with a kitchenette, overlooking the main street, or a room in a boardinghouse. How could she go on being a Cameronian? How could she get to that out-of-the-way church unless she managed to buy a car and learned to drive it? And if she did that she might drive not only to church but to other places. She might go on holidays. She might rent a cottage on a lake for a week, learn to swim, visit a city. She might eat meals in a restaurant, possibly in a restaurant where drinks were served. She might make friends with women who were divorced.

She might meet a man. A friend's widowed brother, perhaps. A man who did not know that she was a Cameronian or what Cameronians were. Who knew nothing of her story. A man who had never heard about the partial painting of the house or the two betrayals, or that it took all her dignity and innocence to keep her from being a joke. He might want to take her dancing, and she would have to explain that she could not go. He would be surprised but not put off – all that Cameronian business might seem quaint to him, almost charming. So it would to everybody. She was brought up in some weird religion, people would say. She lived a long time out on some godforsaken farm. She is a little bit strange but really quite nice. Nice-looking too. Especially since she went and got her hair done.

I might go into a store and find her.

No, no. She would be dead a long time now.

But suppose I had gone into a store – perhaps a department store. I see a place with the brisk atmosphere, the straightforward displays, the old-fashioned modern look of the fifties. Suppose a tall, handsome woman, nicely turned out, had come to wait on me, and I had known, somehow, in spite of the sprayed and puffed hair and the pink or coral lips and fingernails – I had known that this was Flora. I would have wanted to tell her that I knew, I knew her story, though we had never met. I imagine myself trying to tell her. (This is a dream now, I understand it as a dream.) I imagine her listening, with a pleasant composure. But she shakes her head. She smiles at me, and in her smile there is a degree of mockery, a faint, self-assured malice. Weariness, as well. She is not surprised that I am telling her this, but she is weary of it, of me and my idea of her, my information, my notion that I can know anything about her.

Of course it's my mother I'm thinking of, my mother as she was in those dreams, saying, It's nothing, just this little tremor; saying with such astonishing lighthearted forgiveness, Oh, I knew you'd come someday. My mother surprising me, and doing it almost indifferently. Her mask, her fate, and most of her affliction taken away. How relieved I was, and happy. But I now recall that I was disconcerted as well. I would have to say that I felt slightly cheated. Yes. Offended, tricked, cheated, by this welcome turnaround, this reprieve. My mother moving rather carelessly out of her old prison, showing options and powers I never dreamed she had, changes more than her self. She changes the bitter lump of love I have carried all this time into a phantom – something useless and uncalled for, like a phantom pregnancy.

THE CAMERONIANS, I have discovered, are or were an uncompromising remnant of the Covenanters – those Scots who in the seventeenth century bound themselves, with God, to resist prayer books, bishops, any taint of popery or interference by the King. Their name comes from Richard Cameron, an outlawed, or "field," preacher, soon cut down. The Cameronians – for a long time they have preferred to be called the Reformed Presbyterians – went into battle singing the seventy-fourth and the seventy-eighth Psalms. They hacked the haughty Bishop of St. Andrews to death on the highway and rode their horses over his body. One of their ministers, in a mood of firm rejoicing at his own hanging, excommunicated all the other preachers in the world.

MENESETEUNG

I

Columbine, bloodroot,
And wild bergamot,
Gathering armfuls,
Giddily we go.

OFFERINGS, the book is called. Gold lettering on a dull-blue cover. The author's full name underneath: Almeda Joynt Roth. The local paper, the *Vidette*, referred to her as "our poetess." There seems to be a mixture of respect and contempt, both for her calling and for her sex – or for their predictable conjuncture. In the front of the book is a photograph, with the photographer's name in one corner, and the date: 1865. The book was published later, in 1873.

The poetess has a long face; a rather long nose; full, sombre dark eyes, which seem ready to roll down her cheeks like giant tears; a lot of dark hair gathered around her face in droopy rolls and curtains. A streak of gray hair plain to see, although she is, in this picture, only twenty-five. Not a pretty girl but the sort of woman who may age well, who probably won't get fat. She wears a tucked and braid-trimmed dark dress or jacket, with a lacy, floppy arrangement of white material – frills or a bow – filling the deep V at the neck. She also wears a hat, which might be made of velvet, in a dark color to match the dress. It's the untrimmed, shapeless hat, something like a soft beret, that makes me see artistic intentions, or at least a shy and stubborn eccentricity, in this young woman, whose long neck and forward-inclining head indicate as well that she is tall and slender and somewhat awkward. From the waist up, she looks like a young nobleman of another century. But perhaps it was the fashion.

"In 1854," she writes in the preface to her book, "my father brought us – my mother, my sister Catherine, my brother William, and me – to the wilds of Canada West (as it then was). My father was a harness-maker by trade, but a cultivated man who could quote by heart from the Bible, Shakespeare, and the writings of Edmund Burke. He prospered in this newly opened land and was able to set up a harness and leather-goods store, and after a year to build the comfortable house in which I live (alone) today. I was fourteen years old, the eldest of the children, when we came into this country from Kingston, a town whose hand-some streets I have not seen again but often remember. My sister was eleven and my brother nine. The third summer that we lived here, my brother and sister were taken ill of a prevalent fever and died within a few days of each other. My dear mother did not regain her spirits after this blow to our family. Her health declined, and after another three years she died. I then became housekeeper to my father and was happy to make his home for twelve years, until he died suddenly one morning at his shop.

"From my earliest years I have delighted in verse and I have occu-pied myself – and sometimes allayed my griefs, which have been no more, I know, than any sojourner on earth must encounter – with many floundering efforts at its composition. My fingers, indeed, were always too clumsy for crochet-work, and those dazzling productions of embroidery which one sees often today – the overflowing fruit and flower baskets, the little Dutch boys, the bonneted maidens with their watering cans – have likewise proved to be beyond my skill. So I offer instead, as the product of my leisure hours, these rude posies, these ballads, couplets, reflections."

Titles of some of the poems: "Children at Their Games," "The Gypsy Fair," "A Visit to My Family," "Angels in the Snow," "Champlain at the Mouth of the Meneseteung," "The Passing of the Old Forest," and "A Garden Medley." There are other, shorter poems, about birds and wild-flowers and snowstorms. There is some comically intentioned doggerel about what people are thinking about as they listen to the sermon in church.

"Children at Their Games": The writer, a child, is playing with her brother and sister – one of those games in which children on different sides try to entice and catch each other. She plays on in the deepening twilight, until she realizes that she is alone, and much older. Still she hears the (ghostly) voices of her brother and sister calling. *Come over, come over, let Meda come over.* (Perhaps Almeda was called Meda in the family, or perhaps she shortened her name to fit the poem.)

"The Gypsy Fair": The Gypsies have an encampment near the town, a "fair," where they sell cloth and trinkets, and the writer as a child is afraid that she may be stolen by them, taken away from her family. Instead, her family has been taken away from her, stolen by Gypsies she can't locate or bargain with.

"A Visit to My Family": A visit to the cemetery, a one-sided conversation.

"Angels in the Snow": The writer once taught her brother and sister to make "angels" by lying down in the snow and moving their arms to create wing shapes. Her brother always jumped up carelessly, leaving an angel with a crippled wing. Will this be made perfect in Heaven, or will he be flying with his own makeshift, in circles?

"Champlain at the Mouth of the Meneseteung": This poem celebrates the popular, untrue belief that the explorer sailed down the eastern shore of Lake Huron and landed at the mouth of the major river.

"The Passing of the Old Forest": A list of all the trees – their names, appearance, and uses – that were cut down in the original forest, with a general description of the bears, wolves, eagles, deer, waterfowl.

"A Garden Medley": Perhaps planned as a companion to the forest poem. Catalogue of plants brought from European countries, with bits of history and legend attached, and final Canadianness resulting from this mixture.

The poems are written in quatrains or couplets. There are a couple of attempts at sonnets, but mostly the rhyme scheme is simple – *a b a b* or *a b c b*. The rhyme used is what was once called "masculine" ("shore"/"before"), though once in a while it is "feminine" ("quiver"/ "river"). Are those terms familiar anymore? No poem is unrhymed.

II

White roses cold as snow
Bloom where those "angels" lie.
Do they but rest below
Or, in God's wonder, fly?

In 1879, Almeda Roth was still living in the house at the corner of Pearl and Dufferin streets, the house her father had built for his family. The house is there today; the manager of the liquor store lives in it. It's covered with aluminum siding; a closed-in porch has replaced the veranda. The woodshed, the fence, the gates, the privy, the barn – all these are gone. A photograph taken in the 1880s shows them all in place. The house and fence look a little shabby, in need of paint, but perhaps that is just because of the bleached-out look of the brownish photograph. The lace-curtained windows look like white eyes. No big shade tree is in sight, and, in fact, the tall elms that overshadowed the town until the 1950s, as well as the maples that shade it now, are skinny young trees with rough fences around them to protect them from the cows. Without the shelter of those trees, there is a great exposure – back yards, clotheslines, woodpiles, patchy sheds and barns and privies – all bare, exposed, provisional-looking. Few houses would have anything like a lawn, just a patch of plantains and anthills and raked dirt. Perhaps petunias growing on top of a stump, in a round box. Only the main street is gravelled; the other streets are dirt roads, muddy or dusty according to season. Yards must be fenced to keep animals out. Cows are tethered in vacant lots or pastured in back yards, but sometimes they get loose. Pigs get loose too; and dogs roam free or nap in a lordly way on the boardwalks. The town has taken root, it's not going to vanish, yet it still has some of the look of an encampment. And, like an encampment, it's busy all the time – full of people, who, within the town, usually walk wherever they're going; full of animals, which leave horse buns, cow pats, dog turds that ladies have to hitch up their skirts for; full of the noise of building and of drivers shouting at their horses and of the trains that come in several times a day.

I read about that life in the *Vidette.*

The population is younger than it is now, than it will ever be again. People past fifty usually don't come to a raw, new place. There are quite a few people in the cemetery already, but most of them died young, in accidents or childbirth or epidemics. It's youth that's in evidence in town. Children – boys – rove through the streets in gangs. School is compulsory for only four months a year, and there are lots of occasional jobs that even a child of eight or nine can do – pulling flax, holding horses, delivering groceries, sweeping the boardwalk in front of stores. A good deal of time they spend looking for adventures. One day they follow an old woman, a drunk nicknamed Queen Aggie. They get her into a wheelbarrow and trundle her all over town, then dump her into a ditch to sober her up. They also spend a lot of time around the railway station. They jump on shunting cars and dart between them and dare each other to take chances, which once in a while result in their getting maimed or killed. And they keep an eye out for any strangers coming into town. They follow them, offer to carry their bags, and direct them (for a five-cent piece) to a hotel. Strangers who don't look so prosperous are taunted and tormented. Speculation surrounds all of them – it's like a cloud of flies. Are they coming to town to start up a new business, to persuade people to invest in some scheme, to sell cures or gimmicks, to preach on the street corners? All these things are possible any day of the week. Be on your guard, the *Vidette* tells people. These are times of opportunity and danger. Tramps, confidence men, hucksters, shysters, plain thieves are travelling the roads, and particularly the railroads. Thefts are announced: money invested and never seen again, a pair of trousers taken from the clothesline, wood from the woodpile, eggs from the henhouse. Such incidents increase in the hot weather.

Hot weather brings accidents too. More horses run wild then, upsetting buggies. Hands caught in the wringer while doing the washing, a man lopped in two at the sawmill, a leaping boy killed in a fall of lumber at the lumberyard. Nobody sleeps well. Babies wither with summer complaint, and fat people can't catch their breath. Bodies must be buried in a hurry. One day a man goes through the streets ringing a cowbell and calling, "Repent! Repent!" It's not a stranger this time, it's a young man who works at the butcher shop. Take him home, wrap him in cold wet cloths, give him some nerve medicine, keep him in bed, pray for his wits. If he doesn't recover, he must go to the asylum.

Almeda Roth's house faces on Dufferin Street, which is a street of considerable respectability. On this street, merchants, a mill owner, an operator of salt wells have their houses. But Pearl Street, which her back windows overlook and her back gate opens onto, is another story. Workmen's houses are adjacent to hers. Small but decent row houses – that is all right. Things deteriorate toward the end of the block, and the next, last one becomes dismal. Nobody but the poorest people, the unrespectable and undeserving poor, would live there at the edge of a boghole (drained since then), called the Pearl Street Swamp. Bushy and luxuriant weeds grow there, makeshift shacks have been put up, there are piles of refuse and debris and crowds of runty children, slops are flung from doorways. The town tries to compel these people to build privies, but they would just as soon go in the bushes. If a gang of boys goes down there in search of adventure, it's likely they'll get more than they bargained for. It is said that even the town constable won't go down Pearl Street on a Saturday night. Almeda Roth has never walked past the row housing. In one of those houses lives the young girl Annie, who helps her with her house-cleaning. That young girl herself, being a decent girl, has never walked down to the last block or the swamp. No decent woman ever would.

But that same swamp, lying to the east of Almeda Roth's house, presents a fine sight at dawn. Almeda sleeps at the back of the house. She keeps to the same bedroom she once shared with her sister Catherine – she would not think of moving to the large front bedroom, where her mother used to lie in bed all day, and which was later the solitary domain of her father. From her window she can see the sun rising, the swamp mist filling with light, the bulky, nearest trees floating against that mist and the trees behind turning transparent. Swamp oaks, soft maples, tamarack, butternut.

III

Here where the river meets the
   inland sea,
Spreading her blue skirts from the
   solemn wood,
I think of birds and beasts and
   vanished men,
Whose pointed dwellings on these
   pale sands stood.

One of the strangers who arrived at the railway station a few years ago was Jarvis Poulter, who now occupies the next house to Almeda Roth's – separated from hers by a vacant lot, which he has bought, on Dufferin Street. The house is plainer than the Roth house and has no fruit trees or flowers planted around it. It is understood that this is a natural result of Jarvis Poulter's being a widower and living alone. A man may keep his house decent, but he will never – if he is a proper man – do much to decorate it. Marriage forces him to live with more ornament as well as sentiment, and it protects him, also, from the extremities of his own nature – from a frigid parsimony or a luxuriant sloth, from squalor, and from excessive sleeping or reading, drinking, smoking, or freethinking.

In the interests of economy, it is believed, a certain estimable gentleman of our town persists in fetching water from the public tap and supplementing his fuel supply by picking up the loose coal along the railway track. Does he think to repay the town or the railway company with a supply of free salt?

This is the *Vidette,* full of sly jokes, innuendo, plain accusation that no newspaper would get away with today. It's Jarvis Poulter they're talking about – though in other passages he is spoken of with great respect, as a civil magistrate, an employer, a churchman. He is close, that's all. An eccentric, to a degree. All of which may be a result of his single condition, his widower's life. Even carrying his water from the town tap and filling his coal pail along the railway track. This is a decent citizen, prosperous: a tall – slightly paunchy? – man in a dark suit with polished boots. A beard? Black hair streaked with gray. A severe and self-possessed air, and a large pale wart among the bushy hairs of one eyebrow? People talk about a young, pretty, beloved wife, dead in child-birth or some horrible accident, like a house fire or a railway disaster. There is no ground for this, but it adds interest. All he has told them is that his wife is dead.

He came to this part of the country looking for oil. The first oil well in the world was sunk in Lambton County, south of here, in the 1850s. Drilling for oil, Jarvis Poulter discovered salt. He set to work to make the most of that. When he walks home from church with Almeda Roth, he tells her about his salt wells. They are twelve hundred feet deep. Heated water is pumped down into them, and that dissolves the salt. Then the brine is pumped to the surface. It is poured into great evap-orator pans over slow, steady fires, so that the water is steamed off and the pure, excellent salt remains. A commodity for which the demand will never fail.

"The salt of the earth," Almeda says.

"Yes," he says, frowning. He may think this disrespectful. She did not intend it so. He speaks of competitors in other towns who are following his lead and trying to hog the market. Fortunately, their wells are not drilled so deep, or their evaporating is not done so efficiently. There is salt everywhere under this land, but it is not so easy to come by as some people think.

Does this not mean, Almeda says, that there was once a great sea?

Very likely, Jarvis Poulter says. Very likely. He goes on to tell her about other enterprises of his – a brickyard, a lime-kiln. And he explains to her how this operates, and where the good clay is found. He also owns two farms, whose woodlots supply the fuel for his operations.

Among the couples strolling home from church on a recent, sunny Sabbath morning we noted a certain salty gentleman and literary lady, not perhaps in their first youth but by no means blighted by the frosts of age. May we surmise?

This kind of thing pops up in the *Vidette* all the time.

May they surmise, and is this courting? Almeda Roth has a bit of money, which her father left her, and she has her house. She is not too old to have a couple of children. She is a good enough housekeeper, with the tendency toward fancy iced cakes and decorated tarts that is seen fairly often in old maids. (Honorable mention at the Fall Fair.) There is nothing wrong with her looks, and naturally she is in better shape than most married women of her age, not having been loaded down with work and children. But why was she passed over in her earlier, more marriageable years, in a place that needs women to be partnered and fruitful? She was a rather gloomy girl – that may have been the trouble. The deaths of her brother and sister, and then of her mother, who lost her reason, in fact, a year before she died, and lay in her bed talking nonsense – those weighed on her, so she was not lively company. And all that reading and poetry – it seemed more of a drawback, a barrier, an obsession, in the young girl than in the middle-aged woman, who needed something, after all, to fill her time. Anyway, it's five years since her book was published, so perhaps she has got over that. Perhaps it was the proud, bookish father encouraging her?

Everyone takes it for granted that Almeda Roth is thinking of Jarvis Poulter as a husband and would say yes if he asked her. And she is thinking of him. She doesn't want to get her hopes up too much, she doesn't want to make a fool of herself. She would like a signal. If he attended church on Sunday evenings, there would be a chance, during some months of the year, to walk home after dark. He would carry a lantern. (There is as yet no street lighting in town.) He would swing the lantern to light the way in front of the lady's feet and observe their narrow and delicate shape. He might catch her arm as they step off the boardwalk. But he does not go to church at night.

Nor does he call for her, and walk with her *to* church on Sunday mornings. That would be a declaration. He walks her home, past his gate as far as hers; he lifts his hat then and leaves her. She does not invite him to come in – a woman living alone could never do such a thing. As soon as a man and woman of almost any age are alone together within four walls, it is assumed that anything may happen. Spontaneous combustion, instant fornication, an attack of passion. Brute instinct, triumph of the senses. What possibilities men and women must see in each other to infer such dangers. Or, believing in the dangers, how often they must think about the possibilities.

When they walk side by side, she can smell his shaving soap, the barber's oil, his pipe tobacco, the wool and linen and leather smell of his manly clothes. The correct, orderly, heavy clothes are like those she used to brush and starch and iron for her father. She misses that job – her father's appreciation, his dark, kind authority. Jarvis Poulter's garments, his smell, his movements all cause the skin on the side of her body next to him to tingle hopefully, and a meek shiver raises the hairs on her arms. Is this to be taken as a sign of love? She thinks of him coming into her – *their* – bedroom in his long underwear and his hat. She knows this outfit is ridiculous, but in her mind he does not look so; he has the solemn effrontery of a figure in a dream. He comes into the room and lies down on the bed beside her, preparing to take her in his arms. Surely he removes his hat? She doesn't know, for at this point a fit of welcome and submission overtakes her, a buried gasp. He would be her husband.

One thing she has noticed about married women, and that is how many of them have to go about creating their husbands. They have to start ascribing preferences, opinions, dictatorial ways. Oh, yes, they say, my husband is very particular. He won't touch turnips. He won't eat fried meat. (Or he will only eat fried meat.) He likes me to wear blue (brown) all the time. He can't stand organ music. He hates to see a woman go out bareheaded. He would kill me if I took one puff of tobacco. This way, bewildered, sidelong-looking men are made over, made into husbands, heads of households. Almeda Roth cannot imagine herself doing that. She wants a man who doesn't have to be made, who is firm already and determined and mysterious to her. She does not look for companionship. Men – except for her father – seem to her deprived in some way, incurious. No doubt that is necessary, so that they will do what they have to do. Would she herself, knowing that there was salt in the earth, discover how to get it out and sell it? Not likely. She would be thinking about the ancient sea. That kind of speculation is what Jarvis Poulter has, quite properly, no time for.

Instead of calling for her and walking her to church, Jarvis Poulter might make another, more venturesome declaration. He could hire a horse and take her for a drive out to the country. If he did this, she would be both glad and sorry. Glad to be beside him, driven by him, receiving this attention from him in front of the world. And sorry to have the countryside removed for her – filmed over, in a way, by his talk and preoccupations. The countryside that she has written about in her poems actually takes diligence and determination to see. Some things must be disregarded. Manure piles, of course, and boggy fields full of high, charred stumps, and great heaps of brush waiting for a good day for burning. The meandering creeks have been straightened, turned into ditches with high, muddy banks. Some of the crop fields and pasture fields are fenced with big, clumsy uprooted stumps; others are held in a crude stitchery of rail fences. The trees have all been cleared back to the woodlots. And the woodlots are all second growth. No trees along the roads or lanes or around the farmhouses, except a few that are newly planted, young and weedy-looking. Clusters of log barns – the grand barns that are to dominate the countryside for the next hundred years are just beginning to be built – and mean-looking log houses, and every four or five miles a ragged little settlement with a church and school and store and a blacksmith shop. A raw countryside just wrenched from the forest, but swarming with people. Every hundred acres is a farm, every farm has a family, most families have ten or twelve children. (This is the country that will send out wave after wave of settlers – it's already starting to send them – to Northern Ontario and the West.) It's true that you can gather wildflowers in spring in the woodlots, but you'd have to walk through herds of horned cows to get to them.

IV

The Gypsies have departed.
Their camping-ground is bare.
Oh, boldly would I bargain now
At the Gypsy Fair.

Almeda suffers a good deal from sleeplessness, and the doctor has given her bromides and nerve medicine. She takes the bromides, but the drops gave her dreams that were too vivid and disturbing, so she has put the bottle by for an emergency. She told the doctor her eyeballs felt dry, like hot glass, and her joints ached. Don't read so much, he said, don't study; get yourself good and tired out with housework, take exercise. He believes that her troubles would clear up if she got married. He believes this in spite of the fact that most of his nerve medicine is prescribed for married women.

So Almeda cleans house and helps clean the church, she lends a hand to friends who are wallpapering or getting ready for a wedding, she bakes one of her famous cakes for the Sunday-school picnic. On a hot Saturday in August, she decides to make some grape jelly. Little jars of grape jelly will make fine Christmas presents, or offerings to the sick. But she started late in the day and the jelly is not made by nightfall. In fact, the hot pulp has just been dumped into the cheesecloth bag to strain out the juice. Almeda drinks some tea and eats a slice of cake with butter (a childish indulgence of hers), and that's all she wants for supper. She washes her hair at the sink and sponges off her body to be clean for Sunday. She doesn't light a lamp. She lies down on the bed with the window wide open and a sheet just up to her waist, and she does feel wonderfully tired. She can even feel a little breeze.

When she wakes up, the night seems fiery hot and full of threats. She lies sweating on her bed, and she has the impression that the noises she hears are knives and saws and axes – all angry implements chopping and jabbing and boring within her head. But it isn't true. As she comes further awake, she recognizes the sounds that she has heard sometimes before – the fracas of a summer Saturday night on Pearl Street. Usually the noise centers on a fight. People are drunk, there is a lot of protest and encouragement concerning the fight, somebody will scream, "Murder!" Once, there was a murder. But it didn't happen in a fight. An old man was stabbed to death in his shack, perhaps for a few dollars he kept in the mattress.

She gets out of bed and goes to the window. The night sky is clear, with no moon and with bright stars. Pegasus hangs straight ahead, over the swamp. Her father taught her that constellation – automatically, she counts its stars. Now she can make out distinct voices, individual contributions to the row. Some people, like herself, have evidently been wakened from sleep. "Shut up!" they are yelling. "Shut up that caterwauling or I'm going to come down and tan the arse off yez!"

But nobody shuts up. It's as if there were a ball of fire rolling up Pearl Street, shooting off sparks – only the fire is noise; it's yells and laughter and shrieks and curses, and the sparks are voices that shoot off alone. Two voices gradually distinguish themselves – a rising and falling howling cry and a steady throbbing, low-pitched stream of abuse that contains all those words which Almeda associates with danger and depravity and foul smells and disgusting sights. Someone – the person crying out, "Kill me! Kill me now!" – is being beaten. A woman is being beaten. She keeps crying, "Kill me! Kill me!" and sometimes her mouth seems choked with blood. Yet there is something taunting and triumphant about her cry. There is something theatrical about it. And the people around are calling out, "Stop it! Stop that!" or "Kill her! Kill her!" in a frenzy, as if at the theatre or a sporting match or a prizefight. Yes, thinks Almeda, she has noticed that before – it is always partly a charade with these people; there is a clumsy sort of parody, an exaggeration, a missed connection. As if anything they did – even a murder – might be something they didn't quite believe but were powerless to stop.

Now there is the sound of something thrown – a chair, a plank? – and of a woodpile or part of a fence giving way. A lot of newly surprised cries, the sound of running, people getting out of the way, and the commotion has come much closer. Almeda can see a figure in a light dress, bent over and running. That will be the woman. She has got hold of something like a stick of wood or a shingle, and she turns and flings it at the darker figure running after her.

"Ah, go get her!" the voices cry. "Go baste her one!"

Many fall back now; just the two figures come on and grapple, and break loose again, and finally fall down against Almeda's fence. The sound they make becomes very confused – gagging, vomiting, grunting, pounding. Then a long, vibrating, choking sound of pain and self-abasement, self-abandonment, which could come from either or both of them.

Almeda has backed away from the window and sat down on the bed. Is that the sound of murder she has heard? What is to be done, what is she to do? She must light a lantern, she must go downstairs and light a lantern – she must go out into the yard, she must go downstairs. Into the yard. The lantern. She falls over on her bed and pulls the pillow to her face. In a minute. The stairs, the lantern. She sees herself already down there, in the back hall, drawing the bolt of the back door. She falls asleep.

She wakes, startled, in the early light. She thinks there is a big crow sitting on her windowsill, talking in a disapproving but unsurprised way about the events of the night before. "Wake up and move the wheelbarrow!" it says to her, scolding, and she understands that it means something else by "wheelbarrow" – something foul and sorrowful. Then she is awake and sees that there is no such bird. She gets up at once and looks out the window.

Down against her fence there is a pale lump pressed – a body.
Wheelbarrow.

She puts a wrapper over her nightdress and goes downstairs. The front rooms are still shadowy, the blinds down in the kitchen. Something goes *plop, plup,* in a leisurely, censorious way, reminding her of the conversation of the crow. It's just the grape juice, straining overnight. She pulls the bolt and goes out the back door. Spiders have draped their webs over the doorway in the night, and the hollyhocks are drooping, heavy with dew. By the fence, she parts the sticky hollyhocks and looks down and she can see.

A woman's body heaped up there, turned on her side with her face squashed down into the earth. Almeda can't see her face. But there is a bare breast let loose, brown nipple pulled long like a cow's teat, and a bare haunch and leg, the haunch showing a bruise as big as a sunflower. The unbruised skin is grayish, like a plucked, raw drumstick. Some kind of nightgown or all-purpose dress she has on. Smelling of vomit. Urine, drink, vomit.

Barefoot, in her nightgown and flimsy wrapper, Almeda runs away. She runs around the side of her house between the apple trees and the veranda; she opens the front gate and flees down Dufferin Street to Jarvis

Poulter's house, which is the nearest to hers. She slaps the flat of her hand many times against the door.

"There is the body of a woman," she says when Jarvis Poulter appears at last. He is in his dark trousers, held up with braces, and his shirt is half unbuttoned, his face unshaven, his hair standing up on his head. "Mr. Poulter, excuse me. A body of a woman. At my back gate."

He looks at her fiercely. "Is she dead?"

His breath is dank, his face creased, his eyes bloodshot.

"Yes. I think murdered," says Almeda. She can see a little of his cheerless front hall. His hat on a chair. "In the night I woke up. I heard a racket down on Pearl Street," she says, struggling to keep her voice low and sensible. "I could hear this – pair. I could hear a man and a woman fighting."

He picks up his hat and puts it on his head. He closes and locks the front door, and puts the key in his pocket. They walk along the boardwalk and she sees that she is in her bare feet. She holds back what she feels a need to say next – that she is responsible, she could have run out with a lantern, she could have screamed (but who needed more screams?), she could have beat the man off. She could have run for help then, not now.

They turn down Pearl Street, instead of entering the Roth yard. Of course the body is still there. Hunched up, half bare, the same as before.

Jarvis Poulter doesn't hurry or halt. He walks straight over to the body and looks down at it, nudges the leg with the toe of his boot, just as you'd nudge a dog or a sow.

"You," he says, not too loudly but firmly, and nudges again.

Almeda tastes bile at the back of her throat.

"Alive," says Jarvis Poulter, and the woman confirms this. She stirs, she grunts weakly.

Almeda says, "I will get the doctor." If she had touched the woman, if she had forced herself to touch her, she would not have made such a mistake.

"Wait," says Jarvis Poulter. "Wait. Let's see if she can get up."

"Get up, now," he says to the woman. "Come on. Up, now. Up."

Now a startling thing happens. The body heaves itself onto all fours, the head is lifted – the hair all matted with blood and vomit – and the

179

woman begins to bang this head, hard and rhythmically, against Almeda Roth's picket fence. As she bangs her head, she finds her voice and lets out an open-mouthed yowl, full of strength and what sounds like an anguished pleasure.

"Far from dead," says Jarvis Poulter. "And I wouldn't bother the doctor."

"There's blood," says Almeda as the woman turns her smeared face.

"From her nose," he says. "Not fresh." He bends down and catches the horrid hair close to the scalp to stop the head-banging.

"You stop that, now," he says. "Stop it. Gwan home, now. Gwan home, where you belong." The sound coming out of the woman's mouth has stopped. He shakes her head slightly, warning her, before he lets go of her hair. "Gwan home!"

Released, the woman lunges forward, pulls herself to her feet. She can walk. She weaves and stumbles down the street, making intermittent, cautious noises of protest. Jarvis Poulter watches her for a moment to make sure that she's on her way. Then he finds a large burdock leaf, on which he wipes his hand. He says, "There goes your dead body!"

The back gate being locked, they walk around to the front. The front gate stands open. Almeda still feels sick. Her abdomen is bloated; she is hot and dizzy.

"The front door is locked," she says faintly. "I came out by the kitchen." If only he would leave her, she could go straight to the privy. But he follows. He follows her as far as the back door and into the back hall. He speaks to her in a tone of harsh joviality that she has never before heard from him. "No need for alarm," he says. "It's only the consequences of drink. A lady oughtn't to be living alone so close to a bad neighborhood." He takes hold of her arm just above the elbow. She can't open her mouth to speak to him, to say thank you. If she opened her mouth, she would retch.

What Jarvis Poulter feels for Almeda Roth at this moment is just what he has not felt during all those circumspect walks and all his own solitary calculations of her probable worth, undoubted respectability, adequate comeliness. He has not been able to imagine her as a wife. Now that is possible. He is sufficiently stirred by her loosened hair – prematurely gray but thick and soft – her flushed face, her light clothing, which nobody but a husband should see. And by her indiscretion, her agitation, her foolishness, her need?

"I will call on you later," he says to her. "I will walk with you to church."

At the corner of Pearl and Dufferin streets last Sunday morning there was discovered, by a lady resident there, the body of a certain woman of Pearl Street, thought to be dead but only, as it turned out, dead drunk. She was roused from her heavenly — or otherwise — stupor by the firm persuasion of Mr. Poulter, a neighbour and a Civil Magistrate, who had been summoned by the lady resident. Incidents of this sort, unseemly, troublesome, and disgraceful to our town, have of late become all too common.

V

I sit at the bottom of sleep,
As on the floor of the sea.
And fanciful Citizens of the Deep
Are graciously greeting me.

As soon as Jarvis Poulter has gone and she has heard her front gate close, Almeda rushes to the privy. Her relief is not complete, however, and she realizes that the pain and fullness in her lower body come from an accumulation of menstrual blood that has not yet started to flow. She closes and locks the back door. Then, remembering Jarvis Poulter's words about church, she writes on a piece of paper, *I am not well, and wish to rest today.* She sticks this firmly into the outside frame of the little window in the front door. She locks that door too. She is trembling, as if from a great shock or danger. But she builds a fire, so that she can make tea. She boils water, measures the tea leaves, makes a large pot of tea, whose steam and smell sicken her further. She pours out a cup while the tea is still quite weak and adds to it several dark drops of nerve medicine. She sits to drink it without raising the kitchen blind. There, in the middle of the floor, is the cheesecloth bag hanging on its broom handle between the two chairbacks. The grape pulp and juice has stained the swollen cloth a dark purple. *Plop, plup,* into the basin beneath. She can't sit and look at such a thing. She takes her cup, the teapot, and the bottle of medicine into the dining room.

She is still sitting there when the horses start to go by on the way to church, stirring up clouds of dust. The roads will be getting hot as ashes. She is there when the gate is opened and a man's confident steps sound on her veranda. Her hearing is so sharp she seems to hear the paper taken out of the frame and unfolded – she can almost hear him reading it, hear the words in his mind. Then the footsteps go the other way, down the steps. The gate closes. An image comes to her of tombstones – it makes her laugh. Tombstones are marching down the street on their little booted feet, their long bodies inclined forward, their expressions preoccupied and severe. The church bells are ringing.

Then the clock in the hall strikes twelve and an hour has passed.

The house is getting hot. She drinks more tea and adds more medicine. She knows that the medicine is affecting her. It is responsible for her extraordinary languor, her perfect immobility, her unresisting surrender to her surroundings. That is all right. It seems necessary.

Her surroundings – some of her surroundings – in the dining room are these: walls covered with dark-green garlanded wallpaper, lace curtains and mulberry velvet curtains on the windows, a table with a crocheted cloth and a bowl of wax fruit, a pinkish-gray carpet with nosegays of blue and pink roses, a sideboard spread with embroidered runners and holding various patterned plates and jugs and the silver tea things. A lot of things to watch. For every one of these patterns, decorations seems charged with life, ready to move and flow and alter. Or possibly to explode. Almeda Roth's occupation throughout the day is to keep an eye on them. Not to prevent their alteration so much as to catch them at it – to understand it, to be a part of it. So much is going on in this room that there is no need to leave it. There is not even the thought of leaving it.

Of course, Almeda in her observations cannot escape words. She may think she can, but she can't. Soon this glowing and swelling begins to suggest words – not specific words but a flow of words somewhere, just about ready to make themselves known to her. Poems, even. Yes, again, poems. Or one poem. Isn't that the idea – one very great poem that will contain everything and, oh, that will make all the other poems, the poems she has written, inconsequential, mere trial and error, mere rags? Stars and flowers and birds and trees and angels in the snow and dead children at twilight – that is not the half of it. You have to get in the obscene racket on Pearl Street and the polished toe of Jarvis Poulter's boot and the plucked-chicken haunch with its blue-black flower. Almeda is a long way now from human sympathies or fears or cozy household consider-ations. She doesn't think about what could be done for that woman or about keeping Jarvis Poulter's dinner warm and hanging his long under-wear on the line. The basin of grape juice has overflowed and is running over her kitchen floor, staining the boards of the floor, and the stain will never come out.

She has to think of so many things at once – Champlain and the naked Indians and the salt deep in the earth, but as well as the salt the money, the money-making intent brewing forever in heads like Jarvis Poulter's. Also the brutal storms of winter and the clumsy and benighted deeds on Pearl Street. The changes of climate are often violent, and if you think about it there is no peace even in the stars. All this can be borne only if it is channelled into a poem, and the word *channelled* is appropriate, because the name of the poem will be – it *is* – "The Meneseteung." The name of the poem is the name of the river. No, in fact it is the river, the Meneseteung, that is the poem – with its deep holes and rapids and blissful pools under the summer trees and its grinding blocks of ice thrown up at the end of winter and its desolating spring floods. Almeda looks deep, deep into the river of her mind and into the tablecloth, and she sees the crocheted roses floating. They look bunchy and foolish, her mother's crocheted roses – they don't look much like real flowers. But their effort, their floating independence, their pleasure in their silly selves do seem to her so admirable. A hopeful sign. *Meneseteung.*

She doesn't leave the room until dusk, when she goes out to the privy again and discovers that she is bleeding, her flow has started. She will have to get a towel, strap it on, bandage herself up. Never before, in health, has she passed a whole day in her nightdress. She doesn't feel any particular anxiety about this. On her way through the kitchen, she walks through the pool of grape juice. She knows that she will have to mop it up, but not yet, and she walks upstairs leaving purple footprints and smelling her escaping blood and the sweat of her body that has sat all day in the closed hot room. No need for alarm. For she hasn't thought that crocheted roses could float away or that tombstones could hurry down the street. She doesn't mistake that for reality, and neither does she mistake anything else for reality, and that is how she knows that she is sane.

VI

I dream of you by night,
I visit you by day.
Father, Mother, Sister, Brother,
Have you no word to say?

April 22, 1903. At her residence, on Tuesday last, between three and four o'clock in the afternoon, there passed away a lady of talent and refinement whose pen, in days gone by, enriched our local literature with a volume of sensitive, eloquent verse. It is a sad misfortune that in later years the mind of this fine person had become somewhat clouded and her behaviour, in consequence, somewhat rash and unusual. Her attention to decorum and to the care and adornment of her person had suffered, to the degree that she had become, in the eyes of those unmindful of her former pride and daintiness, a familiar eccentric, or even, sadly, a figure of fun. But now all such lapses pass from memory and what is recalled is her excellent published verse, her labours in former days in the Sunday school, her dutiful care of her parents, her noble womanly nature, charitable concerns, and unfailing religious faith. Her last illness was of mercifully short duration. She caught cold, after having become thoroughly wet from a ramble in the Pearl Street bog. (It has been said that some urchins chased her into the water, and such is the boldness and cruelty of some of our youth, and their observed persecution of this lady, that the tale cannot be entirely discounted.) The cold developed into pneumonia, and she died, attended at the last by a former neighbour, Mrs. Bert (Annie) Friels, who witnessed her calm and faithful end.

January, 1904. One of the founders of our community, an early maker and shaker of this town, was abruptly removed from our midst on Monday morning last, whilst attending to his correspondence in the office of his company. Mr. Jarvis Poulter possessed a keen and lively commercial spirit, which was instrumental in the creation of not one but several local enterprises, bringing the benefits of industry, productivity, and employment to our town.

So the *Vidette* runs on, copious and assured. Hardly a death goes undescribed, or a life unevaluated.

I LOOKED FOR Almeda Roth in the graveyard. I found the family stone. There was just one name on it – ROTH. Then I noticed two flat stones in the ground, a distance of a few feet – six feet? – from the upright stone. One of these said PAPA, the other MAMA. Farther out from these I found two other flat stones, with the names WILLIAM and CATHERINE on them. I had to clear away some overgrowing grass and dirt to see the full name of Catherine. No birth or death dates for anybody, nothing about being dearly beloved. It was a private sort of memorializing, not for the world. There were no roses, either – no sign of a rosebush. But perhaps it was taken out. The groundskeeper doesn't like such things; they are a nuisance to the lawnmower, and if there is nobody left to object he will pull them out.

I thought that Almeda must have been buried somewhere else. When this plot was bought – at the time of the two children's deaths – she would still have been expected to marry, and to lie finally beside her husband. They might not have left room for her here. Then I saw that the stones in the ground fanned out from the upright stone. First the two for the parents, then the two for the children, but these were placed in such a way that there was room for a third, to complete the fan. I paced out from CATHERINE the same number of steps that it took to get from CATHERINE to WILLIAM, and at this spot I began pulling grass and scrabbling in the dirt with my bare hands. Soon I felt the stone and knew that I was right. I worked away and got the whole stone clear and I read the name MEDA. There it was with the others, staring at the sky.

I made sure I had got to the edge of the stone. That was all the name there was – Meda. So it was true that she was called by that name in the family. Not just in the poem. Or perhaps she chose her name from the poem, to be written on her stone.

I thought that there wasn't anybody alive in the world but me who would know this, who would make the connection. And I would be the last person to do so. But perhaps this isn't so. People are curious. A few people are. They will be driven to find things out, even trivial things. They will put things together. You see them going around with notebooks, scraping the dirt off gravestones, reading microfilm, just in the hope of seeing this trickle in time, making a connection, rescuing one thing from the rubbish.

And they may get it wrong, after all. I may have got it wrong. I don't know if she ever took laudanum. Many ladies did. I don't know if she ever made grape jelly.

DIFFERENTLY

GEORGIA ONCE TOOK a creative-writing course, and what the instructor told her was: Too many things. Too many things going on at the same time; also too many people. Think, he told her. What is the important thing? What do you want us to pay attention to? Think.

Eventually she wrote a story that was about her grandfather killing chickens, and the instructor seemed to be pleased with it. Georgia herself thought that it was a fake. She made a long list of all the things that had been left out and handed it in as an appendix to the story. The instructor said that she expected too much, of herself and of the process, and that she was wearing him out.

The course was not a total loss, because Georgia and the instructor ended up living together. They still live together, in Ontario, on a farm. They sell raspberries, and run a small publishing business. When Georgia can get the money together, she goes to Vancouver to visit her sons. This fall Saturday she has taken the ferry across to Victoria, where she used to live. She did this on an impulse that she doesn't really trust, and by midafternoon, when she walks up the driveway of the splendid stone house where she used to visit Maya, she has already been taken over some fairly shaky ground.

When she phoned Raymond, she wasn't sure that he would ask her to the house. She wasn't sure that she even wanted to go there. She had no notion of how welcome she would be. But Raymond opens the door before she can touch the bell, and he hugs her around the shoulders and kisses her twice (surely he didn't use to do this?) and introduces his wife, Anne. He says he has told her what great friends they were, Georgia and Ben and he and Maya. Great friends.

Maya is dead. Georgia and Ben are long divorced.

They go to sit in what Maya used to call, with a certain flat cheerfulness, "the family room."

(One evening Raymond had said to Ben and Georgia that it looked as if Maya wasn't going to be able to have any children. "We try our best," he said. "We use pillows and everything. But no luck."

"Listen, old man, you don't do it with pillows," Ben said boisterously. They were all a little drunk. "I thought you were the expert on all the apparatus, but I can see that you and I are going to have to have a little talk."

Raymond was an obstetrician and gynecologist.

By that time Georgia knew all about the abortion in Seattle, which had been set up by Maya's lover, Harvey. Harvey was also a doctor, a surgeon. The bleak apartment in the run-down building, the bad-tempered old woman who was knitting a sweater, the doctor arriving in his shirtsleeves, carrying a brown-paper bag that Maya hysterically believed must contain the tools of his trade. In fact, it contained his lunch – an egg-and-onion sandwich. Maya had the smell of that in her face all the time he and Mme. Defarge were working her over.

Maya and Georgia smiled at each other primly while their husbands continued their playful conversation.)

Raymond's curly brown hair has turned into a silvery fluff, and his face is lined. But nothing dreadful has happened to him – no pouches or jowls or alcoholic flush or sardonic droop of defeat. He is still thin, and straight, and sharp-shouldered, still fresh-smelling, spotless, appropriately, expensively dressed. He'll make a brittle, elegant old man, with an obliging boy's smile. There's that sort of shine on both of them, Maya once said glumly. She was speaking of Raymond and Ben. Maybe we should soak them in vinegar, she said.

The room has changed more than Raymond has. An ivory leather sofa has replaced Maya's tapestry-covered couch, and of course all the old opium-den clutter, Maya's cushions and pampas grass and the gorgeous multicolored elephant with the tiny sewn-on mirrors – that's all gone. The room is beige and ivory, smooth and comfortable as the new blond wife, who sits on the arm of Raymond's chair and maneuvers his arm around her, placing his hand on her thigh. She wears slick-looking white pants and a cream-on-white appliquéd sweater, with gold jewelry. Raymond gives her a couple of hearty and defiant pats.

"Are you going someplace?" he says. "Possibly shopping?"

"Righto," says the wife. "Old times." She smiles at Georgia. "It's okay," she says. "I really do have to go shopping."

When she has gone, Raymond pours drinks for Georgia and himself. "Anne is a worrywart about the booze," he says. "She won't put salt on the table. She threw out all the curtains in the house to get rid of the smell of Maya's cigarettes. I know what you may be thinking: Friend Raymond has got hold of a luscious blonde. But this is actually a very serious girl, and a very steady girl. I had her in my office, you know, quite a while before Maya died. I mean, I had her *working* in my office. I don't mean that the way it sounds! She isn't as young as she looks, either. She's thirty-six."

Georgia had thought forty. She is tired of the visit already, but she has to tell about herself. No, she is not married. Yes, she works. She and the friend she lives with have a farm and a publishing business. Touch and go, not much money. Interesting. A male friend, yes.

"I've lost all track of Ben somehow," Raymond says. "The last I heard, he was living on a boat."

"He and his wife sail around the West Coast every summer," Georgia says. "In the winter they go to Hawaii. The Navy lets you retire early."

"Marvellous," says Raymond.

Seeing Raymond has made Georgia think that she has no idea what Ben looks like now. Has he gone white-haired, has he thickened around the middle? Both of these things have happened to her – she has turned into a chunky woman with a healthy olive skin, a crest of white hair, wearing loose and rather splashy clothes. When she thinks of Ben, she sees him still as a handsome Navy officer, with a perfect Navy look – keen and serious and self-effacing. The look of someone who longed, bravely, to be given orders. Her sons must have pictures of him around – they both see him, they spend holidays on his boat. Perhaps they put the pictures away when she comes to visit. Perhaps they think of protecting these images of him from one who did him hurt.

On the way to Maya's house – Raymond's house – Georgia walked past another house, which she could easily have avoided. A house in Oak Bay, which in fact she had to go out of her way to see.

It was still the house that she and Ben had read about in the real-estate columns of the Victoria *Colonist*. Roomy bungalow under picturesque oak trees. Arbutus, dogwood, window seats, fireplace, diamond-paned windows, character. Georgia stood outside the gate and felt a most predictable pain. Here Ben had cut the grass, here the children had made their paths and hideaways in the bushes, and laid out a graveyard for the birds and snakes killed by the black cat, Domino. She could recall the inside of the house perfectly – the oak floors she and Ben had laboriously sanded, the walls they had painted, the room where she had lain in drugged misery after having her wisdom teeth out. Ben had read aloud to her, from *Dubliners*. She couldn't remember the title of the story. It was about a timid poetic sort of young man, with a mean pretty wife. Poor bugger, said Ben when he'd finished it.

Ben liked fiction, which was surprising in a man who also liked sports, and had been popular at school.

She ought to have stayed away from this neighborhood. Everywhere she walked here, under the chestnut trees with their flat gold leaves, and the red-limbed arbutus, and the tall Garry oaks, which suggested fairy stories, European forests, woodcutters, witches – everywhere her footsteps reproached her, saying *what-for, what-for, what-for*. This reproach was just what she had expected – it was what she courted – and there was something cheap about doing such a thing. Something cheap and useless. She knew it. But *what-for, what-for, what-for, wrong-and-waste, wrong-and-waste* went her silly, censorious feet.

Raymond wants Georgia to look at the garden, which he says was made for Maya during the last months of her life. Maya designed it; then she lay on the tapestry couch (setting fire to it twice, Raymond says, by dozing off with a cigarette lit), and she was able to see it all take shape.

Georgia sees a pond, a stone-rimmed pond with an island in the middle. The head of a wicked-looking stone beast – a mountain goat? – rears up on the island, spouting water. Around the pond a jungle of Shasta daisies, pink and purple cosmos, dwarf pines and cypresses, some other miniature tree with glossy red leaves. On the island, now that she looks more closely, are mossy stone walls – the ruins of a tiny tower.

"She hired a young chap to do the work," Raymond says. "She lay there and watched him. It took all summer. She just lay all day and watched him making her garden. Then he'd come in and they'd have tea, and talk about it. You know, Maya didn't just design that garden. She imagined it. She'd tell him what she'd been imagining about it, and he'd take off from there. I mean, this to them was not just a garden. The pond was a lake in this country they had some name for, and all around the lake were forests and territories where different tribes and factions lived. Do you get the picture?"

"Yes," says Georgia.

"Maya had a dazzling imagination. She could have written fantasy or science fiction. Whatever. She was a creative person, without any doubt about it. But you could not get her to seriously use her creativity. That goat was one of the gods of that country, and the island was like a sacred place with a former temple on it. You can see the ruins. They had the religion all worked out. Oh, and the literature, the poems and the legends and the history – everything. They had a song that the queen would sing. Of course it was supposed to be a translation, from that language. They had some of that figured out too. There had been a queen that was shut up in that ruin. That temple. I forget why. She was getting sacrificed, probably. Getting her heart torn out or some gruesome thing. It was all complicated and melodramatic. But think of the effort that went into it. The creativity. The young chap was an artist by profession. I believe he thought of himself as an artist. I don't know how she got hold of him, actually. She knew people. He supported himself doing this kind of thing, I imagine. He did a good job. He laid the pipes, everything. He showed up every day. Every day he came in when he was finished and had tea and talked to her. Well, in my opinion, they didn't have just tea. To my knowledge, not just tea. He would bring a little substance, they would have a little smoke. I told Maya she should write it all down.

"But you know, the instant he was finished, off he went. Off he went. I don't know. Maybe he got another job. It didn't seem to me that it was my place to ask. But I did think that even if he had got a job he could have come back and visited her now and then. Or if he'd gone off on a trip somewhere he could have written letters. I thought he could have. I expected that much of him. It wouldn't have been any skin off his back. Not as I see it. It would have been nice of him to make her think that it hadn't been just a case of – of hired friendship, you know, all along."

Raymond is smiling. He cannot repress, or perhaps is not aware of, this smile.

"For that was the conclusion she must have come to," he says. "After all that nice time and imagining together and egging each other on. She must have been disappointed. She must have been. Even at that stage, such a thing would matter a lot to her. You and I know it, Georgia. It would have mattered. He could have treated her a little more kindly. It wouldn't have had to be for very long."

MAYA DIED A year ago, in the fall, but Georgia did not hear about it until Christmas. She got the news in Hilda's Christmas letter. Hilda, who used to be married to Harvey, is now married to another doctor, in a town in the interior of British Columbia. A few years ago she and Georgia, both visitors, met by chance on a Vancouver street, and they have written occasional letters since.

Of course you knew Maya so much better than I did, Hilda wrote. *But I've been surprised how often I've thought about her. I've been thinking of all of us, really, how we were, fifteen or so years ago, and I think we were just as vulnerable in some ways as the kids with their acid trips and so on, that were supposed to be marked for life. Weren't we marked – all of us smashing up our marriages and going out looking for adventure? Of course, Maya didn't smash up her marriage, she of all people stayed where she was, so I suppose it doesn't make much sense what I'm saying. But Maya seemed the most vulnerable person of all to me, so gifted and brittle. I remember I could hardly bear to look at that vein in her temple where she parted her hair.*

What an odd letter for Hilda to write, thought Georgia. She remembered Hilda's expensive pastel plaid shirtdresses, her neat, short, fair hair, her good manners. Did Hilda really think she had smashed up her marriage and gone out looking for adventure under the influence of dope and rock music and revolutionary costumes? Georgia's impression was that Hilda had left Harvey, once she found out what he was up to – or some of what he was up to – and gone to the town in the interior where she sensibly took up her old profession of nursing and in due time married another, presumably more trustworthy doctor. Maya and Georgia had never thought of Hilda as a woman like themselves. And Hilda and Maya had not been close – they had particular reason not to be. But Hilda had kept track; she knew of Maya's death, she wrote these generous words. Without Hilda, Georgia would not have known. She would still have been thinking that someday she might write to Maya, there might come a time when their friendship could be mended.

THE FIRST TIME that Ben and Georgia went to Maya's house, Harvey and Hilda were there. Maya was having a dinner party for just the six of them. Georgia and Ben had recently moved to Victoria, and Ben had phoned Raymond, who had been a friend of his at school. Ben had never met Maya, but he told Georgia that he had heard that she was very clever, and weird. People said that she was weird. But she was rich – an heiress – so she could get away with it.

Georgia groaned at the news that Maya was rich, and she groaned again at the sight of the house – the great stone-block house with its terraced lawns and clipped bushes and circular drive.

Georgia and Ben came from the same small town in Ontario, and had the same sort of families. It was a fluke that Ben had been sent to a good private school – the money had come from a great-aunt. Even in her teens, when she was proud of being Ben's girl and prouder than she liked to let on about being asked to the dances at that school, Georgia had a low opinion of the girls she met there. She thought rich girls were spoiled and brainless. She called them twits. She thought of herself as a girl – and then a woman – who didn't much like other girls and women. She called the other Navy wives "the Navy *ladies.*" Ben was sometimes entertained by her opinions of people and at other times asked if it was really necessary to be so critical.

He had an inkling, he said, that she was going to like Maya. This didn't predispose Georgia in Maya's favor. But Ben turned out to be right. He was very happy then, to have come up with somebody like Maya as an offering to Georgia, to have found a couple with whom he and Georgia could willingly link up as friends. "It'll be good for us to have some non-Navy friends," he was to say. "Some wife for you to knock around with who isn't so conventional. You can't say Maya's conventional."

Georgia couldn't. The house was more or less what she had expected – soon she learned that Maya called it "your friendly neighborhood fortress" – but Maya was a surprise. She opened the door herself, barefoot, wearing a long shapeless robe of coarse brown cloth that looked like burlap. Her hair was long and straight, parted high at one temple. It was almost the same dull-brown color as the robe. She did not wear lipstick, and her skin was rough and pale, with marks like faint bird tracks in the hollows of her cheeks. This lack of color, this roughness of texture about her seemed a splendid assertion of quality. How indifferent she looked, how arrogant and indifferent, with her bare feet, her unpainted toenails, her queer robe. The only thing that she had done to her face was to paint her eyebrows blue – to pluck out all the hairs of her eyebrows, in fact, and paint the skin blue. Not an arched line – just a little daub of blue over each eye, like a swollen vein.

Georgia, whose dark hair was teased, whose eyes were painted in the style of the time, whose breasts were stylishly proffered, found all this disconcerting, and wonderful.

Harvey was the other person there whose looks Georgia found impressive. He was a short man with heavy shoulders, a slight potbelly, puffy blue eyes, and a pugnacious expression. He came from Lancashire. His gray hair was thin on top but worn long at the sides – combed over his ears in a way that made him look more like an artist than a surgeon. "He doesn't even look to me exactly clean enough to be a surgeon," Georgia said to Ben afterward. "Wouldn't you think he'd be something like a sculptor? With gritty fingernails? I expect he treats women badly." She was recalling how he had looked at her breasts. "Not like Raymond," she said. "Raymond worships Maya. And he is extremely clean."

(Raymond has the kind of looks everybody's mother is crazy about, Maya was to say to Georgia, with slashing accuracy, a few weeks after this.)

The food that Maya served was no better than you would expect at a family dinner, and the heavy silver forks were slightly tarnished. But Raymond poured good wine that he would have liked to talk about. He did not manage to interrupt Harvey, who told scandalous and indiscreet hospital stories, and was blandly outrageous about necrophilia and masturbation. Later, in the living room, the coffee was made and served with some ceremony. Raymond got everybody's attention as he ground the beans in a Turkish cylinder. He talked about the importance of the aromatic oils. Harvey, halted in mid-anecdote, watched with an unkindly smirk, Hilda with patient polite attention. It was Maya who gave her husband radiant encouragement, hung about him like an acolyte, meekly and gracefully assisting. She served the coffee in beautiful little Turkish cups, which she and Raymond had bought in a shop in San Francisco, along with the coffee grinder. She listened demurely to Raymond talking about the shop, as if she recalled other holiday pleasures.

Harvey and Hilda were the first to leave. Maya hung on Raymond's shoulder, saying goodbye. But she detached herself once they were gone, her slithery grace and wifely demeanor discarded. She stretched out casually and awkwardly on the sofa and said, "Now, don't you go yet. Nobody gets half a chance to talk while Harvey is around – you have to talk after."

And Georgia saw how it was. She saw that Maya was hoping not to be left alone with the husband whom she had aroused – for what-ever purposes – by her showy attentions. She saw that Maya was mournful and filled with a familiar dread at the end of her dinner party. Raymond was happy. He sat down on the end of the sofa, lifting Maya's reluctant feet to do so. He rubbed one of her feet between his hands.

"What a savage," Raymond said. "This is a woman who won't wear shoes."

"Brandy!" said Maya, springing up. "I knew there was something else you did at dinner parties. You drink brandy!"

"He loves her but she doesn't love him," said Georgia to Ben, just after she had remarked on Raymond's worshipping Maya and being very clean. But Ben, perhaps not listening carefully, thought she was talking about Harvey and Hilda.

"No, no, no. There I think it's the other way round. It's hard to tell with English people. Maya was putting on an act for them. I have an idea about why."

"You have an idea about everything," said Ben.

GEORGIA AND MAYA became friends on two levels. On the first level, they were friends as wives; on the second as themselves. On the first level, they had dinner at each other's houses. They listened to their husbands talk about their school days. The jokes and fights, the conspiracies and disasters, the bullies and the victims. Terrifying or pitiable schoolfellows and teachers, treats and humiliations. Maya asked if they were sure they hadn't read all that in a book. "It sounds just like a story," she said. "A boys' story about school."

They said that their experiences were what the books were all about. When they had talked enough about school, they talked about movies, politics, public personalities, places they had travelled to or wanted to travel to. Maya and Georgia could join in then. Ben and Raymond did not believe in leaving women out of the conversation. They believed that women were every bit as intelligent as men.

On the second level, Georgia and Maya talked in each other's kitchens, over coffee. Or they had lunch downtown. There were two places, and only two, where Maya liked to have lunch. One was the Moghul's Court – a seedy, grandiose bar in a large, grim railway hotel. The Moghul's Court had curtains of moth-eaten pumpkin-colored velvet, and desiccated ferns, and waiters who wore turbans. Maya always dressed up to go there, in droopy, silky dresses and not very clean white gloves and amazing hats that she found in secondhand stores. She pretended to be a widow who had served with her husband in various outposts of the Empire. She spoke in fluty tones to the sullen young waiters, asking them, "Could you be so good as to . . ." and then telling them they had been terribly, terribly kind.

She and Georgia worked out the history of the Empire widow, and Georgia was added to the story as a grumpy, secretly Socialistic hired companion named Miss Amy Jukes. The widow's name was Mrs. Allegra Forbes-Bellyea. Her husband had been Nigel Forbes-Bellyea. Sometimes Sir Nigel. Most of one rainy afternoon in the Moghul's Court was spent in devising the horrors of the Forbes-Bellyea honeymoon, in a damp hotel in Wales.

The other place that Maya liked was a hippie restaurant on Blanshard Street, where you sat on dirty plush cushions tied to the tops of stumps and ate brown rice with slimy vegetables and drank cloudy cider. (At the Moghul's Court, Maya and Georgia drank only gin.) When they lunched at the hippie restaurant, they wore long, cheap, pretty Indian cotton dresses and pretended to be refugees from a commune, where they had both been the attendants or concubines of a folk-singer named Bill Bones. They made up several songs for Bill Bones, all mild and tender blue-eyed songs that contrasted appallingly with his greedy and licentious ways. Bill Bones had very curious personal habits.

When they weren't playing these games, they talked in a headlong fashion about their lives, childhoods, problems, husbands.

"That was a horrible place," Maya said. "That school."

Georgia agreed.

"They were poor boys at a rich kids' school," Maya said. "So they had to try hard. They had to be a credit to their families."

Georgia would not have thought Ben's family poor, but she knew that there were different ways of looking at such things.

Maya said that whenever they had people in for dinner or the evening, Raymond would pick out beforehand all the records he thought suitable and put them in a suitable order. "I think sometime he'll hand out conversational topics at the door," Maya said.

Georgia revealed that Ben wrote a letter every week to the great-aunt who had sent him to school.

"Is it a nice letter?" said Maya.

"Yes. Oh, yes. It's very nice."

They looked at each other bleakly, and laughed. Then they announced – they admitted – what weighed on them. It was the innocence of these husbands – the hearty, decent, firm, contented innocence. That is a wearying and finally discouraging thing. It makes intimacy a chore.

"But do you feel badly," Georgia said, "talking like this?"

"Of course," said Maya, grinning and showing her large perfect teeth – the product of expensive dental work from the days before she had charge of her own looks. "I have another reason to feel badly," she said. "But I don't know whether I do. I do and I don't."

"I know," said Georgia, who up until that moment hadn't known, for sure.

"You're very smart," Maya said. "Or I'm very obvious. What do you think of him?"

"A lot of trouble," Georgia said judiciously. She was pleased with that answer, which didn't show how flattered she felt by the disclosure, or how heady she found this conversation.

"You aren't just a-whistlin' 'Dixie,'" Maya said, and she told the story about the abortion. "I am going to break up with him," she said. "Any day now."

But she kept on seeing Harvey. She would relate, at lunch, some very disillusioning facts about him, then announce that she had to go, she was meeting him at a motel out on the Gorge Road, or at the cabin he had on Prospect Lake.

"Must scrub," she said.

She had left Raymond once. Not for Harvey. She had run away with, or to, a musician. A pianist – Nordic and sleepy-looking but bad-tempered – from her society-lady, symphony-benefit days. She travelled with him for five weeks, and he deserted her in a hotel in Cincinnati. She then developed frightful chest pains, appropriate to a breaking heart. What she really had was a gallbladder attack. Raymond was sent for, and he came and got her out of the hospital. They had a little holiday in Mexico before they came home.

"That was it, for me," Maya said. "That was your true and desperate love. Nevermore."

What, then, was Harvey?

"Exercise," said Maya.

*　　*　　*

GEORGIA GOT A part-time job in a bookstore, working several evenings a week. Ben went away on his yearly cruise. The summer turned out to be unusually hot and sunny for the West Coast. Georgia combed her hair out and stopped using most of her makeup and bought a couple of short halter dresses. Sitting on her stool at the front of the store, showing her bare brown shoulders and sturdy brown legs, she looked like a college girl – clever but full of energy and bold opinions. The people who came into the store liked the look of a girl – a woman – like Georgia. They liked to talk to her. Most of them came in alone. They were not exactly lonely people, but they were lonely for somebody to talk to about books. Georgia plugged in the kettle behind the desk and made mugs of raspberry tea. Some favored customers brought in their own mugs. Maya came to visit and lurked about in the background, amused and envious.

"You know what you've got?" she said to Georgia. "You've got a salon! Oh, I'd like to have a job like that! I'd even like an ordinary job in an ordinary store, where you fold things up and find things for people and make change and say thank you very much, and colder out today, will it rain?"

"You could get a job like that," said Georgia.

"No, I couldn't. I don't have the discipline. I was too badly brought up. I can't even keep house without Mrs. Hanna and Mrs. Cheng and Sadie."

It was true. Maya had a lot of servants, for a modern woman, though they came at different times and did separate things and were nothing like an old-fashioned household staff. Even the food at her dinner parties, which seemed to show her own indifferent touch, had been prepared by someone else.

Usually, Maya was busy in the evenings. Georgia was just as glad, because she didn't really want Maya coming into the store, asking for crazy titles that she had made up, making Georgia's employment there a kind of joke. Georgia took the store seriously. She had a serious, secret liking for it that she could not explain. It was a long, narrow store with an old-fashioned funnelled entryway between two angled display windows. From her stool behind the desk Georgia was able to see the reflections in one window reflected in the other. This street was not one of those decked out to receive tourists. It was a wide east-west street filled in the early evening with a faintly yellow light, a light reflected off pale stucco buildings that were not very high, plain storefronts, nearly empty sidewalks. Georgia found this plainness liberating after the winding shady streets, the flowery yards and vine-framed windows of Oak Bay. Here the books could come into their own, as they never could in a more artful and enticing suburban bookshop. Straight long rows of paperbacks. (Most of the Penguins then still had their orange-and-white or blue-and-white covers, with no designs or pictures, just the unadorned, unexplained titles.) The store was a straight avenue of bounty, of plausible promises. Certain books that Georgia had never read, and probably never would read, were important to her, because of the stateliness or mystery of their titles. *In Praise of Folly. The Roots of Coincidence. The Flowering of New England. Ideas and Integrities.*

Sometimes she got up and put the books in stricter order. The fiction was shelved alphabetically, by author, which was sensible but not very interesting. The history books, however, and the philosophy and psychology and other science books were arranged according to certain intricate and delightful rules – having to do with chronology and content – that Georgia grasped immediately and even elaborated on. She did not need to read much of a book to know about it. She got a sense of it easily, almost at once, as if by smell.

At times the store was empty, and she felt an abundant calm. It was not even the books that mattered then. She sat on the stool and watched the street – patient, expectant, by herself, in a finely balanced and suspended state.

She saw Miles' reflection – his helmeted ghost parking his motorcycle at the curb – before she saw him. She believed that she had noted his valiant profile, his pallor, his dusty red hair (he took off his helmet and shook out his hair before coming into the store), and his quick, slouching, insolent, invading way of moving, even in the glass.

It was no surprise that he soon began to talk to her, as others did. He told her that he was a diver. He looked for wrecks, and lost airplanes, and dead bodies. He had been hired by a rich couple in Victoria who were planning a treasure-hunting cruise, getting it together at the moment. Their names, the destination were all secrets. Treasure-hunting was a lunatic business. He had done it before. His home was in Seattle, where he had a wife and a little daughter.

Everything he told her could easily have been a lie.

He showed her pictures in books – photographs and drawings, of mollusks, jellyfish, the Portuguese man-of-war, sargasso weed, the Caribbean flying fish, the girdle of Venus. He pointed out which pictures were accurate, which were fakes. Then he went away and paid no more attention to her, even slipping out of the store while she was busy with a customer. Not a hint of a goodbye. But he came in another evening, and told her about a drowned man wedged into the cabin of a boat, looking out the watery window in an interested way. By attention and avoidance, impersonal conversations in close proximity, by his oblivious prowling, and unsmiling, lengthy, gray-eyed looks, he soon had Georgia in a disturbed and not disagreeable state. He stayed away two nights in a row, then came in and asked her, abruptly, if she would like a ride home on his motorcycle.

Georgia said yes. She had never ridden on a motorcycle in her life. Her car was in the parking lot; she knew what was bound to happen.

She told him where she lived. "Just a few blocks up from the beach," she said.

"We'll go to the beach, then. We'll go and sit on the logs."

That was what they did. They sat for a while on the logs. Then, though the beach was not quite dark or completely deserted, they made love in the imperfect shelter of some broom bushes. Georgia walked home, a strengthened and lightened woman, not in the least in love, favored by the universe.

"My car wouldn't start," she told the baby-sitter, a grandmother from down the street. "I walked all the way home. It was lovely, walking. Lovely. I enjoyed it so much."

Her hair was wild, her lips were swollen, her clothes were full of sand.

HER LIFE FILLED up with such lies. Her car would be parked beside outlying beaches, on the logging roads so conveniently close to the city, on the wandering back roads of the Saanich Peninsula. The map of the city that she had held in her mind up till now, with its routes to shops and work and friends' houses, was overlaid with another map, of circuitous routes followed in fear (not shame) and excitement, of flimsy shelters, temporary hiding places, where she and Miles made love, often within hearing distance of passing traffic or a hiking party or a family picnic. And Georgia herself, watching her children on the roundabout, or feeling the excellent shape of a lemon in her hand at the supermarket, contained another woman, who only a few hours before had been whimpering and tussling on the ferns, on the sand, on the bare ground, or, during a rainstorm, in her own car — who had been driven hard and gloriously out of her mind and drifted loose and gathered her wits and made her way home again. Was this a common story? Georgia cast an eye over the other women at the supermarket. She looked for signs — of dreaminess or flaunting, a sense of drama in a woman's way of dressing, a special rhythm in her movements.

How many, she asked Maya.

"God knows," said Maya. "Do a survey."

Trouble began, perhaps, as soon as they said that they loved each other. Why did they do that — defining, inflating, obscuring whatever it was they did feel? It seemed to be demanded, that was all — just the way changes, variations, elaborations in the lovemaking itself might be demanded. It was a way of going further. So they said it, and that night Georgia couldn't sleep. She did not regret what had been said or think that it was a lie, though she knew that it was absurd. She thought of the way Miles sought to have her look into his eyes during lovemaking — something Ben expressly did not do — and she thought of how his eyes, at first bright and challenging, became cloudy and calm and sombre. That way she trusted him — it was the only way. She thought of being launched out on a gray, deep, baleful, magnificent sea. Love.

"I didn't know this was going to happen," she said in Maya's kitchen the next day, drinking her coffee. The day was warm, but she had put on a sweater to huddle in. She felt shaken, and submissive.

"No. And you don't know," said Maya rather sharply. "Did he say it too? Did he say he loved you too?"

Yes, said Georgia, yes, of course.

"Look out, then. Look out for next time. Next time is always pretty tricky when they've said that."

And so it was. Next time a rift opened. At first they simply tested it, to see if it was there. It was almost like a new diversion to them. But it widened, it widened. Before any words were said to confirm that it was there, Georgia felt it widen, she coldly felt it widen, though she was desperate for it to close. Did he feel the same thing? She didn't know. He too seemed cold – pale, deliberate, glittering with some new malicious intent.

They were sitting recklessly, late at night, in Georgia's car among the other lovers at Clover Point.

"Everybody here in these cars doing the same thing we're doing," Miles had said. "Doesn't that idea turn you on?"

He had said that at the very moment in their ritual when they had been moved, last time, to speak brokenly and solemnly of love.

"You ever think of that?" he said. "I mean, we could start with Ben and Laura. You ever imagine how it would be with you and me and Ben and Laura?"

Laura was his wife, at home in Seattle. He had not spoken of her before, except to tell Georgia her name. He had spoken of Ben, in a way that Georgia didn't like but passed over.

"What does Ben think you do for fun," he'd said, "while he is off cruising the ocean blue?"

"Do you and Ben usually have a big time when he gets back?"

"Does Ben like that outfit as much as I do?"

He spoke as if he and Ben were friends in some way, or at least partners, co-proprietors.

"You and me and Ben and Laura," he said, in a tone that seemed to Georgia insistently and artificially lecherous, sly, derisive. "Spread the joy around."

He tried to fondle her, pretending not to notice how offended she was, how bitterly stricken. He described the generous exchanges that would take place among the four of them abed. He asked whether she was getting excited. She said no, disgusted. Ah, you are but you won't give in to it, he said. His voice, his caresses grew more bullying. What is so special about you, he asked softly, despisingly, with a hard squeeze at her breasts. Georgia, why do you think you're such a queen?

"You are being cruel and you know you're being cruel," said Georgia, pulling at his hands. "Why are you being like this?"

"Honey, I'm not being cruel," said Miles, in a slippery mock-tender voice. "I'm being horny. I'm horny again is all." He began to pull Georgia around, to arrange her for his use. She told him to get out of the car.

"Squeamish," he said, in that same artificially and hatefully tender voice, as if he were licking fanatically at something loathsome. "You're a squeamish little slut."

Georgia told him that she would lean on the horn if he didn't stop. She would lean on the horn if he didn't get out of the car. She would yell for somebody to call the police. She did lean against the horn as they struggled. He pushed her away, with a whimpering curse such as she'd heard from him at other times, when it meant something different. He got out.

She could not believe that such ill will had erupted, that things had so stunningly turned around. When she thought of this afterward – a good long time afterward – she thought that perhaps he had acted for conscience's sake, to mark her off from Laura. Or to blot out what he had said to her last time. To humiliate her because he was frightened. Perhaps. Or perhaps all this seemed to him simply a further, and genuinely interesting, development in lovemaking.

She would have liked to talk it over with Maya. But the possibility of talking anything over with Maya had disappeared. Their friendship had come suddenly to an end.

THE NIGHT AFTER the incident at Clover Point, Georgia was sitting on the living-room floor playing a bedtime card game with her sons. The phone rang, and she was sure that it was Miles. She had been thinking all day that he would call, he would have to call to explain himself, to beg her pardon, to say that he had been testing her, in a way, or had been temporarily deranged by circumstances that she knew nothing about. She would not forgive him immediately. But she would not hang up.

It was Maya.

"Guess what weird thing happened," Maya said. "Miles phoned me. Your Miles. It's okay, Raymond isn't here. How did he even know my name?"

"I don't know," said Georgia.

She had told him it, of course. She had offered wild Maya up for his entertainment, or to point out what a novice at this game she herself was – a relatively chaste prize.

"He says he wants to come and talk to me," Maya said. "What do you think? What's the matter with him? Did you have a fight? . . . Yes? Oh, well, he probably wants me to persuade you to make up. I must say he picked the right night. Raymond's at the hospital. He's got this balky woman in labor; he may have to stay and do a section on her. I'll phone and tell you how it goes. Shall I?"

After a couple of hours, with the children long asleep, Georgia began to expect Maya's call. She watched the television news, to take her mind off expecting it. She picked up the phone to make sure there was a dial tone. She turned off the television after the news, then turned it on again. She started to watch a movie; she watched it through three commercial breaks without going to the kitchen to look at the clock.

At half past midnight she went out and got into her car and drove to Maya's house. She had no idea what she would do there. And she did not do much of anything. She drove around the circular drive with the lights off. The house was dark. She could see that the garage was open and Raymond's car was not there. The motorcycle was nowhere in sight.

She had left her children alone, the doors unlocked. Nothing happened to them. They didn't wake up and discover her defection. No burglar, or prowler, or murderer surprised her on her return. That was a piece of luck that she did not even appreciate. She had gone out leaving the door open and the lights on, and when she came back she hardly recognized her folly, though she closed the door and turned out some lights and lay down on the living-room sofa. She didn't sleep. She lay still, as if the smallest movement would sharpen her suffering, until she saw the day getting light and heard the birds waking. Her limbs were stiff. She got up and went to the phone and listened again for the dial tone. She walked stiffly to the kitchen and put on the kettle and said to herself the words *a paralysis of grief.*

A paralysis of grief. What was she thinking of? That was what she would feel, how she might describe the way she would feel, if one of her children had died. Grief is for serious matters, important losses. She knew that. She would not have bartered away an hour of her children's lives to have had the phone ring at ten o'clock last night, to have heard Maya say, "Georgia, he's desperate. He's sorry; he loves you very much."

No. But it seemed that such a phone call would have given her a happiness that no look or word from her children could give her. Than anything could give her, ever again.

She phoned Maya before nine o'clock. As she was dialling, she thought that there were still some possibilities to pray for. Maya's phone had been temporarily out of order. Maya had been ill last night. Raymond had been in a car accident on his way home from the hospital.

All these possibilities vanished at the first sound of Maya's voice, which was sleepy (pretending to be sleepy?) and silky with deceit. "Georgia? Is that Georgia? Oh, I thought it was going to be Raymond. He had to stay over at the hospital in case this poor wretched woman needed a C-section. He was going to call me—"

"You told me that last night," said Georgia.

"He was going to call me – Oh, Georgia, I was supposed to call you! Now I remember. Yes. I was supposed to call you, but I thought it was probably too late. I thought the phone might wake up the children. I thought, Oh, better just leave it till morning!"

"How late was it?"

"Not awfully. I just thought."

"What happened?"

"What do you mean, what happened?" Maya laughed, like a lady in a silly play. "Georgia, are you in a state?"

"What happened?"

"Oh, Georgia," said Maya, groaning magnanimously but showing an edge of nerves. "Georgia, I'm sorry. It was nothing. It was just nothing. I've been rotten, but I didn't mean to be. I offered him a beer. Isn't that what you do when somebody rides up to your house on a motorcycle? You offer him a beer. But then he came on very lordly and said he only drank Scotch. And he said he'd only drink Scotch if I would drink with him. I thought he was pretty high-handed. Pretty high-handed pose. But I really was doing this for you, Georgia – I was wanting to find out what was on his mind. So I told him to put the motorcycle behind the garage, and I took him to sit in the back garden. That was so if I heard Raymond's car I could chase him out the back way and he could walk the motorcycle down the lane. I am not about to unload anything *new* onto Raymond at this point. I mean even something innocent, which this started out to be."

Georgia, with her teeth chattering, hung up the phone. She never spoke to Maya again. Maya appeared at her door, of course, a little while later, and Georgia had to let her in, because the children were playing in the yard. Maya sat down contritely at the kitchen table and asked if she could smoke. Georgia did not answer. Maya said she would smoke anyway and she hoped it was all right. Georgia pretended that Maya wasn't there. While Maya smoked, Georgia cleaned the stove, dismantling the elements and putting them back together again. She wiped the counters and polished the taps and straightened out the cutlery drawer. She mopped the floor around Maya's feet. She worked briskly, thoroughly, and never quite looked at Maya. At first she was not sure whether she could keep this up. But it got easier. The more earnest Maya became – the further she slipped from sensible remonstrance, half-amused confession, into true and fearful regret – the more fixed Georgia was in her resolve, the more grimly satisfied in her heart. She took care, however, not to appear grim. She moved about lightly. She was almost humming.

She took a knife to scrape out the grease from between the counter tiles by the stove. She had let things get into a bad way.

Maya smoked one cigarette after another, stubbing them out in a saucer that she fetched for herself from the cupboard. She said, "Georgia, this is so stupid. I can tell you, he's not worth it. It was nothing. All it was was Scotch and opportunity."

She said, "I am really sorry. Truly sorry. I know you don't believe me. How can I say it so you will?"

And, "Georgia, listen. You are humiliating me. Fine. Fine. Maybe I deserve it. I do deserve it. But after you've humiliated me enough we'll go back to being friends and we'll laugh about this. When we're old ladies, I swear we'll laugh. We won't be able to remember his name. We'll call him the motorcycle sheikh. We will."

Then, "Georgia, what do you want me to do? Do you want me to throw myself on the floor? I'm about ready to. I'm trying to keep myself from snivelling, and I can't. I'm snivelling, Georgia. Okay?"

She had begun to cry. Georgia put on her rubber gloves and started to clean the oven.

"You win," said Maya. "I'll pick up my cigarettes and go home."

She phoned a few times. Georgia hung up on her. Miles phoned, and Georgia hung up on him too. She thought he sounded cautious but smug. He phoned again and his voice trembled, as if he were striving just for candor and humility, bare love. Georgia hung up at once. She felt violated, shaken.

Maya wrote a letter, which said, in part, *I suppose you know that Miles is going back to Seattle and whatever home fires he keeps burning there. It seems the treasure thing has fallen through. But you must have known he was bound to go sometime and you'd have felt rotten then, so now you've got the rotten feeling over with. So isn't that okay? I don't say this to excuse myself. I know I was weak and putrid. But can't we put it behind us now?*

She went on to say that she and Raymond were going on a long-planned holiday to Greece and Turkey, and that she hoped very much that she would get a note from Georgia before she left. But if she didn't get any word she would try to understand what Georgia was telling her, and she would not make a nuisance of herself by writing again.

She kept her word. She didn't write again. She sent, from Turkey, a pretty piece of striped cloth large enough for a tablecloth. Georgia folded it up and put it away. She left it for Ben to find after she moved out, several months later.

*   *   *

"I'M HAPPY," Raymond tells Georgia. "I'm very happy, and the reason is that I'm content to be an ordinary sort of person with an ordinary calm life. I am not looking for any big revelation or any big drama or any messiah of the opposite sex. I don't go around figuring out how to make things more interesting. I can say to you quite frankly I think Maya made a mistake. I don't mean she wasn't very gifted and intelligent and creative and so on, but she was looking for something – maybe she was looking for something that just is not there. And she tended to despise a lot that she had. It's true. She didn't want the privileges she had. We'd travel, for example, and she wouldn't want to stay in a comfortable hotel. No. She had to go on some trek that involved riding on poor, miserable donkeys and drinking sour milk for breakfast. I suppose I sound very square. Well, I suppose I am. I am square. You know, she had such beautiful silver. Magnificent silver. It was passed down through her family. And she couldn't be bothered to polish it or get the cleaning woman to polish it. She wrapped it all up in plastic and hid it away. She hid it away – you'd think it was a disgrace. How do you think she envisaged herself? As some kind of hippie, maybe? Some kind of free spirit? She didn't even realize it was her money that kept her afloat. I'll tell you, some of the free spirits I've seen pass in and out of this house wouldn't have been long around her without it.

"I did all I could," said Raymond. "I didn't scoot off and leave her, like her Prince of Fantasy Land."

GEORGIA GOT A vengeful pleasure out of breaking with Maya. She was pleased with the controlled manner in which she did it. The deaf ear. She was surprised to find herself capable of such control, such thoroughgoing punishment. She punished Maya. She punished Miles, through Maya, as much as she could. What she had to do, and she knew it, was to scrape herself raw, to root out all addiction to the gifts of those two pale prodigies. Miles and Maya. Both of them slippery, shimmery – liars, seducers, finaglers. But you would have thought that after such scourging she'd have scuttled back into her marriage and locked its doors, and appreciated what she had there as never before.

That was not what happened. She broke with Ben. Within a year, she was gone. Her way of breaking was strenuous and unkind. She told him about Miles, though she spared her own pride by leaving out the part about Miles and Maya. She took no care — she had hardly any wish — to avoid unkindness. On the night when she waited for Maya to call, some bitter, yeasty spirit entered into her. She saw herself as a person surrounded by, living by, sham. Because she had been so readily unfaithful, her marriage was a sham. Because she had gone so far out of it, so quickly, it was a sham. She dreaded, now, a life like Maya's. She dreaded just as much a life like her own before this happened. She could not but destroy. Such cold energy was building in her she had to blow her own house down.

She had entered with Ben, when they were both so young, a world of ceremony, of safety, of gestures, concealment. Fond appearances. More than appearances. Fond contrivance. (She thought when she left that she would have no use for contrivance anymore.) She had been happy there, from time to time. She had been sullen, restless, bewildered, and happy. But she said most vehemently, Never, never. I was never happy, she said.

People always say that.

People make momentous shifts, but not the changes they imagine.

JUST THE SAME, Georgia knows that her remorse about the way she changed her life is dishonest. It is real and dishonest. Listening to Raymond, she knows that whatever she did she would have to do again. She would have to do it again, supposing that she had to be the person she was.

Raymond does not want to let Georgia go. He does not want to part with her. He offers to drive her downtown. When she has gone, he won't be able to talk about Maya. Very likely Anne has told him that she does not want to hear any more on the subject of Maya.

"Thank you for coming," he says on the doorstep. "Are you sure about the ride? Are you sure you can't stay to dinner?"

Georgia reminds him again about the bus, the last ferry. She says no, no, she really wants to walk. It's only a couple of miles. The late afternoon so lovely, Victoria so lovely. I had forgotten, she says.

Raymond says once more, "Thank you for coming."

"Thank you for the drinks," Georgia says. "Thank you too. I guess we never believe we are going to die."

"Now, now," says Raymond.

"No. I mean we never behave – we never behave as if we believed we were going to die."

Raymond smiles more and more and puts a hand on her shoulder. "How should we behave?" he says.

"Differently," says Georgia. She puts a foolish stress on the word, meaning that her answer is so lame that she can offer it only as a joke.

Raymond hugs her, then involves her in a long chilly kiss. He fastens onto her with an appetite that is grievous but unconvincing. A parody of passion, whose intention neither one of them, surely, will try to figure out.

She doesn't think about that as she walks back to town through the yellow-leafed streets with their autumn smells and silences. Past Clover Point, the cliffs crowned with broom bushes, the mountains across the water. The mountains of the Olympic Peninsula, assembled like a blatant backdrop, a cutout of rainbow tissue paper. She doesn't think about Raymond, or Miles, or Maya, or even Ben.

She thinks about sitting in the store in the evenings. The light in the street, the complicated reflections in the windows. The accidental clarity.

CARRIED AWAY

LETTERS

IN THE DINING ROOM of the Commercial Hotel, Louisa opened the
letter that had arrived that day from overseas. She ate steak and potatoes,
her usual meal, and drank a glass of wine. There were a few travellers in
the room, and the dentist who ate there every night because he was a
widower. He had shown an interest in her in the beginning but had told
her he had never before seen a woman touch wine or spirits.

"It is for my health," said Louisa gravely.

The white tablecloths were changed every week and in the meantime were protected by oilcloth mats. In winter, the dining room smelled
of these mats wiped by a kitchen rag, and of coal fumes from the furnace,
and beef gravy and dried potatoes and onions – a smell not unpleasant
to anybody coming in hungry from the cold. On each table was a little
cruet stand with the bottle of brown sauce, the bottle of tomato sauce,
and the pot of horseradish.

The letter was addressed to "The Librarian, Carstairs Public Library,
Carstairs, Ontario." It was dated six weeks before – January 4, 1917.

*Perhaps you will be surprised to hear from a person you don't know and
that doesn't remember your name. I hope you are still the same Librarian
though enough time has gone by that you could have moved on.*

*What has landed me here in Hospital is not too serious. I see worse
all around me and get my mind off of all that by picturing things and
wondering for instance if you are still there in the Library. If you are the
one I mean, you are about of medium size or perhaps not quite, with light
brownish hair. You came a few months before it was time for me to go in
the Army following on Miss Tamblyn who had been there since I first
became a user aged nine or ten. In her time the books were pretty much
every which way, and it was as much as your life was worth to ask her*

for the least help or anything since she was quite a dragon. Then when you came what a change, it was all put into sections of Fiction and Non-Fiction and History and Travel and you got the magazines arranged in order and put out as soon as they arrived, not left to molder away till everything in them was stale. I felt gratitude but did not know how to say so. Also I wondered what brought you there, you were an educated person.

My name is Jack Agnew and my card is in the drawer. The last book I took out was very good – H. G. Wells, Mankind in the Making. *My education was to Second Form in High School, then I went into Douds as many did. I didn't join up right away when I was eighteen so you will not see me as a Brave Man. I am a person tending to have my own ideas always. My only relative in Carstairs, or anyplace, is my father Patrick Agnew. He works for Douds not at the factory but at the house doing the gardening. He is a lone wolf even more than me and goes out to the country fishing every chance he gets. I write him a letter sometimes but I doubt if he reads it.*

After supper Louisa went up to the Ladies' Parlor on the second floor, and sat down at the desk to write her reply.

I am very glad to hear you appreciated what I did in the Library though it was just the normal organization, nothing special.

I am sure you would like to hear news of home, but I am a poor person for the job, being an outsider here. I do talk to people in the Library and in the hotel. The travellers in the hotel mostly talk about how business is (it is brisk if you can get the goods) and a little about sickness, and a lot about the War. There are rumors on rumors and opinions galore, which I'm sure would make you laugh if they didn't make you angry. I will not bother to write them down because I am sure there is a Censor reading this who would cut my letter to ribbons.

You ask how I came here. There is no interesting story. My parents are both dead. My father worked for Eaton's in Toronto in the Furniture Department, and after his death my mother worked there too in Linens. And I also worked there for a while in Books. Perhaps you could say Eaton's was our Douds. I graduated from Jarvis Collegiate. I had some sickness which put me in hospital for a long time, but I am quite well now.

I had a great deal of time to read and my favorite authors are Thomas Hardy, who is accused of being gloomy but I think is very true to life – and Willa Cather. I just happened to be in this town when I heard the Librarian had died and I thought, perhaps that is the job for me.

A good thing your letter reached me today as I am about to be discharged from here and don't know if it would have been sent on to where I am going. I am glad you did not think my letter was too foolish.

If you run into my father or anybody you do not need to say anything about the fact we are writing to each other. It is nobody's business and I know there are plenty of people would laugh at me writing to the Librarian as they did at me going to the Library even, why give them the satisfaction?

I am glad to be getting out of here. So much luckier than some I see that will never walk or have their sight and will have to hide themselves away from the world.

You asked where did I live in Carstairs. Well, it was not anyplace to be proud of. If you know where Vinegar Hill is and you turned off on Flowers Road it is the last house on the right, yellow paint once upon a time. My father grows potatoes, or did. I used to take them around town with my wagon, and every load I sold got a nickel to keep.

You mention favorite authors. At one time I was fond of Zane Grey, but I drifted away from reading fiction stories to reading History or Travel. I sometimes read books away over my head, I know, but I do get something out of them. H.G. Wells I mentioned is one and Robert Ingersoll who writes about religion. They have given me a lot to think about. If you are very religious I hope I have not offended you.

One day when I got to the Library it was a Saturday afternoon and you had just unlocked the door and were putting the lights on as it was dark and raining out. You had been caught out with no hat or umbrella and your hair had got wet. You took the pins out of it and let it come down. Is it too personal a thing to ask if you have it long still or have you cut it? You went over and stood by the radiator and shook your hair on it and the water sizzled like grease in the frying pan. I was sitting reading in the London Illustrated News about the War. We exchanged a smile. (I didn't mean to say your hair was greasy when I wrote that!)

I have not cut my hair though I often think about it. I do not know if it is vanity or laziness that prevents me.

I am not very religious.

I walked up Vinegar Hill and found your house. The potatoes are looking healthy. A police dog disputed with me, is he yours?

The weather is getting quite warm. We have had the flood on the river, which I gather is an annual Spring event. The water got into the hotel basement and somehow contaminated our drinking supply so that we were given free beer or ginger ale. But only if we lived or were staying there. You can imagine there were plenty of jokes.

I should ask if there is anything that I could send you.

I am not in need of anything particular. I get the tobacco and other bits of things the ladies in Carstairs do up for us. I would like to read some books by the authors you have mentioned but I doubt whether I would get the chance here.

The other day there was a man died of a heart attack. It was the News of all time. Did you hear about the man who died of a heart attack? That was all you heard about day and night here. Then everybody would laugh which seems hard-hearted but it just seemed so strange. It was not even a hot time so you couldn't say maybe he was scared. (As a matter of fact he was writing a letter at the time so I had better look out.) Before and after him others have died being shot up or blown up but he is the famous one, to die of a heart attack. Everybody is saying what a long way to come and a lot of expense for the Army to go to, for that.

The summer has been so dry the watering tank has been doing the streets every day, trying to lay the dust. The children would dance along behind it. There was also a new thing in town — a cart with a little bell that went along selling ice cream, and the children were pretty attentive to this as well. It was pushed by the man who had an accident at the factory — you know who I mean, though I can't recall his name. He lost his arm to the elbow. My room at the hotel, being on the third floor, it was like an oven, and I often walked about till after midnight. So did many other people, sometimes in pajamas. It was like a dream. There was still a little water in the river, enough to go out in a rowboat, and the Methodist minister did that on a Sunday in August. He was praying for rain in a public service. But there was a small leak in the boat and the water came in and wet his feet and eventually the boat sank and left him standing in the water, which did not nearly reach his waist. Was it an accident or a malicious trick? The talk was all that his prayers were answered but from the wrong direction.

I often pass the Douds' place on my walks. Your father keeps the lawns and hedges looking beautiful. I like the house, so original and airy-looking. But it may not have been cool even there, because I heard the voice of the mother and baby daughter late at night as if they were out on the lawn.

Though I told you there is nothing I need, there is one thing I would like. That is a photograph of you. I hope you will not think I am overstepping the bounds to ask for it. Maybe you are engaged to somebody or have a sweetheart over here you are writing to as well as me. You are a cut above the ordinary and it would not surprise me if some Officer had spoken for you. But now that I have asked I cannot take it back and will just leave it up to you to think what you like of me.

Louisa was twenty-five years old and had been in love once, with a doctor she had known in the sanatorium. Her love was returned, eventually, costing the doctor his job. There was some harsh doubt in her mind about whether he had been told to leave the sanatorium or had left of his own accord, being weary of the entanglement. He was married, he had children. Letters had played a part that time too. After he left, they were still writing to one another. And once or twice after she was released. Then she asked him not to write anymore and he didn't. But the failure of his letters to arrive drove her out of Toronto and made her take the travelling job. Then there would be only the one disappointment in the week, when she got back on Friday or Saturday night. Her last letter had been firm and stoical, and some consciousness of herself as a heroine of love's tragedy went with her around the country as she hauled her display cases up and down the stairs of small hotels and talked about Paris styles and said that her sample hats were bewitching, and drank her solitary glass of wine. If she'd had anybody to tell, though, she would have laughed at just that notion. She would have said love was all hocus-pocus, a deception, and she believed that. But at the prospect she still felt a hush, a flutter along the nerves, a bowing down of sense, a flagrant prostration.

She had a picture taken. She knew how she wanted it to be. She would have liked to wear a simple white blouse, a peasant girl's smock with the string open at the neck. She did not own a blouse of that description and in fact had only seen them in pictures. And she would have liked to let her hair down. Or if it had to be up, she would have liked it piled very loosely and bound with strings of pearls.

Instead she wore her blue silk shirtwaist and bound her hair as usual. She thought the picture made her look rather pale, hollow-eyed. Her expression was sterner and more foreboding than she had intended. She sent it anyway.

I am not engaged, and do not have a sweetheart. I was in love once and it had to be broken off. I was upset at the time but I knew I must bear it, and now I believe that it was all for the best.

She had wracked her brains, of course, to remember him. She could not remember shaking out her hair, as he said she had done, or smiling at any young man when the raindrops fell on the radiator. He might as well have dreamed all that, and perhaps he had.

She had begun to follow the war in a more detailed way than she had done previously. She did not try to ignore it anymore. She went along the street with a sense that her head was filled with the same exciting and troubling information as everybody else's. Saint-Quentin, Arras, Montdidier, Amiens, and then there was a battle going on at the Somme River, where surely there had been one before? She laid open on her desk the maps of the war that appeared as double-page spreads in the magazines. She saw in colored lines the German drive to the Maine, the first thrust of the Americans at Château-Thierry. She looked at the artist's brown pictures of a horse rearing up during an air attack, of some soldiers in East Africa drinking out of coconuts, and of a line of German prisoners with bandaged heads or limbs and bleak, sullen expressions.

Now she felt what everybody else did – a constant fear and misgiving and at the same time this addictive excitement. You could look up from your life of the moment and feel the world cracking beyond the walls.

I am glad to hear you do not have a sweetheart though I know that is selfish of me. I do not think you and I will ever meet again. I don't say that because I've had a dream about what will happen or am a gloomy person always looking for the worst. It just seems to me it is the most probable thing to happen, though I don't dwell on it and go along every day doing the best I can to stay alive. I am not trying to worry you or get your sympathy either but just explain how the idea I won't ever see Carstairs again makes me think I can say anything I want. I guess it's like being sick with a fever. So I will say I love you. I think of you up on a stool at the Library reaching to put a book away and I come up and put my hands on your waist and lift you down, and you turning around inside my arms as if we agreed about everything.

Every Tuesday afternoon the ladies and girls of the Red Cross met in the Council Chambers, which was just down the hall from the Library. When the Library was empty for a few moments, Louisa went down the hall and entered the room full of women. She had decided to knit a scarf. At the sanatorium she had learned how to knit a basic stitch, but she had never learned or had forgotten how to cast on or off.

The older women were all busy packing boxes or cutting up and folding bandages from sheets of heavy cotton that were spread on the tables. But a lot of girls near the door were eating buns and drinking tea. One was holding a skein of wool on her arms for another to wind.

Louisa told them what she needed to know.

"So what do you want to knit, then?" said one of the girls with some bun still in her mouth.

Louisa said, a muffler. For a soldier.

"Oh, you'll want the regulation wool," another said, more politely, and jumped off the table. She came back with some balls of brown wool, and fished a spare pair of needles out of her bag, telling Louisa they could be hers.

"I'll just get you started," she said. "It's a regulation width too."

Other girls gathered around and teased this girl, whose name was Corrie. They told her she was doing it all wrong.

"Oh, I am, am I?" said Corrie. "How would you like a knitting needle in your eye? Is it for a friend?" she said solicitously to Louisa. "A friend overseas?"

"Yes," said Louisa. Of course they would think of her as an old maid, they would laugh at her or feel sorry for her, according to whatever show they put on, of being kind or brazen.

"So knit up good and tight," said the one who'd finished her bun. "Knit up good and tight to keep him warm!"

ONE OF THE GIRLS in this group was Grace Horne. She was a shy but resolute-looking girl, nineteen years old, with a broad face, thin lips often pressed together, brown hair cut in a straight bang, and an attractively mature body. She had become engaged to Jack Agnew before he went overseas, but they had agreed not to say anything about it.

SPANISH FLU

LOUISA HAD MADE friends with some of the travellers who stayed regularly at the hotel. One of these was Jim Frarey, who sold typewriters and office equipment and books and all sorts of stationery supplies. He was a fair-haired, rather round-shouldered but strongly built man in his middle forties. You would think by the look of him that he sold something heavier and more important in the masculine world, like farm implements.

Jim Frarey kept travelling all through the Spanish flu epidemic, though you never knew then if stores would be open for business or not. Occasionally the hotels too would be closed, like the schools and movie houses and even – Jim Frarey thought this a scandal – the churches.

"They ought to be ashamed of themselves, the cowards," he said to Louisa. "What good does it do anybody to lurk around home and wait for it to strike? Now you never closed the Library, did you?"

Louisa said only when she herself was sick. A mild case, hardly lasting a week, but of course she had to go to the hospital. They wouldn't let her stay in the hotel.

"Cowards," he said. "If you're going to be taken, you'll be taken. Don't you agree?"

They discussed the crush in the hospitals, the deaths of doctors and nurses, the unceasing drear spectacle of the funerals. Jim Frarey lived down the street from an undertaking establishment in Toronto. He said they still got out the black horses, the black carriage, the works, to bury such personages as warranted a fuss.

"Day and night they went on," he said. "Day and night." He raised his glass and said, "Here's to health, then. You look well yourself."

He thought that in fact Louisa was looking better than she used to. Maybe she had started putting on rouge. She had a pale-olive skin, and it seemed to him that her cheeks used to be without color. She dressed with more dash too, and took more trouble to be friendly. She used to be very on-again, off-again, just as she chose. She was drinking whisky now too, though she would not try it without drowning it in water. It used to be only a glass of wine. He wondered if it was a boyfriend that had made the difference. But a boyfriend might perk up her looks without increasing her interest in all and sundry, which was what he was pretty sure had happened. It was more likely time running out and the husband prospects thinned out so dreadfully by the war. That could set a woman stirring. She was smarter and better company and better-looking too than most of the married ones. What happened with a woman like that? Sometimes just bad luck. Or bad judgment at a time when it mattered. A little too sharp and self-assured, in the old days, making the men uneasy?

"Life can't be brought to a standstill all the same," he said. "You did the right thing, keeping the Library open."

This was in the early winter of 1919, when there had been a fresh outbreak of flu after the danger was supposed to be past. They seemed to be all alone in the hotel. It was only about nine o'clock but the hotel-keeper had gone to bed. His wife was in the hospital with the flu. Jim Frarey had brought the bottle of whisky from the bar, which was closed for fear of contagion – and they sat at a table beside the window, in the dining room. A winter fog had collected outside and was pressing against the window. You could barely see the streetlights or the few cars that trundled cautiously over the bridge.

"Oh, it was not a matter of principle," Louisa said. "That I kept the Library open. It was a more personal reason than you think."

Then she laughed and promised him a peculiar story. "Oh, the whisky must have loosened my tongue," she said.

"I am not a gossip," said Jim Frarey.

She gave him a hard laughing look and said that when a person announced they weren't a gossip, they almost invariably were. The same when they promised never to tell a soul.

"You can tell this where and when you like just as long as you leave out the real names and don't tell it around here," she said. "That I hope I can trust you not to do. Though at the moment I don't feel as if I cared. I'll probably feel otherwise when the drink wears off. It's a lesson, this story. It's a lesson in what fools women can make of themselves. So, you say, what's new about that, you can learn it every day!"

She began to tell him about a soldier who had started writing letters to her from overseas. The soldier remembered her from when he used to go into the Library. But she didn't remember him. However, she replied in a friendly way to his first letter and a correspondence sprang up between them. He told her where he had lived in the town and she walked past the house so that she could tell him how things looked there. He told her what books he'd read and she gave some of the same kind of information. In short, they both revealed something of themselves and feelings warmed up on either side. On his side first, as far as any declarations went. She was not one to rush in like a fool. At first, she thought she was simply being kind. Even later, she didn't want to reject and embarrass him. He asked for a picture. She had one taken, it was not to her liking, but she sent it. He asked if she had a sweetheart and she replied truthfully that she did not. He did not send any picture of himself nor did she ask for one, though of course she was curious as to what he looked like. It would be no easy matter for him to have a picture taken in the middle of a war. Furthermore, she did not want to seem like the sort of woman who would withdraw kindness if looks did not come up to scratch.

He wrote that he did not expect to come home. He said he was not so afraid of dying as he was of ending up like some of the men he had seen when he was in the hospital, wounded. He did not elaborate, but she supposed he meant the cases they were just getting to know about now – the stumps of men, the blinded, the ones made monstrous with burns. He was not whining about his fate, she did not mean to imply that. It was just that he expected to die and picked death over some other options and he thought about her and wrote to her as men do to a sweetheart in such a situation.

When the war ended, it was a while since she had heard from him. She went on expecting a letter every day and nothing came. Nothing came. She was afraid that he might have been one of those unluckiest of soldiers in the whole war – one of those killed in the last week, or on the last day, or even in the last hour. She searched the local paper every week, and the names of new casualties were still being printed there till after New Year's but his was not among them. Now the paper began to list as well the names of those returning home, often printing a photo with the name, and a little account of rejoicing. When the soldiers were returning thick and fast there was less room for these additions. And then she saw his name, another name on the list. He had not been killed, he had not been wounded – he was coming home to Carstairs, perhaps was already there.

It was then that she decided to keep the Library open, though the flu was raging. Every day she was sure he would come, every day she was prepared for him. Sundays were a torment. When she entered the Town Hall she always felt he might be there before her, leaning up against the wall awaiting her arrival. Sometimes she felt it so strongly she saw a shadow that she mistook for a man. She understood now how people believed they had seen ghosts. Whenever the door opened she expected to look up into his face. Sometimes she made a pact with herself not to look up till she had counted to ten. Few people came in, because of the flu. She set herself jobs of rearranging things, else she would have gone mad. She never locked up until five or ten minutes after closing time.

And then she fancied that he might be across the street on the Post Office steps, watching her, being too shy to make a move. She worried of course that he might be ill, she always sought in conversation for news of the latest cases. No one spoke his name.

It was at this time that she entirely gave up on reading. The covers of books looked like coffins to her, either shabby or ornate, and what was inside them might as well have been dust.

She had to be forgiven, didn't she, she had to be forgiven for thinking, after such letters, that the one thing that could never happen was that he wouldn't approach her, wouldn't get in touch with her at all? Never cross her threshold, after such avowals? Funerals passed by her window and she gave no thought to them, as long as they were not his. Even when she was sick in the hospital her only thought was that she must get back, she must get out of bed, the door must not stay locked against him. She staggered to her feet and back to work. On a hot afternoon she was arranging fresh newspapers on the racks and his name jumped out at her like something in her feverish dreams.

She read a short notice of his marriage to a Miss Grace Horne. Not a girl she knew. Not a Library user.

The bride wore fawn silk crêpe with brown-and-cream piping, and a beige straw hat with brown velvet streamers.

There was no picture. Brown-and-cream piping. Such was the end, and had to be, to her romance.

But on her desk at the Library, a matter of a few weeks ago, on a Saturday night after everybody had gone and she had locked the door and was turning out the lights, she discovered a scrap of paper. A few words written on it. *I was engaged before I went overseas.* No name, not his or hers. And there was her photograph, partly shoved under the blotter.

He had been in the Library that very evening. It had been a busy time, she had often left the desk to find a book for somebody or to straighten up the papers or to put some books on the shelves. He had been in the same room with her, watched her, and taken his chance. But never made himself known.

I was engaged before I went overseas.

"Do you think it was all a joke on me?" Louisa said. "Do you think a man could be so diabolical?"

"In my experience, tricks like that are far more often indulged in by the women. No, no. Don't you think such a thing. Far more likely he was sincere. He got a little carried away. It's all just the way it looks on the surface. He was engaged before he went overseas, he never expected to get back in one piece but he did. And when he did, there is the fiancée waiting – what else could he do?"

"What indeed?" said Louisa.

"He bit off more than he could chew."

"Ah, that's so, that's so!" Louisa said. "And what was it in my case but vanity, which deserves to get slapped down!" Her eyes were glassy and her expression roguish. "You don't think he'd had a good look at me any one time and thought the original was even worse than that poor picture, so he backed off?"

"I do not!" said Jim Frarey. "And don't you so belittle yourself."

"I don't want you to think I am stupid," she said. "I am not so stupid and inexperienced as that story makes me sound."

"Indeed I don't think you are stupid at all."

"But perhaps you think I am inexperienced?"

This was it, he thought – the usual. Women after they have told one story on themselves cannot stop from telling another. Drink upsets them in a radical way, prudence is out the window.

She had confided in him once before that she had been a patient in a sanatorium. Now she told about being in love with a doctor there. The sanatorium was on beautiful grounds up on Hamilton Mountain, and they used to meet there along the hedged walks. Shelves of limestone formed the steps and in sheltered spots there were such plants as you do not commonly see in Ontario – azaleas, rhododendrons, magnolias. The doctor knew something about botany and he told her this was the Carolinian vegetation. Very different from here, lusher, and there were little bits of woodland too, wonderful trees, paths worn under the trees. Tulip trees.

"Tulips!" said Jim Frarey. "Tulips on the trees!"

"No, no, it is the shape of their leaves!"

She laughed at him challengingly, then bit her lip. He saw fit to continue the dialogue, saying, "Tulips on the trees!" while she said no, it is the leaves that are shaped like tulips, no, I never said that, stop! So they passed into a state of gingerly evaluation – which he knew well and could only hope she did – full of small pleasant surprises, half-sardonic signals, a welling-up of impudent hopes, and a fateful sort of kindness.

"All to ourselves," Jim Frarey said. "Never happened before, did it? Maybe it never will again."

She let him take her hands, half lift her from her chair. He turned out the dining-room lights as they went out. Up the stairs they went, that they had so often climbed separately. Past the picture of the dog on his master's grave, and Highland Mary singing in the field, and the old King with his bulgy eyes, his look of indulgence and repletion.

"It's a foggy, foggy night, and my heart is in a fright," Jim Frarey was half singing, half humming as they climbed. He kept an assured hand on Louisa's back. "All's well, all's well," he said as he steered her round the turn of the stairs. And when they took the narrow flight of steps to the third floor he said, "Never climbed so close to Heaven in this place before!"

But later in the night Jim Frarey gave a concluding groan and roused himself to deliver a sleepy scolding. "Louisa, Louisa, why didn't you tell me that was the way it was?"

"I told you everything," said Louisa in a faint and drifting voice.

"I got a wrong impression, then," he said. "I never intended for this to make a difference to you."

She said that it hadn't. Now without him pinning her down and steadying her, she felt herself whirling around in an irresistible way, as if the mattress had turned into a child's top and was carrying her off. She tried to explain that the traces of blood on the sheets could be credited to her period, but her words came out with a luxurious nonchalance and could not be fitted together.

ACCIDENTS

WHEN ARTHUR CAME home from the factory a little before noon he shouted, "Stay out of my way till I wash! There's been an accident over at the works!" Nobody answered. Mrs. Feare, the housekeeper, was talking on the kitchen telephone so loudly that she could not hear him, and his daughter was of course at school. He washed, and stuffed everything he had been wearing into the hamper, and scrubbed up the bathroom, like a murderer. He started out clean, with even his hair slicked and patted, to drive to the man's house. He had had to ask where it was. He thought it was up Vinegar Hill but they said no, that was the father – the young fellow and his wife live on the other side of town, past where the Apple Evaporator used to be, before the war.

He found the two brick cottages side by side, and picked the left-hand one, as he'd been told. It wouldn't have been hard to pick which house, anyway. News had come before him. The door to the house was open, and children too young to be in school yet hung about in the yard. A small girl sat on a kiddie car, not going anywhere, just blocking his path. He stepped around her. As he did so an older girl spoke to him in a formal way – a warning.

"Her dad's dead. Hers!"

A woman came out of the front room carrying an armload of curtains, which she gave to another woman standing in the hall. The woman who received the curtains was gray-haired, with a pleading face. She had no upper teeth. She probably took her plate out, for comfort, at home. The woman who passed the curtains to her was stout but young, with fresh skin.

"You tell her not to get up on that stepladder," the gray-haired woman said to Arthur. "She's going to break her neck taking down curtains. She thinks we need to get everything washed. Are you the undertaker? Oh, no, excuse me! You're Mr. Doud. Grace, come out here! Grace! It's Mr. Doud!"

"Don't trouble her," Arthur said.

"She thinks she's going to get the curtains all down and washed and up again by tomorrow, because he's going to have to go in the front room. She's my daughter. I can't tell her anything."

"She'll quiet down presently," said a sombre but comfortable-looking man in a clerical collar, coming through from the back of the house. Their minister. But not from one of the churches Arthur knew. Baptist? Pentecostal? Plymouth Brethren? He was drinking tea.

Some other woman came and briskly removed the curtains.

"We got the machine filled and going," she said. "A day like this, they'll dry like nobody's business. Just keep the kids out of here."

The minister had to stand aside and lift his teacup high, to avoid her and her bundle. He said, "Aren't any of you ladies going to offer Mr. Doud a cup of tea?"

Arthur said, "No, no, don't trouble."

"The funeral expenses," he said to the gray-haired woman. "If you could let her know—"

"Lillian wet her pants!" said a triumphant child at the door. "Mrs. Agnew! Lillian peed her pants!"

"Yes. Yes," said the minister. "They will be very grateful."

"The plot and the stone, everything," Arthur said. "You'll make sure they understand that. Whatever they want on the stone."

The gray-haired woman had gone out into the yard. She came back with a squalling child in her arms. "Poor lamb," she said. "They told her she wasn't supposed to come in the house so where could she go? What could she do but have an accident!"

The young woman came out of the front room dragging a rug.

"I want this put on the line and beat," she said.

"Grace, here is Mr. Doud come to offer his condolences," the minister said.

"And to ask if there is anything I can do," said Arthur.

The gray-haired woman started upstairs with the wet child in her arms and a couple of others following.

Grace spotted them.

"Oh, no, you don't! You get back outside!"

"My mom's in here."

"Yes and your mom's good and busy, she don't need to be bothered with you. She's here helping me out. Don't you know Lillian's dad's dead?"

"Is there anything I can do for you?" Arthur said, meaning to clear out.

Grace stared at him with her mouth open. Sounds of the washing machine filled the house.

"Yes, there is," she said. "You wait here."

"She's overwhelmed," the minister said. "It's not that she means to be rude."

Grace came back with a load of books.

"These here," she said. "He had them out of the Library. I don't want to have to pay fines on them. He went every Saturday night so I guess they are due back tomorrow. I don't want to get in trouble about them."

"I'll look after them," Arthur said. "I'd be glad to."

"I just don't want to get in any trouble about them."

"Mr. Doud was saying about taking care of the funeral," the minister said to her, gently admonishing. "Everything including the stone. Whatever you want on the stone."

"Oh, I don't want anything fancy," Grace said.

On Friday morning last there occurred in the sawmill operation of Douds Factory a particularly ghastly and tragic accident. Mr. Jack Agnew, in reaching under the main shaft, had the misfortune to have his sleeve caught by a setscrew in an adjoining flunge, so that his arm and shoulder were drawn under the shaft. His head in consequence was brought in contact with the circular saw, that saw being about one foot in diameter. In an instant the unfortunate young man's head was separated from his body, being severed at an angle below the left ear and through the neck. His death is believed to have been instantaneous. He never spoke or uttered a cry so it was not by any sound of his but by the spurt and shower of his blood that his fellow-workers were horribly alerted to the disaster.

This account was reprinted in the paper a week later for those who might have missed it or who wished to have an extra copy to send to friends or relations out of town (particularly to people who used to live in Carstairs and did not anymore). The misspelling of *flange* was corrected. There was a note apologizing for the mistake. There was also a description of a very large funeral, attended even by people from neighboring towns and as far away as Walley. They came by car and train, and some by horse and buggy. They had not known Jack Agnew when he was alive, but, as the paper said, they wished to pay tribute to the sensational and tragic manner of his death. All the stores in Carstairs were closed for two hours that afternoon. The hotel did not close its doors but that was because all the visitors needed somewhere to eat and drink.

The survivors were a wife, Grace, and a four-year-old daughter, Lillian. The victim had fought bravely in the Great War and had only been wounded once, not seriously. Many had commented on this irony.

The paper's failure to mention a surviving father was not deliberate. The editor of the paper was not a native of Carstairs, and people forgot to tell him about the father until it was too late.

The father himself did not complain about the omission. On the day of the funeral, which was very fine, he headed out of town as he would have done ordinarily on a day he had decided not to spend at Douds. He was wearing a felt hat and a long coat that would do for a rug if he wanted to take a nap. His overshoes were neatly held on his feet with the rubber rings from sealing jars. He was going out to fish for suckers. The season hadn't opened yet, but he always managed to be a bit ahead of it. He fished through the spring and early summer and cooked and ate what he caught. He had a frying pan and a pot hidden out on the riverbank. The pot was for boiling corn that he snatched out of the fields later in the year, when he was also eating the fruit of wild apple trees and grapevines. He was quite sane but abhorred conversation. He could not altogether avoid it in the weeks following his son's death, but he had a way of cutting it short.

"Should've watched out what he was doing."

Walking in the country that day, he met another person who was not at the funeral. A woman. She did not try to start any conversation and in fact seemed as fierce in her solitude as himself, whipping the air past her with long fervent strides.

THE PIANO FACTORY, which had started out making pump organs, stretched along the west side of town, like a medieval town wall. There were two long buildings like the inner and outer ramparts, with a closed-in bridge between them where the main offices were. And reaching up into the town and the streets of workers' houses you had the kilns and the sawmill and the lumberyard and storage sheds. The factory whistle dictated the time for many to get up, blowing at six o'clock in the morning. It blew again for work to start at seven and at twelve for dinnertime and at one in the afternoon for work to recommence, and then at five-thirty for the men to lay down their tools and go home.

Rules were posted beside the time clock, under glass. The first two rules were:

ONE MINUTE LATE IS FIFTEEN MINUTES PAY. BE PROMPT. DON'T TAKE SAFETY FOR GRANTED. WATCH OUT FOR YOURSELF AND THE NEXT MAN.

There had been accidents in the factory and in fact a man had been killed when a load of lumber fell on him. That had happened before Arthur's time. And once, during the war, a man had lost an arm, or part of an arm. On the day that happened, Arthur was away in Toronto. So he had never seen an accident – nothing serious, anyway. But it was often at the back of his mind now that something might happen.

Perhaps he did not feel so sure that trouble wouldn't come near him, as he had felt before his wife died. She had died in 1919, in the last flurry of the Spanish flu, when everyone had got over being frightened. Even she had not been frightened. That was nearly five years ago and it still seemed to Arthur like the end of a carefree time in his life. But to other people he had always seemed very responsible and serious – nobody had noticed much difference in him.

In his dreams of an accident there was a spreading silence, everything was shut down. Every machine in the place stopped making its customary noise and every man's voice was removed, and when Arthur looked out of the office window he understood that doom had fallen. He never could remember any particular thing he saw that told him this. It was just the space, the dust in the factory yard, that said to him *now.*

THE BOOKS STAYED on the floor of his car for a week or so. His daughter Bea said, "What are those books doing here?" and then he remembered.

Bea read out the titles and the authors. *Sir John Franklin and the Romance of the Northwest Passage,* by G. B. Smith. *What's Wrong with the World?,* G. K. Chesterton. *The Taking of Quebec,* Archibald Hendry. *Bolshevism: Practice and Theory,* by Lord Bertrand Russell.

"Bol-*shev*-ism," Bea said, and Arthur told her how to pronounce it correctly. She asked what it was, and he said, "It's something they've got in Russia that I don't understand so well myself. But from what I hear of it, it's a disgrace."

Bea was thirteen at this time. She had heard about the Russian Ballet and also about dervishes. She believed for the next couple of years that Bolshevism was some sort of diabolical and maybe indecent dance. At least this was the story she told when she was grown up.

She did not mention that the books were connected with the man who had had the accident. That would have made the story less amusing. Perhaps she had really forgotten.

THE LIBRARIAN WAS perturbed. The books still had their cards in them, which meant they had never been checked out, just removed from the shelves and taken away.

"The one by Lord Russell has been missing a long time."

Arthur was not used to such reproofs, but he said mildly, "I am returning them on behalf of somebody else. The chap who was killed. In the accident at the factory."

The Librarian had the Franklin book open. She was looking at the picture of the boat trapped in the ice.

"His wife asked me to," Arthur said.

She picked up each book separately, and shook it as if she expected something to fall out. She ran her fingers in between the pages. The bottom part of her face was working in an unsightly way, as if she was chewing at the inside of her cheeks.

"I guess he just took them home as he felt like it," Arthur said.

"I'm sorry?" she said in a minute. "What did you say? I'm sorry."

It was the accident, he thought. The idea that the man who had died in such a way had been the last person to open these books, turn these pages. The thought that he might have left a bit of his life in them, a scrap of paper or a pipe cleaner as a marker, or even a few shreds of tobacco. That unhinged her.

"No matter," he said. "I just dropped by to bring them back."

He turned away from her desk but did not immediately leave the Library. He had not been in it for years. There was his father's picture between the two front windows, where it would always be.

*A. V. Doud, founder of the Doud Organ Factory and
Patron of this Library. A Believer in Progress, Culture,
and Education. A True Friend of the Town of
Carstairs and of the Working Man.*

The Librarian's desk was in the archway between the front and back rooms. The books were on shelves set in rows in the back room. Green-shaded lamps, with long pull cords, dangled down in the aisles between. Arthur remembered years ago some matter brought up at the Council Meeting about buying sixty-watt bulbs instead of forty. This Librarian was the one who had requested that, and they had done it.

In the front room, there were newspapers and magazines on wooden racks, and some round heavy tables, with chairs, so that people could sit and read, and rows of thick dark books behind glass. Dictionaries, probably, and atlases and encyclopedias. Two handsome high windows looking out on the main street, with Arthur's father hanging between them. Other pictures around the room hung too high, and were too dim and crowded with figures for the person down below to interpret them easily. (Later, when Arthur had spent many hours in the Library and had discussed these pictures with the Librarian, he knew that one of them represented the Battle of Flodden Field, with the King of Scotland charging down the hill into a pall of smoke, one the funeral of the Boy King of Rome, and one the Quarrel of Oberon and Titania, from *A Midsummer Night's Dream*.)

He sat down at one of the reading tables, where he could look out the window. He picked up an old copy of the *National Geographic* which was lying there. He had his back to the Librarian. He thought this the tactful thing to do, since she seemed somewhat wrought-up. Other people came in, and he heard her speak to them. Her voice sounded normal enough now. He kept thinking he would leave, but did not.

He liked the high bare window full of the light of the spring evening, and he liked the dignity and order of these rooms. He was pleasantly mystified by the thought of grown people coming and going here, steadily reading books. Week after week, one book after another, a whole life long. He himself read a book once in a while, when somebody recommended it, and usually he enjoyed it, and then he read magazines, to keep up with things, and never thought about reading a book until another one came along, in this almost accidental way.

There would be little spells when nobody was in the Library but himself and the Librarian.

During one of these, she came over and stood near him, replacing some newspapers on the rack. When she finished this, she spoke to him, with a controlled urgency.

"The account of the accident that was printed in the paper – I take it that was more or less accurate?"

Arthur said that it was possibly too accurate.

"Why? Why do you say that?"

He mentioned the public's endless appetite for horrific details. Ought the paper to pander to that?

"Oh, I think it's natural," the Librarian said. "I think it's natural to want to know the worst. People do want to picture it. I do myself. I am very ignorant of machinery. It's hard for me to imagine what happened. Even with the paper's help. Did the machine do something unexpected?"

"No," Arthur said. "It wasn't the machine grabbing him and pulling him in, like an animal. He made a wrong move or at any rate a careless move. Then he was done for."

She said nothing, but did not move away.

"You have to keep your wits about you," Arthur said. "Never let up for a second. A machine is your servant and it is an excellent servant, but it makes an imbecile master."

He wondered if he had read that somewhere, or had thought it up himself.

"And I suppose there are no ways of protecting people?" the Librarian said. "But you must know all about that."

She left him then. Somebody had come in.

The accident was followed by a rush of warm weather. The length of the evenings and the heat of the balmy days seemed sudden and surprising, as if this were not the way winter finally ended in that part of the country, almost every year. The sheets of floodwater shrank magically back into the bogs, and the leaves shot out of the reddened branches, and barnyard smells drifted into town and were wrapped in the smell of lilacs.

Instead of wanting to be outdoors on such evenings, Arthur found himself thinking of the Library, and he would often end up there, sitting in the spot he had chosen on his first visit. He would sit for half an hour, or an hour. He looked at the London *Illustrated News,* or the *National Geographic* or *Saturday Night* or *Collier's.* All of these magazines arrived at his own house and he could have been sitting there, in the den, looking out at his hedged lawns, which old Agnew kept in tolerable condition, and the flower beds now full of tulips of every vivid color and combination. It seemed that he preferred the view of the main street, where the occasional brisk-looking new Ford went by, or some stuttering older-model car with a dusty cloth top. He preferred the Post Office, with its clock tower telling four different times in four different directions – and, as people liked to say, all wrong. Also the passing and loitering on the sidewalk. People trying to get the drinking fountain to work, although it wasn't turned on till the first of July.

It was not that he felt the need of sociability. He was not there for chat, though he would greet people if he knew them by name, and he did know most. And he might exchange a few words with the Librarian, though often it was only "Good evening" when he came in, and "Good night" when he went out. He made no demands on anybody. He felt his presence to be genial, reassuring, and, above all, natural. By sitting here, reading and reflecting, here instead of at home, he seemed to himself to be providing something. People could count on it.

There was an expression he liked. *Public* servant. His father, who looked out at him here with tinted baby-pink cheeks and glassy blue eyes and an old man's petulant mouth, had never thought of himself so. He had thought of himself more as a public character and benefactor. He had operated by whims and decrees, and he had got away with it. He would go around the factory when business was slow, and say to one man and another, "Go home. Go on home now. Go home and stay there till I can use you again." And they would go. They would work in their gardens or go out shooting rabbits and run up bills for whatever they had to buy, and accept that it couldn't be otherwise. It was still a joke with them, to imitate his bark. *Go on home!* He was their hero more than Arthur could ever be, but they were not prepared to take the same treatment today. During the war, they had got used to the good wages and to being always in demand. They never thought of the glut of labor the soldiers had created when they came home, never thought about how a business like this was kept going by luck and ingenuity from one year to the next, even from one season to the next. They didn't like changes – they were not happy about the switch now to player pianos, which Arthur believed were the hope of the future. But Arthur would do what he had to, though his way of proceeding was quite the opposite of his father's. Think everything over and then think it over again. Stay in the background except when necessary. Keep your dignity. Try always to be fair.

They expected all to be provided. The whole town expected it. Work would be provided just as the sun would rise in the mornings. And the taxes on the factory raised at the same time rates were charged for the water that used to come free. Maintenance of the access roads was now the factory's responsibility instead of the town's. The Methodist Church was requesting a hefty sum to build the new Sunday school. The town hockey team needed new uniforms. Stone gateposts were being erected for the War Memorial Park. And every year the smartest boy in the senior class was sent to university, courtesy of Douds.

Ask and ye shall receive.

Expectations at home were not lacking either. Bea was agitating to go away to private school and Mrs. Feare had her eye on some new mixing apparatus for the kitchen, also a new washing machine. All the trim on the house was due to be painted this year. All that wedding-cake decoration that consumed paint by the gallon. And in the midst of this what had Arthur done but order himself a new car – a Chrysler sedan.

It was necessary – he had to drive a new car. He had to drive a new car, Bea had to go away to school, Mrs. Feare had to have the latest, and the trim had to be as fresh as Christmas snow. Else they would lose respect, they would lose confidence, they would start to wonder if things were going downhill. And it could be managed, with luck it could all be managed.

For years after his father's death, he had felt like an impostor. Not steadily, but from time to time he had felt that. And now the feeling was gone. He could sit here and feel that it was gone.

HE HAD BEEN in the office when the accident happened, consulting with a veneer salesman. Some change in noise registered with him, but it was more of an increase than a hush. It was nothing that alerted him – just an irritation. Because it happened in the sawmill, nobody would know about the accident immediately in the shops or in the kilns or in the yard, and work in some places continued for several minutes. In fact Arthur, bending over the veneer samples on his desk, might have been one of the last people to understand that there had been an intervention. He asked the salesman a question, and the salesman did not answer. Arthur looked up and saw the man's mouth open, his face frightened, his salesman's assurance wiped away.

Then he heard his own name being called – both "Mr. Doud!" as was customary and "Arthur, Arthur!" by such of the older men as had known him as a boy. Also he heard "saw" and "head" and "Jesus, Jesus, Jesus!"

Arthur could have wished for the silence, the sounds and objects drawing back in that dreadful but releasing way, to give him room. It was nothing like that. Yelling and questioning and running around, himself in the midst being propelled to the sawmill. One man had fainted, falling in such a way that if they had not got the saw turned off a moment before, it would have got him too. It was his body, fallen but entire, that Arthur briefly mistook for the body of the victim. Oh, no, no. They pushed him on. The sawdust was scarlet. It was drenched, brilliant. The pile of lumber here was all merrily spattered, and the blades. A pile of work clothes soaked in blood lay in the sawdust and Arthur realized that it was the body, the trunk with limbs attached. So much blood had flowed as to make its shape not plain at first – to soften it, like a pudding.

The first thing he thought of was to cover that. He took off his jacket and did so. He had to step up close, his shoes squished in it. The reason no one else had done this would be simply that no one else was wearing a jacket.

"Have they gone a-get the doctor?" somebody was yelling. "Gone a-get the doctor!" a man quite close to Arthur said. "Can't sew his head back on – doctor. Can he?"

But Arthur gave the order to get the doctor; he imagined it was necessary. You can't have a death without a doctor. That set the rest in motion. Doctor, undertaker, coffin, flowers, preacher. Get started on all that, give them something to do. Shovel up the sawdust, clean up the saw. Send the men who had been close by to wash themselves. Carry the man who had fainted to the lunchroom. Is he all right? Tell the office girl to make tea.

Brandy was what was needed, or whisky. But he had a rule against it, on the premises.

Something still lacking. Where was it? There, they said. Over there. Arthur heard the sound of vomiting, not far away. All right. Either pick it up or tell somebody to pick it up. The sound of vomiting saved him, steadied him, gave him an almost lighthearted determination. He picked it up. He carried it delicately and securely as you might carry an awkward but valuable jug. Pressing the face out of sight, as if comforting it, against his chest. Blood seeped through his shirt and stuck the material to his skin. Warm. He felt like a wounded man. He was aware of them watching him and he was aware of himself as an actor must be, or a priest. What to do with it, now that he had it against his chest? The answer to that came too. Set it down, put it back where it belongs, not of course fitted with exactness, not as if a seam could be closed. Just more or less in place, and lift the jacket and tug it into a new position.

He couldn't now ask the man's name. He would have to get it in some other way. After the intimacy of his services here, such ignorance would be an offense.

But he found he did know it – it came to him. As he edged the corner of his jacket over the ear that had lain and still lay upward, and so looked quite fresh and usable, he received a name. Son of the fellow who came and did the garden, who was not always reliable. A young man taken on again when he came back from the war. Married? He thought so. He would have to go and see her. As soon as possible. Clean clothes.

THE LIBRARIAN OFTEN wore a dark-red blouse. Her lips were reddened to match, and her hair was bobbed. She was not a young woman anymore, but she maintained an eye-catching style. He remembered that years ago when they had hired her, he had thought that she got herself up very soberly. Her hair was not bobbed in those days – it was wound around her head, in the old style. It was still the same color – a warm and pleasant color, like leaves – oak leaves, say, in the fall. He tried to think how much she was paid. Not much, certainly. She kept herself looking well on it. And where did she live? In one of the boardinghouses – the one with the schoolteachers? No, not there. She lived in the Commercial Hotel.

And now something else was coming to mind. No definite story that he could remember. You could not say with any assurance that she had a bad reputation. But it was not quite a spotless reputation, either. She was said to take a drink with the travellers. Perhaps she had a boyfriend among them. A boyfriend or two.

Well, she was old enough to do as she liked. It wasn't quite the same as the way it was with a teacher – hired partly to set an example. As long as she did her job well, and anybody could see that she did. She had her life to live, like everyone else. Wouldn't you rather have a nice-looking woman in here than a crabby old affair like Mary Tamblyn? Strangers might drop in, they judge a town by what they see, you want a nice-looking woman with a nice manner.

Stop that. Who said you didn't? He was arguing in his head on her behalf just as if somebody had come along who wanted her chucked out, and he had no intimation at all that that was the case.

What about her question, on the first evening, regarding the machines? What did she mean by that? Was it a sly way of bringing blame?

He had talked to her about the pictures and the lighting and even told her how his father had sent his own workmen over here, paid them to build the Library shelves, but he had never spoken of the man who had taken the books out without letting her know. One at a time, probably. Under his coat? Brought back the same way. He must have brought them back, or else he'd have had a houseful, and his wife would never stand for that. Not stealing, except temporarily. Harmless behavior, but peculiar. Was there any connection? Between thinking you could do things a little differently that way and thinking you could get away with a careless move that might catch your sleeve and bring the saw down on your neck?

There might be, there might be some connection. A matter of attitude.

"That chap – you know the one – the accident–" he said to the Librarian. "The way he took off with the books he wanted. Why do you think he did that?"

"People do things," the Librarian said. "They tear out pages. On account of something they don't like or something they do. They just do things. I don't know."

"Did he ever tear out some pages? Did you ever give him a lecture? Ever make him scared to face you?"

He meant to tease her a little, implying that she would not be likely to scare anybody, but she did not take it that way.

"How could I when I never spoke to him?" she said. "I never saw him. I never saw him, to know who he was."

She moved away, putting an end to the conversation. So she did not like to be teased. Was she one of those people full of mended cracks that you could only see close up? Some old misery troubling her, some secret? Maybe a sweetheart had been lost in the war.

*　　*　　*

ON A LATER EVENING, a Saturday evening in the summer, she brought the subject up herself, that he would never have mentioned again.

"Do you remember our talking once about the man who had the accident?"

Arthur said he did.

"I have something to ask you and you may think it strange."

He nodded.

"And my asking it – I want you to – it is confidential."

"Yes, indeed," he said.

"What did he look like?"

Look like? Arthur was puzzled. He was puzzled by her making such a fuss and secret about it – surely it was natural to be interested in what a man might look like who had been coming in and making off with her books without her knowing about it – and because he could not help her, he shook his head. He could not bring any picture of Jack Agnew to mind.

"Tall," he said. "I believe he was on the tall side. Otherwise I cannot tell you. I am really not such a good person to ask. I can recognize a man easily but I can't ever give much of a physical description, even when it's someone I see on a daily basis."

"But I thought you were the one – I heard you were the one–" she said. "Who picked him up. His head."

Arthur said stiffly, "I didn't think that you could just leave it lying there." He felt disappointed in the woman, uneasy and ashamed for her. But he tried to speak matter-of-factly, keeping reproach out of his voice.

"I could not even tell you the color of his hair. It was all – all pretty much obliterated, by that time."

She said nothing for a moment or two and he did not look at her. Then she said, "It must seem as if I am one of those people – one of those people who are fascinated by these sorts of things."

Arthur made a protesting noise, but it did, of course, seem to him that she must be like that.

"I should not have asked you," she said. "I should not have mentioned it. I can never explain to you why I did. I would like just to ask you, if you can help it, never to think that that is the kind of person I am."

Arthur heard the word "never." She could never explain to him. He was never to think. In the midst of his disappointment he picked up this suggestion, that their conversations were to continue, and perhaps on a less haphazard basis. He heard a humility in her voice, but it was a humility that was based on some kind of assurance. Surely that was sexual.

Or did he only think so, because this was the evening it was? It was the Saturday evening in the month when he usually went to Walley. He was going there tonight, he had only dropped in here on his way, he had not meant to stay as long as he had done. It was the night when he went to visit a woman whose name was Jane MacFarlane. Jane MacFarlane lived apart from her husband, but she was not thinking of getting a divorce. She had no children. She earned her living as a dressmaker. Arthur had first met her when she came to his house to make clothes for his wife. Nothing had gone on at that time, and neither of them had thought of it. In some ways Jane MacFarlane was a woman like the Librarian – good-looking, though not so young, plucky and stylish and good at her work. In other ways, not so like. He could not imagine Jane ever presenting a man with a mystery, and following that up with the information that it would never be solved. Jane was a woman to give a man peace. The submerged dialogue he had with her – sensual, limited, kind – was very like the one he had had with his wife.

The Librarian went to the switch by the door, and turned out the main light. She locked the door. She disappeared among the shelves, turning out the lights there too, in a leisurely way. The town clock was striking nine. She must think that it was right. His own watch said three minutes to.

It was time to get up, time for him to leave, time to go to Walley.

When she had finished dealing with the lights, she came and sat down at the table beside him.

He said, "I would never think of you in any way that would make you unhappy."

Turning out the lights shouldn't have made it so dark. They were in the middle of summer. But it seemed that heavy rain clouds had moved in. When Arthur had last paid attention to the street, he had seen plenty of daylight left: country people shopping, boys squirting each other at the drinking fountain, and young girls walking up and down in their soft, cheap, flowery summer dresses, letting the young men watch them from wherever the young men congregated – the Post Office steps, the front of the feed store. And now that he looked again he saw the street in an uproar from the loud wind that already carried a few drops of rain. The girls were shrieking and laughing and holding their purses over their heads as they ran to shelter, store clerks were rolling up awnings and hauling in the baskets of fruit, the racks of summer shoes, the garden implements that had been displayed on the sidewalks. The doors of the Town Hall banged as the farm women ran inside, grabbing on to packages and children, to cram themselves into the Ladies' Rest Room. Somebody tried the Library door. The Librarian looked over at it but did not move. And soon the rain was sweeping like curtains across the street, and the wind battered the Town Hall roof, and tore at the treetops. That roaring and danger lasted a few minutes, while the power of the wind went by. Then the sound left was the sound of the rain, which was now falling vertically and so heavily they might have been under a waterfall.

If the same thing was happening at Walley, he thought, Jane would know enough not to expect him. This was the last thought he had of her for a long while.

"Mrs. Feare wouldn't wash my clothes," he said, to his own surprise. "She was afraid to touch them."

The Librarian said, in a peculiarly quivering, shamed, and determined voice, "I think what you did – I think that was a remarkable thing to do."

The rain made such a constant noise that he was released from answering. He found it easy then to turn and look at her. Her profile was dimly lit by the wash of rain down the windows. Her expression was calm and reckless. Or so it seemed to him. He realized that he knew hardly anything about her – what kind of person she really was or what kind of secrets she could have. He could not even estimate his own value to her. He only knew that he had some, and it wasn't the usual.

He could no more describe the feeling he got from her than you can describe a smell. It's like the scorch of electricity. It's like burnt kernels of wheat. No, it's like a bitter orange. I give up.

He had never imagined that he would find himself in a situation like this, visited by such a clear compulsion. But it seemed he was not unprepared. Without thinking over twice or even once what he was letting himself in for, he said, "I wish—"

He had spoken too quietly, she did not hear him.

He raised his voice. He said, "I wish we could get married."

Then she looked at him. She laughed but controlled herself.

"I'm sorry," she said. "I'm sorry. It's just what went through my mind."

"What was that?" he said.

"I thought – that's the last I'll see of him."

Arthur said, "You're mistaken."

TOLPUDDLE MARTYRS

THE PASSENGER TRAIN from Carstairs to London had stopped running during the Second World War and even the rails were taken up. People said it was for the War Effort. When Louisa went to London to see the heart specialist, in the mid-fifties, she had to take the bus. She was not supposed to drive anymore.

The doctor, the heart specialist, said that her heart was a little wonky and her pulse inclined to be jumpy. She thought that made her heart sound like a comedian and her pulse like a puppy on a lead. She had not come fifty-seven miles to be treated with such playfulness but she let it pass, because she was already distracted by something she had been reading in the doctor's waiting room. Perhaps it was what she had been reading that had made her pulse jumpy.

On an inside page of the local paper she had seen the headline LOCAL MARTYRS HONORED, and simply to put in the time she had read further. She read that there was to be some sort of ceremony that afternoon at Victoria Park. It was a ceremony to honor the Tolpuddle Martyrs. The paper said that few people had heard of the Tolpuddle Martyrs, and certainly Louisa had not. They were men who had been tried and found guilty for administering illegal oaths. This peculiar offense, committed over a hundred years ago in Dorset, England, had got them transported to Canada and some of them had ended up here in London, where they lived out the rest of their days and were buried without any special notice or commemoration. They were considered now to be among the earliest founders of the Trade Union movement, and the Trade Unions Council, along with representatives of the Canadian Federation of Labor and the ministers of some local churches, had organized a ceremony taking place today on the occasion of the hundred-and-twentieth anniversary of their arrest.

Martyrs is laying it on somewhat, thought Louisa. They were not executed, after all.

The ceremony was to take place at three o'clock and the chief speakers were to be one of the local ministers, and Mr. John (Jack) Agnew, a union spokesman from Toronto.

It was a quarter after two when Louisa came out of the doctor's office. The bus to Carstairs did not leave until six o'clock. She had thought she would go and have tea and something to eat on the top floor of Simpsons, then shop for a wedding present, or if the time fitted go to an afternoon movie. Victoria Park lay between the doctor's office and Simpsons, and she decided to cut across it. The day was hot and the shade of the trees pleasant. She could not avoid seeing where the chairs had been set up, and a small speakers' platform draped in yellow cloth, with a Canadian flag on the one side and what she supposed must be a Labor Union flag on the other. A group of people had collected and she found herself changing course in order to get a look at them. Some were old people, very plainly but decently dressed, the women with kerchiefs around their heads on the hot day, Europeans. Others were factory workers, men in clean short-sleeved shirts and women in fresh blouses and slacks, let out early. A few women must have come from home, because they were wearing summer dresses and sandals and trying to keep track of small children. Louisa thought that they would not care at all for the way she was dressed — fashionably, as always, in beige shantung with a crimson silk tam — but she noticed, just then, a woman more elegantly got up than she was, in green silk with her dark hair drawn tightly back, tied with a green-and-gold scarf. She might have been forty — her face was worn, but beautiful. She came over to Louisa at once, smiling, showed her a chair and gave her a mimeographed paper. Louisa could not read the purple printing. She tried to get a look at some men who were talking beside the platform. Were the speakers among them?

The coincidence of the name was hardly even interesting. Neither the first name nor the last was all that unusual.

She did not know why she had sat down, or why she had come over here in the first place. She was beginning to feel a faintly sickening, familiar agitation. She could feel that over nothing. But once it got going, telling herself that it was over nothing did no good. The only thing to do was to get up and get away from here before any more people sat down and hemmed her in.

The green woman intercepted her, asked if she was all right.

"I have to catch a bus," said Louisa in a croaky voice. She cleared her throat. "An out-of-town bus," she said with better control, and marched away, not in the right direction for Simpsons. She thought in fact that she wouldn't go there, she wouldn't go to Birks for the wedding present or to a movie either. She would just go and sit in the bus depot until it was time for her to go home.

WITHIN HALF A BLOCK of the bus depot she remembered that the bus had not taken her there that morning. The depot was being torn down and rebuilt – there was a temporary depot several blocks away. She had not paid quite enough attention to which street it was on – York Street, east of the real depot, or King? At any rate, she had to detour, because both of these streets were being torn up, and she had almost decided she was lost when she realized she had been lucky enough to come upon the temporary depot by the back way. It was an old house – one of those tall yellow-gray brick houses dating from the time when this was a residential district. This was probably the last use it would be put to before being torn down. Houses all around it must have been torn down to make the large gravelled lot where the buses pulled in. There were still some trees at the edge of the lot and under them a few rows of chairs that she had not noticed when she got off the bus before noon. Two men were sitting on what used to be the veranda of the house, on old car seats. They wore brown shirts with the bus company's insignia but they seemed to be halfhearted about their work, not getting up when she asked if the bus to Carstairs was leaving at six o'clock as scheduled and where could she get a soft drink?

Six o'clock, far as they knew.

Coffee shop down the street.

Cooler inside but only Coke and orange left.

She got herself a Coca-Cola out of the cooler in a dirty little indoor waiting room that smelled of a bad toilet. Moving the depot to this dilapidated house must have thrown everyone into a state of indolence and fecklessness. There was a fan in the room they used as an office, and she saw, as she went by, some papers blow off the desk. "Oh, shit," said the office girl, and stamped her heel on them.

The chairs set up in the shade of the dusty city trees were straight-backed old wooden chairs originally painted different colors – they looked as if they had come from various kitchens. Strips of old carpet and rubber bathroom mats were laid down in front of them, to keep your feet off the gravel. Behind the first row of chairs she thought she saw a sheep lying on the ground, but it turned into a dirty-white dog, which trotted over and looked at her for a moment in a grave semi-official way – gave a brief sniff at her shoes, and trotted away. She had not noticed if there were any drinking straws and did not feel like going back to look. She drank Coke from the bottle, tilting back her head and closing her eyes.

When she opened them, a man was sitting one chair away, and was speaking to her.

"I got here as soon as I could," he said. "Nancy said you were going to catch a bus. As soon as I finished with the speech, I took off. But the bus depot is all torn up."

"Temporarily," she said.

"I knew you right away," he said. "In spite of – well, many years. When I saw you, I was talking to somebody. Then I looked again and you'd disappeared."

"I don't recognize you," said Louisa.

"Well, no," he said. "I guess not. Of course. You wouldn't."

He was wearing tan slacks, a pale-yellow short-sleeved shirt, a cream-and-yellow ascot scarf. A bit of a dandy, for a union man. His hair was white but thick and wavy, the sort of springy hair that goes in ripples, up and back from the forehead, his skin was flushed and his face was deeply wrinkled from the efforts of speechmaking – and from talking to people privately, she supposed, with much of the fervor and persuasiveness of his public speeches. He wore tinted glasses, which he took off now, as if willing that she should see him better. His eyes were a light blue, slightly blood-shot and apprehensive. A good-looking man, still trim except for a little authoritative bulge over the belt, but she did not find these serviceable good looks – the careful sporty clothes, the display of ripply hair, the effective expressions – very attractive. She preferred the kind of looks Arthur had. The restraint, the dark-suited dignity that some people could call pompous, that seemed to her admirable and innocent.

"I always meant to break the ice," he said. "I meant to speak to you. I should have gone in and said goodbye at least. The opportunity to leave came up so suddenly."

Louisa did not have any idea what to say to this. He sighed. He said, "You must have been mad at me. Are you still?"

"No," she said, and fell back, ridiculously, on the usual courtesies. "How is Grace? How is your daughter? Lillian?"

"Grace is not so well. She had some arthritis. Her weight doesn't help it. Lillian is all right. She's married but she still teaches high school. Mathematics. Not too usual for a woman."

How could Louisa begin to correct him? Could she say, No, your wife Grace got married again during the war, she married a farmer, a widower. Before that she used to come in and clean our house once a week. Mrs. Feare had got too old. And Lillian never finished high school, how could she be a high-school teacher? She married young, she had some children, she works in the drugstore. She had your height and your hair, dyed blond. I often looked at her and thought she must be like you. When she was growing up, I used to give her my stepdaughter's outgrown clothes.

Instead of this, she said, "Then the woman in the green dress – that was not Lillian?"

"Nancy? Oh, no! Nancy is my guardian angel. She keeps track of where I'm going, and when, and have I got my speech, and what I drink and eat and have I taken my pills. I tend toward high blood pressure. Nothing too serious. But my way of life's no good. I'm on the go constantly. Tonight I've got to fly out of here to Ottawa, tomorrow I've got a tough meeting, tomorrow night I've got some fool banquet."

Louisa felt it necessary to say, "You knew that I got married? I married Arthur Doud."

She thought he showed some surprise. But he said, "Yes, I heard that. Yes."

"We worked hard too," said Louisa sturdily. "Arthur died six years ago. We kept the factory going all through the thirties even though at times we were down to three men. We had no money for repairs and I remember cutting up the office awnings so that Arthur could carry them up on a ladder and patch the roof. We tried making everything we could think of. Even outdoor bowling alleys for those amusement places. Then the war came and we couldn't keep up. We could sell all the pianos we could make but also we were making radar cases for the Navy. I stayed in the office all through."

"It must have been a change," he said, in what seemed a tactful voice. "A change from the Library."

"Work is work," she said. "I still work. My stepdaughter Bea is divorced, she keeps house for me after a fashion. My son has finally finished university – he is supposed to be learning about the business, but he has some excuse to go off in the middle of every afternoon. When I come home at suppertime, I am so tired I could drop, and I hear the ice tinkling in their glasses and them laughing behind the hedge. Oh, Mud, they say when they see me, Oh, poor Mud, sit down here, get her a drink! They call me Mud because that was my son's name for me when he was a baby. But they are neither of them babies now. The house is cool when I come home – it's a lovely house if you remember, built in three tiers like a wedding cake. Mosaic tiles in the entrance hall. But I am always thinking about the factory, that is what fills my mind. What should we do to stay afloat? There are only five factories in Canada making pianos now, and three of them are in Quebec with the low cost of labor. No doubt you know all about that. When I talk to Arthur in my head, it is always about the same thing. I am very close to him still but it is hardly in a mystical way. You would think as you get older your mind would fill up with what they call the spiritual side of things, but mine just seems to get more and more practical, trying to get something settled. What a thing to talk to a dead man about."

She stopped, she was embarrassed. But she was not sure that he had listened to all of this, and in fact she was not sure that she had said all of it.

"What started me off—" he said. "What got me going in the first place, with whatever I have managed to do, was the Library. So I owe you a great deal."

He put his hands on his knees, let his head fall.

"Ah, rubbish," he said.

He groaned, and ended up with a laugh.

"My father," he said. "You wouldn't remember my father?"

"Oh, yes."

"Well. Sometimes I think he had the right idea."

Then he lifted his head, gave it a shake, and made a pronouncement.

"Love never dies."

She felt impatient to the point of taking offense. This is what all the speechmaking turns you into, she thought, a person who can say things like that. Love dies all the time, or at any rate it becomes distracted, overlaid – it might as well be dead.

"Arthur used to come and sit in the Library," she said. "In the beginning I was very provoked with him. I used to look at the back of his neck and think, Ha, what if something should hit you there! None of that would make sense to you. It wouldn't make sense. And it turned out to be something else I wanted entirely. I wanted to marry him and get into a normal life.

"A normal life," she repeated – and a giddiness seemed to be taking over, a widespread forgiveness of folly, alerting the skin of her spotty hand, her dry thick fingers that lay not far from his, on the seat of the chair between them. An amorous flare-up of the cells, of old intentions. *Oh, never dies.*

Across the gravelled yard came a group of oddly dressed folk. They moved all together, a clump of black. The women did not show their hair – they had black shawls or bonnets covering their heads. The men wore broad hats and black braces. The children were dressed just like their elders, even to the bonnets and hats. How hot they all looked in those clothes – how hot and dusty and wary and shy.

"The Tolpuddle Martyrs," he said, in a faintly joking, resigned, and compassionate voice. "Ah, I guess I'd better go over. I'd better go over there and have a word with them."

That edge of a joke, the uneasy kindness, made her think of somebody else. Who was it? When she saw the breadth of his shoulders from behind, and the broad flat buttocks, she knew who.

Jim Frarey.

Oh, what kind of a trick was being played on her, or what kind of trick was she playing on herself! She would not have it. She pulled herself up tightly, she saw all those black clothes melt into a puddle. She was dizzy and humiliated. She would not have it.

But not all black, now that they were getting closer. She could see dark blue, those were the men's shirts, and dark blue and purple in some of the women's dresses. She could see faces – the men's behind beards, the women's in their deep-brimmed bonnets. And now she knew who they were. They were Mennonites.

Mennonites were living in this part of the country, where they never used to be. There were some of them around Bondi, a village north of Carstairs. They would be going home on the same bus as she was.

He was not with them, or anywhere in sight.

A traitor, helplessly. A traveller.

Once she knew that they were Mennonites and not some lost unidentifiable strangers, these people did not look so shy or dejected. In fact, they seemed quite cheerful, passing around a bag of candy, adults eating candy with the children. They settled on the chairs all around her.

No wonder she was feeling clammy. She had gone under a wave, which nobody else had noticed. You could say anything you liked about what had happened – but what it amounted to was going under a wave. She had gone under and through it and was left with a cold sheen on her skin, a beating in her ears, a cavity in her chest, and revolt in her stomach. It was anarchy she was up against – a devouring muddle. Sudden holes and impromptu tricks and radiant vanishing consolations.

But these Mennonite settlings are a blessing. The plop of behinds on chairs, the crackling of the candy bag, the meditative sucking and soft conversations. Without looking at Louisa, a little girl holds out the bag, and Louisa accepts a butterscotch mint. She is surprised to be able to hold it in her hand, to have her lips shape thank-you, then to discover in her mouth just the taste that she expected. She sucks on it as they do on theirs, not in any hurry, and allows that taste to promise her some reasonable continuance.

Lights have come on, though it isn't yet evening. In the trees above the wooden chairs someone has strung lines of little colored bulbs that she did not notice until now. They make her think of festivities. Carnivals. Boats of singers on the lake.

"What place is this?" she said to the woman beside her.

ON THE DAY OF Miss Tamblyn's death it happened that Louisa was staying in the Commercial Hotel. She was a traveller then for a company that sold hats, ribbons, handkerchiefs and trimmings, and ladies' underwear to retail stores. She heard the talk in the hotel, and it occurred to her that the town would soon need a new Librarian. She was getting very tired of lugging her sample cases on and off trains, and showing her wares in hotels, packing and unpacking. She went at once and talked to the people in charge of the Library. A Mr. Doud and a Mr. Macleod. They sounded like a vaudeville team but did not look it. The pay was poor, but she had not been doing so well on commission, either. She told them that she had finished high school, in Toronto, and had worked in Eaton's Book Department before she switched to travelling. She did not think it necessary to tell them that she had only worked there five months when she was discovered to have t.b., and that she had then spent four years in a sanatorium. The t.b. was cured, anyway, her spots were dry.

The hotel moved her to one of the rooms for permanent guests, on the third floor. She could see the snow-covered hills over the rooftops. The town of Carstairs was in a river valley. It had three or four thousand people and a long main street that ran downhill, over the river, and uphill again. There was a piano and organ factory.

The houses were built for lifetimes and the yards were wide and the streets were lined with mature elm and maple trees. She had never been here when the leaves were on the trees. It must make a great difference. So much that lay open now would be concealed.

She was glad of a fresh start, her spirits were hushed and grateful. She had made fresh starts before and things had not turned out as she had hoped, but she believed in the swift decision, the unforeseen intervention, the uniqueness of her fate.

The town was full of the smell of horses. As evening came on, big blinkered horses with feathered hooves pulled the sleighs across the bridge, past the hotel, beyond the streetlights, down the dark side roads. Somewhere out in the country they would lose the sound of each other's bells.

THE ALBANIAN VIRGIN

IN THE MOUNTAINS, in Maltsia e madhe, she must have tried to tell them her name, and "Lottar" was what they made of it. She had a wound in her leg, from a fall on sharp rocks when her guide was shot. She had a fever. How long it took them to carry her through the mountains, bound up in a rug and strapped to a horse's back, she had no idea. They gave her water to drink now and then, and sometimes *raki*, which was a kind of brandy, very strong. She could smell pines. At one time they were on a boat and she woke up and saw the stars, brightening and fading and changing places – unstable clusters that made her sick. Later she understood that they must have been on the lake. Lake Scutari, or Sckhoder, or Skodra. They pulled up among the reeds. The rug was full of vermin, which got under the rag tied around her leg.

At the end of her journey, though she did not know it was the end, she was lying in a small stone hut that was an outbuilding of the big house, called the *kula*. It was the hut of the sick and dying. Not of giving birth, which these women did in the cornfields, or beside the path when they were carrying a load to market.

She was lying, perhaps for weeks, on a heaped-up bed of ferns. It was comfortable, and had the advantage of being easily changed when fouled or bloodied. The old woman named Tima looked after her. She plugged up the wound with a paste made of beeswax and olive oil and pine resin. Several times a day the dressing was removed, the wound washed out with *raki*. Lottar could see black lace curtains hanging from the rafters, and she thought she was in her room at home, with her mother (who was dead) looking after her. "Why have you hung up those curtains?" she said. "They look horrible."

She was really seeing cobwebs, all thick and furry with smoke – ancient cobwebs, never disturbed from year to year.

Also, in her delirium, she had the sensation of some wide board being pushed against her face – something like a coffin plank. But when she came to her senses she learned that it was nothing but a crucifix, a wooden crucifix that a man was trying to get her to kiss. The man was a priest, a Franciscan. He was a tall, fierce-looking man with black eyebrows and mustache and a rank smell, and he carried, besides the crucifix, a gun that she learned later was a Browning revolver. He knew by the look of her that she was a giaour – not a Muslim – but he did not understand that she might be a heretic. He knew a little English but pronounced it in a way that she could not make out. And she did not then know any of the language of the Ghegs. But after her fever subsided, when he tried a few words of Italian on her, they were able to talk, because she had learned Italian at school and had been travelling for six months in Italy. He understood so much more than anyone else around her that she expected him, at first, to understand everything. What is the nearest city? she asked him, and he said, Skodra. So go there, please, she said – go and find the British Consulate, if there is one. I belong to the British Empire. Tell them I am here. Or if there is no British Consul, go to the police.

She did not understand that under no circumstances would anybody go to the police. She didn't know that she belonged now to this tribe, this *kula*, even though taking her prisoner had not been their intention and was an embarrassing mistake.

It is shameful beyond belief to attack a woman. When they had shot and killed her guide, they had thought that she would turn her horse around and fly back down the mountain road, back to Bar. But her horse took fright at the shot and stumbled among the boulders and she fell, and her leg was injured. Then they had no choice but to carry her with them, back across the border between the Crna Gora (which means Black Rock, or Montenegro) and Maltsia e madhe.

"But why rob the guide and not me?" she said, naturally thinking robbery to be the motive. She thought of how starved they looked, the man and his horse, and of the fluttering white rags of his headdress.

"Oh, they are not robbers!" said the Franciscan, shocked. "They are honest men. They shot him because they were in blood with him. With his house. It is their law."

He told her that the man who had been shot, her guide, had killed a man of this *kula*. He had done that because the man he had killed had killed a man of his *kula*. This would go on, it had been going on for a long time now, there were always more sons being born. They think they have more sons than other people in the world, and it is to serve this necessity.

"Well, it is terrible," the Franciscan concluded. "But it is for their honor, the honor of their family. They are always ready to die for their honor."

She said that her guide did not seem to be so ready, if he had fled to Crna Gora.

"But it did not make any difference, did it?" said the Franciscan. "Even if he had gone to America, it would not have made any difference."

AT TRIESTE SHE had boarded a steamer, to travel down the Dalmatian Coast. She was with her friends Mr. and Mrs. Cozzens, whom she had met in Italy, and their friend Dr. Lamb, who had joined them from England. They put in at the little port of Bar, which the Italians call Antivari, and stayed the night at the European Hotel. After dinner they walked on the terrace, but Mrs. Cozzens was afraid of a chill, so they went indoors and played cards. There was rain in the night. She woke up and listened to the rain and was full of disappointment, which gave rise to a loathing for these middle-aged people, particularly for Dr. Lamb, whom she believed the Cozzenses had summoned from England to meet her. They probably thought she was rich. A transatlantic heiress whose accent they could almost forgive. These people ate too much and then they had to take pills. And they worried about being in strange places – what had they come for? In the morning she would have to get back on the boat with them or they would make a fuss. She would never take the road over the mountains to Cetinge, Montenegro's capital city – they had been told that it was not wise. She would never see the bell tower where the heads of Turks used to hang, or the plane tree under which the Poet-Prince held audience with the people. She could not get back to sleep, so she decided to go downstairs with the first light, and, even if it was still raining, to go a little way up the road behind the town, just to see the ruins that she knew were there, among the olive trees, and the Austrian fortress on its rock and the dark face of Mount Lovchen.

The weather obliged her, and so did the man at the hotel desk, producing almost at once a tattered but cheerful guide and his underfed horse. They set out – she on the horse, the man walking ahead. The road was steep and twisting and full of boulders, the sun increasingly hot and the intervening shade cold and black. She became hungry and thought she must turn back soon. She would have breakfast with her companions, who got up late.

No doubt there was some sort of search for her, after the guide's body was found. The authorities must have been notified – whoever the authorities were. The boat must have sailed on time, her friends must have gone with it. The hotel had not taken their passports. Nobody back in Canada would think of investigating. She was not writing regularly to anyone, she had had a falling-out with her brother, her parents were dead. You won't come home till all your inheritance is spent, her brother had said, and then who will look after you?

When she was being carried through the pine forest, she awoke and found herself suspended, lulled – in spite of the pain and perhaps because of the *raki* – into a disbelieving surrender. She fastened her eyes on the bundle that was hanging from the saddle of the man ahead of her and knocking against the horse's back. It was something about the size of a cabbage, wrapped in a stiff and rusty-looking cloth.

I HEARD THIS STORY in the old St. Joseph's Hospital in Victoria from Charlotte, who was the sort of friend I had in my early days there. My friendships then seemed both intimate and uncertain. I never knew why people told me things, or what they meant me to believe.

I had come to the hospital with flowers and chocolates. Charlotte lifted her head, with its clipped and feathery white hair, toward the roses. "Bah!" she said. "They have no smell! Not to me, anyway. They are beautiful, of course.

"You must eat the chocolates yourself," she said. "Everything tastes like tar to me. I don't know how I know what tar tastes like, but this is what I think."

She was feverish. Her hand, when I held it, felt hot and puffy. Her hair had all been cut off, and this made her look as if she had actually lost flesh around her face and neck. The part of her under the hospital covers seemed as extensive and lumpy as ever.

"But you must not think I am ungrateful," she said. "Sit down. Bring that chair from over there – she doesn't need it."

There were two other women in the room. One was just a thatch of yellow-gray hair on the pillow, and the other was tied into a chair, wriggling and grunting.

"This is a terrible place," said Charlotte. "But we must just try our best to put up with it. I am so glad to see you. That one over there yells all night long," she said, nodding toward the window bed. "We must thank Christ she's asleep now. I don't get a wink of sleep, but I have been putting the time to very good use. What do you think I've been doing? I've been making up a story, for a movie! I have it all in my head and I want you to hear it. You will be able to judge if it will make a good movie. I think it will. I would like Jennifer Jones to act in it. I don't know, though. She does not seem to have the same spirit anymore. She married that mogul.

"Listen," she said. "(Oh, could you haul that pillow up more, behind my head?) It takes place in Albania, in northern Albania, which is called Maltsia e madhe, in the nineteen-twenties, when things were very primitive. It is about a young woman travelling alone. Lottar is her name in the story."

I sat and listened. Charlotte would lean forward, even rock a little on her hard bed, stressing some point for me. Her puffy hands flew up and down, her blue eyes widened commandingly, and then from time to time she sank back onto the pillows, and she shut her eyes to get the story in focus again. Ah, yes, she said. Yes, yes. And she continued.

"Yes, yes," she said at last. "I know how it goes on, but that is enough for now. You will have to come back. Tomorrow. Will you come back?"

I said, yes, tomorrow, and she appeared to have fallen asleep without hearing me.

* * *

THE *KULA* WAS a great, rough stone house with a stable below and the living quarters above. A veranda ran all the way around, and there would always be an old woman sitting there, with a bobbin contraption that flew like a bird from one hand to the other and left a trail of shiny black braid, mile after mile of black braid, which was the adornment of all the men's trousers. Other women worked at the looms or sewed together the leather sandals. Nobody sat there knitting, because nobody would think to sit down to knit. Knitting was what they did while they trotted back and forth to the spring with their water barrels strapped to their backs, or took the path to the fields or to the beech wood, where they collected the fallen branches. They knitted stockings – black and white, red and white, with zigzag patterns like lightning strokes. Women's hands must never be idle. Before dawn they pounded the bread dough in its blackened wooden trough, shaped it into loaves on the backs of shovels, and baked it on the hearth. (It was corn bread, unleavened and eaten hot, which would swell up like a puffball in your stomach.) Then they had to sweep out the *kula* and dump the dirty ferns and pile up arm-loads of fresh ferns for the next night's sleep. This was often one of Lottar's jobs, since she was so unskilled at everything else. Little girls stirred the yogurt so that lumps would not form as it soured. Older girls might butcher a kid and sew up its stomach, which they had stuffed with wild garlic and sage and apples. Or they would go together, girls and women, all ages, to wash the men's white head scarves in the cold little river nearby, whose waters were clear as glass. They tended the tobacco crop and hung the ripe leaves to dry in the darkened shed. They hoed the corn and cucumbers, milked the ewes.

The women looked stern but they were not so, really. They were only preoccupied, and proud of themselves, and eager for competition. Who could carry the heaviest load of wood, knit the fastest, hoe the most rows of cornstalks? Tima, who had looked after Lottar when she was sick, was the most spectacular worker of all. She would run up the slope to the *kula* with a load of wood bound to her back that looked ten times as big as herself. She would leap from rock to rock in the river and pound the scarves as if they were the bodies of enemies. "Oh, Tima, Tima!" the other women cried out in ironic admiration, and "Oh, Lottar, Lottar!" in nearly the same tones, when Lottar, at the other end of a scale of usefulness, let the clothes drift away downstream. Sometimes they whacked Lottar with a stick, as they would a donkey, but this had more exasperation in it than cruelty. Sometimes the young ones would say, "Talk your talk!" and for their entertainment she would speak English. They wrinkled up their faces and spat, at such peculiar sounds. She tried to teach them words – *hand*, *nose*, and so on. But these seemed to them jokes, and they would repeat them to each other and fall about laughing.

Women were with women and men were with men, except at times in the night (women teased about such times were full of shame and denial, and sometimes there would be a slapping) and at meals, when the women served the men their food. What the men did all day was none of the women's business. Men made their ammunition, and gave a lot of care to their guns, which were in some cases very beautiful, decorated with engraved silver. They also dynamited rocks to clear the road, and were responsible for the horses. Wherever they were, there was a lot of laughing, and sometimes singing and firing off of blanks. While they were at home they seemed to be on holiday, and then some of them would have to ride off on an expedition of punishment, or to attend a council called to put an end to some particular bout of killing. None of the women believed it would work – they laughed and said that it would only mean twenty more shot. When a young man was going off on his first killing, the women made a great fuss over his clothes and his haircut, to encourage him. If he didn't succeed, no woman would marry him – a woman of any worth would be ashamed to marry a man who had not killed – and everyone was anxious to have new brides in the house, to help with the work.

One night, when Lottar served one man his food – a guest; there were always guests invited for meals around the low table, the *sofra* – she noticed what small hands he had, and hairless wrists. Yet he was not young, he was not a boy. A wrinkled, leathery face, without a mustache. She listened for his voice in the talk, and it seemed to her hoarse but womanish. But he smoked, he ate with the men, he carried a gun.

"Is that a man?" Lottar said to the woman serving with her. The woman shook her head, not willing to speak where the men might hear them. But the young girls who overheard the question were not so careful. "Is that a man? Is that a man?" they mimicked Lottar. "Oh, Lottar, you are so stupid! Don't you know when you see a Virgin?"

So she did not ask them anything else. But the next time she saw the Franciscan, she ran after him to ask him her question. What is a Virgin? She had to run after him, because he did not stop and talk to her now as he had when she was sick in the little hut. She was always working when he came to the *kula*, and he could not spend much time with the women anyway – he sat with the men. She ran after him when she saw him leaving, striding down the path among the sumac trees, heading for the bare wooden church and the lean-to church house, where he lived.

He said it was a woman, but a woman who had become like a man. She did not want to marry, and she took an oath in front of witnesses that she never would, and then she put on men's clothes and had her own gun, and her horse if she could afford one, and she lived as she liked. Usually she was poor, she had no woman to work for her. But nobody troubled her, and she could eat at the *sofra* with the men.

Lottar no longer spoke to the priest about going to Skodra. She understood now that it must be a long way away. Sometimes she asked if he had heard anything, if anybody was looking for her, and he would say, sternly, no one. When she thought of how she had been during those first weeks – giving orders, speaking English without embarrassment, sure that her special case merited attention – she was ashamed at how little she had understood. And the longer she stayed at the *kula*, the better she spoke the language and became accustomed to the work, the stranger was the thought of leaving. Someday she must go, but how could it be now? How could she leave in the middle of the tobacco-picking or the sumac harvest, or during the preparations for the feast of the Translation of St. Nicholas?

In the tobacco fields they took off their jerkins and blouses and worked half naked in the sun, hidden between the rows of tall plants. The tobacco juice was black and sticky, like molasses, and it ran down their arms and was smeared over their breasts. At dusk they went down to the river and scrubbed themselves clean. They splashed in the cold water, girls and big, broad women together. They tried to push each other off balance, and Lottar heard her name cried then, in warning and triumph, without contempt, like any other name: "Lottar, watch out! Lottar!"

They told her things. They told her that children died here because of the *Striga*. Even grown-up people shrivel and die sometimes, when the *Striga* has put her spell on them. The *Striga* looks like a normal woman, so you do not know who she is. She sucks blood. To catch her, you must lay a cross on the threshold of the church on Easter Sunday when everybody is inside. Then the woman who is the *Striga* cannot come out. Or you can follow the woman you suspect, and you may see her vomit up the blood. If you can manage to scrape up some of this blood on a silver coin, and carry that coin with you, no *Striga* can touch you, ever.

Hair cut at the time of the full moon will turn white.

If you have pains in your limbs, cut some hair from your head and your armpits and burn it – then the pains will go away.

The *oras* are the devils that come out at night and flash false lights to bewilder travellers. You must crouch down and cover your head, else they will lead you over a cliff. Also they will catch the horses and ride them to death.

THE TOBACCO HAD been harvested, the sheep brought down from the slopes, animals and humans shut up in the *kula* through the weeks of snow and cold rain, and one day, in the early warmth of the spring sun, the women brought Lottar to a chair on the veranda. There, with great ceremony and delight, they shaved off the hair above her forehead. Then they combed some black, bubbling dye through the hair that remained. The dye was greasy – the hair became so stiff that they could shape it into wings and buns as firm as blood puddings. Everybody thronged about, criticizing and admiring. They put flour on her face and dressed her up in clothes they had pulled out of one of the great carved chests. What for, she asked, as she found herself disappearing into a white blouse with gold embroidery, a red bodice with fringed epaulets, a sash of striped silk a yard wide and a dozen yards long, a black-and-red wool skirt, with chain after chain of false gold being thrown over her hair and around her neck. For beauty, they said. And they said when they had finished, "See! She is beautiful!" Those who said it seemed triumphant, challenging others who must have doubted that the transformation could be made. They squeezed the muscles in her arms, which she had got from hoeing and wood-carrying, and patted her broad, floured forehead. Then they shrieked, because they had forgotten a very important thing – the black paint that joins the eyebrows in a single line over the nose.

"The priest is coming!" shouted one of the girls, who must have been placed as a lookout, and the woman who was painting the black line said, "Ha, he will not stop it!" But the others drew aside.

The Franciscan shot off a couple of blanks, as he always did to announce his arrival, and the men of the house fired off blanks also, to welcome him. But he did not stay with the men this time. He climbed at once to the veranda, calling, "Shame! Shame! Shame on you all! Shame!

"I know what you have dyed her hair for," he said to the women. "I know why you have put bride's clothes on her. All for a pig of a Muslim!

"You! You sitting there in your paint," he said to Lottar. "Don't you know what it is for? Don't you know they have sold you to a Muslim? He is coming from Vuthaj. He will be here by dark!"

"So what of it?" said one of the women boldly. "All they could get for her was three napoleons. She has to marry somebody."

The Franciscan told her to hold her tongue. "Is this what you want?" he said to Lottar. "To marry an infidel and go to live with him in Vuthaj?"

Lottar said no. She felt as if she could hardly move or open her mouth, under the weight of her greased hair and her finery. Under this weight she struggled as you do to rouse yourself to a danger, out of sleep. The idea of marrying the Muslim was still too distant to be the danger – what she understood was that she would be separated from the priest, and would never be able to claim an explanation from him again.

"Did you know you were being married?" he asked her. "Is it something you want, to be married?"

No, she said. No. And the Franciscan clapped his hands. "Take off that gold trash!" he said. "Take those clothes off her! I am going to make her a Virgin!

"If you become a Virgin, it will be all right," he said to her. "The Muslim will not have to shoot anybody. But you must swear you will never go with a man. You must swear in front of witnesses. *Per quri e per kruch*. By the stone and by the Cross. Do you understand that? I am not going to let them marry you to a Muslim, but I do not want more shooting to start on this land."

It was one of the things the Franciscan tried so hard to prevent – the selling of women to Muslim men. It put him into a frenzy, that their religion could be so easily set aside. They sold girls like Lottar, who would bring no price anywhere else, and widows who had borne only girls.

Slowly and sulkily the women removed all the rich clothes. They brought out men's trousers, worn and with no braid, and a shirt and head scarf. Lottar put them on. One woman with an ugly pair of shears chopped off most of what remained of Lottar's hair, which was difficult to cut because of the dressing.

"Tomorrow you would have been a bride," they said to her. Some of them seemed mournful, some contemptuous. "Now you will never have a son."

The little girls snatched up the hair that had been cut off and stuck it on their heads, arranging various knots and fringes.

Lottar swore her oath in front of twelve witnesses. They were, of course, all men, and looked as sullen as the women about the turn things had taken. She never saw the Muslim. The Franciscan berated the men and said that if this sort of thing did not stop he would close up the churchyard and make them bury their dead in unholy ground. Lottar sat at a distance from them all, in her unaccustomed clothes. It was strange and unpleasant to be idle. When the Franciscan had finished his harangue, he came over and stood looking down at her. He was breathing hard because of his rage, or the exertions of the lecture.

"Well, then," he said. "Well." He reached into some inner fold of his clothing and brought out a cigarette and gave it to her. It smelled of his skin.

*   *   *

A NURSE BROUGHT in Charlotte's supper, a light meal of soup and canned peaches. Charlotte took the cover off the soup, smelled it, and turned her head away. "Go away, don't look at this slop," she said. "Come back tomorrow – you know it's not finished yet."

The nurse walked with me to the door, and once we were in the corridor she said, "It's always the ones with the least at home who turn the most critical. She's not the easiest in the world, but you can't help kind of admiring her. You're not related, are you?"

Oh, no, I said. No.

"When she came in it was amazing. We were taking her things off and somebody said, oh, what lovely bracelets, and right away she wanted to sell them! Her *husband* is something else. Do you know him? They are really quite the characters."

Charlotte's husband, Gjurdhi, had come to my bookstore by himself one cold morning less than a week earlier. He was pulling a wagon full of books, which he had wrapped up in a blanket. He had tried to sell me some books once before, in their apartment, and I thought perhaps these were the same ones. I had been confused then, but now that I was on my own ground I was able to be more forceful. I said no, I did not handle secondhand books, I was not interested. Gjurdhi nodded brusquely, as if I had not needed to tell him this and it was of no importance to our conversation. He continued to pick up the books one by one, urging me to run my hands over the bindings, insisting that I note the beauty of the illustrations and be impressed by the dates of publication. I had to repeat my refusal over and over again, and I heard myself begin to attach some apologies to it, quite against my own will. He chose to understand each rejection as applying to an individual book and would simply fetch out another, saying vehemently, "This too! This is very beautiful. You will notice. And it is very old. Look what a beautiful old book!"

They were travel books, some of them, from the turn of the century. Not so very old, and not so beautiful, either, with their dim, grainy photographs. *A Trek Through the Black Peaks. High Albania. Secret Lands of Southern Europe.*

"You will have to go to the Antiquarian Bookstore," I said. "The one on Fort Street. It isn't far to take them."

He made a sound of disgust, maybe indicating that he knew well enough where it was, or that he had already made an unsuccessful trip there, or that most of these books had come from there, one way or another, in the first place.

"How is Charlotte?" I said warmly. I had not seen her for a while, although she used to visit the store quite often. She would bring me little presents – coffee beans coated with chocolate to give me energy; a bar of pure glycerine soap to counteract the drying effects, on the skin, of having to handle so much paper. A paperweight embedded with samples of rocks found in British Columbia, a pencil that lit up in the dark (so that I could see to write up bills if the lights should go out). She drank coffee with me, talked, and strolled about the store, discreetly occupied, when I was busy. Through the dark, blustery days of fall she wore the velvet cloak that I had first seen her in, and kept the rain off with an oversized, ancient black umbrella. She called it her tent. If she saw that I had become too involved with a customer, she would tap me on the shoulder and say, "I'll just silently steal away with my tent now. We'll talk another day."

Once, a customer said to me bluntly, "Who is that woman? I've seen her around town with her husband. I guess he's her husband. I thought they were peddlers."

Could Charlotte have heard that, I wondered. Could she have detected a coolness in the attitude of my new clerk? (Charlotte was certainly cool to her.) There might have been just too many times when I was busy. I did not actually think that the visits had stopped. I preferred to think that an interval had grown longer, for a reason that might have nothing to do with me. I was busy and tired, anyway, as Christmas loomed. The number of books I was selling was a pleasant surprise.

"I don't want to be any kind of character assassin," the clerk had said to me. "But I think you should know that that woman and her husband have been banned from a lot of stores in town. They're suspected of lifting things. I don't know. He wears that rubber coat with the big sleeves and she's got her cloak. I do know for sure that they used to go around at Christmastime and snip off holly that was growing in people's gardens. Then they took it round and tried to sell it in apartment buildings."

On that cold morning, after I had refused all the books in his wagon, I asked Gjurdhi again how Charlotte was. He said that she was sick. He spoke sullenly, as if it were none of my business.

"Take her a book," I said. I picked out a Penguin light verse. "Take her this – tell her I hope she enjoys it. Tell her I hope she'll be better very soon. Perhaps I can get around to see her."

He put the book into his bundle in the wagon. I thought that he would probably try to sell it immediately.

"Not at home," he said. "In the hospital."

I had noticed, each time he bent over the wagon, a large, wooden crucifix that swung down outside his coat and had to be tucked back inside. Now this happened again, and I said, thoughtlessly, in my confusion and contrition, "Isn't that beautiful! What beautiful dark wood! It looks medieval."

He pulled it over his head, saying, "Very old. Very beautiful. Oak wood. Yes."

He pushed it into my hand, and as soon as I realized what was happening I pushed it back.

"*Wonderful* wood," I said. As he put it away I felt rescued, though full of irritable remorse.

"Oh, I hope Charlotte is not very sick!" I said.

He smiled disdainfully, tapping himself on the chest – perhaps to show me the source of Charlotte's trouble, perhaps only to feel for himself the skin that was newly bared there.

Then he took himself, the crucifix, the books, and the wagon out of my store. I felt that insults had been offered, humiliations suffered, on both sides.

* * *

UP PAST THE tobacco field was a beech wood, where Lottar had often gone to get sticks for the fire. Beyond that was a grassy slope – a high meadow – and at the top of the meadow, about half an hour's climb from the *kula*, was a small stone shelter, a primitive place with no window, a low doorway and no door, a corner hearth without a chimney. Sheep took cover there; the floor was littered with their droppings.

That was where she went to live after she became a Virgin. The incident of the Muslim bridegroom had taken place in the spring, just about a year after she first came to Maltsia e madhe, and it was time for the sheep to be driven to their higher pastures. Lottar was to keep count of the flock and see that they did not fall into ravines or wander too far away. And she was to milk the ewes every evening. She was expected to shoot wolves, if any came near. But none did; no one alive now at the *kula* had ever seen a wolf. The only wild animals Lottar saw were a red fox, once, by the stream, and the rabbits, which were plentiful and unwary. She learned to shoot and skin and cook them, cleaning them out as she had seen the butcher girls do at the *kula* and stewing the meatier parts in her pot over the fire, with some bulbs of wild garlic.

She did not want to sleep inside the shelter, so she fixed up a roof of branches outside, against the wall, this roof an extension of the roof of the building. She had her heap of ferns underneath, and a felt rug she had been given, to spread on the ferns when she slept. She no longer took any notice of the bugs. There were some spikes pushed into the wall between the dry stones. She did not know why they were there, but they served her well for hanging up the milk pails and the few pots she had been provided with. She brought her water from the stream, in which she washed her own head scarf, and herself sometimes, more for relief from the heat than out of concern about her dirtiness.

Everything was changed. She no longer saw the women. She lost her habits of constant work. The little girls came up in the evenings to get the milk. This far away from the *kula* and their mothers, they became quite wild. They climbed up on the roof, often smashing through the arrangement of branches which Lottar had contrived. They jumped into the ferns and sometimes snatched an armful of them to bind into a crude ball, which they threw at one another until it fell apart. They enjoyed themselves so much that Lottar had to chase them away at dusk, reminding them of how frightened they got in the beech wood after dark. She believed that they ran all the way through it and spilled half the milk on their way.

Now and then they brought her corn flour, which she mixed with water and baked on her shovel by the fire. Once they had a treat, a sheep's head – she wondered if they had stolen it – for her to boil in her pot.

She was allowed to keep some of the milk, and instead of drinking it fresh she usually let it go sour, and stirred it to make yogurt to dip her bread in. That was how she preferred it now.

The men often came up through the wood shortly after the little girls had run through it on their way down. It seemed that this was a custom of theirs, in the summer. They liked to sit on the banks of the stream and fire off blanks and drink *raki* and sing, or sometimes just smoke and talk. They were not making this expedition to see how she was getting on. But since they were coming anyway, they brought her presents of coffee and tobacco and were full of competing advice on how to fix up the roof of her shelter so it wouldn't fall down, how to keep her fire going all night, how to use her gun.

Her gun was an old Italian Martini, which had been given to her when she left the *kula*. Some of the men said that gun was unlucky, since it had belonged to a boy who had been killed before he himself had even shot anybody. Others said that Martinis in general were unlucky, hardly any use at all.

Mausers were what you needed, for accuracy and repeating power.

But Mauser bullets were too small to do enough damage. There were men walking around full of Mauser holes – you could hear them whistle as they passed by.

Nothing can really compare with a heavy flintlock that has a good packing of powder, a bullet, and nails.

When they weren't talking about guns, the men spoke of recent killings, and told jokes. One of them told a joke about a wizard. There was a wizard held in prison by a Pasha. The Pasha brought him out to do tricks in front of guests. Bring a bowl of water, said the wizard. Now, this water is the sea. And what port shall I show you on the sea? Show a port on the island of Malta, they said. And there it was. Houses and churches and a steamer ready to sail. Now would you like to see me step on board that steamer? And the Pasha laughed. Go ahead! So the wizard put his foot in the bowl of water and stepped on board the steamer and went to America! What do you think of that!

"There are no wizards, anyway," said the Franciscan, who had climbed up with the men on this evening, as he often did. "If you had said a saint, you might have made some sense." He spoke severely, but Lottar thought he was happy, as they all were, as she too was permitted to be, in their presence and in his, though he paid no attention to her. The strong tobacco that they gave her to smoke made her dizzy and she had to lie down on the grass.

THE TIME CAME when Lottar had to think about moving inside her house. The mornings were cold, the ferns were soaked with dew, and the grape leaves were turning yellow. She took the shovel and cleaned the sheep droppings off the floor, in preparation for making up her bed inside. She began to stuff grass and leaves and mud into the chinks between the stones.

When the men came they asked her what she was doing that for. For the winter, she said, and they laughed.

"Nobody can stay here in the winter," they said. They showed her how deep the snow was, putting hands against their breastbones. Besides, all the sheep would have been taken down.

"There will be no work for you – and what will you eat?" they said. "Do you think the women will let you have bread and yogurt for nothing?"

"How can I go back to the *kula*?" Lottar said. "I am a Virgin, where would I sleep? What kind of work would I do?"

"That is right," they said kindly, speaking to her and then to each other. "When a Virgin belongs to the *kula* she gets a bit of land, usually, where she can live on her own. But this one doesn't really belong to the *kula*, she has no father to give her anything. What will she do?"

Shortly after this – and in the middle of the day, when visitors never came – the Franciscan climbed the meadow, all alone.

"I don't trust them," he said. "I think they will try again to sell you to a Muslim. Even though you have been sworn. They will try to make some money out of you. If they could find you a Christian, it might not be so bad, but I am sure it will be an infidel."

They sat on the grass and drank coffee. The Franciscan said, "Do you have any belongings to take with you? No. Soon we will start."

"Who will milk the ewes?" said Lottar. Some of the ewes were already working their way down the slope; they would stand and wait for her.

"Leave them," said the Franciscan.

In this way she left not only the sheep but her shelter, the meadow, the wild grape and the sumac and mountain ash and juniper bushes and scrub oak she had looked at all summer, the rabbit pelt she had used as a pillow and the pan she had boiled her coffee in, the heap of wood she had gathered only that morning, the stones around her fire – each one of them known to her by its particular shape and color. She understood that she was leaving, because the Franciscan was so stern, but she did not understand it in a way that would make her look around, to see everything for the last time. That was not necessary, anyway. She would never forget any of it.

As they entered the beech wood the Franciscan said, "Now we must be very quiet. I am going to take another path, which does not go so near the *kula*. If we hear anybody on the path, we will hide."

Hours, then, of silent walking, between the beech trees with their smooth elephant bark, and the black-limbed oaks and the dry pines. Up and down, crossing the ridges, choosing paths that Lottar had not known existed. The Franciscan never hesitated and never spoke of a rest. When they came out of the trees at last, Lottar was very surprised to see that there was still so much light in the sky.

The Franciscan pulled a loaf of bread and a knife from some pocket in his garment, and they ate as they walked.

They came to a dry riverbed, paved with stones that were not flat and easily walkable but a torrent, a still torrent of stones between fields of corn and tobacco. They could hear dogs barking, and sometimes people's voices. The corn and tobacco plants, still unharvested, were higher than their heads, and they walked along the dry river in this shelter, while the daylight entirely faded. When they could not walk anymore and the darkness would conceal them, they sat down on the white stones of the riverbed.

"Where are you taking me?" Lottar finally asked. At the start she had thought they must be going in the direction of the church and the priest's house, but now she saw that this could not be so. They had come much too far.

"I am taking you to the Bishop's house," said the Franciscan. "He will know what to do with you."

"Why not to your house?" said Lottar. "I could be a servant in your house."

"It isn't allowed — to have a woman servant in my house. Or in any priest's house. This Bishop now will not allow even an old woman. And he is right, trouble comes from having a woman in the house."

After the moon rose they went on. They walked and rested, walked and rested, but never fell asleep, or even looked for a comfortable place to lie down. Their feet were tough and their sandals well worn, and they did not get blisters. Both of them were used to walking long distances — the Franciscan in his far-flung parish and Lottar when she was following the sheep.

The Franciscan became less stern — perhaps less worried — after a while and talked to her almost as he had done in the first days of their acquaintance. He spoke Italian, though she was now fairly proficient in the language of the Ghegs.

"I was born in Italy," he said. "My parents were Ghegs, but I lived in Italy when I was young, and that was where I became a priest. Once I went back for a visit, years ago, and I shaved off my mustache, I do not know why. Oh, yes, I do know — it was because they laughed at me in the village. Then when I got back I did not dare show my face in the *madhe*. A hairless man there is a disgrace. I sat in a room in Skodra until it grew again."

"It is Skodra we are going to?" said Lottar.

"Yes, that is where the Bishop is. He will send a message that it was right to take you away, even if it is an act of stealing. They are barbarians, in the *madhe*. They will come up and pull on your sleeve in the middle of Mass and ask you to write a letter for them. Have you seen what they put up on the graves? The crosses? They make the cross into a very thin man with a rifle across his arms. Haven't you seen that?" He laughed and shook his head and said, "I don't know what to do with them. But they are good people all the same — they will never betray you."

"But you thought they might sell me in spite of my oath."

"Oh, yes. But to sell a woman is a way to get some money. And they are so poor."

Lottar now realized that in Skodra she would be in an unfamiliar position – she would not be powerless. When they got there, she could run away from him. She could find someone who spoke English, she could find the British Consulate. Or, if not that, the French.

The grass was soaking wet before dawn and the night got very cold. But when the sun came up Lottar stopped shivering and within an hour she was hot. They walked on all day. They ate the rest of the bread and drank from any stream they found that had water in it. They had left the dry river and the mountains far behind. Lottar looked back and saw a wall of jagged rocks with a little green clinging around their bases. That green was the woods and meadows which she had thought so high. They followed paths through the hot fields and were never out of the sound of barking dogs. They met people on the paths.

At first the Franciscan said, "Do not speak to anybody – they will wonder who you are." But he had to answer when greetings were spoken.

"Is this the way to Skodra? We are going to Skodra to the Bishop's house. This is my servant with me, who has come from the mountains."

"It is all right, you look like a servant in these clothes," he said to Lottar. "But do not speak – they will wonder, if you speak."

I HAD PAINTED THE walls of my bookstore a clear, light yellow. Yellow stands for intellectual curiosity. Somebody must have told me that. I opened the store in March of 1964. This was in Victoria, in British Columbia.

I sat there at the desk, with my offerings spread out behind me. The publishers' representatives had advised me to stock books about dogs and horses, sailing and gardening, bird books and flower books – they said that was all anybody in Victoria would buy. I flew against their advice and brought in novels and poetry and books that explained about Sufism and relativity and Linear B. And I had set out these books, when they came, so that Political Science could shade into Philosophy and Philosophy into Religion without a harsh break, so that compatible poets could nestle together, the arrangement of the shelves of books – I believed – reflecting a more or less natural ambling of the mind, in which treasures new and forgotten might be continually surfacing. I had taken all this care, and now what? Now I waited, and I felt like somebody who had got dramatically dressed up for a party, maybe even fetching jewels from the pawnshop or the family vault, only to discover that it was just a few neighbors playing cards. It was just meat loaf and mashed potatoes in the kitchen, and a glass of fizzy pink wine.

The store was often empty for a couple of hours at a time, and then when somebody did come in, it would be to ask about a book remembered from the Sunday-school library or a grandmother's bookcase or left behind twenty years ago in a foreign hotel. The title was usually forgotten, but the person would tell me the story. It is about this little girl who goes out to Australia with her father to mine the gold claims they have inherited. It is about the woman who had a baby all alone in Alaska. It is about a race between one of the old clipper ships and the first steamer, way back in the 1840s.

Oh, well. I just thought I'd ask.

They would leave without a glance at the riches around them.

A few people did exclaim in gratitude, said what a glorious addition to the town. They would browse for half an hour, an hour, before spending seventy-five cents.

It takes time.

I had found a one-room apartment with a kitchenette in an old building at a corner called the Dardanelles. The bed folded up into the wall. But I did not usually bother to fold it up, because I never had any company. And the hook seemed unsafe to me. I was afraid that the bed might leap out of the wall sometime when I was eating my tinned soup or baked-potato supper. It might kill me. Also, I kept the window open all the time, because I believed I could smell a whiff of escaping gas, even when the two burners and the oven were shut off. With the window open at home and the door open at the store, to entice the customers, it was necessary for me to be always bundled up in my black woolly sweater or my red corduroy dressing gown (a garment that had once left its pink tinge on all my forsaken husband's handkerchiefs and underwear). I had difficulty separating myself from these comforting articles of clothing so that they might be washed. I was sleepy much of the time, underfed and shivering.

But I was not despondent. I had made a desperate change in my life, and in spite of the regrets I suffered every day, I was proud of that. I felt as if I had finally come out into the world in a new, true skin. Sitting at the desk, I made a cup of coffee or of thin red soup last an hour, clasping my hands around the cup while there was still any warmth to be got from it. I read, but without purpose or involvement. I read stray sentences from the books that I had always meant to read. Often these sentences seemed so satisfying to me, or so elusive and lovely, that I could not help abandoning all the surrounding words and giving myself up to a peculiar state. I was alert and dreamy, closed off from all particular people but conscious all the time of the city itself – which seemed a strange place.

A small city, here at the western edge of the country. Pockets of fakery for tourists. The Tudor shop fronts and double-decker buses and flower-pots and horse-drawn rides: almost insulting. But the sea light in the street, the spare and healthy old people leaning into the wind as they took their daily walks along the broom-topped cliffs, the shabby, slightly bizarre bungalows with their monkey-puzzle trees and ornate shrubs in the gardens. Chestnut trees blossom as spring comes on, hawthorn trees along the streets bear red-and-white flowers, oily-leaved bushes put out lush pink and rose-red blooms such as you would never see in the hinterlands. Like a town in a story, I thought – like the transplanted seaside town of the story set in New Zealand, in Tasmania. But something North American persists. So many people, after all, have come here from Winnipeg or Saskatchewan. At noon a smell of dinners cooking drifts out of poor, plain apartment buildings. Frying meat, boiling vegetables – farm dinners being cooked, in the middle of the day, in cramped kitchenettes.

How could I tell what I liked so much? Certainly it was not what a new merchant might be looking for – bustle and energy to raise the hope of commercial success. *Not much doing* was the message the town got across to me. And when a person who is opening a store doesn't mind hearing the message *Not much doing*, you could ask, What's going on? People open shops in order to sell things, they hope to become busy so that they will have to enlarge the shop, then to sell more things, and grow rich, and eventually not have to come into the shop at all. Isn't that true? But are there other people who open a shop with the hope of being sheltered there, among such things as they most value – the yarn or the teacups or the books – and with the idea only of making a comfortable assertion? They will become a part of the block, a part of the street, part of everybody's map of the town, and eventually of everybody's memories. They will sit and drink coffee in the middle of the morning, they will get out the familiar bits of tinsel at Christmas, they will wash the windows in spring before spreading out the new stock. Shops, to these people, are what a cabin in the woods might be to somebody else – a refuge and a justification.

Some customers are necessary, of course. The rent comes due and the stock will not pay for itself. I had inherited a little money – that was what had made it possible for me to come out here and get the shop going – but unless business picked up to some extent I could not last beyond the summer. I understood that. I was glad that more people started coming in as the weather warmed up. More books were sold, survival began to seem possible. Book prizes were due to be awarded in the schools at the end of term, and that brought the schoolteachers with their lists and their praise and their unfortunate expectation of discounts. The people who came to browse were buying regularly, and some of them began to turn into friends – or the sort of friends I had here, where it seemed I would be happy to talk to people day after day and never learn their names.

WHEN LOTTAR AND the priest first saw the town of Skodra, it seemed to float above the mud flats, its domes and steeples shining as if they were made of mist. But when they entered it in the early evening all this tranquillity vanished. The streets were paved with big, rough stones and were full of people and donkey carts, roving dogs, pigs being driven somewhere, and smells of fires and cooking and dung and something terrible – like rotten hides. A man came along with a parrot on his shoulder. The bird seemed to be shrieking curses in an unknown language. Several times the Franciscan stopped people and asked the way to the Bishop's house, but they pushed by him without answering or laughed at him or said some words he didn't understand. A boy said that he would show the way, for money.

"We have no money," the Franciscan said. He pulled Lottar into a doorway and there they sat down to rest. "In Maltsia e madhe," he said, "many of these who think so well of themselves would soon sing a different tune."

Lottar's notion of running away and leaving him had vanished. For one thing, she could not manage to ask directions any better than he could. For another, she felt that they were allies who could not survive in this place out of sight of each other. She had not understood how much she depended on the smell of his skin, the aggrieved determination of his long strides, the flourish of his black mustache.

The Franciscan jumped up and said he had remembered – he had remembered now the way to the Bishop's house. He hurried ahead of her through narrow, high-walled back streets where nothing of houses or courtyards could be seen – just walls and gates. The paving stones were thrust up so that walking here was as difficult as in the dry riverbed. But he was right, he gave a shout of triumph, they had come to the gate of the Bishop's house.

A servant opened the gate and let them in, but only after some high-pitched argument. Lottar was told to sit on the ground just inside the gate, and the Franciscan was led into the house to see the Bishop. Soon someone was sent through the streets to the British Consulate (Lottar was not told this), and he came back with the Consul's manservant. It was dark by then, and the Consul's servant carried a lantern. And Lottar was led away again. She followed the servant and his lantern to the consulate.

A tub of hot water for her to bathe in, in the courtyard. Her clothes taken away. Probably burned. Her greasy black, vermin-infested hair cut off. Kerosene poured on her scalp. She had to tell her story – the story of how she came to Maltsia e madhe – and this was difficult, because she was not used to speaking English, also because that time seemed so far away and unimportant. She had to learn to sleep on a mattress, to sit on a chair, to eat with a knife and fork.

As soon as possible they put her on a boat.

Charlotte stopped. She said, "That part is not of interest."

I HAD COME TO Victoria because it was the farthest place I could get to from London, Ontario, without going out of the country. In London, my husband, Donald, and I had rented a basement apartment in our house to a couple named Nelson and Sylvia. Nelson was an English major at the university and Sylvia was a nurse. Donald was a dermatologist, and I was doing a thesis on Mary Shelley — not very quickly. I had met Donald when I went to see him about a rash on my neck. He was eight years older than I was — a tall, freckled, blushing man, cleverer than he looked. A dermatologist sees grief and despair, though the problems that bring people to him may not be in the same class as tumors and blocked arteries. He sees sabotage from within, and truly unlucky fate. He sees how matters like love and happiness can be governed by a patch of riled-up cells. Experience of this sort had made Donald kind, in a cautious, impersonal way. He said that my rash was probably due to stress, and that he could see that I was going to be a wonderful woman, once I got a few problems under control.

We invited Sylvia and Nelson upstairs for dinner, and Sylvia told us about the tiny town they both came from, in Northern Ontario. She said that Nelson had always been the smartest person in their class and in their school and possibly in the whole town. When she said this, Nelson looked at her with a perfectly flat and devastating expression, an expression that seemed to be waiting with infinite patience and the mildest curiosity for some explanation, and Sylvia laughed and said, "Just kidding, of course."

When Sylvia was working late shifts at the hospital, I sometimes asked Nelson to share a meal with us in a more informal way. We got used to his silences and his indifferent table manners and to the fact that he did not eat rice or noodles, eggplant, olives, shrimp, peppers, or avocados, and no doubt a lot of other things, because those had not been familiar foods in the town in Northern Ontario.

Nelson looked older than he was. He was short and sturdily built, sallow-skinned, unsmiling, with a suggestion of mature scorn and handy pugnaciousness laid over his features, so that it seemed he might be a hockey coach, or an intelligent, uneducated, fair-minded, and foul-mouthed foreman of a construction gang, rather than a shy, twenty-two-year-old student.

He was not shy in love. I found him resourceful and determined. The seduction was mutual, and it was a first affair for both of us. I had once heard somebody say, at a party, that one of the nice things about marriage was that you could have real affairs – an affair before marriage could always turn out to be nothing but courtship. I was disgusted by this speech, and frightened to think that life could be so bleak and trivial. But once my own affair with Nelson started, I was amazed all the time. There was no bleakness or triviality about it, only ruthlessness and clarity of desire, and sparkling deception.

Nelson was the one who first faced up to things. One afternoon he turned on his back and said hoarsely and defiantly, "We are going to have to leave."

I thought he meant that he and Sylvia would have to leave, they could not go on living in this house. But he meant himself and me. "We" meant himself and me. Of course he and I had said "we" of our arrangements, of our transgression. Now he had made it the "we" of our decision – perhaps of a life together.

My thesis was supposed to be on Mary Shelley's later novels, the ones nobody knows about. *Lodore*, *Perkin Warbeck*, *The Last Man*. But I was really more interested in Mary's life before she learned her sad lessons and buckled down to raising her son to be a baronet. I loved to read about the other women who had hated or envied or traipsed along: Harriet, Shelley's first wife, and Fanny Imlay, who was Mary's half sister and may have been in love with Shelley herself, and Mary's stepsister, Mary Jane Clairmont, who took my own name – Claire – and joined Mary and Shelley on their unwed honeymoon so that she could keep on chasing Byron. I had often talked to Donald about impetuous Mary and married Shelley and their meetings at Mary's mother's grave, about the suicides of Harriet and Fanny and the persistence of Claire, who had a baby by Byron.

But I never mentioned any of this to Nelson, partly because we had little time for talk and partly because I did not want him to think that I drew some sort of comfort or inspiration from this mishmash of love and despair and treachery and self-dramatizing. I did not want to think so myself. And Nelson was not a fan of the nineteenth century or the Romantics. He said so. He said that he wanted to do something on the Muckrakers. Perhaps he meant that as a joke.

Sylvia did not behave like Harriet. Her mind was not influenced or impeded by literature, and when she found out what had been going on, she went into a wholesome rage.

"You blithering idiot," she said to Nelson.

"You two-faced twit," she said to me.

The four of us were in our living room. Donald went on cleaning and filling his pipe, tapped it and lit it, nursed and inspected it, drew on it, lit it again – all so much the way someone would do in a movie that I was embarrassed for him. Then he put some books and the latest copy of *Maclean's* into his briefcase, went to the bathroom to get his razor and to the bedroom to get his pajamas, and walked out.

He went straight to the apartment of a young widow who worked as a secretary at his clinic. In a letter he wrote to me later, he said that he had never thought of this woman except as a friend until that night, when it suddenly dawned on him what a pleasure it would be to love a kind and sensible, *unwracked-up* sort of person.

Sylvia had to be at work at eleven o'clock. Nelson usually walked her over to the hospital – they did not have a car. On this night she told him that she would rather be escorted by a skunk.

That left Nelson and me alone together. The scene had lasted a much shorter time than I had expected. Nelson seemed gloomy but relieved, and if I felt that short shrift had been given to the notion of love as a capturing tide, a glorious and harrowing event, I knew better than to show it.

We lay down on the bed to talk about our plans and ended up making love, because that was what we were used to doing. Sometime during the night Nelson woke up and thought it best to go downstairs to his own bed.

I got up in the dark, dressed, packed a suitcase, wrote a note, and walked to the phone at the corner, where I called a taxi. I took the six o'clock train to Toronto, connecting with the train to Vancouver. It was cheaper to take the train, if you were willing to sit up for three nights, which I was.

So there I sat, in the sad, shambling morning in the day coach, coming down the steep-walled Fraser Canyon into the sodden Fraser Valley, where smoke hung over the small, dripping houses, the brown vines, the thorny bushes and huddled sheep. It was in December that this earthquake in my life had arrived. Christmas was cancelled for me. Winter with its snow-drifts and icicles and invigorating blizzards was cancelled by this blurred season of muck and rain. I was constipated, I knew that I had bad breath, my limbs were cramped, and my spirits utterly bleak. And did I not think then, What nonsense it is to suppose one man so different from another when all that life really boils down to is getting a decent cup of coffee and room to stretch out in? Did I not think that even if Nelson were sitting here beside me, he would have turned into a gray-faced stranger whose desolation and unease merely extended my own?

No. No. Nelson would still be Nelson to me. I had not changed, with regard to his skin and his smell and his forbidding eyes. It seemed to be the outside of Nelson which came most readily to my mind, and in the case of Donald it was his inner quakes and sympathies, the labored-at kindness and those private misgivings that I had got knowledge of by wheedling and conniving. If I could have my love of these two men together, and settle it on one man, I would be a happy woman. If I could care for everybody in the world as minutely as I did for Nelson, and as calmly, as uncarnally as I now did for Donald, I would be a saint. Instead, I had dealt a twofold, a wanton-seeming, blow.

THE REGULAR CUSTOMERS who had changed into something like friends were: a middle-aged woman who was a chartered accountant but preferred such reading as *Six Existentialist Thinkers*, and *The Meaning of Meaning*; a provincial civil servant who ordered splendid, expensive works of pornography such as I had not known existed (their elaborate Oriental,

Etruscan connections seemed to me grotesque and uninteresting, compared to the simple, effective, longed-for rituals of myself and Nelson); a Notary Public who lived behind his office at the foot of Johnson Street ("I live in the slums," he told me. "Some night I expect a big bruiser of a fellow to lurch around the corner hollering 'Ste-el-la'."); and the woman I knew later as Charlotte – the Notary Public called her the Duchess. None of these people cared much for one another, and an early attempt that I made to bring the accountant and the Notary Public into conversation was a fizzle.

"Spare me the females with the withered, painted faces," the Notary Public said, the next time he came in. "I hope you haven't got her lurking around anywhere tonight."

It was true that the accountant painted her thin, intelligent, fifty-year-old face with a heavy hand, and drew on eyebrows that were like two strokes of India ink. But who was the Notary Public to talk, with his stumpy, nicotined teeth and pocked cheeks?

"I got the impression of a rather superficial fellow," the accountant said, as if she had guessed and bravely discounted the remarks made about herself.

So much for trying to corral people into couples, I wrote to Donald. *And who am I to try?* I wrote to Donald regularly, describing the store, and the city, and even, as well as I could, my own unaccountable feelings. He was living with Helen, the secretary. I wrote also to Nelson, who might or might not be living alone, might or might not be reunited with Sylvia. I didn't think he was. I thought she would believe in inexcusable behavior and definite endings. He had a new address. I had looked it up in the London phone book at the public library. Donald, after a grudging start, was writing back. He wrote impersonal, mildly interesting letters about people we both knew, events at the clinic. Nelson did not write at all. I started sending registered letters. Now I knew at least that he picked them up.

Charlotte and Gjurdhi must have come into the store together, but I did not understand that they were a couple until it was time for them to leave. Charlotte was a heavy, shapeless, but quick-moving woman, with a pink face, bright blue eyes, and a lot of glistening white hair, worn like a girl's, waving down over her shoulders. Though the weather was fairly warm, she was wearing a cape of dark-gray velvet with a scanty gray fur trim – a garment that looked as if it belonged, or had once belonged, on the stage. A loose shirt and a pair of plaid wool slacks showed underneath, and there were open sandals on her broad, bare, dusty feet. She clanked as if she wore hidden armor. An arm reaching up to get a book showed what caused the clanking. Bracelets – any number of them, heavy or slender, tarnished or bright. Some were set with large, square stones, the color of toffee or blood.

"Imagine this old fraud being still on the go," she said to me, as if continuing some desultory and enjoyable conversation.

She had picked up a book by Anaïs Nin.

"Don't pay any attention," she said. "I say terrible things. I'm quite fond of the woman, really. It's him I can't stand."

"Henry Miller?" I said, beginning to follow this.

"That's right." She went on talking about Henry Miller, Paris, California, in a scoffing, energetic, half-affectionate way. She seemed to have been neighbors, at least, with the people she was talking about. Finally, naively, I asked her if this was the case.

"No, no. I just feel I know them all. Not personally. Well – personally. Yes, personally. What other way is there to know them? I mean, I haven't met them, face-to-face. But in their books? Surely that's what they intend? I know them. I know them to the point where they bore me. Just like anybody you know. Don't you find that?"

She drifted over to the table where I had laid out the New Directions paperbacks.

"Here's the new bunch, then," she said. "Oh, my," she said, widening her eyes at the photographs of Ginsberg and Corso and Ferlinghetti. She began reading, so attentively that I thought the next thing she said must be part of some poem.

"I've gone by and I've seen you here," she said. She put the book down and I realized she meant me. "I've seen you sitting in here, and I've thought a young woman would probably like to be outside some of the time. In the sun. I don't suppose you'd consider hiring me to sit there, so you could get out?"

"Well, I would like to –" I said.

"I'm not so dumb. I'm fairly knowledgeable, really. Ask me who wrote Ovid's *Metamorphoses*. It's all right, you don't have to laugh."

"I would like to, but I really can't afford to."

"Oh, well. You're probably right. I'm not very chic. And I would probably foul things up. I would argue with people if they were buying books I thought were dreadful." She did not seem disappointed. She picked up a copy of *The Dud Avocado* and said, "There! I have to buy this, for the title."

She gave a little whistle, and the man it seemed to be meant for looked up from the table of books he had been staring at, near the back of the store. I had known he was there but had not connected him with her. I thought he was just one of those men who wander in off the street, alone, and stand looking about, as if trying to figure out what sort of place this is or what the books are for. Not a drunk or a panhandler, and certainly not anybody to be worried about – just one of a number of shabby, utterly uncommunicative old men who belong to the city somewhat as the pigeons do, moving restlessly all day within a limited area, never looking at people's faces. He was wearing a coat that came down to his ankles, made of some shiny, rubberized, liver-colored material, and a brown velvet cap with a tassel. The sort of cap a doddery old scholar or a clergyman might wear in an English movie. There was, then, a similarity between them – they were both wearing things that might have been discards from a costume box. But close up he looked years older than she. A long, yellowish face, drooping tobacco-brown eyes, an unsavory, straggling mustache. Some faint remains of handsomeness, or potency. A quenched ferocity. He came at her whistle – which seemed half serious, half a joke – and stood by, mute and self-respecting as a dog or a donkey, while the woman prepared to pay.

At that time, the government of British Columbia applied a sales tax to books. In this case it was four cents.

"I can't pay that," she said. "A tax on books. I think it is immoral. I would rather go to jail. Don't you agree?"

I agreed. I did not point out – as I would have done with anybody else – that the store would not be let off the hook on that account.

"Don't I sound appalling?" she said. "See what this government can do to people? It makes them into *orators*."

She put the book in her bag without paying the four cents, and never paid the tax on any future occasion.

I described the two of them to the Notary Public. He knew at once who I meant.

"I call them the Duchess and the Algerian," he said. "I don't know what the background is. I think maybe he's a retired terrorist. They go around the town with a wagon, like scavengers."

I GOT A NOTE asking me to supper on a Sunday evening. It was signed Charlotte, without a surname, but the wording and handwriting were quite formal.

My husband Gjurdhi and I would be delighted –

Up until then I had not wished for any invitations of this sort and would have been embarrassed and disturbed to get one. So the pleasure I felt surprised me. Charlotte held out a decided promise; she was unlike the others whom I wanted to see only in the store.

The building where they lived was on Pandora Street. It was covered with mustard stucco and had a tiny, tiled vestibule that reminded me of a public toilet. It did not smell, though, and the apartment was not really dirty, just horrendously untidy. Books were stacked against the walls, and pieces of patterned cloth were hung up droopily to hide the wallpaper. There were bamboo blinds on the window, sheets of colored paper – surely flammable – pinned over the light bulbs.

"What a darling you are to come," cried Charlotte. "We were afraid you would have tons more interesting things to do than visiting ancient old us. Where can you sit down? What about here?" She took a pile of magazines off a wicker chair. "Is that comfortable? It makes such interesting noises, wicker. Sometimes I'll be sitting here alone and that chair will start creaking and cracking exactly as if someone were shifting around in it. I could say it was a presence, but I'm no good at believing in that rubbish. I've tried."

Gjurdhi poured out a sweet yellow wine. For me a long-stemmed glass that had not been dusted, for Charlotte a glass tumbler, for himself a plastic cup. It seemed impossible that any dinner could come out of the little kitchen alcove, where foodstuffs and pots and dishes were piled helter-skelter, but there was a good smell of roasting chicken, and in a little while Gjurdhi brought out the first course – platters of sliced cucumber, dishes of yogurt. I sat in the wicker chair and Charlotte in the single armchair. Gjurdhi sat on the floor. Charlotte was wearing her slacks, and a rose-colored T-shirt which clung to her unsupported breasts. She had painted her toenails to match the T-shirt. Her bracelets clanked against the plate as she picked up the slices of cucumber. (We were eating with our fingers.) Gjurdhi wore his cap and a dark-red silky dressing gown over his trousers. Stains had mingled with its pattern.

After the cucumber, we ate chicken cooked with raisins in golden spices, and sour bread, and rice. Charlotte and I were provided with forks, but Gjurdhi scooped the rice up with the bread. I would often think of this meal in the years that followed, when this kind of food, this informal way of sitting and eating, and even some version of the style and the untidiness of the room, would become familiar and fashionable. The people I knew, and I myself, would give up – for a while – on dining-room tables, matching wineglasses, to some extent on cutlery or chairs. When I was being entertained, or making a stab at entertaining people, in this way, I would think of Charlotte and Gjurdhi and the edge of true privation, the risky authenticity that marked them off from all these later imitations. At the time, it was all new to me, and I was both uneasy and delighted. I hoped to be worthy of such exoticism but not to be tried too far.

Mary Shelley came to light shortly. I recited the titles of the later novels, and Charlotte said dreamily, "Per-kin War-beck. Wasn't he the one – wasn't he the one who pretended to be a little Prince who was murdered in the Tower?"

She was the only person I had ever met – not a historian, not a *Tudor* historian – who had known this.

"That would make a movie," she said. "Don't you think? The question I always think about Pretenders like that is who do *they* think they are? Do they believe it's true, or what? But Mary Shelley's own life is the movie, isn't it? I wonder there hasn't been one made. Who would play Mary, do you think? No. No, first of all, start with Harriet. Who would play Harriet?

"Someone who would look well drowned," she said, ripping off a golden chunk of chicken. "Elizabeth Taylor? Not a big enough part. Susannah York?

"Who was the father?" she wondered, referring to Harriet's unborn baby. "I don't think it was Shelley. I've never thought so. Do you?"

This was all very well, very enjoyable, but I had hoped we would get to explanations − personal revelations, if not exactly confidences. You did expect some of that, on occasions like this. Hadn't Sylvia, at my own table, told about the town in Northern Ontario and about Nelson's being the smartest person in the school? I was surprised at how eager I found myself, at last, to tell my story. Donald and Nelson − I was looking forward to telling the truth, or some of it, in all its wounding complexity, to a person who would not be surprised or outraged by it. I would have liked to puzzle over my behavior, in good company. Had I taken on Donald as a father figure − or as a parent figure, since both my parents were dead? Had I deserted him because I was angry at *them* for deserting *me*? What did Nelson's silence mean, and was it now permanent? (But I did not think, after all, that I would tell anybody about the letter that had been returned to me last week, marked "Not Known at This Address.")

This was not what Charlotte had in mind. There was no opportunity, no exchange. After the chicken, the wineglass and the tumbler and cup were taken away and filled with an extremely sweet pink sherbet that was easier to drink than to eat with a spoon. Then came small cups of desperately strong coffee. Gjurdhi lit two candles as the room grew darker, and I was given one of these to carry to the bathroom, which turned out to be a toilet with a shower. Charlotte said the lights were not working.

"Some repairs going on," she said. "Or else they have taken a whim. I really think they take whims. But fortunately we have our gas stove. As long as we have a gas stove we can laugh at their whims. My only regret is that we cannot play any music. I was going to play some old political songs − 'I dreamed I saw Joe Hill last night,'" she sang in a mocking baritone. "Do you know that one?"

I did know it. Donald used to sing it when he was a little drunk. Usually the people who sang "Joe Hill" had certain vague but discernible political sympathies, but with Charlotte I did not think this would be so. She would not operate from sympathies, from principles. She would be playful about what other people took seriously. I was not certain what I felt about her. It was not simple liking or respect. It was more like a wish to move in her element, unsurprised. To be buoyant, self-mocking, gently malicious, unquenchable.

Gjurdhi, meanwhile, was showing me some of the books. How had this started? Probably from a comment I made — how many of them there were, something of that sort — when I stumbled over some on my way back from the toilet. He was bringing forward books with bindings of leather or imitation leather — how could I know the difference? — with marbled endpapers, watercolor frontispieces, steel engravings. At first, I believed admiration might be all that was required, and I admired everything. But close to my ear I heard the mention of money — was that the first distinct thing I had ever heard Gjurdhi say?

"I only handle new books," I said. "These are marvellous, but I don't really know anything about them. It's a completely different business, books like these."

Gjurdhi shook his head as if I had not understood and he would now try, firmly, to explain again. He repeated the price in a more insistent voice. Did he think I was trying to haggle with him? Or perhaps he was telling me what he had paid for the book? We might be having a speculative conversation about the price it might be sold for — not about whether I should buy it.

I kept saying no, and yes, trying to juggle these responses appropriately. *No*, I cannot take them for my store. *Yes*, they are very fine. *No*, truly, I'm sorry, I am not the one to judge.

"If we had been living in another country, Gjurdhi and I might have done something," Charlotte was saying. "Or even if the movies in this country had ever got off the ground. That's what I would love to have done. Got work in the movies. As extras. Or maybe we are not bland enough types to be extras, maybe they would have found bit parts for us. I believe extras have to be the sort that don't stand out in a crowd, so you can use them over and over again. Gjurdhi and I are more memorable than that. Gjurdhi in particular — you could *use* that face."

She paid no attention to the second conversation that had developed, but continued talking to me, shaking her head indulgently at Gjurdhi now and then, to suggest that he was behaving in a way she found engaging, though perhaps importunate. I had to talk to him softly, sideways, nodding all the while in response to her.

"Really you should take them to the Antiquarian Bookstore," I said. "Yes, they are quite beautiful. Books like these are out of my range."

Gjurdhi did not whine, his manner was not ingratiating. Peremptory, rather. It seemed as if he would give me orders, and would be most disgusted if I did not capitulate. In my confusion I helped myself to more of the yellow wine, pouring it into my unwashed sherbet glass. This was probably a dire offense. Gjurdhi looked horridly displeased.

"Can you imagine illustrations in modern novels?" said Charlotte, finally consenting to tie the two conversations together. "For instance, in Norman Mailer? They would have to be abstracts. Don't you think? Sort of barbed wire and blotches?"

I went home with a headache and a feeling of jangled inadequacy. I was a prude, that was all, when it came to mixing up buying and selling with hospitality. I had perhaps behaved clumsily, I had disappointed them. And they had disappointed me. Making me wonder why I had been asked.

I was homesick for Donald, because of "Joe Hill."

I also had a longing for Nelson, because of an expression on Charlotte's face as I was leaving. A savoring and contented look that I knew had to do with Gjurdhi, though I hardly wanted to believe that. It made me think that after I walked downstairs and left the building and went into the street, some hot and skinny, slithery, yellowish, indecent old beast, some mangy but urgent old tiger, was going to pounce among the books and the dirty dishes and conduct a familiar rampage.

A day or so later I got a letter from Donald. He wanted a divorce, so that he could marry Helen.

I HIRED A CLERK, a college girl, to come in for a couple of hours in the afternoon, so I could get to the bank, and do some office work. The first time Charlotte saw her she went up to the desk and patted a stack of books sitting there, ready for quick sale.

"Is this what the office managers are telling their minions to buy?" she said. The girl smiled cautiously and didn't answer.

Charlotte was right. It was a book called *Psycho-Cybernetics*, about having a positive self-image.

"You were smart to hire her instead of me," Charlotte said. "She is much niftier-looking, and she won't shoot her mouth off and scare the customers away. She won't have *opinions*."

"There's something I ought to tell you about that woman," the clerk said, after Charlotte left.

THAT PART IS *not of interest.*

"What do you mean?" I said. But my mind had been wandering, that third afternoon in the hospital. Just at the last part of Charlotte's story I had thought of a special-order book that hadn't come in, on Mediterranean cruises. Also I had been thinking about the Notary Public, who had been beaten about the head the night before, in his office on Johnson Street. He was not dead but he might be blinded. Robbery? Or an act of revenge, outrage, connected with a layer of his life that I hadn't guessed at?

Melodrama and confusion made this place seem more ordinary to me, but less within my grasp.

"Of course it is of interest," I said. "All of it. It's a fascinating story."

"Fascinating," repeated Charlotte in a mincing way. She made a face, so she looked like a baby vomiting out a spoonful of pap. Her eyes, still fixed on me, seemed to be losing color, losing their childish, bright, and self-important blue. Fretfulness was changing into disgust. An expression of vicious disgust, she showed, of unspeakable weariness – such as people might show to the mirror but hardly ever to one another. Perhaps because of the thoughts that were already in my head, it occurred to me that Charlotte might die. She might die at any moment. At this moment. Now.

She motioned at the water glass, with its crooked plastic straw. I held the glass so that she could drink, and supported her head. I could feel the heat of her scalp, a throbbing at the base of her skull. She drank thirstily, and the terrible look left her face.

She said, "Stale."

"I think it would make an excellent movie," I said, easing her back onto the pillows. She grabbed my wrist, then let it go.

"Where did you get the idea?" I said.

"From life," said Charlotte indistinctly. "Wait a moment." She turned her head away, on the pillow, as if she had to arrange something in private. Then she recovered, and she told a little more.

CHARLOTTE DID NOT DIE. At least she did not die in the hospital. When I came in rather late, the next afternoon, her bed was empty and freshly made up. The nurse who had talked to me before was trying to take the temperature of the woman tied in the chair. She laughed at the look on my face.

"Oh, no!" she said. "Not that. She checked out of here this morning. Her husband came and got her. We were transferring her to a long-term place out in Saanich, and he was supposed to be taking her there. He said he had the taxi outside. Then we get this phone call that they never showed up! They were in great spirits when they left. He brought her a pile of money, and she was throwing it up in the air. I don't know – maybe it was only dollar bills. But we haven't a clue where they've got to."

I walked around to the apartment building on Pandora Street. I thought they might simply have gone home. They might have lost the instructions about how to get to the nursing home and not wanted to ask. They might have decided to stay together in their apartment no matter what. They might have turned on the gas.

At first I could not find the building and thought that I must be in the wrong block. But I remembered the corner store and some of the houses. The building had been changed – that was what had happened. The stucco had been painted pink; large, new windows and French doors had been put in; little balconies with wrought-iron railings had been attached. The fancy balconies had been painted white, the whole place had the air of an ice-cream parlor. No doubt it had been renovated inside as well, and the rents increased, so that people like Charlotte and Gjurdhi could have no hope of living there. I checked the names by the door, and of course theirs were gone. They must have moved out some time ago.

The change in the apartment building seemed to have some message for me. It was about vanishing. I knew that Charlotte and Gjurdhi had not actually vanished – they were somewhere, living or dead. But for me they had vanished. And because of this fact – not really because of any loss of them – I was tipped into dismay more menacing than any of the little eddies of regret that had caught me in the past year. I had lost my bearings. I had to get back to the store so my clerk could go home, but I felt as if I could as easily walk another way, just any way at all. My connection was in danger – that was all. Sometimes our connection is frayed, it is in danger, it seems almost lost. Views and streets deny knowledge of us, the air grows thin. Wouldn't we rather have a destiny to submit to, then, something that claims us, anything, instead of such flimsy choices, arbitrary days?

I let myself slip, then, into imagining a life with Nelson. If I had done so accurately, this is how it would have gone.

He comes to Victoria. But he does not like the idea of working in the store, serving the public. He gets a job teaching at a boys' school, a posh place where his look of lower-class toughness, his bruising manners, soon make him a favorite.

We move from the apartment at the Dardanelles to a roomy bungalow a few blocks from the sea. We marry.

But this is the beginning of a period of estrangement. I become pregnant. Nelson falls in love with the mother of a student. I fall in love with an intern I meet in the hospital during labor.

We get over all this – Nelson and I do. We have another child. We acquire friends, furniture, rituals. We go to too many parties at certain seasons of the year, and talk regularly about starting a new life, somewhere far away, where we don't know anybody.

We become distant, close – distant, close – over and over again.

As I entered the store, I was aware of a man standing near the door, half looking in the window, half looking up the street, then looking at me. He was a short man dressed in a trenchcoat and a fedora. I had the impression of someone disguised. Jokingly disguised. He moved toward me and bumped my shoulder, and I cried out as if I had received the shock of my life, and indeed it was true that I had. For this really was Nelson, come to claim me. Or at least to accost me, and see what would happen.

We have been very happy.
I have often felt completely alone.
There is always in this life something to discover.
The days and the years have gone by in some sort of blur.
On the whole, I am satisfied.

WHEN LOTTAR WAS leaving the Bishop's courtyard, she was wrapped in a long cloak they had given her, perhaps to conceal her ragged clothing, or to contain her smell. The Consul's servant spoke to her in English, telling her where they were going. She could understand him but could not reply. It was not quite dark. She could still see the pale shapes of roses and oranges in the Bishop's garden.

The Bishop's man was holding the gate open.

She had never seen the Bishop at all. And she had not seen the Franciscan since he had followed the Bishop's man into the house. She called out for him now, as she was leaving. She had no name to call, so she called, "*Xoti! Xoti! Xoti,*" which means "leader" or "master" in the language of the Ghegs. But no answer came, and the Consul's servant swung his lantern impatiently, showing her the way to go. Its light fell by accident on the Franciscan standing half concealed by a tree. It was a little orange tree he stood behind. His face, pale as the oranges were in that light, looked out of the branches, all its swarthiness drained away. It was a wan face hanging in the tree, its melancholy expression quite impersonal and undemanding, like the expression you might see on the face of a devout but proud apostle in a church window. Then it was gone, taking the breath out of her body, as she knew too late.

SHE CALLED HIM and called him, and when the boat came into the harbor at Trieste he was waiting on the dock.

A WILDERNESS STATION

I

MISS MARGARET CRESSWELL, Matron, House of Industry, Toronto, to Mr. Simon Herron, North Huron, January 15, 1852.

Since your letter is accompanied by an endorsement from your minister, I am happy to reply. Requests of your sort are made to us frequently, but unless we have such an endorsement we cannot trust that they are made in good faith.

We do not have any girl at the Home who is of marriageable age, since we send our girls out to make a living usually around the age of fourteen or fifteen, but we do keep track of them for some years or usually until they are married. In cases such as yours we sometimes recommend one of these girls and will arrange a meeting, and then of course it is up to the two parties involved to see if they are suited.

There are two girls eighteen years of age that we are still in touch with. Both are apprenticed to a milliner and are good seamstresses, but a marriage to a likely man would probably be preferred to a lifetime of such work. Further than that cannot be said, it must be left to the girl herself and of course to your liking for her, or the opposite.

The two girls are a Miss Sadie Johnstone and a Miss Annie McKillop. Both were born legitimately of Christian parents and were placed in the Home due to parental deaths. Drunkenness or immorality was not a factor. In Miss Johnstone's case there is however the factor of consumption, and though she is the prettier of the two and a plump rosy girl, I feel I must warn you that perhaps she is not suited to the hard work of a life in the bush. The other girl, Miss McKillop, is of a more durable constitution though of leaner frame and not so good a complexion. She has a waywardness about one eye but it does not interfere with her vision and her sewing is excellent. The darkness of her eyes and hair and brown tinge of her skin is no indication of mixed blood, as both parents were from

Fife. She is a hardy girl and I think would be suited to such a life as you can offer, being also free from the silly timidness we often see in girls of her age. I will speak to her and acquaint her with the idea and will await your letter as to when you propose to meet her.

II

CARSTAIRS *ARGUS*. Fiftieth Anniversary Edition, February 3, 1907. Recollections of Mr. George Herron.

On the first day of September, 1851, my brother Simon and I got a box of bedclothes and household utensils together and put them in a wagon with a horse to pull it, and set out from Halton County to try our fortunes in the wilds of Huron and Bruce, as wilds they were then thought to be. The goods were from Archie Frame that Simon worked for, and counted as part of his wages. Likewise we had to rent the horse off him, and his boy that was about my age came along to take it and the wagon back.

It ought to be said in the beginning that my brother and I were left alone, our father first and then our mother dying of fever within five weeks of landing in this country, when I was three years old and Simon eight. Simon was put to work for Archie Frame that was our mother's cousin, and I was taken on by the schoolteacher and wife that had no child of their own. This was in Halton, and I would have been content to go on living there but Simon being only a few miles away continued to visit and say that as soon as we were old enough we would go and take up land and be on our own, not working for others, as this was what our father had intended. Archie Frame never sent Simon to school as I was sent, so Simon was always bound to get away. When I had come to be fourteen years of age and a husky lad, as was my brother, he said we should go and take up Crown Land north of the Huron Tract.

We only got as far as Preston on the first day as the roads were rough and bad across Nassageweya and Puslinch. Next day we got to Shakespeare and the third afternoon to Stratford. The roads were always getting worse as we came west, so we thought best to get our box sent on to Clinton by the stage. But the stage had quit running due to rains, and they were waiting till the roads froze up, so we told Archie Frame's boy to turn about and return with horse and cart and goods back to Halton. Then we took our axes on our shoulders, and walked to Carstairs.

Hardly a soul was there before us. Carstairs was just under way, with a rough building that was store and inn combined, and there was a German named Roem building a sawmill. One man who got there before us and already had a fair-sized cabin built was Henry Treece, who afterwards became my father-in-law.

We got ourselves boarded at the inn where we slept on the bare floor with one blanket or quilt between us. Winter was coming early with cold rains and everything damp, but we were expecting hardship or at least Simon was. I came from a softer place. He said we must put up with it so I did.

We began to underbrush a road to our piece of land and then we got it marked out and cut the logs for our shanty and big scoops to roof it. We were able to borrow an ox from Henry Treece to draw the logs. But Simon was not of a mind to borrow or depend on anybody. He was minded to try raising the shanty ourselves, but when we saw we could not do it I made my way to Treece's place and with Henry and two of his sons and a fellow from the mill it was accomplished. We started next day to fill up the cracks between the logs with mud and we got some hemlock branches so we would not be out money anymore for staying at the inn but could sleep in our own place. We had a big slab of elm for the door. My brother had heard from some French-Canadian fellows that were at Archie Frame's that in the lumber camps the fire was always in the middle of the shanty. So he said that was the way we should have ours, and we got four posts and were building the chimney on them, house-fashion, intending to plaster it with mud inside and out. We went to our hemlock bed with a good fire going, but waking in the middle of the night we saw our lumber was all ablaze and the scoops burning away briskly also. We tore down the chimney and the scoops being green basswood were not hard to put out. As soon as it came day, we started to build the chimney in the ordinary way in the end of the house and I thought it best not to make any remark.

After the small trees and brush was cleared out a bit, we set to chopping down the big trees. We cut down a big ash and split it into slabs for our floor. Still our box had not come which was to be shipped from Halton so Henry Treece sent us a very large and comfortable bearskin for our cover in bed but my brother would not take the favour and sent it back saying no need. Then after several weeks we got our box and had to ask for the ox to bring it on from Clinton, but my brother said that is the last we will need to ask of any person's help.

We walked to Walley and brought back flour and salt fish on our back. A man rowed us across the river at Manchester for a steep price. There were no bridges then and all that winter not a good enough freeze to make it easy going over the rivers.

Around Christmastime my brother said to me that he thought we had the place in good enough shape now for him to be bringing in a wife, so we should have somebody to cook and do for us and milk a cow when we could afford one. This was the first I had heard of any wife and I said that I did not know he was acquainted with anybody. He said he was not but he had heard that you could write to the Orphanage Home and ask if they had a girl there that was willing to think about the prospect and that they would recommend, and if so he would go and see her. He wanted one between eighteen and twenty-two years of age, healthy and not afraid of work and raised in the Orphanage, not taken in lately, so that she would not be expecting any luxuries or to be waited on and would not be recalling about when things were easier for her. I do not doubt that to those hearing about this nowadays it seems a strange way to go about things. It was not that my brother could not have gone courting and got a wife on his own, because he was a good-looking fellow, but he did not have the time or the money or inclination, his mind was all occupied with establishing our holding. And if a girl had parents they would probably not want her to go far away where there was little in comforts and so much work.

That it was a respectable way of doing things is shown by the fact that the minister Mr. McBain, who was lately come into the district, helped Simon to write the letter and sent word on his own to vouch for him.

So a letter came back that there was a girl that might fit the bill and Simon went off to Toronto and got her. Her name was Annie but her maiden name I had forgotten. They had to ford the streams in Hullet and trudge through deep soft snow after leaving the stage in Clinton, and when they got back she was worn out and very surprised at what she saw, since she said she had never imagined so much bush. She had in her box some sheets and pots and dishes that ladies had given her and that made the place more comfortable.

Early in April my brother and I went out to chop down some trees in the bush at the farthest corner of our property. While Simon was away to get married, I had done some chopping in the other direction towards Treece's, but Simon wanted to get all our boundaries cut clear around and not to go on chopping where I had been. The day started out mild and there was still a lot of soft snow in the bush. We were chopping down a tree where Simon wanted, and in some way, I cannot say how, a branch of it came crashing down where we didn't expect. We just heard the little branches cracking where it fell and looked up to see it and it hit Simon on the head and killed him instantly.

I had to drag his body back then to the shanty through the snow. He was a tall fellow though not fleshy, and it was an awkward task and greatly wearying. It had got colder by this time and when I got to the clearing I saw snow on the wind like the start of a storm. Our footsteps were filled in that we had made earlier. Simon was all covered with snow that did not melt on him by this time, and his wife coming to the door was greatly puzzled, thinking that I was dragging along a log.

In the shanty Annie washed him off and we sat still awhile not knowing what we should do. The preacher was at the inn as there was no church or house for him yet and the inn was only about four miles away, but the storm had come up very fierce so you could not even see the trees at the edge of the clearing. It had the look of a storm that would last two or three days, the wind being from the northwest. We knew we could not keep the body in the shanty and we could not set it out in the snow fearing the bobcats would get at it, so we had to set to work and bury him. The ground was not frozen under the snow, so I dug out a grave near the shanty and Annie sewed him in a sheet and we laid him in his grave, not staying long in the wind but saying the Lord's Prayer and reading one Psalm out of the Bible. I am not sure which one but I remember it was near the end of the Book of Psalms and it was very short.

This was the third day of April, 1852.

That was our last snow of the year, and later the minister came and said the service and I put up a wooden marker. Later on we got our plot in the cemetery and put his stone there, but he is not under it as it is a foolish useless thing in my opinion to cart a man's bones from one place to another when it is only bones and his soul has gone on to Judgment.

I was left to chop and clear by myself and soon I began to work side by side with the Treeces, who treated me with the greatest kindness. We worked all together on my land or their land, not minding if it was the one or the other. I started to take my meals and even to sleep at their place and got to know their daughter Jenny who was about of my age, and we made our plans to marry, which we did in due course. Our life together was a long one with many hardships but we were fortunate in the end and raised eight children. I have seen my sons take over my wife's father's land as well as my own since my two brothers-in-law went away and did well for themselves in the West.

My brother's wife did not continue in this place but went her own way to Walley.

Now there are gravel roads running north, south, east, and west and a railway not a half mile from my farm. Except for woodlots, the bush is a thing of the past and I often think of the trees I have cut down and if I had them to cut down today I would be a wealthy man.

THE REVEREND Walter McBain, Minister of the Free Presbyterian Church of North Huron, to Mr. James Mullen, Clerk of the Peace, Walley, United Counties of Huron and Bruce, September 10, 1852.

I write to inform you, sir, of the probable arrival in your town of a young woman of this district, by the name of Annie Herron, a widow and one of my congregation. This young person has left her home here in the vicinity of Carstairs in Holloway Township, I believe she intends to walk to Walley. She may appear at the Gaol there seeking to be admitted, so I think it my duty to tell you who and what she is and her history here since I have known her.

I came to this area in November of last year, being the first minister of any kind to venture. My parish is as yet mostly bush, and there is nowhere for me to lodge but at the Carstairs Inn. I was born in the west of Scotland and came to this country under the auspices of the Glasgow Mission. After applying to know God's will, I was directed by Him to go to preach wherever was most need of a minister. I tell you this so you may know what sort I am that bring you my account and my view of the affairs of this woman.

She came into the country late last winter as the bride of the young man Simon Herron. He had written on my advice to the House of Industry in Toronto that they might recommend to him a Christian, preferably Presbyterian, female suitable to his needs, and she was the one recommended. He married her straightaway and brought her here to the shanty he had built with his brother. These two young lads had come into the country to clear themselves a piece of land and get possession of it, being themselves orphans and without expectations. They were about this work one day at the end of winter when an accident befell. A branch was loosed while chopping down a tree and fell upon the elder brother so as to cause instant death. The younger lad succeeded in getting the body back to the shanty and since they were held prisoner by a heavy snowstorm they conducted their own funeral and burial.

The Lord is strict in his mercies and we are bound to receive his blows as signs of his care and goodness for so they will prove to be.

Deprived of his brother's help, the lad found a place in a neighbouring family, also members in good standing of my congregation, who have accepted him as a son, though he still works for title to his own land. This family would have taken in the young widow as well, but she would have nothing to do with their offer and seemed to develop an aversion to everyone who would help her. Particularly she seemed so towards her brother-in-law, who said that he had never had the least quarrel with her, and towards myself. When I talked to her, she would not give any answer or sign that her soul was coming into submission. It is a fault of mine that I am not well-equipped to talk to women. I have not the ease to win their trust. Their stubbornness is of another kind than a man's.

I meant only to say that I did not have any good effect on her. She stopped appearing at services, and the deterioration of her property showed the state of her mind and spirit. She would not plant peas and potatoes though they were given to her to grow among the stumps. She did not chop down the wild vines around her door. Most often she did not light a fire so she could have oat-cake or porridge. Her brother-in-law being removed, there was no order imposed on her days. When I visited her the door was open and it was evident that animals came and went in her house. If she was there she hid herself, to mock me. Those who caught sight of her said that her clothing was filthy and torn from scrambling about in the bushes, and she was scratched by thorns and bitten by the mosquito insects and let her hair go uncombed or plaited. I believe she lived on salt fish and bannock that the neighbours or her brother-in-law left for her.

Then while I was still puzzling how I might find a way to protect her body through the winter and deal with the more important danger to her soul, there comes word she is gone. She left the door open and went away without cloak or bonnet and wrote on the shanty floor with a burnt stick the two words: "Walley, Gaol." I take this to mean she intends to go there and turn herself in. Her brother-in-law thinks it would be no use for him to go after her because of her unfriendly attitude to himself, and I cannot set out because of a deathbed I am attending. I ask you therefore to let me know if she has arrived and in what state and how you will deal with her. I consider her still as a soul in my charge, and I will try to visit her before winter if you keep her there. She is a child of the Free Church and the Covenant and as such she is entitled to a minister of her own faith and you must not think it sufficient that some priest of the Church of England or Baptist or Methodist be sent to her.

In case she should not come to the Gaol but wander in the streets, I ought to tell you that she is dark-haired and tall, meagre in body, not comely but not ill-favoured except having one eye that goes to the side.

MR. JAMES MULLEN, Clerk of the Peace, Walley, to the Reverend Walter McBain, Carstairs, North Huron, September 30, 1852.

Your letter to me arrived most timely and appreciated, concerning the young woman Annie Herron. She completed her journey to Walley unharmed and with no serious damage though she was weak and hungry when she presented herself at the Gaol. On its being inquired what she did there, she said that she came to confess to a murder, and to be locked up. There was consultation round and about, I was sent for, and it being near to midnight, I agreed that she should spend the night in a cell. The next day I visited her and got all particulars I could.

Her story of being brought up in the Orphanage, her apprenticeship to a milliner, her marriage, and her coming to North Huron, all accords pretty well with what you have told me. Events in her account begin to differ only with her husband's death. In that matter what she says is this:

On the day in early April when her husband and his brother went out to chop trees, she was told to provide them with food for their midday meal, and since she had not got it ready when they wanted to leave, she agreed to take it to them in the woods. Consequently she baked up some oat-cakes and took some salt fish and followed their tracks and found them at work some distance away. But when her husband unwrapped his food he was very offended, because she had wrapped it in a way that the salty oil from the fish had soaked into the cakes, and they were all crumbled and unpleasant to eat. In his disappointment he became enraged and promised her a beating when he was more at leisure to do it. He then turned his back on her, being seated on a log, and she picked up a rock and threw it at him, hitting him on the head so that he fell down unconscious and in fact dead. She and his brother then carried and dragged the body back to the house. By that time a blizzard had come up and they were imprisoned within. The brother said that they should not reveal the truth as she had not intended murder, and she agreed. They then buried him – her story agreeing again with yours – and that might have been the end of it, but she became more and more troubled, convinced that she had surely been intending to kill him. If she had not killed him, she says, it would only have meant a worse beating, and why should she have risked that? So she decided at last upon confession and as if to prove something handed me a lock of hair stiffened with blood.

This is her tale, and I do not believe it for a minute. No rock that this girl could pick up, combined with the force that she could summon to throw it, would serve to kill a man. I questioned her about this, and she changed her story, saying that it was a large rock that she had picked up in both hands and that she had not thrown it but smashed it down on his head from behind. I said why did not the brother prevent you, and she said, he was looking the other way. Then I said there must indeed be a bloodied rock lying somewhere in the wood, and she said she had washed it off with the snow. (In fact it is not likely a rock would come to hand so easily, with all such depth of snow about.) I asked her to roll up her sleeve that I might judge of the muscles in her arms, to do such a job, and she said that she had been a huskier woman some months since.

I conclude that she is lying, or self-deluded. But I see nothing for it at the moment but to admit her to the Gaol. I asked her what she thought would happen to her now, and she said, well, you will try me and then you will hang me. But you do not hang people in the winter, she said, so I can stay here till spring. And if you let me work here, maybe you will want me to go on working and you will not want me hanged. I do not know where she got this idea about people not being hanged in the winter. I am in perplexity about her. As you may know, we have a very fine new Gaol here where the inmates are kept warm and dry and are decently fed and treated with all humanity, and there has been a complaint that some are not sorry – and at this time of year, even happy – to get into it. But it is obvious that she cannot wander about much longer, and from your account she is unwilling to stay with friends and unable to make a tolerable home for herself. The Gaol at present serves as a place of detention for the Insane as well as criminals, and if she is charged with Insanity, I could keep her here for the winter perhaps with removal to Toronto in the spring. I have engaged for a doctor to visit her. I spoke to her of your letter and your hope of coming to see her, but I found her not at all agreeable to that. She asks that nobody be allowed to see her excepting a Miss Sadie Johnstone, who is not in this part of the country.

I am enclosing a letter I have written to her brother-in-law for you to pass on to him, so that he may know what she has said and tell me what he thinks about it. I thank you in advance for conveying the letter to him, also for the trouble you have been to, in informing me as fully as you have done. I am a member of the Church of England, but have a high regard for the work of other Protestant denominations in bringing an orderly life to this part of the world we find ourselves in. You may believe that I will do what is in my power to do, to put you in a position to deal with the soul of this young woman, but it might be better to wait until she is in favour of it.

THE REVEREND Walter McBain to Mr. James Mullen, November 18, 1852.

I carried your letter at once to Mr. George Herron and believe that he has replied and given you his recollection of events. He was amazed at his sister-in-law's claim, since she had never said anything of this to him or to anybody else. He says that it is all her invention or fancy, since she was never in the woods when it happened and there was no need for her to be, as they had carried their food with them when they left the house. He says that there had been at another time some reproof from his brother to her, over the spoiling of some cakes by their proximity to fish, but it did not happen at this time. Nor were there any rocks about to do such a deed on impulse if she had been there and wished to do it.

My delay in answering your letter, for which I beg pardon, is due to a bout of ill health. I had an attack of the gravel and a rheumatism of the stomach worse than any misery that ever fell upon me before. I am somewhat improved at present and will be able to go about as usual by next week if all continues to mend.

As to the question of the young woman's sanity, I do not know what your Doctor will say but I have thought on this and questioned the Divinity and my belief is this. It may well be that so early in the marriage her submission to her husband was not complete and there would be carelessness about his comfort, and naughty words, and quarrelsome behaviour, as well as the hurtful sulks and silences her sex is prone to. His death occurring before any of this was put right, she would feel a natural and harrowing remorse, and this must have taken hold of her mind so strongly that she made herself out to be actually responsible for his death.

In this way, I think many folk are driven mad. Madness is at first taken on by some as a kind of play, for which shallowness and audacity they are punished later on, by finding out that it is play no longer, and the Devil has blocked off every escape.

It is still my hope to speak to her and make her understand this. I am under difficulties at present not only of my wretched corpus but of being lodged in a foul and noisy place obliged to hear day and night such uproars as destroy sleep and study and intrude even on my prayers. The wind blows bitterly through the logs, but if I go down to the fire there is swilling of spirits and foulest insolence. And outside nothing but trees to choke off every exit and icy bog to swallow man and horse. There was a promise to build a church and lodging but those who made such promise have grown busy with their own affairs and it seems to have been put off. I have not however left off preaching even in my illness and in such barns and houses as are provided. I take heart remembering a great man, the great preacher and interpreter of God's will, Thomas Boston, who in the latter days of his infirmity preached the grandeur of God from his chamber window to a crowd of two thousand or so assembled in the yard below. So I mean to preach to the end though my congregation will be smaller.

Whatsoever crook there is in one's lot, it is of God's making. Thomas Boston.

This world is a wilderness, in which we may indeed get our station changed, but the move will be out of one wilderness station unto another. Ibid.

MR. JAMES MULLEN to the Reverend Walter McBain, January 17, 1853.

I write to you that our young woman's health seems sturdy, and she no longer looks such a scarecrow, eating well and keeping herself clean and tidy. Also she seems quieter in her spirits. She has taken to mending the linen in the prison which she does well. But I must tell you that she is firm as ever against a visit, and I cannot advise you to come here as I think your trouble might be for nothing. The journey is very hard in winter and it would do no good to your state of health.

Her brother-in-law has written me a very decent letter affirming that there is no truth to her story, so I am satisfied on that.

You may be interested in hearing what the doctor who visited her had to say about her case. His belief is that she is subject to a sort of delusion peculiar to females, for which the motive is a desire for self-importance, also a wish to escape the monotony of life or the drudgery they may have been born to. They may imagine themselves possessed by the forces of evil, to have committed various and hideous crimes, and so forth. Sometimes they may report that they have taken numerous lovers, but these lovers will be all imaginary and the woman who thinks herself a prodigy of vice will in fact be quite chaste and untouched. For all this he – the doctor – lays the blame on the sort of reading that is available to these females, whether it is of ghosts or demons or of love escapades with Lords and Dukes and suchlike. For many, these tales are a passing taste given up when life's real duties intervene. For others they are indulged in now and then, as if they were sweets or sherry wine, but for some there is complete surrender and living within them just as in an opium-dream. He could not get an account of her reading from the young woman, but he believes she may by now have forgotten what she has read, or conceals the matter out of slyness.

With his questioning there did come to light something further that we did not know. On his saying to her, did she not fear hanging? she replied, no, for there is a reason you will not hang me. You mean that they will judge that you are mad? said he, and she said, oh, perhaps that, but is it not true also that they will never hang a woman that is with child? The doctor then examined her to find out if this were true, and she agreed to the examination, so she must have made the claim in good faith. He discovered however that she had deceived herself. The signs she took were simply the results of her going so long underfed and in such a reduced state, and later probably of her hysteria. He told her of his findings, but it is hard to say whether she believes him.

It must be acknowledged that this is truly a hard country for women. Another insane female has been admitted here recently, and her case is more pitiful for she has been driven insane by a rape. Her two attack-ers have been taken in and are in fact just over the wall from her in the men's section. The screams of the victim resound sometimes for hours at a stretch, and as a result the prison has become a much less pleasant shelter. But whether that will persuade our self-styled murderess to recant and take herself off, I have no idea. She is a good needlewoman and could get employment if she chose.

I am sorry to hear of your bad health and miserable lodgings. The town has grown so civilized that we forget the hardship of the hinterlands. Those like yourself who choose to endure it deserve our admiration. But you must allow me to say that it seems pretty certain that a man not in robust health will be unable to bear up for long in your situation. Surely your Church would not consider it a defection were you to choose to serve it longer by removing to a more comfortable place.

I enclose a letter written by the young woman and sent to a Miss Sadie Johnstone, on King Street, Toronto. It was intercepted by us that we might know more of the state of her mind, but resealed and sent on. But it has come back marked "Unknown." We have not told the writer of this in hopes that she will write again and more fully, revealing to us something to help us decide whether or not she is a conscious liar.

MRS. ANNIE HERRON, Walley Gaol, United Counties of Huron and Bruce, to Miss Sadie Johnstone, 49 King Street, Toronto, December 20, 1852.

Sadie, I am in here pretty well and safe and nothing to complain of either in food or blankets. It is a good stone building and something like the Home. If you could come and see me I would be very glad. I often talk to you a whole lot in my head, which I don't want to write because what if they are spies. I do the sewing here, the things was not in good repare when I came but now they are pretty good. And I am making curtains for the Opera House, a job that was sent in. I hope to see you. You could come on the stage right to this place. Maybe you would not like to come in the winter but in the springtime you would like to come.

MR. JAMES MULLEN to the Reverend Walter McBain, April 7, 1853.

Not having had any reply to my last letter, I trust you are well and might still be interested in the case of Annie Herron. She is still here and busies herself at sewing jobs which I have undertaken to get her from outside. No more is said of being with child, or of hanging, or of her story. She has written once again to Sadie Johnstone but quite briefly and I enclose her letter here. Do you have an idea who this person Sadie Johnstone might be?

I DON'T GET any answer from you, Sadie, I don't think they sent on my letter. Today is the First of April, 1853. But not April Fool like we used to fool each other. Please come and see me if you can. I am in Walley Gaol but safe and well.

MR. JAMES MULLEN from Edward Hoy, Landlord, Carstairs Inn, April 19, 1853.

Your letter to Mr. McBain sent back to you, he died here at the inn February 25. There is some books here, nobody wants them.

III

ANNIE HERRON, Walley Gaol, to Sadie Johnstone, Toronto. Finder Please Post.

George came dragging him across the snow I thought it was a log he dragged. I didn't know it was him. George said, it's him. A branch fell out of a tree and hit him, he said. He didn't say he was dead. I looked for him to speak. His mouth was part way open with snow in it. Also his eyes part way open. We had to get inside because it was starting to storm like anything. We dragged him in by the one leg each. I pretended to myself when I took hold of his leg that it was still the log. Inside where I had the fire going it was warm and the snow started melting off him. His blood thawed and ran a little around his ear. I didn't know what to do and I was afraid to go near him. I thought his eyes were watching me.

George sat by the fire with his big heavy coat on and his boots on. He was turned away. I sat at the table, which was of half-cut logs. I said, how do you know if he is dead? George said, touch him if you want to know. But I would not. Outside there was terrible storming, the wind

in the trees and over top of our roof. I said, Our Father who art in
Heaven, and that was how I got my courage. I kept saying it every time
I moved. I have to wash him off, I said. Help me. I got the bucket where
I kept the snow melting. I started on his feet and had to pull his boots
off, a heavy job. George never turned around or paid attention or helped
me when I asked. I didn't take the trousers or coat off of him, I couldn't
manage. But I washed his hands and wrists. I always kept the rag between
my hand and his skin. The blood and wet where the snow had melted
off him was on the floor under his head and shoulders so I wanted to
turn him over and clean it up. But I couldn't do it. So I went and pulled
George by his arm. Help me, I said. What? he said. I said we had to turn
him. So he came and helped me and we got him turned over, he was
laying face down. And then I saw, I saw where the axe had cut.

Neither one of us said anything. I washed it out, blood and what else.
I said to George, go and get me the sheet from my box. There was the
good sheet I wouldn't put on the bed. I didn't see the use of trying to take
off his clothes though they were good cloth. We would have had to cut
them away where the blood was stuck and then what would we have but
the rags. I cut off the one little piece of his hair because I remembered
when Lila died in the Home they did that. Then I got George to help me
roll him onto the sheet and I started to sew him up in the sheet. While I
was sewing I said to George, go out in the lee of the house where the
wood is piled and maybe you can get in enough shelter there to dig him
a grave. Take the wood away and the ground is likely softer underneath.

I had to crouch down at the sewing so I was nearly laying on the floor
beside him. I sewed his head in first folding the sheet over it because I
had to look in his eyes and mouth. George went out and I could hear
through the storm that he was doing what I said and pieces of wood were
thrown up sometimes hitting the wall of the house. I sewed on, and every
bit of him I lost sight of I would say even out loud, there goes, there goes.
I had got the fold neat over his head but down at the feet I didn't have
material enough to cover him, so I sewed on my eyelet petticoat I made
at the Home to learn the stitch and that way I got him all sewed in.

I went out to help George. He had got all the wood out of the way
and was at the digging. The ground was soft enough, like I had thought.

He had the spade so I got the broad shovel and we worked away, him digging and loosening and me shovelling.

Then we moved him out. We could not do it now one leg each so George got him at the head and me at the ankles where the petticoat was and we rolled him into the earth and set to work again to cover him up. George had the shovel and it seemed I could not get enough dirt onto the spade so I pushed it in with my hands and kicked it in with my feet any way at all. When it was all back in, George beat it down flat with the shovel as much as he could. Then we moved all the wood back searching where it was in the snow and we piled it up in the right way so it did not look as if anybody had been at it. I think we had no hats on or scarves but the work kept us warm.

We took in more wood for the fire and put the bar across the door. I wiped up the floor and I said to George, take off your boots. Then, take off your coat. George did what I told him. He sat by the fire. I made the kind of tea from catnip leaves that Mrs. Treece showed me how to make and I put a piece of sugar in it. George did not want it. Is it too hot, I said. I let it cool off but then he didn't want it either. So I began, and talked to him.

You didn't mean to do it.

It was in anger, you didn't mean what you were doing.

I saw him other times what he would do to you. I saw he would knock you down for a little thing and you just get up and never say a word. The same way he did to me.

If you had not have done it, some day he would have done it to you.

Listen, George. Listen to me.

If you own up what do you think will happen? They will hang you. You will be dead, you will be no good to anybody. What will become of your land? Likely it will all go back to the Crown and somebody else will get it and all the work you have done will be for them.

What will become of me here if you are took away?

I got some oat-cakes that were cold and I warmed them up. I set one on his knee. He took it and bit it and chewed it but he could not get it down and he spit it onto the fire.

I said, listen. I know things. I am older than you are. I am religious too, I pray to God every night and my prayers are answered. I know what God wants as well as any preacher knows and I know that he does not want a good lad like you to be hanged. All you have to do is say you are sorry. Say you are sorry and mean it well and God will forgive you. I will say the same thing, I am sorry too because when I saw he was dead I did not wish, not one minute, for him to be alive. I will say, God forgive me, and you do the same. Kneel down.

But he would not. He would not move out of his chair. And I said, all right. I have an idea. I am going to get the Bible. I asked him, do you believe in the Bible? Say you do. Nod your head.

I did not see whether he nodded or not but I said, there. There you did. Now. I am going to do what we all used to do in the Home when we wanted to know what would happen to us or what we should do in our life. We would open the Bible any place and poke our finger at a page and then open our eyes and read the verse where our finger was and that would tell you what you needed to know. To make double sure of it just say when you close your eyes, God guide my finger.

He would not raise a hand from his knee, so I said, all right. All right, I'll do it for you. I did it, and I read where my finger stopped. I held the Bible close in to the fire so I could see.

It was something about being old and gray-headed, *oh God forsake me not*, and I said, what that means is that you are supposed to live till you are old and gray-headed and nothing is supposed to happen to you before that. It says so, in the Bible.

Then the next verse was so-and-so went and took so-and-so and conceived and bore him a son.

It says you will have a son, I said. You have to live and get older and get married and have a son.

But the next verse I remember so well I can put down all of it. *Neither can they prove the things of which they now accuse me.*

George, I said, do you hear that? *Neither can they prove the things of which they now accuse me.* That means that you are safe.

You are safe. Get up now. Get up and go and lay on the bed and go to sleep.

He could not do that by himself but I did it. I pulled on him and pulled on him until he was standing up and then I got him across the room to the bed which was not his bed in the corner but the bigger bed, and got him to sit on it then lay down. I rolled him over and back and got his clothes off down to his shirt. His teeth were chattering and I was afraid of a chill or the fever. I heated up the flat-irons and wrapped them in cloth and laid them down one on each side of him close to his skin. There was not whisky or brandy in the house to use, only the catnip tea. I put more sugar in it and got him to take it from a spoon. I rubbed his feet with my hands, then his arms and his legs, and I wrung out clothes in hot water which I laid over his stomach and his heart. I talked to him then in a different way quite soft and told him to go to sleep and when he woke up his mind would be clear and all his horrors would be wiped away.

A tree branch fell on him. It was just what you told me. I can see it falling. I can see it coming down so fast like a streak and little branches and cracking all along the way, it hardly takes longer than a gun going off and you say, what is that? and it has hit him and he is dead.

When I got him to sleep I laid down on the bed beside him. I took off my smock and I could see the black and blue marks on my arms. I pulled up my skirt to see if they were still there high on my legs, and they were. The back of my hand was dark too and sore still where I had bit it.

Nothing bad happened after I laid down and I did not sleep all night but listened to him breathing and kept touching him to see if he was warmed up. I got up in the earliest light and fixed the fire. When he heard me, he waked up and was better.

He did not forget what had happened but talked as if he thought it was all right. He said, we ought to have had a prayer and read something out of the Bible. He got the door opened and there was a big drift of snow but the sky was clearing. It was the last snow of the winter.

We went out and said the Lord's Prayer. Then he said, where is the Bible? Why is it not on the shelf? When I got it from beside the fire he said, what is it doing there? I did not remind him of anything. He did not know what to read so I picked the 131st Psalm that we had to learn at the Home. *Lord my heart is not haughty nor mine eyes lofty. Surely I have behaved and quieted myself as a child that is weaned of his mother, my soul is even as a weaned child.* He read it. Then he said he would shovel out a path and go and tell the Treeces. I said I would cook him some food. He went out and shovelled and didn't get tired and come in to eat like I was waiting for him to do. He shovelled and shovelled a long path out of sight and then he was gone and didn't come back. He didn't come back until near dark and then he said he had eaten. I said, did you tell them about the tree? Then he looked at me for the first time in a bad way. It was the same bad way his brother used to look. I never said anything more to him about what had happened or hinted at it in any way. And he never said anything to me, except he would come and say things in my dreams. But I knew the difference always between my dreams and when I was awake, and when I was awake it was never anything but the bad look.

Mrs. Treece came and tried to get me to go and live with them the way George was living. She said I could eat and sleep there, they had enough beds. I would not go. They thought I would not go because of my grief but I wouldn't go because somebody might see my black and blue, also they would be watching for me to cry. I said I was not frightened to stay alone.

I dreamed nearly every night that one or other of them came and chased me with the axe. It was him or it was George, one or the other. Or sometimes not the axe, it was a big rock lifted in both hands and one of them waiting with it behind the door. Dreams are sent to warn us.

I didn't stay in the house where he could find me and when I gave up sleeping inside and slept outside I didn't have the dream so often. It got warm in a hurry and the flies and mosquitoes came but they hardly bothered me. I would see their bites but not feel them, which was another sign that in the outside I was protected. I got down when I heard anybody coming. I ate berries both red and black and God protected me from any badness in them.

I had another kind of dream after a while. I dreamed George came and talked to me and he still had the bad look but was trying to cover it up and pretend that he was kind. He kept coming into my dreams and he kept lying to me. It was starting to get colder out and I did not want to go back in the shanty and the dew was heavy so I would be soaking when I slept in the grass. I went and opened the Bible to find out what I should do.

And now I got my punishment for cheating because the Bible did not tell me anything that I could understand, what to do. The cheating was when I was looking to find something for George, and I did not read exactly where my finger landed but looked around quick and found something else that was more what I wanted. I used to do that too when we would be looking up our verses in the Home and I always got good things and nobody ever caught me or suspected me at it. You never did either, Sadie.

So now I had my punishment when I couldn't find anything to help me however I looked. But something put it into my head to come here and I did, I had heard them talking about how warm it was and tramps would be wanting to come and get locked up, so I thought, I will too, and it was put into my head to tell them what I did. I told them the very same lie that George told me so often in my dreams, trying to get me to believe it was me and not him. I am safe from George here is the main thing. If they think I am crazy and I know the difference I am safe. Only I would like for you to come and see me.

And I would like for that yelling to stop.

When I am finished writing this, I will put it in with the curtains that I am making for the Opera House. And I will put on it, Finder Please Post. I trust that better than giving it to them like the two letters I gave them already that they never have sent.

IV

MISS CHRISTENA MULLEN, Walley, to Mr. Leopold Henry, Department of History, Queen's University, Kingston, July 8, 1959.

Yes I am the Miss Mullen that Treece Herron's sister remembers coming to the farm and it is very kind of her to say I was a pretty young lady in a hat and veil. That was my motoring-veil. The old lady she mentions was

Mr. Herron's grandfather's sister-in-law, if I have got it straight. As you are doing the biography, you will have got the relationships worked out. I never voted for Treece Herron myself since I am a Conservative, but he was a colorful politician and as you say a biography of him will bring some attention to this part of the country – too often thought of as "deadly dull."

I am rather surprised the sister does not mention the car in particular. It was a Stanley Steamer. I bought it myself on my twenty-fifth birthday in 1907. It cost twelve hundred dollars, that being part of my inheritance from my grandfather James Mullen who was an early Clerk of the Peace in Walley. He made money buying and selling farms.

My father having died young, my mother moved into my grandfather's house with all us five girls. It was a big cut-stone house called Traquair, now a Home for Young Offenders. I sometimes say in joke that it always was!

When I was young, we employed a gardener, a cook, and a sewing-woman. All of them were "characters," all prone to feuding with each other, and all owing their jobs to the fact that my grandfather had taken an interest in them when they were inmates at the County Gaol (as it used to be spelled) and eventually had brought them home.

By the time I bought the Steamer, I was the only one of my sisters living at home, and the sewing-woman was the only one of these old servants who remained. The sewing-woman was called Old Annie and never objected to that name. She used it herself and would write notes to the cook that said, "Tea was not hot, did you warm the pot? Old Annie." The whole third floor was Old Annie's domain and one of my sisters – Dolly – said that whenever she dreamed of home, that is, of Traquair, she dreamed of Old Annie up at the top of the third-floor stairs brandishing her measuring stick and wearing a black dress with long fuzzy black arms like a spider.

She had one eye that slid off to the side and gave her the air of taking in more information than the ordinary person.

We were not supposed to pester the servants with questions about their personal lives, particularly those who had been in the Gaol, but of course we did. Sometimes Old Annie called the Gaol the Home. She said that a girl in the next bed screamed and screamed, and that was why she – Annie – ran away and lived in the woods. She said the girl had been beaten for letting the fire go out. Why were you in jail, we asked her, and she would say, "I told a fib!" So for quite a while we had the impression that you went to jail for telling lies!

Some days she was in a good mood and would play hide-the-thimble with us. Sometimes she was in a bad mood and would stick us with pins when she was evening our hems if we turned too quickly or stopped too soon. She knew a place, she said, where you could get bricks to put on children's heads to stop them growing. She hated making wedding dresses (she never had to make one for me!) and didn't think much of any of the men that my sisters married. She hated Dolly's beau so much that she made some kind of deliberate mistake with the sleeves which had to be ripped out, and Dolly cried. But she made us all beautiful ball gowns to wear when the Governor-General and Lady Minto came to Walley.

About being married herself, she sometimes said she had been and sometimes not. She said a man had come to the Home and had all the girls paraded in front of him and said, "I'll take the one with the coal-black hair." That being Old Annie, but she refused to go with him, even though he was rich and came in a carriage. Rather like Cinderella but with a different ending. Then she said a bear killed her husband, in the woods, and my grandfather had killed the bear, and wrapped her in its skin and taken her home from the Gaol.

My mother used to say, "Now, girls. Don't get Old Annie going. And don't believe a word she says."

I am going on at great length filling in the background but you did say you were interested in details of the period. I am like most people my age and forget to buy milk but could tell you the color of the coat I had when I was eight.

So when I got the Stanley Steamer, Old Annie asked to be taken for a ride. It turned out that what she had in mind was more of a trip. This was a surprise since she had never wanted to go on trips before and refused to go to Niagara Falls and would not even go down to the Harbor to see the fireworks on the First of July. Also she was leery of automobiles and of me as a driver. But the big surprise was that she had somebody she wanted to go and see. She wanted to drive to Carstairs to see the Herron family, who she said were her relatives. She had never received any visits or letters from these people, and when I asked if she had written to ask if we might visit she said, "I can't write." This was ridiculous – she wrote those notes to the cooks and long lists for me of things she wanted me to pick up down on the Square or in the city. Braid, buckram, taffeta – she could spell all of that.

"And they don't need to know beforehand," she said. "In the country it's different."

Well, I loved taking jaunts in the Steamer. I had been driving since I was fifteen but this was the first car of my own and possibly the only Steam car in Huron County. Everybody would run to see it go by. It did not make a beastly loud noise coughing and clanking like other cars but rolled along silently more or less like a ship with high sails over the lake waters and it did not foul the air but left behind a plume of steam. Stanley Steamers were banned in Boston, because of steam fogging the air. I always loved to tell people, I used to drive a car that was banned in Boston!

We started out fairly early on a Sunday in June. It took about twenty-five minutes to get the steam up and all that time Old Annie sat up straight in the front seat as if the show were already on the road. We both had our motoring-veils on, and long dusters, but the dress Old Annie was wearing underneath was of plum-colored silk. In fact it was made over from the one she had made for my grandmother to meet the Prince of Wales in.

The Steamer covered the miles like an angel. It would do fifty miles an hour – great then – but I did not push it. I was trying to consider Old Annie's nerves. People were still in church when we started, but later on the roads were full of horses and buggies making the journey home. I was polite as all get-out, edging by them. But it turned out Old Annie did not want to be so sedate and she kept saying, "Give it a squeeze," meaning the horn, which was worked by a bulb under a mud-guard down at my side.

She must not have been out of Walley for more years than I had been alive. When we crossed the bridge at Saltford (that old iron bridge where there used to be so many accidents because of the turn at both ends), she said that there didn't used to be a bridge there, you had to pay a man to row you.

"I couldn't pay but I crossed on the stones and just hiked up my skirts and waded," she said. "It was that dry a summer."

Naturally I did not know what summer she was talking about.

Then it was, Look at the big fields, where are the stumps gone, where is the bush? And look how straight the road goes, and they're building their houses out of brick! And what are those buildings as big as churches?

Barns, I said.

I knew my way to Carstairs all right but expected help from Old Annie once we got there. None was forthcoming. I drove up and down the main street waiting for her to spot something familiar. "If I could just see the inn," she said, "I'd know where the track goes off behind it."

It was a factory town, not very pretty in my opinion. The Steamer of course got attention, and I was able to call out for directions to the Herron farm without stopping the engine. Shouts and gestures and finally I was able to get us on the right road. I told Old Annie to watch the mailboxes but she was concerned with finding the creek. I spotted the name myself, and turned us in at a long lane with a red-brick house at the end of it and a couple of these barns that had amazed Old Annie. Red-brick houses with verandas and key windows were all the style then, they were going up everywhere.

"Look there!" Old Annie said, and I thought she meant where a herd of cows was tearing away from us in the pasture-field alongside the lane. But she was pointing at a mound pretty well covered with wild grape, a few logs sticking out of it. She said that was the shanty. I said, "Well, good – now let's hope you recognize one or two of the people."

There were enough people around. A couple of visiting buggies were pulled up in the shade, horses tethered and cropping grass. By the time the Steamer stopped at the side veranda, a number were lined up to look at it. They didn't come forward – not even the children ran out to look close up the way town children would have done. They all just stood in a row looking at it in a tight-lipped sort of way.

Old Annie was staring off in the other direction.

She told me to get down. Get down, she said, and ask them if there is a Mr. George Herron that lives here and is he alive yet, or dead?

I did what I was told. And one of the men said, that's right. He is. My father.

Well, I have brought somebody, I told them. I have brought Mrs. Annie Herron.

The man said, that so?

(A pause here due to a couple of fainting-fits and a trip to the hospital. Lots of tests to use up the taxpayers' money. Now I'm back and have read this over, astounded at the rambling but too lazy to start again. I have not even got to Treece Herron, which is the part you are interested in, but hold on, I'm nearly there.)

These people were all dumbfounded about Old Annie, or so I gathered. They had not known where she was or what she was doing or if she was alive. But you mustn't think they surged out and greeted her in any excited way. Just the one young man came out, very mannerly, and helped first her then me down from the car. He said to me that Old Annie was his grandfather's sister-in-law. It was too bad we hadn't come even a few months sooner, he said, because his grandfather had been quite well and his mind quite clear – he had even written a piece for the paper about his early days here – but then he had got sick. He had recovered but would never be himself again. He could not talk, except now and then a few words.

This mannerly young man was Treece Herron.

We must have arrived just after they finished their dinner. The woman of the house came out and asked him – Treece Herron – to ask us if we had eaten. You would think she or we did not speak English. They were all very shy – the women with their skinned-back hair, and men in dark-blue Sunday suits, and tongue-tied children. I hope you do not think I am making fun of them – it is just that I cannot understand for the life of me why it is necessary to be so shy.

We were taken to the dining-room which had an unused smell – they must have had their dinner elsewhere – and were served a great deal of food of which I remember salted radishes and leaf lettuce and roast

chicken and strawberries and cream. Dishes from the china cabinet, not their usual. Good old Indian Tree. They had sets of everything. Plushy living-room suite, walnut dining-room suite. It was going to take them a while, I thought, to get used to being prosperous.

Old Annie enjoyed the fuss of being waited on and ate a lot, picking up the chicken bones to work the last shred of meat off them. Children lurked around the doorways and the women talked in subdued, rather scandalized voices out in the kitchen. The young man, Treece Herron, had the grace to sit down with us and drink a cup of tea while we ate. He chatted readily enough about himself and told me he was a divinity student at Knox College. He said he liked living in Toronto. I got the feeling he wanted me to understand that divinity students were not all such sticks as I supposed or led such a stringent existence. He had been tobogganing in High Park, he had been picnicking at Hanlan's Point, he had seen the giraffe in the Riverdale Zoo. As he talked, the children got a little bolder and started trickling into the room. I asked the usual idiocies . . . How old are you, what book are you in at school, do you like your teacher? He urged them to answer or answered for them and told me which were his brothers and sisters and which his cousins.

Old Annie said, "Are you all fond of each other, then?" which brought on funny looks.

The woman of the house came back and spoke to me again through the divinity student. She told him that Grandpa was up now and sitting on the front porch. She looked at the children and said, "What did you let all them in here for?"

Out we trooped to the front porch, where two straight-backed chairs were set up and an old man settled on one of them. He had a beautiful full white beard reaching down to the bottom of his waistcoat. He did not seem interested in us. He had a long, pale, obedient old face.

Old Annie said, "Well, George," as if this was about what she had expected. She sat on the other chair and said to one of the little girls, "Now bring me a cushion. Bring me a thin kind of cushion and put it at my back."

*   *   *

I SPENT THE afternoon giving rides in the Stanley Steamer. I knew enough about them now not to start in asking who wanted a ride, or bombarding them with questions, such as, were they interested in automobiles? I just went out and patted it here and there as if it was a horse, and I looked in the boiler. The divinity student came behind and read the name of the Steamer written on the side. THE GENTLEMAN'S SPEEDSTER. He asked was it my father's.

Mine, I said. I explained how the water in the boiler was heated and how much steam-pressure the boiler could withstand. People always wondered about that – about explosions. The children were closer by that time and I suddenly remarked that the boiler was nearly empty. I asked if there was any way I could get some water.

Great scurry to get pails and man the pump! I went and asked the men on the veranda if that was all right, and thanked them when they told me, help yourself. Once the boiler was filled, it was natural for me to ask if they would like me to get the steam up, and a spokesman said, it wouldn't hurt. Nobody was impatient during the wait. The men stared at the boiler, concentrating. This was certainly not the first car they had seen but probably the first steam car.

I offered the men a ride first, as it was proper to. They watched skeptically while I fiddled with all the knobs and levers to get my lady going. Thirteen different things to push or pull! We bumped down the lane at five, then ten miles an hour. I knew they suffered somewhat, being driven by a woman, but the novelty of the experience held them. Next I got a load of children, hoisted in by the divinity student telling them to sit still and hold on and not be scared and not fall out. I put up the speed a little, knowing now the ruts and puddle-holes, and their hoots of fear and triumph could not be held back.

I have left out something about how I was feeling but will leave it out no longer, due to the effects of a martini I am drinking now, my late-afternoon pleasure. I had troubles then I have not yet admitted to you because they were love-troubles. But when I had set out that day with Old Annie, I had determined to enjoy myself as much as I could.

It seemed it would be an insult to the Stanley Steamer not to. All my life I found this a good rule to follow – to get as much pleasure as you could out of things even when you weren't likely to be happy.

I told one of the boys to run around to the front veranda and ask if his grandfather would care for a ride. He came back and said, "They've both gone to sleep."

I had to get the boiler filled up before we started back, and while this was being done, Treece Herron came and stood close to me.

"You have given us all a day to remember," he said.

I wasn't above flirting with him. I actually had a long career as a flirt ahead of me. It's quite a natural behavior, once the loss of love makes you give up your ideas of marriage.

I said he would forget all about it, once he got back to his friends in Toronto. He said no indeed, he would never forget, and he asked if he could write to me. I said nobody could stop him.

On the way home I thought about this exchange and how ridiculous it would be if he should get a serious crush on me. A divinity student. I had no idea then of course that he would be getting out of Divinity and into Politics.

"Too bad old Mr. Herron wasn't able to talk to you," I said to Old Annie.

She said, "Well, I could talk to him."

Actually, Treece Herron did write to me, but he must have had a few misgivings as well because he enclosed some pamphlets about Mission Schools. Something about raising money for Mission Schools. That put me off and I didn't write back. (Years later I would joke that I could have married him if I'd played my cards right.)

I asked Old Annie if Mr. Herron could understand her when she talked to him, and she said, "Enough." I asked if she was glad about seeing him again and she said yes. "And glad for him to get to see me," she said, not without some gloating that probably referred to her dress and the vehicle.

So we just puffed along in the Steamer under the high arching trees that lined the roads in those days. From miles away the lake could be seen – just glimpses of it, shots of light, held wide apart in the trees and hills so that Old Annie asked me if it could possibly be the same lake, all the same one that Walley was on?

There were lots of old people going around then with ideas in their heads that didn't add up – though I suppose Old Annie had more than most. I recall her telling me another time that a girl in the Home had a baby out of a big boil that burst on her stomach, and it was the size of a rat and had no life in it, but they put it in the oven and it puffed up to the right size and baked to a good color and started to kick its legs. (Ask an old woman to reminisce and you get the whole ragbag, is what you must be thinking by now.)

I told her that wasn't possible, it must have been a dream.

"Maybe so," she said, agreeing with me for once. "I did used to have the terriblest dreams."

VANDALS

"LIZA, MY DEAR, I have never written you yet to thank you for going out to our house (poor old Dismal, I guess it really deserves the name now) in the teeth or anyway the aftermath of the storm last February and for letting me know what you found there. Thank your husband too, for taking you there on his snowmobile, also if as I suspect he was the one to board up the broken window to keep out the savage beasts, etc. Lay not up treasure on earth where moth and dust not to mention teenagers doth corrupt. I hear you are a Christian now, Liza, what a splendid thing to be! Are you born again? I always liked the sound of that!

"Oh, Liza, I know it's boring of me but I still think of you and poor little Kenny as pretty sunburned children slipping out from behind the trees to startle me and leaping and diving in the pond.

"Ladner had not the least premonition of death on the night before his operation – or maybe it was the night before that, whenever I phoned you. It is not very often nowadays that people die during a simple bypass and also he really did not think about being mortal. He was just worried about things like whether he had turned the water off. He was obsessed more and more by that sort of detail. The one way his age showed. Though I suppose it is not such a detail if you consider the pipes bursting, that would be a calamity. But a calamity occurred anyway. I have been out there just once to look at it and the odd thing was it just looked natural to me. On top of Ladner's death, it seemed almost the right way for things to be. What would seem unnatural would be to get to work and clean it up, though I suppose I shall have to do that, or hire somebody. I am tempted just to light a match and let everything go up in smoke, but I imagine that if I did that I would find myself locked up.

"I wish in a way that I had had Ladner cremated, but I didn't think of it. I just put him here in the Doud plot to surprise my father and my

325

stepmother. But now I must tell you, the other night I had a dream! I dreamed that I was around behind the Canadian Tire Store and they had the big plastic tent up as they do when they are selling bedding-plants in the spring. I went and opened up the trunk of my car, just as if I were getting my annual load of salvia or impatiens. Other people were waiting as well and men in green aprons were going back and forth from the tent. A woman said to me, 'Seven years sure goes by in a hurry!' She seemed to know me but I didn't know her and I thought, Why is this always happening? Is it because I did a little schoolteaching? Is it because of what you might politely call the conduct of my life?

"Then the significance of the seven years struck me and I knew what I was doing there and what the other people were doing there. They had come for the bones. I had come for Ladner's bones; in the dream it was seven years since he had been buried. But I thought, Isn't this what they do in Greece or somewhere, why are we doing it here? I said to some people, Are the graveyards getting overcrowded? What have we taken up this custom for? Is it pagan or Christian or what? The people I spoke to looked rather sullen and offended and I thought, What have I done now. I've lived around here all my life but I can still get this look – is it the word *pagan*? Then one of the men handed me a plastic bag and I took it gratefully and held it, thinking of Ladner's strong leg bones and wide shoulder bones and intelligent skull all washed and polished by some bath-and-brush apparatus no doubt concealed in the plastic tent. This seemed to have something to do with my feelings for him and his for me being purified but the idea was more interesting and subtle than that. I was so happy, though, to receive my load and other people were happy too. In fact some of them became quite jolly and were tossing their plastic bags in the air. Some of the bags were bright blue, but most were green, and mine was one of the regular green ones.

"'Oh,' someone said to me. 'Did you get the little girl?'

"I understood what was meant. The little girl's bones. I saw that my bag was really quite small and light, to contain Ladner. I mean, Ladner's bones. What little girl? I thought, but I was already getting confused about everything and had a suspicion that I might be dreaming. It came into my mind, Do they mean the little boy? Just as I woke up I was thinking of Kenny and wondering, Was it seven years since the accident? (I hope it doesn't hurt you, Liza, that I mention this – also I know that Kenny was no longer little when the accident happened.) I woke up and thought that I must ask Ladner about this. I always know even before I am awake that Ladner's body is not beside me and that the sense of him I have, of his weight and heat and smell, are memories. But I still have the feeling – when I wake – that he is in the next room and I can call him and tell him my dream or whatever. Then I have to realize that isn't so, every morning, and I feel a chill. I feel a shrinking. I feel as if I had a couple of wooden planks lying across my chest, which doesn't incline me to get up. A common experience I'm having. But at the moment I'm not having it, just describing it, and in fact I am rather happy sitting here with my bottle of red wine."

This was a letter Bea Doud never sent and in fact never finished. In her big, neglected house in Carstairs, she had entered a period of musing and drinking, of what looked to everybody else like a slow decline, but to her seemed, after all, sadly pleasurable, like a convalescence.

Bea Doud had met Ladner when she was out for a Sunday drive in the country with Peter Parr. Peter Parr was a science teacher, also the Principal of the Carstairs High School, where Bea had for a while done some substitute teaching. She did not have a teacher's certificate, but she had an M.A. in English and things were more lax in those days. Also, she would be called upon to help with school excursions, herding a class to the Royal Ontario Museum or to Stratford for their annual dose of Shakespeare. Once she became interested in Peter Parr, she tried to keep clear of such involvements. She wished things to be seemly, for his sake. Peter Parr's wife was in a nursing home – she had multiple sclerosis, and he visited her faithfully. Everyone thought he was an admirable man, and most understood his need to have a steady girlfriend (a word Bea said she found appalling), but some perhaps thought that his choice was a pity. Bea had had what she herself referred to as a checkered career. But she settled down with Peter – his decency and good faith and good humor had brought her into an orderly life, and she thought that she enjoyed it.

When Bea spoke of having had a checkered career, she was taking a sarcastic or disparaging tone that did not reflect what she really felt about her life of love affairs. That life had started when she was married. Her husband was an English airman stationed near Walley during the Second World War. After the war she went to England with him, but they were soon divorced. She came home and did various things, such as keeping house for her stepmother, and getting her M.A. But love affairs were the main content of her life, and she knew that she was not being honest when she belittled them. They were sweet, they were sour; she was happy in them, she was miserable. She knew what it was to wait in a bar for a man who never showed up. To wait for letters, to cry in public, and on the other hand to be pestered by a man she no longer wanted. (She had been obliged to resign from the Light Opera Society because of a fool who directed baritone solos at her.) But still she felt the first signal of a love affair like the warmth of the sun on her skin, like music through a doorway, or the moment, as she had often said, when the black-and-white television commercial bursts into color. She did not think that her time was being wasted. She did not think it had been wasted.

She did think, she did admit, that she was vain. She liked tributes and attention. It irked her, for instance, when Peter Parr took her for a drive in the country, that he never did it for the sake of her company alone. He was a well-liked man and he liked many people, even people that he had just met. He and Bea would always end up dropping in on somebody, or talking for an hour with a former student now working at a gas station, or joining an expedition that had been hatched up with some people they had run into when they stopped at a country store for ice-cream cones. She had fallen in love with him because of his sad situation and his air of gallantry and loneliness and his shy, thin-lipped smile, but in fact he was compulsively sociable, the sort of person who could not pass a family volleyball game in somebody's front yard without wanting to leap out of the car and get into the action.

On a Sunday afternoon in May, a dazzling, freshly green day, he said to her that he wanted to drop in for a few minutes on a man named Ladner. (With Peter Parr, it was always a few minutes.) Bea thought that he had already met this man somewhere, since he called him by a single name and seemed to know a great deal about him. He said that Ladner had come out here from England soon after the war, that he had served in the Royal Air Force (yes, like her husband!), had been shot down and had received burns all down one side of his body. So he had decided to live like a hermit. He had turned his back on corrupt and warring and competitive society, he had bought up four hundred acres of unproductive land, mostly swamp and bush, in the northern part of the county, in Stratton Township, and he had created there a remarkable sort of nature preserve, with bridges and trails and streams dammed up to make ponds, and exhibits along the trails of lifelike birds and animals. For he made his living as a taxidermist, working mostly for museums. He did not charge people anything for walking along his trails and looking at the exhibits. He was a man who had been wounded and disillusioned in the worst way and had withdrawn from the world, yet gave all he could back to it in his attention to Nature.

Much of this was untrue or only partly true, as Bea discovered. Ladner was not at all a pacifist – he supported the Vietnam War and believed that nuclear weapons were a deterrent. He favored a competitive society. He had been burned only on the side of his face and neck, and that was from an exploding shell during the ground fighting (he was in the Army) near Caen. He had not left England immediately but had worked for years there, in a museum, until something happened – Bea never knew what – that soured him on the job and the country.

It was true about the property and what he had done with it. It was true that he was a taxidermist.

Bea and Peter had some trouble finding Ladner's house. It was just a basic A-frame in those days, hidden by the trees. They found the driveway at last and parked there and got out of the car. Bea was expecting to be introduced and taken on a tour and considerably bored for an hour or two, and perhaps to have to sit around drinking beer or tea while Peter Parr consolidated a friendship.

Ladner came around the house and confronted them. It was Bea's impression that he had a fierce dog with him. But this was not the case. Ladner did not own a dog. He was his own fierce dog.

Ladner's first words to them were "What do you want?"

Peter Parr said that he would come straight to the point. "I've heard so much about this wonderful place you've made here," he said. "And

I'll tell you right off the bat, I am an educator. I educate high-school kids, or try to. I try to give them a few ideas that will keep them from mucking up the world or blowing it up altogether when their time comes. All around them what do they see but horrible examples? Hardly one thing that is positive. And that's where I'm bold enough to approach you, sir. That's what I've come here to ask you to consider."

Field trips. Selected students. See the difference one individual can make. Respect for nature, cooperation with the environment, opportunity to see at first hand.

"Well, I am not an educator," said Ladner. "I do not give a fuck about your teenagers, and the last thing I want is a bunch of louts shambling around my property smoking cigarettes and leering like half-wits. I don't know where you got the impression that what I've done here I've done as a public service, because that is something in which I have zero interest. Sometimes I let people go through but they're the people I decide on."

"Well, I wonder just about us," said Peter Parr. "Just us, today – would you let us have a look?"

"Out of bounds today," said Ladner. "I'm working on the trail."

Back in the car, heading down the gravel road, Peter Parr said to Bea, "Well, I think that's broken the ice, don't you?"

This was not a joke. He did not make that sort of joke. Bea said something vaguely encouraging. But she realized – or had realized some minutes before, in Ladner's driveway – that she was on the wrong track with Peter Parr. She didn't want any more of his geniality, his good intentions, his puzzling and striving. All the things that had appealed to her and comforted her about him were now more or less dust and ashes. Now that she had seen him with Ladner.

She could have told herself otherwise, of course. But such was not her nature. Even after years of good behavior, it was not her nature.

She had a couple of friends then, to whom she wrote and actually sent letters that tried to investigate and explain this turn in her life. She wrote that she would hate to think she had gone after Ladner because he was rude and testy and slightly savage, with the splotch on the side of his face that shone like metal in the sunlight coming through the trees. She would hate to think so, because wasn't that the way in all the dreary romances – some brute gets the woman tingling and then it's goodbye to Mr. Fine-and-Decent?

No, she wrote, but what she did think – and she knew that this was very regressive and bad form – what she did think was that some women, women like herself, might be always on the lookout for an insanity that could contain them. For what was living with a man if it wasn't living inside his insanity? A man could have a very ordinary, a very unremarkable, insanity, such as his devotion to a ball team. But that might not be enough, not big enough – and an insanity that was not big enough simply made a woman mean and discontented. Peter Parr, for instance, displayed kindness and hopefulness to a fairly fanatical degree. But in the end, for me, Bea wrote, that was not a suitable insanity.

What did Ladner offer her, then, that she could live inside? She didn't mean just that she would be able to accept the importance of learning the habits of porcupines and writing fierce letters on the subject to journals that she, Bea, had never before heard of. She meant also that she would be able to live surrounded by implacability, by ready doses of indifference which at times might seem like scorn.

So she explained her condition, during the first half-year.

Several other women had thought themselves capable of the same thing. She found traces of them. A belt – size 26 – a jar of cocoa butter, fancy combs for the hair. He hadn't let any of them stay. Why them and not me? Bea asked him.

"None of them had any money," said Ladner.

A joke. *I am slit top to bottom with jokes.* (Now she wrote her letters only in her head.)

BUT DRIVING OUT to Ladner's place during the school week, a few days after she had first met him, what was her state? Lust and terror. She had to feel sorry for herself, in her silk underwear. Her teeth chattered. She pitied herself for being a victim of such wants. Which she had felt before – she would not pretend she hadn't. This was not yet so different from what she had felt before.

She found the place easily. She must have memorized the route well. She had thought up a story: She was lost. She was looking for a place up here that sold nursery shrubs. That would suit the time of year. But Ladner was out in front of his trees working on the road culvert, and he greeted her in such a matter-of-fact way, without surprise or displeasure, that it was not necessary to trot out this excuse.

"Just hang on until I get this job done," he said. "It'll take me about ten minutes."

For Bea there was nothing like this – nothing like watching a man work at some hard job, when he is forgetful of you and works well, in a way that is tidy and rhythmical, nothing like it to heat the blood. There was no waste about Ladner, no extra size or unnecessary energy and certainly no elaborate conversation. His gray hair was cut very short, in the style of his youth – the top of his head shone silver like the metallic-looking patch of skin.

Bea said that she agreed with him about the students. "I've done some substitute teaching and taken them on treks," she said. "There have been times when I felt like setting Dobermans on them and driving them into a cesspit.

"I hope you don't think I'm here to persuade you of anything," she said. "Nobody knows I'm here."

He took his time answering her. "I expect you'd like a tour?" he said when he was ready. "Would you? Would you like a tour of the place yourself?"

That was what he said and that was what he meant. A tour. Bea was wearing the wrong shoes – at that time in her life she did not own any shoes that would have been right. He did not slow down for her or help her in any way to cross a creek or climb a bank. He never held out a hand, or suggested that they might sit and rest on any appropriate log or rock or slope.

He led her first on a boardwalk across a marsh to a pond, where some Canada geese had settled and a pair of swans were circling each other, their bodies serene but their necks mettlesome, their beaks letting out bitter squawks. "Are they mates?" said Bea.

"Evidently."

Not far from these live birds was a glass-fronted case containing a stuffed golden eagle with its wings spread, a gray owl, and a snow owl. The case was an old gutted freezer, with a window set in its side and a camouflage of gray and green swirls of paint.

"Ingenious," said Bea.

Ladner said, "I use what I can get."

He showed her the beaver meadow, the pointed stumps of the trees the beavers had chewed down, their heaped, untidy constructions, the two richly furred beavers in their case. Then in turn she looked at a red fox, a golden mink, a white ferret, a dainty family of skunks, a porcupine, and a fisher, which Ladner told her was intrepid enough to kill porcupines. Stuffed and lifelike raccoons clung to a tree trunk, a wolf stood poised to howl, and a black bear had just managed to lift its big soft head, its melancholy face. Ladner said that was a small bear. He couldn't afford to keep the big ones, he said – they brought too good a price.

Many birds as well. Wild turkeys, a pair of ruffed grouse, a pheasant with a bright-red ring around its eye. Signs told their habitat, their Latin names, food preferences, and styles of behavior. Some of the trees were labelled too. Tight, accurate, complicated information. Other signs presented quotations.

NATURE DOES NOTHING USELESSLY.   – ARISTOTLE

NATURE NEVER DECEIVES US; IT IS ALWAYS WE WHO DECEIVE
OURSELVES.   – ROUSSEAU

When Bea stopped to read these, it seemed to her that Ladner was impatient, that he scowled a little. She no longer made comments on anything she saw.

She couldn't keep track of their direction or get any idea of the layout of the property. Did they cross different streams, or the same stream several times? The woods might stretch for miles, or only to the top of a near hill. The leaves were new and couldn't keep out the sun. Trilliums abounded. Ladner lifted a mayapple leaf to show her the hidden flower. Fat leaves, ferns just uncurling, yellow skunk cabbage bursting out of bogholes, all the sap and sunshine around, and the treacherous tree rot underfoot, and then they were in an old apple orchard, enclosed by woods, and he directed her to look for mushrooms – morels. He himself found five, which he did not offer to share. She confused them with last year's rotted apples.

A steep hill rose up in front of them, cluttered with little barbed hawthorn trees in bloom. "The kids call this Fox Hill," he said. "There's a den up here."

Bea stood still. "You have children?"

He laughed. "Not to my knowledge. I mean the kids from across the road. Mind the branches, they have thorns."

By this time lust was lost to her altogether, though the smell of the hawthorn blossoms seemed to her an intimate one, musty or yeasty. She had long since stopped fixing her eyes on a spot between his shoulder blades and willing him to turn around and embrace her. It occurred to her that this tour, so strenuous physically and mentally, might be a joke on her, a punishment for being, after all, such a tiresome vamp and fraud. So she roused her pride and acted as if it were exactly what she had come for. She questioned, she took an interest, she showed no fatigue. As later on – but not on this day – she would learn to match him with some of the same pride in the hard-hearted energy of sex.

She did not expect him to ask her into the house. But he said, "Would you like a cup of tea? I can make you a cup of tea," and they went inside. A smell of hides greeted her, of Borax soap, wood shavings, turpentine. Skins lay in piles, folded flesh-side out. Heads of animals, with empty eyeholes and mouth holes, were set on stands. What she thought at first was the skinned body of a deer turned out to be only a wire armature with bundles of what looked like glued straw tied to it. He told her the body would be built up with papier-mâché.

There were books in the house – a small section of books on taxidermy, the others mostly in sets. The History of the Second World War. The History of Science. The History of Philosophy. The History of Civilization. The Peninsular War. The Peloponnesian Wars. The French and Indian Wars. Bea thought of his long evenings in the winter – his orderly solitude, his systematic reading and barren contentment.

He seemed a little nervous, getting the tea. He checked the cups for dust. He forgot that he had already taken the milk out of the refrigerator, and he forgot that she had already said she did not take sugar. When she tasted the tea, he watched her, asked her if it was all right. Was it too strong, would she like a little hot water? Bea reassured him and thanked him for the tour and mentioned things about it that she had particularly appreciated. Here is this man, she was thinking, not so strange a man after all, nothing so very mysterious about him, maybe nothing even so very interesting. The layers of information. The French and Indian Wars.

She asked for a bit more milk in her tea. She wanted to drink it down faster and be on her way.

He said that she must drop in again if she was ever out in this part of the country with nothing particular to do. "And feel the need of a little exercise," he said. "There is always something to see, whatever the time of year." He spoke of the winter birds and the tracks on the snow and asked if she had skis. She saw that he did not want her to go. They stood in the open doorway and he told her about skiing in Norway, about the tramcars with ski racks on top of them and the mountains at the edge of town.

She said that she had never been to Norway but she was sure she would like it.

She looked back on this moment as their real beginning. They both seemed uneasy and subdued, not reluctant so much as troubled, even sorry for each other. She asked him later if he had felt anything important at the time, and he said yes — he had realized that she was a person he could live with. She asked him if he couldn't say wanted to live with, and he said yes, he could say that. He could say it, but he didn't.

She had many jobs to learn which had to do with the upkeep of this place and also with the art and skill of taxidermy. She would learn, for instance, how to color lips and eyelids and the ends of noses with a clever mixture of oil paint and linseed and turpentine. Other things she had to learn concerned what he would say and wouldn't say. It seemed that she had to be cured of all her froth and vanity and all her old notions of love.

One night I got into his bed and he did not take his eyes from his book or move or speak a word to me even when I crawled out and returned to my own bed, where I fell asleep almost at once because I think I could not bear the shame of being awake.

In the morning he got into my bed and all went as usual.

I come up against blocks of solid darkness.

She learned, she changed. Age was a help to her. Drink also.

And when he got used to her, or felt safe from her, his feelings took a turn for the better. He talked to her readily about what he was interested in and took a kinder comfort from her body.

On the night before the operation they lay side by side on the strange bed, with all available bare skin touching – legs, arms, haunches.

II

LIZA TOLD WARREN that a woman named Bea Doud had phoned from Toronto and asked if they – that is, Warren and Liza – could go out and check on the house in the country, where Bea and her husband lived. They wanted to make sure that the water had been turned off. Bea and Ladner (not actually her husband, said Liza) were in Toronto waiting for Ladner to have an operation. A heart bypass. "Because the pipes might burst," said Liza. This was on a Sunday night in February during the worst of that winter's storms.

"You know who they are," said Liza. "Yes, you do. Remember that couple I introduced you to? One day last fall on the square outside of Radio Shack? He had a scar on his cheek and she had long hair, half black and half gray. I told you he was a taxidermist, and you said, 'What's that?'"

Now Warren remembered. An old – but not too old – couple in flannel shirts and baggy pants. His scar and English accent, her weird hair and rush of friendliness. A taxidermist stuffs dead animals. That is, animal skins. Also dead birds and fish.

He had asked Liza, "What happened to the guy's face?" and she had said, "W. W. Two."

"I know where the key is – that's why she called me," Liza said. "This is up in Stratton Township. Where I used to live."

"Did they go to your same church or something?" Warren said.

"Bea and *Ladner*? Let's not be funny. They just lived across the road.

"It was her gave me some money," Liza continued, as if it was something he ought to know, "to go to college. I never asked her. She just phones up out of the blue and says she wants to. So I think, Okay, she's got lots."

WHEN SHE WAS little, Liza had lived in Stratton Township with her father and her brother Kenny, on a farm. Her father wasn't a farmer. He just rented the house. He worked as a roofer. Her mother was already dead. By the time Liza was ready for high school – Kenny was a year younger and two grades behind her – her father had moved them to Carstairs. He met a woman there who owned a trailer home, and later on he married her. Later still, he moved with her to Chatham. Liza wasn't sure where they were now – Chatham or Wallaceburg or Sarnia. By the time they moved, Kenny was dead – he had been killed when he was fifteen, in one of the big teenage car crashes that seemed to happen every spring, involving drunk, often unlicensed drivers, temporarily stolen cars, fresh gravel on the country roads, crazy speeds. Liza finished high school and went to college in Guelph for one year. She didn't like college, didn't like the people there. By that time she had become a Christian.

That was how Warren met her. His family belonged to the Fellowship of the Saviour Bible Chapel, in Walley. He had been going to the Bible Chapel all his life. Liza started going there after she moved to Walley and got a job in the government liquor store. She still worked there, though she worried about it and sometimes thought that she should quit. She never drank alcohol now, she never even ate sugar. She didn't want Warren eating a Danish on his break, so she packed him oat muffins that she made at home. She did the laundry every Wednesday night and counted the strokes when she brushed her teeth and got up early in the morning to do knee bends and read Bible verses.

337

She thought she should quit, but they needed the money. The small-engines shop where Warren used to work had closed down, and he was retraining so that he could sell computers. They had been married a year.

IN THE MORNING, the weather was clear, and they set off on the snowmobile shortly before noon. Monday was Liza's day off. The plows were working on the highway, but the back roads were still buried in snow. Snowmobiles had been roaring through the town streets since before dawn and had left their tracks across the inland fields and on the frozen river.

Liza told Warren to follow the river track as far as Highway 86, then head northeast across the fields so as to half-circle the swamp. All over the river there were animal tracks in straight lines and loops and circles. The only ones that Warren knew for sure were dog tracks. The river with its three feet of ice and level covering of snow made a wonderful road. The storm had come from the west, as storms usually did in that country, and the trees along the eastern bank were all plastered with snow, clotted with it, their branches spread out like wicker snow baskets. On the western bank, drifts curled like waves stopped, like huge lappings of cream. It was exciting to be out in this, with all the other snowmobiles carving the trails and assaulting the day with such roars and swirls of noise.

The swamp was black from a distance, a long smudge on the northern horizon. But close up, it too was choked with snow. Black trunks against the snow flashed by in a repetition that was faintly sickening. Liza directed Warren with light blows of her hand on his leg to a back road full as a bed, and finally hit him hard to stop him. The change of noise for silence and speed for stillness made it seem as if they had dropped out of streaming clouds into something solid. They were stuck in the solid middle of the winter day.

On one side of the road was a broken-down barn with old gray hay bulging out of it. "Where we used to live," said Liza. "No, I'm kidding. Actually, there was a house. It's gone now."

On the other side of the road was a sign, "Lesser Dismal," with trees behind it, and an extended A-frame house painted a light gray. Liza said that there was a swamp somewhere in the United States called Great Dismal Swamp, and that was what the name referred to. A joke.

"I never heard of it," said Warren.

Other signs said "No Trespassing," "No Hunting," "No Snow-mobiling," "Keep Out."

The key to the back door was in an odd place. It was in a plastic bag inside a hole in a tree. There were several old bent trees – fruit trees, probably – close to the back steps. The hole in the tree had tar around it – Liza said that was to keep out squirrels. There was tar around other holes in other trees, so the hole for the key didn't in any way stand out. "How did you find it, then?" Liza pointed out a profile – easy to see, when you looked closely – emphasized by a knife following cracks in the bark. A long nose, a down-slanting eye and mouth, and a big drop – that was the tarred hole – right at the end of the nose.

"Pretty funny?" said Liza, stuffing the plastic bag in her pocket and turning the key in the back door. "Don't stand there," she said. "Come on in. Jeepers, it's cold as the grave in here." She was always very con-scientious about changing the exclamation "Jesus" to "Jeepers" and "Hell" to "help," as they were supposed to do in the Fellowship.

She went around twirling thermostats to get the baseboard heating going.

Warren said, "We aren't going to hang around here, are we?"

"Hang around till we get warmed up," said Liza.

Warren was trying the kitchen taps. Nothing came out. "Water's off," he said. "It's okay."

Liza had gone into the front room. "What?" she called. "What's okay?"

"The water. It's turned off."

"Oh, is it? Good."

Warren stopped in the front-room doorway. "Shouldn't we ought to take our boots off?" he said. "Like, if we're going to walk around?"

"Why?" said Liza, stomping on the rug. "What's the matter with good clean snow?"

Warren was not a person who noticed much about a room and what was in it, but he did see that this room had some things that were usual and some that were not. It had rugs and chairs and a television and a sofa and books and a big desk. But it also had shelves of stuffed and mounted birds, some quite tiny and bright, and some large and suitable for shooting. Also a sleek brown animal – a weasel? – and a beaver, which he knew by its paddle tail.

Liza was opening the drawers of the desk and rummaging in the paper she found there. He thought that she must be looking for something the woman had told her to get. Then she started pulling the drawers all the way out and dumping them and their contents on the floor. She made a funny noise – an admiring cluck of her tongue, as if the drawers had done this on their own.

"Christ!" he said. (Because he had been in the Fellowship all his life, he was not nearly so careful as Liza about his language.) "Liza? What do you think you're doing?"

"Nothing that is remotely any of your business," said Liza. But she spoke cheerfully, even kindly. "Why don't you relax and watch TV or something?"

She was picking up the mounted birds and animals and throwing them down one by one, adding them to the mess she was making on the floor. "He uses balsa wood," she said. "Nice and light."

Warren did go and turn on the television. It was a black-and-white set, and most of its channels showed nothing but snow or ripples. The only thing he could get clear was a scene from the old series with the blond girl in the harem outfit – she was a witch – and the J. R. Ewing actor when he was so young he hadn't yet become J. R.

"Look at this," he said. "Like going back in time."

Liza didn't look. He sat down on a hassock with his back to her. He was trying to be like a grownup who won't watch. Ignore her and she'll quit. Nevertheless he could hear behind him the ripping of books and paper. Books were being scooped off the shelves, torn apart, tossed on the floor. He heard her go out to the kitchen and yank out drawers, slam cupboard doors, smash dishes. She came back to the front room after a while, and a white dust began to fill the air. She must have dumped out flour. She was coughing.

Warren had to cough too, but he did not turn around. Soon he heard stuff being poured out of bottles – thin, splashing liquid and thick glug-glug-glugs. He could smell vinegar and maple syrup and whisky. That was what she was pouring over the flour and the books and the rugs and the feathers and fur of the bird and animal bodies. Something shattered against the stove. He bet it was the whisky bottle.

"Bull's-eye!" said Liza.

Warren wouldn't turn. His whole body felt as if it was humming, with the effort to be still and make this be over.

Once, he and Liza had gone to a Christian rock concert and dance in St. Thomas. There was a lot of controversy about Christian rock in the Fellowship – about whether there could even be such a thing. Liza was bothered by this question. Warren wasn't. He had gone a few times to rock concerts and dances that didn't even call themselves Christian. But when they started to dance, it was Liza who slid under, right away, it was Liza who caught the eye – the vigilant, unhappy eye – of the Youth Leader, who was grinning and clapping uncertainly on the side-lines. Warren had never seen Liza dance, and the crazy, slithery spirit that possessed her amazed him. He felt proud rather than worried, but he knew that whatever he felt did not make the least difference. There was Liza, dancing, and the only thing he could do was wait it out while she tore her way through the music, supplicated and curled around it, kicked loose, and blinded herself to everything around her.

That's what she's got in her, he felt like saying to them all. He thought that he had known it. He had known something the first time he had seen her at the Fellowship. It was summer and she was wearing the little summer straw hat and the dress with sleeves that all the Fellowship girls had to wear, but her skin was too golden and her body too slim for a Fellowship girl's. Not that she looked like a girl in a magazine, a model or a show-off. Not Liza, with her high, rounded forehead and deep-set brown eyes, her expression that was both childish and fierce. She looked unique, and she was. She was a girl who wouldn't say, "Jesus!" but who would, in moments of down-right contentment and meditative laziness, say, "Well, *fuck!*"

She said she had been wild before becoming a Christian. "Even when I was a kid," she said.

"Wild in what way?" he had asked her. "Like, with guys?"

She gave him a look, as if to say, Don't be dumb.

Warren felt a trickle now, down one side of his scalp. She had sneaked up behind him. He put a hand to his head and it came away green and sticky and smelling of peppermint.

"Have a sip," she said, handing him a bottle. He took a gulp, and the strong mint drink nearly strangled him. Liza took back the bottle and threw it against the big front window. It didn't go through the window but it cracked the glass. The bottle hadn't broken – it fell to the floor, and a pool of beautiful liquid streamed out from it. Dark-green blood. The window glass had filled with thousands of radiating cracks, and turned as white as a halo. Warren was standing up, gasping from the liquor. Waves of heat were rising through his body. Liza stepped delicately among the torn, spattered books and broken glass, the smeared, stomped birds, the pools of whisky and maple syrup and the sticks of charred wood dragged from the stove to make black tracks on the rugs, the ashes and gummed flour and feathers. She stepped delicately, even in her snowmobile boots, admiring what she'd done, what she'd managed so far.

Warren picked up the hassock he had been sitting on and flung it at the sofa. It toppled off; it didn't do any damage, but the action had put him in the picture. This was not the first time he'd been involved in trashing a house. Long ago, when he was nine or ten years old, he and a friend had got into a house on their way home from school. It was his friend's aunt who lived in this house. She wasn't home – she worked in a jewelry store. She lived by herself. Warren and his friend broke in because they were hungry. They made themselves soda-cracker-and-jam sandwiches and drank some ginger ale. But then something took over. They dumped a bottle of ketchup on the tablecloth and dipped their fingers in, and wrote on the wallpaper, "*Beware! Blood!*" They broke plates and threw some food around.

They were strangely lucky. Nobody had seen them getting into the house and nobody saw them leaving. The aunt herself put the blame on some teenagers whom she had recently ordered out of the store.

Recalling this, Warren went to the kitchen looking for a bottle of ketchup. There didn't seem to be any, but he found and opened a can of tomato sauce. It was thinner than ketchup and didn't work as well, but he tried to write with it on the wooden kitchen wall. "*Beware! This is your blood!*"

The sauce soaked into or ran down the boards. Liza came up close to read the words before they blotted themselves out. She laughed. Somewhere in the rubble she found a Magic Marker. She climbed up on a chair and wrote above the fake blood, "*The Wages of Sin is Death.*"

"I should have got out more stuff," she said. "Where he works is full of paint and glue and all kinds of crap. In that side room."

Warren said, "Want me to get some?"

"Not really," she said. She sank down on the sofa – one of the few places in the front room where you could still sit down. "Liza Minnelli," she said peacefully. "Liza Minnelli, stick it in your belly!"

Was that something kids at school sang at her? Or something she made up for herself?

Warren sat down beside her. "So what did they do?" he said. "What did they do that made you so mad?"

"Who's mad?" said Liza, and hauled herself up and went to the kitchen. Warren followed, and saw that she was punching out a number on the phone. She had to wait a little. Then she said, "Bea?" in a soft, hurt, hesitant voice. "Oh, Bea!" She waved at Warren to turn off the television.

He heard her saying, "The window by the kitchen door . . . I think so. Even maple syrup, you wouldn't believe it. . . . Oh, and the beautiful big front window, they threw something at that, and they got sticks out of the stove and the ashes and those birds that were sitting around and the big beaver. I can't tell you what it looks like. . . ."

He came back into the kitchen, and she made a face at him, raising her eyebrows and setting her lips blubbering as she listened to the voice on the other end of the phone. Then she went on describing things, commiserating, making her voice quiver with misery and indignation. Warren didn't like watching her. He went around looking for their helmets.

When she had hung up the phone, she came and got him. "It was her," she said. "I already told you what she did to me. She sent me to college!" That started them both laughing.

But Warren was looking at a bird in the mess on the floor. Its soggy feathers, its head hanging loose, showing one bitter red eye. "It's weird doing that for a living," he said. "Always having dead stuff around."

"They're weird," Liza said.

Warren said, "Do you care if he croaks?"

Liza made croaking noises to stop him being thoughtful. Then she touched her teeth, her pointed tongue to his neck.

III

BEA ASKED LIZA and Kenny a lot of questions. She asked them what their favorite TV shows and colors and ice-cream flavors were, and what kind of animals they would be if they could turn into animals, and what was the earliest thing they remembered. "Eating boogers," said Kenny. He did not mean to be funny.

Ladner and Liza and Bea all laughed – Liza the loudest. Then Bea said, "You know, that's one of the earliest things I can remember myself!"

She's lying, Liza thought. Lying for Kenny's sake, and he doesn't even know it.

"This is Miss Doud," Ladner had told them. "Try to be decent to her."

"Miss Doud," said Bea, as if she had swallowed something surprising. "Bea. Bzzz. My name is Bea."

"Who is that?" Kenny said to Liza, when Bea and Ladner were walking ahead of them. "Is she going to live with him?"

"It's his girlfriend," Liza said. "They are probably going to get married." By the time Bea had been at Ladner's place for a week, Liza could not stand the thought of her ever going away.

THE FIRST TIME that Liza and Kenny had ever been on Ladner's property, they had sneaked in under a fence, as all the signs and their own father had warned them not to do. When they had got so far into the trees that Liza was not sure of the way out, they heard a sharp whistle.

near the other bank and came up gasping, only a yard or
Ladner.
ght in the reeds," she said. "I could have drowned."
luck," said Ladner. He made a pretend grab at her, to get
the legs. At the same time he made a pious, shocked face,
on in his head was having a fit at what his hand might do.
nded not to notice. "Where's Bea?" she said.
oked at the opposite bank. "Maybe up to the house," he
see her go." He was quite ordinary again, a serious work-
fed up with all their foolishness. Ladner could do that. He
from one person to another and make it your fault if you

in a straight line as hard as she could across the pond. She
way out and heavily climbed the bank. She passed the owls
e staring from behind glass. The "Nature does nothing use-

't see Bea anywhere. Not ahead on the boardwalk over the
in the open space under the pine trees. Liza took the path
door of the house. In the middle of the path was a beech
d to go around, and there were initials carved in the smooth
"L" for Ladner, another for Liza, a "K" for Kenny. A foot or
ere the letters "P.D.P." When Liza had first shown Bea the
nny had banged his fist against P.D.P. "Pull down pants!" he
pping up and down. Ladner gave him a serious pretend-rap
d. "Proceed down path," he said, and pointed out the arrow
n the bark, curving around the trunk. "Pay no attention to
ninded juveniles," he said to Bea.
uld not bring herself to knock on the door. She was full of
oreboding. It seemed to her that Bea would have to go away.
d she stay after such an insult – how could she put up with
m? Bea did not understand about Ladner. And how could she?
lf couldn't have described to anybody what he was like. In the
she had with him, what was terrible was always funny, badness
d up with silliness, you always had to join in with dopey faces
s and pretending he was a cartoon monster. You couldn't get

Ladner called them: "You two!" He came out like a murderer on
television, with a little axe, from behind a tree. "Can you two read?"

They were about six and seven at this time. Liza said, "Yes."

"So did you read my signs?"

Kenny said faintly, "A fox run in here." When they were driving with
their father, one time, they had seen a red fox run across the road and
disappear into the trees here. Their father had said, "Bugger's living in
Ladner's bush."

Foxes do not live in the bush, Ladner told them. He took them to see
where the fox did live. A den, he called it. There was a pile of sand beside
a hole on a hillside covered with dry, tough grass and little white flowers.
"Pretty soon those are going to turn into strawberries," Ladner said.

"What will?" said Liza.

"You are a pair of dumb kids," Ladner said. "What do you do all day –
watch TV?"

That was the beginning of their spending Saturdays – and, when
summer came, nearly all days – with Ladner. Their father said it was all
right, if Ladner was fool enough to put up with them. "But you better
not cross him or he'll skin you alive," their father said. "Like he does
with his other stuff. You know that?"

They knew what Ladner did. He had let them watch. They had seen
him clean out a squirrel's skull and fix a bird's feathers to best advantage with delicate wire and pins. Once he was sure that they would be
careful enough, he let them fit the glass eyes in place. They had watched
him skin animals, scrape the skins and salt them, and set them to dry
inside out before he sent them to the tanner's. Tanning put a poison in
them so they would never crack, and the fur would never fall out.

Ladner fitted the skin around a body in which nothing was real. A
bird's body could be all of one piece, carved of wood, but an animal's
larger body was a wonderful construction of wires and burlap and glue
and mushed-up paper and clay.

Liza and Kenny had picked up skinned bodies that were tough as
rope. They had touched guts that looked like plastic tubing. They had
squished eyeballs to jelly. They told their father about that. "But we won't
get any diseases," Liza said. "We wash our hands in Borax soap."

Not all the information they had was about dead things: What does the red-winged blackbird say? *Compan-ee!* What does the Jenny wren say? *Pleasa-pleasa-please, can I have a piece of cheese?*

"Oh, can it!" said their father.

Soon they knew much more. At least Liza did. She knew birds, trees, mushrooms, fossils, the solar system. She knew where certain rocks came from and that the swelling on a goldenrod stem contains a little white worm that can live nowhere else in the world.

She knew not to talk so much about all she knew.

BEA WAS STANDING on the bank of the pond, in her Japanese kimono. Liza was already swimming. She called to Bea, "Come on in, come in!" Ladner was working on the far side of the pond, cutting reeds and clearing the weeds that clogged the water. Kenny was supposed to be helping him. Liza thought, Like a family.

Bea dropped her kimono and stood in her yellow, silky bathing suit. She was a small woman with dark hair, lightly grayed, falling heavily around her shoulders. Her eyebrows were thick and dark and their arched shape, like the sweet sulky shape of her mouth, entreated kindness and consolation. The sun had covered her with dim freckles, and she was just a bit too soft all over. When she lowered her chin, little pouches collected along her jaw and under her eyes. She was prey to little pouches and sags, dents and ripples in the skin or flesh, sunbursts of tiny purplish veins, faint discolorations in the hollows. And it was in fact this collection of flaws, this shadowy damage, that Liza especially loved. Also she loved the dampness that was often to be seen in Bea's eyes, the tremor and teasing and playful pleading in Bea's voice, its huskiness and artificiality. Bea was not measured or judged by Liza in the way that other people were. But this did not mean that Liza's love for Bea was easy or restful — her love was one of expectation, but she did not know what it was that she expected.

Now Bea entered the pond. She did this in stages. A decision, a short run, a pause. Knee-high in the water, she hugged herself and squealed.

"It's not cold," said Liza.

"No, no, I love it!" Bea said

appreciation, to a spot where the

around to face Liza, who had swu

tion of splashing.

"Oh, no, you don't!" Bea cried

pass her hands through the water, f

flower petals. Ineffectually, she spla

Liza turned over and floated on

water toward Bea's face. Bea kept

water Liza kicked, and as she did so

chant. *Oh-woo, oh-woo, oh-woo.* Som

Even though she was lying on h

could see that Ladner had stopped

deep water on the other side of the

watching Bea. Then he too started ju

His body was stiff but he turned his h

ming or patting the water with flutte

carried away with admiration for him

He was imitating Bea. He was do

sillier, uglier way. He was most intentio

of her. See how vain she is, said Ladn

fake. Pretending not to be afraid of t

happy, pretending not to know how w

This was thrilling and shocking. Liz

need to laugh. Part of her wanted to ma

before the damage was done, and part of

the damage Ladner could do, the rippin

Kenny whooped out loud. He had n

Bea had already seen the change in

Kenny. She turned to see what was behin

into the water again, he was pulling up

Liza at once kicked up a distracting sto

to this, she swam out into the deep part

Deep, deep, to where it's dark, where the ca

down there as long as she could. She swa

in the weeds

so away from

"I got cau

"No such

her between

as if the pers

Liza prete

Ladner lo

said. "I didn'

man, slightly

could switch

remembered

Liza swar

splashed her

and the eag

lessly" sign.

She didn

marsh. Not

to the back

tree you ha

bark. One

so below

initials, Ke

shouted, he

on the hea

scratched

the dirty-

Liza co

guilt and

How cou

any of the

Liza herse

secret life

was mixe

and voic

out of it, or even want to, any more than you could stop an invasion of pins and needles.

Liza went around the house and out of the shade of the trees. Barefoot, she crossed the hot gravel road. There was her own house sitting in the middle of a cornfield at the end of a short lane. It was a wooden house with the top half painted white and the bottom half a glaring pink, like lipstick. That had been Liza's father's idea. Maybe he thought it would perk the place up. Maybe he thought pink would make it look as if it had a woman inside it.

There is a mess in the kitchen – spilled cereal on the floor, puddles of milk souring on the counter. A pile of clothes from the Laundromat overflowing the corner armchair, and the dishcloth – Liza knows this without looking – all wadded up with the garbage in the sink. It is her job to clean all this up, and she had better do it before her father gets home.

She doesn't worry about it yet. She goes upstairs where it is baking hot under the sloping roof and gets out her little bag of precious things. She keeps this bag stuffed in the toe of an old rubber boot that is too small for her. Nobody knows about it. Certainly not Kenny.

In the bag there is a Barbie-doll evening dress, stolen from a girl Liza used to play with (Liza doesn't much like the dress anymore, but it has an importance because it was stolen), a blue snap-shut case with her mother's glasses inside, a painted wooden egg that was her prize for an Easter picture-drawing contest in Grade 2 (with a smaller egg inside it and a still smaller egg inside that). And the one rhinestone earring that she found on the road. For a long time she believed the rhinestones to be diamonds. The design of the earring is complicated and graceful, with teardrop rhinestones dangling from loops and scallops of smaller stones, and when hung from Liza's ear it almost brushes her shoulders.

She is wearing only her bathing suit, so she has to carry the earring curled up in her palm, a blazing knot. Her head feels swollen with the heat, with leaning over her secret bag, with her resolution. She thinks with longing of the shade under Ladner's trees, as if that were a black pond.

There is not one tree anywhere near this house, and the only bush is a lilac with curly, brown-edged leaves, by the back steps. Around the house nothing but corn, and at a distance the leaning old barn that Liza and

Kenny are forbidden to go into, because it might collapse at any time. No divisions over here, no secret places – everything is bare and simple.

But when you cross the road – as Liza is doing now, trotting on the gravel – when you cross into Ladner's territory, it's like coming into a world of different and distinct countries. There is the marsh country, which is deep and jungly, full of botflies and jewelweed and skunk cabbage. A sense there of tropical threats and complications. Then the pine plantation, solemn as a church, with its high boughs and needled carpet, inducing whispering. And the dark rooms under the down-swept branches of the cedars – entirely shaded and secret rooms with a bare earth floor. In different places the sun falls differently and in some places not at all. In some places the air is thick and private, and in other places you feel an energetic breeze. Smells are harsh or enticing. Certain walks impose decorum and certain stones are set a jump apart so that they call out for craziness. Here are the scenes of serious instruction where Ladner taught them how to tell a hickory tree from a butternut and a star from a planet, and places also where they have run and hollered and hung from branches and performed all sorts of rash stunts. And places where Liza thinks there is a bruise on the ground, a tickling and shame in the grass.

P.D.P.

Squeegey-boy

Rub-a-dub-dub.

When Ladner grabbed Liza and squashed himself against her, she had a sense of danger deep inside him, a mechanical sputtering, as if he would exhaust himself in one jab of light, and nothing would be left of him but black smoke and burnt smells and frazzled wires. Instead, he collapsed heavily, like the pelt of an animal flung loose from its flesh and bones. He lay so heavy and useless that Liza and even Kenny felt for a moment that it was a transgression to look to him. He had to pull his voice out of his groaning innards, to tell them they were bad.

He clucked his tongue faintly and his eyes shone out of ambush, hard and round as the animals' glass eyes.

Bad-bad-bad.

"The loveliest thing," Bea said. "Liza, tell me – was this your mother's?"

Liza said yes. She could see now that this gift of a single earring might be seen as childish and pathetic – perhaps intentionally pathetic. Even keeping it as a treasure could seem stupid. But if it was her mother's, that would be understandable, and it would be a gift of some importance. "You could put it on a chain," she said. "If you put it on a chain you could wear it around your neck."

"But I was just thinking that!" Bea said. "I was just thinking it would look lovely on a chain. A silver chain – don't you think? Oh, Liza, I am just so proud you gave it to me!"

"You could wear it in your nose," said Ladner. But he said this without any sharpness. He was peaceable now – played out, peaceable. He spoke of Bea's nose as if it might be a pleasant thing to contemplate.

Ladner and Bea were sitting under the plum trees right behind the house. They sat in the wicker chairs that Bea had brought out from town. She had not brought much – just enough to make islands here and there among Ladner's skins and instruments. These chairs, some cups, a cushion. The wineglasses they were drinking out of now.

Bea had changed into a dark-blue dress of very thin and soft material. It hung long and loose from her shoulders. She trickled the rhinestones through her fingers, she let them fall and twinkle in the folds of her blue dress. She had forgiven Ladner, after all, or made a bargain not to remember.

Bea could spread safety, if she wanted to. Surely she could. All that is needed is for her to turn herself into a different sort of woman, a hard-and-fast, draw-the-line sort, clean-sweeping, energetic, and intolerant. *None of that. Not allowed. Be good.* The woman who could rescue them – who could make them all, keep them all, good.

What Bea has been sent to do, she doesn't see.

Only Liza sees.

IV

LIZA LOCKED THE door as you had to, from the outside. She put the key in the plastic bag and the bag in the hole in the tree. She moved towards the snowmobile, and when Warren didn't do the same she said, "What's the matter with you?"

Warren said, "What about the window by the back door?"

Liza breathed out noisily. "Ooh, I'm an idiot!" she said. "I'm an idiot ten times over!"

Warren went back to the window and kicked at the bottom pane. Then he got a stick of firewood from the pile by the tin shed and was able to smash the glass out. "Big enough so a kid could get in," he said.

"How could I be so stupid?" Liza said. "You saved my life."

"Our life," Warren said.

The tin shed wasn't locked. Inside it he found some cardboard boxes, bits of lumber, simple tools. He tore off a piece of cardboard of a suitable size. He took great satisfaction in nailing it over the pane that he had just smashed out. "Otherwise animals could get in," he said to Liza.

When he was all finished with this job, he found that Liza had walked down into the snow between the trees. He went after her.

"I was wondering if the bear was still in there," she said.

He was going to say that he didn't think bears came this far south, but she didn't give him the time. "Can you tell what the trees are by their bark?" she said.

Warren said he couldn't even tell from their leaves. "Well, maples," he said. "Maples and pines."

"Cedar," said Liza. "You've got to know cedar. There's a cedar. There's a wild cherry. Down there's birch. The white ones. And that one with the bark like gray skin? That's a beech. See, it had letters carved on it, but they've spread out, they just look like any old blotches now."

Warren wasn't interested. He only wanted to get home. It wasn't much after three o'clock, but you could feel the darkness collecting, rising among the trees, like cold smoke coming off the snow.

HATESHIP, FRIENDSHIP, COURTSHIP, LOVESHIP, MARRIAGE

YEARS AGO, before the trains stopped running on so many of the branch lines, a woman with a high, freckled forehead and a frizz of reddish hair came into the railway station and inquired about shipping furniture.

The station agent often tried a little teasing with women, especially the plain ones who seemed to appreciate it.

"Furniture?" he said, as if nobody had ever had such an idea before. "Well. Now. What kind of furniture are we talking about?"

A dining-room table and six chairs. A full bedroom suite, a sofa, a coffee table, end tables, a floor lamp. Also a china cabinet and a buffet.

"Whoa there. You mean a houseful."

"It shouldn't count as that much," she said. "There's no kitchen things and only enough for one bedroom."

Her teeth were crowded to the front of her mouth as if they were ready for an argument.

"You'll be needing the truck," he said.

"No. I want to send it on the train. It's going out west, to Saskatchewan."

She spoke to him in a loud voice as if he was deaf or stupid, and there was something wrong with the way she pronounced her words. An accent. He thought of Dutch – the Dutch were moving in around here – but she didn't have the heft of the Dutch women or the nice pink skin or the fair hair. She might have been under forty, but what did it matter? No beauty queen, ever.

He turned all business.

"First you'll need the truck to get it to here from wherever you got it. And we better see if it's a place in Saskatchewan where the train goes through. Otherways you'd have to arrange to get it picked up, say, in Regina."

"It's Gdynia," she said. "The train goes through."

He took down a greasy-covered directory that was hanging from a nail and asked how she would spell that. She helped herself to the pencil that was also on a string and wrote on a piece of paper from her purse: GDYNIA.

"What kind of nationality would that be?"

She said she didn't know.

He took back the pencil to follow from line to line.

"A lot of places out there it's all Czechs or Hungarians or Ukrainians," he said. It came to him as he said this that she might be one of those. But so what, he was only stating a fact.

"Here it is, all right, it's on the line."

"Yes," she said. "I want to ship it Friday – can you do that?"

"We can ship it, but I can't promise what day it'll get there," he said. "It all depends on the priorities. Somebody going to be on the lookout for it when it comes in?"

"Yes."

"It's a mixed train Friday, two-eighteen p.m. Truck picks it up Friday morning. You live here in town?"

She nodded, writing down the address. 106 Exhibition Road.

It was only recently that the houses in town had been numbered, and he couldn't picture the place, though he knew where Exhibition Road was. If she'd said the name McCauley at that time he might have taken more of an interest, and things might have turned out differently. There were new houses out there, built since the war, though they were called "wartime houses." He supposed it must be one of those.

"Pay when you ship," he told her.

"Also, I want a ticket for myself on the same train. Friday afternoon."

"Going same place?"

"Yes."

"You can travel on the same train to Toronto, but then you have to wait for the Transcontinental, goes out ten-thirty at night. You want sleeper or coach? Sleeper you get a berth, coach you sit up in the day car."

She said she would sit up.

"Wait in Sudbury for the Montreal train, but you won't get off there, they'll just shunt you around and hitch on the Montreal cars. Then on to Port Arthur and then to Kenora. You don't get off till Regina, and there you have to get off and catch the branch-line train."

She nodded as if he should just get on and give her the ticket.

Slowing down, he said, "But I won't promise your furniture'll arrive when you do, I wouldn't think it would get in till a day or two after. It's all the priorities. Somebody coming to meet you?"

"Yes."

"Good. Because it won't likely be much of a station. Towns out there, they're not like here. They're mostly pretty rudimentary affairs."

She paid for the passenger ticket now, from a roll of bills in a cloth bag in her purse. Like an old lady. She counted her change, too. But not the way an old lady would count it – she held it in her hand and flicked her eyes over it, but you could tell she didn't miss a penny. Then she turned away rudely, without a good-bye.

"See you Friday," he called out.

She wore a long, drab coat on this warm September day, also a pair of clunky laced-up shoes, and ankle socks.

He was getting a coffee out of his thermos when she came back and rapped on the wicket.

"The furniture I'm sending," she said. "It's all good furniture, it's like new. I wouldn't want it to get scratched or banged up or in any way damaged. I don't want it to smell like livestock, either."

"Oh, well," he said. "The railway's pretty used to shipping things. And they don't use the same cars for shipping furniture they use for shipping pigs."

"I'm concerned that it gets there in just as good a shape as it leaves here."

"Well, you know, when you buy your furniture, it's in the store, right? But did you ever think how it got there? It wasn't made in the store, was it? No. It was made in some factory someplace, and it got shipped to the store, and that was done quite possibly by train. So that being the case, doesn't it stand to reason the railway knows how to look after it?"

She continued to look at him without a smile or any admission of her female foolishness.

"I hope so," she said. "I hope they do."

*   *   *

THE STATION AGENT would have said, without thinking about it, that he knew everybody in town. Which meant that he knew about half of them. And most of those he knew were the core people, the ones who really were "in town" in the sense that they had not arrived yesterday and had no plans to move on. He did not know the woman who was going to Saskatchewan because she did not go to his church or teach his children in school or work in any store or restaurant or office that he went into. Nor was she married to any of the men he knew in the Elks or the Oddfellows or the Lions Club or the Legion. A look at her left hand while she was getting the money out had told him – and he was not surprised – that she was not married to anybody. With those shoes, and ankle socks instead of stockings, and no hat or gloves in the afternoon, she might have been a farm woman. But she didn't have the hesitation they generally had, the embarrassment. She didn't have country manners – in fact, she had no manners at all. She had treated him as if he was an information machine. Besides, she had written a town address – Exhibition Road. The person she really reminded him of was a plainclothes nun he had seen on television, talking about the missionary work she did somewhere in the jungle – probably they had got out of their nuns' clothes there because it made it easier for them to clamber around. This nun had smiled once in a while to show that her religion was supposed to make people happy, but most of the time she looked out at her audience as if she believed that other people were mainly in the world for her to boss around.

ONE MORE THING Johanna meant to do she had been putting off doing. She had to go into the dress shop called Milady's and buy herself an outfit. She had never been inside that shop – when she had to buy anything, like socks, she went to Callaghans Mens Ladies and Childrens Wear. She had lots of clothes inherited from Mrs. Willets, things like this coat that would never wear out. And Sabitha – the girl she looked after, in Mr. McCauley's house – was showered with costly hand-me-downs from her cousins.

In Milady's window there were two mannequins wearing suits with quite short skirts and boxy jackets. One suit was a rusty-gold color and the other a soft deep green. Big gaudy paper maple leaves were scattered round the mannequins' feet and pasted here and there on the window. At the time of year when most people's concern was to rake up leaves and burn them, here they were the chosen thing. A sign written in flowing black script was stuck diagonally across the glass. It said: *Simple Elegance, the Mode for Fall.*

She opened the door and went inside.

Right ahead of her, a full-length mirror showed her in Mrs. Willets's high-quality but shapeless long coat, with a few inches of lumpy bare legs above the ankle socks.

They did that on purpose, of course. They set the mirror there so you could get a proper notion of your deficiencies, right away, and then — they hoped — you would jump to the conclusion that you had to buy something to alter the picture. Such a transparent trick that it would have made her walk out, if she had not come in determined, knowing what she had to get.

Along one wall was a rack of evening dresses, all fit for belles of the ball with their net and taffeta, their dreamy colors. And beyond them, in a glass case so no profane fingers could get at them, half a dozen wedding gowns, pure white froth or vanilla satin or ivory lace, embroidered in silver beads or seed pearls. Tiny bodices, scalloped necklines, lavish skirts. Even when she was younger she could never have contemplated such extravagance, not just in the matter of money but in expectations, in the preposterous hope of transformation, and bliss.

It was two or three minutes before anybody came. Maybe they had a peephole and were eyeing her, thinking she wasn't their kind of customer and hoping she would go away.

She would not. She moved beyond the mirror's reflection — stepping from the linoleum by the door to a plushy rug — and at long last the curtain at the back of the store opened and out stepped Milady herself, dressed in a black suit with glittery buttons. High heels, thin ankles, girdle so tight her nylons rasped, gold hair skinned back from her made-up face.

"I thought I could try on the suit in the window," Johanna said in a rehearsed voice. "The green one."

"Oh, that's a lovely suit," the woman said. "The one in the window happens to be a size ten. Now you look to be – maybe a fourteen?"

She rasped ahead of Johanna back to the part of the store where the ordinary clothes, the suits and daytime dresses, were hung.

"You're in luck. Fourteen coming up."

The first thing Johanna did was look at the price tag. Easily twice what she'd expected, and she was not going to pretend otherwise.

"It's expensive enough."

"It's very fine wool." The woman monkeyed around till she found the label, then read off a description of the material that Johanna wasn't really listening to because she had caught at the hem to examine the workmanship.

"It feels as light as silk, but it wears like iron. You can see it's lined throughout, lovely silk-and-rayon lining. You won't find it bagging in the seat and going out of shape the way the cheap suits do. Look at the velvet cuffs and collar and the little velvet buttons on the sleeve."

"I see them."

"That's the kind of detail you pay for, you just do not get it otherwise. I love the velvet touch. It's only on the green one, you know – the apricot one doesn't have it, even though they're exactly the same price."

Indeed it was the velvet collar and cuffs that gave the suit, in Johanna's eyes, its subtle look of luxury and made her long to buy it. But she was not going to say so.

"I might as well go ahead and try it on."

This was what she'd come prepared for, after all. Clean underwear and fresh talcum powder under her arms.

The woman had enough sense to leave her alone in the bright cubicle. Johanna avoided the glass like poison till she'd got the skirt straight and the jacket done up.

At first she just looked at the suit. It was all right. The fit was all right – the skirt shorter than what she was used to, but then what she was used to was not the style. There was no problem with the suit. The problem was with what stuck out of it. Her neck and her face and her hair and her big hands and thick legs.

"How are you getting on? Mind if I take a peek?"

Peek all you want to, Johanna thought, it's a case of a sow's ear, as you'll soon see.

The woman tried looking from one side, then the other.

"Of course, you'll need your nylons on and your heels. How does it feel? Comfortable?"

"The suit feels fine," Johanna said. "There's nothing the matter with the suit."

The woman's face changed in the mirror. She stopped smiling. She looked disappointed and tired, but kinder.

"Sometimes that's just the way it is. You never really know until you try something on. The thing is," she said, with a new, more moderate conviction growing in her voice, "the thing is you have a fine figure, but it's a strong figure. You have large bones and what's the matter with that? Dinky little velvet-covered buttons are not for you. Don't bother with it anymore. Just take it off."

Then when Johanna had got down to her underwear there was a tap and a hand through the curtain.

"Just slip this on, for the heck of it."

A brown wool dress, lined, with a full skirt gracefully gathered, three-quarter sleeves and a plain round neckline. About as plain as you could get, except for a narrow gold belt. Not as expensive as the suit, but still the price seemed like a lot, when you considered all there was to it.

At least the skirt was a more decent length and the fabric made a noble swirl around her legs. She steeled herself and looked in the glass.

This time she didn't look as if she'd been stuck into the garment for a joke.

The woman came and stood beside her, and laughed, but with relief.

"It's the color of your eyes. You don't need to wear velvet. You've got velvet eyes."

That was the kind of soft-soaping Johanna would have felt bound to scoff at, except that at the moment it seemed to be true. Her eyes were not large, and if asked to describe their color she would have said, "I guess they're a kind of a brown." But now they looked to be a really deep brown, soft and shining.

It wasn't that she had suddenly started thinking she was pretty or anything. Just that her eyes were a nice color, if they had been a piece of cloth.

"Now, I bet you don't wear dress shoes very often," the woman said. "But if you had nylons on and just a minimum kind of pump – And I bet you don't wear jewelry, and you're quite right, you don't need to, with that belt."

To cut off the sales spiel Johanna said, "Well, I better take it off so you can wrap it up." She was sorry to lose the soft weight of the skirt and the discreet ribbon of gold around her waist. She had never in her life had this silly feeling of being enhanced by what she had put on herself.

"I just hope it's for a special occasion," the woman called out as Johanna was hastening into her now dingy-looking regular clothes.

"It'll likely be what I get married in," said Johanna.

She was surprised at that coming out of her mouth. It wasn't a major error – the woman didn't know who she was and would probably not be talking to anybody who did know. Still, she had meant to keep absolutely quiet. She must have felt she owed this person something – that they'd been through the disaster of the green suit and the discovery of the brown dress together and that was a bond. Which was nonsense. The woman was in the business of selling clothes, and she'd just succeeded in doing that.

"Oh!" the woman cried out. "Oh, that's wonderful."

Well, it might be, Johanna thought, and then again it might not. She might be marrying anybody. Some miserable farmer who wanted a workhorse around the place, or some wheezy old half-cripple looking for a nurse. This woman had no idea what kind of man she had lined up, and it wasn't any of her business anyway.

"I can tell it's a love match," the woman said, just as if she had read these disgruntled thoughts. "That's why your eyes were shining in the mirror. I've wrapped it all in tissue paper, all you have to do is take it out and hang it up and the material will fall out beautifully. Just give it a light press if you want, but you probably won't even need to do that."

Then there was the business of handing over the money. They both pretended not to look, but both did.

"It's worth it," the woman said. "You only get married the once. Well, that's not always strictly true –"

"In my case it'll be true," Johanna said. Her face was hotly flushed because marriage had not, in fact, been mentioned. Not even in the last letter. She had revealed to this woman what she was counting on, and that had perhaps been an unlucky thing to do.

"Where did you meet him?" said the woman, still in that tone of wistful gaiety. "What was your first date?"

"Through family," Johanna said truthfully. She wasn't meaning to say any more but heard herself go on. "The Western Fair. In London."

"The Western Fair," the woman said. "In London." She could have been saying "the Castle Ball."

"We had his daughter and her friend with us," said Johanna, thinking that in a way it would have been more accurate to say that he and Sabitha and Edith had her, Johanna, with them.

"Well, I can say my day has not been wasted. I've provided the dress for somebody to be a happy bride in. That's enough to justify my existence." The woman tied a narrow pink ribbon around the dress box, making a big, unnecessary bow, then gave it a wicked snip with the scissors.

"I'm here all day," she said. "And sometimes I just wonder what I think I'm doing. I ask myself, What do you think you're doing here? I put up a new display in the window and I do this and that to entice the people in, but there are days – there are *days* – when I do not see one soul come in that door. I know – people think these clothes are too expensive – but they're *good*. They're good clothes. If you want the quality you have to pay the price."

"They must come in when they want something like those," said Johanna, looking towards the evening dresses. "Where else could they go?"

"That's just it. They don't. They go to the city – that's where they go. They'll drive fifty miles, a hundred miles, never mind the gas, and tell themselves that way they get something better than I've got here. And they haven't. Not better quality, not better selection. Nothing. Just that they'd be ashamed to say they bought their wedding outfits in town.

Or they'll come in and try something on and say they have to think about it. I'll be back, they say. And I think, Oh, yes, I know what that means. It means they'll try to find the same thing cheaper in London or Kitchener, and even if it isn't cheaper, they'll buy it there once they've driven all that way and got sick of looking.

"I don't know," she said. "Maybe if I was a local person it would make a difference. It's very clique-y here, I find. You're not local, are you?"

Johanna said, "No."

"Don't you find it clique-y?"

Cleeky.

"Hard for an outsider to break in, is what I mean."

"I'm used to being on my own," Johanna said.

"But you found somebody. You won't be on your own anymore and isn't that lovely? Some days I think how grand it would be, to be married and stay at home. Of course, I used to be married, and I worked anyway. Ah, well. Maybe the man in the moon will walk in here and fall in love with me and then I'll be all set!"

JOHANNA HAD TO HURRY – that woman's need for conversation had delayed her. She was hurrying to be back at the house, her purchase stowed away, before Sabitha got home from school.

Then she remembered that Sabitha wasn't there, having been carried off on the weekend by her mother's cousin, her Aunt Roxanne, to live like a proper rich girl in Toronto and go to a rich girl's school. But she continued to walk fast – so fast some smart aleck holding up the wall of the drugstore called out to her, "Where's the fire?" and she slowed down a bit, not to attract attention.

The dress box was awkward – how could she have known the store would have its own pink cardboard boxes, with *Milady's* written across them in purple handwriting? A dead giveaway.

She felt a fool for mentioning a wedding, when he hadn't mentioned it and she ought to remember that. So much else had been said – or written – such fondness and yearning expressed, that the actual marrying seemed just to have been overlooked. The way you might speak about getting up in the morning and not about having breakfast, though you certainly intended to have it.

Nevertheless she should have kept her mouth shut.

She saw Mr. McCauley walking in the opposite direction up the other side of the street. That was all right – even if he had met her head-on he would never have noticed the box she carried. He would have raised a finger to his hat and passed her by, presumably noticing that she was his housekeeper but possibly not. He had other things on his mind, and for all anybody knew might be looking at some town other than the one they saw. Every working day – and sometimes, forgetfully, on holidays or Sundays – he got dressed in one of his three-piece suits and his light overcoat or his heavy overcoat, and his gray fedora and his well-polished shoes, and walked from Exhibition Road uptown to the office he still maintained over what had been the harness and luggage store. It was spoken of as an Insurance Office, though it was quite a long time since he had actively sold insurance. Sometimes people climbed the stairs to see him, maybe to ask some question about their policies or more likely about lot boundaries, the history of some piece of real estate in town or farm out in the country. His office was full of maps old and new, and he liked nothing better than to lay them out and get into a discussion that expanded far beyond the question asked. Three or four times a day he emerged and walked the street, as now. During the war he had put the McLaughlin-Buick up on blocks in the barn, and walked everywhere to set an example. He still seemed to be setting an example, fifteen years later. Hands clasped behind his back, he was like a kind landlord inspecting his property or a preacher happy to observe his flock. Of course, half the people that he met had no idea who he was.

The town had changed, even in the time Johanna had been here. Trade was moving out to the highway, where there was a new discount store and a Canadian Tire and a motel with a lounge and topless dancers. Some downtown shops had tried to spruce themselves up with pink or mauve or olive paint, but already that paint was curling on the old brick and some of the interiors were empty. Milady's was almost certain to follow suit.

If Johanna was the woman in there, what would she have done? She'd never have gotten in so many elaborate evening dresses, for a start. What instead? If you made the switch to cheaper clothes you'd only be putting yourself in competition with Callaghans and the discount place, and there probably wasn't trade enough to go around. So what about going into fancy baby clothes, children's clothes, trying to pull in the grandmothers and aunts who had the money and would spend it for that kind of thing? Forget about the mothers, who would go to Callaghans, having less money and more sense.

But if it was her in charge – Johanna – she would never be able to pull in anybody. She could see what needed to be done, and how, and she could round up and supervise people to do it, but she could never charm or entice. Take it or leave it, would be her attitude. No doubt they would leave it.

It was the rare person who took to her, and she'd been aware of that for a long time. Sabitha certainly hadn't shed any tears when she said good-bye – though you could say Johanna was the nearest thing Sabitha had to a mother, since her own mother had died. Mr. McCauley would be upset when she left because she'd given good service and it would be hard to replace her, but that would be all he thought about. Both he and his granddaughter were spoiled and self-centered. As for the neighbors, they would no doubt rejoice. Johanna had had problems on both sides of the property. On one side it was the neighbors' dog digging in her garden, burying and retrieving his supply of bones, which he could better have done at home. And on the other it was the black cherry tree, which was on the McCauleys' property but bore most of its cherries on the branches hanging over into the next yard. In both cases she had raised a fuss, and won. The dog was tied up and the other neighbors left the cherries alone. If she got up on the stepladder she could reach well over into their yard, but they no longer chased the birds out of the branches and it made a difference to the crop.

Mr. McCauley would have let them pick. He would have let the dog dig. He would let himself be taken advantage of. Part of the reason was that these were new people and lived in new houses and so he preferred not to pay attention to them. At one time there had been just three or four large houses on Exhibition Road. Across from them were the fairgrounds, where the fall fair was held (officially called the Agricultural Exhibition, hence the name), and in between were orchard trees, small meadows. A dozen years ago or so that land had been sold off in regular lot sizes and houses had been put up – small houses in alternating styles, one kind with an upstairs and the other kind without. Some were already getting to look pretty shabby.

There were only a couple of houses whose occupants Mr. McCauley knew and was friendly with – the schoolteacher, Miss Hood, and her mother, and the Shultzes, who ran the Shoe Repair shop. The Shultzes' daughter, Edith, was or had been Sabitha's great friend. It was natural, with their being in the same grade at school – at least last year, once Sabitha had been held back – and living near each other. Mr. McCauley hadn't minded – maybe he had some idea that Sabitha would be removed before long to live a different sort of life in Toronto. Johanna would not have chosen Edith, though the girl was never rude, never troublesome when she came to the house. And she was not stupid. That might have been the problem – she was smart and Sabitha was not so smart. She had made Sabitha sly.

That was all over now. Now that the cousin, Roxanne – Mrs. Huber – had shown up, the Schultz girl was all part of Sabitha's childish past.

I am going to arrange to get all your furniture out to you on the train as soon as they can take it and prepaid as soon as they tell me what it will cost. I have been thinking you will need it now. I guess it will not be that much of a surprise that I thought you would not mind it if I went along to be of help to you as I hope I can be.

This was the letter she had taken to the Post Office, before she went to make arrangements at the railway station. It was the first letter she had ever sent to him directly. The others had been slipped in with the letters she made Sabitha write. And his to her had come in the same way, tidily folded and with her name, Johanna, typed on the back of the page so there would be no mistaking. That kept the people in the Post Office from catching on, and it never hurt to save a stamp. Of course, Sabitha could have reported to her grandfather, or even read what was written to Johanna, but Sabitha was no more interested in communicating with the old man than she was in letters – the writing or the receiving of them.

The furniture was stored back in the barn, which was just a town barn, not a real barn with animals and a granary. When Johanna got her first look at everything a year or so ago, she found it grimy with dust and splattered with pigeon droppings. The pieces had been piled in carelessly without anything to cover them. She had hauled what she could carry out into the yard, leaving space in the barn to get at the big pieces she couldn't carry – the sofa and buffet and china cabinet and dining table. The bedstead she could take apart. She went at the wood with soft dus-trags, then lemon oil, and when she was finished it shone like candy. Maple candy – it was bird's-eye maple wood. It looked glamorous to her, like satin bedspreads and blond hair. Glamorous and modern, a total contrast to all the dark wood and irksome carving of the furniture she cared for in the house. She thought of it as *his* furniture then, and still did when she got it out this Wednesday. She had put old quilts over the bottom layer to protect everything there from what was piled on top, and sheets over what was on top to protect that from the birds, and as a result there was only a light dust. But she wiped everything and lemon-oiled it before she put it back, protected in the same way, to wait for the truck on Friday.

Dear Mr. McCauley,
I am leaving on the train this afternoon (Friday). I realize this is without giving my notice to you, but I will waive my last pay, which would be three weeks owing this coming Monday. There is a beef stew on the stove in the double boiler that just needs warming up. Enough there for three meals or maybe could be stretched to a fourth. As soon as it is hot and you have got all you want, put the lid on and put it away in the fridge. Remember, put the lid on at once not to take chances with it getting spoiled. Regards to you and to Sabitha and will probably be in touch when I am settled. Johanna Parry.

P.S. I have shipped his furniture to Mr. Boudreau as he may need it. Remember to make sure when you reheat there is enough water in bottom part of the double boiler.

Mr. McCauley had no trouble finding out that the ticket Johanna had bought was to Gdynia, Saskatchewan. He phoned the station agent and asked. He could not think how to describe Johanna – was she old or young-looking, thin or moderately heavy, what was the color of her coat? – but that was not necessary when he mentioned the furniture.

When this call came through there were a couple of people in the station waiting for the evening train. The agent tried to keep his voice down at first, but he became excited when he heard about the stolen furniture (what Mr. McCauley actually said was "and I believe she took some furniture with her"). He swore that if he had known who she was and what she was up to he would never have let her set foot on the train. This assertion was heard and repeated and believed, nobody asking how he could have stopped a grown woman who had paid for her ticket, unless he had some proof right away that she was a thief. Most people who repeated his words believed that he could and would have stopped her – they believed in the authority of station agents and of upright-walking fine old men in three-piece suits like Mr. McCauley.

The beef stew was excellent, as Johanna's cooking always was, but Mr. McCauley found he could not swallow it. He disregarded the instruction about the lid and left the pot sitting open on the stove and did not even turn off the burner until the water in the bottom pot boiled away and he was alerted by a smell of smoking metal.

This was the smell of treachery.

He told himself to be thankful at least that Sabitha was taken care of and he did not have that to worry about. His niece – his wife's cousin, actually, Roxanne – had written to tell him that from what she had seen of Sabitha on her summer visit to Lake Simcoe the girl was going to take some handling.

"Frankly I don't think you and that woman you've hired are going to be up to it when the boys come swarming around."

She did not go so far as to ask him whether he wanted another Marcelle on his hands, but that was what she meant. She said she would get Sabitha into a good school where she could be taught manners at least.

He turned on the television for a distraction, but it was no use.

It was the furniture that galled him. It was Ken Boudreau.

The fact was that three days before – on the very day that Johanna had bought her ticket, as the station agent had now told him – Mr. McCauley had received a letter from Ken Boudreau asking him to (a) advance some money against the furniture belonging to him (Ken Boudreau) and his dead wife, Marcelle, which was stored in Mr. McCauley's barn, or (b) if he could not see his way to doing that, to sell the furniture for as much as he could get and send the money as quickly as he could to Saskatchewan. There was no mention of the loans that had already been made by father-in-law to son-in-law, all against the value of this furniture and amounting to more than it could ever be sold for. Could Ken Boudreau have forgotten all about that? Or did he simply hope – and this was more probable – that his father-in-law would have forgotten?

He was now, it seemed, the owner of a hotel. But his letter was full of diatribes against the fellow who had formerly owned it and who had misled him as to various particulars.

"If I can just get over this hurdle," he said, "then I am convinced I can still make a go of it." But what was the hurdle? A need for immediate money, but he did not say whether it was owing to the former owner, or to the bank, or to a private mortgage holder, or what. It was the same old story – a desperate, wheedling tone mixed in with some arrogance, some sense of its being what was owed him, because of the wounds inflicted on him, the shame suffered, on account of Marcelle.

With many misgivings but remembering that Ken Boudreau was after all his son-in-law and had fought in the war and been through God-knows-what trouble in his marriage, Mr. McCauley had sat down and written a letter saying that he did not have any idea how to go about getting the best price for the furniture and it would be very difficult for him to find out and that he was enclosing a check, which he would count as an outright personal loan. He wished his son-in-law to acknowledge it as such and to remember the number of similar loans made in the past – already, he believed, exceeding any value of the furniture. He was enclosing a list of dates and amounts. Apart from fifty dollars paid nearly two years ago (with a promise of regular payments to follow), he had received nothing. His son-in-law must surely understand that as a result of these unpaid and interest-free loans Mr.

o good, that's no good," he said. "How can you get blood
e?"

into the Shoe Repair shop and greeted Herman Shultz.
remember those boots you resoled for me, the ones I got
You resoled them four or five years ago."

p was like a cave, with shaded bulbs hanging down over
rkplaces. It was abominably ventilated, but its manly smells –
leather and shoe-blacking and fresh-cut felt soles and rotted
– were comfortable to Mr. McCauley. Here his neighbor
hultz, a sallow, expert, spectacled workman, bent-shouldered,
ed in all seasons – driving in iron nails and clinch nails and,
ked hooked knife, cutting the desired shapes out of leather.
as cut by something like a miniature circular saw. The buffers
uffing noise and the sandpaper wheel made a rasp and the
e on a tool's edge sang high like a mechanical insect and the
chine punched the leather in an earnest industrial rhythm. All
s and smells and precise activities of the place had been famil-
. McCauley for years but never identified or reflected upon
w Herman, in his blackened leather apron with a boot on
, straightened up, smiled, nodded, and Mr. McCauley saw the
ole life in this cave. He wished to express sympathy or admi-
something more that he didn't understand.

do," Herman said. "They were nice boots."

boots. You know I got them on my wedding trip. I got them
d. I can't remember now where, but it wasn't in London."

ember you telling me."

did a fine job on them. They're still doing well. Fine job,
You do a good job here. You do honest work."

's good." Herman took a quick look at the boot on his hand.
auley knew that the man wanted to get back to his work, but
n't let him.

just had an eye-opener. A shock."

e you?"

ld man pulled out the letter and began to read bits of it aloud,
erjections of dismal laughter.

McCauley's income had declined, since he would otherwise have
invested the money.

He had thought of adding, "I am not such a fool as you seem to
think," but decided not to, since that would reveal his irritation and
perhaps his weakness.

And now look. The man had jumped the gun and enlisted Johanna
in his scheme – he would always be able to get around women – and
got hold of the furniture as well as the check. She had paid for the shipping herself, the station agent had said. The flashy-looking modern maple
stuff had been overvalued in the deals already made and they would not
get much for it, especially when you counted what the railway had
charged. If they had been cleverer they would simply have taken something from the house, one of the old cabinets or parlor settees too
uncomfortable to sit on, made and bought in the last century. That, of
course, would have been plain stealing. But what they had done was not
far off.

He went to bed with his mind made up to prosecute.

He woke in the house alone, with no smell of coffee or breakfast
coming from the kitchen – instead, there was a whiff of the burned pot
still in the air. An autumn chill had settled in all the high-ceilinged, forlorn
rooms. It had been warm last evening and on preceding evenings – the
furnace had not been turned on yet, and when Mr. McCauley did turn
it on the warm air was accompanied by a blast of cellar damp, of mold
and earth and decay. He washed and dressed slowly, with forgetful pauses,
and spread some peanut butter on a piece of bread for his breakfast. He
belonged to a generation in which there were men who were said not to
be able even to boil water, and he was one of them. He looked out the
front windows and saw the trees on the other side of the racetrack swallowed up in the morning fog, which seemed to be advancing, not retreat-
ing as it should at this hour, across the track itself. He seemed to see in
the fog the looming buildings of the old Exhibition Grounds – homely,
spacious buildings, like enormous barns. They had stood for years and years
unused – all through the war – and he forgot what happened to them in
the end. Were they torn down, or did they fall down? He abhorred the
races that took place now, the crowds and the loudspeaker and the illegal

drinking and the ruinous uproar of the summer Sundays. When he thought of that he thought of his poor girl Marcelle, sitting on the verandah steps and calling out to grown schoolmates who had got out of their parked cars and were hurrying to see the races. The fuss she made, the joy she expressed at being back in town, the hugging and holding people up, talking a mile a minute, rattling on about childhood days and how she'd missed everybody. She had said that the only thing not perfect about life was missing her husband, Ken, left out west because of his work.

She went out there in her silk pajamas, with straggly, uncombed, dyed-blond hair. Her arms and legs were thin, but her face was somewhat bloated, and what she claimed was her tan seemed a sickly brown color not from the sun. Maybe jaundice.

The child had stayed inside and watched television – Sunday cartoons that she was surely too old for.

He couldn't tell what was wrong, or be sure that anything was. Marcelle went away to London to have some female thing done and died in the hospital. When he phoned her husband to tell him, Ken Boudreau said, "What did she take?"

If Marcelle's mother had been alive still, would things have been any different? The fact was that her mother, when she was alive, had been as bewildered as he was. She had sat in the kitchen crying while their teenage daughter, locked into her room, had climbed out the window and slid down the verandah roof to be welcomed by carloads of boys.

The house was full of a feeling of callous desertion, of deceit. He and his wife had surely been kind parents, driven to the wall by Marcelle. When she had eloped with an airman, they had hoped that she would be all right, at last. They had been generous to the two of them as to the most proper young couple. But it all fell apart. To Johanna Parry he had likewise been generous, and look how she too had gone against him.

He walked to town and went into the hotel for his breakfast. The waitress said, "You're bright and early this morning."

And while she was still pouring out his coffee he began to tell her about how his housekeeper had walked out on him without any warning or provocation, not only left her job with no notice but taken a load of

furniture that had belonged to his ᴐ
belong to his son-in-law but didn't ᴐ
daughter's wedding money. He told ᴐ
an airman, a good-looking, plausibl ᴐ
around the corner.

"Excuse me," the waitress said. "1
waiting on their breakfast. Excuse m

He climbed the stairs to his office,
were the old maps he had been study
exactly the very first burying groun
believed, in 1839). He turned on the
he could not concentrate. After the wa
for a reproof – he hadn't been able to e
He decided to go out for a walk to ca

But instead of walking along in his
passing a few words with them, he fou
The minute anybody asked him how h
a most uncharacteristic, even shameful
like the waitress, these people had busine
and shuffled and made excuses to get aw
be warming up in the way foggy fall m
wasn't warm enough, so he sought the c

People who had known him the longe
had never been anything but reticent – t
his mind on other times, his courtesy a def
was a bit of a joke, because the privilege v
and not apparent to others). He should ha
wrongs or ask for sympathy – he hadn't
when his daughter died – yet here he was, ᴘ
if it wasn't a shame the way this fellow ha
and over again, and even now when he'd ta
the fellow had connived with his houseke
Some thought it was his own furniture h
believed the old man had been left without a
They advised him to go to the police.

"That's
from a stor
He went
"Do you
in England
The sh
various wo
of glue an
old ones
Herman S
was occup
with a wi
The felt v
made a s
emery sto
sewing m
the sound
iar to M
before. N
one hand
man's wh
ration or
"Yes,
"Fine
in Engla
"I ren
"You
Herman
"Tha
Mr. Mc
he coul
"I've
"Hav
The
with in

"Bronchitis. He says he's sick with bronchitis. He doesn't know where to turn. *I don't know who to turn to.* Well he always knows who to turn to. When he's run through everything else, turn to me. *A few hundred just till I get on my feet.* Begging and pleading with me and all the time he's conniving with my housekeeper. Did you know that? She stole a load of furniture and went off out west with it. They were hand in glove. This is a man I've saved the skin of, time and time again. And never a penny back. No, no, I have to be honest and say fifty dollars. Fifty out of hundreds and hundreds. Thousands. He was in the Air Force in the war, you know. Those shortish fellows, they were often in the Air Force. Strutting around thinking they were war heroes. Well, I guess I shouldn't say that, but I think the war spoiled some of those fellows, they never could adjust to life afterwards. But that's not enough of an excuse. Is it? I can't excuse him forever because of the war."

"No you can't."

"I knew he wasn't to be trusted the first time I met him. That's the extraordinary thing. I knew it and I let him rook me all the same. There are people like that. You take pity on them just for being the crooks they are. I got him his insurance job out there, I had some connections. Of course he mucked it up. A bad egg. Some just are."

"You're right about that."

Mrs. Shultz was not in the store that day. Usually she was the one at the counter, taking in the shoes and showing them to her husband and reporting back what he said, making out the slips, and taking the payment when the restored shoes were handed back. Mr. McCauley remembered that she had had some kind of operation during the summer.

"Your wife isn't in today? Is she well?"

"She thought she'd better take it easy today. I've got my girl in."

Herman Shultz nodded towards the shelves to the right of the counter, where the finished shoes were displayed. Mr. McCauley turned his head and saw Edith, the daughter, whom he hadn't noticed when he came in. A childishly thin girl with straight black hair, who kept her back to him, rearranging the shoes. That was just the way she had seemed to slide in and out of sight when she came to his house as Sabitha's friend. You never got a good look at her face.

"You're going to help your father out now?" Mr. McCauley said. "You're through with school?"

"It's Saturday," said Edith, half turning, faintly smiling.

"So it is. Well, it's a good thing to help your father, anyway. You must take care of your parents. They've worked hard and they're good people." With a slight air of apology, as if he knew he was being sententious, Mr. McCauley said, "Honor thy father and thy mother, that thy days may be long in the –"

Edith said something not for him to hear. She said, "Shoe Repair shop."

"I'm taking up your time, I'm imposing on you," said Mr. McCauley sadly. "You have work to do."

"There's no need for you to be sarcastic," said Edith's father when the old man had gone.

HE TOLD EDITH'S mother all about Mr. McCauley at supper.

"He's not himself," he said. "Something's come over him."

"Maybe a little stroke," she said. Since her own operation – for gall-stones – she spoke knowledgeably and with a placid satisfaction about the afflictions of other people.

Now that Sabitha had gone, vanished into another sort of life that had, it seemed, always been waiting for her, Edith had reverted to being the person she had been before Sabitha came here. "Old for her age," diligent, critical. After three weeks at high school she knew that she was going to be very good at all the new subjects – Latin, Algebra, English Literature. She believed that her cleverness was going to be recognized and acclaimed and an important future would open out for her. The past year's silliness with Sabitha was slipping out of sight.

Yet when she thought about Johanna's going off out west she felt a chill from her past, an invasive alarm. She tried to bang a lid down on that, but it wouldn't stay.

As soon as she had finished washing the dishes she went off to her room with the book they had been assigned for literature class. *David Copperfield.*

She was a child who had never received more than tepid reproofs from her parents – old parents to have a child of her age, which was said to account for her being the way she was – but she felt in perfect accord with David in his unhappy situation. She felt that she was one like him, one who might as well have been an orphan, because she would probably have to run away, go into hiding, fend for herself, when the truth became known and her past shut off her future.

IT HAD ALL BEGUN with Sabitha saying, on the way to school, "We have to go by the Post Office. I have to send a letter to my dad."

They walked to and from school together every day. Sometimes they walked with their eyes closed, or backwards. Sometimes when they met people they gabbled away softly in a nonsense language, to cause confusion. Most of their good ideas were Edith's. The only idea Sabitha introduced was the writing down of a boy's name and your own, and the stroking out of all letters that were duplicated and the counting of the remainder. Then you ticked off the counted number on your fingers, saying, *Hateship, friendship, courtship, loveship, marriage,* till you got the verdict on what could happen between you and that boy.

"That's a fat letter," said Edith. She noticed everything, and she remembered everything, quickly memorizing whole pages of the textbooks in a way the other children found sinister. "Did you have a lot of things to write to your dad?" she said, surprised, because she could not credit this – or at least could not credit that Sabitha would get them on paper.

"I only wrote on one page," Sabitha said, feeling the letter.

"A-ha," said Edith. "Ah. Ha."

"Aha what?"

"I bet she put something else in. Johanna did."

The upshot of this was that they did not take the letter directly to the Post Office, but saved it and steamed it open at Edith's house after school. They could do such things at Edith's house because her mother worked all day at the Shoe Repair shop.

Dear Mr. Ken Boudreau,

I just thought I would write and send my thanks to you for the nice things
you said about me in your letter to your daughter. You do not need to worry
about me leaving. You say that I am a person you can trust. That is the
meaning I take and as far as I know it is true. I am grateful to you for saying
that, since some people feel that a person like me that they do not know
the background of is Beyond the Pale. So I thought I would tell you something about myself. I was born in Glasgow, but my mother had to give me
up when she got married. I was taken to the Home at the age of five. I
looked for her to come back, but she didn't and I got used to it there and
they weren't Bad. At the age of eleven I was brought to Canada on a Plan
and lived with the Dixons, working on their Market Gardens. School was
in the Plan, but I didn't see much of it. In winter I worked in the house
for the Mrs. but circumstances made me think of leaving, and being big
and strong for my age got taken on at a Nursing Home looking after the
old people. I did not mind the work, but for better money went and worked
in a Broom Factory. Mr. Willets that owned it had an old mother that came
in to see how things were going, and she and I took to each other some way.
The atmosphere was giving me breathing troubles so she said I should come
and work for her and I did. I lived with her 12 yrs. on a lake called Mourning
Dove Lake up north. There was only the two of us, but I could take care
of everything outside and in, even running the motorboat and driving the
car. I learned to read properly because her eyes were going bad and she
liked me to read to her. She died at the age of 96. You might say what a
life for a young person, but I was happy. We ate together every meal and I
slept in her room the last year and a half. But after she died the family gave
me one wk. to pack up. She had left me some money and I guess they did
not like that. She wanted me to use it for Education but I would have to
go in with kids. So when I saw the ad Mr. McCauley put in the Globe and
Mail I came to see about it. I needed work to get over missing Mrs. Willets.
So I guess I have bored you long enough with my History and you'll be
relieved I have got up to the Present. Thank you for your good opinion
and for taking me along to the Fair. I am not one for the rides or for eating
the stuff but it was still certainly a pleasure to be included.

Your friend, Johanna Parry.

Edith read Johanna's words aloud, in an imploring voice and with a woebegone expression.

"I was born in Glasgow, but my mother had to give me up when she took one look at me —"

"Stop," said Sabitha. "I'm laughing so hard I'll be sick."

"How did she get her letter in with yours without you knowing?"

"She just takes it from me and puts it in an envelope and writes on the outside because she doesn't think my writing is good enough."

Edith had to put Scotch tape on the flap of the envelope to make it stick, since there wasn't enough sticky stuff left. "She's in love with him," she said.

"Oh, puke-puke," said Sabitha, holding her stomach. "She can't be. Old Johanna."

"What did he say about her, anyway?"

"Just about how I was supposed to respect her and it would be too bad if she left because we were lucky to have her and he didn't have a home for me and Grandpa couldn't raise a girl by himself and blah-blah. He said she was a lady. He said he could tell."

"So then she falls in lo-ove."

The letter remained with Edith overnight, lest Johanna discover that it hadn't been posted and was sealed with Scotch tape. They took it to the Post Office the next morning.

"Now we'll see what he writes back. Watch out," said Edith.

NO LETTER CAME for a long time. And when it did, it was a disappointment. They steamed it open at Edith's house, but found nothing inside for Johanna.

Dear Sabitha,

Christmas finds me a bit short this year, sorry I don't have more than a two-dollar bill to send you. But I hope you are in good health and have a Merry Christmas and keep up your schoolwork. I have not been feeling so well myself, having got Bronchitis, which I seem to do every winter, but this is the first time it landed me in bed before Christmas. As you see by the address I am in a new place. The apartment was in a very noisy location and too many people dropping in hoping for a party. This is a boardinghouse, which suits me fine as I was never good at the shopping and the cooking.

Merry Christmas and love, Dad.

"Poor Johanna," said Edith. "Her heart will be broken."

Sabitha said, "Who cares?"

"Unless we do it," Edith said.

"What?"

"*Answer* her."

They would have to type their letter, because Johanna would notice that it was not in Sabitha's father's handwriting. But the typing was not difficult. There was a typewriter in Edith's house, on a card table in the front room. Her mother had worked in an office before she was married and she sometimes earned a little money still by writing the sort of letters that people wanted to look official. She had taught Edith the basics of typing, in the hope that Edith too might get an office job someday.

"Dear Johanna," said Sabitha, "I am sorry I cannot be in love with you because you have got those ugly spots all over your face."

"I'm going to be serious," said Edith. "So shut up."

She typed, "I was so glad to get the letter —" speaking the words of her composition aloud, pausing while she thought up more, her voice becoming increasingly solemn and tender. Sabitha sprawled on the couch, giggling. At one point she turned on the television, but Edith said, "Pul-eeze. How can I concentrate on my e-motions with all that shit going on?"

Edith and Sabitha used the words "shit" and "bitch" and "Jesus Christ" when they were alone together.

Dear Johanna,

I was so glad to get the letter you put in with Sabitha's and to find out about your life. It must often have been a sad and lonely one though Mrs. Willets sounds like a lucky person for you to find. You have remained industrious and uncomplaining and I must say that I admire you very much. My own life has been a checkered one and I have never exactly settled down. I do not know why I have this inner restlessness and loneliness, it just seems to be my fate. I am always meeting people and talking to people but sometimes I ask myself, Who is my friend? Then comes your letter and you write at the end of it, Your friend. So I think, Does she really mean that? And what a very nice Christmas present it would be for me if Johanna would tell me that she is my friend. Maybe you just thought it was a nice way to end a letter and you don't really know me well enough. Merry Christmas anyway.

Your friend, Ken Boudreau.

The letter went home to Johanna. The one to Sabitha had ended up being typed as well because why would one be typed and not the other? They had been sparing with the steam this time and opened the envelope very carefully so there would be no telltale Scotch tape.

"Why couldn't we type a new envelope? Wouldn't he do that if he typed the letter?" said Sabitha, thinking she was being clever.

"Because a new *envelope* wouldn't have a *postmark* on it. Dumb-dumb."

"What if she answers it?"

"We'll read it."

"Yah, what if she answers it and sends it direct to *him*?"

Edith didn't like to show she had not thought of that.

"She won't. She's sly. Anyway, you write him back right away to give her the idea she can slip it in with yours."

"I hate writing stupid letters."

"Go on. It won't kill you. Don't you want to see what she says?"

Dear Friend,

You ask me do I know you well enough to be your friend and my answer is that I think I do. I have only had one Friend in my life, Mrs. Willets who I loved and she was so good to me but she is dead. She was a lot older than me and the trouble with Older Friends is they die and leave you. She was so old she would call me sometimes by another person's name. I did not mind it though.

I will tell you a strange thing. That picture that you got the photographer at the Fair to take, of you and Sabitha and her friend Edith and me, I had it enlarged and framed and set in the living room. It is not a very good picture and he certainly charged you enough for what it is, but it is better than nothing. So the day before yesterday I was dusting around it and I imagined I could hear you say Hello to me. Hello, you said, and I looked at your face as well as you can see it in the picture and I thought, Well, I must be losing my mind. Or else it is a sign of a letter coming. I am just fooling, I don't really believe in anything like that. But yesterday there was a letter. So you see it is not asking too much of me to be your friend. I can always find a way to keep busy but a true Friend is something else again.

Your Friend, Johanna Parry.

Of course, that could not be replaced in the envelope. Sabitha's father would spot something fishy in the references to a letter he had never written. Johanna's words had to be torn into tiny pieces and flushed down the toilet at Edith's house.

WHEN THE LETTER came telling about the hotel it was months and months later. It was summer. And it was just by luck that Sabitha had picked that letter up, since she had been away for three weeks, staying at the cottage on Lake Simcoe that belonged to her Aunt Roxanne and her Uncle Clark.

Almost the first thing Sabitha said, coming into Edith's house, was, "Ugga-ugga. This place stinks."

"Ugga-ugga" was an expression she had picked up from her cousins. Edith sniffed the air. "I don't smell anything."

"It's like your dad's shop, only not so bad. They must bring it home on their clothes and stuff."

Edith attended to the steaming and opening. On her way from the Post Office, Sabitha had bought two chocolate eclairs at the bakeshop. She was lying on the couch eating hers.

"Just one letter. For you," said Edith. "Pore old Johanna. Of course he never actually *got* hers."

"Read it to me," said Sabitha resignedly. "I've got sticky guck all over my hands."

Edith read it with businesslike speed, hardly pausing for the periods.

Well, Sabitha, my fortunes have taken a different turn, as you can see I am not in Brandon anymore but in a place called Gdynia. And not in the employ of my former bosses. I have had an exceptionally hard winter with my chest troubles and they, that is my bosses, thought I should be out on the road even if I was in danger of developing pneumonia so this developed into quite an argument so we all decided to say farewell. But luck is a strange thing and just about that time I came into possession of a Hotel. It is too complicated to explain the ins and outs but if your grandfather wants to know about it just tell him a man who owed me money which he could not pay let me have this hotel instead. So here I am moved from one room in a boardinghouse to a twelve-bedroom building and from not even owning the bed I slept in to owning several. It's a wonderful thing to wake up in the morning and know you are your own boss. I have some fixing up to do, actually plenty, and will get to it as soon as the weather warms up. I will need to hire somebody to help and later on I will hire a good cook to have a restaurant as well as the beverage room. That ought to go like hotcakes as there is none in this town. Hope you are well and doing your schoolwork and developing good habits.

Love, Your Dad.

Sabitha said, "Have you got some coffee?"

"Instant," said Edith. "Why?"

Sabitha said that iced coffee was what everybody had been drinking at the cottage and they were all crazy about it. She was crazy about it too. She got up and messed around in the kitchen, boiling the water and stirring up the coffee with milk and ice cubes. "What we really ought to have is vanilla ice cream," she said. "Oh, my Gad, is it ever wonderful. Don't you want your eclair?"

Oh, my Gad.

"Yes. All of it," said Edith meanly.

All these changes in Sabitha in just three weeks – during the time Edith had been working in the shop and her mother recovering at home from her operation. Sabitha's skin was an appetizing golden-brown color, and her hair was cut shorter and fluffed out around her face. Her cousins had cut it and given her a permanent. She wore a sort of playsuit, with shorts cut like a skirt and buttons down the front and frills over the shoulders in a becoming blue color. She had got plumper, and when she leaned over to pick up her glass of iced coffee, which was on the floor, she displayed a smooth, glowing cleavage.

Breasts. They must have started growing before she went away, but Edith had not noticed. Maybe they were just something you woke up with one morning. Or did not.

However they came, they seemed to indicate a completely unearned and unfair advantage.

Sabitha was full of talk about her cousins and life at the cottage. She would say, "Listen, I've got to tell you about this, it's a scream –" and then ramble on about what Aunt Roxanne said to Uncle Clark when they had the fight, how Mary Jo drove with the top down and without a license in Stan's car (who was Stan?) and took them all to a drive-in – and what was the scream or the point of the story somehow never became clear.

But after a while other things did. The real adventures of the summer. The older girls – that included Sabitha – slept in the upstairs of the boathouse. Sometimes they had tickling fights – they would all gang up on someone and tickle her till she shrieked for mercy and agreed to pull her pajama pants down to show if she had hair. They told stories about girls at boarding school who did things with hairbrush handles, toothbrush handles. *Ugga-ugga.* Once a couple of cousins put on a show – one girl got on top of the other and pretended to be the boy and they wound their legs around each other and groaned and panted and carried on.

Uncle Clark's sister and her husband came to visit on their honeymoon, and he was seen to put his hand inside her swimsuit.

"They really loved each other, they were at it day and night," said Sabitha. She hugged a cushion to her chest. "People can't help it when they're in love like that."

One of the cousins had already done it with a boy. He was one of the summer help in the gardens of the resort down the road. He took her out in a boat and threatened to push her out until she agreed to let him do it. So it wasn't her fault.

"Couldn't she swim?" said Edith.

Sabitha pushed the cushion between her legs. "Oooh," she said. "Feels so nice."

Edith knew all about the pleasurable agonies Sabitha was feeling, but she was appalled that anybody would make them public. She herself was frightened of them. Years ago, before she knew what she was doing, she had gone to sleep with the blanket between her legs and her mother had discovered her and told her about a girl she had known who did things like that all the time and had eventually been operated on for the problem.

"They used to throw cold water on her, but it didn't cure her," her mother had said. "So she had to be cut."

Otherwise her organs would get congested and she might die.

"Stop," she said to Sabitha, but Sabitha moaned defiantly and said, "It's nothing. We all did it like this. Haven't you got a cushion?"

Edith got up and went to the kitchen and filled her empty iced-coffee glass with cold water. When she got back Sabitha was lying limp on the couch, laughing, the cushion flung on the floor.

"What did you think I was doing?" she said. "Didn't you know I was kidding?"

"I was thirsty," Edith said.

"You just drank a whole glass of iced coffee."

"I was thirsty for water."

"Can't have any fun with you." Sabitha sat up. "If you're so thirsty why don't you drink it?"

They sat in a moody silence until Sabitha said, in a conciliatory but disappointed tone, "Aren't we going to write Johanna another letter? Let's write her a lovey-dovey letter."

Edith had lost a good deal of her interest in the letters, but she was gratified to see that Sabitha had not. Some sense of having power over Sabitha returned, in spite of Lake Simcoe and the breasts. Sighing, as if reluctantly, she got up and took the cover off the typewriter.

"My darlingest Johanna –" said Sabitha.

"No. That's too sickening."

"She won't think so."

"She will so," said Edith.

She wondered whether she should tell Sabitha about the danger of congested organs. She decided not to. For one thing, that information fell into a category of warnings she had received from her mother and never known whether to wholly trust or distrust. It had not fallen as low, in credibility, as the belief that wearing foot-rubbers in the house would ruin your eyesight, but there was no telling – someday it might.

And for another thing Sabitha would just laugh. She laughed at warnings – she would laugh even if you told her that chocolate eclairs would make her fat.

"Your last letter made me so happy –"

"Your last letter filled me with rap-ture –" said Sabitha.

"– made me so happy to think I did have a true friend in the world, which is you –"

"I could not sleep all night because I was longing to crush you in my arms –" Sabitha wrapped her arms around herself and rocked back and forth.

"*No.* Often I have felt so lonely in spite of a gregarious life and not known where to turn –"

"What does that mean – 'gregarious'? She won't know what it means."

"*She* will."

That shut Sabitha up and perhaps hurt her feelings. So at the end Edith read out, "'I must say good-bye and the only way I can do it is to imagine you reading this and blushing –' Is that more what you want?"

"Reading it in bed with your nightgown on," said Sabitha, always quickly restored, "and thinking how I would crush you in my arms and I would suck your titties –"

My Dear Johanna,

Your last letter made me so happy to think I have a true friend in the world, which is you. Often I have felt so lonely in spite of a gregarious life and not known where to turn.

Well, I have told Sabitha in my letter about my good fortune and how I am going into the hotel business. I did not tell her actually how sick I was last winter because I did not want to worry her. I do not want to worry you, either, dear Johanna, only to tell you that I thought of you so often and longed to see your dear sweet face. When I was feverish I thought that I really did see it bending over me and I heard your voice telling me I would soon be better and I felt the ministrations of your kind hands. I was in the boardinghouse and when I came to out of my fever there was a lot of teasing going on as to, who is this Johanna? But I was sad as could be to wake and find you were not there. I really wondered if you could have flown through the air and been with me, even though I knew that could not have happened. Believe me, believe me, the most beautiful movie star could not have been as welcome to me as you. I don't know if I should tell you the other things you were saying to me because they were very sweet and intimate but they might embarrass you. I hate to end this letter because it feels now as if I have my arms around you and I am talking to you quietly in the dark privacy of our room, but I must say good-bye and the only way I can do it is to imagine you reading this and blushing. It would be wonderful if you were reading it in bed with your nightgown on and thinking how I would like to crush you in my arms.

L-v-, Ken Boudreau.

Somewhat surprisingly, there was no reply to this letter. When Sabitha had written her half-page, Johanna put it in the envelope and addressed it and that was that.

WHEN JOHANNA GOT off the train there was nobody to meet her. She did not let herself worry about that – she had been thinking that her letter might not, after all, have got here before she did. (In fact it had, and was lying in the Post Office, uncollected, because Ken Boudreau, who had not been seriously sick last winter, really did have bronchitis now and for several days had not come in for his mail. On this day it had been joined by another envelope, containing the check from Mr. McCauley. But payment on that had already been stopped.)

What was of more concern to her was that there did not appear to be a town. The station was an enclosed shelter with benches along the walls and a wooden shutter pulled down over the window of the ticket office. There was also a freight shed – she supposed it was a freight shed – but the sliding door to it would not budge. She peered through a crack between the planks until her eyes got used to the dark in there, and she saw that it was empty, with a dirt floor. No crates of furniture there. She called out, "Anybody here? Anybody here?" several times, but she did not expect a reply.

She stood on the platform and tried to get her bearings.

About half a mile away there was a slight hill, noticeable at once because it had a crown of trees. And the sandy-looking track that she had taken, when she saw it from the train, for a back lane into a farmer's field – that must be the road. Now she saw the low shapes of buildings here and there in the trees – and a water tower, which looked from this distance like a toy, a tin soldier on long legs.

She picked up her suitcase – this would not be too difficult; she had carried it, after all, from Exhibition Road to the other railway station – and set out.

There was a wind blowing, but this was a hot day – hotter than the weather she had left in Ontario – and the wind seemed hot as well. Over her new dress she was wearing her same old coat, which would have taken up too much room in the suitcase. She looked with longing to the shade of the town ahead, but when she got there she found that the trees were either spruce, which were too tight and narrow to give much shade, or raggedy thin-leaved cottonwoods, which blew about and let the sun through anyway.

There was a discouraging lack of formality, or any sort of organization, to this place. No sidewalks, or paved streets, no imposing buildings except a big church like a brick barn. A painting over its door, showing the Holy Family with clay-colored faces and staring blue eyes. It was named for an unheard-of saint – Saint Voytech.

The houses did not show much forethought in their situation or planning. They were set at different angles to the road, or street, and most of them had mean-looking little windows stuck here and there, with snow porches like boxes round the doors. Nobody was out in the yards, and why should they be? There was nothing to tend, only clumps of brown grass and once a big burst of rhubarb, gone to seed.

The main street, if that's what it was, had a raised wooden walk on one side only, and some unconsolidated buildings, of which a grocery store (containing the Post Office) and a garage seemed to be the only ones functioning. There was one two-story building that she thought might be the hotel, but it was a bank and it was closed.

The first human being she saw – though two dogs had barked at her – was a man in front of the garage, busy loading chains into the back of his truck.

"Hotel?" he said. "You come too far."

He told her that it was down by the station, on the other side of the tracks and along a bit, it was painted blue and you couldn't miss it.

She set the suitcase down, not from discouragement but because she had to have a moment's rest.

He said he would ride her down there if she wanted to wait a minute. And though it was a new kind of thing for her to accept such an offer, she soon found herself riding in the hot, greasy cab of his truck, rocking down the dirt road that she had just walked up, with the chains making a desperate racket in the back.

"So – where'd you bring this heat wave from?" he said.

She said Ontario, in a tone that promised nothing further.

"Ontario," he said regretfully. "Well. There 'tis. Your hotel." He took one hand off the wheel. The truck gave an accompanying lurch as he waved to a two-story flat-roofed building that she hadn't missed but had seen from the train, as they came in. She had taken it then for a large and fairly derelict, perhaps abandoned, family home. Now that she had seen the houses in town, she knew that she should not have dismissed it so readily. It was covered with sheets of tin stamped to look like bricks and painted a light blue. There was the one word HOTEL, in neon tubing, no longer lit, over the doorway.

"I am a dunce," she said, and offered the man a dollar for the ride.

He laughed. "Hang on to your money. You never know when you'll need it."

Quite a decent-looking car, a Plymouth, was parked outside this hotel. It was very dirty, but how could you help that, with these roads?

There were signs on the door advertising a brand of cigarettes, and of beer. She waited till the truck had turned before she knocked – knocked because it didn't look as if the place could in any way be open for business. Then she tried the door to see if it was open, and walked into a little dusty room with a staircase, and then into a large dark room in which there was a billiard table and a bad smell of beer and an unswept floor. Off in a side room she could see the glimmer of a mirror, empty shelves, a counter. These rooms had the blinds pulled tightly down. The only light she saw was coming through two small round windows, which turned out to be set in double swinging doors. She went on through these into a kitchen. It was lighter, because of a row of high – and dirty – windows, uncovered, in the opposite wall. And here were the first signs of life – somebody had been eating at the table and had left a plate smeared with dried ketchup and a cup half full of cold black coffee.

One of the doors off the kitchen led outside – this one was locked – and one to a pantry in which there were several cans of food, one to a broom closet, and one to an enclosed stairway. She climbed the steps, bumping her suitcase along in front of her because the space was narrow. Straight ahead of her on the second floor she saw a toilet with the seat up.

The door of the bedroom at the end of the hall was open, and in there she found Ken Boudreau.

She saw his clothes before she saw him. His jacket hanging up on a corner of the door and his trousers on the doorknob, so that they trailed on the floor. She thought at once that this was no way to treat good clothes, so she went boldly into the room – leaving her suitcase in the hall – with the idea of hanging them up properly.

He was in bed, with only a sheet over him. The blanket and his shirt were lying on the floor. He was breathing restlessly as if about to wake up, so she said, "Good morning. Afternoon."

The bright sunlight was coming in the window, hitting him almost in the face. The window was closed and the air horribly stale – smelling, for one thing, of the full ashtray on the chair he used as a bed table.

He had bad habits – he smoked in bed.

He did not wake up at her voice – or he woke only part way. He began to cough.

She recognized this as a serious cough, a sick man's cough. He struggled to lift himself up, still with his eyes closed, and she went over to the bed and hoisted him. She looked for a handkerchief or a box of tissues, but she saw nothing so she reached for his shirt on the floor, which she could wash later. She wanted to get a good look at what he spat up.

When he had hacked up enough, he muttered and sank down into the bed, gasping, the charming cocky-looking face she remembered crumpled up in disgust. She knew from the feel of him that he had a fever.

The stuff that he had coughed out was greenish-yellow – no rusty streaks. She carried the shirt to the toilet sink, where rather to her surprise she found a bar of soap, and washed it out and hung it on the door hook, then thoroughly washed her hands. She had to dry them on the skirt of her new brown dress. She had put that on in another little toilet – the *Ladies* on the train – not more than a couple of hours ago. She had been wondering then if she should have got some makeup.

In a hall closet she found a roll of toilet paper and took it into his room for the next time he had to cough. She picked up the blanket and covered him well, pulled the blind down to the sill and raised the stiff window an inch or two, propping it open with the ashtray she had emptied. Then she changed, out in the hall, from the brown dress into old clothes from her suitcase. A lot of use a nice dress or any makeup in the world would be now.

She was not sure how sick he was, but she had nursed Mrs. Willets – also a heavy smoker – through several bouts of bronchitis, and she thought she could manage for a while without having to think about getting a doctor. In the same hall closet was a pile of clean, though worn and faded, towels, and she wet one of these and wiped his arms and legs, to try to get his fever down. He came half awake at this and began to cough again. She held him up and made him spit into the toilet paper, examined it once more and threw it down the toilet and washed her hands. She had a towel now to dry them on. She went downstairs and found a glass in the kitchen, also an empty, large ginger-ale bottle, which she filled with water. This she attempted to make him drink. He took a little, protested, and she let him lie down. In five minutes or so she tried again. She kept doing this until she believed he had swallowed as much as he could hold without throwing up.

Time and again he coughed and she lifted him up, held him with one arm while the other hand pounded on his back to help loosen the load in his chest. He opened his eyes several times and seemed to take in her presence without alarm or surprise – or gratitude, for that matter. She sponged him once more, being careful to cover immediately with the blanket the part that had just been cooled.

She noticed that it had begun to get dark, and she went down into the kitchen, found the light switch. The lights and the old electric stove were working. She opened and heated a can of chicken-with-rice soup, carried it upstairs and roused him. He swallowed a little from the spoon. She took advantage of his momentary wakefulness to ask if he had a bottle of aspirin. He nodded yes, then became very confused when trying to tell her where. "In the wastebasket," he said.

"No, no," she said. "You don't mean wastebasket."

"In the – in the –"

He tried to shape something with his hands. Tears came into his eyes.

"Never mind," Johanna said. "Never mind."

His fever went down anyway. He slept for an hour or more without coughing. Then he grew hot again. By that time she had found the aspirin – they were in a kitchen drawer with such things as a screwdriver and some lightbulbs and a ball of twine – and she got a couple into him. Soon he had a violent coughing fit, but she didn't think he threw them up. When he lay down she put her ear to his chest and listened to the wheezing. She had already looked for mustard to make a plaster with, but apparently there wasn't any. She went downstairs again and heated some water and brought it in a basin. She tried to make him lean over it, tenting him with towels, so that he could breathe the steam. He would cooperate only for a moment or so, but perhaps it helped – he hacked up quantities of phlegm.

His fever went down again and he slept more calmly. She dragged in an armchair she had found in one of the other rooms and she slept too, in snatches, waking and wondering where she was, then remembering and getting up and touching him – his fever seemed to be staying down – and tucking in the blanket. For her own cover she used the everlasting old tweed coat that she had Mrs. Willets to thank for.

He woke. It was full morning. "What are you doing here?" he said, in a hoarse, weak voice.

"I came yesterday," she said. "I brought your furniture. It isn't here yet, but it's on its way. You were sick when I got here and you were sick most of the night. How do you feel now?"

He said, "Better," and began to cough. She didn't have to lift him, he sat up on his own, but she went to the bed and pounded his back. When he finished, he said, "Thank you."

His skin now felt as cool as her own. And smooth – no rough moles, no fat on him. She could feel his ribs. He was like a delicate, stricken boy. He smelled like corn.

"You swallowed the phlegm," she said. "Don't do that, it's not good for you. Here's the toilet paper, you have to spit it out. You could get trouble with your kidneys, swallowing it."

"I never knew that," he said. "Could you find the coffee?"

The percolator was black on the inside. She washed it as well as she could and put the coffee on. Then she washed and tidied herself, wondering what kind of food she should give him. In the pantry there was a box of biscuit mix. At first she thought she would have to mix it with water, but she found a can of milk powder as well. When the coffee was ready she had a pan of biscuits in the oven.

AS SOON AS HE heard her busy in the kitchen, he got up to go to the toilet. He was weaker than he'd thought – he had to lean over and put one hand on the tank. Then he found some underwear on the floor of the hall closet where he kept clean clothes. He had figured out by now who this woman was. She had said she came to bring him his furniture, though he hadn't asked her or anybody to do that – hadn't asked for the furniture at all, just the money. He should know her name, but he couldn't remember it. That was why he opened her purse, which was on the floor of the hall beside her suitcase. There was a name tag sewn to the lining.

Johanna Parry, and the address of his father-in-law, on Exhibition Road.

Some other things. A cloth bag with a few bills in it. Twenty-seven dollars. Another bag with change, which he didn't bother to count. A bright blue bankbook. He opened it up automatically, without expectations of anything unusual.

A couple of weeks ago Johanna had been able to transfer the whole of her inheritance from Mrs. Willets into her bank account, adding it to the amount of money she had saved. She had explained to the bank manager that she did not know when she might need it.

The sum was not dazzling, but it was impressive. It gave her substance. In Ken Boudreau's mind, it added a sleek upholstery to the name Johanna Parry.

"Were you wearing a brown dress?" he said, when she came up with the coffee.

"Yes, I was. When I first got here."

"I thought it was a dream. It was you."

"Like in your other dream," Johanna said, her speckled forehead turning fiery. He didn't know what that was all about and hadn't the energy to inquire. Possibly a dream he'd wakened from when she was here in the night – one he couldn't now remember. He coughed again in a more reasonable way, with her handing him some toilet paper.

"Now," she said, "where are you going to set your coffee?" She pushed up the wooden chair that she had moved to get at him more easily. "There," she said. She lifted him under the arms and wedged the pillow in behind him. A dirty pillow, without a case, but she had covered it last night with a towel.

"Could you see if there's any cigarettes downstairs?"

She shook her head, but said, "I'll look. I've got biscuits in the oven."

KEN BOUDREAU WAS in the habit of lending money, as well as borrowing it. Much of the trouble that had come upon him – or that he had got into, to put it another way – had to do with not being able to say no to a friend. Loyalty. He had not been drummed out of the peacetime Air Force, but had resigned out of loyalty to the friend who had been hauled up for offering insults to the C.O. at a mess party. At a mess party, where everything was supposed to be a joke and no offense taken – it was not fair. And he had lost the job with the fertilizer company because he took a company truck across the American border without permission, on a Sunday, to pick up a buddy who had got into a fight and was afraid of being caught and charged.

Part and parcel of the loyalty to friends was the difficulty with bosses. He would confess that he found it hard to knuckle under. "Yes, sir," and "no, sir" were not ready words in his vocabulary. He had not been fired from the insurance company, but he had been passed over so many times that it seemed they were daring him to quit, and eventually he did.

Drink had played a part, you had to admit that. And the idea that life should be a more heroic enterprise than it ever seemed to be nowadays.

He liked to tell people he'd won the hotel in a poker game. He was not really much of a gambler, but women liked the sound of that. He didn't want to admit that he'd taken it sight unseen in payment of a debt. And even after he saw it, he told himself it could be salvaged. The idea of being his own boss did appeal to him. He did not see it as a place where people would stay – except perhaps hunters, in the fall. He saw it as a drinking establishment and a restaurant. If he could get a good cook. But before anything much could happen money would have to be spent. Work had to be done – more than he could possibly do himself though he was not unhandy. If he could live through the winter doing what he could by himself, proving his good intentions, he thought maybe he could get a loan from the bank. But he needed a smaller loan just to get through the winter, and that was where his father-in-law came into the picture. He would rather have tried somebody else, but nobody else could so easily spare it.

He had thought it a good idea to put the request in the form of a proposal to sell the furniture, which he knew the old man would never bestir himself enough to do. He was aware, not very specifically, of loans still outstanding from the past – but he was able to think of those as sums he'd been entitled to, for supporting Marcelle during a period of bad behavior (hers, at a time when his own hadn't started) and for accepting Sabitha as his child when he had his doubts. Also, the McCauleys were the only people he knew who had money that nobody now alive had earned.

I brought your furniture.

He was unable to figure out what that could mean for him, at present. He was too tired. He wanted to sleep more than he wanted to eat when she came with the biscuits (and no cigarettes). To satisfy her he ate half of one. Then he fell dead asleep. He came only half awake when she rolled him on one side, then the other, getting the dirty sheet out from under him, then spreading the clean one and rolling him onto that, all without making him get out of bed or really wake up.

"I found a clean sheet, but it's thin as a rag," she said. "It didn't smell too good, so I hung it on the line awhile."

Later he realized that a sound he'd been hearing for a long time in a dream was really the sound of the washing machine. He wondered how that could be – the hot-water tank was defunct. She must have heated tubs of water on the stove. Later still, he heard the unmistakable sound of his own car starting up and driving away. She would have got the keys from his pants pocket.

She might be driving away in his only worthwhile possession, deserting him, and he could not even phone the police to nab her. The phone was cut off, even if he'd been able to get to it.

That was always a possibility – theft and desertion – yet he turned over on the fresh sheet, which smelled of prairie wind and grass, and went back to sleep, knowing for certain that she had only gone to buy milk and eggs and butter and bread and other supplies – even cigarettes – that were necessary for a decent life, and that she would come back and be busy downstairs and that the sound of her activity would be like a net beneath him, heaven-sent, a bounty not to be questioned.

There was a woman problem in his life right now. Two women, actually, a young one and an older one (that is, one of about his own age) who knew about each other and were ready to tear each other's hair out. All he had got from them recently was howling and complaining, punctuated with their angry assertions that they loved him.

Perhaps a solution had arrived for that, as well.

WHEN SHE WAS buying groceries in the store, Johanna heard a train, and driving back to the hotel, she saw a car parked at the railway station. Before she had even stopped Ken Boudreau's car she saw the furniture crates piled up on the platform. She talked to the agent – it was his car there – and he was very surprised and irritated by the arrival of all these big crates. When she had got out of him the name of a man with a truck – a clean truck, she insisted – who lived twenty miles away and sometimes did hauling, she used the station phone to call the man and half bribed, half ordered him to come right away. Then she impressed upon the agent that he must stay with the crates till the truck arrived. By suppertime the truck had come, and the man and his son had unloaded all the furniture and carried it into the main room of the hotel.

The next day she took a good look around. She was making up her mind.

The day after that she judged Ken Boudreau to be able to sit up and listen to her, and she said, "This place is a sinkhole for money. The town is on its last legs. What should be done is to take out everything that can bring in any cash and sell it. I don't mean the furniture that was shipped in, I mean things like the pool table and the kitchen range. Then we ought to sell the building to somebody who'll strip the tin off it for junk. There's always a bit to be made off stuff you'd never think had any value. Then – What was it you had in mind to do before you got hold of the hotel?"

He said that he had had some idea of going to British Columbia, to Salmon Arm, where he had a friend who had told him one time he could have a job managing orchards. But he couldn't go because the car needed new tires and work done on it before he could undertake a long trip, and he was spending all he had just to live. Then the hotel had fallen into his lap.

"Like a ton of bricks," she said. "Tires and fixing the car would be a better investment than sinking anything into this place. It would be a good idea to get out there before the snow comes. And ship the furniture by rail again, to make use of it when we get there. We have got all we need to furnish a home."

"It's maybe not all that firm of an offer."

She said, "I know. But it'll be all right."

He understood that she did know, and that it was, it would be, all right. You could say that a case like his was right up her alley.

Not that he wouldn't be grateful. He'd got to a point where gratitude wasn't a burden, where it was natural – especially when it wasn't demanded.

Thoughts of regeneration were starting. *This is the change I need.* He had said that before, but surely there was one time when it would be true. The mild winters, the smell of the evergreen forests and the ripe apples. *All we need to make a home.*

HE HAS HIS PRIDE, she thought. That would have to be taken account of. It might be better never to mention the letters in which he had laid himself open to her. Before she came away, she had destroyed them. In fact she had destroyed each one as soon as she'd read it over well enough to know it by heart, and that didn't take long. One thing she surely didn't want was for them ever to fall into the hands of young Sabitha and her shifty friend. Especially the part in the last letter, about her nightgown, and being in bed. It wasn't that such things wouldn't go on, but it might be thought vulgar or sappy or asking for ridicule, to put them on paper.

She doubted they'd see much of Sabitha. But she would never thwart him, if that was what he wanted.

This wasn't really a new experience, this brisk sense of expansion and responsibility. She'd felt something the same for Mrs. Willets – another fine-looking, flighty person in need of care and management. Ken Boudreau had turned out to be a bit more that way than she was prepared for, and there were the differences you had to expect with a man, but surely there was nothing in him that she couldn't handle.

After Mrs. Willets her heart had been dry, and she had considered it might always be so. And now such a warm commotion, such busy love.

MR. MCCAULEY DIED about two years after Johanna's departure. His funeral was the last one held in the Anglican church. There was a good turnout for it. Sabitha – who came with her mother's cousin, the Toronto woman – was now self-contained and pretty and remarkably, unexpectedly slim. She wore a sophisticated black hat and did not speak to anybody unless they spoke to her first. Even then, she did not seem to remember them.

The death notice in the paper said that Mr. McCauley was survived by his granddaughter Sabitha Boudreau and his son-in-law Ken Boudreau, and Mr. Boudreau's wife Johanna, and their infant son Omar, of Salmon Arm, B.C.

Edith's mother read this out – Edith herself never looked at the local paper. Of course, the marriage was not news to either of them – or to Edith's father, who was around the corner in the front room, watching television. Word had got back. The only news was Omar.

"Her with a *baby*," Edith's mother said.

Edith was doing her Latin translation at the kitchen table. *Tu ne quaesieris, scire nefas, quem mihi, quem tibi –*

In the church she had taken the precaution of not speaking to Sabitha first, before Sabitha could not speak to her.

She was not really afraid, anymore, of being found out – though she still could not understand why they hadn't been. And in a way, it seemed only proper that the antics of her former self should not be connected with her present self – let alone with the real self that she expected would take over once she got out of this town and away from all the people who thought they knew her. It was the whole twist of consequence that dismayed her – it seemed fantastical, but dull. Also insulting, like some sort of joke or inept warning, trying to get its hooks into her. For where, on the list of things she planned to achieve in her life, was there any mention of her being responsible for the existence on earth of a person named Omar?

Ignoring her mother, she wrote, "You must not ask, it is forbidden for us to know —"

She paused, chewing her pencil, then finished off with a chill of satisfaction, "— what fate has in store for me, or for you —"

SAVE THE REAPER

THE GAME THEY played was almost the same one that Eve had played with Sophie, on long dull car trips when Sophie was a little girl. Then it was spies – now it was aliens. Sophie's children, Philip and Daisy, were sitting in the backseat. Daisy was barely three and could not understand what was going on. Philip was seven, and in control. He was the one who picked the car they were to follow, in which there were newly arrived space travellers on their way to the secret headquarters, the invaders' lair. They got their directions from the signals offered by plausible-looking people in other cars or from somebody standing by a mailbox or even riding a tractor in a field. Many aliens had already arrived on earth and been translated – this was Philip's word – so that anybody might be one. Gas station attendants or women pushing baby carriages or even the babies riding in the carriages. They could be giving signals.

Usually Eve and Sophie had played this game on a busy highway where there was enough traffic that they wouldn't be detected. (Though once they had got carried away and ended up in a suburban drive.) On the country roads that Eve was taking today that wasn't so easy. She tried to solve the problem by saying that they might have to switch from following one vehicle to another because some were only decoys, not heading for the hideaway at all, but leading you astray.

"No, that isn't it," said Philip. "What they do, they suck the people out of one car into another car, just in case anybody is following. They can be like inside one body and then they go *schlup* through the air into another body in another car. They go into different people all the time and the people never know what was in them."

"Really?" Eve said. "So how do we know which car?"

"The code's on the license plate," said Philip. "It's changed by the electrical field they create in the car. So their trackers in space can

399

follow them. It's just one simple little thing, but I can't tell you."

"Well no," said Eve. "I suppose very few people know it."

Philip said, "I am the only one right now in Ontario."

He sat as far forward as he could with his seat belt on, tapping his teeth sometimes in urgent concentration and making light whistling noises as he cautioned her.

"Unh-unh, watch out here," he said. "I think you're going to have to turn around. Yeah. Yeah. I think this may be it."

They had been following a white Mazda, and were now, apparently, to follow an old green pickup truck, a Ford. Eve said, "Are you sure?"

"Sure."

"You felt them sucked through the air?"

"They're translated simultaneously," Philip said. "I might have said 'sucked,' but that's just to help people understand it."

What Eve had originally planned was to have the headquarters turn out to be in the village store that sold ice cream, or in the playground. It could be revealed that all the aliens were congregated there in the form of children, seduced by the pleasures of ice cream or slides and swings, their powers temporarily in abeyance. No fear they could abduct you − or get into you − unless you chose the one wrong flavor of ice cream or swung the exact wrong number of times on the designated swing. (There would have to be some remaining danger, or else Philip would feel let down, humiliated.) But Philip had taken charge so thoroughly that now it was hard to manage the outcome. The pickup truck was turning from the paved county road onto a gravelled side road. It was a decrepit truck with no topper, its body eaten by rust − it would not be going far. Home to some farm, most likely. They might not meet another vehicle to switch to before the destination was reached.

"You're positive this is it?" said Eve. "It's only one man by himself, you know. I thought they never travelled alone."

"The dog," said Philip.

For there was a dog riding in the open back of the truck, running back and forth from one side to the other as if there were events to be kept track of everywhere.

"The dog's one too," Philip said.

*　　*　　*

THAT MORNING, when Sophie was leaving to meet Ian at the Toronto airport, Philip had kept Daisy occupied in the children's bedroom. Daisy had settled down pretty well in the strange house – except for wetting her bed every night of the holiday – but this was the first time that her mother had gone off and left her behind. So Sophie had asked Philip to distract her, and he did so with enthusiasm (happy at the new turn events had taken?). He shot the toy cars across the floor with angry engine noises to cover up the sound of Sophie's starting the real rented car and driving away. Shortly after that he shouted to Eve, "Has the B.M. gone?"

Eve was in the kitchen, clearing up the remains of breakfast and disciplining herself. She walked into the living room. There was the boxed tape of the movie that she and Sophie had been watching last night.

The Bridges of Madison County.

"What does mean 'B.M.'?" said Daisy.

The children's room opened off the living room. This was a cramped little house, fixed up on the cheap for summer rental. Eve's idea had been to get a lakeside cottage for the holiday – Sophie's and Philip's first visit with her in nearly five years and Daisy's first ever. She had picked this stretch of the Lake Huron shore because her parents used to bring her here with her brother when they were children. Things had changed – the cottages were all as substantial as suburban houses, and the rents were out of sight. This house half a mile inland from the rocky, unfavored north end of the usable beach had been the best she could manage. It stood in the middle of a cornfield. She had told the children what her father had once told her – that at night you could hear the corn growing.

Every day when Sophie took Daisy's hand-washed sheets off the line, she had to shake out the corn bugs.

"It means 'bowel movement,'" said Philip with a look of sly challenge at Eve.

Eve halted in the doorway. Last night she and Sophie had watched Meryl Streep sitting in the husband's truck, in the rain, pressing down on the door handle, choking with longing, as her lover drove away. Then they had turned and had seen each other's eyes full of tears and shook their heads and started laughing.

"Also it means 'Big Mama,'" Philip said in a more conciliatory tone. "Sometimes that's what Dad calls her."

"Well then," said Eve. "If that's your question, the answer to your question is yes."

She wondered if he thought of Ian as his real father. She hadn't asked Sophie what they'd told him. She wouldn't, of course. His real father had been an Irish boy who was travelling around North America trying to decide what to do now that he had decided not to be a priest. Eve had thought of him as a casual friend of Sophie's, and it seemed that Sophie had thought of him that way too, until she seduced him. ("He was so shy I never dreamed it would take," she said.) It wasn't until Eve saw Philip that Eve could really picture what the boy had looked like. Then she saw him faithfully reproduced – the bright-eyed, pedantic, sensitive, scornful, fault-finding, blushing, shrinking, arguing young Irishman. Something like Samuel Beckett, she said, even to the wrinkles. Of course as the baby got older, the wrinkles tended to disappear.

Sophie was a full-time archaeology student then. Eve took care of Philip while she was off at her classes. Eve was an actress – she still was, when she could get work. Even in those days there were times when she wasn't working, or if she had daytime rehearsals she could take Philip along. For a couple of years they all lived together – Eve and Sophie and Philip – in Eve's apartment in Toronto. It was Eve who wheeled Philip in his baby carriage – and, later on, in his stroller – along all the streets between Queen and College and Spadina and Ossington, and during these walks she would sometimes discover a perfect, though neglected, little house for sale in a previously unknown to her two-block-long, tree-shaded, dead-end street. She would send Sophie to look at it; they would go round with the real-estate agent, talk about a mortgage, discuss what renovations they would have to pay for, and which they could do themselves. Dithering and fantasizing until the house was sold to somebody else, or until Eve had one of her periodic but intense fits of financial prudence, or until somebody persuaded them that these charming little side streets were not half so safe for women and children as the bright, ugly, brash, and noisy street that they continued to live on.

Ian was a person Eve took even less note of than she had of the Irish boy. He was a friend; he never came to the apartment except with others. Then he went to a job in California – he was an urban geographer – and Sophie ran up a phone bill which Eve had to speak to her about, and there was a change altogether in the atmosphere of the apartment. (Should Eve not have mentioned the bill?) Soon a visit was planned, and Sophie took Philip along, because Eve was doing a summer play in a regional theater.

Not long afterwards came the news from California. Sophie and Ian were going to get married.

"Wouldn't it be smarter to try living together for a while?" said Eve on the phone from her boarding house, and Sophie said, "Oh, no. He's weird. He doesn't believe in that."

"But I can't get off for a wedding," Eve said. "We run till the middle of September."

"That's okay," said Sophie. "It won't be a *wedding* wedding."

And until this summer, Eve had not seen her again. There was the lack of money at both ends, in the beginning. When Eve was working she had a steady commitment, and when she wasn't working she couldn't afford anything extra. Soon Sophie had a job, too – she was a receptionist in a doctor's office. Once Eve was just about to book a flight, when Sophie phoned to say that Ian's father had died and that he was flying to England for the funeral and bringing his mother back with him.

"And we only have the one room," she said.

"Perish the thought," said Eve. "Two mothers-in-law in one house, let alone in one room."

"Maybe after she's gone?" said Sophie.

But that mother stayed till after Daisy was born, stayed till they moved into the new house, stayed eight months in all. By then Ian was starting to write his book, and it was difficult for him if there were visitors in the house. It was difficult enough anyway. The time passed during which Eve felt confident enough to invite herself. Sophie sent pictures of Daisy, the garden, all the rooms of the house.

Then she announced that they could come, she and Philip and Daisy could come back to Ontario this summer. They would spend three weeks with Eve while Ian worked alone in California. At the end of that time he would join them and they would fly from Toronto to England to spend a month with his mother.

"I'll get a cottage on the lake," said Eve. "Oh, it will be lovely."

"It will," said Sophie. "It's crazy that it's been so long."

And so it had been. Reasonably lovely, Eve had thought. Sophie hadn't seemed much bothered or surprised by Daisy's wetting the bed. Philip had been finicky and standoffish for a couple of days, responding coolly to Eve's report that she had known him as a baby, and whining about the mosquitoes that descended on them as they hurried through the shoreline woods to get to the beach. He wanted to be taken to Toronto to see the Science Centre. But then he settled down, swam in the lake without complaining that it was cold, and busied himself with solitary projects – such as boiling and scraping the meat off a dead turtle he'd lugged home, so he could keep its shell. The turtle's stomach contained an undigested crayfish, and its shell came off in strips, but none of this dismayed him.

Eve and Sophie, meanwhile, developed a pleasant, puttering routine of morning chores, afternoons on the beach, wine with supper, and late-evening movies. They were drawn into half-serious speculations about the house. What could be done about it? First strip off the living-room wallpaper, an imitation of imitation-wood panelling. Pull up the linoleum with its silly pattern of gold fleurs-de-lis turned brown by ground-in sand and dirty scrub water. Sophie was so carried away that she loosened a bit of it that had rotted in front of the sink and discovered pine floorboards that surely could be sanded. They talked about the cost of renting a sander (supposing, that is, that the house was theirs) and what colors they would choose for the paint on the doors and wood-work, shutters on the windows, open shelves in the kitchen instead of the dingy plywood cupboards. What about a gas fireplace?

And who was going to live here? Eve. The snowmobilers who used the house for a winter clubhouse were building a place of their own, and the landlord might be happy to rent it year-round. Or maybe sell it very cheaply, considering its condition. It could be a retreat, if Eve got the job she was hoping for, next winter. And if she didn't, why not sublet the apartment and live here? There'd be the difference in the rents, and the old-age pension she started getting in October, and the money that still came in from a commercial she had made for a diet supplement. She could manage.

"And then if we came in the summers we could help with the rent," said Sophie.

Philip heard them. He said, "Every summer?"

"Well you like the lake now," Sophie said. "You like it here now."

"And the mosquitoes, you know they're not as bad every year," Eve said. "Usually they're just bad in the early summer. June, before you'd even get here. In the spring there are all these boggy places full of water, and they breed there, and then the boggy places dry up, and they don't breed again. But this year there was so much rain earlier, those places didn't dry up, so the mosquitoes got a second chance, and there's a whole new generation."

She had found out how much he respected information and preferred it to her opinions and reminiscences.

Sophie was not keen on reminiscence either. Whenever the past that she and Eve had shared was mentioned – even those months after Philip's birth that Eve thought of as some of the happiest, the hardest, the most purposeful and harmonious, in her life – Sophie's face took on a look of gravity and concealment, of patiently withheld judgments. The earlier time, Sophie's own childhood, was a positive minefield, as Eve discovered, when they were talking about Philip's school. Sophie thought it a little too rigorous, and Ian thought it just fine.

"What a switch from Blackbird," Eve said, and Sophie said at once, almost viciously, "Oh, Blackbird. What a farce. When I think that you paid for that. You *paid*."

Blackbird was an ungraded alternative school that Sophie had gone to (the name came from "Morning Has Broken"). It had cost Eve more than she could afford, but she thought it was better for a child whose mother was an actress and whose father was not in evidence. When Sophie was nine or ten, it had broken up because of disagreements among the parents.

"I learned Greek myths and I didn't know where Greece was," said Sophie. "I didn't know *what* it was. We had to spend art period making antinuke signs."

Eve said, "Oh, no, surely."

"We did. And they literally badgered us – they badgered us – to talk about sex. It was verbal molestation. You *paid*."

"I didn't know it was as bad as all that."

"Oh well," said Sophie. "I survived."

"That's the main thing," Eve said shakily. "Survival."

SOPHIE'S FATHER WAS from Kerala, in the southern part of India. Eve had met him, and spent her whole time with him, on a train going from Vancouver to Toronto. He was a young doctor studying in Canada on a fellowship. He had a wife already, and a baby daughter, at home in India.

The train trip took three days. There was a half-hour stop in Calgary. Eve and the doctor ran around looking for a drugstore where they could buy condoms. They didn't find one. By the time they got to Winnipeg, where the train stopped for a full hour, it was too late. In fact – said Eve, when she told their story – by the time they got to the Calgary city limits, it was probably too late.

He was travelling in the day coach – the fellowship was not generous. But Eve had splurged and got herself a roomette. It was this extravagance – a last-minute decision – it was the convenience and privacy of the roomette that were responsible, Eve said, for the existence of Sophie and the greatest change in her, Eve's, life. That, and the fact that you couldn't get condoms anywhere around the Calgary station, not for love or money.

In Toronto she waved goodbye to her lover from Kerala, as you would wave to any train acquaintance, because she was met there by the man who was at that time the serious interest and main trouble in her life. The whole three days had been underscored by the swaying and rocking of the train – the lovers' motions were never just what they contrived themselves, and perhaps for that reason seemed guiltless, irresistible. Their feelings and conversations must have been affected, too. Eve remembered these as sweet and generous, never solemn or desperate. It would have been hard to be solemn when you were dealing with the dimensions and the projections of the roomette.

She told Sophie his Christian name – Thomas, after the saint. Until she met him, Eve had never heard about the ancient Christians in southern India. For a while when she was in her teens Sophie had taken an interest in Kerala. She brought home books from the library and took to going to parties in a sari. She talked about looking her father up, when she got older. The fact that she knew his first name and his special study – diseases of the blood – seemed to her possibly enough. Eve stressed to her the size of the population of India and the chance that he had not even stayed there. What she could not bring herself to explain was how incidental, how nearly unimaginable, the existence of Sophie would be, necessarily, in her father's life. Fortunately the idea faded, and Sophie gave up wearing the sari when all those dramatic, ethnic costumes became too commonplace. The only time she mentioned her father, later on, was when she was carrying Philip, and making jokes about keeping up the family tradition of flyby fathers.

NO JOKES LIKE that now. Sophie had grown stately, womanly, graceful, and reserved. There had been a moment – they were getting through the woods to the beach, and Sophie had bent to scoop up Daisy, so that they might move more quickly out of range of the mosquitoes – when Eve had been amazed at the new, late manifestation of her daughter's beauty. A full-bodied, tranquil, classic beauty, achieved not by care and vanity but by self-forgetfulness and duty. She looked more Indian now, her creamed-coffee skin had darkened in the California sun, and she bore under her eyes the lilac crescents of a permanent mild fatigue.

But she was still a strong swimmer. Swimming was the only sport she had ever cared for, and she swam as well as ever, heading it seemed for the middle of the lake. The first day she had done it she said, "That was wonderful. I felt so free." She didn't say that it was because Eve was watching the children that she had felt that way, but Eve understood that it didn't need to be said. "I'm glad," she said – though in fact she had been frightened. Several times she had thought, Turn around now, and Sophie had swum right on, disregarding this urgent telepathic message. Her dark head became a spot, then a speck, then an illusion tossed among the steady waves. What Eve feared, and could not think about, was not a failure of strength but of the desire to return. As if this new Sophie, this grown woman so tethered to life, could be actually more indifferent to it than the girl Eve used to know, the young Sophie with her plentiful risks and loves and dramas.

"WE HAVE TO GET that movie back to the store," Eve said to Philip. "Maybe we should do it before we go to the beach."

Philip said, "I'm sick of the beach."

Eve didn't feel like arguing. With Sophie gone, with all plans altered, so that they were leaving, all of them leaving later in the day, she was sick of the beach, too. And sick of the house – all she could see now was the way this room would look tomorrow. The crayons, the toy cars, the large pieces of Daisy's simple jigsaw puzzle, all swept up and taken away. The storybooks gone that she knew by heart. No sheets drying outside the window. Eighteen more days to last, by herself, in this place.

"How about we go somewhere else today?" she said.

Philip said, "Where is there?"

"Let it be a surprise."

EVE HAD COME home from the village the day before, laden with provisions. Fresh shrimp for Sophie – the village store was actually a classy supermarket these days, you could find almost anything – coffee, wine, rye bread without caraway seeds because Philip hated caraway, a ripe melon, the dark cherries they all loved, though Daisy had to be watched with the stones, a tub of mocha-fudge ice cream, and all the regular things to keep them going for another week.

Sophie was clearing up the children's lunch. "Oh," she cried. "Oh, what'll we do with all that stuff?"

Ian had phoned, she said. Ian had phoned and said he was flying into Toronto tomorrow. Work on his book had progressed more quickly than he had expected; he had changed his plans. Instead of waiting for the three weeks to be up, he was coming tomorrow to collect Sophie and the children and take them on a little trip. He wanted to go to Quebec City. He had never been there, and he thought the children should see the part of Canada where people spoke French.

"He got lonesome," Philip said.

Sophie laughed. She said, "Yes. He got lonesome for us."

Twelve days, Eve thought. Twelve days had passed of the three weeks. She had had to take the house for a month. She was letting her friend Dev use the apartment. He was another out-of-work actor, and was in such real or imagined financial peril that he answered the phone in various stage voices. She was fond of Dev, but she couldn't go back and share the apartment with him.

Sophie said that they would drive to Quebec in the rented car, then drive straight back to the Toronto airport, where the car was to be turned in. No mention of Eve's going along. There wasn't room in the rented car. But couldn't she have taken her own car? Philip riding with her, perhaps, for company. Or Sophie. Ian could take the children, if he was so lonesome for them, and give Sophie a rest. Eve and Sophie could ride together as they used to in the summer, travelling to some town they had never seen before, where Eve had got a job.

That was ridiculous. Eve's car was nine years old and in no condition to make a long trip. And it was Sophie Ian had got lonesome for – you could tell that by her warm averted face. Also, Eve hadn't been asked.

"Well that's wonderful," said Eve. "That he's got along so well with his book."

"It is," said Sophie. She always had an air of careful detachment when she spoke of Ian's book, and when Eve had asked what it was about she had said merely, "Urban geography." Perhaps this was the correct behavior for academic wives – Eve had never known any.

"Anyway you'll get some time by yourself," Sophie said. "After all this circus. You'll find out if you really would like to have a place in the country. A retreat."

Eve had to start talking about something else, anything else, so that she wouldn't bleat out a question about whether Sophie still thought of coming next summer.

"I had a friend who went on one of those real retreats," she said. "He's a Buddhist. No, maybe a Hindu. Not a real Indian." (At this mention of Indians Sophie smiled in a way that said this was another subject that need not be gone into.) "Anyway, you could not speak on this retreat for three months. There were other people around all the time, but you could not speak to them. And he said that one of the things that often happened and that they were warned about was that you fell in love with one of these people you'd never spoken to. You felt you were communicating in a special way with them when you couldn't talk. Of course it was a kind of spiritual love, and you couldn't do anything about it. They were strict about that kind of thing. Or so he said."

Sophie said, "So? When you were finally allowed to speak what happened?"

"It was a big letdown. Usually the person you thought you'd been communicating with hadn't been communicating with you at all. Maybe they thought they'd been communicating that way with somebody else, and they thought —"

Sophie laughed with relief. She said, "So it goes." Glad that there was to be no show of disappointment, no hurt feelings.

Maybe they had a tiff, thought Eve. This whole visit might have been tactical. Sophie might have taken the children off to show him something. Spent time with her mother, just to show him something. Planning future holidays without him, to prove to herself that she could do it. A diversion.

And the burning question was, Who did the phoning?

"Why don't you leave the children here?" she said. "Just while you drive to the airport? Then just drive back and pick them up and take off. You'd have a little time to yourself and a little time alone with Ian. It'll be hell with them in the airport."

Sophie said, "I'm tempted."

So in the end that was what she did.

Now Eve had to wonder if she herself had engineered that little change just so she could get to talk to Philip.

(Wasn't it a big surprise when your dad phoned from California?
He didn't phone. My mom phoned him.
Did she? Oh I didn't know. What did she say?
She said, "I can't stand it here, I'm sick of it, let's figure out some plan to
get me away.")

EVE DROPPED HER voice to a matter-of-fact level, to indicate an interruption of the game. She said, "Philip. Philip, listen. I think we've got to
stop this. That truck just belongs to some farmer and it's going to turn
in someplace and we can't go on following."

"Yes we can," Philip said.

"No we can't. They'd want to know what we were doing. They might
be very mad."

"We'll call up our helicopters to come and shoot them."

"Don't be silly. You know this is just a game."

"They'll shoot them."

"I don't think they have any weapons," said Eve, trying another tack.
"They haven't developed any weapons to destroy aliens."

Philip said, "You're wrong," and began a description of some kind of
rockets, which she did not listen to.

WHEN SHE WAS a child staying in the village with her brother and
her parents, Eve had sometimes gone for drives in the country with her
mother. They didn't have a car – it was wartime, they had come here
on the train. The woman who ran the hotel was friends with Eve's
mother, and they would be invited along when she drove to the country
to buy corn or raspberries or tomatoes. Sometimes they would stop to
have tea and look at the old dishes and bits of furniture for sale in some
enterprising farm woman's front parlor. Eve's father preferred to stay
behind and play checkers with some other men on the beach. There was
a big cement square with a checkerboard painted on it, a roof protecting it but no walls, and there, even in the rain, the men moved oversized checkers around in a deliberate way, with long poles. Eve's brother

watched them or went swimming unsupervised – he was older. That was all gone now – the cement, even, was gone, or something had been built right on top of it. The hotel with its verandas extending over the sand was gone, and the railway station with its flower beds spelling out the name of the village. The railway tracks too. Instead there was a fake-old-fashioned mall with the satisfactory new supermarket and wineshop and boutiques for leisure wear and country crafts.

When she was quite small and wore a great hair bow on top of her head, Eve was fond of these country expeditions. She ate tiny jam tarts and cakes whose frosting was stiff on top and soft underneath, topped with a bleeding maraschino cherry. She was not allowed to touch the dishes or the lace-and-satin pincushions or the sallow-looking old dolls, and the women's conversations passed over her head with a temporary and mildly depressing effect, like the inevitable clouds. But she enjoyed riding in the backseat imagining herself on horseback or in a royal coach. Later on she refused to go. She began to hate trailing along with her mother and being identified as her mother's daughter. My daughter, Eve. How richly condescending, how mistakenly possessive, that voice sounded in her ears. (She was to use it, or some version of it, for years as a staple in some of her broadest, least accomplished acting.) She detested also her mother's habit of dressing up, wearing large hats and gloves in the country, and sheer dresses on which there were raised flowers, like warts. The oxford shoes, on the other hand – they were worn to favor her mother's corns – appeared embarrassingly stout and shabby.

"What did you hate most about your mother?" was a game that Eve would play with her friends in her first years free of home.

"Corsets," one girl would say, and another would say, "Wet aprons."

Hair nets. Fat arms. Bible quotations. "Danny Boy."

Eve always said. "Her corns."

She had forgotten all about this game until recently. The thought of it now was like touching a bad tooth.

Ahead of them the truck slowed and without signalling turned into a long tree-lined lane. Eve said, "I can't follow them any farther, Philip," and drove on. But as she passed the lane she noticed the gateposts. They were unusual, being shaped something like crude minarets and decorated with whitewashed pebbles and bits of colored glass. Neither one of them was straight, and they were half hidden by goldenrod and wild carrot, so that they had lost all reality as gateposts and looked instead like lost stage props from some gaudy operetta. The minute she saw them Eve remembered something else – a whitewashed outdoor wall in which there were pictures set. The pictures were stiff, fantastic, childish scenes. Churches with spires, castles with towers, square houses with square, lopsided, yellow windows. Triangular Christmas trees and tropical-colored birds half as big as the trees, a fat horse with dinky legs and burning red eyes, curly blue rivers, like lengths of ribbon, a moon and drunken stars and fat sunflowers nodding over the roofs of houses. All of this made of pieces of colored glass set into cement or plaster. She had seen it, and it wasn't in any public place. It was out in the country, and she had been with her mother. The shape of her mother loomed in front of the wall – she was talking to an old farmer. He might only have been her mother's age, of course, and looked old to Eve.

Her mother and the hotel woman did go to look at odd things on those trips; they didn't just look at antiques. They had gone to see a shrub cut to resemble a bear, and an orchard of dwarf apple trees.

Eve didn't remember the gateposts at all, but it seemed to her that they could not have belonged to any other place. She backed the car and swung around into the narrow track beneath the trees. The trees were heavy old Scotch pines, probably dangerous – you could see dangling half-dead branches, and branches that had already blown down or fallen down were lying in the grass and weeds on either side of the track. The car rocked back and forth in the ruts, and it seemed that Daisy approved of this motion. She began to make an accompanying noise. *Whoppy. Whoppy. Whoppy.*

This was something Daisy might remember – all she might remember – of this day. The arched trees, the sudden shadow, the interesting motion of the car. Maybe the white faces of the wild carrot that brushed at the windows. The sense of Philip beside her – his incomprehensible serious excitement, the tingling of his childish voice brought under unnatural control. A much vaguer sense of Eve – bare, freckly, sun-wrinkled arms, gray-blond frizzy curls held back by a black hairband. Maybe a smell. Not of cigarettes anymore, or of the touted creams and cosmetics on which Eve once spent so much of her money. Old skin? Garlic? Wine? Mouthwash? Eve might be dead when Daisy remembered this. Daisy and Philip might be estranged. Eve had not spoken to her own brother for three years. Not since he said to her on the phone, "You shouldn't have become an actress if you weren't equipped to make a better go of it."

There wasn't any sign of a house ahead, but through a gap in the trees the skeleton of a barn rose up, walls gone, beams intact, roof whole but flopping to one side like a funny hat. There seemed to be pieces of machinery, old cars or trucks, scattered around it, in the sea of flowering weeds. Eve had not much leisure to look – she was busy controlling the car on this rough track. The green truck had disappeared ahead of her – how far could it have gone? Then she saw that the lane curved. It curved; they left the shade of the pines and were out in the sunlight. The same sea foam of wild carrot, the same impression of rusting junk strewed about. A high wild hedge to one side, and there was the house, finally, behind it. A big house, two stories of yellowish-gray brick, an attic story of wood, its dormer windows stuffed with dirty foam rubber. One of the lower windows shone with aluminum foil covering it on the inside.

She had come to the wrong place. She had no memory of this house. There was no wall here around mown grass. Saplings grew up at random in the weeds.

The truck was parked ahead of her. And ahead of that she could see a patch of cleared ground where gravel had been spread and where she could have turned the car around. But she couldn't get past the truck to do that. She had to stop, too. She wondered if the man in the truck had stopped where he did on purpose, so that she would have to explain herself. He was now getting out of the truck in a leisurely way. Without looking at her, he released the dog, which had been running back and forth and barking with a great deal of angry spirit. Once on the ground, it continued to bark, but didn't leave the man's side. The man wore a cap that shaded his face, so that Eve could not see his expression. He stood by the truck looking at them, not yet deciding to come any closer.

Eve unbuckled her seat belt.

"Don't get out," said Philip. "Stay in the car. Turn around. Drive away."

"I can't," said Eve. "It's all right. That dog's just a yapper, he won't hurt me."

"Don't get out."

She should never have let that game get so far Out of control. A child of Philip's age could get too carried away. "This isn't part of the game," she said. "He's just a man."

"I know," said Philip. "But *don't get out.*"

"Stop that," said Eve, and got out and shut the door.

"Hi," she said. "I'm sorry. I made a mistake. I thought this was somewhere else."

The man said something like "Hey."

"I was actually looking for another place," said Eve. "It was a place where I came once when I was a little girl. There was a wall with pictures on it all made with pieces of broken glass. I think a cement wall, whitewashed. When I saw those pillars by the road, I thought this must be it. You must have thought we were following you. It sounds so silly."

She heard the car door open. Philip got out, dragging Daisy behind him. Eve thought he had come to be close to her, and she put out her arm to welcome him. But he detached himself from Daisy and circled round Eve and spoke to the man. He had brought himself out of the alarm of a moment before and now he seemed steadier than Eve was.

"Is your dog friendly?" he said in a challenging way.

"She won't hurt you," the man said. "Long as I'm here, she's okay. She gets in a tear because she's not no more than a pup. She's still not no more than a pup."

He was a small man, no taller than Eve. He was wearing jeans and one of those open vests of colorful weave, made in Peru or Guatemala. Gold chains and medallions sparkled on his hairless, tanned, and muscular chest. When he spoke he threw his head back and Eve could see that his face was older than his body. Some front teeth were missing.

"We won't bother you anymore," she said. "Philip, I was just telling this man we drove down this road looking for a place I came when I was a little girl, and there were pictures made of colored glass set in a wall. But I made a mistake, this isn't the place."

"What's its name?" said Philip.

"Trixie," the man said, and on hearing her name the dog jumped up and bumped his arm. He swatted her down. "I don't know about no pictures. I don't live here. Harold, he's the one would know."

"It's all right," said Eve, and hoisted Daisy up on her hip. "If you could just move the truck ahead, then I could turn around."

"I don't know no pictures. See, if they was in the front part the house I never would've saw them because Harold, he's got the front part of the house shut off."

"No, they were outside," said Eve. "It doesn't matter. This was years and years ago."

"Yeah. Yeah. Yeah," the man was saying, warming to the conversation. "You come in and get Harold to tell you about it. You know Harold? He's who owns it here. Mary, she owns it, but Harold he put her in the Home, so now he does. It wasn't his fault, she had to go there." He reached into the truck and took out two cases of beer. "I just had to go to town, Harold sent me into town. You go on. You go in. Harold be glad to see you."

"Here Trixie," said Philip sternly.

The dog came yelping and bounding around them, Daisy squealed with fright and pleasure and somehow they were all on the route to the house, Eve carrying Daisy, and Philip and Trixie scrambling around her up some earthen bumps that had once been steps. The man came close behind them, smelling of the beer that he must have been drinking in the truck.

"Open it up, go ahead in," he said. "Make your way through. You don't mind it's got a little untidy here? Mary's in the Home, nobody to keep it tidied up like it used to be."

Massive disorder was what they had to make their way through – the kind that takes years to accumulate. The bottom layer of it made up of chairs and tables and couches and perhaps a stove or two, with old bed-clothes and newspapers and window shades and dead potted plants and ends of lumber and empty bottles and broken lighting fixtures and curtain rods piled on top of that, up to the ceiling in some places, blocking nearly all the light from outside. To make up for that, a light was burning by the inside door.

The man shifted the beer and got that door open, and shouted for Harold. It was hard to tell what sort of room they were in now – there were kitchen cupboards with the doors off the hinges, some cans on the shelves, but there were also a couple of cots with bare mattresses and rumpled blankets. The windows were so successfully covered up with furniture or hanging quilts that you could not tell where they were, and the smell was that of a junk store, a plugged sink, or maybe a plugged toilet, cooking and grease and cigarettes and human sweat and dog mess and unremoved garbage.

Nobody answered the shouts. Eve turned around – there was room to turn around here, as there hadn't been in the porch – and said, "I don't think we should –" but Trixie got in her way and the man ducked round her to bang on another door.

"Here he is," he said – still at the top of his voice, though the door had opened. "Here's Harold in here." At the same time Trixie rushed forward, and another man's voice said, "Fuck. Get that dog out of here."

"Lady here wants to see some pictures," the little man said. Trixie whined in pain – somebody had kicked her. Eve had no choice but to go on into the room.

This was a dining room. There was the heavy old dining-room table and the substantial chairs. Three men were sitting down, playing cards. The fourth man had got up to kick the dog. The temperature in the room was about ninety degrees.

"Shut the door, there's a draft," said one of the men at the table.

The little man hauled Trixie out from under the table and threw her into the outer room, then closed the door behind Eve and the children.

"Christ. Fuck," said the man who had got up. His chest and arms were so heavily tattooed that he seemed to have purple or bluish skin. He shook one foot as if it hurt. Perhaps he had also kicked a table leg when he kicked Trixie.

Sitting with his back to the door was a young man with sharp narrow shoulders and a delicate neck. At least Eve assumed he was young, because he wore his hair in dyed golden spikes and had gold rings in his ears. He didn't turn around. The man across from him was as old as Eve herself, and had a shaved head, a tidy gray beard, and bloodshot blue eyes. He looked at Eve without any friendliness but with some intelligence or comprehension, and in this he was unlike the tattooed man, who had looked at her as if she was some kind of hallucination that he had decided to ignore.

At the end of the table, in the host's or the father's chair, sat the man who had given the order to close the door, but who hadn't looked up or otherwise paid any attention to the interruption. He was a large-boned, fat, pale man with sweaty brown curls, and as far as Eve could tell he was entirely naked. The tattooed man and the blond man were wearing jeans, and the gray-bearded man was wearing jeans and a checked shirt buttoned up to the neck and a string tie. There were glasses and bottles on the table. The man in the host's chair – he must be Harold – and the gray-bearded man were drinking whiskey. The other two were drinking beer.

"I told her maybe there was pictures in the front but she couldn't go in there you got that shut up," the little man said.

Harold said, "You shut up."

Eve said, "I'm really sorry." There seemed to be nothing to do but go into her spiel, enlarging it to include staying at the village hotel as a little girl, drives with her mother, the pictures in the wall, her memory of them today, the gateposts, her obvious mistake, her apologies. She spoke directly to the graybeard, since he seemed the only one willing to listen or capable of understanding her. Her arm and shoulder ached from the weight of Daisy and from the tension which had got hold of her entire body. Yet she was thinking how she would describe this – she'd say it was like finding yourself in the middle of a Pinter play. Or like all her nightmares of a stolid, silent, hostile audience.

The graybeard spoke when she could not think of any further charming or apologetic thing to say. He said, "I don't know. You'll have to ask Harold. Hey. Hey Harold. Do you know anything about some pictures made out of broken glass?"

"Tell her when she was riding around looking at pictures I wasn't even born yet," said Harold, without looking up.

"You're out of luck, lady," said the graybeard.

The tattooed man whistled. "Hey you," he said to Philip. "Hey kid. Can you play the piano?"

There was a piano in the room behind Harold's chair. There was no stool or bench – Harold himself taking up most of the room between the piano and the table – and inappropriate things, such as plates and over-coats, were piled on top of it, as they were on every surface in the house.

"No," said Eve quickly. "No he can't."

"I'm asking him," the tattooed man said. "Can you play a tune?"

The graybeard said, "Let him alone."

"Just asking if he can play a tune, what's the matter with that?"

"Let him alone."

"You see I can't move until somebody moves the truck," Eve said.

She thought, There is a smell of semen in this room.

Philip was mute, pressed against her side.

"If you could just move –" she said, turning and expecting to find the little man behind her. She stopped when she saw he wasn't there, he wasn't in the room at all, he had got out without her knowing when. What if he had locked the door?

She put her hand on the knob and it turned, the door opened with a little difficulty and a scramble on the other side of it. The little man had been crouched right there, listening.

Eve went out without speaking to him, out through the kitchen, Philip trotting along beside her like the most tractable little boy in the world. Along the narrow pathway on the porch, through the junk, and when they reached the open air she sucked it in, not having taken a real breath for a long time.

"You ought to go along down the road ask down at Harold's cousin's place," the little man's voice came after her. "They got a nice place. They got a new house, she keeps it beautiful. They'll show you pictures or anything you want, they'll make you welcome. They'll sit you down and feed you, they don't let nobody go away empty."

He couldn't have been crouched against the door all the time, because he had moved the truck. Or somebody had. It had disappeared altogether, been driven away to some shed or parking spot out of sight.

Eve ignored him. She got Daisy buckled in. Philip was buckling himself in, without having to be reminded. Trixie appeared from somewhere and walked around the car in a disconsolate way, sniffing at the tires.

Eve got in and closed the door, put her sweating hand on the key. The car started, she pulled ahead onto the gravel – a space that was surrounded by thick bushes, berry bushes she supposed, and old lilacs, as well as weeds. In places these bushes had been flattened by piles of old tires and bottles and tin cans. It was hard to think that things had been thrown out of that house, considering all that was left in it, but apparently they had. And as Eve swung the car around she saw, revealed by this flattening, some fragment of a wall, to which bits of whitewash still clung.

She thought she could see pieces of glass embedded there, glinting.

She didn't slow down to look. She hoped Philip hadn't noticed – he might want to stop. She got the car pointed towards the lane and drove past the dirt steps to the house. The little man stood there with both arms waving and Trixie was wagging her tail, roused from her scared docility sufficiently to bark farewell and chase them partway down the lane. The chase was only a formality; she could have caught up with them if she wanted to. Eve had had to slow down at once when she hit the ruts.

She was driving so slowly that it was possible, it was easy, for a figure to rise up out of the tall weeds on the passenger side of the car and open the door – which Eve had not thought of locking – and jump in.

It was the blond man who had been sitting at the table, the one whose face she had never seen.

"Don't be scared. Don't be scared anybody. I just wondered if I could hitch a ride with you guys, okay?"

It wasn't a man or a boy; it was a girl. A girl now wearing a dirty sort of undershirt.

Eve said, "Okay." She had just managed to hold the car in the track.

"I couldn't ask you back in the house," the girl said. "I went in the bathroom and got out the window and run out here. They probably don't even know I'm gone yet. They're boiled." She took hold of a handful of the undershirt which was much too large for her and sniffed at it. "Stinks," she said. "I just grabbed this of Harold's, was in the bathroom. Stinks."

Eve left the ruts, the darkness of the lane, and turned onto the ordinary road. "Jesus I'm glad to get out of there," the girl said. "I didn't know nothing about what I was getting into. I didn't know even how I got there, it was night. It wasn't no place for me. You know what I mean?"

"They seemed pretty drunk all right," said Eve.

"Yeah. Well. I'm sorry if I scared you."

"That's okay."

"If I hadn't've jumped in I thought you wouldn't stop for me. Would you?"

"I don't know," said Eve. "I guess I would have if it got through to me you were a girl. I didn't really get a look at you before."

"Yeah. I don't look like much now. I look like shit now. I'm not saying I don't like to party. I like to party. But there's party and there's party, you know what I mean?"

She turned in the seat and looked at Eve so steadily that Eve had to take her eyes from the road for a moment and look back. And what she saw was that this girl was much more drunk than she sounded. Her dark-brown eyes were glazed but held wide open, rounded with effort, and they had the imploring yet distant expression that drunks' eyes get, a kind of last-ditch insistence on fooling you. Her skin was blotched in some places and ashy in others, her whole face crumpled with the effects of a mighty bingeing. She was a natural brunette – the gold spikes were intentionally and provocatively dark at the roots – and pretty enough, if you disregarded her present dinginess, to make you wonder how she had ever got mixed up with Harold and Harold's crew. Her way of living and the style of the times must have taken fifteen or twenty natural pounds off her – but she wasn't tall and she really wasn't boyish. Her true inclination was to be a cuddly chunky girl, a darling dumpling.

"Herb was crazy bringing you in there like that," she said. "He's got a screw loose, Herb."

Eve said, "I gathered that."

"I don't know what he does around there, I guess he works for Harold. I don't think Harold uses him too good, neither."

Eve had never believed herself to be attracted to women in a sexual way. And this girl in her soiled and crumpled state seemed unlikely to appeal to anybody. But perhaps the girl did not believe this possible – she must be so used to appealing to people. At any rate she slid her hand along

Eve's bare thigh, just getting a little way beyond the hem of her shorts. It was a practiced move, drunk as she was. To spread the fingers, to grasp flesh on the first try, would have been too much. A practiced, automatically hopeful move, yet so lacking in any true, strong, squirmy, comradely lust that Eve felt that the hand might easily have fallen short and caressed the car upholstery.

"I'm okay," the girl said, and her voice, like the hand, struggled to put herself and Eve on a new level of intimacy. "You know what I mean? You understand me. Okay?"

"Of course," said Eve briskly, and the hand trailed away, its tired whore's courtesy done with. But it had not failed – not altogether. Blatant and halfhearted as it was, it had been enough to set some old wires twitching.

And the fact that it could be effective in any way at all filled Eve with misgiving, flung a shadow backwards from this moment over all the rowdy and impulsive as well as all the hopeful and serious, the more or less unrepented-of, couplings of her life. Not a real flare-up of shame, a sense of sin – just a dirty shadow. What a joke on her, if she started to hanker now after a purer past and a cleaner slate.

But it could be just that still, and always, she hankered after love.

She said, "Where is it you want to go?"

The girl jerked backwards, faced the road. She said, "Where you going? You live around here?" The blurred tone of seductiveness had changed, as no doubt it would change after sex, into a mean-sounding swagger.

"There's a bus goes through the village," Eve said. "It stops at the gas station. I've seen the sign."

"Yeah but just one thing," the girl said. "I got no money. See, I got away from there in such a hurry I never got to collect my money. So what use would it be me getting on a bus without no money?"

The thing to do was not to recognize a threat. Tell her that she could hitchhike, if she had no money. It wasn't likely that she had a gun in her jeans. She just wanted to sound as if she might have one.

But a knife?

The girl turned for the first time to look into the backseat.

"You kids okay back there?" she said.

No answer.

"They're cute," she said. "They shy with strangers?"

How stupid of Eve to think about sex, when the reality, the danger, were elsewhere.

Eve's purse was on the floor of the car in front of the girl's feet. She didn't know how much money was in it. Sixty, seventy dollars. Hardly more. If she offered money for a ticket the girl would name an expensive destination. Montreal. Or at least Toronto. If she said, "Just take what's there," the girl would see capitulation. She would sense Eve's fear and might try to push further. What was the best she could do? Steal the car? If she left Eve and the children beside the road, the police would be after her in a hurry. If she left them dead in some thicket, she might get farther. Or if she took them along while she needed them, a knife against Eve's side or a child's throat.

Such things happen. But not as regularly as on television or in the movies. Such things don't often happen.

Eve turned onto the county road, which was fairly busy. Why did that make her feel better? Safety there was an illusion. She could be driving along the highway in the midst of the day's traffic taking herself and the children to their deaths.

The girl said, "Where's this road go?"

"It goes out to the main highway."

"Let's drive out there."

"That's where I am driving," Eve said.

"Which way's the highway go?"

"It goes north to Owen Sound or up to Tobermory where you get the boat. Or south to – I don't know. But it joins another highway, you can get to Sarnia. Or London. Or Detroit or Toronto if you keep going."

Nothing more was said until they reached the highway. Eve turned onto it and said, "This is it."

"Which way you heading now?"

"I'm heading north," Eve said.

"That the way you live then?"

"I'm going to the village. I'm going to stop for gas."

"You got gas," the girl said. "You got over half a tank."

That was stupid. Eve should have said groceries.

Beside her the girl let out a long groan of decision, maybe of relinquishment.

"You know," she said, "you know. I might as well get out here if I'm going to hitch a ride. I could get a ride here as easy as anyplace."

Eve pulled over onto the gravel. Relief was turning into something like shame. It was probably true that the girl had run away without collecting any money, that she had nothing. What was it like to be drunk, wasted, with no money, at the side of the road?

"Which way you said we're going?"

"North," Eve told her again.

"Which way you said to Sarnia?"

"South. Just cross the road, the cars'll be headed south. Watch out for the traffic."

"Sure," the girl said. Her voice was already distant; she was calculating new chances. She was half out of the car as she said, "See you." And into the backseat, "See you guys. Be good."

"Wait," said Eve. She leaned over and felt in her purse for her wallet, got out a twenty-dollar bill. She got out of the car and came round to where the girl was waiting. "Here," she said. "This'll help you."

"Yeah. Thanks," the girl said, stuffing the bill in her pocket, her eyes on the road.

"Listen," said Eve. "If you're stranded I'll tell you where my house is. It's about two miles north of the village and the village is about half a mile north of here. North. This way. My family's there now, but they should be gone by evening, if that bothers you. It's got the name Ford on the mailbox. That's not my name, I don't know why it's there. It's all by itself in the middle of a field. It's got one ordinary window on one side of the front door and a funny-looking little window on the other. That's where they put in the bathroom."

"Yeah," the girl said.

"It's just that I thought, if you don't get a ride —"

"Okay," the girl said. "Sure."

When they had started driving again, Philip said, "Yuck. She smelled like vomit."

A little farther on he said, "She didn't even know you should look at the sun to tell directions. She was stupid. Wasn't she?"

"I guess so," Eve said.

"Yuck. I never ever saw anybody so stupid."

As they went through the village he asked if they could stop for ice-cream cones. Eve said no.

"There's so many people stopping for ice cream it's hard to find a place to park," she said. "We've got enough ice cream at home."

"You shouldn't say 'home,'" said Philip. "It's just where we're staying. You should say 'the house.'"

The big hay rolls in a field to the east of the highway were facing ends-on into the sun, so tightly packed they looked like shields or gongs or faces of Aztec metal. Past that was a field of pale soft gold tails or feathers.

"That's called barley, that gold stuff with the tails on it," she said to Philip.

He said, "I know."

"The tails are called beards sometimes." She began to recite, "'But the reapers, reaping early, in among the bearded barley –'"

Daisy said, "What does mean 'pearly'?"

Philip said, "Bar-ley."

"'Only reapers, reaping early,'" Eve said. She tried to remember. "'Save the reapers, reaping early –'" "Save" was what sounded best. Save the reapers.

SOPHIE AND IAN had bought corn at a roadside stand. It was for dinner. Plans had changed – they weren't leaving till morning. And they had bought a bottle of gin and some tonic and limes. Ian made the drinks while Eve and Sophie sat husking the corn. Eve said, "Two dozen. That's crazy."

"Wait and see," said Sophie. "Ian loves corn."

Ian bowed when he presented Eve with her drink, and after she had tasted it she said, "This is most heavenly."

Ian wasn't much as she had remembered or pictured him. He was not tall, Teutonic, humorless. He was a slim fair-haired man of medium height, quick moving, companionable. Sophie was less assured, more tentative in all she said and did, than she had seemed since she'd been here. But happier, too.

Eve told her story. She began with the checkerboard on the beach, the vanished hotel, the drives into the country. It included her mother's city-lady outfits, her sheer dresses and matching slips, but not the young Eve's feelings of repugnance. Then the things they went to see – the dwarf orchard, the shelf of old dolls, the marvellous pictures made of colored glass.

"They were a little like Chagall?" Eve said.

Ian said, "Yep. Even us urban geographers know about Chagall."

Eve said, "Sor-ry." Both laughed.

Now the gateposts, the sudden memory, the dark lane and ruined barn and rusted machinery, the house a shambles.

"The owner was in there playing cards with his friends," Eve said. "He didn't know anything about it. Didn't know or didn't care. And my God, it could have been nearly sixty years ago I was there – think of that."

Sophie said, "Oh, Mom. What a shame." She was glowing with relief to see Ian and Eve getting on so well together.

"Are you sure it was even the right place?" she said.

"Maybe not," said Eve. "Maybe not."

She would not mention the fragment of wall she had seen beyond the bushes. Why bother, when there were so many things she thought best not to mention? First, the game that she had got Philip playing, overexciting him. And nearly everything about Harold and his companions. Everything, every single thing about the girl who had jumped into the car.

There are people who carry decency and optimism around with them, who seem to cleanse every atmosphere they settle in, and you can't tell such people things, it is too disruptive. Ian struck Eve as being one of those people, in spite of his present graciousness, and Sophie as being someone who thanked her lucky stars that she had found him. It used to be older people who claimed this protection from you, but now it seemed more and more to be younger people, and someone like Eve had to try not to reveal how she was stranded in between. Her whole life liable to be seen as some sort of unseemly thrashing around, a radical mistake.

She could say that the house smelled vile, and that the owner and his friends looked altogether boozy and disreputable, but not that Harold was naked and never that she herself was afraid. And never what she was afraid of.

Philip was in charge of gathering up the corn husks and carrying them outside to throw them along the edge of the field. Occasionally Daisy picked up a few on her own, and took them off to be distributed around the house. Philip had added nothing to Eve's story and had not seemed to be concerned with the telling of it. But once it was told, and Ian (interested in bringing this local anecdote into line with his professional studies) was asking Eve what she knew about the breakup of older patterns of village and rural life, about the spread of what was called agribusiness, Philip did look up from his stooping and crawling work around the adults' feet. He looked at Eve. A flat look, a moment of conspiratorial blankness, a buried smile, that passed before there could be any need for recognition of it.

What did this mean? Only that he had begun the private work of storing and secreting, deciding on his own what should be preserved and how, and what these things were going to mean to him, in his unknown future.

IF THE GIRL CAME looking for her, they would all still be here. Then Eve's carefulness would go for nothing.

The girl wouldn't come. Much better offers would turn up before she'd stood ten minutes by the highway. More dangerous offers perhaps, but more interesting, likely to be more profitable.

The girl wouldn't come. Unless she found some homeless, heartless wastrel of her own age. (*I know where there's a place we can stay, if we can get rid of the old lady.*)

Not tonight but tomorrow night Eve would lie down in this hollowed-out house, its board walls like a paper shell around her, willing herself to grow light, relieved of consequence, with nothing in her head but the rustle of the deep tall corn which might have stopped growing now but still made its live noise after dark.

RUNAWAY

CARLA HEARD THE car coming before it topped the little rise in the road that around here they called a hill. It's her, she thought. Mrs. Jamieson – Sylvia – home from her holiday in Greece. From the barn door – but far enough inside that she could not readily be seen – she watched the road Mrs. Jamieson would have to drive by on, her place being half a mile farther along the road than Clark and Carla's.

If it was somebody getting ready to turn in at their gate it would be slowing down by now. But still Carla hoped. *Let it not be her.*

It was. Mrs. Jamieson turned her head once, quickly – she had all she could do maneuvering her car through the ruts and puddles the rain had made in the gravel – but she didn't lift a hand off the wheel to wave, she didn't spot Carla. Carla got a glimpse of a tanned arm bare to the shoulder, hair bleached a lighter color than it had been before, more white now than silver-blond, and an expression that was determined and exasperated and amused at her own exasperation – just the way Mrs. Jamieson would look negotiating such a road. When she turned her head there was something like a bright flash – of inquiry, of hopefulness – that made Carla shrink back.

So.

Maybe Clark didn't know yet. If he was sitting at the computer he would have his back to the window and the road.

But Mrs. Jamieson might have to make another trip. Driving home from the airport, she might not have stopped for groceries – not until she'd been home and figured out what she needed. Clark might see her then. And after dark, the lights of her house would show. But this was July, and it didn't get dark till late. She might be so tired that she wouldn't bother with the lights, she might go to bed early.

On the other hand, she might telephone. Any time now.

*　　*　　*

THIS WAS THE summer of rain and more rain. You heard it first thing in the morning, loud on the roof of the mobile home. The trails were deep in mud, the long grass soaking, leaves overhead sending down random showers even in those moments when there was no actual downpour from the sky and the clouds looked like clearing. Carla wore a high, wide-brimmed old Australian felt hat every time she went outside, and tucked her long thick braid down her shirt.

Nobody showed up for trail rides, even though Clark and Carla had gone around posting signs in all the camping sites, in the cafes, and on the tourist office billboard and anywhere else they could think of. Only a few pupils were coming for lessons and those were regulars, not the batches of schoolchildren on vacation, the busloads from summer camps, that had kept them going through last summer. And even the regulars that they counted on were taking time off for holiday trips, or simply cancelling their lessons because of the weather being so discouraging. If they called too late, Clark charged them for the time anyway. A couple of them had complained, and quit for good.

There was still some income from the three horses that were boarded. Those three, and the four of their own, were out in the field now, poking around in the grass under the trees. They looked as if they couldn't be bothered to notice that the rain was holding off for the moment, the way it often did for a while in the afternoon. Just enough to get your hopes up – the clouds whitening and thinning and letting through a diffuse brightness that never got around to being real sunshine, and was usually gone before supper.

Carla had finished mucking out in the barn. She had taken her time – she liked the rhythm of her regular chores, the high space under the barn roof, the smells. Now she went over to the exercise ring to see how dry the ground was, in case the five o'clock pupil did show up.

Most of the steady showers had not been particularly heavy, or borne on any wind, but last week there had come a sudden stirring and then a blast through the treetops and a nearly horizontal blinding rain. In a quarter of an hour the storm had passed over. But branches lay across the road, hydro lines were down, and a large chunk of the plastic roofing over the ring had been torn loose. There was a puddle like a lake at that end of the track, and Clark had worked until after dark, digging a channel to drain it away.

The roof had not yet been repaired. Clark had strung fence wire across to keep the horses from getting into the mud, and Carla had marked out a shorter track.

On the Web, right now, Clark was hunting for someplace to buy roofing. Some salvage outlet, with prices that they could afford, or somebody trying to get rid of such material secondhand. He would not go to Hy and Robert Buckley's Building Supply in town, which he called Highway Robbers Buggery Supply, because he owed them too much money and had had a fight with them.

Clark had fights not just with the people he owed money to. His friendliness, compelling at first, could suddenly turn sour. There were places he would not go into, where he always made Carla go, because of some row. The drugstore was one such place. An old woman had pushed in front of him – that is, she had gone to get something she'd forgotten and come back and pushed in front, rather than going to the end of the line, and he had complained, and the cashier had said to him, "She has emphysema," and Clark had said, "Is that so? I have piles, myself," and the manager had been summoned, to say that was uncalled-for. And in the coffee shop out on the highway the advertised breakfast discount had not been allowed, because it was past eleven o'clock in the morning, and Clark had argued and then dropped his takeout cup of coffee on the floor – just missing, so they said, a child in its stroller. He said the child was half a mile away and he dropped the cup because no cuff had been provided. They said he had not asked for a cuff. He said he shouldn't have had to ask.

"You flare up," said Carla.

"That's what men do."

She had not said anything to him about his row with Joy Tucker. Joy Tucker was the librarian from town who boarded her horse with them. The horse was a quick-tempered little chestnut mare named Lizzie – Joy Tucker, when she was in a jokey mood, called her Lizzie Borden.

Yesterday she had driven out, not in a jokey mood at all, and complained about the roof's not being fixed yet, and Lizzie looking miserable, as if she might have caught a chill.

There was nothing the matter with Lizzie, actually. Clark had tried – for him – to be placating. But then it was Joy Tucker who flared up and said that their place was a dump, and Lizzie deserved better, and Clark said, "Suit yourself." Joy had not – or not yet – removed Lizzie, as Carla had expected. But Clark, who had formerly made the little mare his pet, had refused to have anything more to do with her. Lizzie's feelings were hurt, in consequence – she was balky when exercised and kicked up a fuss when her hoofs had to be picked out, as they did every day, lest they develop a fungus. Carla had to watch out for nips.

But the worst thing as far as Carla was concerned was the absence of Flora, the little white goat who kept the horses company in the barn and in the fields. There had not been any sign of her for two days. Carla was afraid that wild dogs or coyotes had got her, or even a bear.

She had dreamt of Flora last night and the night before. In the first dream Flora had walked right up to the bed with a red apple in her mouth, but in the second dream – last night – she had run away when she saw Carla coming. Her leg seemed to be hurt but she ran anyway. She led Carla to a barbed-wire barricade of the kind that might belong on some battlefield, and then she – Flora – slipped through it, hurt leg and all, just slithered through like a white eel and disappeared.

The horses had seen Carla go across to the ring and they had all moved up to the fence – looking bedraggled in spite of their New Zealand blankets – so that she would take notice of them on her way back. She talked quietly to them, apologizing for coming empty-handed. She stroked their necks and rubbed their noses and asked whether they knew anything about Flora.

Grace and Juniper snorted and nuzzled up, as if they recognized the name and shared her concern, but then Lizzie butted in between them and knocked Grace's head away from Carla's petting hand. She gave the hand a nip for good measure, and Carla had to spend some time scolding her.

*　　*　　*

UP UNTIL THREE years ago Carla never really looked at mobile homes. She didn't call them that, either. Like her parents, she would have thought "mobile home" pretentious. Some people lived in trailers, and that was all there was to it. One trailer was no different from another. When Carla moved in here, when she chose this life with Clark, she began to see things in a new way. After that she started saying "mobile home" and she looked to see how people had fixed them up. The kind of curtains they had hung, the way they had painted the trim, the ambitious decks or patios or extra rooms that had been built on. She could hardly wait to get at such improvements herself.

Clark had gone along with her ideas, for a while. He had built new steps, and spent a lot of time looking for an old wrought-iron railing for them. He didn't make any complaint about the money spent on paint for the kitchen and bathroom or the material for curtains. Her paint job was hasty – she didn't know, at that time, that you should take the hinges off the cupboard doors. Or that you should line the curtains, which had since faded.

What Clark balked at was tearing up the carpet, which was the same in every room and the thing that she had most counted on replacing. It was divided into small brown squares, each with a pattern of darker brown and rust and tan squiggles and shapes. For a long time she had thought these were the same squiggles and shapes, arranged in the same way, in each square. Then when she had had more time, a lot of time, to examine them, she decided that there were four patterns joined together to make identical larger squares. Sometimes she could pick out the arrangement easily and sometimes she had to work to see it.

She did this when it was raining outside and Clark's mood weighted down all their inside space, and he did not want to pay attention to anything but the computer screen. But the best thing to do then was to invent or remember some job to do in the barn. The horses would not look at her when she was unhappy, but Flora, who was never tied up, would come and rub against her, and look up with an expression that was not quite sympathy – it was more like comradely mockery – in her shimmering yellow-green eyes.

Flora had been a half-grown kid when Clark brought her home from a farm where he had gone to bargain for some horse tackle. The people there were giving up on the country life, or at least on the raising of animals – they had sold their horses but failed to get rid of their goats. He had heard about how a goat was able to bring a sense of ease and comfort into a horse stable and he wanted to try it. They had meant to breed her someday but there had never been any signs of her coming into heat.

At first she had been Clark's pet entirely, following him everywhere, dancing for his attention. She was quick and graceful and provocative as a kitten, and her resemblance to a guileless girl in love had made them both laugh. But as she grew older she seemed to attach herself to Carla, and in this attachment she was suddenly much wiser, less skittish – she seemed capable, instead, of a subdued and ironic sort of humor. Carla's behavior with the horses was tender and strict and rather maternal, but the comradeship with Flora was quite different, Flora allowing her no sense of superiority.

"Still no sign of Flora?" she said, as she pulled off her barn boots. Clark had posted a Lost Goat notice on the Web.

"Not so far," he said, in a preoccupied but not unfriendly voice. He suggested, not for the first time, that Flora might have just gone off to find herself a billy.

No word about Mrs. Jamieson. Carla put the kettle on. Clark was humming to himself as he often did when he sat in front of the computer.

Sometimes he talked back to it. *Bullshit*, he would say, replying to some challenge. Or he would laugh – but could not remember what the joke was, when she asked him afterwards.

Carla called, "Do you want tea?" and to her surprise he got up and came into the kitchen.

"So," he said. "So, Carla."

"What?"

"So she phoned."

"Who?"

"Her Majesty. Queen Sylvia. She just got back."

"I didn't hear the car."

"I didn't ask you if you did."

"So what did she phone for?"

434

"She wants you to go and help her straighten up the house. That's what she said. Tomorrow."

"What did you tell her?"

"I told her sure. But you better phone up and confirm."

Carla said, "I don't see why I have to, if you told her." She poured out their mugs of tea. "I cleaned up her house before she left. I don't see what there could be to do so soon."

"Maybe some coons got in and made a mess of it while she was gone. You never know."

"I don't have to phone her right this minute," she said. "I want to drink my tea and I want to have a shower."

"The sooner the better."

Carla took her tea into the bathroom, calling back, "We have to go to the laundromat. Even when the towels dry out they smell moldy."

"We're not changing the subject, Carla."

Even after she'd got in the shower he stood outside the door and called to her.

"I am not going to let you off the hook, Carla."

She thought he might still be standing there when she came out, but he was back at the computer. She dressed as if she was going to town – she hoped that if they could get out of here, go to the laundromat, get a takeout at the cappuccino place, they might be able to talk in a different way, some release might be possible. She went into the living room with a brisk step and put her arms around him from behind. But as soon as she did that a wave of grief swallowed her up – it must have been the heat of the shower, loosening her tears – and she bent over him, all crumbling and crying.

He took his hands off the keyboard but sat still.

"Just don't be mad at me," she said.

"I'm not mad. I hate when you're like this, that's all."

"I'm like this because you're mad."

"Don't tell me what I am. You're choking me. Start supper."

That was what she did. It was obvious by now that the five o'clock person wasn't coming. She got out the potatoes and began to peel them, but her tears would not stop and she could not see what she was doing. She wiped her face with a paper towel and tore off a fresh one to take with her and went out into the rain. She didn't go into the barn because it was too miserable in there without Flora. She walked along the lane back to the woods. The horses were in the other field. They came over to the fence to watch her. All of them except Lizzie, who capered and snorted a bit, had the sense to understand that her attention was elsewhere.

IT HAD STARTED when they read the obituary, Mr. Jamieson's obituary. That was in the city paper, and his face had been on the evening news. Up until the year before, they had known the Jamiesons only as neighbors who kept to themselves. She taught Botany at the college forty miles away, so she had to spend a good deal of her time on the road. He was a poet.

Everybody knew that much. But he seemed to be occupied with other things. For a poet, and for an old man – perhaps twenty years older than Mrs. Jamieson – he was rugged and active. He improved the drainage system on his place, cleaning out the culvert and lining it with rocks. He dug and planted and fenced a vegetable garden, cut paths through the woods, looked after repairs on the house.

The house itself was an odd-looking triangular affair that he had built years ago, with some friends, on the foundation of an old wrecked farm-house. Those people were spoken of as hippies – though Mr. Jamieson must have been a bit old for that, even then, before Mrs. Jamieson's time. There was a story that they grew marijuana in the woods, sold it, and stored the money in sealed glass jars, which were buried around the property. Clark had heard this from the people he got to know in town. He said it was bullshit.

"Else somebody would have got in and dug it up, before now. Somebody would have found a way to make him tell where it was."

When they read the obituary Carla and Clark learned for the first time that Leon Jamieson had been the recipient of a large prize, five years before his death. A prize for poetry. Nobody had ever mentioned this. It seemed that people could believe in dope money buried in glass jars, but not in money won for writing poetry.

Shortly after this Clark said, "We could've made him pay."

Carla knew at once what he was talking about, but she took it as a joke.

"Too late now," she said. "You can't pay once you're dead."

"He can't. She could."

"She's gone to Greece."

"She's not going to stay in Greece."

"She didn't know," said Carla more soberly.

"I didn't say she did."

"She doesn't have a clue about it."

"We could fix that."

Carla said, "No. No."

Clark went on as if she had not spoken.

"We could say we're going to sue. People get money for stuff like that all the time."

"How could you do that? You can't sue a dead person."

"Threaten to go to the papers. Big-time poet. The papers would eat it up. All we have to do is threaten and she'd cave in."

"You're just fantasizing," Carla said. "You're joking."

"No," said Clark. "Actually, I'm not."

Carla said she did not want to talk about it anymore and he said okay.

But they talked about it the next day, and the next and the next. He sometimes got notions like this that were not practicable, which might even be illegal. He talked about them with growing excitement and then – she wasn't sure why – he dropped them. If the rain had stopped, if this had turned into something like a normal summer, he might have let this idea go the way of the others. But that had not happened, and during the last month he had harped on the scheme as if it was perfectly feasible and serious. The question was how much money to ask for. Too little, and the woman might not take them seriously, she might be inclined to see if they were bluffing. Too much might get her back up and she might become stubborn.

Carla had stopped saying that it was a joke. Instead she told him that it wouldn't work. She said that for one thing, people expected poets to be that way. So it wouldn't be worth paying out money to cover it up.

He said that it would work if it was done right. Carla was to break down and tell Mrs. Jamieson the whole story. Then Clark would move in, as if it had all been a surprise to him, he had just found out. He would be outraged, he would talk about telling the world. He would let Mrs. Jamieson be the one who first mentioned money.

"You were injured. You were molested and humiliated and I was injured and humiliated because you are my wife. It's a question of respect."

Over and over again he talked to her in this way and she tried to deflect him but he insisted.

"Promise," he said. "Promise."

THIS WAS BECAUSE of what she had told him, things she could not now retract or deny.

Sometimes he gets interested in me?

The old guy?

Sometimes he calls me into the room when she's not there?

Yes.

When she has to go out shopping and the nurse isn't there either.

A lucky inspiration of hers, one that instantly pleased him.

So what do you do then? Do you go in?

She played shy.

Sometimes.

He calls you into his room. So? Carla? So, then?

I go in to see what he wants.

So what does he want?

This was asked and told in whispers, even if there was nobody to hear, even when they were in the neverland of their bed. A bedtime story, in which the details were important and had to be added to every time, and this with convincing reluctance, shyness, giggles, *dirty, dirty*. And it was not only he who was eager and grateful. She was too. Eager to please and excite him, to excite herself. Grateful every time it still worked.

And in one part of her mind it *was* true, she saw the randy old man, the bump he made in the sheet, bedridden indeed, almost beyond speech but proficient in sign language, indicating his desire, trying to nudge and finger her into complicity, into obliging stunts and intimacies. (Her refusal a necessity, but also perhaps strangely, slightly disappointing, to Clark.)

Now and then came an image that she had to hammer down, lest it spoil everything. She would think of the real dim and sheeted body, drugged and shrinking every day in its rented hospital bed, glimpsed only a few times when Mrs. Jamieson or the visiting nurse had neglected to close the door. She herself never actually coming closer to him than that.

In fact she had dreaded going to the Jamiesons', but she needed the money, and she felt sorry for Mrs. Jamieson, who seemed so haunted and bewildered, as if she was walking in her sleep. Once or twice Carla had burst out and done something really silly just to loosen up the atmosphere. The kind of thing she did when clumsy and terrified first-time horseback riders were feeling humiliated. She used to try that too when Clark was stuck in his moods. It didn't work with him anymore. But the story about Mr. Jamieson had worked, decisively.

THERE WAS NO way to avoid the puddles in the path or the tall soaked grass alongside it, or the wild carrot which had recently come into flower. But the air was warm enough so that she didn't get chilly. Her clothes were soaked through as if by her own sweat or the tears that ran down her face with the drizzle of rain. Her weeping petered out in time. She had nothing to wipe her nose on – the paper towel now soggy – but she leaned over and blew it hard into a puddle.

She lifted her head and managed the long-drawn-out, vibrating whistle that was her signal – Clark's too – for Flora. She waited a couple of minutes and then called Flora's name. Over and over again, whistle and name, whistle and name.

Flora did not respond.

It was almost a relief, though, to feel the single pain of missing Flora, of missing Flora perhaps forever, compared to the mess she had got into concerning Mrs. Jamieson, and her seesaw misery with Clark. At least Flora's leaving was not on account of anything that she – Carla – had done wrong.

*　　*　　*

AT THE HOUSE, there was nothing for Sylvia to do except to open the windows. And to think – with an eagerness that dismayed without really surprising her – of how soon she could see Carla.

All the paraphernalia of illness had been removed. The room that had been Sylvia and her husband's bedroom and then his death chamber had been cleaned out and tidied up to look as if nothing had ever happened in it. Carla had helped with all that during the few frenzied days between the crematorium and the departure for Greece. Every piece of clothing Leon had ever worn and some things he hadn't, including gifts from his sisters that had never been taken out of their packages, had been piled in the backseat of the car and delivered to the Thrift Shop. His pills, his shaving things, unopened cans of the fortified drink that had sustained him as long as anything could, cartons of the sesame seed snaps that at one time he had eaten by the dozens, the plastic bottles full of the lotion that had eased his back, the sheepskins on which he had lain – all of that was dumped into plastic bags to be hauled away as garbage, and Carla didn't question a thing. She never said, "Maybe somebody could use that," or pointed out that whole cartons of cans were unopened. When Sylvia said, "I wish I hadn't taken the clothes to town. I wish I'd burned them all up in the incinerator," Carla had shown no surprise.

They cleaned the oven, scrubbed out the cupboards, wiped down the walls and the windows. One day Sylvia sat in the living room going through all the condolence letters she had received. (There was no accumulation of papers and notebooks to be attended to, as you might have expected with a writer, no unfinished work or scribbled drafts. He had told her, months before, that he had pitched everything. *And no regrets.*)

The south-sloping wall of the house was made up of big windows. Sylvia looked up, surprised by the watery sunlight that had come out – or possibly surprised by the shadow of Carla, bare-legged, bare-armed, on top of a ladder, her resolute face crowned with a frizz of dandelion hair that was too short for the braid. She was vigorously spraying and scrubbing the glass. When she saw Sylvia looking at her she stopped and flung out her arms as if she was splayed there, making a silly gargoyle-like face. They both began to laugh. Sylvia felt this laughter running all through her like a playful stream. She went back to her letters as Carla resumed the cleaning. She decided that all of these kind words – genuine or perfunctory, the tributes and regrets – could go the way of the sheepskins and the crackers.

When she heard Carla taking the ladder down, heard boots on the deck, she was suddenly shy. She sat where she was with her head bowed as Carla came into the room and passed behind her on her way to the kitchen to put the pail and the cloths back under the sink. Carla hardly halted, she was quick as a bird, but she managed to drop a kiss on Sylvia's bent head. Then she went on whistling something to herself.

That kiss had been in Sylvia's mind ever since. It meant nothing in particular. It meant *Cheer up*. Or *Almost done*. It meant that they were good friends who had got through a lot of depressing work together. Or maybe just that the sun had come out. That Carla was thinking of getting home to her horses. Nevertheless, Sylvia saw it as a bright blossom, its petals spreading inside her with tumultuous heat, like a menopausal flash.

Every so often there had been a special girl student in one of her botany classes – one whose cleverness and dedication and awkward egotism, or even genuine passion for the natural world, reminded her of her young self. Such girls hung around her worshipfully, hoped for some sort of intimacy they could not – in most cases – imagine, and they soon got on her nerves.

Carla was nothing like them. If she resembled anybody in Sylvia's life, it would have to be certain girls she had known in high school – those who were bright but never too bright, easy athletes but not strenuously competitive, buoyant but not rambunctious. Naturally happy.

"WHERE I WAS, this little village, this little tiny village with my two old friends, well, it was the sort of place where the very occasional tourist bus would stop, just as if it had got lost, and the tourists would get off and look around and they were absolutely bewildered because they weren't anywhere. There was nothing to buy."

Sylvia was speaking about Greece. Carla was sitting a few feet away from her. The large-limbed, uncomfortable, dazzling girl was sitting there at last, in the room that had been filled with thoughts of her. She was faintly smiling, belatedly nodding.

"And at first," Sylvia said, "at first I was bewildered too. It was so hot. But it's true about the light. It's wonderful. And then I figured out what there was to do, and there were just these few simple things but they could fill the day. You walk half a mile down the road to buy some oil and half a mile in the other direction to buy your bread or your wine, and that's the morning, and you eat some lunch under the trees and after lunch it's too hot to do anything but close the shutters and lie on your bed and maybe read. At first you read. And then it gets so you don't even do that. Why read? Later on you notice the shadows are longer and you get up and go for a swim.

"Oh," she interrupted herself. "Oh, I forgot."

She jumped up and went to get the present she had brought, which in fact she had not forgotten about at all. She had not wanted to hand it to Carla right away, she had wanted the moment to come more naturally, and while she was speaking she had thought ahead to the moment when she could mention the sea, going swimming. And say, as she now said, "Swimming reminded me of this because it's a little replica, you know, it's a little replica of the horse they found under the sea. Cast in bronze. They dredged it up, after all this time. It's supposed to be from the second century B.C."

When Carla had come in and looked around for work to do, Sylvia had said, "Oh, just sit down a minute, I haven't had anybody to talk to since I got back. Please." Carla had sat down on the edge of a chair, legs apart, hands between her knees, looking somehow desolate. As if reaching for some distant politeness she had said, "How was Greece?"

Now she was standing, with the tissue paper crumpled around the horse, which she had not fully unwrapped.

"It's said to represent a racehorse," Sylvia said. "Making that final spurt, the last effort in a race. The rider, too, the boy, you can see he's urging the horse on to the limit of its strength."

She did not mention that the boy had made her think of Carla, and she could not now have said why. He was only about ten or eleven years old. Maybe the strength and grace of the arm that must have held the reins, or the wrinkles in his childish forehead, the absorption and the pure effort there was in some way like Carla cleaning the big windows last spring. Her strong legs in her shorts, her broad shoulders, her big swipes at the glass, and then the way she had splayed herself out as a joke, inviting or even commanding Sylvia to laugh.

"You can see that," Carla said, now conscientiously examining the little bronzy-green statue. "Thank you very much."

"You are welcome. Let's have coffee, shall we? I've just made some. The coffee in Greece was quite strong, a little stronger than I liked, but the bread was heavenly. And the ripe figs, they were astounding. Sit down another moment, please do. You should stop me going on and on this way. What about here? How has life been here?"

"It's been raining most of the time."

"I can see that. I can see it has," Sylvia called from the kitchen end of the big room. Pouring the coffee, she decided that she would keep quiet about the other gift she had brought. It hadn't cost her anything (the horse had cost more than the girl could probably guess), it was only a beautiful small pinkish-white stone she had picked up along the road.

"This is for Carla," she had said to her friend Maggie, who was walking beside her. "I know it's silly. I just want her to have a tiny piece of this land."

She had already mentioned Carla to Maggie, and to Soraya, her other friend there, telling them how the girl's presence had come to mean more and more to her, how an indescribable bond had seemed to grow up between them, and had consoled her in the awful months of last spring.

"It was just to see somebody – somebody so fresh and full of health coming into the house."

Maggie and Soraya had laughed in a kindly but annoying way.

"There's always a girl," Soraya said, with an indolent stretch of her heavy brown arms, and Maggie said, "We all come to it sometime. A crush on a girl."

Sylvia was obscurely angered by that dated word – *crush*.

"Maybe it's because Leon and I never had children," she said. "It's stupid. Displaced maternal love."

Her friends spoke at the same time, saying in slightly different ways something to the effect that it might be stupid but it was, after all, love.

BUT THE GIRL was not, today, anything like the Carla Sylvia had been remembering, not at all the calm bright spirit, the carefree and generous young creature who had kept her company in Greece.

She had been hardly interested in her gift. Almost sullen as she reached out for her mug of coffee.

"There was one thing I thought you would have liked a lot," said Sylvia energetically. "The goats. They were quite small even when they were full-grown. Some spotty and some white, and they were leaping around up on the rocks just like – like the spirits of the place." She laughed in an artificial way, she couldn't stop herself. "I wouldn't be surprised if they'd had wreaths on their horns. How is your little goat? I forget her name."

Carla said, "Flora."

"Flora."

"She's gone."

"Gone? Did you sell her?"

"She disappeared. We don't know where."

"Oh, I'm sorry. I'm sorry. But isn't there a chance she'll turn up again?"

No answer. Sylvia looked directly at the girl, something that up to now she had not quite been able to do, and saw that her eyes were full of tears, her face blotchy – in fact it looked grubby – and that she seemed bloated with distress.

She didn't do anything to avoid Sylvia's look. She drew her lips tight over her teeth and shut her eyes and rocked back and forth as if in a soundless howl, and then, shockingly, she did howl. She howled and wept and gulped for air and tears ran down her cheeks and snot out of her nostrils and she began to look around wildly for something to wipe with. Sylvia ran and got handfuls of Kleenex.

"Don't worry, here you are, here, you're all right," she said, thinking that maybe the thing to do would be to take the girl in her arms. But she had not the least wish to do that, and it might make things worse. The girl might feel how little Sylvia wanted to do such a thing, how appalled she was in fact by this noisy fit.

Carla said something, said the same thing again.

"Awful," she said. "Awful."

"No it's not. We all have to cry sometimes. It's all right, don't worry."

"It's awful."

And Sylvia could not help feeling how, with every moment of this show of misery, the girl made herself more ordinary, more like one of those soggy students in her – Sylvia's – office. Some of them cried about their marks, but that was often tactical, a brief unconvincing bit of whimpering. The more infrequent, real waterworks would turn out to have something to do with a love affair, or their parents, or a pregnancy.

"It's not about your goat, is it?"

"No. No."

"You better have a glass of water," said Sylvia.

She took time to run it cold, trying to think what else she should do or say, and when she returned with it Carla was already calming down.

"Now. Now," Sylvia said as the water was being swallowed. "Isn't that better?"

"Yes."

"It's not the goat. What is it?"

Carla said, "I can't stand it anymore."

What could she not stand?

It turned out to be the husband.

He was mad at her all the time. He acted as if he hated her. There was nothing she could do right, there was nothing she could say. Living with him was driving her crazy. Sometimes she thought she already was crazy. Sometimes she thought he was.

"Has he hurt you, Carla?"

No. He hadn't hurt her physically. But he hated her. He despised her. He could not stand it when she cried and she could not help crying because he was so mad.

She did not know what to do.

"Perhaps you do know what to do," said Sylvia.

"Get away? I would if I could." Carla began to wail again. "I'd give anything to get away. I can't. I haven't any money. I haven't anywhere in this world to go."

"Well. Think. Is that altogether true?" said Sylvia in her best counselling manner. "Don't you have parents? Didn't you tell me you grew up in Kingston? Don't you have a family there?"

Her parents had moved to British Columbia. They hated Clark. They didn't care if she lived or died.

Brothers or sisters?

One brother nine years older. He was married and in Toronto. He didn't care either. He didn't like Clark. His wife was a snob.

"Have you ever thought of the Women's Shelter?"

"They don't want you there unless you've been beaten up. And everybody would find out and it would be bad for our business."

Sylvia gently smiled.

"Is this a time to think about that?"

Then Carla actually laughed. "I know," she said, "I'm insane."

"Listen," said Sylvia. "Listen to me. If you had the money to go, would you go? Where would you go? What would you do?"

"I would go to Toronto," Carla said readily enough. "But I wouldn't go near my brother. I'd stay in a motel or something and I'd get a job at a riding stable."

"You think you could do that?"

"I was working at a riding stable the summer I met Clark. I'm more experienced now than I was then. A lot more."

"You sound as if you've figured this out," said Sylvia thoughtfully.

Carla said, "I have now."

"So when would you go, if you could go?"

"Now. Today. This minute."

"All that's stopping you is lack of money?"

Carla took a deep breath. "All that's stopping me," she said.

"All right," said Sylvia. "Now listen to what I propose. I don't think you should go to a motel. I think you should take the bus to Toronto and go to stay with a friend of mine. Her name is Ruth Stiles. She has a big house and she lives alone and she won't mind having somebody to stay. You can stay there till you find a job. I'll help you with some money. There must be lots and lots of riding stables around Toronto."

"There are."

"So what do you think? Do you want me to phone and find out what time the bus goes?"

Carla said yes. She was shivering. She ran her hands up and down her thighs and shook her head roughly from side to side.

"I can't believe it," she said. "I'll pay you back. I mean, thank you. I'll pay you back. I don't know what to say."

Sylvia was already at the phone, dialling the bus depot.

"Shh, I'm getting the times," she said. She listened, and hung up. "I know you will. You agree about Ruth's? I'll let her know. There's one problem, though." She looked critically at Carla's shorts and T-shirt. "You can't very well go in those clothes."

"I can't go home to get anything," said Carla in a panic. "I'll be all right."

"The bus will be air-conditioned. You'll freeze. There must be something of mine you could wear. Aren't we about the same height?"

"You're ten times skinnier."

"I didn't use to be."

In the end they decided on a brown linen jacket, hardly worn – Sylvia had considered it to be a mistake for herself, the style too brusque – and a pair of tailored tan pants and a cream-colored silk shirt. Carla's sneakers would have to do with this outfit, because her feet were two sizes larger than Sylvia's.

Carla went to take a shower – something she had not bothered with in her state of mind that morning – and Sylvia phoned Ruth. Ruth was going to be out at a meeting that evening, but she would leave the key with her upstairs tenants and all Carla would have to do was ring their bell.

"She'll have to take a cab from the bus depot, though. I assume she's okay to manage that?" Ruth said.

Sylvia laughed. "She's not a lame duck, don't worry. She is just a person in a bad situation, the way it happens."

"Well good. I mean good she's getting out."

"Not a lame duck at all," said Sylvia, thinking of Carla trying on the tailored pants and linen jacket. How quickly the young recover from a fit of despair and how handsome the girl had looked in the fresh clothes.

The bus would stop in town at twenty past two. Sylvia decided to make omelettes for lunch, to set the table with the dark-blue cloth, and to get down the crystal glasses and open a bottle of wine.

"I hope you're hungry enough to eat something," she said, when Carla came out clean and shining in her borrowed clothes. Her softly freckled skin was flushed from the shower, and her hair was damp and darkened, out of its braid, the sweet frizz now flat against her head. She said she was hungry, but when she tried to get a forkful of the omelette to her mouth her trembling hands made it impossible.

"I don't know why I'm shaking like this," she said. "I must be excited. I never knew it would be this easy."

"It's very sudden," said Sylvia. "Probably it doesn't seem quite real."

"It does, though. Everything now seems really real. Like the time before now, that's when I was in a daze."

"Maybe when you make up your mind to something, when you really make up your mind, that's how it is. Or that's how it should be."

"If you've got a friend," said Carla with a self-conscious smile and a flush spreading over her forehead. "If you've got a true friend. I mean like you." She laid down the knife and fork and raised her wineglass awkwardly with both hands. "Drinking to a true friend," she said, uncomfortably. "I probably shouldn't even take a sip, but I will."

"Me too," said Sylvia with a pretense of gaiety. She drank, but spoiled the moment by saying, "Are you going to phone him? Or what? He'll have to know. At least he'll have to know where you are by the time he'd be expecting you home."

"Not the phone," said Carla, alarmed. "I can't do it. Maybe if you —"

"No," said Sylvia. "No."

"No, that's stupid. I shouldn't have said that. It's just hard to think straight. What I maybe should do, I should put a note in the mailbox. But I don't want him to get it too soon. I don't want us to even drive past there when we're going into town. I want to go the back way. So if I write it – if I write it, could you, could you maybe slip it in the box when you come back?"

Sylvia agreed to this, seeing no good alternative.

She brought pen and paper. She poured a little more wine. Carla sat thinking, then wrote a few words.

I HAVE GONE AWAY. I will be all write.

These were the words that Sylvia read when she unfolded the paper, on her way back from the bus depot. She was sure Carla knew *right* from *write*. It was just that she had been talking about *writing* a note, and she was in a state of exalted confusion. More confusion perhaps than Sylvia had realized. The wine had brought out a stream of talk, but it had not seemed to be accompanied by any particular grief or upset. She had talked about the horse barn where she had worked and met Clark when she was eighteen and just out of high school. Her parents wanted her to go to college, and she had agreed as long as she could choose to be a veterinarian. All she really wanted, and had wanted all her life, was to work with animals and live in the country. She had been one of those dorky girls in high school, one of those girls they made rotten jokes about, but she didn't care.

Clark was the best riding teacher they had. Scads of women were after him, they would take up riding just to get him as their teacher. Carla teased him about his women and at first he seemed to like it, then he got annoyed. She apologized and tried to make up for it by getting him talking about his dream – his plan, really – to have a riding school, a horse stable, someplace out in the country. One day she came into the stable and saw him hanging up his saddle and realized she had fallen in love with him.

Now she considered it was sex. It was probably just sex.

WHEN FALL CAME and she was supposed to quit working and leave for college in Guelph, she refused to go, she said she needed a year off.

Clark was very smart but he hadn't waited even to finish high school. He had altogether lost touch with his family. He thought families were like a poison in your blood. He had been an attendant in a mental hospital, a disc jockey on a radio station in Lethbridge, Alberta, a member of a road crew on the highways near Thunder Bay, an apprentice barber, a salesman in an Army Surplus store. And those were only the jobs he told her about.

She had nicknamed him Gypsy Rover, because of the song, an old song her mother used to sing. Now she took to singing it around the house all the time and her mother knew something was up.

> *"Last night she slept in a feather bed*
> *With a silken quilt for cover*
> *Tonight she'll sleep on the cold hard ground —*
> *Beside her gypsy lo-ov-ver."*

Her mother said, "He'll break your heart, that's a sure thing." Her stepfather, who was an engineer, did not even grant Clark that much power. "A loser," he called him. "One of those drifters." As if Clark was a bug he could just whisk off his clothes.

So Carla said, "Does a drifter save up enough money to buy a farm? Which, by the way, he has done?" and he only said, "I'm not about to argue with you." She was not his daughter anyway, he added, as if that was the clincher.

So, naturally, Carla had to run away with Clark. The way her parents behaved, they were practically guaranteeing it.

"Will you get in touch with your parents after you're settled?" Sylvia said. "In Toronto?"

Carla lifted her eyebrows, pulled in her cheeks and made a saucy O of her mouth. She said, "Nope."

Definitely a little drunk.

BACK HOME, having left the note in the mailbox, Sylvia cleaned up the dishes that were still on the table, washed and polished the omelette pan, threw the blue napkins and tablecloth in the laundry basket, and opened the windows. She did this with a confusing sense of regret and irritation.

She had put out a fresh cake of apple-scented soap for the girl's shower and the smell of it lingered in the house, as it had in the air of the car.

The rain was holding off. She could not stay still, so she went for a walk along the path that Leon had cleared. The gravel he had dumped in the boggy places had mostly washed away. They used to go walking every spring, to look for wild orchids. She taught him the name of every wildflower – all of which, except for trillium, he forgot. He used to call her his Dorothy Wordsworth.

Last spring she went out once and picked him a small bunch of dog's-tooth violets, but he looked at them – as he sometimes looked at her – with mere exhaustion, disavowal.

She kept seeing Carla, Carla stepping onto the bus. Her thanks had been sincere but already almost casual, her wave jaunty. She had got used to her salvation.

Back in the house, at around six o'clock, Sylvia put in a call to Toronto, to Ruth, knowing that Carla would not have arrived yet. She got the answering machine.

"Ruth," said Sylvia. "Sylvia. It's about this girl I sent you. I hope she doesn't turn out to be a bother to you. I hope it'll be all right. You may find her a little full of herself. Maybe it's just youth. Let me know. Okay?"

She phoned again before she went to bed but got the machine, so she said, "Sylvia again. Just checking," and hung up. It was between nine and ten o'clock, not even really dark. Ruth must still be out and the girl would not want to pick up the phone in a strange house. She tried to think of the name of Ruth's upstairs tenants. They surely wouldn't have gone to bed yet. But she could not remember. And just as well. Phoning them would have meant making too much of a fuss, being too anxious, going too far.

She got into the bed but it was impossible to stay there, so she took a light quilt and went out to the living room and lay down on the sofa, where she had slept for the last three months of Leon's life. She did not think it likely that she would get to sleep there either – there were no curtains on the bank of windows and she could tell by the look of the sky that the moon had risen, though she could not see it.

The next thing she knew she was on a bus somewhere – in Greece? – with a lot of people she did not know, and the engine of the bus was making an alarming knocking sound. She woke to find the knocking was at her front door.

Carla?

CARLA HAD KEPT her head down until the bus was clear of town. The windows were tinted, nobody could see in, but she had to guard herself against seeing out. Lest Clark appear. Coming out of a store or waiting to cross the street, all ignorant of her abandoning him, thinking this an ordinary afternoon. No, thinking it the afternoon when their scheme – his scheme – was put in motion, eager to know how far she had got with it.

Once they were out in the country she looked up, breathed deeply, took account of the fields, which were slightly violet-tinted through the glass. Mrs. Jamieson's presence had surrounded her with some kind of remarkable safety and sanity and had made her escape seem the most rational thing you could imagine, in fact the only self-respecting thing that a person in Carla's shoes could do. Carla had felt herself capable of an unaccustomed confidence, even of a mature sense of humor, revealing her life to Mrs. Jamieson in a way that seemed bound to gain sympathy and yet to be ironic and truthful. And adapted to live up to what, as far as she could see, were Mrs. Jamieson's – Sylvia's – expectations. She did have a feeling that it would be possible to disappoint Mrs. Jamieson, who struck her as a most sensitive and rigorous person, but she thought that she was in no danger of doing that.

If she didn't have to be around her for too long.

The sun was shining, as it had been for some time. When they sat at lunch it had made the wineglasses sparkle. No rain had fallen since early morning. There was enough of a wind blowing to lift the roadside grass, the flowering weeds, out of their drenched clumps. Summer clouds, not rain clouds, were scudding across the sky. The whole countryside was changing, shaking itself loose, into the true brightness of a July day. And as they sped along she was able to see not much trace at all of the recent past – no big puddles in the fields, showing where the seed had washed out, no miserable spindly cornstalks or lodged grain.

It occurred to her that she must tell Clark about this – that perhaps they had chosen what was for some freakish reason a very wet and dreary corner of the country, and there were other places where they could have been successful.

Or could be yet?

Then it came to her of course that she would not be telling Clark anything. Never again. She would not be concerned about what happened to him, or to Grace or Mike or Juniper or Blackberry or Lizzie Borden. If by any chance Flora came back, she would not hear of it.

This was her second time to leave everything behind. The first time was just like the old Beatles song – her putting the note on the table and slipping out of the house at five o'clock in the morning, meeting Clark in the church parking lot down the street. She was actually humming that song as they rattled away. *She's leaving home, bye-bye.* She recalled now how the sun was coming up behind them, how she looked at Clark's hands on the wheel, the dark hairs on his competent forearms, and breathed in the smell of the inside of the truck, a smell of oil and metal, tools and horse barns. The cold air of the fall morning blew in through the truck's rusted seams. It was the sort of vehicle that nobody in her family ever rode in, that scarcely ever appeared on the streets where they lived.

Clark's preoccupation on that morning with the traffic (they had reached Highway 401), his concern about the truck's behavior, his curt answers, his narrowed eyes, even his slight irritation at her giddy delight – all of that thrilled her. As did the disorder of his past life, his avowed loneliness, the tender way he could have with a horse, and with her. She saw him as the architect of the life ahead of them, herself as captive, her submission both proper and exquisite.

"You don't know what you're leaving behind," her mother wrote to her, in that one letter that she received, and never answered. But in those shivering moments of early-morning flight she certainly did know what she was leaving behind, even if she had rather a hazy idea of what she was going to. She despised her parents, their house, their backyard, their photo albums, their vacations, their Cuisinart, their *powder room*, their walk-in closets, their underground lawn-sprinkling system. In the brief note she had written she had used the word *authentic*.

I have always felt the need of a more authentic kind of life. I know I cannot expect you to understand this.

The bus had stopped now at the first town on the way. The depot was a gas station. It was the very station she and Clark used to drive to, in their early days, to buy cheap gas. In those days their world had included several towns in the surrounding countryside and they had sometimes behaved like tourists, sampling the specialties in grimy hotel bars. Pigs' feet, sauerkraut, potato pancakes, beer. And they would sing all the way home like crazy hillbillies.

But after a while all outings came to be seen as a waste of time and money. They were what people did before they understood the realities of their lives.

She was crying now, her eyes had filled up without her realizing it. She set herself to thinking about Toronto, the first steps ahead. The taxi, the house she had never seen, the strange bed she would sleep in alone. Looking in the phone book tomorrow for the addresses of riding stables, then getting to wherever they were, asking for a job.

She could not picture it. Herself riding on the subway or streetcar, caring for new horses, talking to new people, living among hordes of people every day who were not Clark.

A life, a place, chosen for that specific reason – that it would not contain Clark.

The strange and terrible thing coming clear to her about that world of the future, as she now pictured it, was that she would not exist there. She would only walk around, and open her mouth and speak, and do this and do that. She would not really be there. And what was strange about it was that she was doing all this, she was riding on this bus in the hope of recovering herself. As Mrs. Jamieson might say – and as she herself might with satisfaction have said – *taking charge of her own life*. With nobody glowering over her, nobody's mood infecting her with misery.

But what would she care about? How would she know that she was alive?

While she was running away from him – now – Clark still kept his place in her life. But when she was finished running away, when she just went on, what would she put in his place? What else – who else – could ever be so vivid a challenge?

She had managed to stop crying, but she had started to shake. She was in a bad way and would have to take hold, get a grip on herself. "Get a grip on yourself," Clark had sometimes told her, passing through a room where she was scrunched up, trying not to weep, and that indeed was what she must do.

They had stopped in another town. This was the third town away from the one where she had got on the bus, which meant that they had passed through the second town without her even noticing. The bus must have stopped, the driver must have called out the name, and she had not heard or seen anything in her fog of fright. Soon enough they would reach the major highway, they would be tearing along towards Toronto.

And she would be lost.

She would be lost. What would be the point of getting into a taxi and giving the new address, of getting up in the morning and brushing her teeth and going into the world? Why should she get a job, put food in her mouth, be carried by public transportation from place to place?

Her feet seemed now to be at some enormous distance from her body. Her knees, in the unfamiliar crisp pants, were weighted with irons. She was sinking to the ground like a stricken horse who will never get up.

Already the bus had loaded on the few passengers and the parcels that had been waiting in this town. A woman and a baby in its stroller were waving somebody good-bye. The building behind them, the cafe that served as a bus stop, was also in motion. A liquefying wave passed through the bricks and windows as if they were about to dissolve. In peril of her life, Carla pulled her huge body, her iron limbs, forward. She stumbled, she cried out, "Let me off."

The driver braked, he called out irritably, "I thought you were going to Toronto?" People gave her casually curious looks, nobody seemed to understand that she was in anguish.

"I have to get off here."

"There's a washroom in the back."

"No. No. I have to get off."

"I'm not waiting. You understand that? You got luggage underneath?"

"No. Yes. No."

"No luggage?"

A voice in the bus said, "Claustrophobia. That's what's the matter with her."

"You sick?" said the driver.

"No. No. I just want off."

"Okay. Okay. Fine by me."

"COME AND GET ME. Please. Come and get me."

"I will."

SYLVIA HAD FORGOTTEN to lock her door. She realized that she should be locking it now, not opening it, but it was too late, she had it open.

And nobody there.

Yet she was sure, sure, the knocking had been real.

She closed the door and this time she locked it.

There was a playful sound, a tinkling tapping sound, coming from the wall of windows. She switched the light on, but saw nothing there, and switched it off again. Some animal – maybe a squirrel? The French doors that opened between windows, leading to the patio, had not been locked either. Not even really closed, having been left open an inch or so from her airing of the house. She started to close them and somebody laughed, nearby, near enough to be in the room with her.

"It's me," a man said. "Did I scare you?"

He was pressed against the glass, he was right beside her.

"It's Clark," he said. "Clark from down the road."

She was not going to ask him in, but she was afraid to shut the door in his face. He could grab it before she could manage that. She didn't want to turn on the light, either. She slept in a long T-shirt. She should have pulled the quilt from the sofa and wrapped it around herself, but it was too late now.

"Did you want to get dressed?" he said. "What I got in here, it could be the very things you need."

He had a shopping bag in his hand. He thrust it at her, but did not try to come with it.

"What?" she said in a choppy voice.

"Look and see. It's not a bomb. There, take it."

She felt inside the bag, not looking. Something soft. And then she recognized the buttons of the jacket, the silk of the shirt, the belt on the pants.

"Just thought you'd better have them back," he said. "They're yours, aren't they?"

She tightened her jaws so that her teeth wouldn't chatter. A fearful dryness had attacked her mouth and throat.

"I understood they were yours," he said softly.

Her tongue moved like a wad of wool. She forced herself to say, "Where's Carla?"

"You mean my wife Carla?"

Now she could see his face more clearly. She could see how he was enjoying himself.

"My wife Carla is home in bed. Asleep in bed. Where she belongs."

He was both a handsome man and a silly-looking man. Tall, lean, well built, but with a slouch that seemed artificial. A contrived, self-conscious air of menace. A lock of dark hair falling over his forehead, a vain little moustache, eyes that appeared both hopeful and mocking, a boyish smile perpetually on the verge of a sulk.

She had always disliked the sight of him – she had mentioned her dislike to Leon, who said that the man was just unsure of himself, just a bit too friendly.

The fact that he was unsure of himself would not make her any safer now.

"Pretty worn out," he said. "After her little adventure. You should've seen your face – you should've seen the look on you when you recognized those clothes. What did you think? Did you think I'd murdered her?"

"I was surprised," said Sylvia.

"I bet you were. After you were such a big help to her running away."

457

"I helped her —," Sylvia said with considerable effort, "I helped her because she seemed to be in distress."

"Distress," he said, as if examining the word. "I guess she was. She was in very big distress when she jumped off that bus and got on the phone to me to come and get her. She was crying so hard I could hardly make out what it was she was saying."

"She wanted to come back?"

"Oh yeah. You bet she wanted to come back. She was in real hysterics to come back. She is a girl who is very up and down in her emotions. But I guess you don't know her as well as I do."

"She seemed quite happy to be going."

"Did she really? Well, I have to take your word for it. I didn't come here to argue with you."

Sylvia said nothing.

"I came here to tell you I don't appreciate you interfering in my life with my wife."

"She is a human being," said Sylvia, though she knew it would be better if she could keep quiet. "Besides being your wife."

"My goodness, is that so? My wife is a human being? Really? Thank you for the information. But don't try getting smart with me. *Sylvia.*"

"I wasn't trying to get smart."

"Good. I'm glad you weren't. I don't want to get mad. I just have a couple of important things to say to you. One thing, that I don't want you sticking your nose in anywhere, anytime, in my and my wife's life. Another, that I'm not going to want her coming around here anymore. Not that she is going to particularly want to come, I'm pretty sure of that. She doesn't have too good an opinion of you at the moment. And it's time you learned how to clean your own house.

"Now," he said. "Now. Has that sunk in?"

"Quite sufficiently."

"Oh, I really hope it has. I hope so."

Sylvia said, "Yes."

"And you know what else I think?"

"What?"

"I think you owe me something."

"What?"

"I think you owe me – maybe – you owe me an apology."

Sylvia said, "All right. If you think so. I'm sorry."

He shifted, perhaps just to put out his hand, and with the movement of his body she shrieked.

He laughed. He put his hand on the doorframe to make sure she didn't close it.

"What's that?"

"What's what?" he said, as if she was trying out a trick and it would not work. But then he caught sight of something reflected in the window, and he snapped around to look.

Not far from the house was a wide shallow patch of land that often filled up with night fog at this time of year. The fog was there tonight, had been there all this while. But now at one point there was a change. The fog had thickened, taken on a separate shape, transformed itself into something spiky and radiant. First a live dandelion ball, tumbling forward, then condensing itself into an unearthly sort of animal, pure white, hell-bent, something like a giant unicorn, rushing at them.

"Jesus Christ," Clark said softly and devoutly. And grabbed hold of Sylvia's shoulder. This touch did not alarm her at all – she accepted it with the knowledge that he did it either to protect her or to reassure himself.

Then the vision exploded. Out of the fog, and out of the magnifying light – now seen to be that of a car travelling along this back road, probably in search of a place to park – out of this appeared a white goat. A little dancing white goat, hardly bigger than a sheepdog.

Clark let go. He said, "Where the Christ did you come from?"

"It's your goat," said Sylvia. "Isn't it your goat?"

"Flora," he said. "Flora."

The goat had stopped a yard or so away from them, had turned shy and hung her head.

"Flora," Clark said. "Where the hell did you come from? You scared the shit out of us."

Us.

Flora came closer but still did not look up. She butted against Clark's legs.

"Goddamn stupid animal," he said shakily. "Where'd you come from?"

"She was lost," said Sylvia.

"Yeah. She was. Never thought we'd see her again, actually."

Flora looked up. The moonlight caught a glitter in her eyes.

"Scared the shit out of us," Clark said to her. "Were you off looking for a boyfriend? Scared the shit. Didn't you? We thought you were a ghost."

"It was the effect of the fog," Sylvia said. She stepped out of the door now, onto the patio. Quite safe.

"Yeah."

"Then the lights of that car."

"Like an apparition," he said, recovering. And pleased that he had thought of this description.

"Yes."

"The goat from outer space. That's what you are. You are a goddamn goat from outer space," he said, patting Flora. But when Sylvia put out her free hand to do the same – her other hand still held the bag of clothes that Carla had worn – Flora immediately lowered her head as if to prepare for some serious butting.

"Goats are unpredictable," Clark said. "They can seem tame but they're not really. Not after they grow up."

"Is she grown-up? She looks so small."

"She's big as she's ever going to get."

They stood looking down at the goat, as if expecting she would provide them with more conversation. But this was apparently not going to happen. From this moment they could go neither forward nor back. Sylvia believed that she might have seen a shadow of regret cross his face that this was so.

But he acknowledged it. He said, "It's late."

"I guess it is," said Sylvia, just as if this had been an ordinary visit.

"Okay, Flora. Time for us to go home."

"I'll make other arrangements for help if I need it," she said. "I probably won't need it now, anyway." She added almost laughingly, "I'll stay out of your hair."

"Sure," he said. "You better get inside. You'll get cold."

"People used to think night fogs were dangerous."

"That's a new one on me."

"So good night," she said. "Good night, Flora."

The phone rang then.

"Excuse me."

He raised a hand and turned away. "Good night."

It was Ruth on the phone.

"Ah," Sylvia said. "A change in plans."

SHE DID NOT SLEEP, thinking of the little goat, whose appearance out of the fog seemed to her more and more magical. She even wondered if, possibly, Leon could have had something to do with it. If she was a poet she would write a poem about something like this. But in her experience the subjects that she thought a poet could write about did not appeal to Leon.

CARLA HAD NOT heard Clark go out but she woke when he came in. He told her that he had just been out checking around the barn.

"A car went along the road a while ago and I wondered what they were doing here. I couldn't get back to sleep till I went out and checked whether everything was okay."

"So was it?"

"Far as I could see."

"And then while I was up," he said, "I thought I might as well pay a visit up the road. I took the clothes back."

Carla sat up in bed.

"You didn't wake her up?"

"She woke up. It was okay. We had a little talk."

"Oh."

"It was okay."

"You didn't mention any of that stuff, did you?"

"I didn't mention it."

"It really was all made-up. It really was. You have to believe me. It was all a lie."

"Okay."

"You have to believe me."

"Then I believe you."

"I made it all up."

"Okay."

He got into bed.

"Your feet are cold," she said. "Like they got wet."

"Heavy dew."

"Come here," he said. "When I read your note, it was just like I went hollow inside. It's true. If you ever went away, I'd feel like I didn't have anything left in me."

THE BRIGHT WEATHER had continued. On the streets, in the stores, in the Post Office, people greeted each other by saying that summer had finally arrived. The pasture grass and even the poor beaten crops lifted up their heads. The puddles dried up, the mud turned to dust. A light warm wind blew and everybody felt like doing things again. The phone rang. Inquiries about trail rides, about riding lessons. Summer camps were interested now, having cancelled their trips to museums. Minivans drew up, with their loads of restless children. The horses pranced along the fences, freed from their blankets.

Clark had managed to get hold of a large enough piece of roofing at a good price. He had spent the whole first day after Runaway Day (that was how they referred to Carla's bus trip) fixing the roof of the exercise ring.

For a couple of days, as they went about their chores, he and Carla would wave at each other. If she happened to pass close to him, and there was nobody else around, Carla might kiss his shoulder through the light material of his summer shirt.

"If you ever try to run away on me again I'll tan your hide," he said to her, and she said, "*Would* you?"

"What?"

"Tan my hide?"

"Damn right." He was high-spirited now, irresistible as when she had first known him.

Birds were everywhere. Red-winged blackbirds, robins, a pair of doves that sang at daybreak. Lots of crows, and gulls on reconnoitering missions from the lake, and big turkey buzzards that sat in the branches of a dead oak about half a mile away, at the edge of the woods. At first they just sat there, drying out their voluminous wings, lifting themselves occasionally for a trial flight, flapping around a bit, then composing themselves to let the sun and the warm air do their work. In a day or so they were restored, flying high, circling and dropping to earth, disappearing over the woods, coming back to rest in the familiar bare tree.

Lizzie's owner – Joy Tucker – showed up again, tanned and friendly. She had just got sick of the rain and gone off on her holidays to hike in the Rocky Mountains. Now she was back.

"Perfect timing weatherwise," Clark said. He and Joy Tucker were soon joking as if nothing had happened.

"Lizzie looks to be in good shape," she said. "But where's her little friend? What's her name – Flora?"

"Gone," said Clark. "Maybe she took off to the Rocky Mountains."

"Lots of wild goats out there. With fantastic horns."

"So I hear."

FOR THREE OR FOUR days they had been just too busy to go down and look in the mailbox. When Carla opened it she found the phone bill, some promise that if they subscribed to a certain magazine they could win a million dollars, and Mrs. Jamieson's letter.

My Dear Carla,

I have been thinking about the (rather dramatic) events of the last few days and I find myself talking to myself but really to you, so often that I thought I must speak to you, even if – the best way I can do now – only in a letter. And don't worry – you do not have to answer me.

Mrs. Jamieson went on to say that she was afraid that she had involved herself too closely in Carla's life and had made the mistake of thinking somehow that Carla's happiness and freedom were the same thing. All she cared for was Carla's happiness and she saw now that she – Carla – must find that in her marriage. All she could hope was that perhaps Carla's flight and turbulent emotions had brought her true feelings to the surface and perhaps a recognition in her husband of his true feelings as well.

She said that she would perfectly understand if Carla had a wish to avoid her in the future and that she would always be grateful for Carla's presence in her life during such a difficult time.

The strangest and most wonderful thing in this whole string of events seems to me the reappearance of Flora. In fact it seems rather like a miracle. Where had she been all the time and why did she choose just that moment for her reappearance? I am sure your husband has described it to you. We were talking at the patio door and I – facing out – was the first to see this white something – descending on us out of the night. Of course it was the effect of the ground fog. But truly terrifying. I think I shrieked out loud. I had never in my lift felt such bewitchment, in the true sense. I suppose I should be honest and say fear. There we were, two adults, frozen, and then out of the fog comes little lost Flora.

There has to be something special about this. I know of course that Flora is an ordinary little animal and that she probably spent her time away in getting herself pregnant. In a sense her return has no connection at all with our human lives. Yet her appearance at that moment did have a profound effect on your husband and me. When two human beings divided by hostility are both, at the same time, mystified – no, frightened – by the same apparition, there is a bond that springs up between them, and they find themselves united in the most unexpected way. United in their humanity – that is the only way I can describe it. We parted almost as friends. So Flora has her place as a good angel in my life and perhaps also in your husband's life and yours.

With all my good wishes, Sylvia Jamieson

As soon as Carla had read this letter she crumpled it up. Then she burned it in the sink. The flames leapt up alarmingly and she turned on the tap, then scooped up the soft disgusting black stuff and put it down the toilet as she should have done in the first place.

She was busy for the rest of that day, and the next, and the next. During that time she had to take two parties out on the trails, she had

to give lessons to children, individually and in groups. At night when Clark put his arms around her – busy as he was now, he was never too tired, never cross – she did not find it hard to be cooperative.

It was as if she had a murderous needle somewhere in her lungs, and by breathing carefully, she could avoid feeling it. But every once in a while she had to take a deep breath, and it was still there.

SYLVIA HAD TAKEN an apartment in the college town where she taught. The house was not up for sale – or at least there wasn't a sign out in front of it. Leon Jamieson had got some kind of posthumous award – news of this was in the papers. There was no mention this time of any money.

AS THE DRY GOLDEN days of fall came on – an encouraging and profitable season – Carla found that she had got used to the sharp thought that had lodged in her. It wasn't so sharp anymore – in fact, it no longer surprised her. And she was inhabited now by an almost seductive notion, a constant low-lying temptation.

She had only to raise her eyes, she had only to look in one direction, to know where she might go. An evening walk, once her chores for the day were finished. To the edge of the woods, and the bare tree where the buzzards had held their party.

And then the little dirty bones in the grass. The skull with perhaps some shreds of bloodied skin clinging to it. A skull that she could hold like a teacup in one hand. Knowledge in one hand.

Or perhaps not. Nothing there.

Other things could have happened. He could have chased Flora away. Or tied her in the back of the truck and driven some distance and set her loose. Taken her back to the place they'd got her from. Not to have her around, reminding them.

She might be free.

The days passed and Carla didn't go near that place. She held out against the temptation.

THE BEAR CAME OVER THE MOUNTAIN

FIONA LIVED IN her parents' house, in the town where she and Grant went to university. It was a big, bay-windowed house that seemed to Grant both luxurious and disorderly, with rugs crooked on the floors and cup rings bitten into the table varnish. Her mother was Icelandic – a powerful woman with a froth of white hair and indignant far-left politics. The father was an important cardiologist, revered around the hospital but happily subservient at home, where he would listen to strange tirades with an absentminded smile. All kinds of people, rich or shabby-looking, delivered these tirades, and kept coming and going and arguing and conferring, sometimes in foreign accents. Fiona had her own little car and a pile of cashmere sweaters, but she wasn't in a sorority, and this activity in her house was probably the reason.

Not that she cared. Sororities were a joke to her, and so was politics, though she liked to play "The Four Insurgent Generals" on the phonograph, and sometimes also she played the "Internationale," very loud, if there was a guest she thought she could make nervous. A curly-haired, gloomy-looking foreigner was courting her – she said he was a Visigoth – and so were two or three quite respectable and uneasy young interns. She made fun of them all and of Grant as well. She would drolly repeat some of his small-town phrases. He thought maybe she was joking when she proposed to him, on a cold bright day on the beach at Port Stanley. Sand was stinging their faces and the waves delivered crashing loads of gravel at their feet.

"Do you think it would be fun –" Fiona shouted. "Do you think it would be fun if we got married?"

He took her up on it, he shouted yes. He wanted never to be away from her. She had the spark of life.

*   *   *

JUST BEFORE THEY left their house Fiona noticed a mark on the kitchen floor. It came from the cheap black house shoes she had been wearing earlier in the day.

"I thought they'd quit doing that," she said in a tone of ordinary annoyance and perplexity, rubbing at the gray smear that looked as if it had been made by a greasy crayon.

She remarked that she would never have to do this again, since she wasn't taking those shoes with her.

"I guess I'll be dressed up all the time," she said. "Or semi dressed up. It'll be sort of like in a hotel."

She rinsed out the rag she'd been using and hung it on the rack inside the door under the sink. Then she put on her golden-brown fur-collared ski jacket over a white turtle-necked sweater and tailored fawn slacks. She was a tall, narrow-shouldered woman, seventy years old but still upright and trim, with long legs and long feet, delicate wrists and ankles and tiny, almost comical-looking ears. Her hair, which was light as milk-weed fluff, had gone from pale blond to white somehow without Grant's noticing exactly when, and she still wore it down to her shoulders, as her mother had done. (That was the thing that had alarmed Grant's own mother, a small-town widow who worked as a doctor's receptionist. The long white hair on Fiona's mother, even more than the state of the house, had told her all she needed to know about attitudes and politics.)

Otherwise Fiona with her fine bones and small sapphire eyes was nothing like her mother. She had a slightly crooked mouth which she emphasized now with red lipstick – usually the last thing she did before she left the house. She looked just like herself on this day – direct and vague as in fact she was, sweet and ironic.

OVER A YEAR AGO Grant had started noticing so many little yellow notes stuck up all over the house. That was not entirely new. She'd always written things down – the title of a book she'd heard mentioned on the radio or the jobs she wanted to make sure she did that day. Even her morning schedule was written down – he found it mystifying and touching in its precision.

7 a.m. Yoga. 7:30–7:45 teeth face hair. 7:45–8:15 walk. 8:15 Grant and Breakfast.

The new notes were different. Taped onto the kitchen drawers – Cutlery, Dishtowels, Knives. Couldn't she have just opened the drawers and seen what was inside? He remembered a story about the German soldiers on border patrol in Czechoslovakia during the war. Some Czech had told him that each of the patrol dogs wore a sign that said *Hund*. Why? said the Czechs, and the Germans said, Because that is a *hund*.

He was going to tell Fiona that, then thought he'd better not. They always laughed at the same things, but suppose this time she didn't laugh?

Worse things were coming. She went to town and phoned him from a booth to ask him how to drive home. She went for her walk across the field into the woods and came home by the fence line – a very long way round. She said that she'd counted on fences always taking you somewhere.

It was hard to figure out. She said that about fences as if it was a joke, and she had remembered the phone number without any trouble.

"I don't think it's anything to worry about," she said. "I expect I'm just losing my mind."

He asked if she had been taking sleeping pills.

"If I have I don't remember," she said. Then she said she was sorry to sound so flippant.

"I'm sure I haven't been taking anything. Maybe I should be. Maybe vitamins."

Vitamins didn't help. She would stand in doorways trying to figure out where she was going. She forgot to turn on the burner under the vegetables or put water in the coffeemaker.

She asked Grant when they'd moved to this house.

"Was it last year or the year before?"

He said that it was twelve years ago.

She said, "That's shocking."

"She's always been a bit like this," Grant said to the doctor. "Once she left her fur coat in storage and just forgot about it. That was when we were always going somewhere warm in the winters. Then she said it was unintentionally on purpose, she said it was like a sin she was leaving behind. The way some people made her feel about fur coats."

He tried without success to explain something more – to explain how Fiona's surprise and apologies about all this seemed somehow like routine courtesy, not quite concealing a private amusement. As if she'd stumbled on some adventure that she had not been expecting. Or was playing a game that she hoped he would catch on to. They had always had their games – nonsense dialects, characters they invented. Some of Fiona's made-up voices, chirping or wheedling (he couldn't tell the doctor this), had mimicked uncannily the voices of women of his that she had never met or known about.

"Yes, well," the doctor said. "It might be selective at first. We don't know, do we? Till we see the pattern of the deterioration, we really can't say."

In a while it hardly mattered what label was put on it. Fiona, who no longer went shopping alone, disappeared from the supermarket while Grant had his back turned. A policeman picked her up as she walked down the middle of the road, blocks away. He asked her name and she answered readily. Then he asked her the name of the prime minister of the country.

"If you don't know that, young man, you really shouldn't be in such a responsible job."

He laughed. But then she made the mistake of asking if he'd seen Boris and Natasha.

These were the Russian wolfhounds she had adopted some years ago as a favor to a friend, then devoted herself to for the rest of their lives. Her taking them over might have coincided with the discovery that she was not likely to have children. Something about her tubes being blocked, or twisted – Grant could not remember now. He had always avoided thinking about all that female apparatus. Or it might have been after her mother died. The dogs' long legs and silky hair, their narrow, gentle, intransigent faces made a fine match for her when she took them out for walks. And Grant himself, in those days, landing his first job at the university (his father-in-law's money welcome in spite of the political taint), might have seemed to some people to have been picked up on another of Fiona's eccentric whims, and groomed and tended and favored. Though he never understood this, fortunately, until much later.

SHE SAID TO HIM, at suppertime on the day of the wandering-off at the supermarket, "You know what you're going to have to do with me, don't you? You're going to have to put me in that place. Shallowlake?"

Grant said, "Meadowlake. We're not at that stage yet."

"Shallowlake, Shillylake," she said, as if they were engaged in a playful competition. "Sillylake. Sillylake it is."

He held his head in his hands, his elbows on the table. He said that if they did think of it, it must be as something that need not be permanent. A kind of experimental treatment. A rest cure.

THERE WAS A RULE that nobody could be admitted during the month of December. The holiday season had so many emotional pitfalls. So they made the twenty-minute drive in January. Before they reached the highway the country road dipped through a swampy hollow now completely frozen over. The swamp-oaks and maples threw their shadows like bars across the bright snow.

Fiona said, "Oh, remember."

Grant said, "I was thinking about that too."

"Only it was in the moonlight," she said.

She was talking about the time that they had gone out skiing at night under the full moon and over the black-striped snow, in this place that you could get into only in the depths of winter. They had heard the branches cracking in the cold.

So if she could remember that so vividly and correctly, could there really be so much the matter with her?

It was all he could do not to turn around and drive home.

THERE WAS ANOTHER rule which the supervisor explained to him. New residents were not to be visited during the first thirty days. Most people needed that time to get settled in. Before the rule had been put in place, there had been pleas and tears and tantrums, even from those who had come in willingly. Around the third or fourth day they would start lamenting and begging to be taken home. And some relatives could be susceptible to that, so you would have people being carted home who would not get on there any better than they had before. Six months later or sometimes only a few weeks later, the whole upsetting hassle would have to be gone through again.

"Whereas we find," the supervisor said, "we find that if they're left on their own they usually end up happy as clams. You have to practically lure them into a bus to take a trip to town. The same with a visit home. It's perfectly okay to take them home then, visit for an hour or two – they're the ones that'll worry about getting back in time for supper. Meadowlake's their home then. Of course, that doesn't apply to the ones on the second floor, we can't let them go. It's too difficult, and they don't know where they are anyway."

"My wife isn't going to be on the second floor," Grant said.

"No," said the supervisor thoughtfully. "I just like to make everything clear at the outset."

THEY HAD GONE over to Meadowlake a few times several years ago, to visit Mr. Farquar, the old bachelor farmer who had been their neighbor. He had lived by himself in a drafty brick house unaltered since the early years of the century, except for the addition of a refrigerator and a television set. He had paid Grant and Fiona unannounced but well-spaced visits and, as well as local matters, he liked to discuss books he had been reading – about the Crimean War or Polar explorations or the history of firearms. But after he went to Meadowlake he would talk only about the routines of the place, and they got the idea that their visits, though gratifying, were a social burden for him. And Fiona in particular hated the smell of urine and bleach that hung about, hated the perfunctory bouquets of plastic flowers in niches in the dim, low-ceilinged corridors.

Now that building was gone, though it had dated only from the fifties. Just as Mr. Farquar's house was gone, replaced by a gimcrack sort of castle that was the weekend home of some people from Toronto. The new Meadowlake was an airy, vaulted building whose air was faintly pleasantly pine-scented. Profuse and genuine greenery sprouted out of giant crocks.

Nevertheless, it was the old building that Grant would find himself picturing Fiona in during the long month he had to get through without seeing her. It was the longest month of his life, he thought – longer than the month he had spent with his mother visiting relatives in Lanark County, when he was thirteen, and longer than the month that Jacqui Adams spent on holiday with her family, near the beginning of their affair. He phoned Meadowlake every day and hoped that he would get the nurse whose name was Kristy. She seemed a little amused at his constancy, but she would give him a fuller report than any other nurse he got stuck with.

Fiona had caught a cold, but that was not unusual for newcomers.

"Like when your kids start school," Kristy said. "There's a whole bunch of new germs they're exposed to, and for a while they just catch everything."

Then the cold got better. She was off the antibiotics, and she didn't seem as confused as she had been when she came in. (This was the first time Grant had heard about either the antibiotics or the confusion.) Her appetite was pretty good, and she seemed to enjoy sitting in the sunroom. She seemed to enjoy watching television.

One of the things that had been so intolerable about the old Meadowlake had been the way the television was on everywhere, overwhelming your thoughts or conversation wherever you chose to sit down. Some of the inmates (that was what he and Fiona called them then, not residents) would raise their eyes to it, some talked back to it, but most just sat and meekly endured its assault. In the new building, as far as he could recall, the television was in a separate sitting room, or in the bedrooms. You could make a choice to watch it.

So Fiona must have made a choice. To watch what?

During the years that they had lived in this house, he and Fiona had watched quite a bit of television together. They had spied on the lives of every beast or reptile or insect or sea creature that a camera was able to reach, and they had followed the plots of what seemed like dozens of rather similar fine nineteenth-century novels. They had slid into an infatuation with an English comedy about life in a department store and had watched so many reruns that they knew the dialogue by heart. They mourned the disappearance of actors who died in real life or went off to other jobs, then welcomed those same actors back as the characters were born again. They watched the floorwalker's hair going from black to gray and finally back to black, the cheap sets never changing. But these, too, faded; eventually the sets and the blackest hair faded as if dust from the London streets was getting in under the elevator doors, and there was a sadness about this that seemed to affect Grant and Fiona more than any of the tragedies on *Masterpiece Theatre*, so they gave up watching before the final end.

Fiona was making some friends, Kristy said. She was definitely coming out of her shell.

What shell was that? Grant wanted to ask, but checked himself, to remain in Kristy's good graces

.

IF ANYBODY PHONED, he let the message go onto the machine. The people they saw socially, occasionally, were not close neighbors but people who lived around the countryside, who were retired, as they were, and who often went away without notice. The first years that they had lived here Grant and Fiona had stayed through the winter. A country winter was a new experience, and they had plenty to do, fixing up the house. Then they had gotten the idea that they too should travel while they could, and they had gone to Greece, to Australia, to Costa Rica. People would think that they were away on some such trip at present.

He skied for exercise but never went as far as the swamp. He skied around and around in the field behind the house as the sun went down and left the sky pink over a countryside that seemed to be bound by waves of blue-edged ice. He counted off the times he went round the field, and then he came back to the darkening house, turning the television news on while he got his supper. They had usually prepared supper together. One of them made the drinks and the other the fire, and they talked about his work (he was writing a study of legendary Norse wolves and particularly of the great Fenris wolf who swallows up Odin at the end of the world) and about whatever Fiona was reading and what they had been thinking during their close but separate day. This was their time of liveliest intimacy, though there was also, of course, the five or ten minutes of physical sweetness just after they got into bed – something that did not often end up in sex but reassured them that sex was not over yet.

IN A DREAM Grant showed a letter to one of his colleagues whom he had thought of as a friend. The letter was from the roommate of a girl he had not thought of for a while. Its style was sanctimonious and hostile, threatening in a whining way – he put the writer down as a latent lesbian. The girl herself was someone he had parted from decently, and it seemed unlikely that she would want to make a fuss, let alone try to kill herself, which was what the letter was apparently, elaborately, trying to tell him.

The colleague was one of those husbands and fathers who had been among the first to throw away their neckties and leave home to spend every night on a floor mattress with a bewitching young mistress, coming to their offices, their classes, bedraggled and smelling of dope and incense. But now he took a dim view of such shenanigans, and Grant recollected that he had in fact married one of those girls, and that she had taken to giving dinner parties and having babies, just as wives used to do.

"I wouldn't laugh," he said to Grant, who did not think he had been laughing. "And if I were you I'd try to prepare Fiona."

So Grant went off to find Fiona in Meadowlake – the old Meadowlake – and got into a lecture theater instead. Everybody was waiting there for him to teach his class. And sitting in the last, highest row was a flock of cold-eyed young women all in black robes, all in mourning, who never took their bitter stares off him and conspicuously did not write down, or care about, anything he was saying.

Fiona was in the first row, untroubled. She had transformed the lecture room into the sort of corner she was always finding at a party – some high-and-dry spot where she drank wine with mineral water, and smoked ordinary cigarettes and told funny stories about her dogs. Holding out there against the tide, with some people who were like herself, as if the dramas that were being played out in other corners, in bedrooms and on the dark verandah, were nothing but childish comedy. As if charity was chic, and reticence a blessing.

"Oh, phooey," Fiona said. "Girls that age are always going around talking about how they'll kill themselves."

But it wasn't enough for her to say that – in fact, it rather chilled him. He was afraid that she was wrong, that something terrible had happened, and he saw what she could not – that the black ring was thickening, drawing in, all around his windpipe, all around the top of the room.

HE HAULED HIMSELF out of the dream and set about separating what was real from what was not.

There had been a letter, and the word "RAT" had appeared in black paint on his office door, and Fiona, on being told that a girl had suffered from a bad crush on him, had said pretty much what she said in the dream. The colleague hadn't come into it, the black-robed women had never appeared in his classroom, and nobody had committed suicide. Grant hadn't been disgraced, in fact he had got off easily when you thought of what might have happened just a couple of years later. But word got around. Cold shoulders became conspicuous. They had few Christmas invitations and spent New Year's Eve alone. Grant got drunk, and without its being required of him – also, thank God, without making the error of a confession – he promised Fiona a new life.

The shame he felt then was the shame of being duped, of not having noticed the change that was going on. And not one woman had made him aware of it. There had been the change in the past when so many women so suddenly became available – or it seemed that way to him – and now this new change, when they were saying that what had happened was not what they had had in mind at all. They had collaborated because they were helpless and bewildered, and they had been injured by the whole thing, rather than delighted. Even when they had taken the initiative they had done so only because the cards were stacked against them.

Nowhere was there any acknowledgement that the life of a philanderer (if that was what Grant had to call himself – he who had not had half as many conquests or complications as the man who had reproached him in his dream) involved acts of kindness and generosity and even sacrifice. Not in the beginning, perhaps, but at least as things went on. Many times he had catered to a woman's pride, to her fragility, by offering more affection – or a rougher passion – than anything he really felt. All so that he could now find himself accused of wounding and exploiting and destroying self-esteem. And of deceiving Fiona – as of course he had deceived her – but would it have been better if he had done as others had done with their wives and left her?

He had never thought of such a thing. He had never stopped making love to Fiona in spite of disturbing demands elsewhere. He had not stayed away from her for a single night. No making up elaborate stories in order to spend a weekend in San Francisco or in a tent on Manitoulin Island. He had gone easy on the dope and the drink and he had continued to publish papers, serve on committees, make progress in his career. He had never had any intention of throwing up work and marriage and taking to the country to practice carpentry or keep bees.

But something like that had happened after all. He took an early retirement with a reduced pension. The cardiologist had died, after some bewildered and stoical time alone in the big house, and Fiona had inherited both that property and the farmhouse where her father had grown up, in the country near Georgian Bay. She gave up her job, as a hospital co-ordinator of volunteer services (in that everyday world, as she said, where people actually had troubles that were not related to drugs or sex or intellectual squabbles). A new life was a new life.

Boris and Natasha had died by this time. One of them got sick and died first – Grant forgot which one – and then the other died, more or less out of sympathy.

He and Fiona worked on the house. They got cross-country skis. They were not very sociable, but they gradually made some friends. There were no more hectic flirtations. No bare female toes creeping up under a man's pants leg at a dinner party. No more loose wives.

Just in time, Grant was able to think, when the sense of injustice wore down. The feminists and perhaps the sad silly girl herself and his cowardly so-called friends had pushed him out just in time. Out of a life that was in fact getting to be more trouble than it was worth. And that might eventually have cost him Fiona.

ON THE MORNING of the day when he was to go back to Meadowlake for the first visit, Grant woke early. He was full of a solemn tingling, as in the old days on the morning of his first planned meeting with a new woman. The feeling was not precisely sexual. (Later, when the meetings had become routine, that was all it was.) There was an expectation of discovery, almost a spiritual expansion. Also timidity, humility, alarm.

He left home too early. Visitors were not allowed before two o'clock. He did not want to sit out in the parking lot, waiting, so he made himself turn the car in a wrong direction.

There had been a thaw. Plenty of snow was left, but the dazzling hard landscape of earlier winter had crumbled. These pocked heaps under a gray sky looked like refuse in the fields.

In the town near Meadowlake he found a florist's shop and bought a large bouquet. He had never presented flowers to Fiona before. Or to anyone else. He entered the building feeling like a hopeless lover or a guilty husband in a cartoon.

"Wow. Narcissus this early," Kristy said. "You must've spent a fortune." She went along the hall ahead of him and snapped on the light in a closet, or sort of kitchen, where she searched for a vase. She was a heavy young woman who looked as if she had given up in every department except her hair. That was blond and voluminous. All the puffed-up luxury of a cocktail waitress's style, or a stripper's, on top of such a workaday face and body.

"There, now," she said, and nodded him down the hall. "Name's right on the door."

So it was, on a nameplate decorated with bluebirds. He wondered whether to knock, and did, then opened the door and called her name.

She wasn't there. The closet door was closed, the bed smoothed. Nothing on the bedside table, except a box of Kleenex and a glass of water. Not a single photograph or picture of any kind, not a book or a magazine. Perhaps you had to keep those in a cupboard.

He went back to the nurses' station, or reception desk, or whatever it was. Kristy said "No?" with a surprise that he thought perfunctory.

He hesitated, holding the flowers. She said, "Okay, okay – let's set the bouquet down here." Sighing, as if he was a backward child on his first day at school, she led him along a hall, into the light of the huge sky windows in the large central space, with its cathedral ceiling. Some people were sitting along the walls, in easy chairs, others at tables in the middle of the carpeted floor. None of them looked too bad. Old – some of them incapacitated enough to need wheelchairs – but decent. There used to be some unnerving sights when he and Fiona went to visit Mr. Farquar. Whiskers on old women's chins, somebody with a bulged-out eye like a rotted plum. Dribblers, head wagglers, mad chatterers. Now it looked as if there'd been some weeding out of the worst cases. Or perhaps drugs, surgery had come into use, perhaps there were ways of treating disfigurement, as well as verbal and other kinds of incontinence – ways that hadn't existed even those few years ago.

There was, however, a very disconsolate woman sitting at the piano, picking away with one finger and never achieving a tune. Another woman, staring out from behind a coffee urn and a stack of plastic cups, looked bored to stone. But she had to be an employee – she wore a pale-green pants outfit like Kristy's.

"See?" said Kristy in a softer voice. "You just go up and say hello and try not to startle her. Remember she may not – Well. Just go ahead."

He saw Fiona in profile, sitting close up to one of the card tables, but not playing. She looked a little puffy in the face, the flab on one cheek hiding the corner of her mouth, in a way it hadn't done before. She was watching the play of the man she sat closest to. He held his cards tilted so that she could see them. When Grant got near the table she looked up. They all looked up – all the players at the table looked up, with displeasure. Then they immediately looked down at their cards, as if to ward off any intrusion.

But Fiona smiled her lopsided, abashed, sly, and charming smile and pushed back her chair and came round to him, putting her fingers to her mouth.

"Bridge," she whispered. "Deadly serious. They're quite rabid about it." She drew him towards the coffee table, chatting. "I can remember being like that for a while at college. My friends and I would cut class and sit in the common room and smoke and play like cutthroats. One's name was Phoebe, I don't remember the others."

"Phoebe Hart," Grant said. He pictured the little hollow-chested, black-eyed girl, who was probably dead by now. Wreathed in smoke, Fiona and Phoebe and those others, rapt as witches.

"You knew her too?" said Fiona, directing her smile now towards the stone-faced woman. "Can I get you anything? A cup of tea? I'm afraid the coffee isn't up to much here."

Grant never drank tea.

He could not throw his arms around her. Something about her voice and smile, familiar as they were, something about the way she seemed to be guarding the players and even the coffee woman from him – as well as him from their displeasure – made that not possible.

"I brought you some flowers," he said. "I thought they'd do to brighten up your room. I went to your room, but you weren't there."

"Well, no," she said. "I'm here."

Grant said, "You've made a new friend." He nodded towards the man she'd been sitting next to. At this moment that man looked up at Fiona and she turned, either because of what Grant had said or because she felt the look at her back.

"It's just Aubrey," she said. "The funny thing is I knew him years and years ago. He worked in the store. The hardware store where my grandpa used to shop. He and I were always kidding around and he could not get up the nerve to ask me out. Till the very last weekend and he took me to a ball game. But when it was over my grandpa showed up to drive me home. I was up visiting for the summer. Visiting my grandparents – they lived on a farm."

"Fiona. I know where your grandparents lived. It's where we live. Lived."

"Really?" she said, not paying full attention because the card-player was sending her his look, which was not one of supplication but command. He was a man of about Grant's age, or a little older. Thick coarse white hair fell over his forehead, and his skin was leathery but pale, yellowish-white like an old wrinkled-up kid glove. His long face was dignified and melancholy, and he had something of the beauty of a powerful, discouraged, elderly horse. But where Fiona was concerned he was not discouraged.

"I better go back," Fiona said, a blush spotting her newly fattened face. "He thinks he can't play without me sitting there. It's silly, I hardly know the game anymore. I'm afraid you'll have to excuse me."

"Will you be through soon?"

"Oh, we should be. It depends. If you go and ask that grim-looking lady nicely she'll get you some tea."

"I'm fine," Grant said.

"So I'll leave you then, you can entertain yourself? It must all seem strange to you, but you'll be surprised how soon you get used to it. You'll get to know who everybody is. Except that some of them are pretty well off in the clouds, you know – you can't expect them all to get to know who *you* are."

She slipped back into her chair and said something into Aubrey's ear. She tapped her fingers across the back of his hand.

Grant went in search of Kristy and met her in the hall. She was pushing a cart on which there were pitchers of apple juice and grape juice.

"Just one sec," she said to him, as she stuck her head through a doorway. "Apple juice in here? Grape juice? Cookies?"

He waited while she filled two plastic glasses and took them into the room. Then she came back and put two arrowroot cookies on paper plates.

"Well?" she said. "Aren't you glad to see her participating and everything?"

Grant said, "Does she even know who I am?"

* * *

HE COULD NOT DECIDE. She could have been playing a joke. It would not be unlike her. She had given herself away by that little pretense at the end, talking to him as if she thought perhaps he was a new resident.

If that was what she was pretending. If it was a pretense.

But would she not have run after him and laughed at him then, once the joke was over? She would not have just gone back to the game, surely, and pretended to forget about him. That would have been too cruel.

Kristy said, "You just caught her at sort of a bad moment. Involved in the game."

"She's not even playing," he said.

"Well, but her friend's playing. Aubrey."

"So who is Aubrey?"

"That's who he is. Aubrey. Her friend. Would you like a juice?"

Grant shook his head.

"Oh, look," said Kristy. "They get these attachments. That takes over for a while. Best buddy sort of thing. It's kind of a phase."

"You mean she really might not know who I am?"

"She might not. Not today. Then tomorrow – you never know, do you? Things change back and forth all the time and there's nothing you can do about it. You'll see the way it is once you've been coming here for a while. You'll learn not to take it all so serious. Learn to take it day by day."

DAY BY DAY. But things really didn't change back and forth, and he didn't get used to the way they were. Fiona was the one who seemed to get used to him, but only as some persistent visitor who took a special interest in her. Or perhaps even as a nuisance who must be prevented, according to her old rules of courtesy, from realizing that he was one. She treated him with a distracted, social sort of kindness that was successful in holding him back from the most obvious, the most necessary question. He could not demand of her whether she did or did not remember him as her husband of nearly fifty years. He got the impression that she would be embarrassed by such a question – embarrassed not for herself but for him. She would have laughed in a fluttery way and mortified him with her politeness and bewilderment, and somehow she would have ended up not saying either yes or no. Or she would have said either one in a way that gave not the least satisfaction.

Kristy was the only nurse he could talk to. Some of the others treated the whole thing as a joke. One tough old stick laughed in his face. "That Aubrey and that Fiona? They've really got it bad, haven't they?"

Kristy told him that Aubrey had been the local representative of a company that sold weed killer – "and all that kind of stuff" – to farmers.

"He was a fine person," she said, and Grant did not know whether this meant that Aubrey was honest and openhanded and kind to people, or that he was well spoken and well dressed and drove a good car. Probably both.

And then when he was not very old or even retired – she said – he had suffered some unusual kind of damage.

"His wife is the one takes care of him usually. She takes care of him at home. She just put him in here on temporary care so she could get a break. Her sister wanted her to go to Florida. See, she's had a hard time, you wouldn't ever have expected a man like him – They just went on a holiday somewhere and he got something, like some bug, that gave him a terrible high fever? And it put him in a coma and left him like he is now."

He asked her about these affections between residents. Did they ever go too far? He was able now to take a tone of indulgence that he hoped would save him from any lectures.

"Depends what you mean," she said. She kept writing in her record book while deciding how to answer him. When she finished what she was writing she looked up at him with a frank smile.

"The trouble we have in here, it's funny, it's often with some of the ones that haven't been friendly with each other at all. They maybe won't even know each other, beyond knowing, like, is it a man or a woman? You'd think it'd be the old guys trying to crawl in bed with the old women, but you know half the time it's the other way round. Old women going after the old men. Could be they're not so worn out, I guess."

Then she stopped smiling, as if she was afraid she had said too much, or spoken callously.

"Don't take me wrong," she said. "I don't mean Fiona. Fiona is a lady."

Well, what about Aubrey? Grant felt like saying. But he remembered that Aubrey was in a wheelchair.

"She's a real lady," Kristy said, in a tone so decisive and reassuring that Grant was not reassured. He had in his mind a picture of Fiona, in one of her long eyelet-trimmed blue-ribboned night-gowns, teasingly lifting the covers of an old man's bed.

"Well, I sometimes wonder —" he said.

Kristy said sharply, "You wonder what?"

"I wonder whether she isn't putting on some kind of a charade."

"A what?" said Kristy.

MOST AFTERNOONS THE pair could be found at the card table. Aubrey had large, thick-fingered hands. It was difficult for him to manage his cards. Fiona shuffled and dealt for him and sometimes moved quickly to straighten a card that seemed to be slipping from his grasp. Grant would watch from across the room her darting move and quick, laughing apology. He could see Aubrey's husbandly frown as a wisp of her hair touched his cheek. Aubrey preferred to ignore her as long as she stayed close.

But let her smile her greeting at Grant, let her push back her chair and get up to offer him tea — showing that she had accepted his right to be there and possibly felt a slight responsibility for him — and Aubrey's face took on its look of sombre consternation. He would let the cards slide from his fingers and fall on the floor, to spoil the game.

So that Fiona had to get busy and put things right.

If they weren't at the bridge table they might be walking along the halls, Aubrey hanging on to the railing with one hand and clutching Fiona's arm or shoulder with the other. The nurses thought that it was a marvel, the way she had got him out of his wheelchair. Though for longer trips — to the conservatory at one end of the building or the television room at the other — the wheelchair was called for.

The television seemed to be always turned to the sports channel and Aubrey would watch any sport, but his favorite appeared to be golf. Grant didn't mind watching that with them. He sat down a few chairs away. On the large screen a small group of spectators and commentators followed the players around the peaceful green, and at appropriate moments broke into a formal sort of applause. But there was silence everywhere as the player made his swing and the ball took its lonely, appointed journey across the sky. Aubrey and Fiona and Grant and possibly others sat and held their breaths, and then Aubrey's breath broke out first, expressing satisfaction or disappointment. Fiona's chimed in on the same note a moment later.

In the conservatory there was no such silence. The pair found themselves a seat among the most lush and thick and tropical-looking plants – a bower, if you like – which Grant had just enough self-control to keep from penetrating. Mixed in with the rustle of the leaves and the sound of splashing water was Fiona's soft talk and her laughter.

Then some sort of chortle. Which of them could it be?

Perhaps neither – perhaps it came from one of the impudent flashy-looking birds who inhabited the corner cages.

Aubrey could talk, though his voice probably didn't sound the way it used to. He seemed to say something now – a couple of thick syllables. *Take care. He's here. My love.*

On the blue bottom of the fountain's pool lay some wishing coins. Grant had never seen anybody actually throwing money in. He stared at these nickels and dimes and quarters, wondering if they had been glued to the tiles – another feature of the building's encouraging decoration.

TEENAGERS AT THE baseball game, sitting at the top of the bleachers out of the way of the boy's friends. A couple of inches of bare wood between them, darkness falling, quick chill of the evening late in the summer. The skittering of their hands, the shift of haunches, eyes never lifted from the field. He'll take off his jacket, if he's wearing one, to lay it around her narrow shoulders. Underneath it he can pull her closer to him, press his spread fingers into her soft arm.

Not like today when any kid would probably be into her pants on the first date.

Fiona's skinny soft arm. Teenage lust astonishing her and flashing along all the nerves of her tender new body, as the night thickens beyond the lighted dust of the game.

*   *   *

MEADOWLAKE WAS SHORT on mirrors, so he did not have to catch sight of himself stalking and prowling. But every once in a while it came to him how foolish and pathetic and perhaps unhinged he must look, trailing around after Fiona and Aubrey. And having no luck in confronting her, or him. Less and less sure of what right he had to be on the scene but unable to withdraw. Even at home, while he worked at his desk or cleaned up the house or shovelled snow when necessary, some ticking metronome in his mind was fixed on Meadowlake, on his next visit. Sometimes he seemed to himself like a mulish boy conducting a hopeless courtship, sometimes like one of those wretches who follow celebrated women through the streets, convinced that one day these women will turn around and recognize their love.

He made a great effort, and cut his visits down to Wednesdays and Saturdays. Also he set himself to observing other things about the place, as if he was a sort of visitor at large, a person doing an inspection or a social study.

Saturdays had a holiday bustle and tension. Families arrived in clusters. Mothers were usually in charge, they were like cheerful but insistent sheepdogs herding the men and children. Only the smallest children were without apprehension. They noticed right away the green and white squares on the hall floors and picked one color to walk on, the other to jump over. The bolder ones might try to hitch rides on the back of wheelchairs. Some persisted in these tricks in spite of scolding, and had to be removed to the car. And how happily, then, how readily, some older child or father volunteered to do the removing, and thus opt out of the visit.

It was the women who kept the conversation afloat. Men seemed cowed by the situation, teenagers affronted. Those being visited rode in a wheelchair or stumped along with a cane, or walked stiffly, unaided, at the procession's head, proud of the turnout but somewhat blank-eyed, or desperately babbling, under the stress of it. And now surrounded by a variety of outsiders these insiders did not look like such regular people after all. Female chins might have had their bristles shaved to the roots and bad eyes might be hidden by patches or dark lenses, inappropriate utterances might be controlled by medication, but some glaze remained, a haunted rigidity – as if people were content to become memories of themselves, final photographs.

Grant understood better now how Mr. Farquar must have felt. People here – even the ones who did not participate in any activities but sat around watching the doors or looking out the windows – were living a busy life in their heads (not to mention the life of their bodies, the portentous shifts in their bowels, the stabs and twinges everywhere along the line), and that was a life that in most cases could not very well be described or alluded to in front of visitors. All they could do was wheel or somehow propel themselves about and hope to come up with something that could be displayed or talked about.

There was the conservatory to be shown off, and the big television screen. Fathers thought that was really something. Mothers said the ferns were gorgeous. Soon everybody sat down around the little tables and ate ice cream – refused only by the teenagers, who were dying of disgust. Women wiped away the dribble from shivery old chins and men looked the other way.

There must be some satisfaction in this ritual, and perhaps even the teenagers would be glad, one day, that they had come. Grant was no expert on families.

No children or grandchildren appeared to visit Aubrey, and since they could not play cards – the tables being taken over for the ice cream parties – he and Fiona stayed clear of the Saturday parade. The conservatory was far too popular then for any of their intimate conversations.

Those might be going on, of course, behind Fiona's closed door. Grant could not manage to knock, though he stood there for some time staring at the Disney birds with an intense, a truly malignant dislike.

Or they might be in Aubrey's room. But he did not know where that was. The more he explored this place, the more corridors and seating spaces and ramps he discovered, and in his wanderings he was still apt to get lost. He would take a certain picture or chair as a landmark, and the next week whatever he had chosen seemed to have been placed somewhere else. He didn't like to mention this to Kristy, lest she think he was suffering some mental dislocations of his own. He supposed this constant change and rearranging might be for the sake of the residents – to make their daily exercise more interesting.

He did not mention either that he sometimes saw a woman at a distance that he thought was Fiona, but then thought it couldn't be, because of the clothes the woman was wearing. When had Fiona ever gone in for bright flowered blouses and electric blue slacks? One Saturday he looked out a window and saw Fiona – it must be her – wheeling Aubrey along one of the paved paths now cleared of snow and ice, and she was wearing a silly woolly hat and a jacket with swirls of blue and purple, the sort of thing he had seen on local women at the supermarket.

The fact must be that they didn't bother to sort out the wardrobes of the women who were roughly the same size. And counted on the women not recognizing their own clothes anyway.

They had cut her hair, too. They had cut away her angelic halo. On a Wednesday, when everything was more normal and card games were going on again, and the women in the Crafts Room were making silk flowers or costumed dolls without anybody hanging around to pester or admire them, and when Aubrey and Fiona were again in evidence so that it was possible for Grant to have one of his brief and friendly and maddening conversations with his wife, he said to her, "Why did they chop off your hair?"

Fiona put her hands up to her head, to check.

"Why – I never missed it," she said.

HE THOUGHT HE should find out what went on on the second floor, where they kept the people who, as Kristy said, had really lost it. Those who walked around down here holding conversations with themselves or throwing out odd questions at a passerby ("Did I leave my sweater in the church?") had apparently lost only some of it.

Not enough to qualify.

There were stairs, but the doors at the top were locked and only the staff had the keys. You could not get into the elevator unless somebody buzzed for it to open, from behind the desk.

What did they do, after they lost it?

"Some just sit," said Kristy. "Some sit and cry. Some try to holler the house down. You don't really want to know."

Sometimes they got it back.

"You go in their rooms for a year and they don't know you from Adam. Then one day, it's oh, hi, when are we going home. All of a sudden they're absolutely back to normal again."

But not for long.

"You think, wow, back to normal. And then they're gone again." She snapped her fingers. "Like so."

IN THE TOWN where he used to work there was a bookstore that he and Fiona had visited once or twice a year. He went back there by himself. He didn't feel like buying anything, but he had made a list and picked out a couple of the books on it, and then bought another book that he noticed by chance. It was about Iceland. A book of nineteenth-century watercolors made by a lady traveller to Iceland.

Fiona had never learned her mother's language and she had never shown much respect for the stories that it preserved – the stories that Grant had taught and written about, and still did write about, in his working life. She referred to their heroes as "old Njal" or "old Snorri." But in the last few years she had developed an interest in the country itself and looked at travel guides. She read about William Morris's trip, and Auden's. She didn't really plan to travel there. She said the weather was too dreadful. Also – she said – there ought to be one place you thought about and knew about and maybe longed for – but never did get to see.

WHEN GRANT FIRST started teaching Anglo-Saxon and Nordic Literature he got the regular sort of students in his classes. But after a few years he noticed a change. Married women started going back to school. Not with the idea of qualifying for a better job or for any job but simply to give themselves something more interesting to think about than their usual housework and hobbies. To enrich their lives. And perhaps it followed naturally that the men who taught them these things would become part of the enrichment, that these men would seem to these women more mysterious and desirable than the men they still cooked for and slept with.

The studies chosen were usually Psychology or Cultural History or English Literature. Archaeology or Linguistics was picked sometimes but dropped when it turned out to be heavy going. Those who signed up for Grant's courses might have a Scandinavian background, like Fiona, or they might have learned something about Norse mythology from Wagner or historical novels. There were also a few who thought he was teaching a Celtic language and for whom everything Celtic had a mystic allure.

He spoke to such aspirants fairly roughly from his side of the desk.

"If you want to learn a pretty language, go and learn Spanish. Then you can use it if you go to Mexico."

Some took his warning and drifted away. Others seemed to be moved in a personal way by his demanding tone. They worked with a will and brought into his office, into his regulated, satisfactory life, the great surprising bloom of their mature female compliance, their tremulous hope of approval.

He chose the woman named Jacqui Adams. She was the opposite of Fiona – short, cushiony, dark-eyed, effusive. A stranger to irony. The affair lasted for a year, until her husband was transferred. When they were saying good-bye, in her car, she began to shake uncontrollably. It was as if she had hypothermia. She wrote to him a few times, but he found the tone of her letters overwrought and could not decide how to answer. He let the time for answering slip away while he became magically and unexpectedly involved with a girl who was young enough to be her daughter.

For another and more dizzying development had taken place while he was busy with Jacqui. Young girls with long hair and sandalled feet were coming into his office and all but declaring themselves ready for sex. The cautious approaches, the tender intimations of feeling required with Jacqui were out the window. A whirlwind hit him, as it did many others, wish becoming action in a way that made him wonder if there wasn't something missed. But who had time for regrets? He heard of simultaneous liaisons, savage and risky encounters. Scandals burst wide open, with high and painful drama all round but a feeling that somehow it was better so. There were reprisals – there were firings. But those fired went off to teach at smaller, more tolerant colleges or Open Learning Centers, and many wives left behind got over the shock and took up the costumes, the sexual nonchalance of the girls who had tempted their men. Academic parties, which used to be so predictable, became a minefield. An epidemic had broken out, it was spreading like the Spanish flu. Only this time people ran after contagion, and few between sixteen and sixty seemed willing to be left out.

Fiona appeared to be quite willing, however. Her mother was dying, and her experience in the hospital led her from her routine work in the registrar's office into her new job. Grant himself did not go overboard, at least in comparison with some people around him. He never let another woman get as close to him as Jacqui had been. What he felt was mainly a gigantic increase in well-being. A tendency to pudginess that he had had since he was twelve years old disappeared. He ran up steps two at a time. He appreciated as never before a pageant of torn clouds and winter sunset seen from his office window, the charm of antique lamps glowing between his neighbors' living-room curtains, the cries of children in the park at dusk, unwilling to leave the hill where they'd been tobogganing. Come summer, he learned the names of flowers. In his classroom, after coaching by his nearly voiceless mother-in-law (her affliction was cancer of the throat), he risked reciting and then translating the majestic and gory ode, the head-ransom, the Hofuolausn, composed to honor King Eric Blood-axe by the skald whom that king had condemned to death. (And who was then, by the same king – and by the power of poetry – set free.) All applauded – even the peaceniks in the class whom he'd cheerfully taunted earlier, asking if they would like to wait in the hall. Driving home that day or maybe another he found an absurd and blasphemous quotation running around in his head.

And so he increased in wisdom and stature –
And in favor with God and man.

That embarrassed him at the time and gave him a superstitious chill. As it did yet. But so long as nobody knew, it seemed not unnatural.

HE TOOK THE BOOK with him, the next time he went to Meadowlake. It was a Wednesday. He went looking for Fiona at the card tables and did not see her.

A woman called out to him, "She's not here. She's sick." Her voice sounded self-important and excited – pleased with herself for having recognized him when he knew nothing about her. Perhaps also pleased with all she knew about Fiona, about Fiona's life here, thinking it was maybe more than he knew.

"He's not here either," she said.

Grant went to find Kristy.

"Nothing, really," she said, when he asked what was the matter with Fiona. "She's just having a day in bed today, just a bit of an upset."

Fiona was sitting straight up in the bed. He hadn't noticed, the few times that he had been in this room, that this was a hospital bed and could be cranked up in such a way. She was wearing one of her high-necked maidenly gowns, and her face had a pallor that was not like cherry blossoms but like flour paste.

Aubrey was beside her in his wheelchair, pushed as close to the bed as it could get. Instead of the nondescript open-necked shirts he usually wore, he was wearing a jacket and a tie. His natty-looking tweed hat was resting on the bed. He looked as if he had been out on important business.

To see his lawyer? His banker? To make arrangements with the funeral director?

Whatever he'd been doing, he looked worn out by it. He too was gray in the face.

They both looked up at Grant with a stony, grief-ridden apprehension that turned to relief, if not to welcome, when they saw who he was.

Not who they thought he'd be.

They were hanging on to each other's hands and they did not let go. The hat on the bed. The jacket and tie.

It wasn't that Aubrey had been out. It wasn't a question of where he'd been or whom he'd been to see. It was where he was going.

Grant set the book down on the bed beside Fiona's free hand.

"It's about Iceland," he said. "I thought maybe you'd like to look at it."

"Why, thank you," said Fiona. She didn't look at the book. He put her hand on it.

"Iceland," he said.

She said, "Ice-land." The first syllable managed to hold a tinkle of interest, but the second fell flat. Anyway, it was necessary for her to turn her attention back to Aubrey, who was pulling his great thick hand out of hers.

"What is it?" she said. "What is it, dear heart?"

Grant had never heard her use this flowery expression before.

"Oh, all right," she said. "Oh, here." And she pulled a handful of tissues from the box beside her bed.

Aubrey's problem was that he had begun to weep. His nose had started to run, and he was anxious not to turn into a sorry spectacle, especially in front of Grant.

"Here. Here," said Fiona. She would have tended to his nose herself and wiped his tears – and perhaps if they had been alone he would have let her do it. But with Grant there Aubrey would not permit it. He got hold of the Kleenex as well as he could and made a few awkward but lucky swipes at his face.

While he was occupied, Fiona turned to Grant.

"Do you by any chance have any influence around here?" she said in a whisper. "I've seen you talking to them –"

Aubrey made a noise of protest or weariness or disgust. Then his upper body pitched forward as if he wanted to throw himself against her. She scrambled half out of bed and caught him and held on to him. It seemed improper for Grant to help her, though of course he would have done so if he'd thought Aubrey was about to tumble to the floor.

"Hush," Fiona was saying. "Oh, honey. Hush. We'll get to see each other. We'll have to. I'll go and see you. You'll come and see me."

Aubrey made the same sound again with his face in her chest, and there was nothing Grant could decently do but get out of the room.

"I just wish his wife would hurry up and get here," Kristy said. "I wish she'd get him out of here and cut the agony short. We've got to start serving supper before long and how are we supposed to get her to swallow anything with him still hanging around?"

Grant said, "Should I stay?"

"What for? She's not sick, you know."

"To keep her company," he said.

Kristy shook her head.

"They have to get over these things on their own. They've got short memories usually. That's not always so bad."

Kristy was not hard-hearted. During the time he had known her Grant had found out some things about her life. She had four children. She did not know where her husband was but thought he might be in Alberta. Her younger boy's asthma was so bad that he would have died one night in January if she had not got him to the emergency ward in time. He was not on any illegal drugs, but she was not so sure about his brother.

To her, Grant and Fiona and Aubrey too must seem lucky. They had got through life without too much going wrong. What they had to suffer now that they were old hardly counted.

Grant left without going back to Fiona's room. He noticed that the wind was actually warm that day and the crows were making an uproar. In the parking lot a woman wearing a tartan pants suit was getting a folded-up wheelchair out of the trunk of her car.

THE STREET HE WAS driving down was called Black Hawks Lane. All the streets around were named for teams in the old National Hockey League. This was in an outlying section of the town near Meadowlake. He and Fiona had shopped in the town regularly but had not become familiar with any part of it except the main street.

The houses looked to have been built all around the same time, perhaps thirty or forty years ago. The streets were wide and curving and there were no sidewalks – recalling the time when it was thought unlikely that anybody would do much walking ever again. Friends of

Grant's and Fiona's had moved to places something like this when they began to have their children. They were apologetic about the move at first. They called it "going out to Barbecue Acres."

Young families still lived here. There were basketball hoops over garage doors and tricycles in the driveways. But some of the houses had gone downhill from the sort of family homes they were surely meant to be. The yards were marked by car tracks, the windows were plastered with tinfoil or hung with faded flags.

Rental housing. Young male tenants – single still, or single again.

A few properties seemed to have been kept up as well as possible by the people who had moved into them when they were new – people who hadn't had the money or perhaps hadn't felt the need to move on to someplace better. Shrubs had grown to maturity, pastel vinyl siding had done away with the problem of repainting. Neat fences or hedges gave the sign that the children in the houses had all grown up and gone away, and that their parents no longer saw the point of letting the yard be a common run-through for whatever new children were loose in the neighborhood.

The house that was listed in the phone book as belonging to Aubrey and his wife was one of these. The front walk was paved with flagstones and bordered by hyacinths that stood as stiff as china flowers, alternately pink and blue.

FIONA HAD NOT got over her sorrow. She did not eat at mealtimes, though she pretended to, hiding food in her napkin. She was being given a supplementary drink twice a day – someone stayed and watched while she swallowed it down. She got out of bed and dressed herself, but all she wanted to do then was sit in her room. She wouldn't have taken any exercise at all if Kristy or one of the other nurses, and Grant during visiting hours, had not walked her up and down in the corridors or taken her outside.

In the spring sunshine she sat, weeping weakly, on a bench by the wall. She was still polite – she apologized for her tears, and never argued with a suggestion or refused to answer a question. But she wept. Weeping had left her eyes raw-edged and dim. Her cardigan – if it was hers – would be buttoned crookedly. She had not got to the stage of leaving her hair unbrushed or her nails uncleaned, but that might come soon.

Kristy said that her muscles were deteriorating, and that if she didn't improve soon they would put her on a walker.

"But you know once they get a walker they start to depend on it and they never walk much anymore, just get wherever it is they have to go."

"You'll have to work at her harder," she said to Grant. "Try and encourage her."

But Grant had no luck at that. Fiona seemed to have taken a dislike to him, though she tried to cover it up. Perhaps she was reminded, every time she saw him, of her last minutes with Aubrey, when she had asked him for help and he hadn't helped her.

He didn't see much point in mentioning their marriage, now.

She wouldn't go down the hall to where most of the same people were still playing cards. And she wouldn't go into the television room or visit the conservatory.

She said that she didn't like the big screen, it hurt her eyes. And the birds' noise was irritating and she wished they would turn the fountain off once in a while.

So far as Grant knew, she never looked at the book about Iceland, or at any of the other – surprisingly few – books that she had brought from home. There was a reading room where she would sit down to rest, choosing it probably because there was seldom anybody there, and if he took a book off the shelves she would allow him to read to her. He suspected that she did that because it made his company easier for her – she was able to shut her eyes and sink back into her own grief. Because if she let go of her grief even for a minute it would only hit her harder when she bumped into it again. And sometimes he thought she closed her eyes to hide a look of informed despair that it would not be good for him to see.

So he sat and read to her out of one of these old novels about chaste love, and lost-and-regained fortunes, that could have been the discards of some long-ago village or Sunday school library. There had been no attempt, apparently, to keep the contents of the reading room as up-to-date as most things in the rest of the building.

The covers of the books were soft, almost velvety, with designs of leaves and flowers pressed into them, so that they resembled jewelry boxes or chocolate boxes. That women – he supposed it would be women – could carry home like treasure.

THE SUPERVISOR CALLED him into her office. She said that Fiona was not thriving as they had hoped.

"Her weight is going down even with the supplement. We're doing all we can for her."

Grant said that he realized they were.

"The thing is, I'm sure you know, we don't do any prolonged bed care on the first floor. We do it temporarily if someone isn't feeling well, but if they get too weak to move around and be responsible we have to consider upstairs."

He said he didn't think that Fiona had been in bed that often.

"No. But if she can't keep up her strength, she will be. Right now she's borderline."

He said that he had thought the second floor was for people whose minds were disturbed.

"That too," she said.

HE HADN'T REMEMBERED anything about Aubrey's wife except the tartan suit he had seen her wearing in the parking lot. The tails of the jacket had flared open as she bent into the trunk of the car. He had got the impression of a trim waist and wide buttocks.

She was not wearing the tartan suit today. Brown belted slacks and a pink sweater. He was right about the waist – the tight belt showed she made a point of it. It might have been better if she hadn't, since she bulged out considerably above and below.

She could be ten or twelve years younger than her husband. Her hair was short, curly, artificially reddened. She had blue eyes – a lighter blue than Fiona's, a flat robin's-egg or turquoise blue – slanted by a slight puffiness. And a good many wrinkles made more noticeable by a walnut-stain makeup. Or perhaps that was her Florida tan.

He said that he didn't quite know how to introduce himself.

"I used to see your husband at Meadowlake. I'm a regular visitor there myself."

"Yes," said Aubrey's wife, with an aggressive movement of her chin.

"How is your husband doing?"

The "doing" was added on at the last moment. Normally he would have said, "How is your husband?"

"He's okay," she said.

"My wife and he struck up quite a close friendship."

"I heard about that."

"So. I wanted to talk to you about something if you had a minute."

"My husband did not try to start anything with your wife, if that's what you're getting at," she said. "He did not molest her in any way. He isn't capable of it and he wouldn't anyway. From what I heard it was the other way round."

Grant said, "No. That isn't it at all. I didn't come here with any complaints about anything."

"Oh," she said. "Well, I'm sorry. I thought you did."

That was all she was going to give by way of apology. And she didn't sound sorry. She sounded disappointed and confused.

"You better come in, then," she said. "It's blowing cold in through the door. It's not as warm out today as it looks."

So it was something of a victory for him even to get inside. He hadn't realized it would be as hard as this. He had expected a different sort of wife. A flustered homebody, pleased by an unexpected visit and flattered by a confidential tone.

She took him past the entrance to the living room, saying, "We'll have to sit in the kitchen where I can hear Aubrey." Grant caught sight of two layers of front-window curtains, both blue, one sheer and one silky, a matching blue sofa and a daunting pale carpet, various bright mirrors and ornaments.

Fiona had a word for those sort of swooping curtains – she said it like a joke, though the women she'd picked it up from used it seriously. Any room that Fiona fixed up was bare and bright – she would have been astonished to see so much fancy stuff crowded into such a small space. He could not think what that word was.

From a room off the kitchen – a sort of sunroom, though the blinds were drawn against the afternoon brightness – he could hear the sounds of television.

Aubrey. The answer to Fiona's prayers sat a few feet away, watching what sounded like a ball game. His wife looked in at him. She said, "You okay?" and partly closed the door.

"You might as well have a cup of coffee," she said to Grant.

He said, "Thanks."

"My son got him on the sports channel a year ago Christmas, I don't know what we'd do without it."

On the kitchen counters there were all sorts of contrivances and appliances – coffeemaker, food processor, knife sharpener, and some things Grant didn't know the names or uses of. All looked new and expensive, as if they had just been taken out of their wrappings, or were polished daily.

He thought it might be a good idea to admire things. He admired the coffeemaker she was using and said that he and Fiona had always meant to get one. This was absolutely untrue – Fiona had been devoted to a European contraption that made only two cups at a time.

"They gave us that," she said. "Our son and his wife. They live in Kamloops. B.C. They send us more stuff than we can handle. It wouldn't hurt if they would spend the money to come and see us instead."

Grant said philosophically, "I suppose they're busy with their own lives."

"They weren't too busy to go to Hawaii last winter. You could understand it if we had somebody else in the family, closer at hand. But he's the only one."

The coffee being ready, she poured it into two brown-and-green ceramic mugs that she took from the amputated branches of a ceramic tree trunk that sat on the table.

"People do get lonely," Grant said. He thought he saw his chance now. "If they're deprived of seeing somebody they care about, they do feel sad. Fiona, for instance. My wife."

"I thought you said you went and visited her."

"I do," he said. "That's not it."

Then he took the plunge, going on to make the request he'd come to make. Could she consider taking Aubrey back to Meadowlake maybe just one day a week, for a visit? It was only a drive of a few miles, surely it wouldn't prove too difficult. Or if she'd like to take the time off – Grant hadn't thought of this before and was rather dismayed to hear himself suggest it – then he himself could take Aubrey out there, he wouldn't mind at all. He was sure he could manage it. And she could use a break.

While he talked she moved her closed lips and her hidden tongue as if she was trying to identify some dubious flavor. She brought milk for his coffee, and a plate of ginger cookies.

"Homemade," she said as she set the plate down. There was challenge rather than hospitality in her tone. She said nothing more until she had sat down, poured milk into her coffee and stirred it.

Then she said no.

"No. I can't do that. And the reason is, I'm not going to upset him."

"Would it upset him?" Grant said earnestly.

"Yes, it would. It would. That's no way to do. Bringing him home and taking him back. Bringing him home and taking him back, that's just confusing him."

"But wouldn't he understand that it was just a visit? Wouldn't he get into the pattern of it?"

"He understands everything all right." She said this as if he had offered an insult to Aubrey. "But it's still an interruption. And then I've got to get him all ready and get him into the car, and he's a big man, he's not so easy to manage as you might think. I've got to maneuver him into the car and pack his chair along and all that and what for? If I go to all that trouble I'd prefer to take him someplace that was more fun."

"But even if I agreed to do it?" Grant said, keeping his tone hopeful and reasonable. "It's true, you shouldn't have the trouble."

"You couldn't," she said flatly. "You don't know him. You couldn't handle him. He wouldn't stand for you doing for him. All that bother and what would he get out of it?"

Grant didn't think he should mention Fiona again.

"It'd make more sense to take him to the mall," she said. "Where he could see kids and whatnot. If it didn't make him sore about his own two grandsons he never gets to see. Or now the lake boats are starting to run again, he might get a charge out of going and watching that."

She got up and fetched her cigarettes and lighter from the window above the sink.

"You smoke?" she said.

He said no thanks, though he didn't know if a cigarette was being offered.

"Did you never? Or did you quit?"

"Quit," he said.

"How long ago was that?"

He thought about it.

"Thirty years. No – more."

He had decided to quit around the time he started up with Jacqui. But he couldn't remember whether he quit first, and thought a big reward was coming to him for quitting, or thought that the time had come to quit, now that he had such a powerful diversion.

"I've quit quitting," she said, lighting up. "Just made a resolution to quit quitting, that's all."

Maybe that was the reason for the wrinkles. Somebody – a woman – had told him that women who smoked developed a special set of fine facial wrinkles. But it could have been from the sun, or just the nature of her skin – her neck was noticeably wrinkled as well. Wrinkled neck, youthfully full and up-tilted breasts. Women of her age usually had these contradictions. The bad and good points, the genetic luck or lack of it, all mixed up together. Very few kept their beauty whole, though shadowy, as Fiona had done.

And perhaps that wasn't even true. Perhaps he only thought that because he'd known Fiona when she was young. Perhaps to get that impression you had to have known a woman when she was young.

So when Aubrey looked at his wife did he see a high-school girl full of scorn and sass, with an intriguing tilt to her robin's-egg blue eyes, pursing her fruity lips around a forbidden cigarette?

"So your wife's depressed?" Aubrey's wife said. "What's your wife's name? I forget."

"It's Fiona."

"Fiona. And what's yours? I don't think I ever was told that."

Grant said, "It's Grant."

She stuck her hand out unexpectedly across the table.

"Hello, Grant. I'm Marian."

"So now we know each other's name," she said, "there's no point in not telling you straight out what I think. I don't know if he's still so stuck on seeing your – on seeing Fiona. Or not. I don't ask him and he's not telling me. Maybe just a passing fancy. But I don't feel like taking him back there in case it turns out to be more than that. I can't afford to risk it. I don't want him getting hard to handle. I don't want him upset and carrying on. I've got my hands full with him as it is. I don't have any help. It's just me here. I'm it."

"Did you ever consider – it *is* very hard for you –" Grant said – "did you ever consider his going in there for good?"

He had lowered his voice almost to a whisper, but she did not seem to feel a need to lower hers.

"No," she said. "I'm keeping him right here."

Grant said, "Well. That's very good and noble of you."

He hoped the word "noble" had not sounded sarcastic. He had not meant it to be.

"You think so?" she said. "Noble is not what I'm thinking about."

"Still. It's not easy."

"No, it isn't. But the way I am, I don't have much choice. If I put him in there I don't have the money to pay for him unless I sell the house. The house is what we own outright. Otherwise I don't have anything in the way of resources. I get the pension next year, and I'll have his pension and my pension, but even so I could not afford to keep him there and hang on to the house. And it means a lot to me, my house does."

"It's very nice," said Grant.

"Well, it's all right. I put a lot into it. Fixing it up and keeping it up."

"I'm sure you did. You do."

"I don't want to lose it."

"No."

"I'm not *going* to lose it."

"I see your point."

"The company left us high and dry," she said. "I don't know all the ins and outs of it, but basically he got shoved out. It ended up with them saying he owed them money and when I tried to find out what was what he just went on saying it's none of my business. What I think is he did something pretty stupid. But I'm not supposed to ask, so I shut up. You've been married. You are married. You know how it is. And in the middle of me finding out about this we're supposed to go on this trip with these people and can't get out of it. And on the trip he takes sick from this virus you never heard of and goes into a coma. So that pretty well gets *him* off the hook."

Grant said, "Bad luck."

"I don't mean exactly that he got sick on purpose. It just happened. He's not mad at me anymore and I'm not mad at him. It's just life."

"That's true."

"You can't beat life."

She flicked her tongue in a cat's businesslike way across her top lip, getting the cookie crumbs. "I sound like I'm quite the philosopher, don't I? They told me out there you used to be a university professor."

"Quite a while ago," Grant said.

"I'm not much of an intellectual," she said.

"I don't know how much I am, either."

"But I know when my mind's made up. And it's made up. I'm not going to let go of the house. Which means I'm keeping him here and I don't want him getting it in his head he wants to move anyplace else. It was probably a mistake putting him in there so I could get away, but I wasn't going to get another chance, so I took it. So. Now I know better."

She shook out another cigarette.

"I bet I know what you're thinking," she said. "You're thinking there's a mercenary type of a person."

"I'm not making judgments of that sort. It's your life."

"You bet it is."

He thought they should end on a more neutral note. So he asked her if her husband had worked in a hardware store in the summers, when he was going to school.

"I never heard about it," she said. "I wasn't raised here."

DRIVING HOME, he noticed that the swamp hollow that had been filled with snow and the formal shadows of tree trunks was now lighted up with skunk lilies. Their fresh, edible-looking leaves were the size of platters. The flowers sprang straight up like candle flames, and there were so many of them, so pure a yellow, that they set a light shooting up from the earth on this cloudy day. Fiona had told him that they generated a heat of their own as well. Rummaging around in one of her concealed pockets of information, she said that you were supposed to be able to put your hand inside the curled petal and feel the heat. She said that she had tried it, but she couldn't be sure if what she felt was heat or her imagination. The heat attracted bugs.

"Nature doesn't fool around just being decorative."

He had failed with Aubrey's wife. Marian. He had foreseen that he might fail, but he had not in the least foreseen why. He had thought that all he'd have to contend with would be a woman's natural sexual jealousy – or her resentment, the stubborn remains of sexual jealousy.

He had not had any idea of the way she might be looking at things. And yet in some depressing way the conversation had not been unfamiliar to him. That was because it reminded him of conversations he'd had with people in his own family. His uncles, his relatives, probably even his mother, had thought the way Marian thought. They had believed that when other people did not think that way it was because they were kidding themselves – they had got too airy-fairy, or stupid, on account of their easy and protected lives or their education. They had lost touch with reality. Educated people, literary people, some rich people like Grant's socialist in-laws had lost touch with reality. Due to an unmerited good fortune or an innate silliness. In Grant's case, he suspected, they pretty well believed it was both.

That was how Marian would see him, certainly. A silly person, full of boring knowledge and protected by some fluke from the truth about life. A person who didn't have to worry about holding on to his house and could go around thinking his complicated thoughts. Free to dream up the fine, generous schemes that he believed would make another person happy.

What a jerk, she would be thinking now.

Being up against a person like that made him feel hopeless, exasperated, finally almost desolate. Why? Because he couldn't be sure of holding on to himself against that person? Because he was afraid that in the end they'd be right? Fiona wouldn't feel any of that misgiving. Nobody had beat her down, narrowed her in, when she was young. She'd been amused by his upbringing, able to think its harsh notions quaint.

Just the same, they have their points, those people. (He could hear himself now arguing with somebody. Fiona?) There's some advantage to the narrow focus. Marian would probably be good in a crisis. Good at survival, able to scrounge for food and able to take the shoes off a dead body in the street.

Trying to figure out Fiona had always been frustrating. It could be like following a mirage. No – like living in a mirage. Getting close to Marian would present a different problem. It would be like biting into a litchi nut. The flesh with its oddly artificial allure, its chemical taste and perfume, shallow over the extensive seed, the stone.

HE MIGHT HAVE married her. Think of it. He might have married some girl like that. If he'd stayed back where he belonged. She'd have been appetizing enough, with her choice breasts. Probably a flirt. The fussy way she had of shifting her buttocks on the kitchen chair, her pursed mouth, a slightly contrived air of menace – that was what was left of the more or less innocent vulgarity of a small-town flirt.

She must have had some hopes, when she picked Aubrey. His good looks, his salesman's job, his white-collar expectations. She must have believed that she would end up better off than she was now. And so it often happened with those practical people. In spite of their calculations, their survival instincts, they might not get as far as they had quite reasonably expected. No doubt it seemed unfair.

In the kitchen the first thing he saw was the light blinking on his answering machine. He thought the same thing he always thought now. Fiona.

He pressed the button before he got his coat off.

"Hello, Grant. I hope I got the right person. I just thought of something. There is a dance here in town at the Legion supposed to be for singles on Saturday night, and I am on the supper committee, which means I can bring a free guest. So I wondered whether you would happen to be interested in that? Call me back when you get a chance."

A woman's voice gave a local number. Then there was a beep, and the same voice started talking again.

"I just realized I'd forgot to say who it was. Well you probably recognized the voice. It's Marian. I'm still not so used to these machines. And I wanted to say I realize you're not a single and I don't mean it that way. I'm not either, but it doesn't hurt to get out once in a while. Anyway, now I've said all this I really hope it's you I'm talking to. It did sound like your voice. If you are interested you can call me and if you are not you don't need to bother. I just thought you might like the chance to get out. It's Marian speaking. I guess I already said that. Okay, then. Good-bye."

Her voice on the machine was different from the voice he'd heard a short time ago in her house. Just a little different in the first message, more so in the second. A tremor of nerves there, an affected nonchalance, a hurry to get through and a reluctance to let go.

Something had happened to her. But when had it happened? If it had been immediate, she had concealed it very successfully all the time he was with her. More likely it came on her gradually, maybe after he'd gone away. Not necessarily as a blow of attraction. Just the realization that he was a possibility, a man on his own. More or less on his own. A possibility that she might as well try to follow up.

But she'd had the jitters when she made the first move. She had put herself at risk. How much of herself, he could not yet tell. Generally a woman's vulnerability increased as time went on, as things progressed. All you could tell at the start was that if there was an edge of it now, there'd be more later.

It gave him a satisfaction – why deny it? – to have brought that out in her. To have roused something like a shimmer, a blurring, on the surface of her personality. To have heard in her testy, broad vowels this faint plea.

He set out the eggs and mushrooms to make himself an omelette. Then he thought he might as well pour a drink.

Anything was possible. Was that true – was anything possible? For instance, if he wanted to, would he be able to break her down, get her to the point where she might listen to him about taking Aubrey back to Fiona? And not just for visits, but for the rest of Aubrey's life. Where could that tremor lead them? To an upset, to the end of her self-preservation? To Fiona's happiness?

It would be a challenge. A challenge and a creditable feat. Also a joke that could never be confided to anybody – to think that by his bad behavior he'd be doing good for Fiona.

But he was not really capable of thinking about it. If he did think about it, he'd have to figure out what would become of him and Marian, after he'd delivered Aubrey to Fiona. It would not work – unless he could get more satisfaction than he foresaw, finding the stone of blameless self-interest inside her robust pulp.

You never quite knew how such things would turn out. You almost knew, but you could never be sure.

She would be sitting in her house now, waiting for him to call. Or probably not sitting. Doing things to keep herself busy. She seemed to be a woman who would keep busy. Her house had certainly shown the benefits of nonstop attention. And there was Aubrey – care of him had to continue as usual. She might have given him an early supper – fitting his meals to a Meadowlake timetable in order to get him settled for the night earlier and free herself of his routine for the day. (What would she do about him when she went to the dance? Could he be left alone or would she get a sitter? Would she tell him where she was going, introduce her escort? Would her escort pay the sitter?)

She might have fed Aubrey while Grant was buying the mushrooms and driving home. She might now be preparing him for bed. But all the time she would be conscious of the phone, of the silence of the phone.

Maybe she would have calculated how long it would take Grant to drive home. His address in the phone book would have given her a rough idea of where he lived. She would calculate how long, then add to that time for possible shopping for supper (figuring that a man alone would shop every day). Then a certain amount of time for him to get around to listening to his messages. And as the silence persisted she would think of other things. Other errands he might have had to do before he got home. Or perhaps a dinner out, a meeting that meant he would not get home at suppertime at all.

She would stay up late, cleaning her kitchen cupboards, watching television, arguing with herself about whether there was still a chance.

What conceit on his part. She was above all things a sensible woman. She would go to bed at her regular time thinking that he didn't look as if he'd be a decent dancer anyway. Too stiff, too professorial.

He stayed near the phone, looking at magazines, but he didn't pick it up when it rang again.

"Grant. This is Marian. I was down in the basement putting the wash in the dryer and I heard the phone and when I got upstairs whoever it was had hung up. So I just thought I ought to say I was here. If it was you and if you are even home. Because I don't have a machine obviously, so you couldn't leave a message. So I just wanted. To let you know.

"Bye."

The time was now twenty-five after ten.

Bye.

He would say that he'd just got home. There was no point in bringing to her mind the picture of his sitting here, weighing the pros and cons.

Drapes. That would be her word for the blue curtains – drapes. And why not? He thought of the ginger cookies so perfectly round that she'd had to announce they were homemade, the ceramic coffee mugs on their ceramic tree. A plastic runner, he was sure, protecting the hall carpet. A high-gloss exactness and practicality that his mother had never achieved but would have admired – was that why he could feel this twinge of bizarre and unreliable affection? Or was it because he'd had two more drinks after the first?

The walnut-stain tan – he believed now that it was a tan – of her face and neck would most likely continue into her cleavage, which would be deep, crepey-skinned, odorous and hot. He had that to think of, as he dialled the number that he had already written down. That and the practical sensuality of her cat's tongue. Her gemstone eyes.

FIONA WAS IN her room but not in bed. She was sitting by the open window, wearing a seasonable but oddly short and bright dress. Through the window came a heady, warm blast of lilacs in bloom and the spring manure spread over the fields.

She had a book open in her lap.

She said, "Look at this beautiful book I found, it's about Iceland. You wouldn't think they'd leave valuable books lying around in the rooms. The people staying here are not necessarily honest. And I think they've got the clothes mixed up. I never wear yellow."

"Fiona . . . ," he said.

"You've been gone a long time. Are we all checked out now?"

"Fiona, I've brought a surprise for you. Do you remember Aubrey?"

She stared at him for a moment, as if waves of wind had come beating into her face. Into her face, into her head, pulling everything to rags.

"Names elude me," she said harshly.

Then the look passed away as she retrieved, with an effort, some bantering grace. She set the book down carefully and stood up and lifted her arms to put them around him. Her skin or her breath gave off a faint new smell, a smell that seemed to him like that of the stems of cut flowers left too long in their water.

"I'm happy to see you," she said, and pulled his earlobes.

"You could have just driven away," she said. "Just driven away without a care in the world and forsook me. Forsooken me. Forsaken."

He kept his face against her white hair, her pink scalp, her sweetly shaped skull. He said, Not a chance.